Freya gave up a PhD
For four years she t
who pleaded with h
the dole and did a succession of freelance and temping jobs to support her writing days. In 1995, throwing caution to the wind, Freya sent three chapters and a page of completely fabricated reviews to a top literary agent, and met with success: five publishers entered a bidding war for her books. In 1996 *Sally* was published to great acclaim and Freya was heralded as a fresh voice in fiction. Her next books, *Chloë*, *Polly*, *Cat*, *Fen*, *Pip* and *Love Rules* have all been bestsellers. She lives in London with her family.

For more information on Freya North, visit her website at www.freyanorth.co.uk.

Visit www.AuthorTracker.co.uk for exclusive updates on Freya North.

By the same author:

Sally
Chloë
Polly
Cat
Fen
Pip

FREYA NORTH

Love Rules
Home Truths

HARPER

Harper*CollinsPublishers*
77–85 Fulham Palace Road,
Hammersmith, London W6 8JB

www.harpercollins.co.uk

This omnibus edition published by HarperCollins*Publishers* 2008
Reprinted 2008

A catalogue record for this book
is available from the British Library

Set in Sabon by Palimpsest Book Production Ltd, Polmont, Stirlingshire

Printed and bound in Great Britain by
Clays Ltd, St Ives plc

Love Rules

For Lucy Smouha, Kirsty Johnson and Clare Grogan
My glory is I have such friends.

Something's gotten hold of my heart
Keeping my soul and my senses apart

Greenaway/Cook

Mark and Saul and Alice and Thea

Mark Sinclair liked to think that there was an inevitability to happy-ever-afters. He believed that they were granted to those who were good in life, to people whose thoughts were honourable, who had worthy goals, whose deeds and dealings were principled. However, at the age of thirty, Mark Sinclair understood that he would need to modify his belief, revise his dream and compromise. He intended to do this without turning into a cynic or allowing his ethics to suffer. He'd just have to let his dream of twenty years fade. It wasn't going to be easy. But there again, the dream wasn't going to come true, no matter how virtuous he was.

Mark Sinclair's dream was Alice Heggarty. But she had gone and fallen in love with someone who wasn't him. Again. Just as she had at the age of twenty-five. And at twenty-three. And before that, annually at university. And before that, with the captain of the first XV at his school. The girl Mark had loved for so long had gone and fallen in love again but this time Alice was nearly twenty-nine. Mark knew she'd have made a calculated decision that this love ought to take her into her thirties and onwards, into matrimony and children and a house in NWsomewhere. The time was right for her own happy-ever-after. 'So dream on,' Mark told himself sternly, 'dream on.'

In the two decades he'd known Alice, Mark had always had hope because he'd always had the dream because, being a man of patience and principles, he'd taken a philosophical view on waiting. He theorized that Alice had never broken his dream because he'd never brought it out into the open. Besides, she'd been so busy, permanently falling madly in love and despairingly out of love with all those other men. At the time, Mark felt this to be a positive thing and he did not regret keeping his own feelings secret. After all, it meant that Alice had never made a decision against him, she'd never turned him down, never ditched him in favour of another, never suggested they revert to being 'just good friends'.

As lovers charged in and stormed out of her life, and as

girlfriends breezed into his and left quietly, their friendship had remained unscathed. Alice was never possessive of Mark and Mark accepted her periodic disappearance into the fast eddies of new love-lust. Indeed, Mark had always found it encouraging that Alice went for a type – and that the type she went for was the antithesis of him. It meant she'd never fallen for someone like Mark; she'd always gone for men who were diametrically opposed to all that he was. Tall, loud, movie-blond beefy blokes with heartbreaker reputations or ice-beautiful arrogance Alice was convinced she could conquer and melt. Consequently, Mark could not feel jealous of the men in Alice's life though he envied them Alice. Rather, he was irked that they were delaying his personal happy-ever-after.

Very very privately, he was also relieved that invariably it was they who left her. Looking after Alice with her heart all hurt was actually even more rewarding than being in her company when she was hyper-effervescent with the distractions of love. Though it scorched Mark's soul to see her distraught, he knew he could make her feel better. It was a job he could do brilliantly. And it augmented his hope. Because when his dream came true, he'd never leave her. Of that she could be as sure as he was.

Whereas Alice rushed headlong into love affairs, Mark merely dabbled in what he believed to be just an interim after all. Now, with Alice in love once more, yet again not with Mark, and given their respective ages, he acknowledged, sensibly, that an interim was a period between two points and that there really was no point in holding out for Alice. Because he loved her, and because he'd been privy to her teenage turmoil and twenties torment, he wanted only peace and fulfilment for her in her thirties and beyond. Even if her joy and contentment meant he'd never have her cry on his shoulder again.

Mark was happy for Alice, but he was not so altruistic not to be sad for himself. He had believed, mistakenly, that if he lived well and worked hard, if he was honourable in his thoughts and actions, his reward would be all he had dreamt of. Reluctantly, he had to accept that good behaviour and a belief in the potential of one's wishes ultimately might not win the prize. Neither Alice, nor the Man Who Will Marry Her, were at fault or to blame. And, just because he now no longer believed in happy-ever-after didn't mean the future need be misery-for-evermore.

He was going to moderate his desire without seeing compromise as a tragedy. He'd have to stop letting down gently all those lovely girls after the fourth or fifth date. He'd need to see the wider picture and take a view. There had been two or three he had liked enormously. Previously, when he'd reached the stage of thinking of them fondly, planning holidays, masturbating in their honour, browsing Liberty for trinkets of his affection, an image of Alice glancing at her watch had always sprung to mind. As if she was waiting for him. And though the lovely girls were let down gently, all wished to remain friends. Mark, as Alice once told a girlfriend who was single, was one of life's great good guys.

Mark was a good person because for twenty years he had always believed that if you are a good boy, all your dreams come true.

* * *

Saul Mundy stumbled on his Road to Damascus at roughly the same time that Mark Sinclair stepped resignedly onto his. Saul had been with Emma for three years when he met a pretty and friendly blonde in a bar. They chatted and smiled and flirted lightly. Saul had no true desire for her, no intention of asking for her number or grabbing a furtive snog. Until that night, he had quite enjoyed the occasional, harmless, forgettable flirt because his affection for Emma and monogamy had remained unsullied. That night, however, it wasn't that he wanted the blonde, it was that he didn't want Emma.

He blanked the blonde, made hasty excuses to his friends and stumbled out in a daze onto Tottenham Court Road. The sudden clarity of the situation was ugly but he knew he mustn't look away. If he did, complacency would wheedle in soon enough and honesty would be replaced by betrayal. Saul wouldn't let that happen. He believed in doing the right thing and he was going home directly to do so. He had to, he was committed. It would be far easier to stay than split, far easier to act fine than confess, to hide than confide, but Saul's belief in his relationship had gone and the only honourable thing he could do was go too. Waiting for a taxi, he shivered and sheltered in a shop doorway, gazing at the rain-sluiced pavement. It looked polished to perfection, like a meticulously varnished floor. Actually, it was just grey concrete that was wet and grimy. The truth was it was dull, no matter what tried to cover it. Surface details were worthless if the integrity of structure was lacking. Saul couldn't believe that the last three years of his life amounted to a comparison with London pavement.

That morning, he had left the house to go to work. Now he was returning only to leave home. Had he kissed Emma that morning? He couldn't remember. Would the offer of just good friendship be a possibility or a cowardly digression? Would she believe him when he said that he was so sorry, that he did love her and felt wretched for hurting her? That it wasn't her, it was him? Would she believe him that he truly felt she deserved more than he could give? That he didn't mean to sound exactly like all those articles in the women's mags she pored over in her long bubble baths and that he browsed through when he'd forgotten to buy an *Evening Standard*? He doubted it.

He had the taxi drop him off on Upper Street and he walked, reluctant but resigned, towards the house, to Emma blissfully unaware, sitting beside the home-fire she'd kept burning.

'I don't burn for you any more,' Saul whispered, eyes closed, forehead resting against the door frame, 'and I should. It's a prerequisite. I can't compromise.' He couldn't even summon a spark of it from the deepest recess of his soul. His heart might be warm for her, and would continue to be, but he was absolutely sure that it wasn't enough. He wished there was a kinder way of being so seemingly cruel. But to use a cool head to decipher his heart would give the cleanest cut, though he knew that all Emma would read written all over his face was Heartless. Saul put his key in the front door for the last time.

* * *

A decade before Mark and Saul had their epiphanies, Thea Luckmore had hers when Joshua Brown ditched her at Alice Heggarty's eighteenth birthday party. It was irrelevant that he proceeded to snog Rachel Hutton in the kitchen. It didn't matter that Alice, incensed, had poured Woodpecker cider over his head and told him he was a wanker who should fucking fuck off. It wasn't even that Joshua no longer wanted her, it was that Thea was still in love with him. She didn't ask Alice how she could win him back, instead she asked her what she should do with all the feelings of love.

Alice suggested getting off with Joshua's mate to piss him off.

'But I don't feel anything for him,' Thea had qualified.

'Exactly, it'll be easy,' Alice had encouraged.

'Alice,' Thea balked, 'I can't kiss someone I don't feel something for.'

Though Joshua Brown's friend would have done anything for a snog off Thea, Thea decided then and there that unless she experienced a shudder of desire for someone, unless she could detect potential, unless her heart swelled approvingly, she'd be keeping her kisses. Warmth or revenge were not enough. She realized that it was the love she had for Joshua that was the point. Despite the fact that he was a cad. She'd read enough Austen to know that love was a good thing and, whether it made one feel wonderful or wretched, it was her ultimate requirement for a fulfilled life.

It was the dyed-dark drama student who captured Thea's heart during her second year at Manchester University. Though she was never quite sure whether he was proclaiming his innermost feelings or reciting his lines, she adored him and was glad to lavish love on him. They smoked dope. They had his-and-hers unkempt pony-tails. They made vast vats of ratatouille. They found deep and meaningful tenets in Joy Division. They rejoiced in the intensity of their world of Us. They went InterRailing together during the summer vacation and slept on beaches, watched sunsets and professed to truly understand e. e. cummings. He fell out of love with Thea just before her finals a year later, citing that love was life's torment and proclaiming the wring of his feelings was a headfuck.

'Did he actually say "headfuck", Thea?' Alice asked, not sure whether it was interference on the Cambridge–Manchester phone line or Thea's sobbing.

'Yes,' Thea said, 'but he also said that his love for me was so all consuming—'

'– that it threatened to devour him?' Alice interrupted. 'Life is love's torment or vice versa?'

'Yes!' Thea gasped, comforted that Alice had obviously been in such a situation herself, no doubt with that third year from Trinity with the double-barrelled surname.

'Did he say something about only the winds of time could determine where his seed would fall and take root?' Alice asked.

Thea paused. 'Yes,' she said, hesitant.

Alice continued gently. 'Do you remember that God-awful theatre-thing, that art-performance-bollocks you dragged me to when I visited just before Christmas?'

'Yes,' Thea wavered.

'He was performing his friend's prose poem?' Thea didn't reply. 'You were gazing at him too adoringly to actually hear any of it, weren't you?'

Thea's broken heart clanked heavily against a sudden twist of mortification in her stomach. She was speechless.

'Thea,' Alice continued quietly but firmly, 'I promise you, you'll find love again. And I promise you one day you'll laugh about this one. We both will. We'll laugh until we pee our pants. Trust me.'

Alice always kept her promises and she was the one person Thea always trusted. Alice, it turned out, was quite right. Memories of Headfuck Boy continue to provide them with much mirth and they can still quote his friend's prose poem verbatim. Headfuck Boy did not cause Thea any lasting damage, nor did he in any way alter her belief in the virtue and value of falling head over heels in love. Thea Luckmore was not one to compromise.

* * *

Alice had her epiphany over a bowl of soup, ten years later – just a few months after Mark and Saul had theirs. She left her office near Tower Bridge, grabbing new issues of magazines just arrived from the printers. Though she'd never intended to take public transport anyway, the whip of November chill that accosted her outside further justified the taxi.

'Chiltern Street, please,' she told the cabbie, 'the Paddington Street end. You know, off Baker Street.'

'And do you tell your granny how to suck eggs?' the cabbie teased her. Alice looked confused. 'It's my job, love,' he continued jovially, 'the Knowledge? Short cuts? Crafty back-doubles? Bus lanes? I do know Chiltern Street – amazingly enough.'

'Sorry,' Alice said meekly, 'I didn't mean to.'

She thought how Bill absolutely detested her habit of giving directions if she wasn't driving. In their early days, he had gently teased her, even indulged her. A year on, it now irritated him supremely. 'Which way do you want to go then?' he'd give a henpecked sigh before they'd set off. And if Alice's route proved circuitous, or with a proliferation of speed bumps, or beset by roadworks or vengeful traffic lights, he'd let his stony silence yell his disapproval and annoyance.

'I'm not a control freak,' Alice said out loud, not intentionally to the cab driver but not out of context either. 'It's not an obsession, it's just a trait of my character.' She gazed out of the window, about to ask him why he was going along the Embankment rather than via Farringdon at this time of day. But she bit her lip. Was it a loathsome quirk of her personality? Should it be something she should resolve to change? She could feel her tears smarting and prickling. She'd kept them in check all morning and her throat ached from the effort. 'Here!' she unintentionally barked at the taxi driver who swerved and shunted to a standstill in response.

'Can you tell Thea I'm here,' she said to the receptionist in Thea's building.

Thea's 'there there' was precisely what Alice had come halfway across London in her lunch hour to hear. The sound of it triggered the tears. 'There there,' said Thea again, and Alice cried all the more. 'Let's get some soup in you,' Thea soothed, guiding Alice to Marylebone High Street.

Alice sipped obediently. 'I'm going to sound like Headfuck Boy,' she admitted, after a few spoonfuls, 'but if I don't end it now, it's going to consume me. And I'll end up all spat out. Again. I'm just so tired.' Though Thea knew her friend's face by rote, objectively she noted a sallowness to the complexion, a flatness to the eyes, cheekbones now too sharp to be handsome, a thinness attributable to stress rather than vanity. 'I'm nearly thirty,' Alice concluded in a forlorn whisper. 'When am I going to learn?'

'You're not fretting about *that*, are you?' Thea asked, due to turn thirty a month before Alice.

'Look at this,' Alice said, showing Thea the new copy of *Lush* magazine. 'It's the "Alice Heggarty This is Your Life" issue.'

Thea read the cover lines out loud. '*More Shoes Than Selfridges.*' She looked at Alice. 'But I've never known you to buy a pair and not wear them out. '*A Chef in the Kitchen, A Whore in the Bedroom.*' Thea patted the cover of the magazine: 'Why, that's a skill others envy you.'

'Look!' Alice declared. '*Falling For Mr Wrong.*' She jabbed her finger at the magazine. '*Passion Drove Me Insane*,' she proclaimed, '*Lovelorn or Lustaholic.* For fuck's sake, I'm meant to be the publisher – not the inspiration for every sodding article.' She sighed and continued in a quieter voice, '*Lush* is directed at the early-twenties market, Thea. I'm basically thirty and *still* slave to all these insecurities and issues.'

'Bill,' Thea said darkly, buttering a doorstep of bread and dunking it, watching the satisfying ooze of butter slither off the bread and dissolve into the soup.

Alice covered her face with her hands. 'If I say it out loud, it has to be real,' she said, 'if I look you in the eye, I can't hide from the truth.' She laid her hands in her lap and regarded Thea. 'He's Mr Wrong,' she whispered, 'it's as simple as that. I'm exhausted. I'm a lovelorn lustaholic and passion is driving me insane.'

'Gentle sympathy or hard advice?' Thea asked.

'You're my best friend, I need you to tell me what I need to know,' Alice said, 'even if it's not what I want to hear.'

Thea regarded Alice levelly. She tipped her head to one side. 'You're right,' she shrugged, 'Bill is Mr Wrong.' Momentarily, Alice felt like springing to Bill's defence only Thea jumped in first. 'In Bill's defence,' she said, 'he's a gorgeous and charming man. With a great car. Physically, you make a beautiful couple. But your relationship is ugly.' She'd witnessed enough blazing rows, spiked sarcasm, hostile silences and relentless bickering to speak with authority.

'It's been such hard work,' said Alice, stirring her soup as though it was a cup of well-sugared tea, 'constantly trying to safeguard his love and lust for me. Even though, sometimes when I get it, I don't actually want it,' Alice confided. 'I hate feeling so pathetically insecure, when actually I don't think I really like him anyway.'

'He is what he is,' said Thea fairly, 'gorgeous and aloof and rich and a sod.'

'It seems we're always playing some horrid power game – either I'm the one who's pissed him off or else I'm in a manipulative sulk with him.' Alice paused. 'We just ricochet from his stony silences to my flouncy strops. It's exhausting.'

'The renowned playboy,' Thea told her, 'he was captivated by your feistiness but to be honest, he'd be better suited with a bimbo or a mousy-wifey.'

'Could change?' Alice said meekly and with some ambiguity.

'You or him?' Thea asked pointedly. 'Don't you dare go compromising. And what would you change *him* into? And don't say a frog.'

But Alice was off on a tangent, gazing into the middle distance, reinventing Bill. Or, rather, creating an entirely different man simply clad in Bill's likeness. 'Someone calm. Someone who adores me and I'll never doubt it. Someone who won't mind the way I'm a back-seat driver. Someone who makes me feel safe, someone who won't cause me panic when I find their mobile phone is switched off. Someone who won't play games.

Or play around. Someone who won't flirt in front of me. Or when I'm not around.'

Or with your friends, Thea thought to herself remembering more than one occasion when Bill had paid her a little too much attention. They scraped their soup bowls with their spoons and then used the last of the bread to swab them dry.

'I would have finished it months ago,' Alice said, dropping her voice to a whisper, 'but in some ways it was easy to become addicted to the fabulous passionate making-up sex which always concludes our rows. But you know what? We rarely have sex unless it's concluding an argument. And we've never, ever, made love.'

Thea snorted. 'I haven't had sex, made love, shagged, fornicated, humped or mated for eleven months!'

'You and your daft standards.' Alice laughed a little. 'I'm surprised you don't just take yourself to a nunnery and be done with it.'

'Christ,' said Thea, who was actually an atheist, 'I love sex. I'm dying for a fuck. I'm just not so desperate as to lower my standards.'

'Do they actually have to proclaim their romantic intentions, their degree of wholesome love before you'll permit entry?' Alice teased.

'Piss off!' Thea joshed. 'You've missed my point. *They* can feel all they like, they can compose poems and do the bended-knee routine. But if *I* don't burn for them, if *I* don't feel that spark – no chance.'

They ordered tea for two and cake to share.

'You're in love with love,' Alice said, dividing the gateau with her fork and offering Thea the choice of portions, 'while I lust for lust.'

'Sounds like a magazine article, if ever there was one,' Thea said, choosing the end of the wedge, rather than the point.

Alice glanced down at the cover of *Lush* and gave a little snort. '*From Heartbreak to Happy-Ever-After – 7 Steps to Take You There*.' She paused. 'Perhaps I ought to practise what I publish.'

The girls skimmed through the relevant article. Neither of them thought that Number 1 *Time for a New You – Go for a Funky New Hairdo!!* was the answer. Nor was Number 2 *Flirt with Your Best Mate's Brother!!* a remotely feasible idea. Thea's older brother was a densely bearded academic who rather unnerved both girls. Numbers 3 and 4 dealt predictably with *Take Time and Make Time for Me Time!!!!* and *Rebound Repercussions – A Quick Shag is Not a Long-Term Fix!!!*

'Number 5 is interesting, though,' Thea remarked, '*It's Not* Who *You Love It's* How *You Love!!!*'

'I detest exclamation marks,' Alice said. 'I'll have to have a word with editorial.'

'*Change What's on Your Wish List!!!*' Thea read out Number 6. 'Perhaps there is some sense in rejigging your requirements, Alice?'

'What about you?' Alice retorted. 'Why do I have to do all this personality-dissection, inner-feeling workshopping?'

'Because I'm happy being celibate while true love eludes me.'

'You must have the Rolls Royce of vibrators,' Alice murmured.

'Well, you'd know,' Thea countered brightly, 'you bought it me.'

'Got it free,' Alice stuck her tongue out.

'Should've kept it for yourself then,' Thea gurned back.

'Number 7,' Alice returned to the article, '*Blink!!! He Might be Standing There, Staring You in the Face!!!!*'

'The postman!' Thea gasped with mock eagerness.

'That guy from the ad agency we use,' said Alice, with genuine enthusiasm. Thea regarded Alice sternly, but Alice licked her lips and winked. And then, like a mist descending, anxiety dulled her eyes and turned her mouth downwards. It was just a magazine article anyway, with too many exclamation marks and a target market half a decade younger than them. 'I'll finish it with Bill tonight,' Alice said, quietly but decisively, 'I bet he won't even care.'

'I think he does care about you,' Thea said, 'but I think you're doing the right thing. I'd better go, I have a client in five minutes and I mustn't have cold hands.'

'Will you be around later?' Alice said, her face fragile and her voice wavering. 'In case I need you?'

'Of course,' Thea shrugged, as if it was the daftest question to even think of asking your closest friend.

* * *

So it turned out that Mark Sinclair was right. He was so right that, for some time, he would quietly wonder if something must be wrong. Alice Heggarty *was* to be married, just as he predicted, by the time she was thirty. Actually, she would turn thirty-one on honeymoon because her meticulous attention to detail and aversion to compromise meant the wedding was shunted to accommodate seamstress, florist, venue and cake-maker. Though, normally, she liked to have her birthday planned to perfection too, she didn't actually know where she would be when she turned thirty-one. That was up to the groom and she had relinquished some responsibility to him in return for assurances of untold luxury. After all, she was not so secretly dreaming of the Caribbean.

All that Mark had wrong was her choice of groom. Alice wasn't going to marry Bill. In all other respects, though, Mark had been absolutely right. It turned out that if you are good, you can indeed earn yourself a happy-ever-after. Obviously, Mark Sinclair must have been very very good. Because Alice Heggarty was going to marry him.

Thea Luckmore

Thea Luckmore's twelve-o'clock client, a fit man in his mid-thirties, groaned under her. She kept the pressure steady and insistent until she could feel him yield, sense the tautness of his body ebb away, the grimace on his face ease into an expression of relief. She rolled his flesh between her fingers. Under her hands, he now felt as soft as his appreciative sigh. She lightened her touch and changed rhythm and direction as a wind-down. Finally, she placed both palms on his bare back, between his shoulder blades, and inhaled deeply. She closed her eyes, feeling warmth interchange between them. She exhaled quietly but deeply and opened her eyes.

'OK,' she said softly, lifting her hands away very slowly, 'there you go.' She wondered if he had fallen asleep.

'Can't move,' he muffled, his face buried in the bed, 'amazing.'

'I'll leave you to rest and get dressed,' said Thea as she closed the door quietly behind her and went to wash her hands. She ran her damp fingers through her hair, giving her short, gamine crop what her mother termed 'an Audrey Hepburn nonchalance, darling – if Audrey had been mouse-brown'. Thea hadn't had hair long enough for a pony-tail since Headfuck Boy of her student days.

'God, that was good,' her client grinned, handing over £50 though he would gladly have doubled it. 'Can I have you again next week?'

The session had drained Thea; her bones felt soft and her joints felt stiff. Often, the clients for whom her treatment had the most extreme results were those whose negative energy she absorbed in the process. Which is why they felt so energized and she felt so sapped. She flicked her hands as if trying to fling something away, shook her arms and legs and splashed cold water on her face. She could climb on the bed and sleep for an hour, which was tempting, or she could pull herself together and step out into a gorgeous spring day. Thea Luckmore always tried to do what she felt was right, even if it wasn't quite what she felt like. So she opened the sash window to air the room and went out for a brisk walk. With an extravagantly stuffed sandwich from Pret a Manger, she strolled to Paddington Street Gardens and had an impromptu picnic with a copy of *Heat* magazine for company and light relief.

Her phone showed two missed calls from Giles. And a voicemail message. Thea felt burdened. Giles was nice enough. 'But not nice *enough*,' Thea explained to a pigeon who was bobbing at a respectful distance within pecking reach of any crumb she might dispense. 'I've tried telling him that I value our friendship too much to jeopardize it by taking it further, but he saw that as a challenge rather than a gentle let-down.' Filling from her sandwich dropped to the ground. The pigeon, it seemed, didn't care for avocado. Patiently, it continued to bob and coo. 'I like him but I don't fizz for him. No spark – no point.' A slice of tomato was tried and rejected so Thea gave the pigeon more bread. 'I'm just going to have to be blunt with him. Tell him he's simply not my type. Not that I really have a type.' She watched the pigeon wrestle with her chewy granary crust, fending off the pestering of other birds. 'Just a feeling.'

Thea wasn't expecting her six o'clock to come early – she'd expected him to be at least ten minutes late. She'd developed a theory, based on ample evidence over the years, that her clients tended to be early in the winter months, when inclement weather and darkness by teatime saw them jump in cabs to arrive early yet apologetic, as if sitting quietly in the waiting room, thawing out, was somehow taking a liberty. Come the spring, her clients would stroll to her, or jump off the bus a couple of stops early. They were simply not in so much of a rush to be indoors from outside. With this March being one of the warmest on record, Thea's clients were not turning up on time. Apart from this one. It was unexpected. But not half as unexpected as seeing Alice in reception too. Alice and the client were standing side by side awkwardly, both fixing her with a beseeching gaze like puppies in a pet shop competing for her attention. Thea mouthed 'one minute' to her client and with a tilt of her head, she beckoned Alice through to the kitchenette. Maintaining the mime, she raised one eyebrow to invite an explanation from Alice who thought, just then, that her best friend would make a very good headmistress. Indeed, Alice suddenly felt a little bashful, turning up and surprising Thea while her six o'clock loitered. She proffered a clutch of magazines. 'Here,' she said in a contrived, sheepish voice and a don't-beat-me look on her face, 'these are for your waiting room.'

'Are you all right?' Thea enquired in a discreet whisper.

'Fine,' Alice tried to whisper back but found that her smile of prodigious proportions caused her voice to squeak. 'I have something to tell you.'

'I'll be an hour,' Thea told her, glancing at the clock and seeing it was now six, 'perhaps quicker. He may not need the full session today.'

Alice waited in the kitchenette while Thea led her client upstairs, small talk accompanying their footsteps. Then she returned to the waiting room and removed magazines by any rival publisher, arranging her copies of *BoyRacer*, *HotSpots*, *GoodGolfing*, *FilmNow*, *YachtUK*, and *Vitesse*. Something to cater for all of Thea's clients, she hoped. She sat and waited, fidgeting with her hair, twisting her pony-tail up into a chignon, then French plaiting it, letting it fall in billows around her shoulders. She smiled, remembering how, when they were young and horse mad, Thea would marvel that Alice's flaxen hair really was like a pony's tail.

'It's so thick and amazing!' Thea would say.

'It's a bother,' Alice would rue, 'I'd prefer your soft silky hair.' Thea would brush Alice's hair smooth, utilizing a technique they'd been taught at the riding school – holding the bunch in one hand whilst softly, gradually, rhythmically, sweeping strands away. Finally, she'd take the bunch in one hand and spin it before letting it fall, wafting down into a tangle-free fan.

'If we were ponies, you'd be a palomino and I'd just be a boring old roan,' Thea had said, without rancour.

'Then pull out any dark hairs!' Alice exclaimed. 'Apparently, palominos can't have more than twelve dark hairs in their tail.'

Even now, Thea automatically searched Alice's hair. Though, if there were any rogue dark hairs to pluck, Alice gave her West End colourist an earful. She was still flaxen, but the glint and shine of her pre-teen hair now required strips of tinfoil and banter with the colourist about holidays and soap operas, for two hours and a small fortune every two months.

Thea's six o'clock all but floated down the stairs at ten to seven and paid cash for the Cloud Nine privilege. Alice waited behind a copy of *BoyRacer* until Thea came to her.

'Ready?' she asked.

'Nearly,' Thea replied, 'I just have to tidy my room.'

'Shall I come?' Alice suggested. 'Help?'

'If you want!' Thea laughed.

Thea's room, at the top of the building, though small in terms of square footage, appeared airy and more spacious because of the oddly angled walls and Velux windows. It was also painted a very matt white which appeared to obscure the precise surface of the walls and gave the small room a sense of space. Underfoot was a pale beech laminate floor. A simple white small melamine desk with two plain chairs in white frosted plastic were positioned under an eave. The bed was in the centre of the room. Shelves had been built in the alcove and they were piled with white towels. Three baskets, lined in calico, were placed on the bottom shelf and filled with potions and lotions in gorgeous dark blue glass bottles.

'It's lovely since it's been redone,' Alice said. 'Did all the rooms get the same makeover?'

Thea nodded. 'New beds too. It's a great space to work in – our client base has soared.'

Alice pressed down onto the bed as if testing it. Then she looked beseechingly at Thea. 'Go on, then,' Thea sighed, raising her eyebrows in mock exasperation, 'just a quickie.'

'Is that what you say to your clients?' Alice retorted. 'Seriously,' she whispered, 'do they *never* get the wrong idea?'

'What?' Thea balked. 'And ask for "extras"?'

'Most of your clients seem to be gorgeous sporty blokes,' Alice commented.

'Fuck off!' Thea objected. 'I'm a masseuse, I specialize in sports injuries, I barely notice what clients look like – all I'm interested in is the body under my hands and how I can help to put it right. Anyway, sporty beefy isn't my type.'

'Yes, yes – you don't have a type,' Alice said, 'just a feeling.' She and Thea caught eyes and laughed. 'Well, I tell you, I wouldn't mind copping a feel of some of your clients.'

'Well, you're a filthy cow,' Thea said, 'and I'm a professional with standards.'

'Have you let Giles into your pants yet?' Alice asked, taking off her top.

'No way,' said Thea, 'not my type.'

'You'll be a virgin again soon,' Alice remarked as she silently slipped her shoes off and unzipped her skirt. She eased herself onto the bed, lying on her stomach. She placed her face into the hole of the padded doughnut-ring at the head end.

'OK,' Thea said softly, 'let's have a feel of you.' She placed her hands lightly on Alice and then began to work. Within moments, it felt to Alice as though a troupe of fairies was travelling all over her back, lifting her shoulder blades and dusting underneath, doing synchronized roly-polys down her spine, breathing relief in between her vertebrae, unfurling the muscles around her neck, marching over her biceps, soothing her scapulae, giving her hip-joints a good spring clean. She hadn't had a massage from Thea in ages. Guiltily, she recalled how dismissive she had been when Thea had announced years ago that despite her first-class geography degree, she was going to train as a masseuse.

'Pilates has had a really positive effect on your back,' Thea declared, bringing Alice back to the present, 'but you should check the ergonomics of your desk, chair and screen at work.'

Slowly, Alice sat up. Her face was flushed and her eyes were gently glazed with relaxation. 'You're a genius,' she declared woozily, 'you have healing hands.'

Thea, however, snorted almost derisively. 'Don't be daft,' she said, 'they're just "helpful hands" – if you want truly healing hands, you want to have Reiki with Maria. Or Souki's acupuncture. Or have Lars tutor you in the basics of Feldenkrais. My massage is more a satisfying after-dinner mint to the main course served by the other practitioners.'

'Would you just give yourself some bloody credit, girl,' Alice said, almost angrily. 'You didn't see the look on your last client's face. Blissed-out is an understatement.'

'I didn't need to,' Thea shrugged, 'I felt his back say thank you all by itself.'

'Can I make one tiny suggestion?' Alice asked. 'Ditch the plinky-plinky rainforest music in reception. It made me want to yell and wee simultaneously.'

Later that night, Thea sat up in bed, flicked on the bedside light and looked at the clock. It was in fact the early hours of the next day. She couldn't sleep and she knew the worst place to be was her bed. She pulled on her fleece dressing gown and padded out of the room. The brutal change from soft carpet to cold floor tiles still unnerved her though she'd lived with it for four years. By the time she reached her small kitchen – a matter of only a few steps – her feet had acclimatized to the tiles. She made a cup of tea and went through to the sitting room and the comfort of carpet once more. Her mother liked to say that the flat was placed around a sixpence and it made her quite dizzy. The perpetually cold central hallway, small indeed and basically circular, was the hub off which the other rooms radiated. The bedroom, the kitchen, the sitting room, the bathroom. Standing in the hallway with all the other doors shut and surrounding you was a slightly disorientating experience. But Thea loved it. 'It's my little slice of Lewis Carroll Living,' she'd proclaimed to her mother when begging her for a loan for her deposit. Viewed from the pavement, the side of the building where Thea's flat was located was a turreted, cylindrical add-on to an otherwise unremarkable Victorian exterior.

'A satisfying expression of Gothick-with-a-k,' Thea's usually serious and conservative older brother had declared with surprising approval, 'don't you think so, Alice?'

'I reckon your sister just wants her Rapunzel moment!' Alice had said.

Thea scrunched her toes into her shaggy rug and sat down, hugging her knees. She didn't drink the tea – the ritual of making it and cupping her hands around it had been the thing. She saw her mobile phone on the sofa and reached for it. It was on and a text message was unopened.

u r happy 4 me?!! Say u r!! xxx

course I am!!! Thea replied. brill news – u deserve hap-ev-aft! Xxx

Though Alice's news was undoubtedly brilliant, Thea was still somewhat overwhelmed by the shock of it. She thought back to Alice linking arms with her and hauling her off to Blandford Street for sushi.

Guess what!

What?

You'll never guess!

What?

Guess!

What? Don't tell me! Don't tell me! That bloke from your ad agency?

I'm getting married!

That bloke from your ad agency?

No, silly. No! Mark Sinclair!

Mark Sinclair?

Yes!

Mark Sinclair?

Yes! *Yes*!

Mark Sinclair?

Yes, Thea, Mark Sinclair!

Does he know?

Alice hadn't met someone. She'd found someone. Those had been her words and she was effervescing with excitement, exclamation marks now peppering her speech.

'I found someone! I'm getting married. Fucking hell! Can you believe it! I've *found* someone!'

Initially Thea was gobsmacked into jaw-dropped silence but Alice's animation was infectious. Though baffled by the simple facts that Alice was now engaged, that Mark Sinclair was fiancé, and though stunned by the speed of it all, Thea soon spun into Alice's excitement. She sketched wedding-dress possibilities on serviettes while Alice, flushed and gesticulating, re-enacted the entire proposal before launching into list-making.

'You know what? I can't believe I didn't think of him earlier. I mean, I've known him for ever! I've always loved him. Because he's always *always* been there for me.'

Thea agreed. Mark Sinclair had always always been there. She knew him, of course, without really knowing him at all.

The lovely guy who always made Alice feel better, who had always been there for her when some cad or other had done her wrong. With hindsight, Thea recalled the gaze he'd bestowed on Alice now and then over the years which, at the time, she'd interpreted as brotherly affection. After all, it was Mark who had shared with Thea the job of looking after Alice when some Lothario had broken her heart again. Mark who had gladly taken Alice out to lovely restaurants or opening nights at the theatre when she was without a date and down in the doldrums. Mark who'd been at the other end of the phone as Alice's late-night insecurity guard. Mark who assured Alice that not all men were bastards, that there were fish in the sea aplenty and she was the prize catch. Thea had been grateful to him for this. Without ever really having had the forum to tell him so. Well, she could now. Here was one man she'd never have to take to one side to threaten that if he hurt her friend she'd kill him. He was the absolute antithesis of Alice's previous pick. That's why it was such a shock. Such a revelation.

And yet it made sense. Since breaking up with Bill, Alice had indeed had a quiet, sometimes pensive few months. Maybe she had made a conscientious decision to practise what she published. Perhaps it really was as easy as reassessing her wish list. Blinking and seeing that the man to marry was standing right in front of her. Learning it's not who you love, it's how.

'But how long have you been seeing him? I mean, how come I didn't know you've even been seeing him?'

'Two weeks. Don't shout at me, Thea!'

'Two *weeks*? And now you're *engaged*?'

'Be happy for me – or you can't be bridesmaid.'

'Of course I'm happy for you, idiot. Ecstatic. I'm just shocked. Two weeks?'

'He's perfect. What was the point of waiting? Kind, considerate, calm – there are no safer hands in the world for handling me.'

'Are you madly in love with him? With Mark Sinclair?'

Alice looked at Thea. 'You do know that feeling of "madly in love" is merely phenylethylamine, Thea?' Alice said with a sigh. 'It's just a natural amphetamine – which is why it's addictive. It's the same hormone that's released during high-risk sports and eating chocolate.'

'Whatever,' said Thea, 'but you need to be in love with someone to actually marry them.'

'So fiction and films would have us believe,' Alice said.

'There's more to marriage than being head over heels. In fact, my feet are firmly rooted and my head is now out of the clouds and firmly on my shoulders – that's why I know it's going to work. I'm ready for this.'

'And you do love him,' Thea said.

'Everyone loves Mark,' Alice smiled, 'he's one of life's good guys.'

'And you love him,' said Thea.

'I'm the love of his life. And he's my love for life. That's why we're marrying. What more could I ask for?'

Now, contemplating quietly in the conducive early hours, Thea likened it to Alice having a good tidy-up and coming across something she'd forgotten all about. Like something never worn, bought on impulse, never even tried on, pushed to the back of a cupboard, then rediscovered. A perfect fit, it transpired. A delightful surprise. What disconcerted Thea was that she hadn't ever thought that when Alice did her tidy-up, she'd find Mark. What unnerved her most – and she could now admit it in the silence and privacy of her space – was that she was actually slightly taken aback. Alice had brought Thea the best news in the world. But for the first time in their friendship, she'd done so without the need to ask Thea's advice or seek her opinion first.

Mark Sinclair

Mark Sinclair had an aptitude for diplomacy and an instinct for manners. They hadn't been drilled into him at home, he hadn't learnt them at school or been trained in them after university. They were simply part of his personality and throughout his thirty-two years they had won him friends and influence. These qualities, combined with a head for figures and a heart with a strong work ethic, saw his rapid promotion through the hierarchies at ADS Internationale for whom he worked as an investment analyst. He was invaluable to them. He could speak languages, keep calm under the pressure of City finance, didn't get drunk over business lunches, never fell out with colleagues or associates, travelled uncomplainingly and trained his immediate team into an efficient, likeable unit. The company had no need to incentivize him and every reason to reward him which they did, handsomely.

Whoever met Mark, wished to befriend him. It helped that he was fluent in Spanish and French, passable in German and Italian, and that his work took him abroad frequently. A full Filofax and a packed Palm Pilot kept track of his worldwide friendships. He was a terrific host when people came to London. He'd stock the fridge for them, tailor a list of sights to see, and provide his membership cards for a variety of museums. He'd meet them after work, having secured great seats at theatres or enviable tables in top restaurants. Mark was also a wonderful guest – as comfortable sleeping on the bottom bunk of his godson's bed in Didsbury as he was staying in palatial grandeur in a suite at the Peninsula, Hong Kong. He loved hiking hard in Skye with his old friends the McLeods and he enjoyed putting the world to rights in French with his new friend at the Paris office, Pierre. He went on safari by himself in Kenya and made Jeep-loads of new friends there. He was a Friend of the Royal Academy of Arts and soon made friends at the Royal Academy. He had friends who'd invite him to Glyndebourne and others he'd accompany to Glastonbury. Mark Sinclair was open-minded, kind-hearted and plain good company. He hated confrontations and far preferred to bite his tongue than fall out with anyone he cared for. An even keel was what he aimed for. Which is why he had so many friends but not actually one best one.

Alice looked at Mark expectantly. She smoothed her white shirt, flicked her hair back, cocked her head and regarded him again.

'Are you ready?' he asked, while patting his pockets to double-check on keys, wallet, mobile phone. 'Shall we go?'

'But how do I *look*?' Alice said, standing her ground a little petulantly. 'Will they approve? Do you think I should wear a skirt instead?'

'You look gorgeous,' Mark assured her, congratulating himself on the earrings he'd bought her. 'You look – brown?'

'Thea did my fake tan,' Alice said, with no embarrassment. 'I felt a bit pale and peaky from my cold last week – I don't want your mum to think you're not looking after me. Do you think your parents will approve? Do you think they'll like me? I hope your mum is a good cook – I'm *starving*.'

'Of course they will,' said Mark, 'who wouldn't. Come on. Mum's Sunday Roast is legendary – but don't touch the white wine. They only do Liebfraumilch.'

Gail Sinclair busied off to the kitchen to prepare the dessert, turning down Alice's keen offer to help. Gail was delighted. Better still, she was charmed.

'Charmed, absolutely charmed,' she practised quietly to herself in the kitchen whilst decanting Marks & Spencer custard into a jug and carefully transferring their cherry Bakewell onto her best cake dish. *Charmed*, she continued in a whisper, *Alice is delightful, Hazel. Absolutely winning to look at. A magazine person. She brought us copies – a real variety, Mary. She dotes on Mark, Carole – absolutely dotes on him. Chris and I couldn't be more happy.*

'She's a cracker,' Chris Sinclair, who'd never mastered the art of the whisper, told his son; while Alice sat to his right and tried to look as though she wasn't eavesdropping. Gail heard, even though she was at a clatter changing their everyday crockery for the best china. *Chris thinks she's a cracker, Joyce, and I know you'll agree once you've met her.*

Alice reckoned Chris to be in his mid-sixties, dapper despite the patterned sweater and corduroy slippers. Thinning silvery hair cut neatly, bright eyes, elegant hands and a healthy complexion due to his love of golf and gardening. She reckoned Gail to be five years younger, her hair cut into a short, neat style appropriate for her age, any grey expensively masked by an overall coppery sheen. While Mark talked to his father about PELS and Gail poured Marks & Spencer's coulis into another jug, Alice thought how best to describe Mark's parents and his childhood home to Thea. 'Refreshingly nice,' she would probably say, 'just normal, nice people.' She stifled giggles into her serviette, predicting how she and Thea would then analyse the mothers of boyfriends past. Callum's mother who wore the same Whistles jeans as her own but a size smaller, Finlay's mother who'd insisted Alice call her Mrs Jones despite allowing them to sleep together. Tom's mother who was insanely jealous of his affection for Alice and would thus drape herself over him quite alarmingly for the duration of their visits. But Mark's parents seemed to be simply nice, ordinary people.

'You look like your dad,' Alice suddenly announced though

it momentarily halted conversation and fixed Gail's cake slice mid-air. Alice was happy to predict that in thirty years or so, the man seated opposite her, whom she was soon to marry, would look a little like the gentleman currently seated to her left.

Charmed, Gail thought to herself again, *charmed*.

Chris and Mark browsed the Sunday papers while Gail poured coffee and Alice effervesced over the beauty of their garden.

'God, I completely love your verbena.'

'Viburnum,' Gail corrected lightly. 'Have you a garden?'

'Well, at the moment, I'm restricted to what the lifestyle mags call *patio living*,' Alice said. 'It's basically a small, glorified back yard covered with cream gravel and pots with plants that die on me on an annual basis. And twisty wire furniture that looks amazing, cost a bloody fortune and is bloody uncomfortable.'

Gail looked at Alice without expression at much the same time that Alice thought to herself shit! Is 'bloody' swearing? And Mark jerked up from the *Sunday Times* thinking oh shit, she bloody swore.

'Perhaps once you're married, you'll find a house with a garden,' Gail said diplomatically. 'Herbaceous borders pretty much look after themselves and perennials do just what they're meant to do.' She took a thoughtful sip of coffee. 'They needn't be expensive either.' See, no need for 'bloody'.

'Lovely idea,' said Alice warmly, helping herself to another chocolate because she noted that Gail was on her third.

'Now, I want to hear all about the proposal,' Gail said expectantly, 'all the romantic details.'

'Mum –' Mark remonstrated, raising his eyebrow at his father for sympathy and assistance.

'Did he get down on bended knee?' Gail asked. 'Did he take you to a restaurant and have the *maître d'* present you with a diamond ring?' Mark groaned but Alice giggled. She thought Gail probably had the makings of a rather good mother-in-law. 'Perhaps he whisked you off to Venice for the weekend and popped the question aboard a gondola?'

'Last week,' Alice grinned over to Mark who was attempting to disappear behind the *Sunday Times*, 'at Mark's flat. He was cooking that amazing chorizo and butterbean casserole thing with the six cloves of garlic. We had a glass of Rioja. I was eating a carrot.'

Gail had never been a fan of garlic, let alone Spanish peasant fare, but she tried to look enthusiastic.

'It struck me, it simply struck me that it was the best idea ever,' Alice said dreamily.

'Yes, but how was the question itself *popped*?' Gail persisted. 'Mark's father whisked *me* to Paris expressly to propose.'

Alice grinned. 'It was quite matter of fact, actually,' she said, 'I had to turn down the radio to be heard. It all made such perfect sense. Even though I had a mouth full of carrot, I just looked at Mark and said "Marry me, Mark, marry me." He looked at me as if he was having difficulty understanding my language. So I swallowed the carrot, repeated the question and added "please". Still he stared. And then he said yes.'

Gail stared at Alice as if she had difficulty understanding her language. Chris just stared. 'What's that on your shirt?' Gail exclaimed, looking horrified. 'On the collar and cuffs? It's brown.'

'What?' Alice looked at her collar and cuffs. 'Oh bugger!' she declared. 'It's fake tan. I'll bloody kill Thea.'

'Do you think they liked me?' Alice asked Mark as they drove away.

'Of course,' Mark assured her, concentrating on the road, biting his tongue on being cut up by a man with a sharp haircut driving a car that was obviously meant to look like a Porsche but was glaringly not. Alice gazed out of the car. She pressed her cheek against the passenger window. She needn't have had the fake tan – the wine at lunchtime, the effort of being on best behaviour had made her feel quite warm. She looked at the trees, some bursting into leaf, others in full blossom. She'd learn the names of lots of plants by the time she next met Mark's parents. And she'd try not to swear.

Saul Mundy

Saul Mundy had assumed he'd buy a sensible two-bedroom house in a popular postcode, take out a mortgage with Emma and have a leg-up onto the London property ladder. He had been thinking about Brondesbury or Tufnell Park or Ealing as safe bets. But then he hadn't been thinking about breaking up with Emma. Twelve hours after the relationship ended, Saul signed a short let on a top-floor space in central London, a location he'd previously never considered as residential. It was uncompromisingly open plan, and he reckoned the landlord had probably marketed it variously as office space, storage space, apartment or studio according to the potential tenant's requirements. Saul chanced upon it en route to a meeting in Baker Street and rented it because it was available that afternoon and had a view he knew he'd never tire of, a privileged panorama of the city from a vantage point available to few. He need never elbow his way onto a crowded Tube again. And with upmarket delicatessens such as Villandry on his doorstep, he need never resort to frozen meals again.

When the short let expired six months later, Saul bought the place, having unexpectedly fallen for the charms of city-centre living and having learnt to cook at an evening course run by Divertimenti a stroll away. Twelve months on, Saul has become a dab hand at property improvement and is quite the house-proud DIY-er. He partitioned the expansive area with a curved wall of opalescent glass blocks, dividing the space by a sinuous line into attractive and practical zones. Privacy in an arc for sleeping; an ample and quirkily curved section in which to relax and a clever paisley-shaped bud concealing his home office. He'd mosaiced the bathroom, laid funky rubber flooring in the kitchen, and given great thought to lighting. He loved it.

And he loved the location. He hadn't stepped on the Northern Line for eighteen months. He swiftly attained an enviable knowledge of the capital's hidden secrets and the added advantage of living so centrally was that soon enough he was known and warmly welcomed at them all. Consequently, he was never ripped off at a convenience store. He had no need for a car and therefore never had parking fines or the Congestion Charge hanging over him. Marco, who owned the sandwich shop and deli, let Saul park his scooter under cover for free. He was always guaranteed a table for breakfast at Bernard's Café, usually with the day's papers presented to him too. At lunchtime, Marco always over-filled Saul's sandwich and if it was Maria serving, she'd slip in a chocolate brownie for free. He never suffered a lousy curry. Or a dodgy Thai. Or disappointing sushi. Even if he was out of change, Dave on the corner would still have Saul's *Evening Standard* for him, ready folded. He was able to secure just what he wanted, at the best possible price, during the sales, before crowd-swamping made shopping unbearable. He never had to resort to an All Bar One. He'd never been in a Pitcher & Piano. He didn't have to fight his way through bars thronging with over-excited and over-made-up office girls, or over-indulged and over-the-limit City smart arses. He could have the liveliest and latest of nights out without ever being ripped off by a minicab, he could just stroll home. So, when Saul's friend Ian Ashford called and suggested a night out, Saul was able to say that he knew a great little place to meet.

The Swallow, nestled between a printing shop and an iron-monger's along one of the little streets forming the tight clasp east of Great Portland Street, was an old-fashioned hostelry. It appeared unprepossessing enough from the outside to safe-guard against clientele other than locals and regulars. The drab paint, the windows seemingly in need of a basic wash to say nothing of new frames, were a shrewd exterior to protect an interior that was actually bright, cosy and spruce. The place was not big and resembled an elongated sitting room; the bar itself was confined to one corner and cramped enough for the staff to be unable to serve side by side necessitating an intricate but effective *pas de deux*. Whilst one pulled a pint or reached for a whisky glass or discussed the runners at Kempton Park, the other would look over his shoulder to take the next order. And then they'd change position with a courteous glide. A coal fire murmured away constantly from November until March. From May until September, the back door was permanently open to a small patio complete with its own grapevine, increasing the pub's interior capacity of twenty-eight seated and six standing to a further twelve standing. On Tuesdays, Wednesdays and Thursdays, sausages and mash were available. At other times, peanuts and crisps were complimentary.

At the Swallow, though no one actually knew what anyone actually did or where they lived, the atmosphere was congenial and every now and then, a sense of community emerged. Arthur gave everyone a great tip for shares to be bought in a new Internet start-up. Lynton offered Marlboro cigarettes for less than half the shop price. When Barry's flat was broken into, his home was restocked courtesy of the staff and clients at the Swallow. Eddie's cousin owned a locksmith's concession and sorted out new security. Anne ran up two new pairs of curtains for Barry because the burglars had ripped down his to use as sacks. Lynton knew someone who did CD players on the cheap and as they owed him a favour, he secured one for Barry for free. But Saul earned himself complimentary pints for a month. Not that free drinks were Saul's motivation to provide Barry with more CDs than he'd owned in the first place, an electric shaver, an electric toothbrush that retailed at twice the price of the shaver, a digital camera, an Alessi teapot and a lava lamp.

'Blimey, mate,' Keith the landlord had marvelled, pulling Saul a Guinness on the house, 'is all that kosher?'

'You got a little shop or something?' asked Barry, hugely grateful but also quietly wondering what else Saul had. 'Or you got the back of a lorry?'

'Knock-off?' Lynton quizzed, defensive but interested.

Saul had laughed. 'It's kosher, Lynton, your patch is safe, mate! I'm a writer,' he shrugged, knowing he'd told them before at some point. 'I'm sent stuff all the time to test and review. Mostly, they don't ask for it back. I've had a 42-inch plasma since the summer.' Barry glanced up hopefully from behind the ziggurat of CDs. 'They've only just asked for it back,' Saul continued, 'they're talking about installing a home cinema for me to test next.' Saul was called everything from lucky geezer to jammy bastard and the wish-lists of the staff and clients at the Swallow were discreetly presented to him.

So, when Ian Ashford phoned Saul, Saul suggested the Swallow as perfect for a mid-November, mid-week drink, with perhaps sausages and mash if they fancied.

'Jesus, it's been a while.' Ian shook Saul's hand warmly, nodded and grinned. 'What'll you drink?' he asked, glancing around the Swallow and nodding approvingly.

'I'll have a Stella, thanks,' Saul replied, reciprocating Ian's amiable nodding with a friendly punch to the bicep. 'Good to see you,' Saul said warmly, 'it's been bloody ages. Where've you been?'

'Otherwise engaged,' said Ian. He watched Saul take a long drink. 'Literally,' he added. He winked, sighed and took a swig of beer. 'Engaged.'

'Work been a bitch, then?' Saul enquired.

'Work?' Ian said. 'I'm *engaged.*' Again he winked and raised his eyebrows along with his glass when he saw the penny drop for Saul.

'Christ!' Saul exclaimed. 'Bloody hell,' he raised his glass and drank urgently before chinking Ian's, 'bloody hell – and there was I thinking you've been up to your eyes in some crucial trial at the Old Bailey when all the while you were waltzing up the road to eternal love and heading down the aisle to domesticity!'

'You sound just like your column,' Ian protested, 'don't you go featuring me.'

'Here's to you and Liz. Congratulations,' Saul said, with genuine affection.

'Er, I'm engaged to Karen,' said Ian. 'Lizzie and I broke up.'

'Bloody hell,' Saul said. Though he hadn't expected Ian to be engaged, he certainly hadn't reckoned on it being to anyone other than Liz.

'I left Liz for her,' Ian said lightly.

'Bloody hell,' Saul said darkly.

'I know,' said Ian guiltily, 'I know.' He sipped at his beer and looked into the middle distance. 'I always thought it would be Lizzie. Then I met Karen and there was no contest. No conscience, even. It's what you'd call a "no-brainer" – I had to be with her. Simple.'

'Bloody hell,' Saul said, his vocabulary sorely limited by the shock of Ian's news. He downed his drink thirstily. 'Another pint?' He went to the bar, ordering sausages and mash at the same time. 'How's work?' Saul asked Ian on his return, a packet of crisps between his teeth.

'Oh fine,' said Ian, 'manic. Karen's a lawyer too so she totally understands the stress and long hours issue. She works in Litigation. At Tate Scot Wade.'

'Right,' said Saul, 'right.' He didn't want to dislike Karen before he'd even met her, he didn't want his affection for Liz to colour his acceptance of her. But he couldn't help but resent Ian's surprise fiancée for dominating the conversation thus far and for having monopolized his friend in recent months.

'How about you?' Ian asked. 'What's happening?'

'More work than I can do – but I can't turn any of it down,' Saul laughed. 'I love it. Mostly.'

'Karen's a fan of your column,' Ian said, 'we both are.'

'Which one?' Saul asked, genuinely flattered.

'*ES* magazine – it's so much more than a consumer low-down. It's like a little slice of your life – very self-effacing and engaging. Well written, too.' Ian chinked his glass. 'I chuckle but you have Karen in stitches.'

'Cheers, mate,' Saul said, 'cheers.'

'And you still have your regular slots in the men's mags?'

'Yes,' said Saul, '*GQ* have expanded my section. I do the gadgets pages for that new mag, *Edition*, my columns for the weeklies and the odd bit of roving reporter here and there, some editorial consultancy for launches on the side.'

'Don't suppose you've any iPods knocking around?' said Ian, who could easily afford one but loved the idea of a freebie. 'Any cool press trips? Golf in the Algarve? Scuba anywhere?'

'Just the one iPod,' Saul said, 'and as for press trips, there was Bermuda for sailing and Sweden for sledding. By husky. And a lost weekend in Prague with Sonja from the Tourist Office.'

'You jammy bastard,' Ian laughed.

'Three thousand words, though I had to censor most of it, thanks to Sonja,' Saul said, as if it was an occupational hazard.

'And how about *you*?' Ian asked again, with a concern Karen had taught him how to access. Saul tucked into his sausages, nodded and shrugged. He'd rather have his mouth full than talk. 'Are you seeing anyone?' Ian asked, partly because Karen had told him to.

Saul chewed thoughtfully. He shook his head. 'Not at the moment,' he said, wishing for more mash.

'Anyone on the horizon?'

'Why?' Saul laughed. 'Has Karen a queue of luscious friends?'

'Actually,' said Ian, 'yes.'

Saul shrugged. 'Cool,' he said, 'why not. There hasn't been anyone since Emma. I'm not sure if I count the tryst with Sonja.'

'Blimey,' Ian said, 'we're talking a good eighteen months, mate. Sounds like celibacy to me.'

Saul shrugged again. 'You know me,' he said quietly, 'I can be quite choosy.'

'Mind you,' Ian theorized, 'your social life is pretty lively and there are always relatively funky work do's on. I bet you don't even notice the absence of a girlfriend.'

Saul considered Ian's overview. 'Actually, it's not so much that,' he said thoughtfully. 'I'm quite into the idea of a steady partner – even the concept of commitment. However, I just can't be bothered with doing the singles-circuit-dating games. It's too contrived.'

'Too time consuming,' Ian agreed, 'and expensive.' God,

he thanked his luck for Karen. 'Mind you, celibacy must be a bit bloody frustrating.' He raised an eyebrow.

'I do what a lot of other blokes do,' shrugged Saul.

Ian shrugged back. He also made a mental note to provide Karen with a current description of Saul to circulate amongst her friends. He'd heard Karen refer admiringly to similar hair-styles as 'bed hair' and no doubt she'd declare the colour of Saul's to be like caramel or something. He noted his friend still had a thing about trendy footwear and approved his Oris watch as an indication that Saul's career was going very well indeed. Armani soft black jeans. And a shirt he'd tell Karen was Paul Smith. They were already compiling their guest list for the wedding. It would be cosy if by then Saul attended with a girlfriend who happened to be a friend of Karen's. Ian glanced at his watch. 'I'd better be going, mate. Does this place not have last orders?'

'It's when the last person orders,' Saul informed him.

'It's good to see you,' Ian said, 'let's not make it so long, next time. Come over to ours. Karen is a great cook. You'll love her. I'll call you.'

Saul sat on alone in the Swallow with another pint. Lynton sat by himself too. And Barry was on his own tonight as well. They all nodded amiably at each other but were quietly content to sit separately. That was what Saul loved about the Swallow, its concept of relaxed companionship, that it wasn't necessary to cramp around the same table to be in warm company. Saul looked over to Eleni, snuggled against her boyfriend. He reckoned he was their age or thereabouts. When Anne, the wife of the landlord, had brought over the two plates of sausage and mash, she'd ruffled Saul's hair maternally. He reckoned she was close to his mother in age.

Saul walked around the corner back to his flat. He scanned through the draft of the article he'd be writing the next day and then logged off his laptop, content. There was nothing watchable on television. He thought he ought to run a bath – he'd been sent products by Clarins For Men to test. All that talk of women and wives and girlfriends and his own barren situation had left him quite hollow and horny. So he decided to do what a lot of other blokes do. He'd lie in a bath later. He grabbed his jacket and went back out into the night.

Alice Heggarty

I keep singing the corniest of songs. 'I'm Getting Married in the Morning!' In the daftest of voices. 'Going to the Chapel and We're Going to Get Ma-ha-ha-rid.' The daftest of songs in the silliest of accents. I even sang 'Nights in White Satin' in the cab today. It struck me, for the first time, that it was actually 'nights' and not 'knights'. And then I was absorbed for at least an hour wondering why it had never previously crossed my mind that a knight got up in white satin would be pretty odd in a heterosexual love song.

Anyway, I am *going to be married in the morning. Thanks in no small part to the girls on* Dream Weddings *magazine and Mark indulging me, it's going to be a fairy-tale wedding. I'm feeling deliriously excited – but a bit stressed too. I'm even feeling a bit pissed off – like I want everyone to continually pat me on the back and acknowledge how much hard work I've put into it all. We only got engaged in March, after all. Eight months later, and I've researched and secured the flowers, the dresses, the venue, held auditions for the band, even written the vows. I want it to be the best day of my life. And Mark's too. And I want it to go down in the annals of the guests as the best wedding they've ever been to.*

I must pack for honeymoon. Initially I wanted the destination to be a surprise, but I pointed out to Mark that I'd be a stroppy cow if I packed salopettes and we arrived in Bermuda. Actually, I just pressed and pestered him because I really did need *to know. It's not that I'm a control freak, though I suppose I am, it's just that I know myself well enough to admit that I'm a nightmare if I'm disappointed. So, if I was going to be disappointed, at least I could've had the chance to get over it in advance. Shit, OK, if I have to admit it, I might have subtly persuaded Mark to change the plans if need be! Anyway, bless him, Mark must have picked up on all my not-so-subtle hints and he is whisking me away to St Lucia. A helicopter to the Jalousie Plantation between those two iconic Piton mountains you see in the films, in the brochures. They know we're honey-*

mooning so hopefully they'll lay on all sorts of little extras. I am going to be princess for a fortnight. And why not – because when we get home, I'll be just boring old Mrs Sinclair!

They gave me a great send-off at work. They must have had quite some whip-round as they've gone for the Gaggia coffee machine from the wedding list. Anyway, all my mags will be fine – they can spare me for a fortnight but if they need me, I've told them they can phone the Jalousie.

I'm getting married in the morning. Bloody bloody hell. Ding dong. I really really am. I'll be thirty years old. And fifty-one weeks. I, Alice Rose Heggarty, am going to marry Mark Oliver Sinclair in approximately twenty-three hours' time. How do I feel? Still a touch peaky from my hen-night! I feel ready, actually. Everything is going according to plan. All I need to do is turn up and say 'I do' and look ravishing. I want Mark to feel that he's the luckiest bloke alive. I feel good. There really is no better man for me to marry. Lovely dearest Mark. He'll look after me and cherish me and keep me safe. None of those other wankers ever did. It's so lovely not to worry. It's a novelty for me. It's so wonderful to be loved so unequivocally. Unconditionally. No one could possibly love me more – so what more could I possibly ask for? Tomorrow I'm going to be the bride of his dreams. I'll make sure I cry a little when I say 'I do' because I know he'll love that.

I'm so happy Thea is staying over with me tonight. I can't wait to snuggle up with her and have hot chocolate with marshmallows and reminisce about our olden days. My best, beautiful friend. My bridesmaid. My only bridesmaid. Me being me, I'm glad out of the two of us I'm the first to wed. Just recently, though, I've been hoping that perhaps she'll not be too long behind. Whereas I'm now the first to admit I used to fall in love with a type – and the wrong one – I've seen that my path to happiness necessitated me walking off course. And in doing so, I came across my kind, gentle Mark. Who'd have thought it? Who'd have thought!

I think, at our age, after the highs and lows experienced through our twenties, the time comes to alter your focus, a shift in perspective. I decided to turn my back on a view which actually gave me little joy. I want Thea to take a leaf out of my book – we're similar and yet so different. I hated ever being single – I used to wait until a replacement was a dead cert before breaking off an already failed relationship. Thea, though, would rather be all on her tod than dally with someone she doesn't experience her elusive spark for. It's actually infuriating – I've introduced her to a couple of Mark's friends who are really nice, successful, balanced blokes. But in each instance Thea has said 'He's really nice – but he doesn't do it for me.' I know she's hardly on the shelf, but still I don't think she should be so choosy. I wish for her all that I'm headed for. Though, if I'm honest, as nice and successful and gentlemanly as Mark's friends are, I concede they are just the tiniest bit dull. Just the tiniest. Well, I'm not marrying them, I'm marrying Mark Oliver Sinclair.

I've just thought – when Thea marries, I won't be called her 'bridesmaid'. What is the term? Something like Lady of Honour? No no – that can't be right – that sounds like an eighteenth-century hooker attempting to turn her life around. Lady in Waiting? No no – that's what royalty have and although I'm princess for a day tomorrow, my delusions of grandeur are not *on that scale! Matron of Honour? Damn and bugger. That's it, that's what married women in bridesmaid capacities are called. Bloody Matron. God, it sounds horrendously frumpy. But there again, by the time Thea gets her act together, I'll be the definitive boring old housewife! Maybe we can fix her up with Mark's American cousin tomorrow.*

Thea will *so fixate on the notion of a dashing hero – it's her yardstick and she resolutely refuses to alter the scale. I've tried to tell her that in my experience – and especially my discovery through Mark – it doesn't really work like that. But she won't believe me. She doesn't want to think that growing up is about understanding that love's no longer about falling in love. I say to her ah, but look where it's got me – getting married in the morning and deliriously happy about it. She'll figure it out, I guess, like I did.*

* * *

Jesus, it's here. It's the day of my wedding. I have exactly seven hours to go. How on earth am I going to make time pass? I only need to have my hair done and put my make-up on and then my dress. Not even I can make that last seven hours. I slept pretty well, actually. Thea's the best bed-partner a girl can have because she doesn't snore, she doesn't toss and turn and she always recounts the funniest dreams. Last night she dreamt that the groom was Bill but that I didn't notice and she couldn't make her voice heard because my veil was

30 feet long and wafted all around her like cheap bubble bath and tasted like marshmallow.

We tried for ages to find some deep significance to her dream but we concluded she ought to keep away from sugary snacks and that Bill wants to be where Mark will be but will die a lonely old bachelor. Thea brought me breakfast in bed; a tray laden with pain au chocolat, orange juice, tea and a blush-coloured rose. She keeps calling me Miss Almost Sinclair and Nearly Mrs. I told her I wished I could take her on honeymoon – and I do! I want to be able to run around the bathroom with Thea getting over-excited about all the gorgeous toiletries and sumptuous thick towels.

People keep phoning and asking if I have last-minute doubts, or if I'm a bag of nerves. Actually, I feel pretty level-headed about everything. I'm excited. About my dress. About seeing all the people. OK, yes – about being the centre of attention. Bring it on, I say – all is planned to perfection so bring it on. Yes, I'm full of butterflies but they're fluttering in excitement and anticipation, not swarming with trepidation or nerves. This isn't just my big day, it's huge. I'm going to a wedding in four hours' time and it's my own and I can't wait.

I'm meant to be having a lie-down – that's what Thea suggested. She's just in the bath – she was happy to have my bath water. I do love my flat but it does make sense for Mark and me to sell our flats and buy a marital home. One with a hot water tank big enough for more than just one bathful. A house with a ready-matured herbaceous border in the garden. Tell me there isn't a catch. That life can be this blessed. I need to double-check the cab to take us to the hairdresser's.

I love my hair! Manuel is amazing. Thea's looks gorgeous too. She actually had hers trimmed today – I just had the blow-dry of my life. Her hair is gleaming, slightly shorter than usual, cut into the nape of her neck and tucked behind her ears. I hate the way she says it's boring and mousy. Anyway, she looks like a fusion of Audrey Hepburn and Isabella Rossellini. I've had this beautiful grip made for her – a single orchid. I can't wait to see her in her frock. We chose A-line in crushed velvet the colour of buttermilk; slightly empire under the bust, a low, square-cut neck and wide straps just off the shoulder. I seriously almost wept when I saw her in it. She looks divine. My mum just phoned in some unnecessary flap or other. I *spoke to Dad and diplomatically asked him to intervene on any further calls she might be tempted to make. I'm glad the car will take just Dad and me. And I know Thea will cope fine with Mum. I wonder how Mark is. We spoke when Thea was in the bath. I was meant to be having a little lie-down but I couldn't keep my mind still enough for my body to relax. He sounded fine. He said yes to every single thing on my Double-Triple-Check And Check Again List. He was laughing. He loves my quirks. I hope he likes my hair all heaped up like this. In fact, I wonder whether to warn him in advance that if he touches it, it's grounds for an immediate annulment. Whoever thought that hair could feel so heavy! Maybe it's the little pearls that they've pinned into it. Fake. Not that you'd know. In fact, I'm getting a stiff neck from admiring the back view in the mirror.*

Thea came to say it's time to get dressed. She's a glorious vision in the pretty panties and bra we bought from Fenwicks for her. We bought my undies from Agent Provocateur. Mark will blush. I love it that Mark blushes at my sexiness. If he wore glasses, he'd be the type they'd steam up on. Thea and I have set the dress out on my bed and we have twice gone through the precise order that things must go on, be stepped into, have laced up and smoothed down. So I'm stepping in. And slipping my arms through the sleeves. And Thea is lacing me up. And smoothing me down. We've gone quiet. We're listening to some play on Radio 4 but I couldn't tell you what it's about. I don't know how to describe the feeling of my dress. I don't want to use clichés. It's duchesse satin, blush coloured – the colour you'd imagine a child's kiss would equate to. The sensation on my body is like a loved one gently, adoringly, whispering to my skin. I almost daren't look in the mirror. Thea's finished the lacing and smoothing and her eyes are welling up. She's just nodding at me. Nodding. And biting her lip. And nodding some more. With her eyes all watery and her nose now red. I'll have a look. In a minute. I'll turn around. I'll have a look now. I'll have a little look at Alice Heggarty in her wedding dress.

Hullo, Daddy. Hullo, hullo. Oh my God – the car is amazing! Let's tell the driver to drive round the block a couple of times. I ought to be five minutes late. Ten, preferably. And we must remember not to stride up the aisle. Mum will kill us. And please please don't say anything to me that'll make me cry. Don't call me your little girl. I am your little girl but if I hear it from you today, I'll cry and want to run all the way home.

I can't hear. I can't hear a thing. I'm watching lips move over the vows I helped pen. I know it all off by heart. But I can't hear. I'm ever so warm. Actually I feel a bit hot. Mark is saying things. Pardon? It's my turn. I have to say something. Something for everyone to hear. I know this bit. I know what to say. Please don't let my voice croak.

'I DO.'

Thea and Saul

Thea Luckmore had a remarkable constitution when it came to alcohol. Guts of iron, Alice called it. For some, this would be their downfall. For Thea, it was no big deal. She didn't regard it as a skill, or a gift; nor as a demon to keep at bay, or an affliction to be wary of. She could simply drink as much as she liked, become talkative and effervescent until the small hours yet maintain the presence of mind not to snog indiscriminately, to remember where she lived, to take off her mascara before she went to sleep and to awaken with energy, a clear head and a fresh complexion. Just occasionally, however, a hangover befell her which reminded her that alcohol could be rather a bore. A hangover for Thea bore no relevance to the amount drunk the night before, it was attributable solely to champagne. And at Mark and Alice's wedding, Veuve Clicquot flowed as if it were lemonade.

So, while Alice was trying to procure an upgrade from Club to First on her first morning as a married woman, Thea was creaking open an eyelid, groaning and praying for numb sleep. When Alice and Mark left Heathrow, First Class, two hours later, Thea managed to creep carefully to her bathroom, take two Nurofen and tolerate an invigoratingly cool shower.

Although it felt as if the inside of her skull and the rims of her eye-sockets were being maliciously rubbed with industrial sandpaper, that sawdust had stuck her tongue to her tonsils and that her stomach would never absorb any kind of food again, Thea was staggered to see from the mirror that she looked as if she'd had eight hours' sleep, a macrobiotic supper the night before and a challenging Pilates session.

She gave herself a stern look and vowed never to drink champagne again. She let the telephone ring and listened to Alice leave a message.

'Thea? I'm on the plane! I am 38,000 feet high! We're in First Class. Which isn't the reason I'm calling – well, it is. But also, would you mind popping into mine while I'm away – twitch the curtains and all the etceteras? Thanks, babes. Oh! By the way, one of Mark's cousins from America thought you were "hot". And I've given him your email address – apparently, he's over in Britain on business quite often.'

'I can't remember him,' said Thea, wondering if a warmer shower might be good for the cold sweat now gripping her.

'And if you can't remember him, he was the one you danced with on Top Table to "Lady's Night".'

'I was dancing on Top Table? Oh my God.' Thea groaned.

'You also danced with Jeff, one of my features editors. But despite his passion for mascara and glossy lippy, I don't think you were aware that he is in fact gay. And shorter than you. Anyway, must fly – oh, I already am! There's in-flight massage! Bye, darling, bye.'

A purpose was a very good idea. Thea had a purpose to the day. And after she checked on Alice's flat, she walked sedately to the top of Primrose Hill. The air was cold and cut through the fog in her head. The wind sliced across her face and elicited tears which refreshed her eyes. She was under-dressed for the weather but every time she shivered, she found that her nausea quelled. So she stood on the top of Primrose Hill, tears coursing down her face, shuddering violently at irregular intervals. And that was when Saul Mundy first saw Thea Luckmore, all silent tears and harsh, spasmodic shuddering. She was staring in the vague direction of St Paul's Cathedral but to Saul it seemed she was gazing deep into the nub of whatever it was that irked her so. It immediately struck him as peculiar that a seemingly unhinged person he'd never met was in fact capturing his attention. Even more bizarre was his instinct to take off his jacket and place it around her shoulders. He wanted to buy her soup. To sit her down. Though disconcerted, he felt compelled to linger. She seemed oblivious to her surroundings yet at the mercy of the elements. Trembling. Tears. Pale.

'Hullo,' said Saul, whether it was a good idea or not, 'chilly, isn't it.' He couldn't believe he'd chosen the weather as his opening gambit, but he was not in the habit of striking up conversation with a complete stranger, albeit an attractive woman who appeared intriguingly sorrowful. The only other thing he thought of saying was 'nice view', but he managed to resist.

Thea didn't dare turn her head for fear of upsetting the fragile balance she'd achieved. Even glancing down the hill, five minutes before, had made her feel dizzy.

'Look, excuse me for asking,' Saul continued, 'but are you all right?' *Fuck, now I sound like a bloody Samaritan.*

'Thanks,' Thea mumbled, 'I'm fine.'

'I don't mean to pry,' Saul said, though it would appear he was doing just that. She said nothing. She didn't look at him. This was so not his style and yet on he rabbited, grimacing at himself for sounding like an insipid do-gooder. 'I just don't like to see people crying and shivering and alone on a cold November afternoon.'

Oh for fuck's sake, thought Thea, *can't I just have my hangover in peace?*

'I'm fine, OK?' she grumbled. 'I have a sodding hangover. That's all. Go and rescue souls somewhere else, please. The devil's had mine and I'm a lost cause.'

Saul tipped his head back and laughed. 'I take back all my sympathy then,' he joshed. 'I was going to offer you my jacket. But hey, it's Armani. And anyway, your suffering is self-inflicted, enjoy!'

Carefully, Thea turned to regard the sartorial Samaritan. And she caught her breath. She had just discovered another component for Luckmore's Elixir for the Over-Indulged. Fresh air. Nurofen. Primrose Hill altitude. And a rather handsome guardian angel. 'Who are you? Some zealot Methodist?' she sparred back.

Again the man laughed. 'I'm Saul,' he answered, extending his hand which, to his surprise, she took, 'and Jesus Christ do you have the coldest hands. I can't lead you to the Lord because I don't know the way myself. Just take my damn jacket, would you?'

'I'm Thea and if it's all right with you, I will just have a quick go of your jacket.' Saul placed his jacket around Thea's shoulders. She thanked him with a slight smile that obviously caused her a little discomfort but was rewarding for him. 'It was my best friend's wedding yesterday. Champagne,' she said by way of an explanation and shrugged.

'And today you are resolving never to drink again,' Saul said, knowingly.

'Did you know they have telephones on planes,' Thea marvelled. 'Alice phoned me from 38,000 feet.'

'Technology, hey!' teased Saul, who'd made a few calls from even higher altitudes in his time.

'Amazing,' said Thea, earnestly.

'Sit down,' Saul said lightly, as if the park bench was his own for the offering. 'You'll find some Opal Fruits in my jacket pocket. They've changed the name to something else so if you're decades younger than me you won't know what an Opal Fruit is.'

'I'm thirty-one,' Thea said, sitting down gratefully, 'and I only like the red or yellow ones.'

The sugar rush from the sweets worked wonders. She must patent this cure. Fresh air, Nurofen, Primrose Hill altitude, a handsome guardian angel bearing Opal Fruits. It worked – Thea found she could turn her head with ease. Saul sat beside her. She gladly zipped up his jacket and settled into it. It was soft brown leather, lined with something warm. 'Gorgeous jacket,' she said gratefully.

'Don't you run off with it,' Saul cautioned, eyeing it as if regretting his generosity.

'Yes yes, it's Armani,' said Thea. 'Well, one thing's for sure – I am not capable of running anywhere today.'

'Are there any sweeties left?' Saul asked and Thea delighted in his childish terminology.

'Two greens and a red,' said Thea.

'Well, I'll be having the greens then,' Saul said with exaggerated selflessness.

Thea sucked the red Opal Fruit and hummed. '*Starburst*,' she said, 'that's what they're called now. What a rubbish name for them.'

'*Opal Fruits*,' Saul sang the advert of old.

'*Made to make your mouth water*,' Thea sang back.

'Er, would you like to go for a drink?' Saul suggested.

Thea looked as if she might cry. 'I shall never touch alcohol again,' she declared, 'even the term "hair of the dog" makes me feel nauseous.'

'Why do Americans call it "norshus"?' Saul pondered, unsure whether Thea had turned him down outright.

'I don't know,' Thea mused, 'norshus nauseous.'

'But there again, why do they say "math" and "sports" and we say "maths" and "sport"?' Saul digressed. 'Anyway, how about I buy you some carbohydrates and protein cooked in a pan over a flame?'

'Pardon?'

'I was worried the term *fry-up* might make you nauseous or even norshus,' Saul said, 'but I can recommend a nice greasy sausage, two eggs slightly runny, a mound of chips, a squirt of brown sauce and a blob of red as an excellent cure for the common hangover.' Thea groaned and paled visibly. Saul was amused but also disappointed. He quite fancied a cooked breakfast. Even at almost teatime.

'Perhaps more sweeties?' Thea suggested.

Saul regarded her and she regarded him straight back. She was accepting his advance. He'd struck lucky on Primrose Hill. Good God. 'You'd like me to buy you some sweets?' he verified. He looked at her. *Those eyes aren't watering, they're sparkling, the minx.* 'Opal Fruits?'

'Do you know what I'd really like? Refreshers! Do you remember them? They come in a roll, little fizzy things. Like compacted sherbet. If you chew a few at once, they fizz up and fill your mouth and bubble through your lips.' And Thea settled further into his jacket, dipping her face so that the collar came over her nose. *I can't believe I'm being chatted up on Primrose Hill.* 'Anyway, that's what I'd like: Refreshers.'

'Can I trust you to sit still and not bugger off in my jacket?' Saul asked. 'It's Armani.'

'So you keep saying,' said Thea. 'Are you sure it's not knock-off?' and she scrutinized the cuffs suspiciously.

'Fuck off,' said Saul because he knew she'd stay. He headed off down the hill, thanking God for hangovers and for friends' flats and for phones at 38,000 feet. As he walked back up Primrose Hill, a roll of Refreshers in his back pocket, her smile floated down to him.

'Refreshers, milady,' he announced, proffering them to her.

'I only like the yellow and pink ones,' she said.

'Suck or crunch?'

'Crunch.'

'Me too.'

They crunched and hummed and stifled the burps that scoffing the entire packet in a matter of minutes created.

'I'm thawing out now,' Thea said, 'and I ought to go home, I'm exhausted.'

'Thea,' Saul said, 'take my jacket. Seriously. Every man should have one Sir Walter Ralegh moment in his life. Please allow me mine. My mum would be so proud.'

Thea giggled at the thought of this man rushing home: *Mum! Mum! I was a gentleman today, I lent my jacket to a chilly waif. Do I get more pocket money? Can I stay up late?* 'But I'm fine,' she continued gratefully, 'my car is just over there.'

Saul shrugged and nodded. 'Yeah, but if I lend you my jacket, you'll have to return it,' he concluded with a hopeful trump card. Thea glanced at him and knew she blushed. 'Perhaps same place, same time, a week from now?' he suggested, unfolding and folding the foil from the sweets.

'OK,' said Thea, thinking to herself how Alice's mags would tell her to decline and play hard to get, or to suppress her grin for demure procrastination at the very least. But sod Alice's magazines. 'Same time, same place, next Sunday then,' she said.

'Good,' said Saul, smiling openly. He slid his hand into the jacket pocket, felt over and under Thea's fingers and retrieved his keys. Then he pulled the zip down halfway and slipped his hand into the inner breast pocket, taking his mobile phone. He could feel Thea's breath on his wrist as he pulled the zip up. He looked at her and thought he might suddenly find himself kissing her. But he shook hands with her formally instead.

'Until next week, then,' said Saul, standing.

'Next week,' Thea confirmed, making to move off.

'By the way, where do you live?' he asked.

'Crouch End,' she replied, walking off a step or two. 'You?'

'The West End, actually,' he said, heading down the hill. 'And what do you do?'

'I'm a masseuse,' she said, over her shoulder. 'You?'

'I write.'

Saul spent Monday against a deadline for an article on the new generation iPods whilst trying not to be interrupted by engaging images of Thea. On Tuesday with no deadlines looming, Saul searched 'massage north london' on Google but was led to questionable sites he didn't dare enter for fear of jinxing his PC with a sexually transmitted computer virus. By Wednesday, Saul thought sod it, it's only a jacket and it was a freebie anyway. Thursday came and he strolled to Armani to check prices on leather jackets. Jesus, that Thea better show up with it. He filed his column for the *Observer* and accepted a commission from the *Express* magazine. Saul spent Friday daytime avoiding thinking about jackets and Thea and Primrose Hill, and wrote all day. He went out in the evening with friends and confided to one that he'd met a girl in a park who looked cold and sad and said she had a hangover so he'd lent her his Armani jacket.

'The brown leather one?'

'Yeah.'

'You twat!'

On Saturday night, Ian Ashford invited Saul to meet Karen. And Karen had invited her friend Jo to meet Ian's friend Saul. And Ian and Karen had also invited Angus and Anna so that Saul and Jo wouldn't feel it was all a bit of a set-up. And dinner had been fun and Saul reckoned that if Fate was Friend not Foe, Thea would fit in well with his circle. And Jo was smitten and hoped Saul would phone her within the next few days.

Thea felt somewhat at a loss without Alice. Sally Stonehill was a close friend but Thea longed for Alice's take on the situation, for the dozen scenarios good, bad and downright fanciful she'd hatch. Thea was appalled at herself for daring to quietly resent Alice – or Mark rather – for their inconveniently timed honeymoon. However, Sally delighted in Thea's challenge and told her to return to Primrose Hill as arranged, but to hide behind a tree early and double-check Saul was worth handing back the gorgeous jacket. 'But if he's wearing black leather gloves – run,' said Sally seriously. 'Psycho.'

Sally's husband Richard thought Saul sounded shady, with or without black leather gloves, and told Thea not to go. Richard reckoned Thea should give the jacket to him instead and put a lonely-hearts in *Time Out* if she was that desperate.

'Or my mate Josh,' Richard suggested, 'he's still single.'

'I'm not that desperate,' Thea declined, while Sally made throwing-up faces behind Richard.

On the Tuesday, Mark's American cousin emailed Thea politely suggesting dinner when he was next over on business. Thea was still unable to conjure a memory of him but replied accidentally-on-purpose forgetting to give her phone number as requested. The next day, she went to Prospero's Books in Crouch End on the off chance that a book by a bloke called Saul might catch her eye. There appeared to be none on the shelves.

'Sally,' said Thea, 'have you heard of a writer called Saul someone?'

'Bellow?' Sally said. 'But your Saul may have a nom de plume, of course.'

'Say he's an axe-wielding homicidal maniac,' said Thea, 'and the police find bits of me all over Primrose Hill on Monday morning?'

'Well, as I said, steer clear of black leather gloves.'

'Maybe I won't go,' Thea said gloomily.

'Say he's not a book writer,' Sally mooted, because she liked the sound of Saul and his sweets, 'perhaps he's a journalist.'

'Maybe I'll go,' Thea said, non-committally.

On Thursday, Thea phoned her mother in Chippenham and suggested lunch on Sunday.

'Darling, I'm going to the Craig-Stewarts' for lunch this Sunday,' her mother said, a little baffled that her daughter was willing to drive down just for the day when Christmas was only six weeks away. Feeling slightly demoralized and in need of unequivocal advice, Thea wondered what Alice would say. She reckoned Alice herself would hide behind another tree on Primrose Hill and keep watch. If she wasn't otherwise engaged. More than engaged – fundamentally married and lying on the white sands of St Bloody Lucia.

'You're still all right to babysit Molly tomorrow?' Lynne phoned Saul on Saturday evening as he was leaving for Ian's. 'We can't take her to the Clarksons' wedding.'

Saul had forgotten. But actually, babysitting Molly was a very good idea. It was a cunning Plan B. He'd be on Primrose Hill whether or not Thea decided to turn up. 'No problem,' he told Lynne.

'We'll drop her round at yours first thing,' said Lynne gratefully.

* * *

Nothing conspired against Saul and Thea planning their trips to Primrose Hill a week to the day that they'd first met. Neither had nightmares the night before. Both had slept well and awoken feeling fine. The weather was glorious, a degree or two warmer than the previous week and sunny too. An autumn day in winter, as precious as an Indian summer in autumn. Thea decided she'd check on Alice's flat en route to further justify her trip. At Alice's flat, she took the liberty of borrowing her friend's cashmere jumper the shade of bluebells, leaving her own boring navy lambswool polo neck in return. She also helped herself to a spritz of Alice's Chanel perfume in case her own had faded by now. Thea checked her reflection and gave herself an approving grin. She had an inkling that this might be fun; a long-held belief in serendipity said it might be a good idea. She zipped up her jacket and folded Saul's over her arm. She held it to her face and inhaled. Then she stiffly told herself not to be so daft.

* * *

'Come on, Molly,' said Saul, 'best behaviour, now.'

* * *

Thea didn't have time to hide behind a tree. As she approached the crest of Primrose Hill, she could see Saul was already there, jacketless and grinning. She picked up her pace and walked towards him, quickly congratulating herself on how handsome he was, axe-wielding homicidal maniac or not. She saw he was gloveless and at that point she smiled and waved. However, when he waved back, it appeared he was carrying a belt in his hand. She was just about to read great tomes into this, wondering what definition Sally would give belt-brandishing, when Molly appeared. Hurtling. Yapping. Running tight rings around Thea. Thea screamed.

'Molly!' Saul half-laughed, half-shouted, loping down the hill towards them. 'Get down, your paws are all muddy and Thea – And Thea. And Thea – is crying.'

'Get the dog away!' she sobbed. 'Get it *away*.'

Saul was not used to being torn between the needs of two women. But there was no way that, just then, on Primrose Hill, he could relinquish either. All he could do was call out both their names, imploring Molly to come and Thea to stay. He wanted Molly to be still and Thea not to bolt. What would

Barbara Woodhouse have said? Heel? Down? Crazy hound? Paul bloody McKenna would be better.

'Molly!' Saul hollered. 'Heel! Come! Down! Stay! Sit, you crazy hound!' To Molly this was double Dutch, to the bona-fide dog owners within earshot, this was comedy. Molly was now careering around at speed, zipping through people's legs, barking joyously and returning to yap and skittle and leap at Thea who stood stock still, her fists squeezed together and clasped under her chin.

'She's not mine,' Saul shouted as if that made the situ-ation better. Molly was now transfixed by the backside of a King Charles Spaniel some way off and Saul crept over to capture her.

By the time Molly was safely on her lead, Saul could but watch Thea hurry out of the park. Beyond earshot. With his jacket.

'That'll teach me to talk to strangers,' Saul told Molly. 'I should know to steer clear of hysterical types who drink.' He decided to think of her no more. Nice jacket, though. That was a shame.

Barefaced Bloke and the Girl with the Scar

Thea went to Alice's flat to prepare it for the newly-weds' imminent return from their fortnight in Caribbean paradise. She took flowers, fresh milk and bread, opened windows, bleached the toilet, changed the linen and stacked the mail. Then she lit a scented candle and sat down with the *Observer* and a Starbucks cappuccino. It was nice to have a Sunday when she felt healthy and clear-headed, with no plans and no need of Primrose Hill. And it was comforting to think of Alice winging her way back. There was something relaxing about reading the papers in someone else's home, no distractions of chores that ought to be done or calls that should be made or fridges that needed restocking or tax returns lurking on the table.

The *Observer* on a Sunday was an institution; familiar, entertaining, non-taxing and sometimes vaguely irritating, like an old friend with whom Thea conversed once a week. She read it in a very particular order; main paper first, 'Review' second, then 'Escape'. 'Sport', 'Business' and 'Cash' were never read but not wasted, kept instead under the kitchen sink to absorb the slow drip from the washing-machine hose. This week, an interview with David Bowie in the bonus 'Music Monthly' magazine was particularly absorbing, rekindling memories of the shrine she and Alice had built in honour of Mr Bowie during their teenage years. Thea pulled out the article and placed it on top of Alice's post. The 'OM' magazine was Thea's favourite component, savoured last. The voices within the pages were as familiar to her as those on Radio 4. A restaurant close to where she worked was reviewed favourably so she tore that page out and folded it into her Filofax. The cartoon made her laugh out loud, so she ripped that out too and stuck it to Alice's fridge. Sage advice from Barefoot Doctor made her think. Mariella Frostrup made her murmur in agreement. But Barefaced Bloke's opening line made her swear out loud.

It was meant to be my Sir Walter Ralegh moment.

'Oh good God!'

Instead, it turned into a Dog Day Afternoon.

Barefaced Bloke was Saul. Saul Mundy. It said so in black and white. And a black-and-white photo confirmed it.

This week I give you the sorry tale of the Barefaced Bloke, the Gorgeous Thief, a Terrorizing Terrier and My Armani Jacket.

'He thinks I'm a thief!'

Well, you are, Thea. But he also says you're gorgeous.

I'm through with good deeds. I'm done with dog-sitting. I'll bet Sir Walter's jacket wasn't Armani.

'Sally,' Thea whispered down the phone, having speed-read the article, 'look at the *Observer* mag – and tell Richard I need that jacket back.'

At the time of writing, I can't tell you which way the tide will turn. Will Barefaced Bloke turn into Soft Git and clamber up Primrose Hill for the third Sunday running, hopeful but chilly? Or has Barefaced Bloke turned into Sod It Saul and stayed warm indoors with his X Box not giving a 4X?

'Saul Mundy is a *spunk*!' Sally declared. 'I *love* his column – and he doesn't look half bad either. Saul Bloody Mundy – can you believe it? Aren't you the lucky one!'

'I don't know whether to feel flattered or used,' Thea said sanctimoniously, 'and I'm not sure what to do.'

'Tell her I'm keeping the bloody jacket,' Thea could hear Richard in the background.

'Oh shut up!' Sally derided to both Thea and her husband.

Thea was actually fizzing with excitement but it seemed both arrogant and fate-tempting to admit it to herself, let alone Sally Stonehill, so she maintained her contrived ambivalence.

'Yes, but—' Thea attempted.

'Gracious Good Lord, girl, you're being flirted with through the pages of a national newspaper. It's possibly the most romantic thing I've ever heard of!' Sally said impatiently. 'Away with you to Primrose Hill! It seems to me his balls are in your court.'

Thea paced Alice's flat, then she sat down and reread the article.

I hope she likes the jacket. She looked far better in it than I ever did anyway.

Was he making a pass or taking the piss? Should she read between the lines or disbelieve what she read? Alice hurry home!

Ultimately, what could the Gorgeous Thief do but tramp up Primrose Hill for the third Sunday in a row?

He wasn't there.

What could she have been thinking?

Of course he wasn't there.

'I made good copy, that's all,' Thea said with reluctant resignation, having loitered for half an hour. Overhead, a scruff of crows littered the sky, like flits of charcoal coughed up by a bonfire. Thea found herself wondering if the crows were somehow goading the birds caged in the London Zoo aviary, just down the hill and over the road. Perhaps she'd take herself off to the zoo right now. She hadn't been for years. And it wouldn't make her afternoon seem so wasted. Did people go to the zoo alone? she wondered. Were you let in if you didn't have a child in tow?

'Where's my sodding jacket, you gorgeous thief?' a voice behind her halted her meanderings.

Thea did not turn to face him. 'My friend's husband has

now nicked it,' she replied, her eyes tracing the rise and fall of the aviary.

'Sod my Sir Walter Ralegh Moment,' said Saul, now pressing up close, enfolding his arms around her waist, 'and sod my image – I'm going for full-blown Mills & Boon.' And with that Saul turned Thea to face him, cupped her head in his hands and kissed her.

* * *

'Champagne, madam?' the stewardess asked Alice who was pressing all the buttons on her vast First Class seat whilst rummaging in its capacious pockets too.

'Absolutely!' said Alice. 'And can you pop my name down for the massage?'

'Certainly – would you like a massage too, sir?'

'No, thanks very much, but no,' Mark declined.

'Champagne?' he was offered.

'Thanks – but no.'

'Paper?'

'Yes,' said Mark, '*Sunday Telegraph*, please.'

'Madam?'

'*Observer*, thanks,' said Alice. '*Tory-graph*!' she teased Mark.

'Limp lefty!' he sparred back. Without having to be asked, he handed over his luxury complimentary travel pack for his wife to rifle through. By the time Alice had reached Saul's article, laughing aloud a couple of times, 38,000 feet below, the author of it was scrutinizing her best friend's scars.

* * *

'Fifty-four stitches,' Thea told him, 'from a weedy little terrier. The bizarre thing is, at the time, I was far more distressed that the dog was destroyed.'

Thea Luckmore had never before jumped into bed on a first date, let alone slept with a relative stranger. Moreover, she had hitherto guarded her scars as fiercely as her perceived chastity. Yet here she was, naked and post-coitally languid above the covers on Saul Mundy's bed, feeling more than fine while he traced the snaking line of scar that scored her waist and the top of her right thigh. He found the site and sight of her injury disturbing but intriguing. The scar was like a single line of pale pink silk braid laid in a particular route. It was obvious where the dog's jaws had clamped, where the teeth had punctured her, where her flesh had been ripped away and the flap carefully sewn back down. It was almost a cartoon scar, so perfect was the impression of the bite.

'I was twelve years old,' Thea continued, 'and it was Alice's dog. Tiddler. I've been petrified of terriers ever since.'

Saul rolled over and dipped his face down to her stomach. 'I'm not surprised,' he murmured, dipping his nose into her navel.

'I'm not too bad with Rottweilers, oddly enough,' Thea added while Saul let his lips touch her lightly, so gently that when she closed her eyes she couldn't tell if he was kissing scar or skin. 'Big dogs tend to lollop, little terriers just go berserk.'

'Your scar suits you,' he said. 'It tells a story – vulnerability behind the feistiness. If that doesn't sound too corny.'

'Corny?' Thea smiled. 'Anyone would think you were trying to get into my knickers. Again.'

'Horny,' Saul confessed, 'again. And anyway, where *are* your knickers?' he asked, glancing up at her from stroking her bush before returning his gaze and snuffling his nose down.

'I think you flung them off somewhere in your living room,' Thea giggled, but Saul was now too preoccupied to reply. He needed his tongue and his lips to explore Thea's sex. And Thea was now rendered speechless by the pleasure of it all. Their easy chatter gave way to gasps and moans and the seductive sound of her own wetness against Saul's mouth. She ran her fingers through Saul's hair, bending her knees up, shifting her hips and tilting her pelvis, rocking and undulating herself against his face. Instinctively, he let her dictate the pace and he didn't change what he was doing. His lips brushed her, his nose nudged her, his tongue flicked over and inside her. She looked down at him and he looked up at her briefly before closing his eyes to focus better. From previous experience, Thea had presumed cunnilingus merely to be a man's way to expedite lubrication and permit swifter entry. But Saul seemed to be enjoying himself very much if his appreciative hums were anything to go by. Thea eased his head away from her crotch to kiss and suck his face. They rolled and romped over his bed, his straining cock pressing hopefully, pressingly, against her. She pushed him onto his back, slithered on top of him, her sex just tantalizingly beyond the reach of his penis, her nipples a few inches away from his desperate mouth. She licked her own lips, then darted her tongue along his.

'For Christ's sake, fuck me,' Saul whispered.

'Condom,' Thea whispered, hoping he had another.

It occurred to both of them that it wasn't even yet evening. It was Sunday teatime. How decadent. It meant they could do this all night. Quietly, it occurred to both Saul and Thea that, actually, they could indeed do this as long as they liked. They had no commitments, after all. Not that evening. Nor the next. Not to anyone – nor had either for some time. It was all above board, with no complications. Out of the blue, from a chance daft meeting on Primrose Hill, the saga of a lent leather jacket, the fiasco with a lent harmless terrier, Saul Mundy and Thea Luckmore found each other.

Mr and Mrs Sinclair

'Bye-bye, Mr Sinclair,' said Alice over a cup of strong coffee, struggling to counteract the light-headed nausea that a night of jet-lagged semi-sleep had caused, 'hurry home to me, won't you?'

'Of course, darling,' said Mark, kissing the top of her head, grabbing a slice of toast, his jacket and his briefcase. 'I'm horrendously late, I really must go.'

'Don't!' Alice implored plaintively. 'Please bunk off! Go on, I dare you. Phone in sick or something. Please stay. I don't want you to go. You could work from home! I've had you all to myself for a fortnight – I don't want to be alone.'

Mark smiled at his wife, gazing at him all wide-eyed and winsome despite the bags around her eyes and her hair all mussed up. 'Why don't you go in yourself?' he asked.

'Because I don't have to!' Alice remonstrated. 'I'm not due in until tomorrow. Anyway, John Lewis are coming with all our wedding-list goodies.'

'Give Thea a call,' Mark suggested.

'Already have – it's her day off but she doesn't seem to be at home,' Alice said with contrived petulance.

'Why not go and register with some estate agents?' Mark kissed the top of her head again. 'I must go.'

'Will you phone me?' Alice pleaded. 'Don't you miss me already?'

'Alice,' said Mark, happily exasperated, 'have a shower, get dressed, go to Sainsbury's, track down Thea, sign your flat up for sale with Benham and Reeves and put our wish-list out to all agents covering NW3 and N6. Three bedrooms, garden, no galley kitchens or PVC windows.' He blew her a kiss and left. He floated down the escalator at Belsize Park and grinned intermittently while the Northern Line took him and a packed carriage of scowling commuters to Moorgate. How nice to have a wife, a beautiful wife, who clung to his shirt-tails begging him to play hooky from work to stay with her. Alice Heggarty had married him, was sending him to work with a kiss and would be waiting for him to come home later – could life be much sweeter? Mark arrived at the office, answered his PA's misty-eyed questions about his wedding and honeymoon, checked his diary, noted there were 288 emails in his in-box, rescheduled the lunch that was booked, set up two meetings for before lunch and three for the afternoon and called his team to the boardroom for an update. His PA made a note to buy him sandwiches because she knew he'd be too busy to remember to eat otherwise.

Alice did as she was told. She had a shower, dressed, went to the supermarket and phoned estate agents. She also continued to call Thea but her mobile phone was off and there was still no answer at her home. It had been warm and welcoming to return to a sweetly scented apartment, fresh linen and neat piles of post, a fridge stocked with necessities, and Alice now longed to see Thea, to thank her at the very least. She was also tiring of her own company. Alice had never been a disciple of the cult of Me-Time though the magazines she published frequently extolled it as a necessary indulgence. Alice functioned best in company, an audience even. Peace, quiet and solitude were overrated, in Alice's book. If one had time on one's hands, why not spend it wisely in company – the return was far greater than silent navel-gazing home alone. If Thea still wasn't in, maybe she would go into work for the afternoon. She dialled Thea's mobile again.

'Hullo?'

'Thea! Where the fuck have you been – I've been trying you for ages! I'm back!'

'Alice! Alice! Oh my God, how *are* you? How's Mark? I've missed you! Did you get upgraded again?'

'First Class – but I'm still jet lagged which I think is outrageous. Wait till you see my tan. Amazing place – you must go. God, I have so much to tell you – shall I come over right now?'

'Um.'

'Thea?'

'I'm – a bit, busy.'

'When, then?'

'Um.'

'Hang on – doing *what*? Busy doing what? You usually chill out on your day off – you and your me-time. Well, have your me-time with me! It feels like ages since I saw you – I'm an old married woman! Wait till you hear about First Class!'

'Er . . .'

'Is it your tax return? Fuck it – it can wait! I can't!'

'Alice—'

'What's that?'

'What?'

'*That*! In the background. I can hear someone – is there someone there? There *is* someone there. I can hear a *bloke*?'

'Er . . .'

'Thea! Thea! Tell me, you cow! Why am I whispering? I can hear a man! Can I? Can I hear a man in your flat?'

'I'm not in my flat.'

'Where are you? Are you in a bloke's flat? Thea!'

'Yes. Yes, I am.'

'Who, tell me, *who*!'

'Saul.'

'Who the hell is Saul! Oh my God, who the *fuck* is Saul!'

'My boyfriend.'

'Your *boy*friend? You don't *have* a boyfriend! Who the hell is Saul? You're meant to be seeing Mark's American cousin. You're going to marry him and then we can be related sort of. I've been planning so all honeymoon. You don't *have* a boyfriend. Thea! Since when?'

'Since yesterday.'

'Stop giggling! What are you talking about, woman? I don't understand. What do you mean *since yesterday*? A boyfriend called Saul? I *have* to see you!'

'I'll come to you later, Alice. In a couple of hours, say.'

'A couple of *hours*? I can't wait that long!'

'You'll have to. I haven't even got out of bed, let alone showered.'

'Thea, for Christ's sake! Promise you'll be here in a couple of hours then? No more than three, tops. I can't wait. I can't wait! Saul? I don't know a Saul! And up until my wedding, neither did *you*.'

Alice had wisely anticipated that returning home from honeymoon would be a comedown, that jet lag would drag her down lower, that her wedding day would seem a dream ago. However, apart from the January magazines already replacing the Christmas issues though it was still December, she hadn't expected any other changes. In fact, sitting with a cup of tea, waiting for Thea to help her unpack the wedding gifts towering in John Lewis boxes around her, Alice admitted that she had been depending on everything being exactly as she'd left it a fortnight before. She had wanted her world to wait and to long for her return, to crave photos and Technicolor detail of her interlude in St Lucia. She hadn't expected the world to stop turning but she had hoped it might revolve around her for a little while longer. She was, after all, still the blushing bride, the newly-wed, just married, just home from honeymoon; she had hoped to enjoy the status for at least a few more days yet.

Alice couldn't work out how Thea had gone off and found a boyfriend when she hadn't even been looking for one in the first place. How could this have happened when she hadn't been around to advise her? Thea Luckmore had never been one for the thrill of strangers. So who on earth was this Saul person?

'How did she manage to do it without me?' Alice wondered aloud and then listened to how awful that sounded. 'Not that I'm her chaperone,' she murmured quickly, unpacking some boxes from John Lewis and wondering if it would be all right to do thank-you notes on the computer, 'it's just I've always known everything about her. I've known when she's feeling lonely, lovelorn, playful, horny or shy. And I've always been aware of names and dates. Because she always, *always* consults me for a plan of action.' Alice unwrapped a bulky item and then cursed friends of her parents for deviating from the wedding list in favour of an unnecessarily patterned soup tureen of staggering dimensions. 'My generation don't do soup tureens – our soup comes fresh in a carton from Marks & Sparks.' She knew she sounded spoilt and ungrateful so she blamed jet lag and post-honeymoon blues and wrote a gushing thank-you note straight away proclaiming soup making to be one of Mark's favourite pastimes.

'Thea's always methodically talked through potential entanglements with me first. That was half the fun – analysing it all and digging for signs and significance,' Alice muttered whilst wondering why she had chosen cream Egyptian cotton towels when between Mark and herself, they already owned more than a full complement of towels and linen. She felt just a little like a fraud, as if she was playing at being a grown-up, dressing up in her mother's lifestyle. Soup tureens and Royal Doulton crockery. Why had she ordered 'best china' when she and Mark tended to turn to Marks & Spencer ready-meals during the week? She felt a little embarrassed, she worried that she sounded horribly materialistic even to herself. There's more to marriage than wedding gifts. Where would all this stuff go? She made a mental note that ample storage should be a prerequisite on their house-hunting wish-list. 'I do love my flat,' Alice sighed, 'but Mark is right, it is time for us both to move and set up a new home together. How weird that quality plumbing and storage space should suddenly be my priority. But then, I'm not a single girl in my twenties gadding about any more.' She laughed out loud at how ludicrous she sounded. 'What am I like – I've only been married for two weeks and I've been thirty-one for just ten days!'

Alice hung on Thea's every word. They sat together on the floor, drinking tea, eating double-chocolate muffins, admiring the gifts and fidgeting with the polystyrene packing nuggets. Alice lapped up all the details Thea gave. They marvelled that there was no need for Thea to embellish the facts, to take liberties with details or overdo adjectives.

'It's like a film!' Alice declared. 'I can practically hear a Morcheeba and Jimi Hendrix soundtrack. Someone like Anna Friel playing you.'

'I swear to God,' Thea shrugged, 'it is exactly as I'm telling you.'

'And he *licked* your scar?' Alice whispered. 'You actually *let* him?'

Thea nodded. 'It even turned me on.'

'Jesus, I must meet him. Saul Mundy,' said Alice, 'his name

does ring a bell – in the industry. And of course I know his column from the *Observer*. But tell me again about the sex – that thing with his tongue and finger.'

'Thumb,' Thea corrected.

'I think I might drop a hint or two to Mark,' Alice planned.

'Is married sex a bore and chore already?' Thea teased. 'Is it all "Mr Sinclair, prithee do attend to my heaving bosom"? Is it missionary with lights out? And "That was most satisfactory, dear husband but now please away to your own chamber"? Conjugal obligations?'

Alice laughed. 'For your information, married sex is lovely,' she declared a little defensively, 'it's warm and considerate and we synchronize our climax. Mark's a very attentive lover. True, it's without that element of wild abandon you're describing.'

'Yes, but I'm in the throes of the first flush, remember,' Thea defined wisely.

'I know,' Alice replied softly, 'but Mark and I go back so long that there's never been a first flush. No fireworks, just a gorgeous glow. It's different with Mark,' Alice said with a contented shrug, 'it's what I want – passion was a health hazard for me. I prefer it this way – sex with Mark makes me feel cosy, rather than racked with insecurity.'

'Yet here's me,' Thea said, 'a stickler for old-fashioned romance and the sanctity of monogamy – now jumping into and onto and half-on half-off the bed on a first date and shagging in all manner of contortions for twenty-four hours non-stop.'

'Good for you!' Alice laughed. 'I can't wait to meet him. I mean – you really think this'll be a goer? More than a fling?'

'Alice Heggarty,' Thea chastised, 'when have I *ever* had a fling – let alone a one-night stand? When have I ever even snogged – never mind slept with – a man who I haven't felt an emotional pull towards?'

'You're right in that respect,' said Alice, 'but wrong in another – it's Alice *Sinclair*, remember.'

'*Mrs* Sinclair,' Thea practised.

'Miss Luckmore,' Alice cautioned, 'you must admit it does all seem pretty fast. And with a perfect stranger.'

'There's the rub,' said Thea, 'he *was* a stranger – but already he has the potential to be perfect. He's not strange in the slightest. The real beauty of it is that it all appears to be so uncomplicated. We're both single, we're a similar age, our worlds appear to be complementary – I'm surprised our paths haven't crossed before. We just happened to meet in the open air unexpectedly.'

'So it's headlong into the whole boyfriend–girlfriend thing? You don't fancy an exploratory period of *I-won't-call-him-for-four-days*? You're not going to phone me to fret about bollocks like your bum looking big in this or that? You don't feel the need for us to *workshop* a long list of what-ifs and what-do-you-thinks?'

'Nope,' said Thea, 'as Saul said to me this morning, "I could do that thing of not calling you for a few days to keep you keen, but then I'd be denying myself the pleasure of you in the interim and where's the sense in that?" So, he's asked me to go to his place straight after work tomorrow and I'll be there. Funny how you can feel you know someone off by heart before I've even committed his mobile phone number to memory.'

'Thea *Mundy*,' Alice mused, 'it has a certain ring to it!'

'Fuck off!' Thea laughed, giving her friend a gentle shove. They chuckled and sighed and contemplated the ugly soup tureen. 'Do you remember how we'd do that?' Thea said. 'Tag a boy's surname to our names before we'd even managed to kiss them?'

'*You* did,' Alice corrected, 'you always did a lot of thinking and planning prior to kissing. In fact, sometimes you'd conclude against kissing altogether. If the surname didn't scan satisfactorily. I just went for the snog and then despaired afterwards at the ghastly phonetics of Alice Sissons or Alice Hillace.'

'Jesus,' Thea covered her face with her hands, 'Ben Sissons – he was the one with the bleached quiff!'

'He used his mum's Jolene facial bleach to achieve it,' Alice said, 'rather enterprising, really. Until the hairs started snapping off.'

'And Richard Hillace,' Thea reminisced, 'I quite fancied him myself, actually.'

'I know you did,' said Alice, 'and you could have had him later, but you were so irritatingly principled about my offer of hand-me-downs.'

'Funny to think out of all of them, Good Old Mark Sinclair was the one to ultimately land you,' said Thea, trying to fathom the use of a peculiar-looking kitchen tool.

'*Land* me,' mused Alice, taking the utensil from Thea. 'It's a mandolin – Mark chose it, he knows how it works. *Land me* – yes, I do feel grounded at last.'

'I like to think of hearts breaking amongst all those exbeaux of yours,' Thea smiled, stroking the towel pile. '*Mark Sinclair*? they are probably weeping, *lucky lucky bastard*.'

'Oh, Thea,' Alice said, throwing a handful of polystyrene squiggles into the air, 'let's promise that marriage and Mark, passion and Saul won't come between us!'

'You daft cow,' said Thea, throwing up the packaging as if it was confetti, 'how could anything, ever, come between *us*?'

'Christ help us,' Alice murmured, having just unwrapped an odd-shaped item, 'it's a gravy boat and it matches the soup tureen.'

Under duress from his fiancée, Ian Ashford phoned Saul for the umpteenth time that day. Finally, the mobile phone had been switched on.

'Saul! Ian.'

'Ian! How's it going?'

'Er, listen mate, Karen's been on to me suggesting we all go out one evening.'

'Cool. Love to. When?'

'This week perhaps? Friday maybe?'

'Yes, looks fine to me.'

'And Jo. We'll bring Jo, shall we? She loved meeting you.'

'The thing is – I mean, please tell Karen I thought Jo was a great girl – hot too – but I actually have a girlfriend now. Thea.'

'Sorry?'

'Jo – great girl. But Thea – greatest yet.'

'You have a *girl*friend? Since when?'

'Since Sunday.'

'It's Monday.'

'And you can see for yourself on Friday then. You'll love her.'

'Hullo, Mrs Sinclair,' Mark phoned Alice.

'Hullo, husband,' Alice replied, glancing at the clock and marvelling how writing thank-yous could make the time fly, 'where are you?'

'Office,' Mark apologized. 'I'm almost finished – I promise. Another hour. Home by nine. I'm knackered.'

Alice quickly advised herself to be neither disappointed nor pissed off. Remember the jet lag. Remember post-wedding blues. 'Soup for supper?' Alice suggested, half wondering whether to decant a carton into the tureen.

Alice felt a little flat. Her place was a mess and the piles of presents suddenly irritated her. She longed for St Lucia. She tried to phone Thea but the line was busy. Alice didn't doubt that she was talking to Saul. They'd probably been chatting for ages and she reckoned they would be for some time yet. Telling each other about their lives, loves and quirks. They'd be laughing and marvelling and nattering nineteen to the dozen. Ah, the joys and the intricacy of the human mating dance. The thought made Alice feel warm. And just a little lonely.

Mundy, Luckmore & Co.

Saul soon gained everyone's seal of approval. Sally Stonehill considered various adjectives before deciding on 'dashing' to best describe him. Richard Stonehill liked him enough to return the Armani jacket and Saul liked Richard enough to consider telling him to keep it. Instead, he bought him a pint over which they discovered they both played squash. They arranged a game and their standards were so level that it soon became a weekly fixture with the obligatory post-match praise and pints which they enjoyed just as much as time on court.

Mark Sinclair didn't play squash but he was happy to guide Saul on playing the stock market. Mark was more than flattered when Saul asked to interview him for *GQ* magazine, an article entitled 'Barrow Boys and Bowler Hats: Who Stocks the Stock Market' and they had a jocular but productive lunch on expenses. The other therapists Thea worked alongside at the Being Well welcomed Saul's impromptu visits. He usually came bearing gifts: fresh juice and brownies, a poinsettia for reception, magazines for the waiting room, a smile to Thea's face. He also made it his business to recommend the clinic to friends and colleagues moaning about bad backs, tiredness and stress.

Alice had rehearsed an acerbic soliloquy starting 'Let me tell you about Thea' and ending 'so, hurt her and I'll kill you'. However, she was actually pleasantly surprised that she took to Saul, though it meant her soliloquy remained unperformed. She decided not to be suspicious of his good looks and she detected no cockiness in the fact that he was naturally outgoing. She respected him for sparring back when she tried to provoke him. She liked it that they could talk about their industry. Most importantly, he appeared very taken with Thea. How fortunate that her best friend's boyfriend had the potential to become a friend in his own right too.

Thea was instantly liked by all to whom Saul introduced her. Karen Soon-to-be-Ashford had to concede to Jo that Thea was great and would fit right into one of their girls' nights out. Even Lynne took to her, despite having to keep Molly shut in the downstairs toilet for the duration of her visit. Lynne's husband was so impressed with a five-minute speed treatment Thea gave his interminably stiff shoulder that he booked an appointment, then another and also gladly took Thea's advice to see Souki the acupuncturist. Staff and patrons at the Swallow gave her a warm nod of acceptance. Marco from the Deli slipped her a complimentary muffin and slid Saul a knowing wink underscored by appreciative insinuations in throaty Italian. Dave the paper man soon called out to her by name whether or not she was buying an *Evening Standard*. None of them resented Saul taking his custom to Crouch End for half the week. It evened out anyway, because Thea invariably accompanied him when he returned home.

Thea surprised herself at holding her own amongst Saul's editors and fellow writers at dos down in Soho, even calling the bluff of one cocky columnist who asked her if she gave 'extras' with her massage. 'Of course I do. But I don't *give* them,' said Thea most levelly, 'they cost.' He was just about to lick his lips and ask for a price list when those standing near roared with laughter and called him a dickhead. Alice was at that party. Neither married life for her, nor new relationship fervour for Thea, had imposed any constriction on their friendship. Alice decided it was serendipitous that Thea had met someone whose path crossed naturally with her own. And with Mark travelling so regularly it seemed daft not to attend events when Thea and Saul would be there too. What would she do otherwise? Work late? Sit at home showing people around her flat? Simultaneously, Alice's world became smaller and Thea's broadened.

* * *

'Saul,' Alice phoned Saul out of the blue, 'can I tickle your fancy?'

'That's a rather tempting offer on a grim February morning,' Saul laughed.

'Let me buy you lunch and whet your appetite,' Alice continued, her desk diary open, red pen to hand, prepared to rearrange anything already booked.

'Wednesday?' Saul suggested.

'Perfect,' said Alice.

'It's a date,' said Saul, tapping the details into a Palm Pilot.

'Top secret,' said Alice.

'You can trust me,' said Saul.

Quentin

'No one knows about Quentin,' Alice told Saul over a covert sushi lunch near Liverpool Street. She lit a cigarette and replenished her green tea, aware that puffing one and sipping the other was vaguely contradictory.

'I thought you only ever smoked at parties,' Saul remarked.

'And over clandestine lunches about top-secret things,' Alice said, her eyes glinting. 'Don't tell Mark. He hates cigarettes.'

Saul pulled an imaginary zip across his lips. 'OK, Mrs Sinclair,' he said, 'tell me about Quentin and where I come in?'

'Heggarty today,' said Alice, 'I've kept Heggarty for half my life. And Quentin, well, Quentin is my baby.'

Saul popped slippery edamame beans out of their salty pods. 'Quentin,' he mused.

'Code-name: Project Quentin,' she whispered, adding hastily, 'you know – after Tarantino, rather than Crisp.'

'So, we're talking a men's mag, hetero rather than homo,' Saul surmised. He split his wooden chopsticks and rubbed the one against the other to smooth any shards.

'Yes,' said Alice, 'we all know the market for men's mags is huge. We're not going for anything ground breaking. The main focus is absolutely no compromise on quality. From clothes to cars, columnists to celebrities – quality.'

'Quality?' Saul remarked. 'Sounds pretty ground breaking to me when you think of the tat that makes up most lads' mags. Talking of tat, where do you stand on tits?'

'Again,' shrugged Alice, 'quality breasts. But not on the cover. We're pitching at a slightly older market – ABC1 men, thirty to fifty. Not too blokey, but not too staid, of course. Men like you. The covers will be icons, not babes. Someone has practically guaranteed us Clint Eastwood for the first issue if we get the go-ahead.'

Saul raised an eyebrow. 'Pierce Brosnan had acupuncture with Souki at the Being Well when he was in town.'

Alice raised her green tea. 'Pierce can have issue two, then.'

'And David Bowie's mum and my mum were at school together,' Saul said.

'David Bowie?' Alice had to swallow a squeal. 'Has Thea told you how complete our teenage love was for David darling Bowie?'

'Yes,' Saul confirmed with an overly compassionate expression and a tone of utter pity, 'I know all about sending red roses to his dressing room at Wembley; that you both promptly fainted when the show began and spent the entire concert sipping tea with the St John's Ambulance crew.'

'And the mural,' Alice laughed, 'did Thea not tell you about our mural?'

'No,' Saul said patiently, 'though she told me you both saved all your pocket money to buy one pair of blue contact lenses to share between you so you could both have Bowie eyes.' He poked the tip of his chopstick into the lurid green wasabe. The horseradish shot tears into his eyes and fizzed heat through the bridge of his nose. Fantastic.

'We did this incredible mural on my bedroom wall – based on the "Scary Monsters" LP cover,' Alice reminisced. 'My mum went berserk. Mind you, we hadn't even been able to smuggle in the paint pots past Thea's mum at her house. Anyway, if we had Bowie as cover for issue three, I'd be happy to sweep floors for the rest of my career. But I digress. Project Quentin is our big secret – and potentially the company's biggest launch to date.'

'What's the timescale?' Saul asked.

Alice cleared her throat. 'Dummy in six weeks, then into research, and if we get the green light, first issue will be June out May.'

Saul calculated dates and weeks in his head. 'Who else

knows?' he asked. 'Nat Mags? IPC? Because I know that EMAP are developing too, at the moment.'

'Will you tell me?' Alice asked with a coquettish pout and a beguiling wriggle in her chair. 'Tell me about silly old EMAP? I promise I won't tell a soul. I swear on David Bowie's life. Trust me?'

'Absolutely not!' Saul laughed, inadvertently shaking a piece of sashimi at her. 'Like I said – if I'm given a secret, I keep it. No matter how absolute your love for Bowie is. Suffice it to say, I'm not involved.'

Alice contrived to look sulky and offended but her enthusiasm for her project soon overtook. 'Initially, I was hoping you'd work on the dummy with us, Saul,' she said, still in a whisper, 'basically oversee editorial – it would mean committing three days a week for the next month or so. Take the dummy into research, then head up the launch issue if we get the go-ahead. With, of course, absolutely no guarantee of a staff position at the end.'

Saul laughed. 'I know the score,' he said, 'and I'd love to be involved.'

'Fan-bloody-tastic,' Alice beamed.

'Alice, you haven't eaten a thing,' Saul observed.

'I can't eat when I'm excited,' Alice declared. 'Great for weight loss, though.'

Saul thought aren't girls silly sometimes.

Apart from Thea, of course. Saul didn't think her silly at all. Her fear of dogs was understandable, her propensity for weeping during *ER* or re-runs of *Cold Feet* he found quite endearing, her belief in drinking only juice until noon each day he thought eccentric. But he didn't think her silly.

'She's not a calorie-counting, chardonnay-swilling, Mui-Mui obsessive,' he quantified to Ian Ashford over a pile of poppadams and a mound of chutney, 'but then neither is she a drink-your-own-pee, salute-the-sun and wear-hessian-to-Pilates type either.'

'Does she do Pilates?' Ian asked.

'Yes, with her mates Sally and Alice,' said Saul, 'and she has a gorgeous figure because of it. But my point is she may drink only juice until lunchtime but she's also partial to a Marlboro Light with her vodka-tonics after dark. She makes soup with organic produce – but her preferred lunch is Pret a Manger egg mayo sandwiches and a Coca-Cola.'

'What's with the juice-till-noon thing?' Ian asked, wondering whether it might be a good regime for his acid and thinking that the madras he ordered probably wasn't.

'She simply doesn't have an appetite until then,' Saul explained. 'I bought her a juicer for Christmas because she was spending a fortune on smoothies.'

'What you're talking about is balance,' Ian said, spooning pilau rice onto his plate.

'I am,' said Saul, 'a girl who balances M&S socks and a top she's had for ever with an Anya Hindmarsh handbag. Do you know how much those bags cost? But balance, yes – she connects with the yin and yang and whole shebang of meridians and energy flow and shiatsu stuff – but her CD collection is more the White Stripes than whale music.'

'She's at ease with herself,' Ian defined, passing the dhal to Saul.

'It's one of the most attractive things about her,' Saul nodded, passing the Bombay aloo to Ian.

'Does she keep *Men are from Mars and Women are from Venus* under her bed?' Ian asked suspiciously.

'No,' Saul laughed, '*Heat* magazine.'

'So what's she like in the sack?' Ian posed, working his fork dexterously through the curry and rice like a bricklayer trowelling cement.

'She's great,' said Saul evenly, 'for all the same reasons – sometimes it's deep and meaningful lovemaking. Other times it's fast and furious shagging. She doesn't pester me to whisper sweet nothings but she writhes when I talk dirty. She doesn't sulk to the other end of the bed if all I want to do post-coitally is roll over and snore, and I'm just as likely to wake up to a blow-job as to Radio 4.'

'Sounds like you've hit the jackpot, mate,' said Ian. 'I'd suggest you snap her up and put your name on her, quick.'

'You know how with some women you end up playing along with them just for peace and quiet,' Saul mused, 'and you find yourself apologizing for the bits that make us blokes?' Ian nodded with the weight of someone most familiar with such a syndrome. 'You know how some women fulfil one part of our criteria but are so sorely lacking in other aspects?' Saul continued. 'Beautiful but boring? Interesting but just not sexy? Horny as hell but dumb as fuck? Well, it seems incredibly simple, but I like all of her a lot.'

'To Thea,' said Ian, raising his bottle of Kingfisher beer

and telling himself he really did not need that last rip of nan bread. He'd do juice until noon the next day, he decided.

'I wasn't looking,' Saul mused wistfully, 'I was just on Primrose Hill and she came into view.'

'Good luck,' said Ian, presuming the evening to be subliminal payback for the time he'd droned on about Karen.

'It is,' Saul agreed, 'it is very good luck.'

'So that's it then?' Ian said slyly. 'Temptation can lead you by the balls and you'll resist?'

'Thea inspires fidelity.' Saul paused. 'In my heart and mind, at least!'

Ian and Saul looked at each other for a moment and then chuckled into the last of their curry.

'Not on a full stomach – surely not!' Ian said.

* * *

'Your wife's footing the tab,' Saul laughed, taking Mark to a restaurant that still believed in starched linen at lunchtime. 'How was Hong Kong?'

'Knackering,' Mark said quietly, 'but essential. Hong Kong is crazy – but the business is a dream for us at the moment. Tokyo next week.'

'I guess the bonus will be your bonus?' Saul said.

Mark tipped his head and chinked glasses with Saul. 'I need to keep my wife in Jimmy Shoes.'

Saul wasn't sure whether to correct Mark. He let it go. 'You get what you pay for!' he said lightly instead.

'Actually, Alice is brilliant at blagging,' Mark confessed. 'I always offer to buy stuff but she always declines and says she can call in favours at work. I think she gets more of a thrill from getting a bargain or freebie than from the item itself. Have you seen those monstrous rocks in her ears?'

'The diamonds?' Saul said. 'You can't really fail to notice them.'

'Three carats?' Mark suggested. Saul shrugged. He had never bought a diamond. 'QVC,' Mark said triumphantly.

'Is that the sparkle factor or the colour clarity?' Saul asked, trying to sound like someone who'd bought diamonds.

Mark roared with laughter. 'QVC – the shopping channel! Alice is forever buying stuff from QVC. Those earrings were £29.95 – and she got a hideous suedette presentation box for being one of the first hundred callers.'

'Are the Jimmy *Choos* fake too?' Saul said subtly.

'Unfortunately not,' Mark groaned, 'they're bona-fide Jimmy Shoes shoes.'

'I suppose it evens out,' Saul said lightly. 'Think how much you'd pay at Tiffany for gems that size.'

'Hey, I'm not complaining,' said Mark, 'Christ no. I have the most beautiful wife – I was about to say "I could ever dream of" but in fact she *is* the beautiful wife I always dreamt of.'

'You've known each other ages,' Saul recalled.

'Since school days,' Mark said, 'friends for years. Confidants. And then one day, Alice says to me, "If you ask me, I'll say yes." I hadn't a clue what she was on about. I mean, I hadn't even kissed the girl, let alone taken her to bed. I just stared at her gormlessly. She proposed. It wasn't a leap year. I hadn't bought diamonds from Tiffany or QVC. I was washing up and, calm as you like, she turns to me and asks me to marry her.'

'And you still can't believe your luck?' Saul laughed.

'That's just it,' said Mark, 'it's not about luck. To me, the more you love someone, the more you deserve them – and I'd loved her for a long, long time. Albeit from afar. I hadn't resented the fuckwits she dated though I hated them when they hurt her. I hadn't found anyone special and was happy to see women in a non-committal way. And then Alice decided she'd like to marry me.'

'So, you have this gorgeous woman, successful in her career, who buys her own diamonds, no matter how fake they are, and simply stings you for a pair of Jimmy *Choos* every now and then,' Saul quantified. 'Can life get much better?'

'Well, I'm looking forward to the bonus,' Mark laughed, 'which will hopefully coincide with the next Jimmy Shoes sale!' He glanced at his watch. 'Anyway, are we here about Quentin?' he murmured covertly, with a wink and a surreptitious tap of his nose.

'We are,' Saul nodded, privately bemused that such an expensive restaurant hadn't bothered to fillet his monkfish. 'Now, because we're pitching at a slightly older market – not so much aspirational, as can afford it anyway – I was thinking of a City section. You know, investments, portfolios, gift horse and traps; lively overviews on finance and our times, a note of light relief from the *Financial Times*.'

Mark nodded. 'Interesting,' he said, 'how can I help?' He glanced at his watch again. 'I'll need to make tracks in half an hour, Saul. But I'm back from Tokyo at the weekend.'

* * *

'You bastard,' Richard Stonehill panted, hands on his knees, his squash racket between his feet, 'you bastard. You're just a jammy bastard.'

'And you're a bad loser,' Saul laughed, wiping sweat from his brow onto his T-shirt. 'My game, my match – your round.'

'Let's make it the best out of seven then,' Richard said, slashing a ball against the court.

'Fuck off,' Saul laughed, returning the shot perfectly. 'What would your wife say when I call her to say you've thrown yourself into Highgate Ponds with concrete in your pockets because you lost five–two?'

'Yeah, yeah,' Richard said, 'you're younger than me. Anyway, I have a cold coming. But next week I'm going to roast you, mate, *roast* you. Annihilation.'

'I look forward to it,' Saul said, slicing the ball and intentionally missing Richard by a hair's breadth.

'You won't even *make* it to Highgate Ponds,' Richard said, returning Saul's ball impressively, 'you'll do the hara-kiri thing right here on court.'

'And on that note,' Saul said, 'let's go for a drink.'

For a moment or two, both men just gazed at the pints of pale, chilled lager with unreserved affection before raising the glasses to their lips and taking a long, well-earned drink. They said 'cheers' to each other, chinked glasses and then downed what was left. 'My round,' said Richard, going to the bar at the Swallow and ordering sausages and mash for them both. 'How's Thea?' he asked, on returning.

'I had a set of my keys cut for her just today,' Saul grinned. 'And Sally?'

'It's our wedding anniversary this weekend,' Richard said, 'five years.'

'Cheers!' said Saul, with admiration.

'Who'd have thought a crazy fling would lead to marriage,' Richard marvelled wistfully.

'Are you whisking her off to Paris?' Saul enquired.

Richard laughed but shook his head.

'Venice?' Saul tried. 'Barcelona? Babington House? No? Well. I assume you've been to Tiffany's.'

'No,' Richard groaned, 'not yet.'

'Mark Sinclair was telling me Alice buys her own jewels,' Saul said.

'Really?' Richard responded, 'but on his credit card probably. She has some fuck-off diamonds, that girl.'

'No, she buys them herself,' Saul revealed. 'They're *fake*,' he said, 'fake! How cool is that?' He really was more impressed than he would have been had they been genuine. 'She buys them for small change from the shopping channel.'

Richard laughed. 'Seriously? Bloody hell. She certainly wears them well. Perhaps I'll ask her to order double – I'm sure I could pop them into a Tiffany box.'

'Talking of Alice,' Saul said, dropping his voice, 'I'm working on a project with her – top secret. But I have an idea for a property section. I'm not talking estate agents' advertorials. I'm not talking Laurence Llewelyn-Bowen makeovers. I was thinking of a section that is part DIY, part property improvements, part investment savvy. You know, kitchen extensions or loft conversions or knocking through – a how to, how much, how long.'

'Sounds good,' Richard nodded.

'You're an architect,' Saul shrugged, 'can I pick your brains?'

'Cool,' Richard nodded, 'sure. What's it called?'

'Top secret,' said Saul.

'That's a bit naff,' said Richard.

'The *title* is top secret,' Saul said very slowly. 'I'm not telling you the title because I can't. I'm sworn to secrecy.'

'Code-name?' Richard asked.

'Quentin,' Saul revealed rather reluctantly.

'Gay?'

'No – as in *Tarantino*,' Saul explained. And he and Richard proceeded to quote salient lines from *Pulp Fiction* until their sausages arrived.

Beth and Hope

When Beth Godwin and Hope Johnson set up their Pilates studio in Crouch End, Sally Stonehill joined on a whim because there was an introductory offer on. Thea signed up on the recommendation of Lars, the Feldenkrais practitioner at the Being Well. Alice joined on account of the effect of Pilates on the physique of Elizabeth Hurley. Mostly, the three of them synchronized their sessions. It hardly mattered, though. They were so busy concentrating on engaging their pelvic floor and pursuing core stability that they barely said a word to each other apart from 'great Pikes, Thea' or 'your reverse-monkey looked good, Alice' or 'I'm finished with the Reformer, Sally'.

Invariably, if they'd been training together, they'd go for a meal afterwards, determined to consolidate the merits of Pilates with healthy salads or bowls of hearty soup and glasses of mineral water. Usually, though, there was some reason for a glass of wine too – from it being good for the blood, to it being necessary to toast one of the girls for something or other. However even the one glass of wine, when mixed with the endorphins of exercise, led to the inevitable ordering of chips. To share, of course. Just to pick at. And mayonnaise too, please. Who's for ketchup? Anyone for HP Sauce?

'A large bottle of sparkling mineral water,' Alice ordered.

'It's my wedding anniversary this weekend,' Sally remarked, with intent.

'Is it? Right then,' Alice responded, 'a bottle of Sauvignon too, please.'

'I'll have the avocado and mung bean salad,' Thea told the waitress with scant enthusiasm.

'Grilled trout for me, please,' ordered Alice, 'no butter.'

'I think I'll go for the stir-fried veg,' Sally muttered.

'Anything else?' the waitress asked casually.

'Oh, one portion of chips,' Thea added as an afterthought.

'Actually, make that two,' Alice said, 'to share between the three of us.'

'And some mayo, please,' Sally called after the waitress.

'Cheers!' said Alice, raising her glass. 'Here's to you and Richard and to marriage in general.'

'I'll drink to that,' said Sally, 'here's to my husband and five lovely years.'

'Cheers,' said Thea, 'here's to – chips.'

'You'll be next,' Alice nudged Thea and winked at Sally.

'I hardly see the boy,' Thea remonstrated, tapping the prongs of her fork against the pad of her thumb before pointing her cutlery at Alice. 'You have him working all bloody hours on your hush-hush project.'

'How's that going?' Sally asked Alice. 'Richard likes to think of himself as Editor of Architecture and Interiors or something. The prat.'

'We're launching next month,' Alice said triumphantly.

'Will there be a glamorous party?' Sally asked hopefully.

'Of course,' Alice said.

'And may lowly primary school teachers attend?' Sally asked.

'You may,' Alice confirmed graciously.

'And will there be room on the guest list for a sports masseuse?' Thea asked.

'God no,' Alice laughed in mock shock, 'but I might turn a blind eye to the girlfriend of the editorial consultant sneaking in.'

'Cow,' Thea stuck her tongue out at Alice.

'How are things with Alice's Editorial Consultant?' Sally asked Thea. 'Richard has spent a small fortune on a new squash racquet. Bad workmen, tools and blame, springs to mind.'

'Lovely,' Thea grinned, 'it's fun. It's cosy. It's sexy. It's everything I want. And everything I need.'

'You mean it's love,' Sally deduced.

'Yes,' Thea confirmed, 'yes, it is.'

'Six months after I started seeing Richard, we were already engaged,' Sally recalled. 'Mind you, six months after *you* started seeing Mark you were practically married, Ms Heggarty.'

'Mrs Sinclair to you,' Alice retorted. 'Actually, the craziest thing about it all was that I didn't even start seeing Mark *until* we were engaged. Chaste is an understatement.'

'Chaste is overrated,' Sally said with a wink, confessing she'd bought Richard, for their anniversary, some peculiar-looking love beads which apparently he was to use on her – if they could figure out how and where.

'Did you go into a sex shop on your own?' Alice asked, slightly unnerved by an image of petite Sally unchaperoned amongst stacks of gadgets and racks of hardcore.

'Mail order,' Sally giggled.

'Of course, Saul and I have absolutely no need for gizmos on account of his stupendous natural equipment and our exceptionally resourceful technique,' Thea began primly. 'But actually,' she added in a sly whisper, 'we have a particularly well-stocked toy chest as well.'

'Dirty girl,' Alice marvelled.

'That was one kinky shopping trip,' Thea reminisced. 'I happened to make just a passing remark I'd never been in a sex shop. A week or so later, we were heading back to Saul's from a restaurant in Soho when he suddenly bundled me through a doorway. Slap bang into this den of iniquity and plastic things.'

'You never told me!' Alice objected.

'Well, it was hardly Joseph or Whistles,' Thea reasoned. 'Actually, it was a peculiar experience. Down a really seedy side street yet inside it was all bright lights and the most normal-looking customers imaginable. Though I seem to recall the sales assistant being quite alarmingly tattooed.'

'Did you giggle like mad?' Sally asked.

'At first,' Thea admitted, 'but actually, everyone was browsing the wares so casually that I soon found myself assessing the merits of one dildo against another as I would ready-meals at Tesco. Saul spent a fortune. We couldn't wait to get back to his to try things in.'

'On,' the editor in Alice corrected automatically.

'No,' Thea laughed, 'I really do mean *in*!'

'Do you have any of these bead things?' Sally asked, now regarding Thea as the doyenne of kinky paraphernalia.

Thea went through a lengthy, though obviously mostly fabricated, inventory. 'No,' she apologized at length, 'no beads. My advice would be, if it fits, wear it out.'

'Mark doesn't know I have a vibrator,' Alice confessed, half wondering whether he ought, yet unable to predict how he'd react. 'In fact, I can't imagine using toys with him. The thing is, our sex is admittedly pretty straightforward but actually all the more satisfying for it. I had boyfriends who couldn't get it up unless they could get something battery-operated up first. God, sometimes I used to crave simple, quick missionary in the dark.'

'I guess I bought these plastic things to sustain the spice,' Sally said, 'not because our sex life is lacking or uninspired. I like surprising Richie – though nowadays I sometimes have to remind myself to – because I know he loves it. The day I can't be bothered is the day to worry.'

'Keeping the marriage alive?' Thea asked.

'No, it's not that,' Sally declared, 'no need to – all is dreamy. I just like to envisage Richard thinking to himself that he's a lucky boy. I like to think of him all distracted and hot under the collar at work by knowing what's under my pillow.'

'It's funny,' Alice mused, 'how you and I have actually contrived our relationships. You ensure that you maintain the allure of a vamp all these years into your marriage. I eschew my previous incarnation as feisty temptress to secure the stability and fidelity that defines Mark. I guess you could say I'm in an arranged marriage which I arranged.'

'Richard proposed out of the blue, when we were still at the height of our heady falling-in-love phase,' Sally reminisced. 'Me being ludicrously dramatic, I ran away from him to hide in the wilds of Scotland, broke my bloody leg and he then turned up and wrote "will you?" on my plaster cast.'

'It's such a great story,' Thea laughed.

'God, my proposal is mundane in comparison,' Alice admitted. 'I asked Mark to marry me with a carrot in my mouth.'

'I bet it wasn't mundane to him,' Sally said.

'Funnily enough, it's the mundanity that I love now,' Alice defined. 'Christ, when I think of all that passion I used to put myself through.' She paused to privately recall it. 'It was so damned draining; replete with suspicions. Now I am loved unconditionally. I can just be myself and I'm adored for it. It's such a relief that my worries are now confined solely to work or to trivial things like whether we made a mistake using Cath Kidston florals in the bedroom with the rest of the house so minimalist.'

'How is your new house?' Sally asked Alice.

'Gorgeous,' Thea enthused on Alice's behalf, 'it's so grown-up!'

'It really is gorgeous,' Alice agreed. 'I'm very lucky.'

'I love being married,' Sally enthused with no smugness. 'Richard is my best friend, my best shag, my confidant.'

'I love it that to the outside world there's this normal bloke called Saul – but in my eyes I see this knight in shining armour,' Thea said proudly, 'a man I burn for. I lavish my love and lust on him and it's reciprocated. That's the best thing – finally with Saul it's this gorgeous two-way rally. Like a ball caught between flingers in a pinball machine – affection, lust, empathy, friendship, love ricocheting between the two of us.'

'You're a hopeless romantic,' Alice said fondly, 'the first person to compare love to a pinball machine, that's for sure. And how many times do I have to tell you there's no magic or mystique in your feeling of "burning" for a man – it's just sudden surges of adrenalin and dopamine released in your brain.'

'Oh shut up, Alice,' Thea laughed.

'Let the girl enjoy her chemical reaction!' Sally said.

The food arrived and they picked at the salad and polished off the chips. Alice raised her glass and lowered her voice. 'Look at that gaggle over there at that table.' Thea and Sally glanced surreptitiously to a table of three women much like themselves. 'Short of actually eavesdropping or lip-reading, I'll bet you anything they're bemoaning all men are sods and stuff. They look miserable. Down in the doldrums, drowning their discontent.' Alice replenished their glasses and raised hers, chinking it against Sally's and Thea's. 'We're bloody lucky, us three. We each have what we want and life ticks along happily because we're blessed with precisely what makes us tick.'

Girls and Boys

Alice sat up in bed; coddled by cloud-plump pillows and finest goose down, bedecked tastefully with Cath Kidston roses, in a waft around her. Her hair tumbled in a breeze-soft fan over her shoulders, glints of spun gold splaying over the creaminess of her skin. She looked like something out of a Merchant Ivory film, Mark thought to himself. Actually, Alice felt playful and horny and was surreptitiously fingering herself lightly as she watched Mark undress. She smiled at how particular his routine was. The order in which he took off his clothes, checked the pockets of his suit jacket before hanging it on a broad wooden hanger, rolled his belt up and put it in his drawer of rolled-up belts and took his dirty laundry through to the basket in their ensuite bathroom. Alice noted her skirt draped over the back of the chair, over jeans she'd worn at the weekend, her jumper strewn on the seat, her knickers scrunched on the floor. She wondered whether she was slovenly or if Mark was particularly fastidious. She wondered if her disregard for end-of-the-day neatness and order irked him.

'Mark,' she asked quietly, 'do you despair of me being a mucky pup?'

'Mucky pup?' Mark frowned, slipping cedar shoe horns into his shoes. Alice gestured to her discarded clothes. 'Don't be daft,' he smiled, selecting tomorrow's shirt. 'When I wake up, whichever way I'm facing, I see Alice rumpled. I like that.' He picked up her jumper. 'But this is cashmere and you really should fold it.' He did it for her. 'Which drawer?'

Alice looked over to the chest of drawers. 'Middle one,' she said, suddenly remembering her vibrator was in the drawer beneath. And then she wondered whether perhaps tonight was as good a time as any to introduce Mark to her bright pink, battery-operated friend. 'Not the middle drawer,' she announced, 'I mean the one below.' Find it! Don't find it!

Mark didn't find it. Alice didn't know whether she was disappointed or relieved. He continued his bedtime routine, inching the curtains back and looking down to the street, up to the sky. 'Clear night,' he assessed. It had been cloudy yesterday. Blustery the day before. He flicked his bedside light on, went back to the doorway and switched the main light off, hung his robe on the back of the door, rolled his head to either side while he walked over to the bed. He plumped his pillow, took off his watch and wound it up, checked the alarm clock though he never changed the setting. Though he always awoke moments in advance of the bell, he'd never not set it. He liked the physical act of silencing it just before it trilled so as not to disturb Alice. He reached for his Ian Rankin and skim-read the last paragraph from the night before, settling himself further into his pillow to read a chapter tonight.

He sighed. 'Long day,' he said, smiling apologetically at Alice, 'long day.'

Alice put her novel down. She reached for him, ran her fingertips along his forearm, stroked her hand up to his biceps, rested her touch tenderly on his shoulder. She nestled against him. He stretched out his arm and draped it round her shoulders though this made page-turning a little awkward. He kissed the top of her head. She kissed his chest in reply. Kissed it again, optimistically. Put her mouth over his nipple and changed her kiss to a suck. She looked up at Mark, he looked down from his book. He looked tired.

'Are you tired?' she whispered, her fingers tantalizingly tiptoeing a path down his chest and over his stomach.

'I am a little,' he admitted, 'work is a bit of a bitch at the moment. I'm carrying all David's while he's convalescing.'

'When he's back, why don't we take a week off?' Alice suggested, her hand resting lightly on his stomach while the conversation remained prosaic.

'Hopefully,' said Mark, deciding not to tell her about the imminence of trips to Singapore, Australia and Japan.

Alice decided distraction was good action. She traversed his torso with the palm of her hand. His nipples sprung to attention. 'Mark,' she murmured, licking her lips lasciviously, eyes asparkle, 'are you *tired* tired? Or just tired tired?'

He laughed through his nose. 'Are you laying claim to your conjugal rights, Mrs Sinclair?'

'I most certainly am,' Alice winked and kissed him on the chin, his mouth, nibbling his lower lip, 'if you're up to it.'

'I'm tired, but *he*'s certainly up to it,' Mark said as he led Alice's hand down his body, underneath the duvet to his hardening cock. Alice closed her eyes, closed her hand around him, felt him grow and stiffen and felt herself start to melt and moisten.

Mark held her head in his hands and kissed her softly all over her face. Alice rated him a very good kisser but actually, just then, she didn't want lips romantic and gentle, she wanted him to thrust his tongue into her mouth and gorge. Gently and evenly, he fondled each breast in turn before sliding his hand down her stomach, over the undulations of waist and hips, lightly over her bush and as far down her thigh as he could reach without breaking off from kissing her. She hungered for his mouth to feast on her breasts, she wanted his teeth to rasp against her nipples, she wanted his hands to knead her buttocks, she craved his fingers to delve greedily inside her. She pulled her face away and tried to guide his head down and his hand up. But he buried his face in her neck and nuzzled her there instead, cupped his hand over her sex without exploring further, stroking and stroking the length of her body. Desire for what he wasn't doing was heightening her arousal far more than what he was doing to her. It was as if her body was screaming and he couldn't hear it, so engrossed was he in his slow, tender lovemaking. The deafer he became, the more desperate her longing. It was strangely fantastic and frustrating.

Mark brought his face level with hers and gazed deep into Alice's eyes. 'You're so beautiful,' he told her. Gently, he parted her legs with his knee and, without taking his eyes off her, he carefully pushed his way inside her. He was pleasingly hard and Alice could sense her sex wanting to suck him in deeply. Her body tried to buck and grind against him but he had her securely enfolded in his arms and was setting a dignified, rhythmic pace. He moved inside her, gyrating subtly, moved and gyrated intoxicatingly slowly. She wanted to yell out fuck me you bastard but her mouth was plugged with his. She wanted him to thrust into her as if he had no self-control but he maintained his quiet, measured rhythm. He rolled her on top of him, sweeping her long hair from his face, scooping it up behind her head, holding her gaze. 'You feel so good,' he murmured. She sat up, the change in angle making her gasp. He stroked the fronts of her thighs whilst marvelling at the sight of her; the dip of her waist, the toned run of her stomach, the soft weight of her breasts, the eagerness of her nipples, the grace of her neck, the beauty of her face. 'I love you,' he whispered, 'God, I love you.' She was starting to pick up her pace, rotating and pumping as she straddled him. Mark pulled her down, rolled her over and kissed her and kissed her as he came. Deftly, Alice moved against him, the sudden rush of stickiness within her facilitating her own orgasm.

'That'll put me to sleep with a smile on my face,' he grinned at her. She smiled back. She could see how sleepy the orgasm had left him yet it had energized her.

'Did you know that the national average for sex amongst cohabiting couples is less than twice a week?' Alice announced, the jollity of her voice, as much as her topic, causing Mark's eyes to spring open.

He had a head for figures. 'Well, darling, we're above average, then.'

'Did you know that 50 per cent of women own vibrators?' Alice said, glancing at her chest of drawers, her heartbeat picking up a little.

'They must be the ones who are restricted to the national average,' Mark deduced.

Alice wasn't very good with figures and presumed Mark to have calculated some statistic, so she changed her tack. 'Have you ever used a vibrator on a woman?' she asked carefully.

He looked at her with a quick frown. 'Why?'

She gave him a sly smile. 'Just wondered.' Again, he frowned. 'You have!' she exclaimed, triumphantly. 'You have! Who? Tell me who!'

'No,' he said quite sternly, 'I assure you I haven't.' Because

Alice believed him, she suddenly wasn't sure how to progress the conversation.

'Anyway,' Mark said, 'aren't vibrators used in lieu of the real thing?' Alice was about to suggest they needn't be restricted to such times and would you like me to show you mine; but she sensed that Mark was mid-sentence. 'Or ridiculous props in dodgy vids,' he remarked.

'Have you ever filmed yourself?' Alice probed with a mischievous glint to her voice and eye.

'Christ, Alice!' Mark exclaimed, looking at her as if she was suffering sudden manic insanity.

'Might be fun?' Alice prompted coyly.

'Vibrators?' Mark said. 'Camcorders? Do I not satisfy you?' He regarded her with a flicker of suspicion to his gaze. Actually, he looked hurt and it shocked her. 'Do you find our sex life lacking?' he asked.

'No!' she protested. 'Not at all.'

'Am I travelling too much? Is that what's brought on this talk of vibrators? Were you faking your orgasm just now?'

'No,' Alice said, 'no. I was just— For an article. I was just editing out loud. Thinking.'

'I can't see how a shuddering lump of rubber could possibly better what's great as it is,' Mark said defensively. 'Wouldn't it detract from the intensity and meaning of our lovemaking – cheapen it?'

Alice felt badly. She hadn't anticipated Mark's hurt. She'd thought, at most, he'd be endearingly embarrassed and grateful for her dominance and initiative. Or else regard her as harmlessly kinky without taking offence. 'I was just editing an article,' she lied again, 'that's why I brought it up. That's all.'

He nodded. Full of surprises, his wife. He kissed her. 'Goodnight, Alice,' he said, 'I love you.'

* * *

'If you peel onions under a running tap, your eyes don't water.'

Saul watched Thea peeling onions under a running tap. 'How do you want the aubergine?' he asked. 'Sliced or diced?'

'Sliced, please.'

'Under running water?'

'No need. But spread them out then sprinkle salt over them to take away any bitterness.'

Saul sliced the aubergine. He reached up to take the salt

from the cupboard. Thea sensed the closeness of his body just behind her. His shirtsleeves were rolled to the elbow. Just a glance at his forearm, the soft hairs spattering down to his wrist, the delineation of muscle, shot desire through to her stomach. She could smell him and the pleasure of it flickered her eyes shut. Saul brushed his hand fleetingly between her shoulder blades and then set about salting his sliced aubergine. Pass the butter, please. Fingertips touched and electrical impulses charged. Eye contact. Adrenalin. You have flour on your cheek. I'll just brush it away for you. Thank you – here, let me feed you a fingerful of home-made mayonnaise. I need to reach up for that casserole dish. Yes, and when you do, I get to see your stomach lengthen and tauten and when you bring your arms down, your breasts swell.

'Saul, can you pass me that tea towel? Thanks.'

'Glass of wine? Red? Budge over – the corkscrew is in that drawer.'

Saul gently moved Thea to one side, his hands either side of her hips. She leant back lightly against his body and the proximity of his bulk sent a shiver of anticipatory pleasure through her. Suddenly Saul forgot about corkscrews. It seemed his reason for being there, behind Thea, was expressly to have his hands on her hips, his lips at the ultra-sensitive kiss of skin behind her ear. She pressed back against his chest and turned her cheek quickly; his lips leaving her neck and travelling over her jaw line to her mouth, her lips parted and her tongue tip was eager to dance with his. Behind her, rocking against her, her neck twisted round to reach his face, Saul gorged on her mouth. Something clanged down to the floor but they only half heard it. Thea whipped herself around so that she was facing him, her arms now thrown around his neck, her fingers enmeshed in his hair, urging his face against hers. He had a hand in the small of her back, his other clasping her right buttock. He pressed against her and she pulled herself up at him. The seam of her jeans was catching the swell of her sex and she parted her legs to find Saul's thigh for further friction. He backed her up against the fridge, his leg wedged between both of hers, his hands now in her hair, over her breasts, pulling and grabbing; the smattering of his evening bristles rasping against her cheeks, her chin, her neck.

Thea tried to unbutton Saul's shirt but it was taking too long so he pulled it over his head, undid his belt and ripped down his trousers to his knees. At the same time, Thea wriggled from her T-shirt and Saul pulled her bra straps down over her arms, not bothering with the clasp, not minding that it remained on, just as long as her tits were exposed for him to feel, to see and to suck. Thea's hand worked energetically over and under his boxer shorts, at last liberating his straining, leaping cock. They crumpled themselves down onto the rubber floor, romping and humping and snogging and sucking. Saul tugged Thea's jeans down, freeing her right leg. He moved her knickers to one side and took his mouth down to her. He could have spent hours feasting on her juice but tasting the rush of her moistness gave an urgency to the moment. With his trousers around his ankles, eyes closed, breathing fast and audible, Saul thrust into Thea and she ground against him. They humped and bucked and grunted and fucked, coming simultaneously; eyes scrunched shut, voices loud, faces racked into near-grimaces with the intensity of it all while their bodies spurted and sponged. And then they rolled apart, lay on the rubber floor, sticky and slippery and sweaty and satisfied, unable to speak while they let their heartbeats settle down.

'Jesus Christ,' Saul exclaimed on rolling towards Thea, his eyes slightly bloodshot. Just a few centimetres to the right of her face, a Sabatier knife lay glinting.

'Christ,' Thea agreed, her face flushed, a rash to one corner of her mouth. She reached her hand to Saul's face and gently flicked chopped parsley from his hair.

* * *

'Ouch!'

'Sorry, babe.'

'I don't think the beads go *there*, Richard.'

'I'm sure I saw it on some porn vid once. All right, how about here?'

'Well, they fit – but I can't say my world is shuddering. Porn vid? What porn vid?'

'How about if I try this with them? Hang on.'

'Do what with them where?'

'This! I'm doing it!'

'Are you? Oh.'

'Hang on, what about—'

'Don't you dare!'

'We're kind of running out of orifices, Sal.'

'Do you think it's orifices or orificii?'

'Wait a sec, let's try – this. Move that leg a bit. A bit more. There.'

'Ouch. Give them here. *You* roll over.'

'You must be bloody joking!'

'Look, shall we just bin the beads and have a good old shag?'

'Now you're talking.'

'Happy anniversary, big boy.'

Adam

Seven months after Alice and Mark were married, after Saul and Thea had formed a couple, Adam came into the world. Until then, Alice had hailed her wedding as marking the zenith of her creative and organizational talent. But Adam surpassed all of that. Adam was Alice's baby. Her true love. Her life's work. Her future ambition. Her past achievement, her present success. Her key to larger offices two floors above.

Just before her first wedding anniversary, Alice won Launch of the Year for *Adam* at a prestigious industry awards ceremony. The trophy, a rather dramatic slash of perspex in a gravity-defying swoop into a lump of softwood, shared pride of shelf-space in her executive office two floors up, alongside a framed first issue of *Adam* – the one with Clint Eastwood on the cover.

'Our project name was Quentin,' Alice told a packed Grosvenor House ballroom at that awards night, 'but as we kept having to stress "as in Tarantino, not Crisp" we needed something synonymous with Alpha Male. So our magazine became *Adam*. Biblical connotations end with the title – as we all know, publishing is no Garden of Eden, it's a men's mag jungle out there. However, with our spectacular circulation figures – and now with this major award – *Adam* reigns supreme.'

As she returned to her table, carried on a cushion of generous applause, the trophy pleasingly heavy, a reassuring ache in her arches from her Jimmy Choos, Alice believed the moment to mark the apotheosis of her career. Unfortunately, there was no Mark to the moment – he was in Hong Kong and she couldn't even phone him because of the time difference. With no husband to cuddle up to, Alice intended to get justifiably drunk on the company credit card and stay out ridiculously late.

'Mr Mundy,' she said whilst leaning around their round table topping up her team's glasses, 'Mr Mundy, you are a dickhead.'

'Thank you, Miss Heggarty,' Saul acquiesced, chinking glasses and sharing a raised eyebrow with the fashion editor and advertising manager.

'I mean,' Alice qualified, 'if you'd only come off your free-lance high horse and join the mag as staff, you'd be up there awarded Editor of the Year.' The fashion editor and ad manager nodded earnestly.

'That's kind of you,' Saul said, pausing to applaud a woman on stage receiving her jag of perspex for being Specialist Editor of the Year, 'but I've told you, I don't want to trade my freedom – my access to variety – for commuting, office politics and a lump of plastic.'

'It's perspex!' Alice retorted. 'It's sculpture!'

'Sure,' said Saul, 'but if I did *Adam* full-time I'd have to relinquish all my other work. And I'm a loyal bastard.' He clapped with everyone though he had no idea of the award just won.

'But me pay top dollar,' Alice said in a peculiar Japanese accent.

'Your dollars can't buy my desire for diversity, Alice,' Saul said, tonguing the words theatrically. 'I spend more time on *Adam* than on any of my other commitments. But I like my tutti-frutti life. I like dipping my finger in a fair few pies. *ES* mag versus the *Observer*, *T3* versus *GQ*. *MotorMonth* versus *Get Gadget*. I *need* variety.'

Another award was won, this time by a former colleague of Alice's so she wolf-whistled through her fingers – a raucous skill amusingly at odds with her sartorial grace and sleek deportment. 'Desire for diversity?' she balked, turning again to Saul. 'finger-dipping?' Alice wagged her finger at him. 'Your need for variety better not go beyond your professional life, Mr Mundy.'

Saul laughed. 'I may flirt my working way around publishing circles – but at play I'm working on being all Thea's. In my mind, in my heart,' he said, 'I'm all hers.'

'Promiscuous by pen is fine, promiscuous by penis – not!' Alice declared, rather pleased with that and wondering if she could regurgitate it in print. Not for *Adam*, obviously. *Lush*, perhaps.

'Has it escaped you that your first wedding anniversary also marks my first year with Thea?' Saul said defensively.

They chinked glasses.

'To Thea,' Saul drank, 'I couldn't love her more.'

'I love my husband, I love my job, I love my posh house, I love the plants I can't pronounce in my garden,' Alice proclaimed with regular sips, 'I love *Adam*. I love Thea. I love you!'

'This isn't the Oscars,' Saul laughed.

'It's the champagne,' Alice rued, 'it makes me emotional.'

'Switch to water,' Saul suggested.

'Bugger off!' Alice retorted, topping up everyone's glasses.

Mark flew back from the Far East and was immensely proud of Alice's Launch of the Year award, so much so that he persuaded her to bring it back home from the office at weekends. Until one weekend when he was abroad on business and Alice didn't bother. His excessive travelling and deal-mongering paid dividends in the form of a large and timely bonus. He whisked Alice off to Prague for their first anniversary and replaced Alice's shopping-channel paste earrings with genuine diamonds. Only larger. And set in platinum. She'd bought him a papier mâché globe because the girls on *Dream Weddings* reminded her that the first anniversary is paper. Alice was overwhelmed by Mark's gift. In fact, she was a little taken aback.

'I feel too young for such fuck-off rocks,' she confided to Thea, 'like I've sneaked my mum's for dressing up. Only my mum doesn't have diamonds even half this size. I have to keep them in a safe when I'm not wearing them or else they're not insured.'

'They're *stunning*,' Thea marvelled, privately thinking that, despite their dazzle, they were almost too big to be attractive or actually look real.

'They're serious,' Alice assessed. 'The fun of the fakes was that they were cheap tat. A joke where I had the last laugh. Do you want them?'

'Sure!' Thea said. 'Which ones?' she added.

*

'Where can I take you?' Saul asked Thea, a few days before their first anniversary. 'Cartier? TopShop?'

'Memory Lane,' Thea answered decisively.

'Is that some spa in Barbados?' Saul half joked.

'Primrose Hill,' Thea laughed. 'I want to retrace our steps.'

'Christ, you're soppy,' Saul said.

'I just want to walk hand in hand on Primrose Hill!' Thea protested.

'And if it's raining?'

'We'll get wet.'

'Can't I whisk you off to Babington House or somewhere, in a top-of-the-range Jag?' Saul all but pleaded.

'You don't have a car,' Thea reminded him patiently, 'you have a scooter.'

'Actually, that's where you're wrong. I've been given said Jag for the weekend – to take for a spin and assess for *MotorMonth*.'

'What colour is it?' Thea asked, slightly tempted.

'Racing green,' Saul shrugged, 'cream leather.'

'But I *want* to go to Primrose Hill to *our* bench,' Thea said with a petulant pout Saul couldn't resist.

So they compromised. They drove the mile or so to Primrose Hill and paid-and-displayed for two hours at great expense. At the top of the hill, Saul pulled out a roll of Refreshers and a family-size pack of Opal Fruits though it said Starburst on the packet. For Thea, the gesture was far more romantic than a country hideaway accessed by sports car. As an expression of her gratitude, she took off her jumper, and with no bra beneath her T-shirt, her nipples stood to Saul's attention, reminding him instantly of a year ago, when she was up there, all cold and hungover. He stroked her arms, giving her far stronger goose bumps than the November air.

Thea gazed at him, marvelling to herself that she hadn't noticed the slate-grey flecks to his irises. 'I love you, Saul Mundy,' she said.

'Happy First Whatever,' he grinned, 'Happy Us.'

* * *

When did you stop qualifying your age with *and a quarter*, or *and a half*, or *and three-quarters*? Thea continued until she hit her teens. In her mid-twenties, Alice was still in the habit of saying 'next year I'll be . . .' which, according to the time of year, enabled her to add up to two years onto her current age. However, the precise notch in the scale of their thirties soon seemed of little concern to others, it was the age of their relationships which generated interest now. Though both Alice and Thea had loved their first year with Mark and Saul, they were impatient for their first anniversaries to give their relationships status. As soon as Alice had passed the six-months mark, she took to saying she'd been married 'almost a year'. Thea spoke in terms of seasons rather than months. She'd say she and Saul had been together 'since last autumn' – which, by the following summer, seemed a distant time indeed. Thea did theorize to herself that November probably qualified as winter, but last November – *their* November – really had been mild. On average. According to meteorologists. According to high-street retailers. Hadn't ornithologists been concerned that certain birds hadn't yet flown south?

By the close of their first year, Thea was deeply in love with Saul and Alice loved being married very much. Alice rejoiced in believing that she knew everything there was to know about Mark. That there were no surprises was a blessing. She didn't envy Thea always learning something new about Saul, be it grey flecks to his eyes, or his expulsion at fifteen from boarding school, or his threesome with two Danish girls in his twenties on his first press trip. No, Alice was happy to embrace predictability at the expense of thrills. Thrills, her experience had taught her, were far too costly. If her head was now not for turning, it followed that her heart could not be for breaking.

Mark continued to be all she'd had a feeling he'd be – that hunch on the back of which she had proposed in his kitchen through a mouthful of carrot. He was a husband perfect for her. Loving, straight and responsible. And, now that she'd managed subtly to supervise his entire wardrobe, dapper too. Nice even brown eyes, unblemished education and career history, no deviations from the sexual norm. They didn't argue, there was nothing to fall out about. Tolerance was a key quality of Mark's and it sat well with his belief in the attraction of opposites. He never reacted when Alice over-reacted, he gladly sprang to his duty to calm and cool her down. Anyway, such times usually transpired only when work interfered. And it flattered and touched Mark that Alice should care so much and need him so. Best of all, he loved the baby-voiced, doleful-eyed ways she had of pleading with him not to stay late at work, not to fly to Hong Bloody Kong again.

Though Alice herself adored her job and was as ambitious and committed to her career as Mark, it seemed the pressures of Mark's job were actually more challenging to Alice than to him. No matter how demanding his day, how fraught the financial world, how difficult the deal, he always came home with an easy smile, eager and energized by his role as husband. The frequent travel he undertook was strenuous for him, yet it appeared to be far tougher on Alice. He just had jet lag to contend with, the vagaries of business etiquette around the world, the precarious threads that deals hung by, the tedium of chain hotels no matter how luxurious; his timetable was so full there was rarely an opportunity to think, let alone relax. Alice, however, was left with only half her home; all the trimmings of marriage but with no husband. It wasn't that she actually moped for Mark, nor that she felt forsaken. It simply wasn't much fun playing home alone.

Their house in Hampstead, with all its gadgets and gorgeousness, was meant to be their Wonderland. However, Alice didn't feel in Wonderland when she was on her own; she felt she shrank in the house, as though she had downed some Carrollian Drink-Me potion. Her luxury kitchen suddenly seemed stage-set oversized with its echoey French limestone floor, cavernous American fridge, catering-standard range cooker and abundant bespoke units. Had she not sourced the designer bath precisely on account of its curves and capaciousness being calibrated for two, not one? The surround-sound system connected to the vast plasma screen in the sitting room was too technical for her. Their bed was so enormous it seemed downright daft to sleep in it alone when Mark was away, so Alice would take to her old double bed, now in the smaller of their two other bedrooms. Consequently, she usually ate heartily at lunchtime on the days when Mark wouldn't be home, having just a packet of crisps or a KitKat or two in the evening, curling up on his lounger watching a DVD on the Mac in his study until she was too sleepy to take a bath which would have taken too long to run anyway.

Alice did not like it when Mark travelled. She didn't like it when he travelled because she didn't like living alone. She also didn't like it when he travelled because she didn't like it when he returned. She didn't like it when he travelled because she didn't like it when he returned because she couldn't prevent herself from being snappish and ungracious. She didn't like it when he returned because, though he was the one justified in being scuppered by jet lag and drained by the pressure of transatlantic deals done or lost, he was always calm and delighted to see her. She was the one who was inexcusably ratty. She'd sullenly turn down dinner, in or out, claiming no appetite. She'd yawn that she was too tired to talk on any of his thoughtfully chosen topics. She'd go to bed early and pretend to be asleep; feign headaches and exhaustion when he deserved a soothing back rub or craved an affirming blow-job. She'd pretend to be too deeply asleep even to acknowledge, never mind reciprocate, his affectionate kiss goodnight.

Mark always brought her something – from fabulous Hong Kong kitsch (a luminous limited-edition Hello Kitty digital watch) to trinkets from Barney's, New York; from gorgeous toiletries brazenly swiped from the housekeeping trolley at Hotel Costes in Paris, to the catalogue from a Paul Klee exhibition just opened in Chicago. Invariably, Alice initially accepted the gifts with a startling lack of grace, ignoring her conscience until the next day when she'd phone or email or text Mark to say she loved him and that she was wishing away the hours on her Hello Kitty watch until home time. And then she'd prepare a gorgeous supper and have Mark in stitches with anecdotes from work. She'd run a bath for two with Costes bath foam and have candles lit in the bedroom. She'd lavish attention on his body, faking her own orgasm if necessary, ensuring Mark went to sleep with an exhausted smile on his face.

One of the mags Alice published ran an article defining Reverse Punishment Syndrome – '*he's trying to be nice but you're just nasty*'. Perhaps that's me, she thought. But the piece went to repetitive lengths (she'd scold the features editor) to tell her not to bollock her bloke for having a few beers down the pub with the boys, not to punish her fella for playing footie with the lads every single Sunday, not to hassle her man for inviting his mates round for Xbox marathons. Mark, however, didn't play football, didn't own an Xbox, pubs weren't his thing and he preferred a good burgundy to beer. She could never accuse him of choosing over her. She never had cause to doubt that she was absolutely the love of his life, the axis around which his world revolved.

'Is it that you don't like being on your own? Do you resent his job? Because you often work long hours too. Or is it that you simply miss him when he's not around? They're interlinked, undoubtedly, but fundamentally separate issues,' Thea asked, whilst wrestling with the home-cinema system one night when Mark was in Chicago.

'You actually *choose* to have nights off from Saul, don't you?' Alice digressed. 'You choose to spend time apart.'

'I like my flat. I saved for ages. I like to escape into my own little slice of Lewis Carroll Living,' Thea qualified, 'and you've avoided a direct answer. Look, do you really no longer have anything as dependable and old-fashioned as a video?'

'Not any more,' said Alice.

'Jesus, how many remote controls does a girl need?' Thea despaired, fiddling with another one.

'You'd think just the one,' said Alice.

Thea had been in love previously, but prior to Saul, love had lacked balance. It was only now, through the equilibrium and reciprocation achieved between the two of them, that she could see this. In the past, she had invested far more affection and trust, loyalty and generosity, than was ever returned to her. She'd attributed virtues and qualities not present to past boyfriends, in the deluded hope that if she believed they were faithful, loyal and as in love with her as she was with them, then perhaps they would be. Her dogged veneration of the concept of Romantic Love saw her turn a blind eye even when transgressions had leered back at her directly. Though her heart had been hurt, she had never let the pain harden her; she never questioned her belief that true love makes the world go round, she'd never lost hope that love could conquer all.

Before she met Saul, Thea had believed that the deeper the love the more wrought with complexity it ought to be. However, she also thought that great art was only born of angst until Saul took her to a Matisse exhibition at Tate Modern. And so it was with Saul that Thea discovered to her amazement that love could be the simplest thing in one's life. Being in love with Saul introduced her to the balance necessary for longevity. With this heaped magnificently on one side of the scale, Thea found all the other elements and concerns of life were invested with correct weight and proportions on the other. She was in love with Saul and he was just as in love with her and the plain fact was enough to keep a steady equilibrium in her life. All the love she gave him, he gave right back to her.

She loved Saul's spontaneous visits to the Being Well armed with orange juice or the new issue of *Heat*; how he'd pop in for a kiss en route to a meeting, drop off a raisin-and-biscuit Yorkie on his way back from an editorial brainstorming session. She loved how he would occasionally materialize behind her in the lunchtime queue at Pret a Manger, murmuring 'they say that banana cake is an aphrodisiac' or 'gissa bite of your baguette, love'. His text messages arrived at all hours and she never knew whether they'd be chatty, romantic or downright dirty. Sometimes he'd make love to her with great tenderness, taking time to stroke her, absorbed in just looking at her, watching the effect that altering the angle or a subtle variation in pace could have on the flush to her cheeks or the dilation of her pupils. And sometimes he'd fuck her most carnally, his eyes screwed shut as he screwed her, clenching his teeth as he grabbed her buttocks and bucked forcefully into her until he came. Sometimes, he was as sated purely through cunnilingus as she was; though she'd sleepily offer to return the favour, he'd hush her with a goodnight kiss, turn out the light and spoon tenderly against her. Thea didn't mind that he was grumpy when he woke up, that his farts were noxious and that he could snore for Britain. It didn't bother her that his timekeeping was lousy, that he'd snap at her if she talked during films, that their taste in music had few overlaps, that sometimes he bolted his food. She was glad to love him enough to allow him his personality. She had no higher ideal to project onto him. 'Rounded with rough edges,' she defined to Alice, 'he's not perfect and so he's ideal.' At last, Thea had fallen in love with someone she had no inclination, no need, to deify. Alice's wish for Thea had only ever been that someone would find her who deserved the depth of the love she had to give.

Thea and Saul could have frantic late nights gallivanting around the bars of Soho, or they could plunder Villandry and go home for extravagant carpet picnics. They could be the loved-up couple at dinners hosted by friends, or they could arrive together at parties but socialize separately, with the occasional grin or wink over to each other. They'd have backgammon tournaments which became quite tense, Scrabble sessions that were downright serious or raucous evenings watching DVDs of Spinal Tap or the Blues Brothers, aided by shots of home-made Mars Bar vodka. Then there were the evenings when they were so engrossed in their own thing that they hardly knew the other was there; the Saturdays when Thea ironed for most of the day and Saul tapped away at his laptop in her bedroom; the Sundays spent in affable silence over the newspapers. There were also Saul's evenings at the Swallow with Ian or Richard that Thea had no intention of gatecrashing. And evenings when Saul smiled at the thought of Thea all by herself, unplugging her phone so she could watch *ER* uninterrupted.

Thea read everything Saul wrote, but only once it was in print.

'Shall I start putting you in my columns?' Saul mused.

'What – Michael Winner style?' Thea looked up from the *Sunday Times*. 'Christ!'

Saul laughed. 'I was thinking more *à la* A. A. Gill, hon.'

But he didn't. Barefaced Bloke's readers had heard no more about the Gorgeous Thief since that article published the day they first kissed. Saul Mundy had a public voice and a private side. And when he finished writing an article with laddish overtones for one mag, or a column infused with sarcasm for another, or a review so cleverly barbed it was downright spiky, what he found most satisfying was to log off, look up and see Thea. Engrossed in a book, or quietly sipping a cup of tea, or embroiled in a text-messaging marathon with Alice, or simply daydreaming.

'She's my mate,' Saul qualified one evening to Ian, 'in every sense of the word. Soulmate, best mate, bed mate.'

'Flatmate?' Ian posed.

Saul sipped thoughtfully at his pint. 'Not yet,' he said cautiously, 'but there again, we've only been together a year.'

A Year Between the Sheets

ADAM

January, Issue 8

Jack Nicholson cover

- Is this the coolest man in the world?
- The year in preview – wear it, see it, hear it, buy it
- Health & fitness: six weeks to a six-pack

- Motors – penis extension or life support?
- Sex – do it
- Money – make it
- Property – live it
- Win! Gadgets and gear up for grabs

ADAM
February, Issue 9
Nicole Kidman cover

- Nicole, we love you, marry us
- Hot property – buy abroad, get a tan, make a profit
- Fitness: back your back
- Hand-made shoes and bespoke suits, every wardrobe should have them
- Sex – it's good for you, fact
- Tool kits and WD40: every woman loves a handyman
- Plus! Reviews – we've seen 'em, read 'em, heard 'em, tasted 'em and played 'em
- Win! Sail into the sunset: two weeks on a luxury yacht

ADAM
March, Issue 10
Sean Connery cover

- Connery – the real McCoy
- There's something about Mary, Isla and Jen – supermodels with brains *and* bod
- Prison – it's a step closer than you'd think
- Double your money in half a year
- Bachelor pad or disaster area: architects, designers, cleaners show us how
- Love handles? Man boobs? Stop it with the names and get rid of them in 4 weeks
- Sex – come together or drift apart
- Win! Top seats at Top 10 sporting fixtures

'Thea, I've blocked out your eleven-o'clock slot,' Souki put her hand over the telephone receiver and told Thea, who was arranging magazines for the waiting room and flowers for the reception. 'New client – sounds desperate.'

'Sure,' said Thea.

'That's fine,' Souki told the caller. 'May I take your name? Mr Sewell. Lovely, we'll see you in a couple of hours. Yes, Baker Street Tube. That's right. Goodbye.' Souki filled in the appointments diary and turned to Thea. 'Cup of tea?'

'I was half hoping Saul might pop by with lattes all round,' Thea remarked.

'Two days on the trot might be wishful thinking,' Souki said. 'Do you think we could offer Saul free fortnightly massage in return for daily lattes?'

'I'll put it to him,' Thea said, 'though he claims to hate massage. Says it makes him feel uncomfortable and exposed.'

'Just wait till he puts his back out through squash or something – he'll be begging for it,' Souki declared. 'Earl Grey or Red Bush?'

'RB, please. So who's the eleven o'clock?'

'A Mr Sewell – said he's done his back in,' Souki informed Thea, 'but as Brent and Dan are fully booked, I reckoned yours were the second-safest hands.'

Mr Sewell arrived ten minutes early. He was far younger than Thea had expected. In fact, he looked like Peter O'Toole in his Lawrence of Arabia period, which was a very pleasant surprise. Though dressed smartly, the pain from his back caused his suit to hang oddly, as if he'd forgotten to remove the hanger. Likewise, his face had an exaggerated angularity caused by teeth clenching; what appeared to be extraordinary blue eyes were dulled.

'Usually, clients who refer to themselves as Mr or Mrs Such-and-Such are older,' Thea remarked by way of small talk as she led the way to her room at the top. He didn't say his name was Gabriel until Thea took his details and asked for it outright. She noted him shift gingerly in the seat, a greyness flood his face as he did so. If pain was this visible, the poor man must be in torment, she thought. In her experience, men in pain either exaggerated its intensity or downplayed it entirely.

'Tell me about the pain,' Thea said, pen poised.

'Oh, it's nothing,' Mr Sewell lied.

From Mr Sewell's personal details, Thea considered his lifestyle and its possible ramifications on his current predicament. Gabriel Sewell was thirty-eight years old with a home in Clapham and an office in Mayfair. He was an actuary by profession – Thea didn't know what this entailed but ascertained it was sedentary and high-powered. He appeared to be relatively fit, playing five-a-side once a week, plus regular golf and occasional cycling. It seemed he was fairly healthy, good diet, good weight, just a social smoker and a regular but not heavy drinker.

'So,' Thea said, 'tell me about your back.'

'I'm sure it's nothing,' Mr Sewell began.

But it wasn't nothing. It transpired that leaving his wife over the weekend and hauling suitcases out of the loft and personal possessions out of the marital home had conspired to cause Mr Sewell's spasm.

'OK,' Thea said after working on him for an hour, 'I'll leave you for a moment. Take your time.'

She hovered outside her room, listening to silence followed by a sigh and the sound of Mr Sewell dressing. She knocked and after a moment, entered. He was sitting in the chair, gazing out over rooftops. His expression was unreadable but to Thea's trained eye, the tenseness in his neck had dissolved and the greyness of his complexion had lifted. She asked how he felt, if the treatment had helped, if the pain was diminished, but Mr Sewell expressed any gratitude in a monosyllabic way.

'I'd like you to come again,' Thea advised, 'towards the end of this week, preferably. I'd also like you to see one of our osteopaths for some manipulation.'

'Fine,' Mr Sewell said, 'OK.'

'I'll book you in downstairs,' Thea said, leading the way.

'Thank you, Miss –?' Mr Sewell waited to be informed.

'Thea,' Thea assured him, 'Thea's fine.'

He nodded and left.

'Thea darling! I'm late, I know – I'm sorry, honey, but I've had a bitch of a morning. A total *bitch*. And my back's killing me. Total fucking nightmare.'

Thea's twelve o'clock arrived quarter of an hour late with his usual flurry of excuses. Because he was a regular, she would overrun her lunch hour to honour a full session for him. 'Don't worry, it's not a problem, Peter,' she acquiesced, 'come on up and let's get cracking.'

'I thought only osteos could do that,' Peter joked.

'*Let's get petrissaging* doesn't have quite the same ring to it,' Thea said over her shoulder as she climbed the stairs.

Peter Glass had been a client of Thea's for a year or so. He came in now for 'monthly maintenance' as he termed it, though he regularly phoned for 'crisis sessions' in between. This was meant to be a maintenance visit but it was obvious from his stilted gait that a crisis now superseded it.

'How are you, Peter?' Thea asked him, wondering how long it would take the serene atmosphere of her room to calm him. Peter was usually busy to the point of being manic – an upmarket estate agent earning on commission only, with a complex love life, a love of material goods and a propensity for changing his car as frequently as his girlfriend.

'Work's mental – good mental. Life's crazy – cool crazy. New squeeze, new Beemer.'

'What's Beemer?' Thea asked.

Peter laughed. 'BMW – Beemer, you know? Like Merc? Alpha?'

'Skoda?' Thea said.

'You don't!' Peter exclaimed.

'I don't,' Thea assured him, 'I have a Fiat Panda.'

'You *don't*!' Peter exclaimed with genuine horror.

'Eleven years old,' Thea said proudly. 'Now, how are you?' She glanced at the clock, knowing that he'd talk at her throughout the session anyway.

'Nightmare,' Peter groaned theatrically but with justification. 'Do you want me down to my Jockeys?'

'Yes, please,' said Thea, skimming her notes on Peter's last session, 'and then face down on the table.'

'How's your love life, babes?' Peter enquired, his voice muffled as Thea started the massage.

'This feels tight.' Thea ignored his question, pressing into his lower trapezius until she felt it yield.

'If I was single, I'd wine and dine you, honey,' Peter told her with an appreciative groan.

'If I was single, I'd turn you down,' Thea responded though immediately wished she hadn't.

'So you *do* have a love life,' Peter commented, 'but do you have a love nest? I can show you some gorgeous properties.'

'You haven't been doing those stretches I showed you, have you?' Thea chastised, glad to change the subject.

'Not enough hours in the day, babes,' Peter rued. 'Stretching takes too long.'

'Peter!' Thea admonished. 'That series I showed you takes a maximum ten minutes, on weekdays only. You can do them *anywhere*.'

'Not long but *slow*,' Peter qualified, 'I mean they feel like they take too long because they're so slow. All that holding and breathing. I don't do slow – not in my life.'

Reluctantly, Thea understood. He was a character, Peter Glass, a wide boy and charmer but self-deprecating and thus likeable. For all his bravura and bullshit, bragging of Beemers and calling every woman 'babes', he was a decent bloke contending with vicious pain.

'You do make me feel better,' Peter told her, knotting his Gucci tie. 'If I could afford the time I'd come to you every bloody week. Twice, maybe. It's only here that I slow down and unwind a little while you untie all those crap muscles of mine.'

'Let's book you in for next week,' Thea said.

'Cool, babes,' said Peter, 'but I may have to cancel last minute.'

'Zay say zat avocado makes a lady ripe for lurve. Zay say zat carrot cake makes a lady hot. Zay say zat cheesy crisps make a lady juicy.'

Thea stood in the queue at Pret a Manger, thrilled at the surprise of Saul whispering in her ear, with his improbable accent and bizarre theories on foodstuffs.

'Lady,' he continued, murmuring throatily, his voice an octave lower than his regular English accent, 'zay say zat a lady who likes avocado and cheesy crisps and cake of carrot, she is lady who do much sexy sex.'

'Piss off,' Thea whispered, giggling. Saul stood close behind her and kissed insistently behind her ear and along the curve of her neck. 'Stop it,' Thea hissed, 'we're in public.'

'Exactly,' whispered Saul. 'God, I'm horny.'

'I'm on a short lunch,' Thea apologized, now feeling quite horny herself.

'I'll walk you back,' Saul said, 'as long as the tent pole in my trousers doesn't get me arrested en route.'

It had snowed overnight and though the pavements were clear of it, a dusting still sprinkled the shrubs, iced the lawns and cushioned the benches in Paddington Street Gardens. Dogs trotted through the park with elevated action and children scampered around trying to snowball all spare snow.

'It always seems bizarre to be planning summer issues when it's February and freezing,' Saul commented, 'but that's my afternoon – top beaches and barbecue tips. And a haircut – look at me, Christ!'

'After my morning of men,' Thea told him, 'I have an afternoon of girls – my ballet dancer, two pregnant women and my little old lady. But I'd really better make tracks and warm my hands or I'll lose all my clients.'

'And then you'll come to mine?' Saul asked. 'Movie? Villandry carpet picnic? Rude sex?'

'Reverse order, preferably,' Thea said. She looked at Saul and bit her bottom lip with coquettish intent. 'Who'd've thought that cheesy crisps were an aphrodisiac.'

Saul took Thea at face value and didn't dare say he'd made it up. 'Let's sneak up to your room for a quickie,' he said instead, 'you know you want it, you dirty thing!'

'You're incorrigible. I'm not remotely tempted,' Thea scolded him playfully, kissing him teasingly with her tongue before flouncing into the Being Well with a provocative wiggle.

'Christ, I need a shag,' Saul muttered to himself, putting beaches and barbecues on the back burner, the haircut on hold.

ADAM

April, Issue 11

Vic Reeves/Bob Mortimer cover

- Why British comedy rocks
- Rock – why British rock is comedy
- Sex – rock hard
- Vinnie Jones – still rock hard
- Travel – Gibraltar, Brighton and Australia – and other famous rocks
- Sport – rock climbing
- Win! Some rocks, courtesy of De Beers

ADAM

May, Issue 12

Emmanuelle Beart/Vanessa Paradis double cover

- It's in the Cannes – the sexiest film festival, now and then
- Secrets, lies and big big bucks – what keeps the film industry rolling
- Muscle in – steroid abuse: coming to your high-street chemist soon
- Sex addiction – bona-fide illness or top excuse
- Air guitar, shadow boxing and imaginary golf swings – good for your health
- Property how-to: it doesn't cost much and it won't hurt your back
- Win! A line in Danny Boyle's new film

Saul sat in Alice's office and they both swivelled in the chairs, Saul tapping a Biro gently against his teeth, Alice furrowing her brow and twitching her lip, while they brainstormed features for future issues.

'How about,' Alice mused, 'sex advice through the eyes of – hang on – a porn star, a sex therapist and a—'

'Housewife,' Saul suggested.

'Brilliant,' Alice said, her fingers scuttling over her keyboard.

'I was thinking,' Saul said, 'the Tour de France for the July issue – *the world's best athletes or drugged-up cheats*.'

'Yep,' said Alice, 'I like it. How's the August issue going?'

Saul twitched his lip. He looked sidelong at Alice, swivelled a complete revolution, rolled up the sleeves on his shirt, ran his fingers through his hair, rubbed his chin and then leant forward. 'I'm going to hear by the end of the week if we've got Bowie for the cover,' he said nonchalantly.

'Oh, Good Lord,' Alice exclaimed, blushing visibly, clasping her hand to her heart. She reached across her desk and grabbed Saul's wrists, her eyes darting around his. 'Seriously?' she whispered. 'Because you know you really must never joke about something like that.' Saul raised an eyebrow in affirmation. 'Oh, Good Lord,' Alice exclaimed. She slumped back in her chair. 'I'm coming to the photo shoot,' she declared. 'Have you told Thea?'

Saul shook his head. 'It's not confirmed,' he cautioned, 'and the shoot will be in New York.'

'Well, I feel a business trip coming on,' Alice proclaimed, 'and I'll need an assistant, of course.'

'I'm far too busy,' Saul declared.

'Not you, idiot boy, *Thea*!' Alice retorted, quietly wondering if an enduring crush on an ageing icon was in any way unsuitable for a married woman. She swiftly decided it was not.

'Anyway, Bowie or not, the issue's coming on fine,' Saul assured her, 'it'll be the biggest yet and the ad team are storming their targets already.'

'Brilliant,' said Alice. 'Bowie. Oh, my God. Right. Yes. Moving on – how about something on relationship dynamics, you know, who has power.'

'Who has the balls, who wears the trousers,' Saul said, 'that's good – I'll try and commission someone like Jeff Green to write it. Oh, Richard Stonehill is putting me in touch with a guy who has a self-build company – I thought that would make an interesting piece.'

'Certainly,' said Alice, 'and Ben from the music division is working on Liam Gallagher. Come on, let's go for lunch. Thea said you had an amazing weekend in Brighton. You were lucky with the weather – May bank holiday is usually a washout.'

Saul gathered his things and followed Alice through the building. He smiled to himself, recalling Thea that previous weekend, stripping off nonchalantly on a quiet spot on the beach. It was only when she was down to her knickers that he clarified it was Bournemouth, not Brighton, that had the nudist beach.

'Saul thinks we'll have Bowie for the August issue,' Alice told Mark as he loaded the dishwasher. 'Can you believe that?'

'Believe what, darling?' Mark asked distractedly.

'That we'll have Bowie for the August issue,' Alice frowned.

'Well done,' Mark said, straightening up and rubbing the small of his back. 'I think I'll take some paracetamol.'

'So I may go to New York for the shoot,' Alice said, though she feared tempting fate by being presumptuous.

'New York?' Mark said, rummaging through his briefcase for painkillers. 'No, San Francisco next week, home via Chicago.'

'I give up,' Alice muttered, turning her back on Mark and her attention to the *Evening Standard*, flipping noisily through the pages.

'Alice,' Mark protested quietly, 'I just really want to knock the Gerber–Klein deal on the head – precisely so there won't be so much travelling.'

'Until the next deal,' Alice said under her breath. 'Actually, I was talking about *me*, Mark – *I* may have to go to New York.'

'For work?' Mark asked.

'Yes, Mark, we're shooting Bowie for the August issue and he's personally requested I attend,' Alice said with cutting nonchalance, though she was now convinced she'd probably jinxed the deal completely.

'Well, that's a feather to your cap,' Mark said ingenuously, wondering why his wife looked cross when her news was so good. He swallowed the paracetamol. 'John and Lisa have invited us to dinner next Friday,' Mark changed the subject brightly, 'and Leo and Nadia want to know if we'd like to accompany them to the Barbican the following week – *Madame Butterfly*.'

Alice tried to bite her tongue but she missed, snapping at Mark instead. 'Oh, great. Dull dinners with your boss and sodding opera with your dreary clients.'

'Alice!' Mark exclaimed, unprepared for her reaction. 'I thought you liked Lisa – you said she's a marvellous cook. And you've been saying recently how you'd like us to go out more, do things.'

'I'm more than just your corporate wife, you know,' Alice said, unfairly as Mark had never treated her as such. Mark, bewildered that a dinner invite and concert tickets could have such an adverse effect on Alice, started cleaning the coffee machine.

With her back towards Mark, she lowered her voice. 'I'm

thirty-two, Mark. I don't want to do boring dinner parties and stuffy concerts all the time.'

'Come on,' Mark said, 'it's hardly all the time.'

Alice turned to face him, her hands on her hips. 'That's true,' she said, 'because the rest of the time you're invariably away.'

'Alice, that's not fair,' Mark objected, 'I work hard because I work for *us*.' He waved his hand around vaguely to signify their home.

'And I'm just the little wifey keeping your home fire burning?' Alice asked spikily.

Mark ran his hands through his hair, though they were full of coffee grains. He was hurt. But very clear. 'You know what, Alice,' Mark said, 'for me that is precisely one of the joys of marriage – knowing you *are* my home. Wherever I am in the world, whatever time it is, no matter how stressful my day or how hectic my schedule, there's this underlying warmth and security which makes sense of everything – the knowledge of my wife, my home.'

Alice flounced off to bed early, in the spare room, in her old bed. She dreamt of New York and David Bowie; that she and Thea brought roses to the shoot, which liquefied into green gloop. In the small hours, she awoke with her heart racing, acutely aware of the hurt and confusion she'd caused the man who loved her most. She felt ashamed. Mark's love was unconditional and she told herself that she should aim to love him likewise. She waited a while and then tiptoed to their bedroom, to their vast bed and said sorry.

Mark was finding it difficult to sleep. His back hurt, the Gerber Klein deal was a lingering headache and it pained him that he'd upset Alice. He welcomed her with open arms and a tender kiss to her forehead.

Alice had seemed distracted at Pilates, cutting her session short to sit quietly in the reception area, browsing back issues of *Hello* magazine. Even suggesting the bistro on a balmy May evening had taken Thea some doing. Assessing the menu, she remarked that Alice seemed tired.

'I'm not tired,' Alice said.

'Hungry?' Thea asked, beckoning the waitress.

'Not particularly,' Alice said, glancing at the specials board.

'Oh, my God, are you pregnant?' Thea gasped because Sally

had recently announced that she was and *she* looked tired and had gone off Pilates and chips.

'I am most certainly not pregnant,' Alice declared flatly.

'Is it work?' Thea presumed.

'No, Thea,' Alice said, 'it's Mark.'

'Mark?' Thea balked, ignoring the chips, which had just arrived. She stared at Alice who was gazing into the middle distance of the restaurant. 'Alice?'

'Yes,' said Alice, prodding the pasta without looking, 'Mark.'

'What's he done?' Thea demanded, heaping Greek salad onto her fork.

'Nothing,' Alice said despondently, twirling the pasta to such a degree that it unwound from the fork completely.

'Nothing?' Thea repeated, with her mouth full.

'Yes, nothing,' Alice sighed, lifting her empty fork and putting it in her mouth, 'and that's the point. It's just nothingy.' She shrugged. 'All work and no play make Mark a dull, dull boy.' Though she felt instantly disloyal, she was just a little relieved too. 'I'm scared that I'm bored,' Alice confided, looking genuinely alarmed. 'I'm worried, Thea. Actually, perhaps it's not Mark. Perhaps it's me.'

Thea didn't want to hear this and didn't know what to make of it, let alone how to comment. 'Mark is all that you've wanted and he is all that you need, he's what you never had and you married him precisely for his commitment and his soberness,' she told Alice sternly.

'But his commitment is to work and he's so sober it's a bore,' Alice muttered. 'Corporate dinners and bloody opera, Thea, that's the sum of it.'

'What are his workmates like?' Thea asked, trying to be positive.

'Mark doesn't have "mates", Thea,' Alice said, 'he has colleagues and clients. They're fine – I mean, a similar age – but dull.'

'Well, I love Mark,' Thea said warmly. 'Let's organize some evenings together, the four of us. How about salsa? Or that hysterical pub quiz you and I used to go to? I don't know, ice-skating at Ally Pally?'

Alice shrugged. 'Can you honestly see Mark salsa dancing? Do you really think he'd leave work on time for a pub quiz?'

'Come on,' Thea said gently, 'perhaps you're a little stressed yourself – work?'

Alice laughed harshly. 'I have David Bowie as my cover boy – how can I be stressed?'

'Maybe Mark's stress is rubbing off on you?' Thea tried, knowing she didn't sound convincing.

'Mark is ticking along just fine, Thea – it's *me*,' Alice whispered. 'Suddenly he seems so much older than me.' She couldn't say it so she mouthed it, staring at the table. *Boring*.

Thea didn't want to hear this. Mark Sinclair was Alice's salvation, the yin to her yang. Alice, it seemed to Thea, had done the grown-up thing when she married Mark; she'd set the standard and embraced the rules. Alice being unhappy made Thea feel discomfited. That Alice was bored caused Thea to worry. As her best friend, she didn't think twice about reprimanding Alice.

'You need to remember all your reasons for marrying Mark,' Thea told her, 'and you need to remember that your playboy exes actually made you miserable. You need to think logically about marriage, Alice, because by definition, you're in it for the long haul. Of course there are going to be fluctuations in temperature – cold currents, heatwaves, warm periods. Maybe you should look on it as just being a little unsettled at the moment,' Thea concluded, hoping to sound reassuring, 'and know that it'll abate and be fine.'

'I'm starting to feel stifled, Thea,' Alice said quietly, wondering when her best friend had become a meteorologist and marriage counsellor. 'There seems to be no frisson between me and Mark. No fizz. It's all gone a bit flat.'

'Alice, I'm the diehard romantic here but even I can acknowledge that there's more to marriage than raunchy sex or just being in love,' Thea said. 'Anyway, I thought you said frissons and fizz were just phenyl-something.'

'Phenylethylamine,' Alice muttered. She felt irritated. It wasn't as if Thea was even living with Saul, so on what authority could she lecture? 'I mean, of course I want to grow old with Mark – I just don't want to be old while I'm still youngish.'

'It'll be *fine*,' Thea said, because she really couldn't start thinking it could possibly be anything other. She believed in the mystical sanctity of being in love; she didn't like the way Alice dissected it into chemical components, albeit light-heartedly. But just then, Thea prayed for surges of adrenalin and dopamine and that phenyl-something for her best friend, so that Alice could feel love flushed and happy to be Mrs Sinclair once more.

Later that night, after sending a text message to Alice assuring her that everything would be OK and that she was there for her, Thea rang Saul to say goodnight. He wasn't in and his mobile was switched off. She tried again ten minutes later. And then ten minutes after that, when his mobile was back on.

'Hullo,' said Thea, hearing traffic in the background, 'where are you?'

'I've just nipped out for a pint of milk and some chocolate biscuits,' Saul said. Thea was surprised he hadn't come across the milk she'd replenished that morning and the KitKats and Hobnobs. 'Oh,' Saul faltered, 'did you? Thanks. How was Pilates?'

'Good,' Thea said, settling into bed for a chat.

'What was it tonight – Rioja and chips?' Saul laughed, obviously walking briskly.

'Alice seemed a bit tired, actually,' said Thea, 'off her chips. Tell you what, why not call me from the land line in a mo'?'

Actually, it took half an hour for Saul to return Thea's call when it transpired he hadn't nipped to *that* corner shop but actually one further afield.

'Can I ask you something?' she asked him.

'Shoot,' said Saul, clattering around his flat.

'Mark –' Thea started. 'You get on with him, don't you?'

'Of course,' said Saul, 'who wouldn't.'

'But you *really* get on well with Richard, don't you?'

'Yes,' Saul qualified easily, 'Richard's a really good bloke.'

'Is Mark not a good bloke, then?' Thea asked.

Saul paused. 'Mark's more of a nice guy than a good bloke,' he explained.

ADAM
June, Issue 13
1st Anniversary special edition
Beautiful Britain cover

- Celebrate!
- It's a tough job, but someone has to do it: Britain's top-selling men's mag one year on
- *Models, actors, singers, whatever – the best of British*
- Power couples – who has the balls may not be who wears the trousers
- High street or haute couture – who can tell?
- Build muscle, lose fat, eat like a horse, no catch
- She told me she was 16 – and other nightmare scenarios
- Wear it, hear it, read it, see it – cutting edge and lead the pack

All the news-stands at Heathrow Airport were awash with the anniversary issue of *Adam*. Because Alice hadn't been able to justify a trip to New York for the Bowie shoot and because Mark himself had stayed longer than anticipated in the States, he was whisking his wife off to Marbella for the weekend as a consolation prize, a gesture. And also, a celebration – he'd finally secured the Gerber–Klein deal. He'd propped her passport and plane ticket against her toothbrush when he'd left early for work.

Mark picked up a copy of *Adam* and bought it. Alice looked puzzled. 'I bring copies home, Mark.'

'Ah, but I want the pleasure of buying my own. Anyone who's anyone buys *Adam*,' Mark said sweetly, 'it's the ultimate accessory. Anyway, a little subliminal marketing never goes amiss – I can always tuck my copy of the *Economist* inside the cover.'

Alice smiled and went in search of a paperback. She needed a break. They both did.

ADAM

July, Issue 14

Tour de France cover

- Superhumans or simple junkies – peddling and pedalling with the peloton
- The porn star, the housewife, the sex therapist – three women set you homework
- Beach buff – crash course to boost confidence and tone
- Next year, we'll be mostly wearing . . . the fashion industry laid bare
- I earn, I live, I'm broke – stretch it without feeling the pinch
- The best – and worst – jobs in the world
- The house that Jack built – self-build successes . . . and nightmares
- Win! £50,000 of watches waiting

ADAM

August, Issue 15

Double cover: David Bowie/Iman

- Beautiful couple – Mr and Mrs Bowie, as good as it gets
- A shark ate my homework . . . and my arm – facing near-death with a sense of humour
- All buy yourself – online investing made simple
- Cooking – have her begging for more
- I'm 30 and I know I'll never have sex again
- Liam Gallagher, icon or scally?
- Property – buy or rent, sell or let?
- Scrutinized! New releases – buy it, or don't. Trust us

Alice and Thea were concentrating on Sally's abdomen. Sally sighed and poked herself in different spots. They all stared for a while longer. She stood, shifted around, sat down heavily and placed her palms all over her bump. 'Perform – or I'll dock your pocket money!' Sally growled at her belly.

'Was that something?' Thea gasped.

'No,' Sally said. 'But that is! Quick, give me your hands!'

Thea and Alice had their hands against Sally's stomach and stayed that way for quite some time to no avail. 'I know, I'll eat some pickled onion crisps – that usually has the wriglet cartwheeling.' But she'd eaten her way through an industrial supply recently and there were no packets left.

'Let's do the ring test,' Alice suggested. 'Sally, give me your wedding ring – and Thea, let me have your necklace. Then we dangle it over Sally's bump and if it swings back and forth, it's a boy. Circles – and it's a girl.'

'Oh, my God, it's twins!' Thea declared as the ring swung this way and that.

'Flatulence, more like,' laughed Sally.

Alice took the necklace from Thea. 'Seriously,' she said with a face so straight the other two laughed, 'it works – my grandma told me.'

'Your grandma also told you if you ate your crusts your hair would curl,' Thea reminisced, 'but despite living on toast you still had to resort to that terrifying perm when you were sixteen.'

'Shut up,' Alice said, 'watch – the ring is going round and round. You're having a girl. Oh. Hang on. No, it's not. What's it doing now? It's a boy.'

Soon enough, they were swinging the ring over the cat (who was male, according to the ring, though her kittens born two years previously would seem to disprove it), a picture of Prince Charles on the *Radio Times* ('Boy!' Alice proclaimed triumphantly) and Richard's shoes ('*Boy*! See!' Alice laughed). Even the floorboards had gender according to the swing of the ring.

'When are you and Mark going to breed?' Sally asked Alice, telling herself not to panic that the ring didn't appear to move at all when she dangled it.

Alice took the ring and assessed the sex of a cushion tucked up Thea's jumper. 'I don't know,' she said cautiously, 'I mean, when we were engaged we'd talk dreamily of babies and sand-pits and Winnie-the-Pooh. When we bought the house we allocated "kids' rooms". But actually, we haven't mentioned it.'

'There again, I've been married to Richard for nearly seven years,' Sally said, 'and you two are still pretty much newly-weds.'

'Coming up to two years, actually,' Alice corrected. She gave Sally back her ring and hooked Thea's necklace around her neck. 'I guess I don't feel ready. I guess *Adam*'s been my baby. I guess you have to have sex to conceive and my husband is invariably in a different time zone and continent to me.'

'Mark would make a lovely father,' Sally projected. 'How about you and Saul, Thea?'

'Us?' Thea said, looking up from a pregnancy magazine. 'We're not even living together, let alone married.' Her glum pout surprised Alice.

'But you've been together for ages,' Sally declared.

Thea shrugged.

'You're not waiting for him to ask, are you?' Sally probed, as if the notion was so old-fashioned as to be far-fetched.

Thea shrugged again.

'Ever the romantic, our Thea,' Alice said fondly, giving her arm a reassuring squeeze.

'So?' said Thea, resolutely.

ADAM

September, Issue 16

Willem Dafoe cover

- The quiet hero – Dafoe defines cool
- Sex – learn the language of talking dirty
- Perfect 'V' – hone your physique in a month
- Divas, sparrows, angels, fruitcakes – female rock goddesses
- Yeah man, I was there: Woodstock, Isle of Wight, Glastonbury
- Big Brother – 130 CCTVs log your daily movements
- Fast-food nation – terrifying facts that'll have you reaching for the alfalfa
- Toys, gadgets and gizmos – we don't need them, but we love them

ADAM

October, Issue 17

The Survivor's Guide. Underwater cover

- How to love and have lust survive
- How to do platonic sex and have the friendship survive
- How to dive with sharks and survive
- How to play the stock market and survive
- How to cook a banquet and have your guests survive
- How to renovate your house – and have the building survive
- How to win a survival course in the Pyrenees

Mark stroked Alice's stomach, turned away from *Newsnight* and tucked a lock of her hair behind her ear. 'When is Sally's baby due?' he asked.

'Couple of months,' Alice told him, her eyes on the vast television screen, 'I think her due date is Boxing Day.'

'You'd look glorious pregnant,' Mark anticipated. Alice was quiet. 'Maybe we should think about trying?' Mark said. 'We are married, after all. And we are ageing rapidly. And we do rattle around this big place. And I don't know about you but maybe the cogs of my biological clock are starting to turn.'

Alice wanted to cry and she hadn't a clue why. She invented a coughing fit and rushed to the kitchen for a long drink of water.

ADAM

November, Issue 18

Mick Jagger cover

- Old enough to be your dad, cool enough to be your mate, rich enough to buy a continent – Sir Mick, we salute you!
- Stay or stray? When love loses lust
- Lizzie Jagger – what *would* her dad say?
- Undercover in Afghanistan
- Armani or Burton – who suits you?
- Fitness – prepare now for your mum's Christmas cooking
- Sex and drugs – don't try this at home
- Money – save or spend: is it worth it?

Kiki had worked in the West End for three years, from the time she came to Britain from Indonesia at the age of seventeen. She liked it. The money was good. Her colleagues were now as close as family. Her clients were mostly fine. Her accommodation exceeded her expectations. She felt she had much to be thankful for because she knew she was much luckier than some. Kiki chose not to take much time off, limiting herself to one morning and one afternoon a week but never a whole day. It didn't seem worth it; her plan was to save and not spend and she didn't hate her job enough to run from it whenever she could. She'd seen quite early on how not much business came in on Monday afternoons and Sundays so these were the times she decided not to work.

In the first year of her life in London, she had spent her Sundays and Monday afternoons too overwhelmed by the scale of the capital city, the pace of it all, to do much else than go from McDonald's to McDonald's, splitting a meal between establishments and giving herself an allowance that stretched to a further soft drink and two cups of tea to fill her free time. It wasn't that Kiki became braver, but as time passed the city seemed smaller; her awe simply dwindled and her penchant for McDonald's ceased altogether. As her English improved and she found *Time Out* fairly easy to read, she took to venturing further afield. She started with the major museums and galleries, then she sought out smaller collections, traversing London from east to west, north to south as she did so.

She went on a tour of the Thames Barrier and walked around Hampstead with a group of strangers and a guide dressed as Charles Dickens. She lay on her back alongside other visitors at an installation at Tate Modern and craned her neck during a walking tour of the financial district. She went backstage at the Royal Opera House and down into the orchestra pit at the Barbican. She pressed the buttons in the Science Museum and rode the small train at Kew Bridge Steam Museum. She walked around a candlelit restored Huguenot property in Folgate Street in reverential silence and sang 'My Old Man Said Follow the Van' raucously at a living Music Hall museum. From fans to dolls, musical to medical instruments, from wine to buses – it seemed to Kiki there was a museum to celebrate everything.

Kiki had never heard the shipping forecast. The radio at work, when on, was set to Heart FM and softly at that. But she'd read about an exhibition called 'The Shipping Forecast' showing at a gallery space within Spitalfields market and, though she didn't know her North from her South Utsire, it was a rainy October Sunday so she decided to go along.

'At school, Alice and I did a project called The Shipping Forecast in our second year,' Thea told Saul. 'It was our first and – if I don't count our David Bowie collage – our last foray into mixed media.' Saul laughed and unfurled his umbrella to protect them both from a sudden squall. 'Don't laugh,' Thea protested, 'we sewed and stuck and modelled and carved all the stations on the forecast. We spent ages on it. And though we spelt German Bight incorrectly and treated Lundy Fastnet as a single location – overall, it looked good.'

'So do those burgers,' Saul salivated as they walked through Spitalfields, 'look at the size of them.'

'Culture first,' Thea said, 'then I'll buy you lunch.'

The exhibition was small; just one photo per location, but the space was cleverly subdivided by walls and screens to create a journey for the viewer. This also served to give a sense of private viewing time in front of each image, the chatter of the market merely a muffled background thrum. Saul was leaving Dogger and Thea was approaching Biscay when Kiki moved away from South-east Iceland.

'Hullo.'

Thea glanced round but the greeting appeared to be directed at Saul. She narrowed her eyes and tipped her head, regarding the girl. She knew her from somewhere. 'Hullo,' Thea said.

'Oh, hi!' the girl exclaimed, blushing. She bade Saul and Thea goodbye and off she went, with the shy smile that had enabled Thea to place her.

'It's clicked,' Thea said to Saul.

'Sorry?' Saul said. 'Great photo, this one of Rockall – look at the quality of the light.'

'The girl – that girl,' Thea continued, thinking the photo Saul referred to was actually quite ordinary.

'What?' Saul looked confused and was moving over to Bailey.

'That girl,' Thea said, 'just then – who said hullo to you and me.'

Saul pointed to the photo of Malin. 'Now this,' he said, still pointing, 'this I like.'

Thea stood alongside him and slipped her hand into his. 'I prefer that one behind there, of Portland,' she said, guiding Saul through with her hands in the back pockets of his jeans. 'She works a couple of doors down from the Being Well – in that dodgy sauna-massage place!'

'Really?' Saul said, peering at the Hebrides.

'You've probably seen her without realizing it,' Thea said, 'en route to visiting me.'

Saul turned away from Cromarty. 'Shall we go for that burger now?' he suggested, putting his arm around Thea's shoulders and guiding her away from Viking back through to the market.

ADAM

December, Issue 19

Julia Roberts as Christmas Fairy cover

- All we want for Christmas is Julia
- Christmas parties – seasonal snogging, festive favours, misplaced mistletoe
- Christmas bonus – mine's bigger than yours
- Christmas crap – we sift through the tat so you don't have to
- Christmas cheer – your round
- Christmas dinner – dos
- Christmas carols – don'ts
- Christmas present – free CD: the year's hottest sounds
- Christmas past – how to do a great New Year's Eve

'Do you know, I've been married for exactly two years and this is the first time I've used this particular Le Creuset casserole,' Alice declared to Thea, peeling a label from the lid.

'Is that because you're a ready-meal kind of girl,' Thea teased her, 'or because you eat out an inordinate amount?'

Alice laughed. 'Actually, it's because I put one of absolutely every Le Creuset product on the wedding list so I simply have had no need of this dish thus far.'

'I assume this corkscrew was a wedding present too,' Thea grumbled, 'it's so state-of-the-art I haven't a clue how to use it. In fact, I'm assuming it *is* a corkscrew, right?'

Alice gave Thea the onions to peel while she wrestled with the corkscrew. 'Bloody thing,' she said at length, 'I'm sure the regular old one is at the back of a drawer.'

'And which drawer would that be?' Thea remarked, eyeing the impressive run of them.

'Your guess is as good as mine,' Alice sighed. 'You rummage through those over there and these here, and I'll wade my way through those and these.'

'Bingo,' Thea said after a good five minutes' clattering, fulminating and rediscovering items Alice had thought she'd lost. She uncorked the Rioja and poured two glasses, adding a slosh to the sauce bubbling gently in a small Le Creuset saucepan. 'When's Mark back?'

'Friday,' Alice said.

'Christ, that's cutting it fine for Christmas shopping, isn't it?' Thea declared.

'That's why he'd better find time to shop in Singapore,'

Alice reasoned, 'or else I'll make him suffer for it during the January sales.'

'Did I tell you I'm going to Saul's folks for Boxing Day?' Thea said, sitting herself up on one of the many work surfaces while Alice arranged orange slices and cinnamon sticks on top of the chicken. 'It's weird, in London, and as I know him, Saul seems so self-contained, so independent, at harmony with his environment – as if he's always been this age, living in his pad, doing his job.' She raised her legs so Alice could retrieve a zester from a drawer beneath her. 'Yet back in Nottingham there are graduation photos and junior-school woodwork examples and tennis trophies belonging to someone called Saul Mundy who I don't know. And parents. I find them peculiar too – though actually they're completely normal and really pretty nice. I simply can't connect Saul to them.' Thea shifted slightly so that Alice could check the recipe propped up behind her. 'It's as if seeing him in his family home rids him of some of the identity I associate with him.'

'Mark hasn't changed a jot,' Alice said fondly, shutting the oven door and wiping her hands on her jeans. 'It'll be an hour and a half, shall we have some nibbles while we wait?' Alice and Thea sat and chatted, sipped wine and munched tortilla chips. 'The bloke in my wedding photograph is identical to the photo on his parents' mantelpiece of the twelve-year-old collecting his Junior Chess Champion medal from Peter Purves,' Alice said, stretching out on her sofa and placing her feet on Thea's lap. 'Mind you, I suppose I've known Mark for almost as many years so there are unlikely to be surprises or skeletons.' They chinked wineglasses and suddenly she missed him very much. 'I feel bad,' she confided. 'He goes away and I denounce him – yet then I think of his Junior Chess Champion medal or the way he folds everything away every night and I long for him.'

'Friday is only the day after the day after tomorrow,' Thea soothed.

'I'll probably be a stroppy cow when he's back,' Alice said, resigned, 'poor old Mark.'

'Mark thinks he's the luckiest bloke in the world,' Thea told Alice.

'I think we should do our New Year's resolutions tonight, you and me,' Alice declared, 'because we won't see each other till next year, after all. I kind of wish Mark hadn't booked

Paris for New Year's Eve – but there's no way I can complain, let alone cancel.'

Over a fabulous Moroccan chicken casserole with saffron rice and roasted butternut squash, and Christmas crackers from Heals, Alice laid out her hopes for the next year.

'I want to win Publisher of the Year,' she listed, straightening her paper crown, 'I want *Adam* to outsell *GQ*.'

'Those aren't resolutions,' Thea told her, testing the plastic whistle that came in her cracker, 'they're goals.'

'Top of my wish-list,' Alice shrugged, reading the cracker joke and deciding swiftly it wasn't worth repeating out loud.

'What about you and Mark?' Thea asked.

'I suppose,' Alice said cautiously, 'it would be to spend more time together. But then that was my aim last year. I suppose, it's for me to be less narky with him. And to develop a taste for opera.'

'And thoughts of babies, perhaps?' Thea suggested.

'I'm going to see Sally tomorrow,' said Alice, changing track but not the subject. 'I bought the dearest present for baby Juliette.'

'Well, if you do have any thoughts about babies,' Thea said, 'for goodness' sake tell Sally not to tell you her birth story.'

'Shitting a watermelon?' Alice asked.

'With spikes on,' Thea whispered.

'Anyway, I'm not thinking of having babies,' Alice whispered back.

'But Mark is,' Thea said quietly.

Over Marks & Spencer's Christmas pudding and fresh lychees, Thea divulged her thoughts for the coming year. 'I'm going to redecorate my flat – a room a month,' she said, 'and I'm going to go running every other lunch hour. I'm going to do my tax on time and pay my credit cards off each month.' She chinked Alice's wineglass.

'And Saul?' Alice asked. 'Where do you see the both of you this time next year? Will you have wed and bred?'

Thea fell silent. She pressed the back of her fork down hard onto the pudding, squashing it flat. 'Actually,' she said, 'I'm hoping for some sense of planning. A strategy.' She took a second helping of Christmas pudding and ate a couple of spoonfuls thoughtfully before peeling another lychee. 'You know lychees are known as "babies' bottoms" too?' she remarked.

'It still doesn't make me broody,' said Alice, analysing the fruit.

'I don't doubt Saul's love for me,' Thea explained, 'but we never really assess it. Neither of us has a problem with commitment – but we haven't ever sat down and analysed where we're at. We just stroll from day to day, ambling along, hand in hand.'

'It sounds idyllic to me,' said Alice, 'and anyway, you know how it's sometimes counterproductive to analyse a relationship – the whole "let's talk about Us" syndrome.'

'I know. Believe me, from experience, I do know that. But I wouldn't mind hearing Saul proclaim that I'm the girl for him.' Thea shrugged at Alice.

'I know what it is,' Alice said, pouring them both some Cointreau. 'You have no shadow of doubt that Saul is indeed your knight in shining armour. But what you want is for him to behave like one,' she declared.

'Rose between his teeth, bended knee – the lot,' Thea laughed, her fist to the table. 'God, you know me well – if you weren't already married, I'd suggest you and I wed.'

'Would you say yes, then, if Saul asked?' Alice probed.

'I don't need him to ask me to marry him,' Thea said, 'that's not the point at all.'

'You are funny – funny peculiar,' Alice said, 'you're such a sucker for extreme romance and yet marriage just isn't on your agenda, is it?'

'But you're just as funny peculiar,' Thea sparred, 'because you can explain the sensation of love in chemical terms yet you marched down the aisle in a traditional frock with a great big grin on your face.'

'Perhaps it's because my parents set me an excellent example of marriage, but yours didn't,' Alice said.

'Perhaps,' said Thea, 'but fundamentally, I regard being in love as so intrinsically, mystically sublime that the man-made institution of marriage seems irrelevant. I think the awesome aspect of true love is trivialized by signing a piece of paper.'

'Well, I think marriage is an excellent idea,' Alice declared. She thought for a moment. 'I suppose where you don't see marriage as being the point of love, I don't see love as being the point of marriage,' said Alice.

'But you do love Mark,' Thea cautioned, 'don't you?'

'Of course I do!' said Alice. 'Will you please stop going on at me about that.'

The Isley Brothers

'You should practise what you preach,' Alice tells Saul nonchalantly while they pore over contact sheets of a recent shoot with Kate Winslet for a forthcoming cover. She bends over the light box, giving a skilled twist to her hair and fixing it against her head with a Biro to keep it out of the way. She lowers her right eye to the loupe and deftly scans the shots. With a yellow chinagraph pencil, she marks off four or five frames, sits back satisfied and hands the loupe to Saul.

'Can you just remind me what I've preached?' Saul humours her while he inspects the contact sheets even faster than Alice, ultimately agreeing with her preliminary selection.

'Well, the figures coming in for the last issue suggest it was our biggest seller yet,' Alice informs him, while marking the chosen images of Miss Winslet to be cropped, 'and I do believe it was your idea to call it the Romance Issue; that you coined the spine quote: "Warmth can be cool – rock on, Valentine". In a nutshell, the slant on love and all its panoply was your call.'

'Which you tried to overrule!' Saul quips, with a raised eyebrow. 'You thought the February issue should have a completely sarcastic and ironic take. Which it then transpired *GQ* and *Arena* and *FHM* all took. Boring.'

'Anyway,' says Alice, rather primly, 'you should put your name to it.'

'You're not still on at me to join your sodding staff, are you?' Saul sighs, surreptitiously trying to read one of Alice's memos, albeit upside down.

'Christ no, you'd cost me far too much in annual salary and perks now, Mr Mundy,' Alice exclaims. She regards him contemplatively, her head tipped to one side, her hair starting to escape anarchically from her improvised Biro clasp. 'I'm talking about taking your work home.'

'If you are telling me to work from home, you're hardly practising what *you* preach,' Saul says. 'You give Mark a hard time if he even skims through the *Economist* after seven p.m.'

'Not in that respect, you noodle,' Alice says affectionately, 'I'm simply suggesting that you redirect a little of the focus you laid on romance for February's *Adam*, to your home life.'

'Alice,' Saul says with exaggerated exasperation, 'what the fuck are you going on about? You're talking so cryptically I can't work out if you're telling me off, telling me to work less from your office or telling me to become a torch-bearer for Romance.'

'Yes!' Alice exclaims, triumphant, her hair in a sudden swoosh around her shoulders, the Biro on the floor. 'Romantic hero! That's *precisely* what I'm suggesting. With a capital R.'

Saul frowns and then regards Alice suspiciously. 'Are you talking about Thea?'

'Sort of,' Alice confesses, 'but if you tell her, I'll bloody kill you and *then* I'll sack you.'

'If. I. Tell. Thea. What?'

'It's just I know that recently, privately, she's been hoping for some declaration of intent,' Alice shrugs, 'and Saul, you're bright enough to figure out what I'm on about.'

It was a freakishly balmy late February and Saul eschewed ordering a cab in favour of the bus but soon enough jumped from that at the lights to indulge in a long and cathartic walk home from his meeting with Alice. Figuring out what she was on about was alternately unnerving yet stirring. When the thinking became too onerous, he'd pop into a newsagent to check stock and positioning of the titles he worked for, on occasion phoning the publishers to report his findings. One shop still had their Valentine's Day display up, but all the cards and trinkets were half price. Saul found himself browsing, tempted to buy a card – not because it was cheap but simply because it had a cheery photo of two amorous tortoises which he thought Thea would like. Actually, Saul had given her a large envelope filled with Loveheart sweets for Valentine's Day, though he'd painstakingly removed any with inappropriate inscriptions like 'Big Boy' or 'Hunky'. Saul put the rutting tortoises card back. He checked the magazine stock, repositioned *Adam* to the front of the rack, and walked on. He was a little troubled. Was Thea unhappy? But she hadn't given him any cause to think so. He was gently perplexed. Had he ever given her reason not to trust him or believe in his commitment and affection for her? He was sure that he hadn't. What he did acknowledge was that two years and three months into their relationship, he felt so completely comfortable with Thea being an integral part of his life that he really didn't give the matter much thought any more.

Perhaps that was the crux of it; the rub for Thea that Alice alluded to. Though he always looked forward to being with her – and a night apart was rare now – just then he accepted that he never actually told her so. It didn't occur to him to. Wouldn't it seem contrived? And anyway, wasn't the proof in the sweet pudding of their combined lives? He had as many clothes at her place as she had at his, their social circle was so fully integrated that he would need to concertedly recall whose friends were whose originally. Thea's new Hoover was bought by Saul and he'd retiled her bathroom with as much pernickety pride as if it was his own. Often, she changed his linen as a matter of course, stocked his food cupboards and thought nothing of answering his phone, land line or mobile, if he was out of earshot. So many other signs illustrated a love so legible that surely it didn't need to be spelt out too? Everyone knew Saul and Thea were a team. It was such an oft-pronounced phrase that it sounded as though they were no longer two distinct people; the 'd' was dropped and the words fused: Saulan-Thea. The balance between them was such that little rocked their proverbial boat. They got along too well for that, liked each other so much that they never found reason to disagree, or much point in arguing.

Do I take Thea for granted? Is that what Alice implied?

When Saul finally walked up Great Portland Street it was gone six o'clock. He'd been walking for three hours and his feet were sore, his mind still fugged. Was he doing something wrong or just not doing right enough? He meandered circuitously to his street. From the corner, he looked up and saw that his lights were on. He stood still for a while and regarded the run of his windows, stopping to thoroughly analyse what he normally gave no second thought to. Thea Jessica Luckmore, aged thirty-three, was up there. That was a fact. Five feet four inches high, around nine stones in weight, natural mousy hair, hazel eyes, slightly skew bottom teeth, impressive scars from a vicious dog, favourite colour turquoise, favourite book *Black Beauty*, all-time favourite song 'Cygnet Committee' by David Bowie, favourite film *Jules et Jim*, favourite animal tortoise. Supports Chelsea FC but prefers watching rugby. Electric toothbrushes make her gag. Drinks hot Marmite when she has a cold. Once performed a tap dance on *Blue Peter*. All facts he knew off by heart. At that very moment, she was in his flat. Probably watching the early-evening news or taking a shower. Or perhaps she was just sitting quietly letting the physical tensions she'd massaged from her clients all day ebb away from her. Saul walked a few paces closer but stopped again, looking up at his flat.

I don't know what she's doing up there, actually, but the fact is that I much prefer returning home to a flat full of Thea than one devoid of her. She is part of my world. She is synonymous with Home. She lights my life. She makes my space personal. She defines it.

He continued to loiter on the corner, engrossed in thoughts about light bulbs. They were on in his flat and, as if in a cartoon strip, Saul envisaged one suddenly sparking into light atop his head. As if he'd just had the best idea in the world. Like the answer to life itself had clicked on. How many feminists does it take to change a light bulb? Just one, actually – and I don't think that's very funny. How many Theas does it take to change a light bulb? None, actually. Saul had systematically gone through her flat just that weekend and replaced the lot.

February may have been unseasonably mild but Saul acknowledged it was downright deluded to have the Isley Brothers' 'Summer Breeze' soaring through his mind. Over the years, when discussing his Desert Island Discs with friends or compiling his Top 8 by himself in the bath, it had been the only mainstay on his list. It was one of those songs that in his head he sang perfectly but out loud, when he so wanted to put the power into his voice that the song instilled in him, the result was discordant and cringeworthy. Just then, though, it wasn't the summer breeze per se, nor the bizarre notion of having jasmine in one's mind; it wasn't the sweet and melodious tune nor the joyous vocals. For Saul, the immediate connection was with a man returning home; knowing from the mere hang of the curtains, from the little light shining in the window, that his love was there, with her arms reaching out to hold him, to make his world all right. More than all right. The blissful domesticity of it all. What more could a man want?

And I come home from a hard day's work
And you're waitin' there
Not a care in the world
See the smile a-waitin' in the kitchen
Food cookin' and the plates for two
Feel the arms that reach out to hold me
In the evening when the day is through

Saul takes the stairs, two at a time, music filling his soul, mirroring his feelings, reverberating around his head, providing the answer. He bursts through the door and Thea looks up. There she is. There she is. Sitting on the sofa with her feet on the coffee table. Painting her toenails. Wearing a T-shirt of his, inside out. A mug and a screwed-up KitKat wrapper by the bottle of nail polish. *The Simpsons* on the television with the volume turned down. David Bloody Bloody Bowie on the stereo.

'Hullo,' she says, 'I'm painting my toenails. It's a freebie from Alice – it's Chanel. I've cooked us something delicious. It'll be ready in an hour. How was your day?'

Saul doesn't know what to say because he hasn't a clue where to start or how to say it. The Isley Brothers desert him. All he can do, just now, is nod and say hi, kiss the top of her head and kick himself, as he passes by on the way to the fridge for a beer.

'Are you all right?' Thea asked him, a couple of hours later. She regarded him with a softly suspicious expression.

'Fine,' Saul assured her. 'God – why?'

'I don't know,' Thea said lightly, 'you've seemed a little pensive and you keep looking at me when you think I won't notice. Makes me think I have a Biro mark on my chin or a stray bogey.'

Saul drew her against him, enfolding his arms around her, and gently placed his lips to her temple while they watched the nine o'clock news.

He slept fitfully that night. They'd had intercourse by frantic fucking rather than refined lovemaking more akin to his earlier mood. He should have been worn out after that, drained after all his thinking on top of a long walk home. But he'd drift off then wake up, every hour or so. At two a.m. he awoke to the Isley Brothers playing again and again in his head. Be quiet. At four a.m. he woke again because he could no longer hear the Isley Brothers, his heartbeat drowned it out. And Alice. Oh shut up, Alice. I can think for myself. By five a.m. Saul had reached a turning point.

I'm confident I haven't done anything wrong – but perhaps, just perhaps, it really is time to do the right thing.

The notion made him feel exhilarated and terrified and like waking Thea right there and then. However, at some point, he must have slumped down into a soundless, dreamless sleep because when he woke with start at eight o'clock, he felt exhausted and fuggy and, as a consequence, non-communicative.

'See you later, grumpy,' Thea said, kissing his cheek as she left for work.

* * *

Shall I email her?

Ask her by text message?

But not over the phone.

Should I write a love letter or dictate a message to a florist and have it sent in someone else's handwriting with a huge bouquet?

Shall I just stride into the Being Well, burst in on her and ask her outright?

Perhaps I should whisper it to her while we make love?

Or ask her nonchalantly after we've had sex?

I could do it over dinner – a ready-meal or after sausages at the Swallow or even a table at Sheekey's?

I could call to her from my window when I see her approach.

Ought I to whisk her away and do it on some glorious bridge in Venice or Paris or Las Vegas even?

Blag an Aston Martin DB7, take her for a spin and then ask?

Should I run any of this past Alice?

Or Ian?

Should I let Barefaced Bloke do the talking for me in my piece this Sunday?

How about a singing telegram?

Balloons in a box?

Icing – literally – on a cake, spelling it out?

First thing in the morning? So how about tomorrow?

Last thing at night? What about tonight, then?

No time like the present? Then fuck it – why don't I just jump on my scooter and nip up to Crouch End right now?

Serenade outside her Gothick tower?

Rapunzel, Rapunzel – I have something to say.

Did David Bowie say anything on the matter? Hang on, I'll just do a Google search to find out.

But what will she say?
What will she say?
And will she say yes?

Crowded House

It's raining. It's pouring. It's bucketing down cats, dogs and hailstones on a day when really it shouldn't. It is the first day of spring and it also happens to be Juliette Celia Stonehill's baby blessing. Her daddy is pissed off because he hired an awning, paid caterers, organized everything impeccably but forgot to even hope the weather would be fine. Her mummy is in a bit of a flap because she doesn't know quite how to position sixty people on the ground floor of a Highgate terrace house.

'Sally!' Thea pipes up. 'Brainwave – you, Richard and Baby Ju stand on the landing at the top of the stairs, godparents on the steps below, then close family for the few steps down and then we'll all shove and scrum around the lower steps or out in the hallway.'

'Genius!' Sally exclaims. 'But – oh.'

'What?'

'Come with me a sec – you stand at the bottom there. Now, look up at me standing at the top from different angles and check you can't see up my skirt.'

'Great knees, Sally – but that's all you're giving me.'

'Cool, great. But – oh. Do you think it's rude to ask everyone to take their shoes off – the carpets are new?'

'Yes – but no one would put it past you to.'

'OK, everyone! Everyone. We're having the ceremony on the stairs and can you all take your shoes off, please. Pass it on. Pass it on, Thea – can you spread the word?'

When Saul Mundy had split from Emma all those years ago, one of the things that upset her most was the fact that he didn't cry. One of the things that made the ordeal easier for Saul was an inkling at the time that Emma was actually charging her waterworks with a torrent not entirely commensurate with her distress. He'd since written a couple of pieces as Barefaced Bloke on the whole subject of men and tears. He'd focused on the tears shed and embraces shared by grown men when Spurs lost to Arsenal in the last minute. Another time, he claimed that contrary to popular belief, heterosexual blokes cry frequently and easily. The perfect trigger of Bruce Springsteen songs, for example. Whisky, in certain amounts. *Raging Bull* and *Chariots of Fire*. Wrestling with IKEA shelving. Getting pubic hair caught in a zip – not necessarily one's own. Zip, that is.

Saul himself did not subscribe to stiff-upper-lipness yet he did not cry often. Recently, Springsteen had got to him. And Spurs losing, of course. But that day, the first day of spring, in his socks at the Stonehills' house in Highgate, he did. It was as if all the most cherished components that made up his world were colliding – yet on impact they were cloaking him in cloud-soft warmth and affirmation.

Life is really, really good. I am thirty-five years old and that baby girl is so tiny and beautiful. And her very existence makes sense of all the things we take for granted and don't bother to think about or don't treasure and acknow-ledge enough. Sex is fun but baby making is what it's all about. And my friend Richard made that little Juliette. And he wasn't a friend until I met him through the woman I love. And I met him because she'd given him the jacket I'd lent her up on Primrose Hill one November afternoon that seems an age ago.

'Saul?' Thea whispers. 'You OK?' He turns to look at her and nods and grins with eyes that are bloodshot from the pressure of welling tears; his nose crackling with snot. Thea looks simultaneously embarrassed but moved. 'Shh!' she hushes because Saul's sniff makes heads turn away from the action on the stairs. She hands him a tissue, which Alice has passed her with a nudge and a raised eyebrow.

'Soft git!' Alice whispers carefully to Thea. Thea giggles.

*

'Saul,' Thea finds him knocking back champagne as though it's lemonade, 'you OK?'

'Fine!' he declares. 'Thirsty.'

'Were you OK?' Thea asks him tenderly, putting her arms around him. 'Back there?'

'Back there?' Saul frowns, feigning confusion.

Thea tips her head to one side and regards him quizzically.

'Champagne?' he offers.

'Piss off!' Thea retorts. 'You know champagne and I don't mix. Evil stuff.'

'You would think that after a lifetime as a hack, he could take his drink by now,' Thea apologized to Sally an hour later while Saul swayed around the hallway, peering at framed photos unsteadily.

'Don't worry about it,' Sally laughed, 'take him home and put him to bed with a bucket nearby.'

'Thanks,' said Thea, rolling her eyes, 'Mark and Alice are giving us a lift.'

'Thea, is everything OK there?' Sally lowered her voice. 'Alice seems a little – I don't know. Distant? Preoccupied?'

Thea thought for a moment. 'She's fine,' she said, 'she's Alice. Mark's been abroad a lot and she's feeling a little – needy.'

'We need to make tracks,' Alice said, her coat already on, 'Mark's got to go into the sodding office.'

'You could stay? Cab it home later?' Thea suggested.

'I think I'll just catch up on a little work myself,' Alice said flatly. 'If you two still want a lift, we're going now.'

'Bye Alice, bye Mark, bye Thea,' Sally kissed them all and waved them off from her doorstep. 'Bye Saul. Oops – easy there, tiger. Christ, is he all right?'

'Fuck bollocks, my knee. Ouch. Wank,' Saul fulminated in a stagger towards Mark's very nice Lexus.

Although Thea focused on Saul for the journey over to Crouch End, noting with alarm a green-tinged pallor permeate his face by the top of Coolhurst Road, she was also able to observe her best friend gazing out of the window in a quiet world of her own, a downward sigh to her shoulders. Just then, she wished she was sitting with her arms around Alice, rather than serving as a buttress to the slumping Saul. Thea also noticed that Mark drove with deliberate attentiveness to the route and road sense, thereby counteracting any chance for chat.

He's probably just worried Saul will throw up on the cream leather, Thea told herself, *or thinking about the hassles awaiting him at the office, perhaps.*

Thea put Saul in her bed with a bucket at the side and a jug of water and a packet of Nurofen on the bedside table.

'I love you, Thea,' he slurred while she bustled around him, undressing him and plumping pillows, 'I really love you and want to get you for ever.'

'Now, let's go and have a pee, yes?' she said in a matronly manner. 'Come along.'

'I don't want to have a pee,' he mumbled petulantly.

'Come on,' she said as she hauled him through to the bathroom and pulled down his boxers, 'have a nice pee.'

'I don't want to have a pee,' said Saul sulkily while it gushed out with Thea's guidance.

'Now let's get you into bed.'

'I don't want to go to bed,' Saul objected, bashing his shoulder into the door frame but appearing not to notice. 'Come for a cuddle? A nice shag?'

'Have a snooze first,' Thea cooed, thinking just then that she really did not want to cuddle let alone shag this beery leery lump.

'I don't want to have a snooze,' Saul pouted as she shoved and pushed him to a safe place at the centre of her bed.

'Do you feel OK?' Thea asked. 'Because there's water right here – and a bucket just there if you don't.'

'I feel very OK,' Saul muttered with his eyes closed and a frown he couldn't correct. 'Room going dizzy.'

'Oh shit,' Thea whispered under her breath while closing her nose to his. She flicked his cheeks and shook him. 'Saul. Saul! Open your eyes and sit up. Now. Hey you! Up!'

Saul's eyes opened in sluggish succession and he lumbered himself up into a seated position of sorts. He brought his face in the approximate direction of where he thought Thea's voice had come from and, finding she had quite a few faces, he tried to keep his glazed eyes anchored to some of hers. She didn't really know his face at all just then and she wasn't sure whether she was amused or actually a little repelled. 'I love you, Thea,' Saul slurred, his eyes welling, 'marry me, Thea, marry me.'

'Drink some water, Saul,' Thea said, 'here – sip. That's right – it's a lovely pint of beer. Sip some more. OK. Do you feel

OK? Sip some more. Do you want to pee again? Yes? Right, come on then. No, you can't pee in the bucket. Oh Christ. No no! Not on the carpet – in the bucket, then. There. Good boy. Finished? Good. Oh shit, not finished – careful! OK, now back into bed. More sips of water. I mean beer. Little sips. Don't gulp. I'm going to wash out the bucket and bring it back. Are you going to puke? No? Well, I'm going to bring the bucket back just in case.'

'I love you Thea and I want to live with us for ever and ever.'

Thea patted his forehead and went to rinse out the bucket and replenish the glass of water.

Saul had been so drunk he couldn't remember a word he'd said to Thea. Saul had been so drunk Thea hadn't bothered to believe a word he'd said.

Peter, Gabriel

'Thea? Sorry to phone so early – it's Mark.'

'Hullo, Mark – I was up actually. I slept on the sofa – Saul's sleeping it off in my bed, drunken bum. Is everything OK?'

'I've done something to my neck – that's why I'm ringing so early – I just wondered if you could squeeze me in? I'm in pain and I can't move it much.'

'I don't have my appointments diary – I'll be at work at nine – I could call you then? I can assess you but you may need an osteo.'

'*Nine*? Oh. It's just I have a meeting and I was wondering—'

'Oh. Yes, of course. Can you make eight? In fact, I could probably be there for seven forty-five.'

'Thanks, petal.'

'Don't be daft! Oh, is Alice there? Can I have a quick word?'

'She's still asleep, Thea. My neck – you know – anyway, so she slept in the spare room. So as not to disturb me, you see.'

'Sometimes spasms are only partly physiological,' Thea advised Mark gently as she assessed his predicament an hour later. 'The pressure of stress can greatly exacerbate even mild twinges.'

'There's a fair bit going on at the moment,' he told her.

Thea nodded.

'At work,' Mark added, lest she should probe.

Thea nodded again. Over the years, she'd found that simply nodding whilst looking down at her notepad, pen poised, often encouraged her clients to elaborate with greater honesty than if she asked them outright. She looked down at her notepad and waited for a moment before nodding again. But Mark said no more.

'I would really like you to see one of our osteopaths,' Thea recommended, 'Dan and Brent are both excellent. But you have to promise me not to cancel – I know you're busy but believe me, it's a false economy to turn your back on the odd hour of osteopathy. I can ask the guys if they can schedule you in for an early or a late. Failing that, I'll ask if they know of a practitioner nearer to your work.'

'Thanks, Thea,' Mark said, 'I appreciate it.' He bent down gingerly to pick up his briefcase.

'Lower yourself, don't bend! Lower like a child does – they squat, keeping their backs straight, they never stoop. And lift like a weightlifter – face straight ahead.'

Thea insisted Mark put his briefcase back down and they made a few practice lowers and lifts. He marvelled at the simplicity but efficacy of the technique. He did it again. 'Christ – thanks, Thea.'

'No problem,' Thea smiled, 'and don't roll your neck like that!'

'Sorry,' Mark said sheepishly.

'Buy a packet of frozen peas on your way to work, wrap it in a towel and plonk it on your neck,' Thea suggested.

'Peas?'

'Sweetcorn will do too. And take it easy, please,' Thea said gently, 'or just a little easier. At work and at home.'

However, by then Mark had put his jacket on and his guard up.

*

There was nothing a good full English breakfast couldn't cure and though Saul had woken with a cracking hangover, two sausages, eggs, beans, bacon and fried bread later he felt revived and clear-headed. He'd just go back and tidy Thea's flat and then make his way into town. As miserable and rainy as the previous day had been, it was now a sparkling spring day. With the aesthetic wizardry of sunlight and clear skies on a March Monday, Crouch End resembled a bustling, self-contained, relatively picturesque market town. Strangers greeted one another cheerily, mothers promenaded cutting-edge buggies boasting babies resplendent in bright knits and cute hats, pensioners dawdled happily, catching up on the price of this and the cost of that and wasn't yesterday's weather *atrocious*. Pairs jogged to and from Priory Park, shopkeepers stood outside their premises grinning at nothing in particular and friends gossiped as they made their way to Banners for smoothies and comfort food. Saul thought how Hollywood would pay big bucks for such a scene; quintessentially English due to the balance of local architecture, local colour and local characters. As if on cue, a talented young television actor passed by Saul and said 'All right, mate?' as he went. 'Hiya,' Saul replied. He was in a very good mood.

Peter Glass wasn't. Peter Glass was actually in a full-blown foul temper. He'd invested hours each day, over a number of weeks, in a potential buyer who that morning had pulled out at the last minute without so much as an apology, let alone an explanation. So the luxury trip to the Seychelles was off. And so was upgrading the Beemer.

'All right, babes?' Peter said to Thea in a hollow voice and with a face like thunder. 'If you can massage away the aggression I feel, I'll pay you double.'

'You don't need to pay me double,' Thea assured him, 'just lie down and I'll let your body guide me. Trust me. Try to clear your mind. Try not to talk.'

'I could fall asleep,' Peter murmured, an hour later.

Thea looked at her watch. She had an hour's space before her next client. 'Just relax for a while, Peter, I'll come back in a mo'.' Actually, Thea returned forty minutes later and gently woke him up.

*

One ballet dancer, a pregnant woman and a tennis coach later, Thea's last client for the day is Mr Sewell. She has continued to call him Mr Sewell though he is now a regular client and even occasionally divulges quite personal information with no warning and certainly no prying on her part. Recently, he'd expressed his concern that his neck felt no better though he was much happier in himself having returned to his wife. On his last visit, he'd actually started reciting lines from the new Ricky Gervais television series and had laughed so much the bed had shaken.

Souki meets Thea on her way down to the waiting room. She's holding a latte and a muffin. 'Mr Sewell is here,' she says, 'and so is Saul. With coffee and cakes for us all, bless him.'

'Hullo, Mr Sewell, would you like to go on up and get ready,' Thea says, giving Saul the same nod she gives all her clients, 'I'll be with you in a moment.'

Saul waits for Mr Sewell to disappear upstairs. Thea could murder that muffin. It had been an early start and a long day.

'I'm starving,' she says. She approaches Saul who is offering her the cake. He snatches it back as she's about to take it. 'Hey!' she protests.

'Say yes!' Saul says. 'If you say yes, the muffin is yours.'

'Yes?' says Thea. 'Whatever – yes *please*.'

'But you don't know what you're agreeing to!' Saul exclaims.

'I'm so hungry I'd agree to anything,' Thea assures him.

'Really?' he says, a veritable twinkle to his eye. Thea nods, literally licking her lips. Still he holds the muffin aloft. 'Would you say yes to a Gimp Mask and PVC crotchless knickers?'

Thea regards him as if he's mad. 'Yes, yes, now give me the sodding muffin – I'm going to be late for Mr Sewell.'

'Would you say yes to moving in together?' Saul says, offering her the cake.

Thea's heart leaps into her mouth while her stomach somersaults and Saul's proposal fills her head. Suddenly, there is no room for cake. And she can't find her voice and time stands still and poor Mr Sewell is in his underwear, face down on the bed in the room at the top.

'Well,' Saul says, 'are you going to say yes?'

Thea stares at him.

'Is that a yes?' Saul asks, jiggling the cake temptingly.

Thea gulps.

'Live with me, be with me,' Saul implores, 'let's move in together, live with each other for ever and ever. Live happily ever after.' He picks out a chocolate chip. 'Say yes – and the muffin is yours.'

Thea blinks, grins and nods. Yes, she mouths. 'Yes!' she laughs.

'Fantastic,' Saul says, 'and all for the price of a muffin.' He turns her around to face the stairs. 'Back to work, missy,' he laughs, giving a gentle shove to her bottom, 'see you later.'

Thea is five minutes late for Mr Sewell.

'Sorry to keep you,' she apologizes quietly. She puts the muffin down on the table. She knows that she'll be in a quandary whether to eat it or keep it for sentimental posterity. 'Now,' she says to Mr Sewell, 'how's that back of yours?'

'Not bad,' he says, lifting his head a little, 'how are you?'

It's the first time Mr Sewell has ever asked Thea anything remotely personal. She's slightly taken aback. 'Oh, fine,' she breezes, 'I'm fine, thank you.' She lays her hands lightly on Mr Sewell's back, closes her eyes and inhales deeply. She controls her exhale while she moves her palms up his back to his neck, strokes out along his shoulders, sweeps down and up his arms, squeezes along his upper arms and then swoops her hands back over his shoulders and down his back. He sighs with relief and pleasure. His body feels good to her. Much softer and more receptive than on his last visit. It's an easy massage to give.

Cohen & Howard

Alice held Thea very close as she embraced her. And when she sensed Thea was ready to pull away, she held her tighter still. 'Good,' she said, 'I'm so pleased. It's the right time. It's brilliant news.'

'Do you think I'm doing the right thing?'

'You have to ask?'

'Are you happy for me?'

'You have to ask?'

'You do think that Saul is The One For Me, don't you?'

'You have to *ask*?'

Alice and Thea gazed at each other, manic excitement manifest and contagious in their dancing eyes and slight breathlessness.

'So,' Alice said, 'there we have it. We're all grown up, you and I. God, I'll probably be pregnant by your house-warming party,' Alice said with a slump to her shoulders, 'and I'll be confined to wearing some God-awful kaftan and support tights.'

Thea looked at her thoughtfully. 'I wasn't really thinking of house-warming parties. But are you really thinking about pregnancy?'

'I can't see how my marriage will survive if I don't,' Alice reasoned, a little darkly.

'Shit,' Thea exclaimed, 'don't say that. You're not serious? I mean, I know you've been low – ambivalent even – but we've talked through it all, haven't we. Time and again. Surely you are not considering a baby to hold the answer?'

Alice was quiet. She regarded Thea with a meekly apologetic pursing of her lips. 'I'll never forget your mother begging you to be the glue to keep your father from leaving. How old were you? Fifteen?'

'Fourteen,' Thea corrected.

'When did you last see him?' Alice asked.

'Three years ago?' Thea estimated.

'It's interesting,' Alice said quietly, 'how divorce affects a child by shaping their attitude towards love as adults. Many become totally averse or utterly cynical to long-term relationships. You come from a pretty poor example of marriage and yet it seems it's given you the determination to truly believe in lasting love. It would make an interesting article for *Adam* – how *blokes* are affected by their parents' relationships.'

'Well, it seems you and I have struck lucky with Saul and Mark then, as they both come from good stock,' Thea mused.

'You make them sound like prize rams – in fact, you sound like your mother!' Alice laughed. Her expression changed, she placed the back of her hand against Thea's cheek. 'You have always imposed somewhat fairy-tale proportions onto love and eternity. I know I tease you. And sometimes, it *has* landed you in a pickle. But ultimately, I think it's your greatest strength. I may rib you for being a hopeless romantic but actually I admire you for it.'

'You don't mind that I don't believe in your theory that your phenyl-something is the cause of love?' Alice laughed and shook her head. 'When I was little,' Thea said cautiously, 'the only way to block out the noise of the rows, the only way to put something pretty into my life, was to lose myself in this imagined world of heroes and heroines triumphant in love.'

'Well, now you have your hero in Saul,' Alice said conclusively.

'And you have yours in Mark,' Thea said, adding a note of warning to her voice. 'Do not use a baby as glue, Alice, please.'

Alice regarded her wedding ring thoughtfully. 'Glue, Sellotape, Velcro,' she said quietly, 'some type of weather-tight bonding is needed, that's for sure.'

'Bonding,' Thea said, musing over the word. 'It'll be within you, within the home itself,' she said decisively, 'you'll just have to patiently seek it out.'

'And there ends our correlation between love and sticky stuff,' Alice proclaimed. 'There are only so many metaphors a girl can take in her lunch hour.'

'Love *is* sticky stuff,' Thea shrugged with a wink, 'if we're talking fellatio.'

With his sharp suit, loud tie and verbal swagger, the estate agent at Cohen & Howard reminded Thea of Peter Glass but as Saul didn't know Peter Glass, and as Thea assumed that all estate agents were probably alike, she didn't comment. Just then, with the agent slicking back his already product-laden hair and rolling a fat Mont Blanc pen avariciously as if it were a cigar, Thea wondered whether they should have consulted Peter instead. He'd been in that morning. On a roll. Deposit paid for Seychelles ultra luxury. Upgrading the Beemer to a Merc. Taking a new girlfriend to Chinawhite. Hardly aware of the crick to his neck.

'Miss Luckmore,' the estate agent was saying, 'will Cohen & Howard be handling the sale of your property too? We do have an office in Muswell Hill – and market share in N10, N8, N22.'

'We would consider it,' Saul butted in, enunciating his vowels an octave lower than Thea had heard before, 'for a drop in your commission to 1 per cent, bearing in mind that you'll be handling the sale of my property and most probably arranging our purchase too.' Thea didn't mind that Saul had answered for her. She found it quite touching. Plus he was saving her 1.5 per cent which would probably pay for an IKEA kitchen. 'If we can agree on such a commission,' Saul was saying, 'you may have both premises to market.'

'Immediately?' the agent asked with a lip-lick of gleeful anticipation.

Saul and Thea looked at each other. Saul raised an eyebrow and a smile broadened. Thea bit her lip – not with reservations but to quell a rising chirp of excitement. 'Immediately,' Thea told the agent.

She and Saul left the office with a clutch of property particulars and, with arms linked and a skip to their stride, headed for Patisserie Valerie on Marylebone High Street to peruse the details over coffee and cake. For a day devoted to the exposing of fools, April 1st for Saul and Thea was proving to be a day in which they were making some very wise moves. Saul put his arm around Thea's waist and pulled her close to him, giving her a smacking kiss to her temple. She beamed up at him. 'I'm so excited!' She started babbling about Shaker-style kitchens and granite worktops and Smeg fridges in retro pink. She enthused about Purves & Purves for rugs, that she'd seen Mies van der Rohe style Barcelona chairs on the web for a bargain. With a footstool and no delivery charge. Perhaps in cream. 'Designers Guild for fabrics!' she exclaimed. 'And can we buy a superking-size bed? I love Farrow & Ball paint colours.' She was hopping and weaving in her excitement. 'Bridgewater!' she beamed, standing outside the eponymous shop. 'Oh my God, I *adore* her crockery.' A few steps later, Thea was darting over the road and pulling Saul into the White Company. 'Divine!' she repeated as she ran her hands lightly over the stacks of linen. 'Let's make the bedroom a peaceful haven of muted tones. Mushroom. Ecru. Flax. Calico. Vanilla.'

'His and Hers waffle towelling robes?' Saul suggested, twirling one against himself, his gentle sarcasm totally lost on Thea.

'Actually,' she replied artlessly, 'the Conran Shop's the place for bathrobes – we could look at prices after we've had tea.'

Even an old-fashioned homewares shop caught Thea's attention as they strolled on and she enthused about their exhaustive range of Vileda mops and accessories. Jabbering on about cream carpets, Venetian mirrors and terracotta chimineas for patios, she danced in front of Saul so that he almost tripped, wrapping her arms around his neck and standing slightly on tiptoes to kiss and kiss him some more. Calmly, he encircled her waist with his arms, lifted her up and continued to walk towards Patisserie Valerie while Thea laughed and embraced him as he carried her.

'Oh here, this is for you,' Saul said. 'It's only silver – but I thought it was very you. The jeweller is Ian's sister.'

Outside Waitrose, Thea looked at the ring. It was inscribed.

∞ I have spread my dreams under your feet ∞

'*Tread softly because you tread on my dreams*,' Thea said quietly, completing the stanza. She loved that Yeats poem. She looked at Saul, elated, awash with love and brimful of excitement for their future. Their dreams were shared, their future spread ahead. For Thea, not even the most sumptuous wedding in the world, or the most gorgeous flat on the market, or the most expensive ring from Tiffany, could actually better the dizzying happiness she felt just then.

'Well done, mate,' Richard said to Saul, slipping his racquet into its cover.

'But you *slaughtered* me,' Saul laughed as they headed from the court to the showers.

'I meant about Thea, you prat!' Richard said with a friendly shove. 'Sally told me you're buying a little love nest together.'

'We've signed up our flats with Cohen & Howard,' Saul called over the shower cubicle.

'Wise,' Richard affirmed. 'Did they drop their commission?'

'You bet,' Saul said, 'I mean, both properties should be a doddle to sell. And we both bought at the right time.'

'Well, if you need an architect,' Richard laughed.

'Discount?' Saul joshed, grabbing a towel and throwing one to Richard.

'Yeah, right,' Richard laughed. 'Anyway, what are you looking for and where?'

'I thought I'd have a tough job suggesting Thea relinquish her Crouch End affections,' Saul mused, 'but actually she's really into the idea of central London.'

'There are some great developments near Covent Garden,' Richard informed him, 'the Drury Lane end. I know of one not yet released – I could try and organize a viewing.'

'That would be cool,' Saul thanked him, 'I know Thea likes the idea of Bloomsbury too. But she's seen too many Merchant Ivory films.'

'I have to say, the area you're in at the moment is fabulous,' Richard commented, heading out from the changing room.

'I'll drink to that,' said Saul, clanging shut the locker and following him out of the changing room.

'You'll drink to me trouncing you at squash first,' Richard laughed over his shoulder, as they headed for the bar, 'and then we'll drink to you and Thea.'

'And then we'll wet your baby's head,' Saul elaborated.

'And then we'll raise a glass to my wife,' Richard said.

'I can't believe we haven't been out to celebrate Juliette's birth,' Saul marvelled, 'we must be talking four months or so.'

'Christ, I had to negotiate hard with Sally, let me tell you,' Richard sighed. 'I get tonight off only on the guarantee of a midnight curfew and the assurance of only mild wooziness as opposed to utter inebriation. *And* she's factored into the equation a lie-in on Saturday *and* her own night out with Thea and Alice next Wednesday.'

'She drives a tough bargain, your wife,' Saul commented, raising his glass to her nonetheless.

'I have my two beautiful girls,' Richard declared with a happy shrug, 'they have me wrapped around their little fingers – but I'm a pretty happy captive.'

Hullo, little home. Hullo, my little slice of Lewis Caroll Living. I've entrusted you to some wide-boy estate agent with a dodgy goatee beard. Lance from Cohen & Howard's Muswell Hill office. He says you'll be a breeze to sell. And I have no idea why I feel guilty. Like I'm abandoning you to some unknown fate, like I'm turning my back on you after all the security you've given me. But I like to think of some other Thea chancing upon you, living here and loving it until life moves her along too. Saul says I mustn't become emotional about selling. I walloped him for that – what a daft thing to say. Of course it'll be an emotional process. Do you know he says it would be better for me not to meet potential purchasers? He ganged up with Lance on that one. Saul says he knows me, he says if potential purchasers don't live up to my exacting expectations, I won't sell to them even if they offer the asking price. But to me, that's obvious – to him, that's daft. Lance looked horrified.

This home is an extension of me – an expression of who I am and how I've been; a living photo album, an entire diary of my last five years. All the things these walls have seen! All the comfort I've felt here, the safety of it all – the stains from my tears, the marks of my happiness. I could write a novel about it! I can't possibly sell to someone who won't love this place as I have. I'll always love Crouch End and my memories of my gorgeous first flat will remain vivid and cherished. I was very, very happy here. When I was a single girl. All that time ago.

The first person who walked through Thea's front door made an offer within twenty-four hours. The second person who viewed the property half an hour later, made an offer the next day of the asking price. Lance warned the third person before they went to see the flat that he'd already had two offers within twenty-four hours of the property being on the market. That person saw Thea's flat and offered the asking price there and then, before they'd even stood in the hallway with all the doors closed for maximum Lewis Carroll impact. Thea didn't quite know why she declared she needed a night to think about it. And nor did the potential purchaser, who promptly raised his initial offer of the asking price by a full five thousand pounds, guaranteed a speedy exchange of contracts and volunteered details of his lawyer, his surveyor and his mortgage company. 'Let me sleep on it,' Thea pleaded with Lance.

'Well, sweet dreams, darls,' he said to her, 'but you'd better get an early night because I'm telling you, they'll be on the phone as soon as the office is open tomorrow morning.'

That evening, Thea thought how Peter Glass calling her 'babes' was more classy, more genuinely affectionate than Lance's 'darls'. But she couldn't let that influence her decision. She just wanted a night all alone in her home before she gave the go-ahead. She sent some goodnight kisses in a text message to Saul but it was to Alice that she sent a text: fuck fuck fuck do i sell sell sell??? Tx

The reply was immediate: yes yes yes Axxxxxxxxx

bloke = nice gay guy who sez flat is DIVINE! Thea sent back.

sounds perfct! ;-) Alice wrote.

r u watchng ER? Thea texted back

yes! Alice replied, Carter damn cute

Luka cuter! Thea responded.

fone during ads? Alice wrote.

k xxx texted Thea.

'So, basically, if I accept the offer the whole thing could be done and dusted within a few weeks.' Thea switches the phone to her other ear and changes the subject after a lengthy and thorough dissection of *ER*.

'Look, I know this purchaser isn't in a chain and he's offering top dollar and he's a nice sensitive gay bloke who loves your colour schemes and is into the whole Rapunzel vibe, but don't be pressurized to rush it through,' Alice advises her, tucking the phone under her chin while she runs a bath. 'You and Saul mightn't find somewhere for ages.'

'Yes, but I can move into his place,' Thea theorizes.

'True, but all your stuff would have to go into storage and it is *his* place,' Alice reasons, 'I mean, it may be cool and funky but it's not big.'

'True,' Thea agrees, 'true.'

'You should go for a speedy exchange of contracts,' Alice recommends, 'and then a slightly longer completion – at least that way you have the security of the purchaser's deposit.'

'Makes sense,' Thea agrees, 'I'll sleep on it. Anyway, how are you? Are you packed?'

Alice groans. 'No,' she sighs, 'I mean, what the fuck am I meant to take?'

'I don't know,' Thea says, 'what does one wear on an all-expenses-paid management-bonding trip? I've never been on one – it's not really a perk in my line of work.'

'It's hardly a perk,' Alice groans, 'it's a pain. I mean, we managers all know each other well enough anyway. Why we have to traipse out to France for five days I don't know. I'd get more of a feel-good factor from a hefty bonus or an increase in holiday entitlement.'

'Well, at least you can shop,' Thea says.

'We're in the middle of fuck-knows-where,' Alice says sulkily, 'the nearest town is Arles which is more famous for Van Gogh or Cézanne or someone, than for Prada.'

'Well, at least you may come back with a tan,' Thea says.

'I looked at the weather forecast there just today. *Il pleut*.'

'Come on, Alice,' Thea says, 'it'll probably be a laugh.'

'They've told us to pack "cagoules" – the closest I have is my Agnès B mac and I'm *not* taking *that*!'

'I have a cagoule,' Thea confesses cheerily, 'you could borrow it if you like.'

'Is it repulsive?' Alice asks.

'Fuck off! It's Berghaus, it's cutting edge and it cost a lot.'

'Could I borrow it then?' Alice asks a little sheepishly. 'That would be great – oh, but what colour is it?'

'Black and red,' Thea tells her and Alice can sense she's raising her eyebrows.

'Well, my walking boots are black Gore-tex,' Alice muses.

'See, you *can* be colour coordinated *and* appropriately dressed,' Thea concludes.

'Languedoc, here I come,' Alice says with negligible enthusiasm, 'whoopee-doo.'

'When do you leave on Friday?'

'Some ungodly hour,' Alice moans, 'back next Tuesday. I can think of better ways to spend a long weekend, but there you go.'

'Text me while you're there, won't you?' Thea says.

'If I get a signal in the middle of Cézanne country,' Alice says darkly.

'Is Mark away anyway?'

'Ironically, no – so it's his turn to rattle around the house on his tod,' Alice says with a note of triumph. 'Listen, can you give that cagoule to Saul – he's coming in for a meeting on Wednesday so he could bring it in for me.'

'No problem,' Thea says, 'and Alice – shall I accept the offer then?'

'Yes, yes, you should,' Alice says encouragingly, 'it's time to get the ball rolling, Thea my dear. Time to trade in your little bit of Lewis Carroll Living for something more grown up.'

Alice envisages Thea sitting there, curled on her sofa, looking around her flat, nodding reflectively. She'll text Thea before she goes to sleep, she decides, tell her again that she should go for it. That it's the right decision. That she'll be quids in, in every respect. For now, Alice will drizzle an extravagant amount of Penhaligon's bath oil into her bath and luxuriate – after all, she may well be restricted to lukewarm showers in the depths of Cézanne country.

La Grande Motte

The group flew into Montpellier airport. All of Alice's colleagues had packed rucksacks, two or three even opting for a size small enough to pass as hand luggage. Because it had been traumatic enough for Alice to pack a cagoule, there was no way she was going to forsake her Mulberry grosgrain holdall for a backpack. Her bad mood blackened when her luggage arrived on the baggage reclaim damaged. Off she flounced to the baggage-handlers' office to complain.

'Come on, Alice,' Steven Hunter from the music division called over to her on behalf of the group, 'the coach is waiting.'

With her hands still stroppily on her hips she spun on her heels and glowered to all asunder. 'Coach? *Coach*? Oh, for Christ's sake.'

However, she was happy to concede that with its air conditioning, the lounge-style seating, various refreshments and superb suspension, the coach was a far cry from that which she was expecting: the juddery, slurching vehicles upholstered in the colours of vomit she recalled from school trips. Her appeasement was short-lived and her lifted spirits dove again on arriving at the hotel.

'It's not a hotel,' she hissed to Jeanette Baker from the lifestyle division. 'It makes Center Parcs look like Gleneagles.'

'You're such a snob!' Jeanette teased her. 'Who cares if it's Butlins de la Camargue – the plonk'll be plentiful and we'll be happy campers.'

Alice raised her eyebrows at herself and smiled. 'Do you reckon we'll have mini-bars in our rooms?'

'Rooms?' Jeanette exclaimed. 'You do know we're having to bunk up?'

'Bunk up?' Alice asked.

'Share,' Jeanette elaborated, 'in groups of three.'

Alice laughed heartily and gave Jeanette a jocular nudge. While the lady with the clipboard who'd accompanied them from the airport bustled through to the hotel reception, Alice coolly took stock of the situation. The group consisted of twenty respected managers each on a high and esteemed rung of their company, all justly honoured by PPA, BSME or ACE awards, soaring circulation figures and massive advertising revenue to their credit. In addition, most were married, all were in their thirties or beyond, on top salaries with share options and positions on the board. Of course they were going to have their own rooms, with mini-bars and satellite television.

Oh no, they weren't.

'I thought you were joking,' Alice almost wept to Jeanette, an expression of pleading panic furrowing her face.

'Well, I have my iPod and speakers and Jacquie Duckworth bought duty-free gin and two hundred Marlboro Lights – so our dorm will be rocking,' Jeanette tried to enthuse.

'You bet,' said Jacquie, her duty-free carrier bag clanking in proof. 'Who needs a mini-bar?'

'You're on!' said Alice, hoping her enviable collection of Bobbi Brown cosmetics would be seen as a valid contribution.

'No, you're not,' Ben Starkey butted in darkly, 'they've already designated who's in which room.'

'You are *joking*!' Alice exclaimed hoarsely, while Jacquie almost dropped her fags and lost her bottle.

'He's not,' Jeanette said glumly, trudging off with the publisher of the crafts titles and the director of circulation.

The accommodation was set in the grounds, in rows of gaily painted breeze-blocked cabins, optimistically called chalets. As Alice trudged towards hers, she was suddenly aware of the natural beauty of the landscape and that it was quite at odds with the ugliness of the hotel complex. The sea could be heard but not seen and the big sky of the Petite Camargue, by then streaked with a colour close to apricot, seemed somehow higher and lighter than that above London. Beyond the hotel grounds, inky pine forests fringed the dunes that led to the coast and a distinctive salty tang from the lagoons and marshes permeated the air. However, Alice's appreciation of her new surroundings was negated on arriving at Chalet B27. Pea-green on the outside, the breeze-blocks inside had been painted the colour of lemon curd, jumping to a hue close to tomato ketchup in the bathroom. It was by no means cramped, in fact it was spacious, with an additional toilet and a large hallway doubling as a lounge with peculiar seating modules made from foam blocks covered with bright fleece fabric. However, in the bedroom Alice felt irritated by the organization of space. Why insinuate that the three beds were afforded privacy by placing them at acute angles, partially screened by ugly furniture? Why not just build stud walls and be done with it? Alice rarely smoked and gin was not her tipple, but as she attempted to unpack how she craved a swig from Jacquie's bottle, a lungful of Marlboro Lights.

'Gosh, three coat-hangers between us,' Anita Farrell remarked as if it were a scandal. 'Luckily for you two, I only brought casual clothing so you can share my hanger.'

Alice smiled fleetingly at Anita, who was placing well-worn slippers by the side of her bed. Then she glanced at Rochelle who was arranging framed photos of her horse on the chest of drawers.

Christ and Double Christ.

Alice was in a sulk.

Why wasn't she sharing with Jeanette and Jacquie? How on earth would sharing rickety wardrobe space with a fifty-year-old equestrienne and a slipper-wearing spinster editorial director of the business periodicals augment her career? In what way was any of this going to affirm her affection and fidelity for the company? And how were *Adam* and *Lush* and the rest of her titles to benefit from their publisher spending a week in a ghastly hut with two of the dullest women in the company?

'My church is holding a forum on how the media corrupt our youth,' Anita was saying as she stacked a pile of increasingly khaki clothing on a plastic chair, 'teen mags, lads' mags and the like. Would you be interested in speaking, Alice? Defend *Lush* and the like?'

Christ, Christ and Triple Christ.

'You see,' Rochelle sighed, loading an excessive amount of thick socks into a drawer, 'that's where ponies come in. Did either of you read the research conducted for our Christmas issue of *100% Horse*? It established that youngsters who ride are far less likely to play truant or misbehave. To love a sport at an impressionable age, to embrace the responsibility of caring for an animal – is proven to keep them out of trouble. The readership of *Pony World* is now over 75,000 – so encouraging, don't you think?'

Good God Almighty.

'Rochelle,' Anita fizzed, 'you could be on the panel too! You and Alice could go head to head!'

Sweetest Jesus H Christ.

'When I was a kid,' Alice said to the middle of the room while she attempted to load two Whistles skirts, a Nicole Farhi shirt and a Brora cardigan onto a single hanger, 'I used to ride regularly. I was madly in love with a pony called Percy but for me the main point of it all was snogging Nathan Jones behind the tack room and smoking John Player fags on the muck heap with my best mate Thea.'

Supper, eaten at long refectory tables, preceded something called 'Orientation', according to the printed itinerary handed out with the hors d'oeuvres. Alice sat at one end with Jeanette and Jacquie in a conspiratorial huddle, planning the best time to convene for gin and cigarettes. Their spirits rose with the arrival and constant replenishing of ceramic pitchers of quite palatable rosé table wine throughout the meal.

'What's Orientation, do we think?' Jacquie asked.

'Probably some character-building mountain hike,' groaned Alice.

'In the dark,' Jeanette added.

'But it's in Conference Room B,' Jacquie pointed out.

'Perhaps it's an emotional workshop to scale the metaphorical mountains we've encountered in our working lives,' Alice said.

'Well, we'd better prepare our mind-set then,' said Jeanette, sloshing more rosé into their glasses. They drank to each other, they drank to workshops and mind-sets, they drank to orienteering and orientation. By the time they headed for Conference Room B, they were incapable of walking a straight line, unable to follow arrows and thus couldn't find Conference Room B at all.

It must be here somewhere.

If only they'd taught us orientationeering before supper.

We could always just nip back to mine and have a tiny sip of duty free.

Yes, that is a good idea.

After all, when they realize we are lost, that's where the search party will first look.

Exactly – so we probably won't miss too much orientaling anyway.

Exactly.

Good plan.

Cool.

As the three of them staggered off in the vague direction of Jacquie's cabin, Alice thought how this wasn't too far off a school trip after all. St Trinian's for big girls. Mallory Towers with booze. Just then, she had to concede it might just be a bit of a giggle.

Paul Brusseque

Alice was the last one on the coach the next morning. She didn't dare take off her sunglasses though the day was quite dull. She mumbled an apology to a pair of male feet clad in high-performance hiking boots. She noted Jacquie curled almost foetally in one seat, a decidedly pale Jeanette staring vacantly ahead in another. She saw Anita and Rochelle sitting together, lowering their eyes to their laps as she passed. She found an empty row towards the back, slumped down, closed her eyes and prayed for the Nurofen to kick in. A twangy Australian voice disrupted her need for absolute silence. She assumed it belonged to the hiking-boot man but there was no way she was going to open her eyes to verify this.

'Right guys, we're off to Mont Saint Victoire this morning – immortalized in the paintings of Cézanne. But we're not going to sit there with our watercolours, we're going to climb the fucker.'

'Just you try and make me,' Alice muttered under her breath.

Alice was the last one off the coach. A surreptitious glance around revealed that most of her colleagues – in fact everyone but her, Jeanette and Jacquie, were dressed appropriately for a walk up Cézanne's mountain. Alice, though, was wearing a denim skirt, a velour hooded top the colour of bubblegum and a pair of beige Hogan trainers with no socks.

'OK guys, let's go!' enthused the bloody Australian.

'I'm not a guy,' Alice said to herself, pinching the bridge of her nose to see if that alleviated the throb in her skull, 'so I'm not going.' She turned to face the coach and saw the driver tucking into a hunk of baguette, with slices of ham the size and texture of chamois leather draped over his knees. Her stomach lurched.

'Excuse me?'

Christ. The jolly Antipodean.

Alice turned. 'I'm not going to walk up your mountain,' she said politely to his feet, 'I'm feeling a little fragile. And anyway, none of my mags have anything to do with hiking.' The hiking boots gave one irritated tap. She travelled her eyes up over the laces to ribbed socks rolled down. Above those, tanned shapely lower legs with a masculine smattering of coarse hairs.

'What's your name?'

'I beg your pardon?' Alice balked, looking up a little further and seeing a pair of knees, one of which was grazed.

'Well, Ibegyourpardon, I always find that a stroll in the fresh air clears a hangover far more thoroughly than sunglasses and a sulk.'

Alice's eyes travelled over a pair of thighs so shapely they'd be termed 'thighs to die for' in *Lush* magazine. She stopped for a moment at the jagged fringe of frayed denim shorts. Then looked upwards; over a lean torso clad in a faded T-shirt lauding some obscure rock band, skimmed over tanned forearms, on up to broad shoulders and a strong neck.

'Come on,' he urged quietly, 'it's more of a stroll up an easy incline. And if it *is* too much for you, we'll do some team bonding and make a stretcher from twigs for you, hey? Deal?'

'Oh fucking hell, deal deal deal,' she muttered. Finally, she established eye contact and found herself ensnared by a pair of eyes the colour of cypress trees. She flashed a lascivious smile in automatic response. Miraculously, her hangover was lifting already.

'Who are *you*?' she asked.

'I'm Paul Brusseque,' he said, extending his hand, 'I'm your group's guide.'

Alice was very tempted to remark to Anita, whom she overtook as she strode on to contrive a position closer to Paul for the hike, that there is a God after all.

'Teacher's pet,' Jacquie hisses at Alice with a wink.

'Thought you were married!' Jeanette remarks with an arched eyebrow.

'Fuck off!' Alice retorts, blushing a little.

The afternoon's session, back at the hotel, was a crashing disappointment. Alice had turned up early with a careful slick of mascara and a subtle change of clothes only to discover that the workshop was being taken by a large Belgian psychologist with a peculiar moustache-less beard and an annoying habit of interspersing '*non?*' throughout his sentences. She skimmed through the itinerary and wondered if Paul would be umpiring the pre-supper rounders match.

He was.

Alice had always been good at rounders at school. She and her team were delighted to discover that almost fifteen years later she could still bat magnificently and field like a dream. She was the centre of attention, a place she knew she thrived in. It seemed to her a while since she'd been there and, as she sat at the refectory table talking left, right and centre, she thought how much she loved it. It suited her: she became wittier and more energized. Her words were hung upon, her anecdotes were laughed at, she had something to say about everything and everyone wanted to hear it. She felt popular and attractive and she simply didn't have time to listen all the way through Mark's chatty message on her phone. Everyone was meeting at the bar for the evening. Including the Bearded Belgian and including that Paul bloke.

It was as if cogs of concupiscence, recently dormant, started slowly to turn again in Alice; oiled by bottles of Kronenbourg beer and lubricated by frequent eye contact from Paul Brusseque. She'd absorbed the information that her colleagues' polite chat revealed about him. He worked there each spring and summer and then did the ski season. This was his third year. No, he hadn't been to England but he'd like to. His mum was Australian, his father was French. Originally he was from Cairns and this year would be his first trip home since he left for Europe at the age of twenty-six, three years ago. He was the 'outward-bound bloke' – Fritz the Belgian shrink conducted the formal workshops. And yes, he had a heap of physical activities in store for them. Pont du Gard the next day. A cathedral at Les Baux the following day. Yeah, he lived on site – in a chalet just like the ones guests had, but painted just white. The pay was pretty cool. The region was pretty cool. Hiking the petticoats of Mont Saint Victoire on a weekly basis was pretty cool. Arles and Nîmes were pretty cool towns. Carcassonne was awesome, Montpellier a bit of a dump. The French in general were a pretty cool nation. France on the whole was awesome. French food was fantastic. And French beer was just the best.

'And how about the French ladies?' Alice asked casually but with slyly lingering eye contact.

Paul regarded her levelly. 'Some are pretty cool,' he said, 'some, however, are *hot* – so liberated.' A bolt of desire struck Alice but she quickly swept all evidence behind a coquettish smile. 'You married?' he was asking. Alice wanted to say no. She ought to say yes. But nothing came out. 'That's some fuck-off ring,' Paul commented.

Alice looked down and wished she wasn't wearing it. 'It's fake,' she lied.

'So you're not married?' Paul asked.

'I didn't say that,' Alice said haughtily and saw how it made his pupils darken, 'I said my ring was a fake.' She took a consciously lingering sip at her bottle of beer. 'The real one is in the safe at home.'

Paul held out his hand and raised an eyebrow. Without batting an eyelid, Alice took off the ring and dropped it nonchalantly into his hand. He assessed its weight and held it up to the light. He placed it back on her finger, his thumb travelling suggestively to the centre of her palm as he did so. 'Your husband must earn a fair whack,' Paul commented, chinking his bottle against hers.

'I'm very lucky,' Alice acquiesced.

'He's the lucky one,' Paul said, regarding her squarely and with no ambivalence.

In his terms of engagement, there's probably a rule of involvement.

Alice walks back to her room.

Some code – both contractual and moral. Like teachers and pupils. Liaisons with clients is probably forbidden. It'll be a sackable offence, no doubt. However, there's probably a fine line drawn and delineated in his job description – and his nature – when it comes to flirting. Flirt all you can and thereby boost morale. He's probably being paid to flirt. He's probably been told to pamper my self-esteem.

Somewhat unsteadily, she slips her key into the lock.

Well, I can't remember the last time I was flirted at. And it's certainly one big, long-overdue ego boost. And I liked flirting back. It's fun. I feel bright and sparky and attractive.

Momentarily, she considers going to find Jacquie or Jeanette for a gin and a gossip. But she knows this would be inappropriate, unwise even. It is late anyway. And though she gets on well with them, they aren't exactly close friends, just the closest she has out here, far from home. She looks at the key in the lock. She takes her mobile phone from her pocket. Perhaps she'll just give Thea a quick call.

And say what? Was there actually anything to say?

I haven't done anything and I have no intention of doing anything. So why do I feel precariously close to the edge of my comfort zone? I'm married after all – and that's life's greatest anchor, isn't it? I'm hardly going to lose my head to some bloody outward bounder. An outward bounder and a cad, no doubt. And I'm out of bounds.

She brought up the blank screen on her phone and wondered what to text Thea. She tapped in H. *H*ullo? *H*elp? *H*ow are you? *H*aving a great time? *H*aving a harmless flirt? *H*orny bloke – what'll I do? She deleted the H and switched off her phone.

Harmless flirting can't hurt.

It depends how secure is the base you've come from, Alice. You're a married woman, not 100 per cent happy. Flirting may well be unwise.

Pont du Gard

Paul surreptitiously and adeptly fondled Alice's backside the next morning as she disembarked the coach on arrival in Nîmes. She was so surprised, all she could do was gawp.

'Ever wondered where your jeans come from?' he asked her.

'Whistles,' Alice informed him, appalled that her blush had yet to subside.

'In the nineteenth century, they started producing a hard-wearing cloth right here in Nîmes,' Paul said casually, 'then Levi Strauss started importing it to California, this *Serge de Nîmes*.'

'De *Nîmes*!' Alice exclaimed as the penny dropped and Paul helped himself to another furtive feel. '*Denim*!' At once, Alice justified Paul's precocious assault on her bottom. He was just trying to make a point. Quite well, actually.

Paul addressed the group, informing them to meet back at the coach in two hours to head on to the Pont du Gard. 'You want to get a coffee?' he asked Alice.

'No, thanks,' Alice said, practising what *Lush* preached about playing hard to get. She flounced off with Jeanette and Jacquie; an obvious wiggle to her denimed derrière for Paul's benefit.

*

Alice's stomach had flipped with an excited butterfly or two at Paul's lip-licking smile when she boarded the coach later; however it lurched and her spirits plummeted when she caught sight of the Pont du Gard. Was her knowledge of world-famous architectural landmarks really that poor? Had her History A level meant so little? How could she forget Agrippa's monumental aqueduct? And now, apparently in the name of character building and team bonding, they were going to have to walk its length.

'OK, guys,' Paul held the coach's microphone like a rock singer, 'here she is! 275 metres long, almost 50 metres high and built to transport 20,000 cubic metres of water daily into Nîmes – the Pont du Gard! Watch your step – we're walking right on the top – there are slabs over the channel where the water once flowed, but there are no railings. My advice? Don't look down!'

'I don't do heights!' Alice hissed at Jeanette and Jacquie. 'I'm not walking across *that* – I can't. Seriously. I feel sick just looking at it.'

The previous day, Alice hadn't felt like traipsing up the lower slopes of Mont Saint Victoire because she'd had a cracking hangover and had yet to spy the aesthetic merits of Paul Brusseque. Today, she had been actively looking forward to the day's activities, to banter and eye contact with Paul. However, she was now genuinely alarmed. She didn't want to walk this bridge at all. She did not have a head or the guts for heights.

She had presumed the day would be spent doing things that made her happy, that she could do well at, that would enable her to show off. Like rounders, or being the life and soul. However, now she was faced with a dilemma. If she admitted to her terror and therefore saved herself the trauma of walking across the bridge, she'd thereby deny herself the company of Paul Brusseque. And possibly jeopardize her standing in his affection. But, if she opted for his company and walked the sodding bridge, she'd be a gibbering wreck – which was not a feeling she wanted to feel, nor an image she wanted to project.

'I'm not doing it,' Anita announced, happily decisive, 'no way, José! I had an operation on my knee a couple of months ago.'

'I'll keep you company, I don't mind,' said Alice with hastily deployed altruism. 'I'm staying with Anita,' she told Paul, mouthing that her colleague was scared.

'Anita, do you need Alice to stay with you?' Paul asked because he'd already sensed Alice's anxiety.

'Crumbs, no,' Anita said, 'I'll be fine!'

'Are you sure?' Paul asked.

'Absolutely,' said Anita, 'I have my book to read.'

'Come on, Alice,' Paul said nonchalantly.

With her mind working overtime yet unable to hatch an escape route, Alice followed Paul, feeling sick but desperate to hide the fact.

'See up there?' Paul stopped and came close behind her, pointing ahead so that his inner forearm lightly brushed her cheek. 'Can you see the phallus? Look between those two arches. See it?' Alice looked but her nerves were such that she couldn't make out anything other than the horrible height of it all. 'The Romans carved it as a symbol against bad luck,' Paul told her. Alice made a strange noise in her throat and turned it into a laugh she intended to sound breezy and not too fake.

Alice is 50 metres above the river. And there are no railings. And there are regular, large gaps in the stone. And everyone else apart from Anita is walking across – albeit some more gingerly than others. But they're all making that journey. Alice can't. She simply can't. And now Paul is coming back with an outstretched hand and a sympathetic but strong voice urging her to make that first step. Come on, lady, you can do it, you *can*.

Alice takes a step and freezes. She's going to faint. No, she's not. First, she's going to throw up. No, she's not. She's not going to hold his hand. She doesn't want to hold his hand and she doesn't want to be on this bridge no matter how famous and iconic it is. She's scared, really terrified.

'Face your fear,' Paul implores her, 'come on, hon. Face your fear – and trust me. I'll take you there. You'll feel so fucking great. Let's do it. Go!'

'No, I can't.'

'Oh, you can – you're a strong woman. You can do it.'

'I don't *want* to.'

'*I* want you to.'

'I don't *care* what you want!' Alice declares, suddenly absolutely sure of what she wants. 'I can't and I don't want to and I'm not going to do it. All right?'

Cautiously, she turns away, tears of fear, humiliation and relief catching in her throat. She's shuffling away gingerly;

hating herself, hating Paul and his stupid motivational speak, hating herself for wanting to impress him, hating herself for being too weak to. Face her fears? Why the hell should she do that? Just so she can impress some brawny Australian tour guide? Perhaps owning up to one's fears, admitting to one's limitations, is a strength, not a weakness anyway. She's afraid of heights, everybody. *Compris*? She's *happy* to be afraid of heights. She loves her vertigo, OK?

'Don't give up, Alice,' Paul has come after her again, 'you're made of stronger stuff than that.'

Alice turns and regards his beautiful, tanned face. 'Will you just fuck off!' she growls. 'Just leave me alone.'

She takes refuge by a crop of pine trees nowhere near Anita. It is quiet and the air is warm and fragrant. Her back is turned towards the aqueduct. If she's so relieved not to be walking the Pont du Gard, why does she feel so wretched?

Flamingos look peculiar when they fly; crooked and too rigid to be aerodynamic, surely. In fact, until Alice had seen them fly, she had assumed the birds to be flightless. Like emus and boobies and dodos. She'd always thought of flamingos as comedy birds with their clonking great beaks, one-legged stance and synthetic colouring. Actually, she hadn't thought about them much at all, until just then, sitting on her own by a Camargue lagoon just outside the hotel's perimeter; the glasswort and tamarisk of the whispering marshland providing a protective screen behind which she could indulge in her bruised mood. Flamingos flew purposefully overhead, animating a dusk sky streaked with a colour identical to their plumage.

'Artemia.'

It was Paul's voice and she felt his breath on the back of her neck. He sat down behind her. She hugged her knees close to her chest while he stretched his tanned, shapely legs either side of her.

'Artemia,' he said again, 'they're flamingos' favourite snack – a mollusc that gives them their awesome colour. Do those birds look like crazy fuckers or what!'

I think I'm on the verge of being a crazy fucker quite literally, Alice remarked to herself, though the balance just then tipped a little more towards foreboding than excitement. But her gaze was drawn magnetically to the athletic splendour of Paul's legs and her stomach somersaulted as she recalled the sensation of his grope through her jeans to her bottom and beyond. In an instant, she theorized that she was miles from home, no one need know, and it wouldn't mean anything anyway. The notion of sex with this man shot her adrenal glands into overdrive and her scales of morality and reason tipped suddenly again. Caution and misgivings were now outweighed by pure and reckless desire. Rapidly, she justified that a rampant one-night stand with this stereotypical sex god might even be a rather good thing, a necessary elixir. Mightn't it restore the self-confidence she'd lost over recent months? Couldn't it redress the sexual imbalance that had gone untended at home? Wouldn't it put the spring back in her step? She'd be a nicer person for it. Absolutely everyone would benefit.

So Alice turned a blind eye to Mark smiling sweetly in her mind's eye and replaced it instead with an image of him in Marbella, with his sunburnt forehead and his legs paler and half the size of Paul's. She glanced down again at Paul's legs, regarded his hands with their shapely fingers, his bangle of Mexican silver, the provenance of which most probably involved some daring adventure or other.

Alice turned deaf ears to the clangorous warning bells. Her memory failed her when it came to her marriage vows. Instead, she leant back against Paul and while he gabbled on about molluscs and tamarisk or whatever, she wondered just when they would fuck.

Not that night, it transpired, though their verbal foreplay had been such that if Paul had suggested a shag in the corner of the bar Alice would have complied. Instead, people and particulars provided obstacles. Alice was sure if she'd told Jeanette and Jacquie that she wanted to bed Paul and could they please leave, they'd have done so. But there was absolutely no way she was going to tell a soul. And so Jeanette and Jacquie flirted with Paul themselves, apparently oblivious to the frisson reverberating between him and Alice. Furthermore, the bar was full of her colleagues and his; the pair of them could hardly leave without being noticed. And where would they go anyway? Back to Alice's chalet where no doubt Anita was saying her prayers and Rochelle was text-messaging her bloody horse? Or back to his which he shared with the weirdy-beardy Belgian psychologist who'd have a field day analysing their ravenous coupling? Instead, they had to settle for eye contact of burning intensity, sign language of moistened parted lips, secret signs of fingers touching fleetingly as beer bottles were reached for. Their gaze lingered for dangerous but thrilling seconds. They synchronized their trips to the toilet so that they could brush past each other. Alice stared at herself in the mirror after one such rendezvous, looked hard at her reflection. She glowed. The proximity, the inevitability, of sex with Paul was intoxicating, made all the more so by the hassles and logistics blocking their way.

Alice strolls back to her cabin, alternately whistling and humming, a comely but conscious wiggle to her walk. She looks over her shoulder once or twice to see if Paul is following. He isn't. It's simultaneously frustrating yet thrilling. She is drunk on this cocktail of anticipation and desire. She closes the door to her cabin after a long loiter and a last look down the path for Paul. The bedroom lights are off and she tiptoes around, giggling to herself. She tries to locate her mobile phone, fumbling around her possessions in the dark. She finds it and gets into bed, switching it on under the pillow so as not to waken Anita or Rochelle. Two text messages flash up. She replies to Mark's with a brief goodnight. She opens Thea's.

omigod! acceptd offer on my flat!!!! u ok???? Txxxxxx

Alice sends one back replete with congratulations and kisses. Then she lies in the dark and tunes into how high she feels. She and Thea were often at their happiest at the same times. Thank God, though, that their crises never collided.

Good for Thea. Moving on. It's the right time. She's found her Mr Perfect – someone she can both be madly in love with and deeply lust for and Saul feels the same.

Alice's phone vibrates through another text. It's Thea.

thanx! am taping ER 4 u . . . . !! xxxx

Shall I creep out and phone her? How can I text across all that's happening? But God I'd love to share the thrill of it all with her.

Another text message buzzes its arrival. Thea again.

howz u? bored of brie & team-bonding bollox? don't despair - home v soon!!

It struck Alice like a bolt of lead. The next day was the last.

And we're off to some bloody cathedral. It's now not only a case of when I'll screw Paul, but where?

*

Les Baux

'I can think of better ways of spending my last day than traipsing around some stuffy old cathedral,' Alice murmured to Paul, consciously perking out her breasts and licking her lips lasciviously as she brushed against him on leaving breakfast.

'Get on the coach, wench,' he all but growled, hooking his finger in the back of her skirt as she passed, affording himself a tantalizing glimpse of her underwear.

The coach trundled the party into the heart of the Alpilles, to the Val d'Enfer and the eerily beautiful village of Les Baux. As the group set off on foot, Paul discoursed on how this area, this Hell's Valley, was the inspiration for Dante's *Divine Comedy*. Alice looked around her, captivated by the stunning natural forms, some eroded into strange tortured shapes by the wind, others carved and hacked into stark angularity by the quarrying of dark red bauxite rock and creamy limestone.

Paul stopped. 'No doubt many of you guys reckoned there were better ways of spending your last day than traipsing around some dull old cathedral.' He looked around the group, skipped over an offended Anita to linger his gaze on Alice. 'Well, I'm telling you this is like no cathedral you'll ever have seen but it's a religious experience you won't forget. Welcome, guys, to the Cathédrale d'Images.'

It had been a quarry. But now it was more than a quarry. It had been used as a filmset by Jean Cocteau but it was so much more than a stage. The Val d'Enfer had inspired Dante but it was so much more than a backdrop. Cathédrale d'Images was like a vast gallery, a huge exhibition space, yet the pictures were transitory and did not actually exist at all. The group walked through and down, deep under the mountain, into a gigantic hall sectioned by megalithic columns left by the quarrying as structural support. Every surface had now become a natural screen for the projection of constantly changing images up to 20 metres in size, above, below, side to side, over there, over here, over everyone – 3,000 images. This wasn't an exhibition, this wasn't *son et lumière*, this made IMAX seem singularly unimpressive.

Underfoot, the limestone had been long since ground into a silt-soft powder as fine as flour, as light as goose down, as deep as a beach. Instinctively, many of the group took off their shoes and shrugged off preconceptions and inhibitions. Alice included. All around, images of Africa burst out against the bare rock face, whilst African music both melodic and intensely rhythmic drowned any other sound or the need to talk. The effect was mesmeric, hallucinatory almost. If the purpose of a cathedral is to suck a visitor deep into its very message, then this disused, re-cycled quarry was a cathedral indeed. Where was Alice? In Africa? In France? Was she hearing with her eyes and seeing with her ears? Why hadn't she been anywhere like this in her thirty-three years? Her body began to sway to the hypnotic drum-heavy soundtrack and she sashayed her way, trancelike, through the halls. Sometimes, she was completely alone, images drenching her. Sometimes, she found herself amongst people – her colleagues, strangers, all sharing the space and the experience and moving to the rhythms instinctively. Savannah and fabric and faces and dried river beds and wildlife and blood-red skies enveloped her. She caught sight of Rochelle, dancing quite bizarrely all by herself, but Alice had no inclination to laugh or cringe. Paul was right. This was a cathedral in so much as it was an awe-inspiring space where all who entered experienced an intense and spiritual headiness. Paul was right. Where was he?

He's behind me, he's to my side, he's in front of me. An image of a huge tribal chief swathed in robes the colour of sunburst is superimposed over him. Paul's face is red and yellow. Now there's a flame tree all over him. And now he's up close against me. His lips are hovering near mine. Touch down. Tongue. I'm kissing Paul. And his hands are all over my body, they're squeezing my boobs and fondling my bum and travelling up and down my back. And mine are grappling and groping him. God, his biceps, his six-pack, his tight bum. We're swaying and pulsing to the music, which is deafening and divine. Christ, I'm turned on, not just by his lip–tongue talent, nor the tantalizing bulge of his hard-on or the fact that he's pinching my nipples and nuzzling my neck. It's more. It's the energy of this place. It's the strange contradiction of stone that is soft, powdering its way between my toes. It's the thrumming tribal beat. It's the sultry, rich, ever-changing colours. It's like being stoned. I suppose, in this derelict quarry, we are stoned in a sense. Actually, it's better than being stoned. It's more real. My senses are in overdrive. I'm gorging on Paul's mouth like I've been half starved. I have no idea if people can see us. I don't care if they can. I want to stay in this moment. I want to be in this place.

The wink wink nudge nudging started on the coach. It was as if the unbridled unity the group attained inside the Cathédrale was decimated by the startling sunlight and sudden heat which confronted them on leaving. As if, by shielding their eyes from the sun, they hid from the unexpected spirituality they'd just encountered. As if it was suddenly unseemly for publishing and editorial directors to be seen barefoot and blissed out when they were normally known for their professional poise and thrust. No matter how at ease they had felt within the Cathédrale d'Images, it was a comfort zone they could no longer access once the reality of the day outside had hit them. And so the whispers started. Alice was dismayed. How could something that had tasted so good and felt so right have negative ramifications so quickly? Even Anita seemed to be having a good old gossip with Rochelle as they stood in line to board the coach.

'And what do you have to say on the matter?' Jeanette whispered, slithering into the seat next to Alice, raising an eyebrow while elbowing her in the ribs.

'Yes,' Jacquie said, popping up from the seat in front, 'what's your take, Alice?'

Fuck. Is that it then? Is that where a trance-like snog in some spaced-out quarry gets me? Does my perceived crime really warrant my reputation being compromised? Christ, it was only necking and a bit of a grope – it's not as if we got down and shagged. God, if only we'd've fucked at least it would have made this bit slightly more worthwhile. Hell's Valley indeed.

'Consenting adults,' Alice declared in an uninterested voice. 'People shouldn't judge so sweepingly nor condemn so quickly. Perhaps the behind-the-scenes situation justifies the visual dramatics – you know?'

'Blimey, Alice!' Jacquie said. 'You do surprise me.'

'Me too,' Jeanette agreed. 'After all, she's your main rival at work – and you need him on your side. We all do.'

'God knows I do,' Jacquie sighed, 'but not enough to perform *that* on!'

Alice stared from one woman to the other and as the pennies began to drop like a one-armed bandit spewing the jackpot, she wondered how best to backtrack.

'Isn't she married?' Alice hedged her bets, trying to come across as knowing exactly who – never mind what – they were on about.

'Clare?' Jacquie exclaimed in a whisper. 'Didn't you hear Clare called off her engagement? Even though the Vera Wang was already on order.'

Clare! They're talking about Clare Cabot. Christ alive!

'He's married too, isn't he?' Alice went for broke, now keen to know just who it was that Clare had done what with in the depths of the quarry.

'Geoff is more than married, Alice – Christ, his baby can be only a few months old. A few weeks even.'

Geoff – they're talking about Geoff. Bloody hell, Clare and Geoff. Who could've seen that *coming?*

'I like Geoff,' Alice mused, gazing out of the window as the coach ambled off. She wondered whether she'd ever return to Les Baux. Perhaps the experience should be left as a one-off so as not to dilute the impact.

'Everyone likes Geoff,' Jeanette whispered.

'That's the point,' Jacquie agreed.

'What on earth possessed him to go for *her*?' Alice joined in, for safety's sake.

Yet I do know what possessed them. I empathize. La Cathédrale d'Images possessed them. As it did me. But Clare was caught and I wasn't.

Now that it transpired Alice hadn't been seen, but so easily might have been, her desire for Paul increased tenfold and the danger of being caught made the notion of sex with this man all the more irresistible. It was all she could think about. However, the afternoon was timetabled relentlessly with the Belgian's motivational workshops and role-playing exercises; the evening was centred around the team dinner; their plane was leaving first thing the next morning.

Well, no doubt Beard Man from Bruges will be harping on about believing in the Power of Me. So why don't I just practise what he'll be preaching – I ought to account for my actions and Access the Impact I have on others. Right then. If the point of this trip is to inspire me, I can think of something far more motivational than one of Fritz's daft exercises. I'll be role-playing all right, just not in Conference Room B. If there's one thing that's guaranteed to make me feel good about myself, that will make me think this trip has been worthwhile, that it's given me something positive and memorable to take home, it'll be rampant sex with Paul Brusseque. Surely all managers of my calibre should be encouraged to take matters into their own hands as we see fit? And what matters to me is getting hold of Paul's throbbing cock. See how we fit.

Alice told Anita and Rochelle that the experience of Les Baux had given her a migraine for which the only cure was to lie down, undisturbed, in a darkened room. She told Jeanette and Jacquie she was faking a headache to skive off the afternoon's sessions and she'd meet them in the bar at six. She told Paul she was playing hooky from the afternoon's workshops and to meet her in her room in ten. She told herself that all of this was a very good idea. So she set about tweezering renegade hairs from her bikini line, applying a little perfume in strategic places and putting on fresh underwear, a swipe of mascara and a dirty, dirty smile.

Paul takes off his watch and puts it in his bedside drawer. He washes his hair, showering the limestone from his legs and feet. He must have made over fifty visits to Les Baux over the past three seasons, but still the place captivates him, simultaneously charging and challenging him physically and emotionally. This year's theme of Africa is the best yet, he feels. Last year it was the Seven Wonders of the World. The year before, Ancient Greece. But there is something about this year's display, the entrancing clash of the primitive and the opulent in sound and vision alike. Just as there is something so compelling about Alice – last year he'd had a couple of clients who'd done all the pursuing. Sex had been easy and both women had automatically tipped him handsomely which alone was an unexpected and rather welcome bonus. Getting paid to come when the women were gagging for it anyway – it was as close to being a porn star as he'd ever get. The year before that, his first over here, he'd bedded that older woman – and had then had those pointless few months supposedly dating Nathalie from the tennis club.

Paul dresses. He wonders what state of undress he'll find Alice in. He grins at the thought of her, spread-eagled on a bed, perhaps. He considers how she has everything he rates – looks, intellect, success and spirit. But she's off back to England tomorrow. Paul is horny as hell, as he has been for the last four days. He puts on new boxer shorts and a fresh T-shirt.

Hand relief has provided him temporary respite the last few nights but the sight of Alice each morning has tipped him into a dither of desire all over again. And now he's been summonsed. The imminence of sex, after a couple of celibate months, is stirring his cock already. He checks his reflection and he's looking good.

He knocks and waits for an answer, as if unsure whether anyone is home.

'You're polite,' Alice teases, because she was half looking forward to him bursting in and ravishing her without so much as a greeting. She is in a white T-shirt and jeans. Barefoot and braless. Her nipples are precociously erect and her arse is tantalizingly pert. She smells good and looks great. And his cock is hardening by the minute. Yes, they have all afternoon, but what he actually wants is to fuck her right now and empty the throbbing sack-load of expectant sperm amassed since that morning.

'You're happy to see me,' Alice remarks, eyeing the bulge in his shorts.

'Nah, it's a gun in my pocket,' he quips back.

'Well, take off your holster, cowboy,' says Alice, 'and let's fuck.'

If Alice was to document it all, she'd reprimand herself for a glut of clichés. But actually how else can she describe being wetter than she's ever been? That her sex is throbbing for him? That her lips are engorged with the anticipation of being kissed and her heart is racing from the fire of his intense gaze? Similarly, the simple fact is that his straining cock *is* rock hard, his butt *is* firm and his abs *are* rippling. Her breasts are indisputably heaving and her sex is oozing with the honey he can't lap enough of. They are devouring each other as if their hunger is insatiable.

God, this is kinky. Mark stays a decorous and hygienic distance from my bum on the occasions he does go down on me. It's fantastic that my breasts are tits again, to be manhandled greedily. I can't even recall Mark's term for my genitalia but Paul has just said 'Christ, you have a cute cunt.' I need this – I've missed this. How refreshing to be fucked senseless rather than being made love to conscientiously.

'God, you're a horny bitch,' Paul pants, tonguing her ear lobe and sucking his way down her neck, up her chin and deep into her mouth.

'You're a pretty good fuck yourself,' Alice reciprocates, licking the salty dampness from his torso as she slithers downwards to feast on his cock. His balls are shaven. She is surprised. She likes it. She wants to writhe, she wants to show off and she contorts herself this way and that, taking charge and initiating positions and the pace. Now she wants to be supine and subservient, revelling in this man driven wild with his desire for her. He flips her onto her side and he plunges into her from behind. He hauls her top leg over his waist, her body stretched out to his touch. Craning her neck around, they suck at each other's mouths while he fondles her tits and slips his fingers between the lips of her sex, finding her clitoris and rubbing gently until she's on the brink of orgasm.

'Don't come,' he commands. He pulls out and his lips are feathering over her nipples infuriatingly lightly. Now he's not touching her at all – he's between her legs staring intently at her sex. Alice gives a playful buck of her hips and he takes his face down to her, dabbing his tongue tip gently over the outer lips of her sex. She writhes and spreads her legs, thrusting to glue his mouth to where she wants, but he resists.

'Fuck me, you bastard,' she hisses.

Suddenly, he's sucking her clitoris and plunging a finger deep inside her sex, another up her anus, and the mind-blowing orgasm she's been craving racks her body. While she continues to shudder with spasms of pleasure, he squats over her and she takes his cock in her mouth before he pulls out and pumps his come all over her stomach. Alice takes her fingers down to the sticky lake of his spunk and massages it over her belly. Then she sucks at each finger while remaining eye locked with him. She feels as though she's just starred in her own private porn performance. And she's loved every minute of it. What a great idea this trip was. Look what she has to take home with her!

It wasn't possible for Paul to grab any time with Alice the following morning. When she boarded the coach, he could only shake her hand and say 'Well done.' Just as he shook everyone's hand and congratulated them. He waved them off. He couldn't tell who waved back behind the tinted glass.

He reckoned he'd go down to the beach for the day, unwind and prepare for the arrival of the next group the following day. The group had presented him with a cool pair of O'Neill shorts – he wanted to try them on. April was warming up by the hour and the delicate fragrance of spring was being usurped daily by the denser scent of summer. Waiting for him at reception was a note from Alice. He took it with him, unopened, to the beach.

Dear Paul,

No doubt you're already poncing around in your snazzy new shorts – for the record, I did not contribute to the whip-round for you. I wouldn't want you to think that I was paying you for services rendered – I wouldn't want you to feel like a whore . . . So, here's my mobile phone number – be sure to phone if ever you find yourself in London. I'll be only too pleased to play hooky from work and entertain you in my own inimitable way . . .

Alice Heggarty

The note made him laugh, made him long for Alice. He'd look up 'inimitable' later. First, he'd work on his tan and ponder the logistics of a trip to London some time soon.

Le Retour

Alice could have gone straight into work but she didn't want to, though they arrived back by lunchtime. She could have spent the afternoon at home, reacclimatizing to her life, but she didn't want to do that either. She should have gone to Thea to confide and be guided, but she didn't want to, not yet. What she wanted to do was to be by herself, accountable to no one, for a precious few hours more. She wanted to indulge in memories of the last few days; conjure the look and the taste and the feel of Paul. Transport herself back to Les Baux. Just for a little while longer. Not to daydream. Simply to remember.

So Alice whiled away her afternoon in an Internet café off Tottenham Court Road. She surfed the sights and facts of the Camargue, of the Pont du Gard, of Arles and Nîmes, of Les Baux and flamingos. She visited the O'Neill website and clicked on the same pair of shorts they'd bought Paul. She found the hotel website and clicked on every picture, analysing the tiny, pixillated figures. It was stupid to check the tariff page she told herself as she did just that. She Googled Paul's name but found nothing. He really ought to be nothing, she told herself. It wasn't as if she'd be going back, or would ever see him again. He had to have no role in her memory other than as a one-afternoon stand, a fantastic shag with no strings attached, guilt-free sex, a zipless fuck and best forgotten.

In his closing debrief, Fritz had told the group to 'take what we give you and turn it into new tools for your trade'. She'd do that, she would. She could apply it to her life in general. She wouldn't be deifying Paul. She wouldn't long for him or allow the tricks of memory and the mundanity of everyday life to transform him into anything other than a Franco–Australian beefcake she'd shagged. She'd turn the event to her benefit, she'd make sure she was eternally grateful it had happened. After all, her sexual thirst had been quenched and the spring to her step, the glint to her eye, her verve and her smile, had been restored.

Mark arrives home with a bunch of flowers and a legibly excited smile.

'Hullo, you,' he coos, embracing his wife. 'God, I missed you – I did try to ring.'

'No signal,' Alice shrugs, hugging him back and thinking to herself that he's had a disastrous haircut.

'Did you have a great time?' he asks, taking off his jacket, loosening his tie and top button, rubbing his temples and pinching the bridge of his nose. What a day. Good to be home.

'It was fine,' Alice shrugs again. 'You know these courses – part outward-bound, part bullshit-waffle assertion techniques. We were timetabled to within an inch of our lives.'

'Was it as dull as you were expecting?' Mark asks, leafing through the post and leaving it all unopened.

'I guess not,' Alice says, 'but you'll never guess – they made us share rooms! Can you believe that? Three hangers between us!'

Mark laughs as he selects a good Rioja and hunts for the state-of-the-art corkscrew. 'Well, you look gorgeous, Wife – look at you. You really do. The outward-bound bit must have done you good. All that fresh air and exercise. God knows I could do with some.'

'It was all very picturesque. Like a Stella Artois advert. And actually the workshops weren't too hug-a-tree or primal-screamish. But I didn't walk the Pont du Gard,' Alice admits sheepishly, 'I was too scared.'

'I don't blame you,' Mark says. 'I've done it – and it's pretty hair-raising.'

'You've been?' Alice is stunned, appalled, intrigued.

'During my gap year,' says Mark, still going through endless drawers in search of the corkscrew.

'Did you go to Les Baux?' Alice asks, almost accusatorily.

'Don't think so,' says Mark who's found the corkscrew. 'Was it good?'

'So-so,' Alice shrugs, 'no big deal.'

What?!

When Thea and Alice saw each other a couple of days later, they were each fizzing with excitement, gabbling unexpurgatedly, demanding that the other listen to me me me.

'So the estate agent reckons my buyer will be ready to exchange contracts in the next couple of *weeks*! We're looking to complete perhaps a month or so after that. And this place Saul and I have seen is just amazing.' Thea looked to Alice for a reaction. Her friend was grinning, eyes dancing, stuffing a chocolate éclair into her mouth. Good. 'It's duplex – with a roof terrace! It's like something you'd see on *Grand Designs* – beautiful flow of space and just the most incredible fixtures and fittings. You are going to die when you see the bathroom! And the kitchen is my dream kitchen. The views – oh my God – just you wait!' Alice glowed with excitement, which delighted Thea and spurred her to continue. 'There's just a one-bed flat beneath and guess who lives there? Guess! Rene Overton!'

'Who?'

'Actually, I hadn't a clue who he was either,' Thea laughed

into her tea, 'but we're reliably informed that he's the definitive hairdresser to the stars.'

'So you'll be popping down, not to borrow a cup of sugar, but rather his ceramic straightening irons?'

'My hair's too short for those, silly,' Thea hooted, 'but I *am* hoping that he likes nothing better on his days off than to pop up to the flat above for a quick blow-dry!' Alice and Thea guffawed excessively. 'I'm also hoping never to have to pay for hair products again,' Thea continued, 'so the whack of our mortgage repayments will be beautifully balanced by freebie haircuts and industrial-sized bottles of shampoo. As long as our offer is accepted. Anyway, so the king of hair is on the first floor and the ground floor is a snazzy interiors company.'

'So you're thinking free sofas too?' Alice laughed. 'You could offer your home as a kind of living showroom – in return for full furnishing.'

'Genius!' Thea exclaimed and they chinked teacups and agreed to share another éclair. 'So tell me about France? Was it OK in the end? Oh! I've got the *ER* tape for you – here.'

Alice regarded Thea, twitched her lip and let a lascivious smile spread. 'It was – interesting,' she said, rolling out the word with cunning. 'Have you heard of a place called Les Baux?'

'No?'

'Cathédrale d'Images?'

'No.'

'It's this place, this space – I don't know how to describe it. Dante loved it, Cocteau loved it. You'd love it. It's a defunct quarry – and you walk around while all these massive images are projected all around to amazing music.'

Thea regarded Alice, alarmed. 'You haven't gone all trippy-hippy, have you?'

Alice threw back her head and laughed. 'No, of course not! But it was undeniably atmospheric and intense. And had a bizarre impact on us all. *Anyway*, Clare Cabot – you know, my nemesis – shagged Geoff Sprite. Practically there and then – regardless of their audience.'

'You are *joking*?' Thea gasped. 'Blimey! Talk about scandal – *outrageous*!'

'And I shagged our guide.'

Alice bit her lip, glanced away and then dragged sheepish but sparkling eyes back to Thea. 'This absolutely gorgeous bloke called Paul,' Alice confessed, her brow furrowed above her excited whisper, 'divine looking – the sort of physique you see on a Calvin Klein underwear ad. Incredibly handsome – half French, half Australian – a real mountain-climbing, nature-loving, sex-god stereotype. Bit of a toyboy actually – not even thirty. Does the ski season half the year. Anyway, so we're in the cathedral – *cathédrale* – and there's this thrustingly sexy rhythmic music and all these images of Africa. And Paul and I have been flirting since I arrived and it's obvious he fancies me. And I don't mind saying it made me feel really fantastic. What a boost – attention like that can certainly restore a girl's pout and wiggle! So, there I am, walking around this quarry with the sights and sounds of Africa and watching my colleagues dancing. It's like everyone was stoned (*stoned*? *Quarry*? Do you see!). Anyway, suddenly Paul's there – there's been all this chemistry, days of lingering looks and lip licking and brushing past each other accidentally-on-purpose. And he's there, Thea, right up against me. And he just starts fondling me and snogging me. Real snogging – like we used to do at teenage discos. Greedy, lust-drenched tonguing and groping. It was incredible.'

'*What*?'

Alice regarded Thea. 'Then I shagged him!' Immediately, she covered her face with her hands and groaned.

'Alice! You did *what*?'

Alice peeped at Thea through the cage of her fingers. 'When we returned to the hotel. I bunked off to bonk, basically.' She placed her hands in her lap, chewed at her lip guiltily. 'We snuck off and had the most rampant, filthy, abandoned wild sex of my life!'

'What?'

'Stop saying *what*!'

'But Alice!' Thea protested, her eyes skittering over her best friend's face trying to detect a lie, obvious elaboration. Anything but the dance and sparkle that met her gaze.

'What!' Alice exclaimed, her face twitching between shame and triumph.

'You're *married*!' Thea exclaimed. 'That's what.'

Alice looked at Thea. She had thought Thea would be surprised – stunned, perhaps – but still she had expected her best friend's approval. She was taken aback by Thea's frown. 'So what?' Alice said, with a defensive jerk to her shrug.

'But what about Mark?' Thea asked quietly.

'What about him?' Alice replied evenly. 'He's hardly going to find out, is he. I'm not likely to leave Mark for some tour guide, am I – albeit one with an incredible dick and the last word in sexual athletics. Come on, Thea – get off your moral high horse! I had a one-night stand! That's all! And do you know something? I don't regret it and I don't feel guilty. It's what I needed and I feel fucking great. It completely boosted my self-esteem. There will be no repercussions.'

Thea sipped her tea. It was lukewarm and she grimaced as she swallowed it down. Despite that, she sipped again to give her time to think because, just then, she really didn't know what to say. Thea was gutted by her friend's behaviour. She wanted to whack Alice, to scold her, to say what the hell were you thinking, why the hell did you do that, don't you dare get a taste for it, don't you ever do it again. But she didn't. She couldn't. Just look at Alice – just look at her – gone is the pale complexion of late, the dullness to her eyes, the slump in her demeanour, the fatigued gazing into the middle distance, the disillusionment with her lot. Look at her now – she looks as though she's spent a fortnight being pampered at a world-class spa, she looks as though she's won the lottery, she looks as though she's mid-leap from Cloud 8 to 9, she looks as though she's having the time of her life. She's beautiful and centred and exuding delirious happiness. She's radiating the glow of a well-laid woman.

'You're wicked, you are,' Thea decided to say, acting bright and breezy, though privately it irked her to have to do so, 'you're a slag!'

'I know!' Alice said, surfacing from giggles to sigh at the memory of it all. 'I tell you, if you had to choose between Paul Brusseque and Brad Pitt? No contest whatsoever.'

'And if you had to choose between him and Mark Sinclair?' Thea said with a sternly arched eyebrow.

'Fuck off!' Alice barked defensively, trying to cover it with a beguiling pout. 'It was a one-night stand – that's all. A common, simple, one-night stand. Christ, stop giving it more gravity than it deserves. Anyway, I'm telling you, Miss Sanctimonious – if you were faced with someone even half as horny as Paul Brusseque, far from home and safe in secrecy, I'd defy you not to drop your knickers too.' Alice sucked in her cheeks slightly, as if challenging Thea to retort, to deny if she dared.

'But I have Saul,' Thea said firmly. 'I wouldn't want to.'

'When temptation confronts you, believe me you are a helpless, happy slave.' Alice lowered her voice ominously and wagged her finger with detectable superiority.

It was as if, by being flung far from Alice's conscience, thoughts of Mark were assaulting Thea's. She couldn't rid an image of him from her mind's eye. It was irrelevant that he would not find out about his wife's adultery – still Thea's heart bled for him. She felt like an accessory to Alice's crime. And Thea decreed it a misdemeanour absolute. She deemed sexual fidelity and true love to be inextricably bound. For the latter to exist, the former was unconditional. No one would ever love Alice as much as Mark – and Thea believed he should be loved right back. Just then, Thea didn't know which was worse – the fact that Alice had been unfaithful to Mark or that, as a cuckold, he was to be pitied. On Mark's behalf, Thea felt the humiliation and bewilderment she hoped sincerely that blessed ignorance would keep from him. It was horrible.

'Are you OK?' Saul gently tucks Thea's hair behind her ear. He's concerned – she's been withdrawn all evening, chewing at the skin around her fingernails, fiddling with her ring, frowning suddenly, even wincing once or twice.

'Fine,' Thea nods with minimal eye contact though Saul notes a gauze of sadness clouding her eyes, 'just tired.'

'You sure?' Saul presses because he's rarely known Thea in anything other than her sunny, happy state. Especially recently – she's been infectiously euphoric. He doesn't like to see her unhappy but he doesn't know how to help and it is not his style to pry.

'Honestly,' she says, but unconvincingly because he knows she's trying to inhibit further probing, 'I'm done in. Sometimes, giving massage can invigorate me – sometimes it utterly depletes me. I think I'll go to bed.'

'OK,' Saul says, placing his hand tenderly across her forehead, then tapping the tip of her nose with his finger. 'If you look in my bag, I bought you the new issue of *Grand Designs*.'

'Thanks,' Thea says and she takes the magazine off to bed, grateful for distraction. That's what she'll think of – sinks and fabrics and flooring and ways with light. Not Alice, she won't think of Alice. Or Mark. She'll think about setting up home with Saul. And she smiles at the knowledge that absolutely no one, from Brad Pitt to this Paul Brusseque, could tempt her from Saul.

txt sex

It's peculiar – I almost feel like writing an anonymous piece for Adam *on the merits of infidelity. I want to evangelize the effect that a one-night stand has had on my life. I want to stand up and defend what our society denounces as morally reprehensible. It's not. I was miserable before – doubting the point of marriage, questioning my choice of husband, negative about my lot, pessimistic about my future. And it all came down to sex! Just sex. That instinctive, carnal interchange. Simple sex – that's all. I'm sure of it. One dose of pure sex and I'm cured! Now I'm happy with my husband, my energy and optimism have returned at both work and play and best of all, I feel happier and more centred in myself than I have done for months.*

When Alice felt buoyant, everyone in contact with her was dusted with her jauntiness and vigour. Her team produced work worthy of awards and Mark reaped the benefits of his wife's excellent mood. She was spirited yet affectionate, effervescent but considerate. She didn't glower when he said he'd have to go to Singapore and Tokyo the following week, instead she came home with potions and tonics from the naturopath to alleviate all primary and secondary symptoms of jet lag. Their lovemaking was back up to twice a week and Mark noted with some pride how she wanted to prolong each session, how her eyes were closed throughout as if in utter appreciation of their coupling.

It lasted a week. Then the first text message arrived. And by replying to it (initially she justified it would be impolite not to at least answer, but if she was honest, she fired back her reply in anticipation of another response) Alice somersaulted down into the murky depths of secrecy, lies and betrayal.

'Is that your phone?' Mark said, while ripping something out of the *Financial Times* and tucking it in his suit jacket. 'Bloody hell, it's almost midnight – who's texting you at this time as if I couldn't guess?'

'It's just Thea – fretting about her house sale and stuff,' said Alice, not knowing quite how she was controlling herself, having seen that the number was overseas. 'I'd better reply – I know how stressful the process is.'

'Why don't you just ring her? Your thumb will get RSI!'

'Saul's probably asleep – that'll be why she's texting,' Alice said with a mock yawn. 'I'll go and have a bath and reply.'

'Tell her we thoroughly recommend our conveyancing lawyer.'

'I'll do just that.'

With enormous restraint, Alice resisted running to the bathroom, sauntering away instead with credible nonchalance. As the bath ran, she sat on the edge of the tub and read the message, her stomach flipping with a swarm of manic butterflies, her heart galloping in her throat.

it's late. lying here thinking of u and ur wet pussy. PB x

Alice wanted to squeal and squeak and run around whooping 'It's from Paul, it's from Paul!' What should she say? How should she reply? Should she reply? Or ignore? Should she text Thea and send her four or five possible responses to choose from? Shit – the bath is almost overflowing.

Alice sat in the bath and read Paul's message over and over. Giggling, her thumb set to work.

pussy wet thnkng of u

Did she dare? Did she dare say that? Did she dare send it?

She did.

Come on, come on – reply, damn you!

Come

on!

Replyreplyreply.

Yes!

rock hard – where r u?

She gave a joyous shriek.

'Alice?' Mark called through the door. 'Are you OK?'

'What? I'm fine – I'm fine. It's just Thea being daft.'

in bath – v soapy

She waited a decorous few minutes before sending it.

'Alice?'

Oh for fuck's sake, Mark – what?

'Yes?'

'I wouldn't mind coming in and doing my teeth and stuff.'

Shit, the next message had just buzzed through and she was desperate to read it.

'But the door's locked,' Mark continued.

'God, can't I have a bath in peace,' Alice protested. 'Look, I'll be out in two minutes – all right?'

She heard Mark pad away. She felt relieved rather than guilty. She looked at her phone.

u horny bitch

Paul was right. She was. She was horny. Very excited and extremely horny. Just then she was horny enough not to care that she was a bitch.

Five pence was the cost of it. It occurred to Alice that a 5p text message had bought her an affair. But she didn't stop to think that it might be at the price of her marriage. It was just harmless texting, after all. Virtual sex. Not real. No one need know.

But it wasn't long before Alice was living from text message to text message, becoming decidedly fractious in between. Her moods, a pendulum swinging erratically between high spirits and furtive anticipation; her spiky frustration affecting everyone in spitting distance. She could be impatient and surly at work and short-tempered and snappish with Mark, or inspiring and energetic with her team and affectionate and vivacious at home. It all depended on whether she was owed a text from Paul or not. No one around her could figure out what the problem was and whether or not it lay with them. Because they did not know where they stood, so they tiptoed around her and tried their best to please her.

Thea was dismayed when Alice handed over her mobile

and told her to scroll through. 'You said it was just a one-night stand.'

'It was,' Alice frowned, snatching back her phone and gazing at the screen as if a photo was lodged there. 'God, stop taking everything so seriously, Thea,' she said, 'they're just silly, sexy, harmless texts – but Christ they make my day.'

Once more, Thea felt compromised between her own personal morality and Alice's infectious energy.

'They must be costing you a fortune,' Thea remarked.

'I've started buying those text bundles the phone companies market at teenagers!' Alice exclaimed, her face one lascivious expansive grin.

'Let me see that last one again,' Thea requested because she felt it was expected of her. Though she didn't want to encourage Alice, she knew her duty as the adulteress's best friend was not to alienate her either.

And when Mark flew off to Singapore and Tokyo on business, then the phone sex began. In the house alone, with no intention of asking Thea's approval, permission or advice, Alice phoned Paul. And the outright dirtiness of the text messaging was replaced with naughty giggles and coy referencing and then, surprisingly, five minutes of chit-chat. On a nightly basis.

'He's just a friend,' Alice justified to Thea, having thrust her mobile phone at her friend's ear so she could hear his voice. 'We're just mates.'

'"Mate" being the operative word,' Thea couldn't resist saying. 'You fucked, remember.'

Alice physically swiped the air dismissively. 'He lives in Fucksville France!' Alice breezed, as if Thea's insinuation was ludicrous.

`u awake? can u spk? u alone?`

Yes, Alice was awake but no she couldn't speak because Mark and she were just about to sit down to supper.

'I'm just going to the loo,' Alice told Mark, surreptitiously slipping her phone into her back pocket. 'Can you stir the sauce and switch the rice off in a couple of minutes?'

'Wine? White?' Mark asked, starting the interminable search for the sodding corkscrew.

Alice locks the toilet door.

`not alone - hows u, big boy?`

`coming` the reply announces.

Alice laughs as she sends her reply: `u dirty boy - u'll go blind!`

`coming over` he sends back.

Before Alice has the chance to absorb the information let alone formulate a response, a barrage of messages arrives on her phone.

```
to london
  next tues
    3 nights
      get ready, baby - gonna make u sore
```

Oh
My
God

Sitting on the closed toilet seat, Alice is utterly stuck for text words.

She switches off her phone without replying and leaves it on top of the cistern in irrational fear of Paul suddenly materializing from it like a genie from the lamp.

Oh
My
God

Table for Four

'I can't remember it being this much hassle when I bought my flat five years ago,' Thea declared with a sorry pout around the table.

'You were a first-time buyer,' Mark said soothingly, asking the wine waiter to bring whichever red he'd recommend.

'But it's not like I'm in a chain,' Thea protested, 'my problem is that my buyer is a bloody lawyer and he's being exasperatingly finicky. We could be on the verge of exchanging contracts but he's not going to unless a structural surveyor has checked some minor detail or other.'

'Has your offer been accepted on the place you like?' Mark asked Saul.

'No – we've upped it but they're sitting on it,' Saul told him, squeezing Thea's wrist supportively.

'It's Sod's Law – and it's down to the bloody postcode fiasco. Thea's trying to sell in a buyer's market and yet you're trying to buy in a seller's market. All in the same city,' Mark observed. 'Thea darling, if you sell before you buy, you can always store your stuff at ours.'

'Thanks,' said Thea glumly because it was of little consolation just then. 'They say that moving house is the most stressful thing we encounter after death and divorce.'

'Better not die then – and keep cohabiting, rather than marrying,' Mark laughed. He looked over at Alice who was gazing at her lap. 'Are you OK, darling?'

'What?' She looked up and around the table as if she was startled to find herself there with them. 'I'm fine. I'm fine. Just hassles at work – just had to text one of my editors.' She brandished her mobile phone and then dropped it into her bag. Thea looked away from Alice's fleeting smirk. 'Have you exchanged yet?' Alice asked her. 'Wasn't it meant to be this week?'

Thea groaned, put her head in her hands, looked up and glugged gratefully at the glass of wine. 'Don't ask!' she said hoarsely, and then proceeded to repeat in great detail the stress and minutiae.

'Did you get my text?' Alice asked her, as if she'd not heard a word of Thea's rant.

'What text?'

'About my client?' Alice said.

Thea checked her phone. 'Oh, it's here – I hadn't seen it.'

lover boy's coming 2 UK nxt wk !!!!!!!

Thea read it and read it again. What on earth was she meant to say? Right then? Right there? In an upmarket restaurant with her best friend's husband in eyeshot of her mobile phone. 'Right,' she faltered, 'right.'

'He'd like to see you,' Alice carried on blithely while Thea prayed that Alice's expression of triumphant glee was legible to her alone.

'OK,' Thea nodded slowly, 'OK.'

'Who's this?' Mark asked.

'Paul,' Alice announced lightly, as if jogging Mark's memory that he knew him too. 'I think Thea should assess him.'

'Paul Who?' Saul asked.

'He's not part of the *Adam* team,' Alice replied dismissively, 'different department.'

'What's his problem?' Mark asked politely.

Thea couldn't believe it was she who was starting to redden. Surely it should be Alice. But Alice was having great fun with her hidden meanings. 'I've told him to be careful. I've told him he'll be flat on his back by next week – so I really think he'd benefit from Thea's evaluation.'

Thea's appetite slumped. Luckily for Alice, Mark and Saul presumed Thea had lost it under the pile of faxes and hassle swamping her from the sale of her property.

'Alice was in high spirits,' Saul remarks, peeling off his clothes and slinging them onto the floor.

'Manic, I'd say,' Thea asserts, picking up Saul's clothes and adding them to a pile she's sorted to be washed.

'Are things OK with her and Mark?' Saul asks cautiously.

Thea pretends not to have heard as she heads off with the laundry to the kitchen to load the washing machine, hoping to buy herself some time in which Saul might forget his question. He's in bed, when she returns, reading *FHM*.

'New issue?' Thea asks.

'Do they?' Saul looks up.

'Pardon?'

'Issues – you said Alice and Mark had issues.'

Thea laughs unnecessarily. 'No, no! I asked if that *FHM* was a new issue!'

Saul looks at the front cover and nods. Thea climbs into bed, faces away from him and yawns exaggeratedly at how tired she is. Saul puts down *FHM* and spoons up against her back. 'Don't tell me you're turned on by some soft-porn pics in a bloody lads' mag!' Thea exclaims, feeling Saul's hard-on nudging hopefully at the small of her back.

'Don't be daft,' he murmurs, nuzzling her neck, 'it was the sight of you doing the laundry in the buff. Your gorgeous peach of an arse.' And he is burrowing under the duvet to the object of his desire, kissing her buttocks and unexpectedly spreading her cheeks for a long lick downwards. Thea is pleased to close her eyes and swim into the physical sensations Saul is crafting; to propel herself away from the stress of selling her flat and the disquiet over her best friend's behaviour.

Sometimes, Thea likes to be dominant during sex with Saul; she'll initiate it and call the pace and the positions. At other times, she craves utter synchronicity – that he desires her as much as she does him, that he wants to take her from behind at the exact moment she flips herself over, that she wants to suck his cock without needing to be asked, that their orgasms occur within milliseconds of each other. But there are also times, and just now is one of them, when what she needs is to be made love to. She wants to consciously detect that Saul loves and desires her absolutely, venerates her, to the exclusion of all other thoughts and all other people. And so Thea lies in his arms, being licked and kissed and adored and wanted.

Post-coitally, with Saul on his back panting himself back to a normal heart rate, Thea snuggles against his chest. She cups her hand lightly over his cock still semi-hard and twitching lazily. 'God, that was good,' Saul declares. Thea smiles. Good.

'Saul,' she says in a quiet, little-girl-lost voice she is not in the habit of using blithely, 'promise me we won't ever be like that.' He twists his head down to look at her and she gazes up at him, with a beguiling bat of her eyelashes. 'Like Alice and Mark,' she says very quietly, all wide-eyed and winsome.

'I thought there was something up,' Saul declares. 'What's going on with those two?'

'I don't know,' Thea evades, 'nothing, probably. You know Alice. The point is, I never want us to loiter on that plateau of complacency.'

Saul kisses Thea on the forehead. 'I know what you mean – it was as if Alice was unaware that her husband was dining with us at all. They converse without really communicating – they didn't really chat to each other. They just made up the numbers for a table for four.'

'I just want you and me always to stay close – and always truly feel *in* love,' Thea declares. She kisses Saul back and turns to fall asleep, feeling a little happier and safer.

P.I.C.

'Cover for me!'

Thea's heart dropped and she felt like hanging up the phone. She'd become reluctantly resigned to such a call from Alice, which wasn't to say she hadn't been deludedly hoping Alice might say Paul had changed his mind, or he was staying in Lancashire, or she'd changed her mind and was ignoring his calls.

'Cover for me?' Alice implored. 'Please! Come on – you promised. You must honour our promise to be each other's P.I.C.'

Thea suddenly deeply regretted that fateful school day in the second year when they had snuck behind the science block to smoke – daring each other, declaring they'd be each other's Partner In Crime, swearing solemnly that if one was caught the other would go down with her. But neither was caught and they puffed their way through the packet of Sobranie Cocktail cigarettes over the next eight lunch hours. And after that, when it came to anything which implied risk or wrong, Thea and Alice committed to being each other's P.I.C. I'll do it if you do it. Come on, let's try it! I won't tell if you won't. We'll say it was *both* our ideas! The difference now was that this was the first occasion in eighteen years that the P.I.C. was acting merely as lookout rather than collaborator.

'It would be the one bloody week Mark isn't travelling,' Alice bemoaned, 'so cover for me, Thea. You *have* to.'

'When?' Thea asked out of a sense of duty, an unwilling partner in a crime she did not want committed.

'Tonight! Tomorrow night! The night after!' Alice's effervescence and excellent spirits were seductive and Thea had to sternly remind herself of the deplorable cause of Alice's mirth.

'What's your story?' Thea sighed.

'Pilates tomorrow night – with you. And some late-night preview shopping thing at Heal's on Thursday night – with you. He flies back Friday afternoon.'

'When does he arrive?'

'Late tonight,' Alice enthused.

'You're not going to climb out of your window and steal away to him tonight, are you?' Thea asked flatly.

'No, I'll just about resist!' Alice laughed.

'You *so* owe me, Mrs Sinclair,' Thea told her.

'I think I ought to be Miss Heggarty for the next three days, don't you?'

'I wouldn't mind going to that Heal's thing anyway,' Thea justified. 'Saul and I could look at dining tables.'

'I made it up, silly!'

'Alice,' Thea cautioned, 'are you sure you're doing the right thing here? Isn't it bloody dangerous?'

'Yes,' said Alice, 'it *is* dangerous but I have to do it – I feel compelled to – so in that respect, it must be right even if, on paper, it's wrong and dastardly. I have to rid it from my system.'

'I thought the one-night stand had done that,' Thea reminded her.

'So did I,' Alice said darkly. Then she brightened. 'Guess what!'

'What?'

'I'm going to play hooky from work tomorrow afternoon and Thursday morning.'

'Christ, Alice,' Thea exclaimed, 'you really need to tread carefully.'

'Oh shush, Thea – you know you'll be gagging for details!'

And that was it. That was just it. No matter how greatly Thea deplored Alice's actions and despaired at her abhorrent lack of morality, she did indeed crave details. The whole scenario was car-crash horrific, but like a terrible road accident, one is compelled to look. Because it's bizarrely life-affirming to gasp and recoil from something so appalling you can't believe it's real. And it's sobering to think thank God that's not me. And it's chastening to think I hope it never happens to me.

Miss Heggarty and Mr Brusseque

Alice's first thought was Christ, what on earth am I thinking, let alone doing? This isn't me. This really isn't.

However, her need to live out her fantasy as a foxy temptress, to fulfil her desire for debauchery with the rock-climbing, nature-communing sex god, overruled her crashing dismay at where the dirty deed was to happen. Paul had given an address in Clapham – 23a Blanchard Road. It was the 'a' that unnerved Alice most. As the taxi stuttered its way along Blanchard Road, with the driver and Alice craning to see numbers, she kept her hopes up. The road was pretty. And quiet. That was a good start. The fare was expensive and Alice justified it would be money well spent.

'Number twenny-free, darling.'

Alice noted the scruffy front door and numerous bells and hoped they were but an ironic façade to a *bijou* residence. Perhaps the beer bottles and takeaway cartons tossed aside in the front garden were there as a cunning foil to would-be burglars. As she rang the bell, she lowered her expectations and just prayed that there wouldn't be batik bedspreads pinned up as wall hangings, or Jim Morrison looking down in his Jesus-like way from posters Blu-Tacked to the backs of doors. Please no CND symbols graffitied with marker pen onto the fridge door. And dear God, no patchouli joss-sticks.

You're a snob, Alice.

No, I'm not – I've merely outgrown the 'dope-smoke digs' thing.

Been there done that?

Exactly (though I've never used a bedspread as a wall hanging).

But now you're a married woman of thirty-three living very nicely in Hampstead.

Exactly.

Sloping off work for a little light adultery in the afternoon.

When Paul saw Alice through the spyhole, he hovered and stared. What a great suit. He watched Alice grow impatient, saw her looking with certain disdain around her. He grinned. He'd give her something to moan about. And just then, the expense of his trip over to England, the negotiation it had necessitated at work, the lies he'd told to Brigitte, whom he'd just started seeing, were all worth it.

'It's not the Ritz,' he said as he opened the door, brandishing his easy smile and looking Alice up and down like a tipster evaluating a racehorse, 'but the sheets are clean and no one's here.'

'I could've booked us into a nice hotel for the price of the taxi fare!' Alice pouted, brushing past him and finding herself in a communal hallway badly in need of a Hoover. She primly offered her cheek for the kissing but Paul took her chin between his finger and thumb and turned her face towards his, sinking his mouth over hers, their tongues suddenly in a whirl.

'Let's fuck,' he murmured. Alice's desire to be in bed with him was so strong that she didn't notice the scruff of pizza flyers and general detritus littering the hallway, the rude waft of other people's cooking. It may as well have been the Ritz, for all the attention she gave the surroundings. The flat itself was unkempt with drab, tired furniture and unforgivable features such as the paper lantern with a glaring rip in it, a plate with dried HP Sauce left on the sofa. Alice did note that there were no ethnic bedspreads on the walls and for her, just then, this fact alone both rose-tinted the rest of the flat and justified her illegal exeat from her marriage and her career that afternoon. So, on a mattress on the floor, under two sleeping bags zipped together, Alice romped the afternoon away with her lover.

It was only when she awoke with a start from a doze she couldn't recall slipping into, slightly chilly and aware of the irritating sound of Paul's semi-snoring, that it struck her she was on the other side of London to where she lived and worked and that her surroundings were categorically unpleasant. On any normal Wednesday, she'd be making her way home by now. An image of her sumptuous bathroom, the luxurious fluffy weight of her Egyptian cotton bath sheets came to mind. With it came a stab of guilt. But if she felt guilty it meant she was in the wrong and she wasn't prepared to own up just then. The best thing to do was to put it all out of her mind. And the best way to do that was to give herself something else to think about. So she rolled over and started to kiss and caress Paul. Soon enough they were fucking again and all thoughts of work, marriage and scuzzy bedrooms were flung far from her conscience.

Every time the phone rang, Thea jumped, fearing it was Mark wanting to know if she'd seen his wife. What was tonight meant to be? The Heal's do or Pilates? Saul assumed that Thea's tetchiness was due to her anticipation that the phone would be the estate agent ringing with news, bad or good. She didn't tell him but she was almost relieved when it turned out to be the vendor's agent turning down their revised offer on the new property.

'Come on,' said Saul, 'let's go out – let's go for a few drinks, perhaps a stonking hot curry, and not think about bricks and mortar.'

But Thea worried they might bump into Mark, which was highly unlikely as he wasn't that partial to curry. 'Let's catch a film instead,' she suggested, thinking that she'd be safe in a dark cinema.

'Good idea,' said Saul, 'Arnie's new film would be a welcome distraction. Let's go.'

However, Thea suddenly thought what if Alice needed her? What if all had gone horribly wrong in Clapham? What if her phone didn't have a signal in the cinema? She couldn't risk that. 'No,' she flummoxed, 'curry. Let's go local.' Saul was now a little irritated but it was nothing a karahi chicken couldn't soothe.

As Alice took a taxi all the way back to Hampstead, she began a text message to Thea but stopped mid-word. What was she meant to write? State the obvious – been shagging non-stop and now walking like John Wayne? Perhaps theorize instead – orgasms this good cannot be bad? Instead, she pressed the speed-dial button to phone Thea. But what would she say? We fucked until suppertime and then I tried to have a shower in a bath with scum-marks and one of those rubber shower attachments you bung onto the taps like a milking machine? Was she to tell Thea that the flat was rented by a bloke who was a friend of a friend of Paul's? That some bloke had arrived back at some point and was quietly rolling a joint on the sofa next to the plate with the dried-on sauce when she and Paul surfaced? Which precise details of the afternoon were worth recounting? The only people who knew of her whereabouts were she, Paul and Thea. And they all knew the purpose of the afternoon was solely sex and no matter how mind-blowing the orgasm, the mechanics of sex were pretty straightforward.

All this thinking had passed the journey. Her cab was already travelling through Camden. She decided she'd send Thea a short text before she went to bed, confirming lunch the next day. Please don't let Mark be at home.

Please don't let this be a day when he doesn't have to stay late for some conference call or other.

Thea thought how Alice's teenage fluster and giggle the next day were actually quite endearing. If this Paul bloke was good for anything, it was reinstating her best friend's bounce and spirit.

'God, I can't wait for you to see him!' Alice declared, drumming her fingers on the restaurant table in the safe territory of Maida Vale. 'I'm telling you, he's more gorgeous and sexy than *anyone* you'll ever have seen – in reality or on screen. Honestly!'

'Shut up, you idiot.' Thea poked her. 'You sound like a teenager.'

'He's here – here he is!'

Thea was desperately disappointed. She was a firm believer in beauty being much more than skin deep. But she had to admit that Paul was quite spectacular looking, in a rugged, Timberland-branded sort of way. Not really her type at all – but unquestionably attractive and obviously smitten with Alice. He shook her hand and took Alice's in his which made Thea feel awkward.

'Are you enjoying your trip?' Thea asked him with a stern edge that made Alice kick her under the table.

'Very much,' he said, ruffling his already tousled hair.

'What have you done?' Thea probed, moving her legs out of kicking distance. 'Where have you been?'

'Oh, you know, mainly hanging out in Clap Ham.'

His enunciation of the silent 'h' struck both Thea and Alice but while Alice thought it sweet, Thea let it irritate her supremely.

'You haven't seen the sights then?' Thea challenged him.

'Like Bucking Ham Palace, you mean? Or Saint Paul's Cathedral?'

Silent 'ai', you prat.

'Any of the galleries?' Thea persisted, holding Alice's glare. 'Our glorious parks?'

'Not this time,' Paul said, throwing a furtive smirk over to Alice which Thea intercepted. 'I'm on a tight schedule, you know? Perhaps next time, though.'

'Next time?' Alice exclaimed.

'Next time?' Thea challenged.

'Hey, the trip over was a doddle – why not!'

Alice excused herself and went to splash cold water on her face. Thea and Paul glanced at each other awkwardly.

'So,' Paul said, 'is her man a bit of a bastard then?'

'Who?' Thea shot. 'Mark? A bastard? He's one of the nicest people I know.'

Paul seemed surprised. 'Well, she's obviously not getting what she needs.'

Alice returned before Thea had the chance to respond. 'We could, if you like, go for a stroll in Regent's Park this afternoon,' Alice said to Paul, 'if you felt the need to authenticate your trip.'

Paul shrugged before a thoroughly licentious expression suffused his face, which Alice found thrillingly contagious.

'Thea,' Alice said without taking her eyes off Paul, 'are you staying at Saul's tonight?'

Thea had been busying herself with her French fries. 'Yes, why?'

'Perhaps I really ought to go and *water your house plants*,' Alice said, licking her lips at Paul whilst trying to locate Thea's legs to nudge with her foot.

'Sorry?' Thea knew exactly what Alice was implying but was so taken off her guard as to feel downright insulted.

'Perhaps you'd like me to *stack your post*?' Alice elaborated, slithering a coy giggle over to Paul. '*Do your laundry*?'

'Alice, are you asking to borrow my flat to shag Paul?' Thea barked, hoping to shock some sense of decorum into her and embarrass Paul.

'We'll leave it spick and span,' Paul told her, obviously rubbing at Alice's leg under the table.

'Please?' Alice pleaded with her most winsome, beguiling pout.

'I have to go, I have a client in twenty minutes,' Thea declared, leaving with a blatant glower. Alice stood up to go after her, prepared to demand her door keys, when she saw Thea had left them on her plate already. In a splodge of ketchup.

Alice licked off the sauce with wholly unnecessary suggestiveness. 'Let's go and see the sights of Crouch End,' she declared, snogging Paul while a waitress cleared the table.

Loggerheads

Thea was appalled, incensed and insulted. Poor Peter Glass received a massage so vigorous he was virtually winded and Thea's final client was given a perfunctory forty minutes before being told he was much better despite leaving her room with the stilted gait he'd entered with. Later, Thea snapped at Saul, 'Tell them this is our final offer and they can take it or fucking fuck off.' And then, when she saw she'd missed a call from Mark, she burst into tears.

'Baby,' Saul tried to soothe her, 'baby, what's up?'

'Nothing,' Thea cried.

'Tell me,' Saul said, through lips pressed to the top of her head.

'Alice,' Thea sobbed.

'What's wrong with Alice?' Saul asked, remembering he hadn't seen her in the office that afternoon. 'Is she OK?'

'We've fallen out,' Thea whispered. She felt a sudden stab of acute loneliness at the fact that Alice was actually very happy and utterly unaware that they'd fallen out.

'About what?' Saul said, wiping Thea's nose for her. But Thea didn't want to tell him. She'd been sworn to secrecy, after all. And a part of her could not betray trust placed in her. Another part of her simply didn't want to reveal the crime, the sin, to Saul. He liked Alice. He worked with her. He liked Mark too. It was so hideous she didn't want to talk about it. She didn't want to say out loud that she hated her lifelong best friend for behaving in a manner which threatened to undermine all they were meant to hold sacred, all they were supposed to be striving to achieve. This wasn't playground gallivanting or youthful experimentation. It was full-on promiscuity. It was dangerous and deplorable and Thea didn't want it to be happening. It made her feel unsafe. Why wasn't Alice behaving?

'What about?' Saul repeated.

'Just stupid,' Thea said, wiping her nose gratefully against Saul's shoulder, 'nothing.'

'It'll blow over,' Saul said, kissing her forehead, 'these

things always do. She's your best friend. I bet you she texts you before she goes to sleep tonight. Now, am I really phoning the estate agent declaring our final offer or the vendor can fucking fuck off?'

Thea smiled. 'I love you Saul,' she said with a crackling sniff. 'I'd never do anything to hurt you – even if you might never know about it.'

Saul gave her a puzzled smile. 'Thanks, baby,' he said, 'ditto.' Thea leant towards him and cupped his face in her hands, kissing his mouth with tenderness. 'I'm going to phone the agent,' he said, kissing her back. 'Are we agreed this is our final offer then?' Thea had her eyes closed. She nodded. She did so love Saul. Her home was with him, wherever that might be.

Thea's Twelve O'Clock

'Hullo. I brought your keys back. And a latte.'

'Alice, I don't have time for this – my twelve o'clock is due any moment.'

'I *am* your twelve o'clock, silly.'

'What? You? Why?'

'Because I'm not due in at work until this afternoon and I've just said goodbye to Paul and I could do with a massage after all the vigorous indoor sport I've been doing.'

'Well, you're not having a freebie.'

'I paid in advance, actually. Are you OK, Thea? Has something happened? Is it the flat?'

'Alice, just undress and lie face down on the table. Are you in pain or discomfort anywhere?'

'Not specifically. But I *have* been shagging Paul in a furiously athletic way. And I suppose I have been burning the candle at both ends.'

'Is there any tenderness?' Thea asks, loading the question with ulterior meaning.

'Nope!' Alice declares, rather triumphantly.

'Is there any tenderness, Alice? Any tenderness at all?'

'None whatsoever,' Alice says, 'unless you can locate something I can't feel.'

Thea regards Alice's body, supine and undeniably beautiful. And she is filled with an emotion just short of pure loathing.

'Lie face down, please,' Thea says as she slips off her clogs and pads over to the table. She gazes down at Alice until Alice can feel Thea's calm, measured breathing trickle over her skin. Thea is centred and ready to begin. She knows just the type of massage that would do Alice good. She won't bother with effleurage – the basic light and soothing stroking techniques she'd normally start and end a session with. Effleurage is best used for the reduction of pain and for its relaxing properties. Well, Alice doesn't seem to be in any pain and appears totally at ease. Nor does Thea feel Alice would benefit today from petrissage, the compression or kneading method primarily used to stretch and release muscular tissue – hadn't Alice bragged that shagging Paul had given her a full body workout? Alice certainly doesn't require any lymphatic massage and Thea feels friction methods won't be needed – there's enough friction already. Perhaps some invigorating percussive movements might be useful – hacking, pounding, cupping and flicking could serve Alice well today. Mainly, though, Thea is going to treat Alice with skin rolling – whether Alice considers this a treat will be interesting.

Using a method akin to hand rolling a cigarette, Thea pinches up a sausage of Alice's skin and uses her thumbs to roll it up and over her fingers. The sensation is like being pinched, pulled and scorched. And because the technique is a rolling motion, there is no break, no hands off. Initially Alice says nothing because she assumes it is good for her and assumes the discomfort will lessen. But the discomfort turns to pain and the pain has no let-up.

'Ouch!' Alice gasps. Thea continues to roll her skin, all the way along her back, her waist, her shoulders, her neck.

'Jesus, Thea!' Alice cries out. 'It feels like an inside-out Chinese burn.'

'Just relax,' Thea says in a soothing tone belying the frown Alice can't see.

'Thea – ow!' Alice protests but Thea continues, rolling Alice's skin over and over.

Let me do a weaselly little roll-up. How about a nice thick Vienna sausage? Now I'll roll a joint – carefully and slowly and tightly. Right, I think it's time for some cocktail chipolatas. Another skinny roll-up now. A nice fat Churchill cigar. How about I try to turn your skin right over? As far as it'll go.

'Thea! You're killing me!'

'I'm not killing you,' Thea declares with derision, 'I'm merely working from basal layer to skin surface. I'm using a variant of connective-tissue massage – it is believed that the surface tissues, being a continual membrane, connect to the brain and that one's emotional state can affect the tissues and vice versa. So I'm just seeking to unravel, smooth and repair the myo fascia, OK?'

'But it hurts.'

'Rubbish. Think of it as a powerful neurofascial effect.'

'But I don't know what that means.'

'Alice, stop being so wet. Just lie there and think of England then.'

Thea starts using the technique on Alice's upper arms. Alice twists away. The soreness makes her eyes smart. 'Stop it, all right? I've had enough. Thanks, Thea – OK. You can stop now.'

'Just let me find a couple of trigger points,' Thea says with deceptive gentleness. Alice heaves out a sigh of relief as the skin rolling ceases. And then yelps. She can't define where Thea has just pressed but pain scores at her temples.

'Oh dear,' Thea says, 'I'd say you need further treatment there.' She presses elsewhere and the pain is referred as a stab down Alice's leg. She finds another point and Alice's eyeball feels as though it's been sliced. 'Gosh, Alice,' Thea says, 'I'd suggest intensive therapy. You're in a mess.'

'Seriously, am I in a mess?'

'Yes.'

Alice sits up. Her eyes are watering and her brow is furrowed. Her back feels as if it is covered in seeping blotches, bruises and weals. 'Can I get you struck off some register?' she asks reproachfully as she dresses. 'You're a total sadist!'

'Can I have *you* sacked from *your* job?' Thea retorts over her shoulder, tidying away towels and laying a fresh swathe of paper sheeting over the bed.

'Well, I may give my staff the odd headache but I don't

inflict physical pain,' Alice laughs, 'so under what grounds?'

'Playing truant to play truant from your marriage,' Thea declares, hands on her hips. She's batted her shot with conviction and she is primed for any volley back. Alice stares at her but Thea outstares.

'Thea, is there something you want to say?' Alice asks, bristling.

'Yes, there is,' says Thea, relieved to be invited to let rip. 'I think you're out of order and I'm mad at you for risking all that you have. You're behaving like someone we'd hate. I'm not even going to go into you asking for the keys to my flat.'

Quite suddenly, Alice looks as though she might cry and Thea hopes she will. 'Stop giving me a hard time – you have no right to.' Alice jumps to the defensive, hugging herself and rubbing her upper arms as if Thea has just rolled the skin there again. 'Just because you have it all with Saul – all the loving and all the passion and all the dreams. Don't be so fucking patronizing. You have no idea what it's like. I'm miserable – I can't believe you can't see that, you're meant to be my best friend. I've been miserable for months – you of all people should have known.'

'You have nothing to be miserable about,' Thea announces, now as outraged by Alice's poor defence as by her immoral deed itself. 'Stop trying to come across as the victim. You just got bored.'

'You know what,' Alice spits back, 'you're completely right. Bored is an understatement. Money can buy all the luxury that surrounds me but my body and my soul ache for attention.'

'For Christ's sake!' Thea has to clench her teeth to bite back yelling. 'Mark is madly in love with you. He worships you. You know that. It's why you bloody married him. How can you jeopardize that?'

'Don't you dare go all sanctimonious on me,' Alice warns her.

'I'm not,' Thea says coldly, 'but look at the facts. It's shocking. You've been married less than three years and you're behaving like a slag just because you get sulky that Mark works hard, travels a bit and you can't work the home cinema or find your ridiculous corkscrew.'

'Don't insult me,' Alice barks. 'It wasn't me who put that corkscrew on the wedding list.'

'I'm *so* glad you've brought up the wedding,' Thea says with infuriating calm. 'You can remember who chose what on the list but you can't remember the vows you made to Mark.'

'Whose side are you *on*?' Alice asks with genuine alarm.

'Mark's,' Thea proclaims. 'No one will ever love you more, keep you safe, look after you, put up with you, the way he does. You're an idiot, risking all that you have for some beefcake's dick.'

A fat oily tear oozes from Alice's eye and slicks a slow path down to the tip of her nose. She whispers something.

'Speak up!' Thea demands.

'I know,' Alice croaks. She wipes her nose on the back of her hand. 'Do you know the barrenness of being worshipped by someone you are not in love with?' Alice looks up at her. Thea is stuck for words. She wanted this to be the great reprimand, she wanted to dish out just deserts, to give Alice the ticking-off of her life. 'You're right, Thea, I'm an ungrateful cow. I hope to God Mark never finds out. He doesn't deserve this.' Alice is teary and holds her arms out to Thea, like a child craving a mother's embrace. 'And you're right, Thea, I've turned my back on it all for the transient physical ecstasy of being fucked by a hunk of brawny beefcake. But I can't help it. I crave it. This kind of attention is what makes me tick. I don't think I can survive without it.'

'You said it was just a one-night stand.' Thea squares her shoulders and folds her arms.

'Will you just stop judging me,' Alice shouts. 'You have no idea. You don't know what it's like. Just piss off, will you.'

'You're insane,' Thea laughs harshly. 'Don't bloody come to me when it all goes horribly wrong.'

'Sod off, Thea,' Alice hisses, 'don't flatter yourself.'

Thea's Six O'Clock

It has been a long day. Thea and Saul still have not heard from the estate agent whether their final offer has been accepted, and Haringey council still haven't confirmed the last of the local searches which means Thea won't be exchanging contracts on her old flat this week. Most of all, she's depressed about Alice. For all the vehemence of her disapproval, Thea can still empathize with her best friend for what she's suffering, no matter how twisted she considers her dilemma to be. But Alice stormed off earlier and Thea didn't go after her and they've never fallen out like this before and Thea isn't sure what the etiquette is now.

She has one final appointment. Mr St Clare. Souki has written 'n/p' by the name and Thea wonders if she actually can muster the energy to go through the necessary rigmarole of note-taking, assessment and judging the bony landmarks of a new patient. She slumps her way down the three flights of stairs and fixes a smile on her face before entering the waiting room. Oh bloody bloody hell. Mark is there, looking decidedly pale. Or is that just in comparison with bloody Paul and his bronzed sex-god looks?

'Mark!' says Thea as if it is a lovely surprise and what on earth could he want.

'Hullo, Thea,' he says, rising.

'Er, Mark, the thing is I have a six o'clock booked,' Thea says kindly. 'Is everything all right?' She doesn't know if Mark even knows that Alice has been in for a massage.

'I *am* your six o'clock,' Mark tells her. 'I tried to call your mobile last night but there was no answer and I didn't want any favours like last time so I decided to book myself in officially.'

'St *Clare*,' Thea says. 'They misspelt Sinclair so I didn't click.'

'It's my neck again,' Mark explains, 'see?' He turns his head with good range to the right but can judder only half the distance to the left.

'Come on up,' Thea says. 'Let's see what's going on. And we'll figure out what we can do.'

What Thea would actually like Mark to do is to see Dan or Brent, one of the osteopaths, but both are fully booked a week in advance and actually their therapy might not be quite appropriate today. But there is work she can do on Mark in the meantime. She considers the knot Mark has in his rhomboid muscle and a stiffness around the thoracic, both of which are contributing to the soreness and stiffness he feels in his neck. Under normal circumstances she'd do a deep and lengthy focused palpation with her thumb or finger precisely into the tender nub of the problem which, though intensely painful, usually results in immediate relaxation. However, part of her innate skill as a masseuse is to read her client's situation. And Mark is an open book to Thea, not that he knows it. Thea feels that what he needs today, more than anything, is a simple laying-on of hands; some classic TLC. She needs him to leave her room feeling soothed and relaxed.

'Just pop on the table, Mark,' she says softly, 'and lie face down.' She heats a little geranium essential oil in the amphora and checks that the room is warm enough. She walks over to Mark and stands alongside him. She inhales and exhales and inhales again. She closes her eyes and exhales in a long, controlled, silent breath. OK, Mark, this is for you.

Touch down. Thea places both hands on Mark's back and presses lightly; she begins to rock his body from side to side, from one hand to the other. She keeps the rhythm gentle and consistent and soon feels him yield and allow his body to travel under her guidance. Then, with Mark relaxed and tuned, Thea sweeps her hands gently from the base of his back up and around his shoulders, down again, around again. The effleurage soothes Mark to the extent that Thea can actually see the space between his ears and his shoulders lengthen as he relaxes and lets go. She kneads him sparingly. All she wants to do is instil in him a sense of calm, a feeling of well-being, make him subliminally cosseted by the care and comfort one human can dispense to another. Sometimes, when Thea massages, she experiences negative energy or tensions travelling from her client and into her, leaving her quite enervated. From other clients, the massage can even be mutually invigorating. But from Mark today she detects so little energy of any persuasion that she simply takes to stroking him. As her hands travel their persistent warmth wisely over his body, she closes her eyes and envisages sending affection and hope down through her arms, through her fingers to be absorbed by him.

'Mark, when you're ready, turn onto your back,' Thea tells him, leaving her hands on him constantly. She covers him with fresh towels and walks her way to the head of the table, keeping a hand on him all the while. His eyes are naturally half closed and she's pleased. She rests his head slightly to one side into her hand. 'I'm going to apply a little pressure just with my fingertip to a point near your sternocleidomastoid attachment,' she tells him, doing just that. 'It'll feel nice when I release,' she says, and it does. Then she straightens and cups his head in her hands, placing her fingertips at the base of his skull. 'I'm going to do the same to points in the sub-occipital region,' she tells him. She judges the length of his exhale to be directly proportionate to the tension she's released. Good.

Thea strokes along his neck, down over his shoulders and along the top of his arms. She runs her hands over his scalp, uses her fingertips to walk the skin lightly along the skull, tugging at tufts of his hair like a troupe of industrious fairies on a mass weaving mission. Then with the lightest touch, she changes pace and position and treats the acupressure points on his face in a calm and measured way. She stands and tugs each of his arms in turn, stroking downwards until she reaches his palms where she massages carefully before rubbing along the length of each of his fingers to give a sudden, light fling to each fingertip. To Mark, it feels as though Thea has guided his entire deposit of stress and tension down each arm, and coaxed it out of him. He's sure that if he looked to either side of the bed, he'd see little piles of the negative stuff.

Thea has worked on Mark for over an hour and a half and he's so still he looks dead. She wants to cry. She bites her cheek hard. 'OK?' she asks, implying that, should he say 'not quite', she'd happily work on him some more. Mark is too relaxed to find his voice but he thinks he's given the semblance of a nod. 'OK,' Thea confirms, 'you take your time. As long as you like.' She tiptoes from the room.

When she returns a generous quarter of an hour later, Mark is sitting in one of the plastic chairs, in his suit, tie neatly knotted, briefcase propped against his leg.

'How do you feel?' Thea asks him.

'I tell you, Thea,' Mark says, shaking his head in wonder, 'that was just what I needed.'

'Good,' Thea says, 'but you should have a little osteo too.'

'Can't you teach Alice how to do that?' Mark asks her, laughing. 'Go on, do me a favour.' Thea doesn't think it funny at all, but she's not going to show it so she gives Mark a kiss and tells him to book in with Dan or Brent. As she tidies her room, she reflects on the bizarre parity. Alice doesn't ever think of giving her husband a massage though he'd love it. And Saul never wants Thea to massage him, because he says he simply doesn't get it.

Cold Shoulders

It was strange for Thea to experience something as momentous as exchanging contracts yet have no Alice to effervesce and celebrate with. And it was peculiar for Alice to be totally disinclined to contact Thea though she knew she could well benefit from her advice and support. As high as Thea felt, Alice was low. This zipless-fuck concept wasn't as carefree and uncomplicated as she'd planned. She was unnerved that her sassiness could have been so easily replaced by irritable insecurity directly accountable to the time it took Paul to send a text, to the length and tone of his abbreviated words. She'd even started feeling jealous of Paul's new groups, imagining some gorgeous woman or other sashaying across the Pont du Gard in front of him, or seducing him in the Cathédrale d'Images, or sharing knowledge about the dietary preferences of the flamingo. And though she'd urge herself to practise what she preached, or obey the editors of *Lush* at the very least, she often found herself forsaking the 'play hard to get' or 'treat him mean, keep him keen' philosophies to send Paul texts that sometimes simply said `did u get my last txt??` Her mood towards her staff depended entirely on whether or not Paul had replied. If she was awaiting a response, she was impatient and unfocused. If he replied, she fizzed with energy and creativity. Mark, though, bore the brunt of the length and frequency of Paul's messages. If Alice was expecting a reply, she was sullen and distracted. If his reply was of pleasing length and raunchy content, she'd be offhand with Mark because she resented him for not being Paul. If Paul's text was short and mundane, Alice was even more moody with Mark, begrudging him for being all she had.

Alice needed Thea, she knew how she'd benefit from the two of them 'workshopping' her dilemma through, blasting away unreasonable misgivings, deciding on a constructive way of thinking, a realistic path forward. More than that, Alice just missed Thea. It was lonely confiding to her own reflection; she couldn't give herself any astute answers and if she didn't want to hear certain advice, she could just turn away from the mirror and strop off. Without Thea, Alice didn't have the confidence or the motivation to confront the state of her relationship with Mark, the situation now developing with Paul and what to do with one, the other or the both of them.

Thea quite simply missed Alice; she wanted to have a second opinion when she browsed around the White Company store on Marylebone Road, she wanted Alice to take her to that place she knew near Westbourne Park that did stunning antiqued mirrors. However, Thea was still bristling with indignation that Alice should behave like a careless tart. And Alice was exasperated at what she perceived to be a sanctimonious arrogance and complete lack of understanding on Thea's part. How could they be best friends if their moral codes were indecipherable to each other? What connection could they truly have if their ethics and standards were so diametrically opposed? There was absolutely no attraction in such opposites. The only comfort to Alice was that, despite feeling detested by Thea, she knew her secret was safe. Even through the silence and dislike, she knew Thea was unwaveringly loyal. She doubted whether Thea would even confide in Saul.

Mark and Saul both knew their partners had fallen out. But neither of them knew the reason. Even without a reason, it seemed so daft for two grown women, two childhood friends, two soulmates, not to be speaking. But when Mark tried to ask Alice, and when Saul asked Thea, both men were given such short shrift that they decided not to mention the friend until she was back in favour again. Mark, who came back to Thea for another massage on the osteopath's advice, dared to begin: 'Thea, why aren't you and Alice—' at which point it felt as though his skin was being pinched into corduroy and he thought better of finishing his sentence. Certainly, he didn't dare voice his concern for his marriage to Thea. Anyway, if she wasn't on speaking terms with his wife, she probably wouldn't know why Alice's temper was as it was. Saul, over a brainstorming lunch with Alice, filled her wineglass for the third time and said, 'When the fuck are you and Thea going to kiss and make up?' but Alice had narrowed her eyes and shot steel-cold daggers which told him most emphatically to back off.

Sally knew her two friends weren't speaking but neither Alice nor Thea would tell her any more than a non-committal shrug would permit. Pilates became a place where Alice and Thea, if their sessions had to overlap, tried to out-Pike, out-Elephant, out-Mermaid each other. Sally could only watch – and actually wish her roll-ups were half as good as Thea's, her Swan-dives anywhere near as fluid as Alice's. So everyone around them kept quiet about the situation though they all thought it was bizarre and really quite childish.

Black Beauty

It was one of those balmy May days when the dull drag of winter is forgotten and the promise of summer is at last plausible. Under opalescent skies of Wedgwood blue, gluts of flowers burst from bud and juicy foliage unfurled in a gloss giving the air a clean freshness and warmth that could be tasted and smelt. The day had a clarity which bestowed splendid humour and a spring-cleaned *joie de vivre* on everyone. Alice strode into work in a fabulous mood actually dictated more by the weather and the wearing of sandals for the first time that year, than the kinky message from Paul which had just arrived on her phone. Saul had rattled off an article for the *Evening Standard*, filed his copy for the *Observer* early and banked a number of long-awaited cheques, all ensuring a smile of the broadest dimensions. Mark arrived at work to be called into a meeting with the CEO, VP and MD where he was promoted, given a whopping pay rise and the assurance of more staff and less travel. Thea awoke alone in her flat and turned her face towards a kiss of sunlight filtering in through a gap in the curtains. What a gorgeous day, she thought, what a gorgeous day.

'Morning!' It was Saul.

'I'm on the bus!' Thea tried to whisper into her phone while steadying herself over the bumps and lurches of Kentish Town Road. 'Let me phone you when I'm at work.'

'Is the bus crowded?' Saul asked.

'Yes,' Thea bemoaned, 'standing room only.'

'Do you want to give your fellow passengers something to smile about?'

'Saul,' Thea chided softly, 'let me phone you when I'm at work. It's ever so jolty.'

'Thea – our offer has been accepted. We stand to exchange and complete simultaneously – in a month.'

Suddenly, the pretty passenger with the gamine crop was jumping for joy and whooping with delight, proclaim-ing 'We've got it, we've got it!' breathlessly to every-one. 'Our offer's been accepted!' she was singing. 'We're buying this great flat!' Her fellow passengers grinned at her spontaneous emotion. Just as Saul anticipated they would when he envisaged her reacting in precisely the way she did.

Thea out-talked Peter Glass when he came in for a session at ten. He knew the development Thea spoke of and assured her that the agreed purchase price was a good one. He couldn't really comment on her tumble of ideas for a colour scheme on a theme and variations of taupe but he let her gabble on in the hope that she'd soon return her undivided attention to his frozen shoulder.

'Well, good morning, Gabriel!' Thea greeted a somewhat taken aback Mr Sewell an hour later. 'And how are we, this gorgeous day?'

'I'm fine, Miss Luckmore,' he said rather pointedly which went unnoticed by Thea who practically skipped her way up to her room.

'Come on then!' she smiled expansively at Gabriel. 'Hop on the bed and let's have a look at you.'

I know we haven't exchanged – and I know the process might be beset with hassles and stress but sod it, I have a good vibe and a long lunch hour and it's a beautiful day so I'm going to stroll all the way to the Ruth Aram shop and buy something gorgeous for our new home. A lamp maybe! Perhaps something funky and functional for the kitchen! Or a stunning piece of ceramic just because it's beautiful!

She phones Saul to see if he wants to join her, perhaps even squeeze in a celebratory sandwich lunch somewhere, but his phone is off and she imagines he is either up against a deadline to extol the new generation Bluetooth for *T3* magazine or perhaps out of range in some picture editor's office.

No! No, he's not! He's not doing Bluetooth or pictures because there he is! Just ahead of me! Over there! Saul! Saul! O most auspicious day!

Saul is wending his way down Berwick Street ahead of Thea. The scamp and bustle of the market absorb Thea's voice so she attempts to pick up her pace and weaves between stallholders and browsers to try and catch up with him. She sees him turning left.

'Hey! Saul – Mr Mundy!'

He hasn't heard. And there's a bloke riding a moped on the pavement sending pedestrians scattering like skittles. Thea skips her way on and off the kerb with the deftness of Gene Kelly in *Singing in the Rain* only it's not raining, it's gloriously sunny. She turns the corner just in time to see Saul disappearing into a doorway some yards ahead.

Damn. Quick. Let me try his phone again. Bugger – still off. He must have gone into some meeting. Bluetooth and pictures or what have you.

Momentarily disappointed, Thea decides she'll stroll along this street anyhow because it won't be too much of a detour and, although it's mostly sex shops and dodgy video clubs, there may be some interesting shops further along.

Here. This is where Saul is having his meeting. In here.

Strange.

Doesn't look like an office.

There's no front door!

Well, there is, but it's been propped open. But there's certainly no sign of a reception area with a cold-water dispenser and the company logo on laser-etched glass. The open doorway reveals just a bare hallway and a staircase, with gloss paint chipped like a tart's fingernails.

There are two signs taped to the door jamb, each beneath a buzzer.

BLACK BEAUTY 1ST FLOOR

MODELS! top

Thea stands at the threshold and backs away. How odd – because she's sure this was where Saul went. Positive, in fact. Perhaps it's all very C. S. Lewis, she thinks to herself – you go in one place and come out quite somewhere else. She checks the buildings to either side. One is a minicab office with a sleepy Ugandan sitting on the doorstep with a clipboard on his knee. The other is a business selling perspex of all colours, thicknesses, shapes and sizes. It's closed, though. *Back 1 Hour* the note says. No, this building in between is definitely where Saul went in.

Thea hovers back outside the building. Black Beauty and Top Models. Fleetingly, she imagines Kate Moss and her pals sitting upstairs watching daytime television and the thought is so incongruous she grins. But anyway, it's 'MODELS! top', not 'top models', so Thea lets the image go.

All it says is 'BLACK BEAUTY 1ST FLOOR' *and* 'MODELS! top'. *But there must be someone else, another business, in there because Saul's gone in.*

'Excuse me.' Thea approaches the Ugandan, relaxed on a rickety chair, tapping a Biro on his clipboard.

'You want a cab, lady? Where you going?'

'No, thanks. I'm just. Do you know what else is in that building?' Thea asks. The man glances and shrugs. 'Is there a small studio or company that makes gadgets?' Thea asks. 'You know, boys' toys and the like?' The minicab man chuckles. 'Is there something to do with publishing in there?' Thea persists.

'No. Just the girls,' the man tells her, 'just those girls.'

'Oh,' says Thea, frowning. How peculiar. She stares at the building. There's probably a writer's tiny garret right at the top. Saul's probably gone to commission some freelancer or other. 'Is there a tiny office right at the top?' she asks. The minicab man shrugs and shakes his head. Thea reads this as the man not actually knowing the answer. The perspex shop is still closed. Maybe they have a small storeroom in the next building and Saul needs some perspex.

BLACK BEAUTY.

Wait! Oh my God, Black Beauty!

Thea spins an explanation so plausible and heart-warming that she starts swooning at Saul's thoughtfulness.

He's researched it! It's some book specialist devoted to Anna Sewell's great tome! He's buying me a first edition!

*

Is he?

Is he, Thea?

Is that what he's buying in there?

She sees that the minicab man is putting his chair inside and shutting up shop, walking off towards the market. The street is quiet. There's another man, sauntering up the street, jangling a bunch of keys. Perspex for sale. What kind of a trade is that? How much perspex must you sell in a day to make a living? How long has Thea been there? She has no idea. How long has Saul been in there? She just can't figure it out.

'Exuse me,' she approaches the perspex man as he's unlocking the shop door, 'what's next door?'

'It's a house of ill repute, my dear,' he says theatrically, lightly.

'And what else?' Thea asks. 'Are there any writers in there too? Or small quirky businesses? Anything with anything to do with magazine publishing?'

'No,' the man says, 'just the girls. Try a couple of streets along – there's a few book places and the like around there.' He enters the shop. Thea remains on the pavement. She's starting to feel sick and confused. Come on, *think*. There *must* be an explanation. Why is Saul in there? What's he doing? When is he coming out?

BLACK BEAUTY 1ST FLOOR.
MODELS! top

Where is Saul? Where is he? First floor? Or on top?

There's only so much thinking Thea can do because, after all, there's only the girls in there. And Saul. In painfully slow motion, Thea's life is beginning to fragment into splintered images and fractured memories, half-formed theories and hastily rejected signs and clues, all of which wreak havoc with her ability to acknowledge fact.

* * *

A door closes. Footsteps are descending the staircase. Thea fears she's rooted to the spot and yet suddenly she finds herself inside the perspex shop. Her heart pounds in her throat and head at different rates. Some force hauls her stomach against her spine and evaporates all the moisture in her mouth. Her conscience rails; she yells at herself you horrible cow! how dare you cast aspersions at Saul! how dare you think he could do something like that! something like that to you! look! see! it's not Saul! of course it's not Saul – it's a complete stranger! just some sad old fat bloke in his sixties who lives with his mum in Purley and has never had a girlfriend.

No.

It *is* Saul. It *is* Saul. It *is* Saul.

Thea watches Saul saunter past through her fractured perspex veil. Saul, distorted through this prism of shards and sheets and panes and panels in jewel-like colours and degrees of transparency. Everything is twisted, fragmented; like a Cubist painting. What is real? How do you piece it together? How can the meaning be deciphered?

That was Saul.

It was him.

It really was.

He wasn't casting furtive looks to either side. He didn't skulk away incognito. His head was high and he looked pretty happy.

'I need to use your toilet.'

Mr Perspex has never had a customer ask before and this one doesn't even seem to be a customer but Mr Perspex shrugs and tells Thea it's out the back. She vomits. She throws up everything she has inside her. She flushes it away but suddenly there's more. She flushes again before another churning spasm scorches her stomach and burns her throat as she hurls bile down into the toilet. Flush it away. Flush it away. She heaves and retches but at last there's nothing left. Physically, it's a relief yet still she feels desperately sick.

Nothing's left. There is nothing left.

Alice?

u there, Mr B?

Yes, he is!

howz u? I miss u, u mad sexy bitch! ☺

miss u 2 ☹

'Who are you texting, Alice?'

'No one – I mean, it's just a work matter, Mark.'

'Do you fancy Thai?'

'Sorry?'

'Thai – takeaway?'

'Yes. Sure. Whatever. Just give me a minute, would you, Mark?'

bad timing, txt u L8R xxxxxxxxxxx

'Sorry, Mark. Now, what were you saying?'

'Do you fancy Thai?'

'I'm not hugely hungry, actually.'

'Well, there's nothing in the fridge.'

'I've been busy!'

'I'm not criticizing you, Alice – I just said we've nothing in the house so do you fancy popping out for a meal or ordering a takeaway?'

'Oh. OK. Sure. Order plenty and I'll have a nibble.'

'OK. Unless you'd rather go out?'

'No – takeaway is fine. Just get a takeaway.'

u there, big boy?

yes - thnkng of ur hot bod . . .

my hot bod v v slippry!

me hard & horny - wanna suk?

yum yum cum! come 2 me! come 2 uk??!!

luv 2 but me skint

but I want 2 play with my toyboy . . .

can u fone?

no – not now – not poss xxxxx

'Here we go – I ordered way too much. Are you all right, Alice?'

'Sorry? Yes, I'm fine. Just thinking about work actually.'

'I popped into Blockbuster too.'

'I have some work to do – do you mind if I disappear for an hour or so?'

'No – of course. Here, let me do you a plateful. There you are, darling.'

'Thanks, Mark.'

I cld send u tix . . .

wots 'tix'?

TICKETS – idiot! u r all balls, no brain!! Easyjet/Eurostar etc

but I'm broke Alice!

am sure u can thnk of ways 2 recompense me, Mr D

cld fuck u til you beg for mercy . . .

hmmm that'll do nicely!

seriously, Alice – u serious?

v serious – will research & fone/txt u 2moro xxxxxxxxxxxx

xxxxxxxxxxxx

'How did it go?'

'That was delicious.'

'How did it go? The work – all done?'

'Oh. Yes. It's fine. I just wanted to try to sort something out. Mark – have you any trips booked in the near future?'

'I'm not sure. Why?'

'Oh, nothing. It doesn't matter.'

'I know what you're after – a holiday! Good call, Alice – we haven't been away for ages. Tell you what, I'll mention it tomorrow. What a great idea. How about the Maldives – ultra luxury.'

'But are you going away on business at all? Soon?'

'I don't think so – no plans to. Anyway, you know what – sod it! I'd cancel!'

* * *

u there? X

When Alice's phone buzzed a message through two hours later, her heart skipped but then slumped at not seeing Paul's name flash up. Her heart then picked up its pace a little when she saw it was from Thea. Alice read it and then deleted it.

I am here, Thea. But I'm not quite ready yet, lady.

Thea?

'Hi, babe – just me. I'll leave a message on your land line. Call me when you get this. Bye!'

lunch 2day? Film 2nite? Sx

'Oh, hi hon – it's just me – I'm wondering if you've lost your mobile? Anyway, give me a call as soon as you can. Bye.'

earth 2 Thea, earth 2 Thea . . . Wheres u????
Fone me!! Sxxxx

'Hullo, babe – have you been abducted by aliens? Fallen down a well? Run away? I'm slightly worried now – give us a call. OK. Bye.'

r my txts arriving - is your fone on the blink?? Sxx

'Er. It's just me – Saul – I think you've probably lost your mobile but I'm leaving this message anyway and I'll call your land line again. If you pick up this message, can you phone me, babe? Speak to you soon, bye.'

'Thea, it's gone lunchtime now – can you please phone me as soon as you get this message? Love you.'

'Alice? It's Saul. Yes – I'll be in around three-ish. Listen, I don't suppose you've heard from Thea, have you? No? No – no reason – I think she may have lost her mobile, that's all – daft thing. OK, I'll see you later – yes, I'll bring them in with me.'

'Thea, it's Saul – if you're there can you pick up, please. I popped into the Being Well but you're not there and they don't know where you are either. Can you phone me as soon as you get this? Or text. I'm at home – but the mobile is on, too. Speak soon. Love you.'

'Hi, Alice – it's Saul again. Listen, do you mind if I cancel the meeting – Thea's not at work, there's no answer on her mobile or at home and I'm worried now. Pardon? I saw her two nights ago – I spoke to her yesterday morning and told her about the offer being accepted. She was giggling on the bus. I haven't heard from her since. What? Yes – the offer on the place we like, it's all going ahead. Listen, I think I'm going to go up to Crouch End – I have keys. Is that OK about the meeting then? Cool. Yes. Tomorrow's fine.'

* * *

Shit. Thea's text late last night. Alice grabs her phone and fires off a message.

u ok?

After two minutes too long, she sends another.

u ok? Axx

Thea could cry with relief. Help is at hand. Alice is there.

no. Tx

```
u at home? Axxx

yes - can u come?? need u, v v much Txx

k. on my way - so is Saul
```

Saul? Coming here? No no no! Shit. I don't want to see him. I've got to go.

When Headfuck Boy had dumped Thea, her heart had been broken and the pain had been terrible and exquisite but in a cathartically Brontë-like way. However, Saul hadn't broken her heart. If he'd wilfully broken her heart, at least she could hurl herself into a romantic vortex of grieving, sobbing and deluded hope. Instead, Thea was lumbered with his insidious secret and it was asphyxiating. A broken heart was a walk in the park compared to this. All she'd been able to do for twenty-four hours was pace her flat and hyperventilate, rush to the toilet trying to throw up something other than bile-bitter emptiness. She'd been incapable of rationally assessing what she'd seen, the black-and-white facts had been too mammoth for her mind. So, of course she'd ignored Saul's calls. Of course she'd deleted his goodnight and goodmorning and Thea sweetie, where ARE you messages. And of course she is rushing out of her flat, knowing he is on his way over.

Today, she feels even worse than yesterday; at least yesterday she'd had something to throw up and too much to think about. Today, she feels hollow and doomed and exhausted. There cannot be any explanation, any escape from what she'd seen. The bare facts are emblazoned, as harsh as a neon strip-light; but she can't close her eyes to them, she can't flinch away – they are imprinted on her mind's eye anyway. She feels wretched; beyond distraught. Horror, disbelief, anger and hurt collide cataclysmically. Saul had done something unbelievable but she has to believe it because she saw it with her own eyes. She finds herself alternately repulsed by him yet somehow scared of him too; she swings from yelling out loud that she never wants to see him again, to sobbing silently at the terrifying notion of a future without him.

He isn't who I thought he was. He is someone else. My Saul is gone. Who is this other Saul? Who is this person? A man who does terrible things.

Yesterday Thea reeled from the shock. However, the surges of adrenalin, the unremitting need to throw up, offered a bizarre respite, a temporary distraction, from deciphering the facts and admitting to the meaning. Today, she is consumed by the deceit, mangled by the hideousness of it all. Reality looms large and there is no escape from the truth.

Saul – do that?
Yes.
Him – with them?
Yes.

How dare he claim love and affection for me while paying for sex elsewhere. You cannot do the one and also the other. It is ethically impossible. It is morally reprehensible. Either love has lost its meaning or he never loved me in the first place. You simply cannot have sex with prostitutes and love your partner. And that's a fact. And the fact is that yesterday, at lunchtime, when I fancied a sandwich, Saul fancied a fuck.

Thea stumbles out from her flat. She shivers spasmodically despite the day being even more beautiful than yesterday. With shoulders hunched, she walks clutching her hollow, aching stomach. Her face is ashen, she's wearing slippers and an agitated expression and people stare as if they know what has befallen her, as if she is indelibly branded, stigmatized. Poor wretch – she's just found out her boyfriend uses hookers. Look at the state of her, staggering down Topsfield Parade – she's walking in the road! Is she mad? Is she drunk? Is she ill? No, she's discovered her boyfriend pays for sex. God, how awful.

'Alice?'

'Thea,' Alice answers immediately, 'are you OK? What's going on? I'm on my way, I'm in a cab, in Dartmouth Park – but the traffic is a nightmare. Is Saul there yet?'

'But Alice – I don't want to see Saul.'

Alice is stunned into silence. The thought 'not in a million years did I consider that' scorches her. What has he done, the bastard? She'll kill him. 'Where are you?'

'Outside.'

'Outside where?'

'Outside down a side street.'

'Are you still in Crouch End? Walk to one end of the street and tell me the name. Don't hang up.'

The taxi costs a fortune. The driver doesn't know Crouch End so he's fine with Alice rifling through his A–Z and directing him.

'Left – leftleftleft!' Alice barks. 'There! There she is. Slow down. Just stop, will you? Just stop and wait a sec – well, put your bloody hazard lights on, then. I'm coming back.'

Thea is pacing ten yards one way, then ten yards the other. She looks up at the sound of Alice's footsteps and stands still.

'Come on,' Alice says with calm kindness, her arm around Thea's shoulder, as if assisting a little old lady or a very small child across the road, 'I'm here.'

It was a little like knowing exactly what to do in an emergency. Outside of a dire situation, one fears one will lose the presence of mind to think straight, act on intelligence and do the right thing. However, when such circumstances arise, suddenly one reacts sagaciously and efficiently. And so it was with Alice.

'Alice, is Saul writing something on prostitutes? Are you publishing something in *Adam* about buying sex?'

'No.'

'I saw him go into a brothel yesterday, Alice. I waited for him to come out again. He did.'

Alice knew instinctively not to let the shock show. She knew not to rubbish what Thea claimed, neither to attack or defend Saul just yet, nor to raise or dash Thea's hopes. The recovery position she needed to put Thea in was to calm her down, make her feel safe and listen without prejudice and with minimal comment. Just then, it didn't matter whether Saul had or hadn't, whether he was a bastard deserving castration or a maligned man, whether Thea should go to an STD clinic, whether Thea should confront Saul, whether or not their relationship could survive this. Instead, there were practical measures to be taken which were far more pressing. Alice knew Thea had to eat, needed to sleep, must not be on her own and that Saul had to be fobbed off, temporarily at least. If Alice phoned him on Thea's behalf, he'd know there was a crisis and he would afford them no peace.

'Do you see?' Alice asked Thea, whom she'd taken back to Hampstead, made a hot-water bottle for and made drink flat Coca-Cola. 'It makes sense. You need to call him. And quickly.'

Thea looked at her phone for some time. And then she dialled because Alice kept telling her to.

'Hiya!' she acted for all her worth, contriving to sound as breezy as anything, glancing at Alice for bolstering, hating his stupid lovely voice.

'Thea, thank Christ!' Saul exclaimed. 'Jesus, where have you been?'

'I lost my phone yesterday,' Thea claimed convincingly, 'when I was shopping. And I went to collect it and decided to take the day off.'

'But no one knew where you were!' Saul protested.

'But I phoned work,' Thea lied, 'and left a message on the machine.'

'I couldn't reach you,' Saul said softly, 'I was worried.'

And all those times I couldn't reach you, Saul? Were you really in meetings and up against deadlines? Or are mobiles not allowed in brothels? Perhaps they interfere with the equipment? Put you off your pace?

'I even went over to yours,' Saul was saying. 'I tell you, if you're selling it in three weeks' time, you ought to start having a sort-through. It was a pigsty, young lady.'

Oh, God. My flat goes in three weeks.

Thea had gone cold and shuddered violently at the realization. Alice draped her luxurious shahtoosh around Thea's shoulders.

'Are you coming to mine tonight?' Saul carried on.

'I'm tired,' Thea said truthfully, 'and I do have lots of sorting out to do.'

'I'll phone you later,' Saul said with such warmth in his voice Thea found it difficult not to believe that he really loved her.

At ten o'clock, half an hour after Mark had arrived home and, on raised eyebrow from Alice, had greeted Thea as if her presence was the most normal and expected thing, Thea phoned Saul and said she'd be over shortly.

'Do you think that's wise?' Alice asked her, worried by the distracted glaze to her eyes. She'd rather Thea had another light snack, an aromatherapy bath and an early night as planned.

'I just need to see him,' Thea said. She wasn't going to

confide to Alice that actually she'd suddenly been subsumed by an urgent fear that if Saul was alone he might pop out for a quick cash shag. Was that what he did? Those occasions when they stayed in their respective flats, when she phoned late to say goodnight and he explained he was just out buying biscuits or somesuch from the corner shop?

'Tread carefully,' Alice warned her caringly. 'You're fragile – I wouldn't say anything tonight. You really need to sleep. Would you like a valium?' Thea shook her head. 'We'll work this out, Thea,' Alice told her, 'we'll figure out what to do.'

Alice wasn't in the mood for a furtive text session with Paul. She needed to keep her phone open for Thea. In fact, for the first time, she resented Paul's messages arriving and left them unread. Mark had gone to bed early, with the diaries of Winston Churchill. Alice felt traumatized. How could Saul have done this to Thea? How could it be that Saul was that kind of man? Normal, nice blokes don't do that. Whoever heard of such a thing? And anyway, Saul has Thea, for Christ's sake – could he really abuse her so? Alice felt shaken. And the one person who could soothe her was the one upstairs reading Winston Churchill. Thank God for Mark. Thank God Mark was Mark, straight and steady and there for her. She cuddled up against him, sinking fast into the safety net he provided.

'Is Thea OK?' Mark asked, using his finger for a bookmark in case Alice wanted to talk or there again didn't. 'She looked a fright.'

Alice sighed, grateful for Mark's intuitive care but burdened at the secret she had to guard. 'She'll be fine,' Alice said. She let Mark return to his book for a while. 'Mark?'

'Yes?' he said, his finger bookmark at the ready.

'Nothing.'

'Are you OK, Alice?' he asked, closing the book and laying it down. 'You look a little out of sorts.'

'I feel a little low,' Alice confided in a whisper, the threat of tears a flint-edged pebble catching her voice.

Mark switched off the light and took her in his arms. 'It's OK,' he said, 'there there. Get some sleep. Everything passes.'

It wasn't Mark's simplistic optimism that raised a small smile from Alice, it was that he knew precisely what to do for her just then. He knew not to probe, not to reason. He just had to hold her close and soothingly and so he did just that. It was just right. And she loved him for it. And for the first time she felt searing guilt at her own transgression and profound regret.

To Thea, it seemed glaringly bizarre that Saul should carry on as if nothing had happened. In his eyes, however, nothing *had* happened. Why wouldn't he want to chat about the new place? Why shouldn't he twirl her in his arms and place celebratory kisses on her face? Naturally, he'd want to express the anxiety her disappearance had caused him. And of course he was eager to discuss mortgage minutiae. Of course he was going to ask her if she was all right. Of course he was going to comment that she looked pale and tired and of course he'd automatically place his palm tenderly on her forehead to assess her temperature. And of course Thea wanted to scream you evil deviant sod what the fuck do you think you are doing screwing hookers when you have me?

But she didn't. Not because Alice had told her to bite it back but because suddenly she found herself obsessed with a perverse mission of sorts. When they went to bed, she instigated sex: athletic, urgent, ravenous sex. She had a point, not love, to make. She had to feel him overcome with hunger for her. She needed to sense that his passion for her could send him to the verge of frenzy. So she writhed and gasped and twisted herself in mock abandon. She faked the pleasure of every thrust and grind. She let her voice lie most convincingly. What she sought was to analyse Saul's every move and groan. She needed to assess his response. Was he loving it? Did fucking her absorb and sate him utterly? She scrutinized his every hump and groan, evaluated the length and intensity of his climax and studied his breathing pattern and facial expressions throughout.

There was absolutely no doubt about it, she drove the man wild. Why the hell, then, was he paying for sex elsewhere?

'Christ, that was good,' Saul declared, post-coital triumph softening into affectionate gratitude. He rolled towards Thea, his hand gently cupping her breast while he kissed the tip of her nose.

And do you say that to all the women? Thea wondered, turning away from him, gulping against the swell of nausea.

'That'll certainly put me to sleep with a smile on my face,' Saul chuckled, switching off the light, spooning against her and nuzzling the nape of her neck.

It all felt dirty. As if everything needed a good scrub and a boil wash. Saul's sheets. Saul's bathroom. Saul's crockery. Thea's body.

'I have Pilates three times this week,' she announced after a lengthy, scalding-hot shower the next morning. Actually she had only the one class booked. Saul nodded as he tucked into two croissants on account of Thea claiming no appetite. 'And Alice and I are going to the cinema tonight.'

No, we're not – but Alice'll cover for me.

'Busy bee!' Saul said affectionately. 'You'd better start packing too.'

Oh, God. My flat. I have just over a fortnight.

'Yes,' Thea agreed, 'lots to sort out.'

'But we're off to my parents this weekend, remember?'

'This weekend? Oh. Oh, God. I forgot.'

I did forget. It's true.

'Yes – but it isn't a problem, is it? They're looking forward to seeing you again.'

'It's just that I promised Alice I'd—'

'Oh.'

'Sorry.'

'Don't worry. We'll go another time.'

'But you'll still go? You must, Saul – they'll be so disappointed.'

'Yes – I'll go. See if you can change whatever it is with Alice?'

'I'll try.'

No, I won't.

Thea couldn't leave Saul's flat fast enough, inventing an early booking at the Being Well. Yet, by the time she arrived at work, she sat alone in her room at the top and felt like running all the way back to Saul's. An hour later, she felt intense hatred. By lunchtime she was so confused that she wondered whether she'd imagined it all. During the afternoon, all doubt had been blasted away by pure anger. By teatime she was exhausted. When Saul phoned her, his voice made her shudder. She couldn't possibly countenance seeing him at all while her emotions were so varied and raw. She feigned flu and managed to avoid him for five days.

The Oldest Trade

I never noticed before. I never noticed, but suddenly I see that the world is full of prostitutes. Or is it that I'm becoming obsessed? Only a month ago the world seemed a very nuptial place – everywhere I looked I saw brides and weddings and everything pointed to love and romance. De Beers' adverts on buses. The local church festooned with flowers. Honeymoon special in the 'Escape' section of the Observer. *Now my world is rife with the world's oldest trade. I've just been to my local newsagent's. I never before stopped to read those hand-written cards in the window. I couldn't believe it – an alarming number of them offer 'exotic massage' or 'adult fun' or 'toys and role play'. One advertised 'dominatrix. Nice flat.' What does Mr Patel think he's doing, condoning all of this? And the newspaper I've just bought has three different scandals involving hookers – a politician caught kerb crawling, a police raid on a vice ring in suburbia and a respected actor caught with an escort and Class A drugs in a Leeds hotel. If I'd bought a tabloid, I bet there'd be even more stories.*

Have you ever noticed how every local high street has a dodgy massage/sauna establishment? But have you ever seen anyone actually go in or come out? You should see the phone box near work, it's awash with cards advertising the services of Asian Nymph, Busty Blonde, Thai Princess, Fantasia Twins and scores of other unlikely-named sex workers. Who uses phone boxes nowadays anyway? Doesn't everyone have a mobile? Are they there only as a pinboard for pimps? I noticed that two of the cards have the same photo but with different names and phone numbers. As if, in the end, all the punter requires is a nice, accommodating vagina: surface details are interchangeable or irrelevant. Perhaps it simply doesn't matter what she looks like.

Are they prettier than me?
Are they better in bed than I am?
How much does it cost?
How much does Saul pay?

How much money has he spent, over the years?

I hate him I hate him but how then can I miss him? I haven't seen him for a week. I'm running out of excuses. I've done the imagined flu. Now I'm fobbing him off with make-believe Pilates classes and non-existent arrangements with Alice. I know I can't keep kidding myself that I'll think about it all later, that somehow I'll know what to do. I don't know what to do. I cannot believe this has happened. Maybe it didn't. Perhaps I was mistaken. There's probably a straightforward explanation. There has to be. Saul Mundy does not use prostitutes. It really is the most loathsome and ridiculous notion.

'Alice? Can you meet me for lunch? There's something we need to do.'

'Of course I can.'

It is one of the most bizarre marks of their friendship but also the truest stamp of their intimacy and loyalty that neither Alice nor Thea has thought to acknowledge that they're on speaking terms again. In fact, they've slipped right back into being the closest of friends. There have been no outright apologies, no calm or emotional workshopping of their massive falling-out. Thea is in the midst of a crisis – why wouldn't she turn to Alice for help? And why wouldn't Alice drop everything to be there? Apologize? Who should apologize to whom? Didn't you know that love means never having to say you're sorry?

Thea and Alice retraced her steps of a week ago, or were they Saul's steps, back down Berwick Street. They turned left and stopped outside Black Beauty's stable. There was the doorway, wide open; the shabby staircase leading up.

'Do you want me to go up?' Alice asked.

Thea looked at her as if she was crazy. 'And do what?'

'I don't know,' Alice shrugged. 'Suss it out? Talk to them? Ask them if they know Saul?'

'No!' Thea cried. 'No! I don't even know why I need to be here.'

They crossed the street and loitered. The perspex shop was once again closed for an hour. 'Need any perspex?' Alice asked Thea, while they lingered, as if she was talking about toothpaste or postage stamps. Thea laughed nervously though a frown was stitched to her face. They watched and waited. No one went in or came out of the building.

'Do they have days off, do you think?' Alice pondered.

'What are we doing here?' Thea asked Alice.

'I don't know,' Alice admitted. 'If we loiter much longer, they might think we want a job.'

Thea tittered bravely but then a man went in and wiped her smile away.

'Christ,' Alice hissed, 'he could have been our fathers – did you see him? All suited and dapper and – *normal*?'

'I think I want to go now,' Thea pleaded, walking a few yards this way and then that, 'I don't know what to do.' She started walking away. 'I don't want to wait for him to reappear. I don't want to time him. I don't want to stand here while he's paying – and having – sex right now, yards from where we are.'

Alice linked arms with her and they walked briskly away. She sat Thea down in a café and allowed her as much silence and middle-distance gazing as she needed. Finally, Thea looked up and mouthed, 'I don't know what to do, Alice. I don't know what to do about anything. What do I do with all my plans?'

'Do you love him?'

'Yes.'

'Is it enough?'

'I don't think so.'

'Had you any other doubts, any at all, before you uncovered all this?'

'None whatsoever.'

Alice shook her head and shrugged. 'I know, without asking him or you, that this man loves you absolutely.'

'But he goes to prostitutes!' Thea protested, suddenly objecting to Saul having anything in his defence at all.

'We don't know that,' Alice said, hoping she sounded more convinced than she felt, 'not for sure.'

'I saw him go in! I saw him come out!' Thea declared. 'I don't think Black Beauty runs the Anna Sewell fan club. I don't think "Models! top" sell Plasticine or Hornby toy railways.' Thea was hunched, rocking with the pain of it all. 'I want to run away.'

Alice felt powerless as she tried to comfort her. 'If you run from pain, it will follow you – but if you turn towards it, face it head on, it can only reach halfway,' Alice soothed.

'But that's like saying a problem shared is a problem solved and it's not, Alice, it's not,' Thea sobbed tearlessly. 'I've shared with you that Saul pays for sex, fucks hookers, visits prostitutes, call it what you will and what have I solved? My anguish isn't lessening, it's increasing.'

Alice sucked at her bottom lip thoughtfully. 'Perhaps he doesn't have sex with them, Thea. Maybe he has a perversion he's embarrassed about – maybe he likes to dress as a baby or a nun, perhaps he likes to look but not touch. Maybe he likes to be spanked or spat at or pissed on or God knows what.'

'He has *me*!' Thea bellowed. 'Let him spank me, if that's what he wants. I'll wee on him, if that turns him on. If he satisfies my every desire, why can't I satisfy his?'

Alice paused again. 'I'll do the devil's advocate thing, OK?' She waited for Thea's reluctant shrug before continuing. 'We don't know the specifics but what we do know is that it's Saul's secret. Don't we? Isn't it? A secret he'd categorically hate you to discover. You chanced upon his most private whim, however deviant we decree it. You weren't meant to know. He'd be mortified.'

'No!' Thea all but barked. 'No Alice *no*. Christ, sometimes I pick my nose and eat it, sometimes I waft the duvet and indulge in the stench of my farts, sometimes I fantasize about gang-bangs – those are the secrets of *mine* that I'd hate Saul to discover. Come *on*. No! No correlation.'

'At our age, we all have history,' Alice tried a different tack.

'This isn't history!' Thea objected. 'A week ago is *not* history!'

'The thing I'm sure about,' said Alice, trying to sound balanced and credible, 'is that he's not doing this to hurt you. OK? Can you hear that? Saul wouldn't do anything to hurt you. You *are* the love of his life and I think that you *do* know that. Whatever he's doing, whatever he pays for, it *is* a weird, upsetting, dark predilection – but on paper he's a wonderful boyfriend. You've never doubted him, you've never loved or been loved so deeply, so entirely. So, can you live with it?'

'Turn a blind eye?' Thea was staggered. 'Ignore the fact that the man I honour with my sexual fidelity fucks whores in his lunch hour?' Alice looked down at the table. 'What would you do, Alice,' Thea asked her levelly, just then thinking that Saul wasn't so much dark as the devil incarnate, 'if this was you? If you found out that Mark pays for sex?'

They looked at each other and tears sprang to both sets of eyes. They both knew that Mark simply wouldn't.

'I hate him, I hate him, I hate him,' Thea sobbed.

'The thing is,' Alice said carefully, 'I think you really want to hate him but I don't think you ever can.'

'I never want to see him again.'

'The thing is,' said Alice, 'at some point you're simply going to have to.'

Thea's Two O'Clock

'Hullo, babes.' Peter Glass was waiting in reception, halfway through the *Evening Standard* when Thea arrived back late from her lunch with Alice. Thea was not in the mood to be called babes. Just then she hated the male species without exception.

'How are you, Peter?' Thea asked perfunctorily, as she led the way to her room.

Do you pay for sex, Peter Glass? Is it a toss-up between one kind of massage and another? Did I win or lose today, hey?

'I'm the usual, babes. You know, stressed, overworked,' he laughed. 'It's my sodding lower back today, Thea. The pain is going down my leg – I'm hobbling, it hurts to drive even the Beemer.'

'OK,' Thea said, skimming through her notes on his last visit, 'down to your boxer shorts and onto the bed, please.' In the calm of her room, with something to absorb her, she was soon grateful to Peter for bringing her his aches and pains. For an hour she could take her mind off what irked her and concentrate instead on alleviating someone else's discomfort. It was something she knew how to do. Placing her hands on Peter's back, Thea began to rock his pelvis rhythmically to and fro.

'How are you, babes?' Peter asked, his voice suddenly softer as his body began to unwind under Thea's guidance. 'How's it going? All signed and sealed on the new place? Have you exchanged on yours?'

Thea stopped rocking and for the first time in her career, entirely took her hands away from a client's body mid-massage. Peter felt the chill and isolation and lifted his head, twisting round to look at her. She looked very puzzled. 'Are you all right?' he asked.

'Yes,' she said, though she didn't look it. 'Peter, is it possible for the vendor to unexchange a contract?'

'Revoke?' he balked as if the crime was so heinous as to be virtually unheard of. Thea shrugged. 'Fucking hell, Thea,' he said, returning his head to the hole in the massage bed, 'you'll be sued to within a pound of their entire deposit – they just changed the law to prevent misdemeanours like that.'

'I thought so,' Thea said with forced jollity.

'Cold feet?' Peter asked.

'Nah,' Thea faked her nonchalance, 'I was just wondering.'

She said no more. She rubbed some more ointment between her palms and effleuraged Peter's back with long, smooth strokes. When he wasn't groaning in appreciation and sighing with relief, he was filling her in on the details of his life, professional and personal. He'd pranged the Beemer, he'd chucked the girlfriend, bedded her best mate to make her jealous but since started dating a teacher.

'Not my usual type, Thea,' he marvelled, 'she's a bit older than me and not what I'd call a "stunner". But she's a great girl and she makes me laugh out loud.'

Thea hooked her fingers around the lateral fibres of Peter's latissimus dorsi, lifting and pulling medially. It silenced him for a while and then he started a rant against a rival estate agent. She set about some deep tissue work where he didn't realize he needed it and for the time being, she managed to massage away the stress his adversaries had heaped around his neck and shoulders.

He has a good physique.
Not really my type.
But objectively, he's in good shape.
But I wouldn't say he does it for me.

Thea trails her fingertips lightly up and down Peter's spine. Up and down. And then down some more. Down until she's reached the dimples above his buttocks. Just relax. Just relax. She leaves one hand there and takes her other to his right leg. She strokes up his hamstring and then down. And again. Then, with both hands she starts to massage his legs lightly. Up and down and up some more. She slides her hands around and travels along Peter's inner thighs. And up and down her hands go. This is not massage. This is not ambiguity. This is caressing. She feels nothing. It's easy to trace the hemline of his boxer shorts suggestively with her fingertips.

Peter has gone from being deeply relaxed and utterly motionless to springing up from the table, his face striated with embarrassment. For the first time in his life, he's at a loss for what to say. So he scrabbles into his clothes instead and starts wittering on about Christ is that the time, dear God he has clients waiting.

'I'd better go – thanks for the, er. I feel fine.'

Thea's Four O'Clock

Thea had intended to cancel Gabriel Sewell. She wanted to finish early; she'd had a dreadful headache since Peter's session and it could be a valid excuse not to see Saul for yet another night, to cancel Pilates and just go home, go home and curl up and not do any packing. But her afternoon had been back to back with other people's backache and, at five to four, she went downstairs and found Mr Sewell already there, expressionless as usual.

'Come on, Mr Sewell,' she said, with negligible charm or enthusiasm. He followed her up. 'How have you been?' she asked him cursorily, while helping herself to a long drink of mineral water.

'Not too bad, actually,' Gabriel Sewell replied, thinking he'd like a glass of water too, 'still blocked to the right. But the pain is substantially better.'

For the first time in her career, Thea wasn't remotely interested in her client despite his physical improvement being a direct credit to her. 'Look to the left,' she told him, 'and to the right. And to the left again, please. And to the right once more.'

'It's no longer what I'd term *pain*,' Gabriel defined, 'it's more *discomfort*.'

Well, if it's only discomfort, Mr Sewell, I wish you'd cancelled your appointment and waited another week.

'Down to your underwear and onto your stomach, please,' Thea said with scant interest. Perhaps she'd just give him thirty minutes and charge him half the fee.

Thea commenced a pretty perfunctory massage, like a musician practising scales or a showjumper taking his top horse for a hack around the block. Something to keep it all ticking over. Her mind drifted and she found herself wondering whether any of the girls in massage parlours were actually qualified masseuses. And if so, which skill did they consider their forte? Did they look in the vacancies section of the Job Centre or local paper under 'masseuse' or 'sex worker'? She wondered whether they started off with a cursory shoulder rub to somehow legitimize what came next. Saul always claimed he didn't really rate massage. Is that because he'd never had a good one? Or did he just tell the girls to forget the neck rub and go straight to his dick?

Thea looks down at Mr Sewell. He has a nice back, smooth and slightly freckled over the shoulders. It tapers becomingly to his waist and his legs are muscular and with just the right spread of hairs to be attractively masculine rather than unappetizingly hirsute. Turning deaf ears to the small voice warning her that she's mad, that this isn't going to help, that this is a very bad idea and fundamentally the wrong thing to do, Thea trails her fingertips down Gabriel's spine, just as she had on Peter. And then her hands start to caress his legs, interspersing strong strokes to the hamstrings with a feathered caress of the inner thighs. But at the point where Peter had objected and bolted away and left Thea feeling wretched, Gabriel spreads his legs slightly and Thea finds the signal a horrible but undeniable thrill.

Where else, Mr Sewell, she says silently to herself, *what else can I do for you today?* She is fingering the seam of his jockey pants blatantly. 'Turn over,' she murmurs. God, this is easy.

Mr Sewell's erection is impressive. In fact, it is so impressive that the very sight of it simultaneously excites but appals Thea. The shape of it leers up behind his pants. As bemused as Peter had been, Gabriel is now lying there, proudly tumescent. He is obviously, and quite literally, up for it. He is rock hard and eager and Thea can see his cock twitching expectantly, skewed slightly by the constraint of his underwear. She doesn't know whether to be shocked or titillated that this man, right here, would fuck her right now. He'd be quite happy to pay, there's no doubt about it.

'But I don't even particularly like you,' Thea thinks to herself as she looks down on his expectant body, 'you're not my type at all. You're surly and non-communicative and cold.'

'Miss Luckmore?'

Thea is horrified to see that while she's been deep in thought gazing at his penis, he's been staring at her intently.

'Miss Luckmore,' he repeats, 'is it à la carte – or can I order off menu? What, may I ask, are the specials today?'

Thea is catapulted from her safety zone into dangerous territory. She doesn't like it. Quick. Think of something. Feign innocence. Ignorance. 'I could do you an Indian head massage?' she suggests.

Gabriel smirks, his hand now lolling arrogantly over the mound of his cock. 'I assume that involves giving me head, then?'

'Pardon?' Thea flusters.

Gabriel snaps back to his more usual curt self. 'Look, are you up for it or what?'

Thea wants to cry. She feels mucky. 'I don't date clients,' she mutters. 'The ethics of my job discourage it. Sorry.'

'I wasn't talking about a date,' Gabriel says, 'just a blow-job or something. Whatever. Never mind. I'll try the head massage. Come on.'

I'm going mad. I'm not thinking straight. I'm losing my grip. I need to think but I can't. It's like I won't let myself. I have to decide what to do but I'm incapable of making decisions because I can't think about them. I have less than two weeks before I move out. But how can I think of packing when I don't know where home is any more? I've suddenly acquired so much baggage. I can't move under the weight of it all. Maybe I'll just shove the lot into storage and run away.

Thea and Sally's Six O'Clock

Thea didn't cancel her Pilates class that evening though her head throbbed and she was utterly exhausted from her unbelievable day. However, she knew she was best off devoting an hour to shutting out all that tormented her; indulging in an hour tuning into her own body; centring herself, focusing on breathing, concentrating on all she really was – a skeleton swathed in muscles, joints and ligaments, assembled intricately but logically. She wouldn't be able to think about Peter or Gabriel and what had almost happened, she could forget all about Saul and what had happened. Respite, even for just an hour, was what she craved.

Alice wasn't at Pilates though she'd confirmed their session over lunch. Ultimately, Thea was slightly relieved – she actually didn't want to receive Alice's kindly glances and supportive squeezes and concerned whispers for her welfare. Thea didn't want to workshop her problems and woes over chips and wine after the class. She certainly didn't want to reveal to Alice her bizarre behaviour that afternoon. Thea just wanted to think about her body, about inhaling and exhaling, about maintaining neutral. It was nice, though, to see Sally, and Thea eagerly accepted an invitation to a light supper at the Stonehills'. It would be good to be in Sally's company, she theorized, to have no reason or recourse to talk about 'it'. It would be constructive to simply chat, to natter on topics other than how prostitution and her future seemed inextricably bound. Sally's invite was also a good reason not to go home and have to think about packing and it provided a bona-fide excuse not to see Saul for another night at least. Ultimately, Thea rationalized that to be surrounded by the Stonehills' perfect domesticity would be comforting and affirming.

In Highgate, Sally could harp on all she liked about sleepless nights, the sorry state of her sex life, the demise of her social life and language skills, and the destruction of her clothes by baby puke. However, for Thea, the scent pervading the Stonehill house was uplifting and restorative. Drying laundry. Baby shampoo. Flowers from husband to wife. Home pride. Everything smelt so warm and clean and cosy and complete and grown up. It was a fragrance Thea acknowledged she had always wanted in her life. Just then, she wished she could bottle it. Just in case.

Don't let Sally see me sad. Stop it, Thea, get a grip.

'I wonder where Alice was today?' Sally said, passing Thea tomatoes to slice while she spread oven chips on a baking tray.

Thea shrugged. 'She said she was coming when I saw her at lunch.'

'Have you two buried the hatchet, kissed and made up then?' Sally probed.

'God, yes,' Thea said, busying herself with tearing basil into slivers.

'You're like an old married couple, you two,' Sally laughed, trying to shave parmesan with a potato peeler. 'Talking of marriage, how's Saul? Richard's playing squash with him tonight. He'll be back home soon – he'll give you a lift home, if you like. Providing he managed to stick to just the one post-match pint, of course.'

The door-to-door distance from the Stonehills' house in Highgate to Thea's flat in Crouch End was less than a mile and a half. Just long enough, Richard would have thought, for a quick chat about how the purchase of the new flat was progressing.

'Can I ask you something, Richard?'

'Sure,' he said, presuming his professional capacity as an architect was required.

'Have you ever paid for it?' Thea asked him outright.

'Me?' Richard asked. 'No – we tend to use each other in our company.'

Thea's mind-set was so rigid that momentarily she didn't realize Richard had not grasped her question and she fleetingly imagined a bacchanalian orgy of architects. 'No,' she corrected, 'not architect stuff. Sex. Have you ever paid for sex?'

Richard stared in amazement, wondering if he'd just heard right. Fortuitously, the traffic lights between Archway Road and Shepherd's Hill turned red. Thea repeated the question. 'No,' he replied decisively, 'I haven't. But I do know plenty of blokes who have.'

'Who *have*?' Thea dissected his answer. 'Or who *do*?'

'Christ, Thea!' Richard laughed with a fleeting frown. 'What's this all about?'

'A client of mine,' Thea moulded the truth credibly with cleverly employed ambiguity, 'had the wrong idea about me.'

This seemed plausible to Richard so he continued. 'I know blokes who have paid for it just the once, Thea, but I also know guys who use prostitutes regularly,' he said. 'You'd be surprised.'

'Why?' Thea asked.

'Why do they do it, or why would you be surprised?' Richard countered. Thea, though, just stared at him, simultaneously dreading details but desiring to know more. 'You'd be surprised how many blokes do. Professional guys like me, really,' Richard elaborated, 'with all the same privileges – a good wage, a gorgeous wife, a fabulous home, great kids.'

'Why?' Thea asked again.

'I suppose,' Richard considered, 'simply because they can. It's a "bloke thing", isn't it?'

'Is it?' Thea asked, forlornly.

'It's bizarre and contradictory,' Richard mused, 'but a man's sex drive is infinitely complex by virtue of the fact that it's so primal and base.'

'Virtue?' Thea balked. 'Vice – *virtuous*?'

'I mean – and this is in strictest confidence – there's a bloke in the office, my age, my position. He has a charmed life – great marriage to a gorgeous, fun woman. Anyway, occasionally he fancies a shag in the way I might fancy a sandwich. Morality and risk don't cross his mind. It's a physical requirement. He finds himself hungry and he nips out of the office and satisfies it.'

'Say his wife finds out?' Thea posed, hating this colleague of Richard's intensely.

'She never will,' Richard shrugged, 'unless she puts a private detective on him. But she never would because their relationship is great – you could say, guys who use prostitutes are committing the slightest and most negligible form of infidelity because emotional betrayal doesn't come into it.'

'But say she *did* find out,' Thea pressed, 'this chap's gorgeous fun wife?'

Richard was adamant. 'She wouldn't – you have no idea how easy and discreet it is.'

'Then how do you know he does it,' Thea countered, 'if it's so easy and discreet?'

The lights turned green. Richard drove across Archway Road and pulled in along Shepherd's Hill, by the library, under the gentle orange glow of a waning street lamp.

'This might sound shocking,' he said, 'but one afternoon he basically offered me a recommendation.'

'What?' Thea exclaimed.

'He recommended the services of this new girl he'd just seen.'

'For fuck's sake!' Thea objected, gripped by a violent loathing for this colleague. 'What – like telling you Pret a Manger have a great new sandwich you should try?'

Richard laughed. 'Exactly like that,' he said, 'but in my case, it was like telling this chap thanks, but I don't eat red meat.'

'Fucking bastard!' Thea spat. Richard had never heard her swear, let alone imagined she could be anything other than sweet, temperate Thea.

'This colleague of mine is a really nice bloke,' Richard felt compelled to defend him. He drove on. 'You'd like him. That's the irony.'

'Promise me it's not you?' Thea said with steel in her voice and thunder in her eyes.

Richard glanced at her before indicating right and dipping down the long sweep of Stanhope Road. 'Christ, *of course* it's not me,' he said, obviously offended, 'it's never been me. It's simply *not* me – I just don't fancy it. Not during periods when I've been single. Not after nights out with the lads. Not when I've been far away from home.'

'Promise me,' Thea warned him.

'Thea!' Richard protested, regarding her quizzically. 'What's your problem?'

'It was unbelievably upsetting,' she declared, leaving the car, not checking the passenger door was shut properly, forgetting to thank Richard for the ride.

Thea savours a Lewis Carroll Moment in her hallway, encircled by closed doors. She can't decide where she wants to be, so she sits down where she is, for a long while, until she's quite calmed down. She stays where she is, takes her mobile phone and thinks about calling Alice to tell her what Richard has said. It's strange, what she heard from Richard is ultimately more illuminating than it is shocking. And though the details are deplorable, fundamentally it has been helpful.

I almost feel I now have reasons to forgive Saul; the information by which I can understand him a little better. Facts that should lessen the revulsion and shock of it all. Plausible explanations that could appease my turmoil. Perhaps I should be relieved, perhaps I should try and philosophize that actually it has nothing to do with me – he's just being a bloke. Maybe I should believe that his emotional fidelity to me is sacred to him. That everything really can be quite all right.

'But if Richard Stonehill can choose *not* to use hookers,' Thea shouts, 'why can't Saul?'

Ryanair's 10.10 a.m.

At Carcassonne, all Paul Brusseque knows, as he boards a Ryanair flight he's managed to find the fare for, is that there's this hot chick in England who's occupied his thoughts most of the time. Yeah, so she's married, but so what – from what he can deduce from the little information she's given him about husband and home, he reckons it must be on the rocks. Or else wide open. Something like that. Whatever. If she's up for some no-strings action, he isn't going to get his morals in a knot about it.

Tix. She had said something about sending him tix 2 uk. But she's a tease, this Alice Heggarty, a playful, tease of a flirt. Her text sex has tantalized him to distraction, to desiring the real thing enough to go for broke and board a plane for it. So he's her bit on the side, her bit of rough, her toyboy, her big boy, her fantasy incarnate. So what. It's a damn sight better than being a boring old fart of a husband who most likely can't satisfy her or probably cheats on her the whole time anyway. Is he in love with her? The husband? He'd be a crazy fucker not to be. Is Paul in love with her? Or is he just crazy about fucking her? Crazy enough to scrounge two days' leave and scrape together an air fare to surprise her. Sit back and enjoy the flight. But it's cool to go with the flow. It would be boring to always let your head rule your heart.

'Much better to think with your dick,' Paul laughs to himself.

Paul arrives at Stansted and wonders which way London

is. And where he can change his euros. And when he should contact Alice. And how – text, telephone or just turn up? And where is he going to stay?

Alice's phone made her jump. She thought she'd put it onto silent mode. Her instinct was to hide the document she was reading on her computer. Silly, really, because the caller wouldn't know what was up on screen. In fact, even someone looking over Alice's shoulder would merely note the *Guardian* website and an archive article on British sex workers. Alice doing research. Inspired by her trip to Soho with Thea over lunch. Very up *Adam*'s street, after all.

However, Alice's phone ringing through a message surprised her. Paul. She might've known. He texted her around this time most days. It was strange but in the light of Thea's situation, Alice's pleasure in her extramarital dalliance had dulled a little. Paul's texts were still an ego boost and her replies remained fruity, but it was as if it was all now so fanciful as to be virtually harmless. It was a virtual affair, after all, because she hadn't actually seen or even spoken to him for a good three weeks. Last month, in fact. For Alice, the texts provided light relief from the demands of the day, an ego boost at opportune moments and a little light sauce into the blandness of her home life. Having a secret was still fun; quite safe fun, actually. It was all words and no action and where's the harm in that?

There is an enduring irony that actually there's a time and a place for spontaneity and if they are out of sync, the impact and attraction are severely compromised. Had Paul sprung his surprise visit the previous week, she would have fizzed with the outrageous arrogance of it. She'd have played hooky from work or she'd have smuggled him up to her office or she'd have lied to Mark and invented an industry drinks party that would take up all evening. But Paul's text arrived an hour after Alice had returned to her office from her trip to Soho with Thea. His text bleeped through just as Alice was trawling articles on the Internet, absorbing the facts and figures of the socio-economics of prostitution. Over 50 per cent of men have paid for sex; 50 per cent of those pay for it regularly. Of those, 75 per cent are ABC1 men, 30–60. *Adam*'s circulation was ABC1 men, 30–50. Alice calculated that the majority of *Adam*'s readers had paid for sex, and a fair proportion use prostitutes often. And then she considered her colleagues and wondered who had and who does and who wouldn't. And she couldn't decide; she just couldn't decide. But the statistics indicated that a percentage had to be punters. She wondered whether to impart this information to Thea. Would it help to know that Saul was not a deviant? That he wasn't acting alone? That he wasn't even in much of a minority? Or would it actually be of little comfort and no constructive use at all?

fancy a fuck?

Paul's message raised a short smile until Alice wondered if he'd ever paid for it.

where r u?

She'd reply later. For now, she put her phone onto silent mode. She bookmarked the webpage, logged off the Internet and turned her attention to spreadsheets and her division's budgets. Twenty minutes later she checked her phone.

Oh Paul, haven't you anything better to do today than bombard me with texts? Go and climb Mont Saint Victoire, or something.

nice weather!

Alice glanced out of the window. It was a nice day.

go climb a mountain / have a wank! Alice texted back. me v busy xxx

Her phone rang. 'Alice Heggarty,' she answered, her eyes fixed on a spreadsheet.

'And just how *busy* is "busy"?' Paul was asking.

'Listen, you!' Alice chided. 'I've a job to do!'

'How about a blow-job?' Paul riposted predictably.

'Go and have a *wank* – go and climb a *mountain*! Bugger off.'

'Well, there are no mountains in London,' Paul mused, 'and Leicester Square is not the place for a wank.'

Alice was struck silent. Paul was chuckling. Paul was *here*? There in Leicester Square? How could that be? She hadn't sent him tickets. She hadn't sent for him full stop. It never crossed her mind that he'd come unless she called. In an instant, she had to assess that affairs are not about control at all, but a teeter on the knife edge of chaos.

Paul loved every second of Alice's silence – he envisaged her shocked and delighted, rapidly rearranging all her afternoon meetings and planning the fastest route to him. He wasn't sure where Liverpool Street was in relation to Leicester Square.

'You're *here*?' Alice managed to exclaim at last.

'Yup,' Paul proclaimed.

'But when?' Alice asked. 'And how long for? And why didn't you say? I'd've sent tickets.'

'I wanted to surprise you,' Paul said.

Alice scanned her diary. She had very little on that afternoon and only momentarily did she wonder whether this was a godsend or not. She had no deadlines to oversee, no one to let down and thus no lies to tell – no excuse, really, not to take the afternoon off. Rapidly, she reasoned that the fact that the path to proscribed passion was today paved her way with no obstacles whatsoever was a Sign. It was Fate giving her the nod to go forth and fornicate. She felt almost protected. Surely if it was wrong, it wouldn't be so easy.

Where, when, how?

Crouch End?

Today was absolutely not the day to ask Thea to assist Alice's adulterous proclivities.

'Take the Northern Line to Camden Town and meet me in the shoe shop opposite the Tube in twenty,' Alice whispered covertly, leaping back into her role as adulteress.

Paul hadn't a clue what she meant. 'Is the Tube in Twenty a store too?'

Alice was a little irritated. 'Stupid! The *Tube* – the underground station – in twenty *minutes*.'

'Oh – OK! Cool.'

He'd annoyed her and the thrill of what was meant to be furtive had been diluted and that made her cross.

Is it a Sign pointing the other way, then? A dead-end street with an unmissable No Entry sign? As she packed her handbag, she decided to leave all sobering thoughts and responsibility behind in her office.

It's a quiet day, it's a lovely day, no one will know, why deny myself pure physical pleasure?

Alice was slightly irked to arrive at the shoe shop before Paul. She'd wanted to sashay in with a toss of her hair and beckon him over with the magnetism of her raised eyebrow alone. Instead, she found herself browsing shoes she'd never wear, glancing at her watch and wondering if the shop had done research into whether blaring hip-hop actually increased sales.

Paul was fifteen minutes late. 'Sorry, baby – that Northern

Line is mental! I went too far up and had to jump off at Tough Nell's Something.'

'Tufnell Park,' Alice corrected. 'Hullo.'

'Hiya. Cool trainers,' Paul remarked, picking up a pair. 'How much is £70?'

'Well, let's see,' Alice said coolly, 'I reckon it's about seventy pounds.'

Paul laughed. 'I mean in euros,' he apologized.

'Are you seriously going to buy them?' Alice asked, glancing at her watch. She wasn't in a rush but she was bored of the shop.

Paul had a good look at the trainers. They were funky. But £70 was probably expensive. 'Nah,' he said, putting them back and giving Alice a squeeze. 'You look fab.'

'Come on,' said Alice though she wasn't quite sure where they were going.

They meandered into Inverness Street and walked slowly by the fruit and vegetable stalls. 'What do you want to do?' Alice asked Paul, assuming he didn't really want to buy apples or carrots.

He raised his eyebrow lasciviously and Alice smirked back. 'But let's get something to eat first,' Paul countered prosaically, 'I'm hungry.'

Alice watched him wolf down spaghetti bolognese and diverted her gaze as he chatted with his mouth full. She paid before he could order dessert. She wanted to cut to the sex. Paul Brusseque wasn't meant to be about friendly chit-chat and perusing trendy trainers. He wasn't meant to be a somewhat naive tourist in London. He wasn't meant to turn up late or be bamboozled by the London Underground system and the Euro–Sterling exchange rate. He was only meant to be about raw sex. He should grunt, not chat. He should be naked and manly – not fixated by trendy footwear. Ultimately, he should be her lover; rampant and masculine – not a cheery friend.

Had they been in the West End, she might have been tempted to blow a fortune on a hip hotel room for the afternoon. But they were in Camden Town with not a boutique hotel in sight, let alone walking distance. 'We'll go to mine, it's just up the road,' Alice told him, hailing a cab by whistling through her fingers, which charmed Paul no end. So he told her how cool he thought she was. And kept asking her to whistle like that again. And Alice wished he'd just be quiet. His sex appeal was ebbing away and she was desperate to fuck him before it disappeared entirely.

Come back, Paul, back to how I remember you.

But Alice, this *is* Paul. You want Paul as you've imagined him, as you've reinvented him since your trip to France. After all, a fleeting dalliance deepened by the economy of text messaging leaves plenty of room for fanciful embellishment.

By Belsize Park, to prevent Paul wittering on, Alice started kissing him. He was, after all, still extremely kissable on the surface. She closed her eyes to the familiarity of Haverstock Hill and transported herself back to Les Baux. Back to Clapham. The times and places where Paul had kissed her before. He tasted the same and his expert oscillation turned her on again, much to her relief.

In silence, she paid the taxi and led the way up the steps to her house. She didn't want to note Paul's reaction. No doubt he'd be gobsmacked by the beauty of her home and she didn't want to see the effect on him, didn't want to invite questions, didn't want to think about betraying her husband under his own roof.

'Christ, Alice,' he marvelled in a hush. She plugged his mouth with her tongue while closing the front door with a kick.

'Hullo, Mrs Sinclair.'

Oh, fucking hell.

Wednesday. The cleaner came on Wednesday afternoons.

'Hullo, Carmen,' Alice said to the robust Brazilian lady, relieved to detect that Carmen hadn't witnessed her snogging Paul, 'how are you?'

'Very good, Mrs Sinclair, thank you! I am doing ironing now – the house is very clean.'

'Thank you, Carmen.' Introduce Paul. Think of something. 'This is Paulo – he has come to look at the, at the –' *At the what, for heaven's sake? He's come to look at my tits, Carmen. I wanted him to screw me on the freshly laid linen on my bed, Carmen.* '– at the main bathroom.'

'You change your bathroom, Mrs Sinclair?' Carmen looked horrified. 'But it is very beautiful bathroom. Very new. Very clean.'

'Pressure,' Alice said, 'he's come to check the pressure. This way, Paulo. Follow me.'

Alice took Paul into the bathroom. She thought about pressure and allowed herself an exasperated glance in the mirror. Actually, the water pressure was wonderful, thanks to Mark's insistence on hi-tech pumping. 'Paulo,' Alice said loudly just in case Carmen could hear or was remotely interested, 'this is what I mean.' She ran the bath taps and the water gushed impressively and conspiratorially loudly. Alice turned to Paul and placed her finger over his lips. She unzipped his jeans whilst unbuttoning her blouse. She wanted to fuck and go. She wanted to have sex with him and then she wanted him to go. He fondled her breasts and took his mouth to them greedily while she enmeshed her fingers in his hair and regarded their clinch reflected in the mirror. They looked good. It was a sexy sight. She pulled his face up to hers and they tongued voraciously. Slowly, she knelt and eased down his jeans, pulled down his boxer shorts and took her mouth immediately to his glorious hard-on. She almost gagged. He'd had a long journey. He'd raced around central London. He needed a shower, ideally. A wash at the very least. But there wasn't the time for that. All Alice wanted was fast, urgent sex. 'Do you see what I mean, Paulo?' she suddenly called, for Carmen's benefit.

'Yes!' Paul called out, as Alice sucked his cock and caressed his balls.

Paul pulled Alice up, positioned so she could grab hold of the sink, facing into the mirror. He bent her over slightly, yanked down her knickers and penetrated her. She watched herself being humped, watched his face contorted with intense pleasure. This was precisely what she wanted – to be desired sexually to such a degree that the act itself was greedy, carnal, basic and verging on rough. She observed Paul – his teeth clenched, his eyes screwed shut. He pumped and thrust and came explosively.

'Did you come, baby?' he asked. Alice thought about climaxes and anti-climaxes and decided not to answer directly. She put her finger over her lips and mouthed 'hush' as she switched off the taps. Silence. As she watched Paul pull up his trousers, she felt his semen dribble out of her. They hadn't used a condom. How could she have been so stupid and reckless? What on earth was she thinking? What the fuck was she playing at? Alice detested herself.

'What shall we do now?' Paul asked, thinking along the lines of Bucking-Ham Palace, perhaps. Or Carnaby Street.

'I need to make some work calls,' Alice replied.

'You wouldn't know anyone whose floor I can crash on?' Paul asked. Alice looked confused. 'Clapham's not available – my mate's away and I forgot to ask him for keys.'

'Sorry,' Alice said, 'I don't think I can help.'

'Your mate up in that Crouch place?'

'No! I mean, she's moving soon – so we can't ask her.'

Paul looked at Alice. Alice looked back at him. 'Two nights, right? I'll book you a hotel.'

'Alice, I'm broke.'

'I'll pay for it.'

* * *

Should I go to an STD clinic?

Should I take the morning-after pill?

I desperately need Thea, but no way can I burden her with this. Not only will it upset her but there's far more on her plate at the moment than I could stomach. I wanted my cake but now I'll just have to choke on it. I'll just have to suffer feeling wretched all on my own and accept it as my come-uppance.

Alice doesn't doubt that a slap of humiliation would be cathartic, so she goes to the chemist and forces herself to maintain eye contact as she asks for emergency contraception. She knows that a dose of guilt would be medicinal too. She is subsumed by it when Mark comes strolling home a couple of hours later, with his customary cheery kiss, a lovely bottle of wine and the fresh ingredients for his home-made pesto. She isn't hungry. Her remorse and self-loathing have filled her up.

It is only when she's trying to wash away her shame in a scalding hot bath later that evening that she realizes she forgot all about her Pilates class. She won't get a refund now. It means that lousy, pathetic shag with Paul cost her £45. Plus his hotel bill. Actually, the price she is paying is far higher and she's acutely aware of it. She's taking a bath in the guest bathroom because she just can't face going back into hers. And she's told Mark she's going to sleep in the spare room, fabricating a dose of Thea's phony flu as the reason though in truth she feels she does not deserve to sleep with him in their marital bed. She ought to give Thea a quick call to check she's OK. But Thea's mobile is off because she's currently engrossed in her conversation with Richard Stonehill.

Oh, Thea. Oh, Thea. How can we be in such a mess when we're only in our early thirties and our lives until recently were really so charmed? How did everything plummet from our control so quickly? The major difference is that you're the victim in your situation and I'm the perpetrator in mine. You deserve only salvation and happiness – but privately I just can't see how you'll find this. Look at me with my faithful, adoring husband. What the hell was I doing? Please God don't let my comeuppance depend on Mark finding out. Please God, just don't let Mark find out – it will slaughter him. I don't want Mark to hurt. I never did it to hurt Mark. Please save him from pain. Please God, don't let Mark ever find out what I've done – I promise I'll never do it again. Please God, save Mark the torment – I swear it won't be me getting away with it; my shame and regret will ensure it. Honestly.

But do you know what? I don't actually believe in God.

I'm scared.

I feel sick.

Oh, Thea, I so need to talk all this through with you. But I can't, I can't. You have an unfathomable amount to cope with. My isolation and my remorse must somehow carry me through and teach me to live and love better than I have been.

Saul's Three O'Clock

can i c u?

no - pls undstnd

fuck u! come on! i go 2nite . . .

no Paul - not poss. pls, pls undstnd

i came all this way 4 u . . .

i didn't ask u 2

oh no?

cant - sorry. Ax ps: no more txts etc PLEASE

Etc.? Paul reads reams into the word on his phone. Was Alice referring to sex as an 'etc.'? Arrogant bitch. Paul decided it would be easier to simply hate her than to object, plead or protest. He didn't want to feel his trip was wasted. The fact that he'd ended up paying for his plane ticket slightly irked him – but ordering excessively from the room-service menu and raiding the mini-bar onto Alice's tab at the hotel gave him some satisfaction. There was more to London than Alice bloody Heggarty or St Clair or whoever she was. He'd damn well go to Buckingham Palace and Carnaby Street. He'd put Alice down to experience; after all, he liked plenty of it in his life; it was his chosen mode of living. Toyboy, sex tool, rich bitch's bit on the side? Fine. Whatever. Been there, done that. Tick that one off the list now.

* * *

Saul was looking forward to his three-o'clock meeting with Alice. He loved brainstorming ideas so he prepared well and arrived at the offices early.

'Hiya,' he greeted her, kissing her twice.

'Saul,' Alice responded cordially, offering her cheeks but not kisses. She was tired and she felt on edge. She wanted Paul Brusseque out of the country. She wanted to want her life back yet despite making the decision to cut the contact with Paul, she didn't feel like returning to Mark's warm, simple embrace. And the emotion, or lack of it, bewildered and depressed her. And now she was confronted with the dissolute Saul Mundy.

'Coffee?' she offered, swiftly deciding to fully immerse herself into Alice Heggarty, publisher extraordinaire, and keep her alter egos of cuckolding wife and best friend's keeper firmly out of office hours.

'Thanks,' said Saul. 'How are things?'

'Fine,' Alice declared, trying not to balk at the question or look remotely guilty, 'and you?'

'There's a delay on the purchase of the new place,' Saul bemoaned. 'I daren't tell Thea – she appears to be so overwhelmed by her flat sale next week. I've hardly spoken to her, let alone seen her – have you? Every time I phone she says she's too busy sorting her life out to chat. It's only packing – but Christ, is it taking all her time. She won't let me go over because she says it's all a mess – yet she claims she can't afford the time to stay at mine!' Saul laughed while Alice thought he should have read into Thea's chosen phrases. 'She's a daft thing!' he said affectionately. 'When did you see her last? Pilates?'

'No. Not since the weekend. I had to cancel my class the other day,' Alice said, suddenly keen to swerve away from the subject. She tapped her desk. 'Let's get cracking,' she said. 'How's *Adam*?'

'How about *From Apple to Blackberry – technology gets fruity* – and not just because I'm hoping for a freebie,' Saul smiled.

'I like it,' Alice said, making notes. 'I met Nick Hornby's agent – but rather than a straight interview, I want to pitch for a piece on his experience as parent to an autistic child. I've suggested offering an increased fee as a donation to his TreeHouse Trust charity.'

Saul nodded thoughtfully. 'I was musing over a Fatherhood issue – writers, celebs, Joe Public.'

'I like it!' Alice enthused.

'Iconic father/child relationships,' Saul rolled on, 'from Homer and Bart Simpson, to George Bush Senior and George Dubya, Ringo Starr and Zac Starkey, Prince Charles and Wills, Beckham and Brooklyn.'

'And what about daughters!' Alice protested, raising an eyebrow to challenge Saul.

'Paul and Stella McCartney,' Saul laughed, 'Terry and Gaby Yorath, Jimmy and Lisa Tarbuck, Nigel and Nigella Lawson, Mick and Jade and Lizzie Jagger.'

'Homer and Lisa Simpson,' Alice laughed. 'We could integrate the Nick Hornby idea into such an issue. Good. What next?'

'I love the title *Ripper Ripped Off* for an investigative piece on copycat crimes,' Saul suggested.

'I suppose that would necessitate suitably grisly pics, then?' Alice said hopefully.

'Unquestionably. And how about *Adult Adolescents*?' Saul suggested, 'thinking about that whole resurgence in BMX bikes and skateboards and the Beastie Boys who I reckon are probably older than me. Buy a bike and recapture your youth, kind of thing.'

'Good,' Alice mused, 'good.'

She and Saul sat in affable silence, broken only by the occasional pensive murmur or thoughtful sucking of pens when inspiration alighted. Alice was trying to process a train of thought concerning a great title, *Back from the Brink*, because she'd heard an inspiring interview with a mountaineer who'd lost his limbs to frostbite but lived to climb another peak.

Suddenly her mind's eye beamed up Paul, in his hiking boots, his muscled bronzed legs. She felt taunted and glanced away from the unwelcome intrusion to find her gaze, previously non-focused into the middle distance, fixed on her shelf. The framed first cover of *Adam*. Her award for Launch of the Year – that gravity-defying jag of perspex swooping into the wooden base. Without warning, she was bombarded with the perspex shop connection, next door to that Black Beauty and those Models! top. And out of nowhere, as clear as if he was speaking right then, she recalled verbatim Saul's comments at that very awards night almost two years ago. He'd proclaimed he liked to dip his finger into a 'fair few pies'. He'd said dollars couldn't buy his desire for diversity – well, yes, they obviously could, albeit not in dollars but his pounds sterling bought him pounds of flesh. And though, in hindsight, Alice could find double meaning in the comments he'd made about his career, there was one thing he'd said which leapt from her memory and assaulted her.

He said how much he loved Thea. He said – and it didn't even strike me at the time – that he was faithful to her 'in my mind and in my heart'. Why didn't he say 'body and soul'? Why did he even have to qualify fidelity? He specified his suspect mind, his half a heart while being careful to make no mention of the physical.

She blinked and halted a shudder as she slowly looked at Saul, sitting opposite her, tapping a Biro irritatingly against his lower teeth while he mused over more ideas for the magazine.

'*Paying For It*,' she announced calmly, her level stare belying her racing heart.

Saul was still formulating '*That's Not What I Call Music – our inevitable decline into our parents*' and thus failed to grasp Alice's insinuation. '*Paying For It*,' Saul repeated, as if she had alluded to first-class air travel or NHS prescriptions.

'*Cash for Sex*,' Alice continued. She scrutinized Saul for a reaction but there did not seem to be much of one as yet, he was just looking at her intently. Keep the eye contact, Alice. Keep the pressure. '*Hooked on Hookers*,' she tried. Maintain the momentum. '*Jades and their Johns*.' Saul was nodding slowly. Did she have him? She wasn't sure. '*Prostitutes and their Punters*.' She thought she could detect a slight falter to his nodding. '*Paying For It*,' she said again. Time to raise her eyebrow and then glower. Saul was now taking undue interest in his pen; putting his finger on the ball point. Had she struck a heart chord? Time to go for the jugular. This is for you, Thea. '*A Shag or A Sandwich? Buying sex in your lunch hour*.' Alice paused to maximize the dramatic impact of her volley. 'What do you think, Saul?' She let her question hang, the steel in her voice slicing through. 'This one is right up your street, isn't it? Right up your Soho side street.'

Slowly, Saul looked at Alice. She was shocked. There was no glimmer of guilt. No jump to self-defence. No arrogant denial which she could then batter back. No blithering wreck for her to chastise to the hilt. No tears of remorse she could refuse to mop up. Saul simply looked horrifically ashen; far worse than if he'd seen a ghost – more as though he'd foreseen his own death and it was imminent. '*You* could write this one, Saul, couldn't you?' she continued spikily. '*I have a stunning, gorgeous girlfriend but I pay for sex on the side*. Put it on expenses! I'll go to petty cash right now! Or do you have an account, Saul?'

'Alice,' Saul said, but without protest, more just to request she be quiet.

They sat in the loudest silence; time ticked excruciatingly slowly, reality suspended in a caught moment, their thoughts rocketing far too fast to harness. Nothing could be done. Time couldn't be turned back; neither words nor actions could be taken back.

'She knows,' Alice said quietly, at length.

Saul whipped his head away from the unequivocal meaning of the sentence and stared at Alice's door while unseen tears lacerated his throat like thorns.

'She saw you,' Alice declared hoarsely, her ultimate shot striking the very heart of Saul.

The toxic silence continued to fill Alice's office like an asphyxiating fog. Alice wanted to fire a million questions. Why, you bastard? What were you thinking? How could you? Why on earth would you? How often do you? What's it like? How does it differ? How much do you pay? How much have you spent? When was the last time? Will there be a next time? Why would you want to when you have a girl like Thea? However, Alice's voice was hampered from materializing by her surprise that Saul should dare to look so broken. Her onslaught was somewhat dependent on the assumption that Saul would jump to his defensive, or accuse her of lying, or lie that Thea was mistaken or that they had no proof. Over the last few days, in imagined confrontations, she'd prepared for these responses and had perfected her final self-righteous lunge. Instead, she was confronted by a Saul who was speechless, defenceless and in imminent need of tissues.

Please God, don't let me actually have to comfort the bastard.

'How do you know?' Saul asked quietly. 'How do you know that she knows?'

'She's my best friend,' Alice said through clenched teeth.

'What am I going to do?' Saul said with little hope and negligible energy. He was suddenly devastated to realize that Thea hadn't had flu last week, she probably hadn't been at all those Pilates classes nor had she cancelled the trip to his parents because of a commitment to Alice. The simple truth was that she obviously didn't want to see him, she was actively avoiding him. The rejection was shocking. 'What do you think I can do?' he asked Alice because he had no idea and he desperately sought guidance from the person closest to Thea. Alice shrugged and narrowed her eyes with hostility. Why should she do any thinking on his part – a problem shared was a problem halved and he did not deserve to have his load lessened at all.

'For fuck's sake,' Alice declared, 'you have Thea. Why on earth would you want to even think about jeopardizing that, let alone go forth and fuck and fuck it up irrevocably?'

Saul's frown furrowed deep behind his eyes. 'I never, ever wanted to jeopardize my relationship with Thea nor hurt her in any way,' he declared quietly and with such passion Alice found she could have quite easily believed him.

'Oh, come on,' she rubbished, 'you have *no* excuse.'

'I have no excuse,' Saul agreed, 'you're right. My only defence is an explanation – and that is: I'm a bloke. I guarantee I'm not a deviant, I'm not a bastard – I just do what a hell of a lot of other blokes do. I have the most beautiful girlfriend whom I love deeply and want to share my life with but I also – occasionally – pay for sex. It's just sex.'

Alice was hearing it from his own lips. He was confirming it. He was verifying it. He was admitting it. He was owning up, confessing. She wanted to throw something at him. She wanted to scream at him. She wanted to see him squirm with suffering and be paralysed with pain. She shouldn't let him just sit there and qualify that he was a bloke, *c'est la vie*.

'I couldn't love Thea more,' he was saying while Alice eyed her Rolodex and considered hurling it at him.

'How can you talk of love?' she spat.

'I am telling you, I love that girl more than I have any other – she is my soulmate,' Saul countered emphatically. 'I love her as much as I can – which is more than I thought I could. I adore her. She has never doubted it. And nor have you.'

'Why are you pathologically unfaithful to her, then?' Alice lunged.

'I don't see it that way. It's just sex. It's nothing,' said Saul. 'Unfaithful suggests wilful cruelty and devious disloyalty.'

'Oh, fuck off with your skewed theories,' Alice hurled. A sickening silence throttled them again.

'You know what, Alice, you're right,' Saul said at length. 'You're right – it would make a fascinating article. And maybe I will do it for you, do it for *Adam*, my swansong if you like. You needn't even pay me – donate my fee to Nick Hornby's charity. But I'm warning you I can't write a self-flagellating parable of shame. I could, however, pen you a doctorate on how it is that men can divorce sex from emotion perfectly and yet still desire and believe in love and fidelity totally.'

'Saul!' Alice protested, outraged that he should have a plausible explanation and dispassionately astute grasp of the situation.

'Once in a while I pay for sex, Alice,' Saul said quietly. 'It's hardly a habit and it's not a problem. Nothing illegal, nothing violent. A straightforward quick shag. I don't do it because of Thea – our sex life is fabulous. I don't do it for some macho power drive. I'm not a misogynist and I'm not a sex maniac and I'm not stressed. I don't do it for any reason other than I can.'

'You *can't*,' Alice objected with a screech, 'you *can't* – not when you have Thea.'

'But I *can*. I can make the distinction. I can make the tenderest love to Thea, have passionate and kinky sex with her but very occasionally, if she's not around, if I feel horny or bored and I can't be bothered to wank, I think, I know, I'll go and get £80 out of the cash point and buy a quick fuck.'

'You're a reprehensible con man!' Alice shouted. 'You're a totally selfish, stupid, fucked-up loser.'

'I am going to lose the most precious thing I ever had,' Saul confirmed.

'You bastard!' Alice hissed. 'Who *are* you? Nice guys *don't* – OK? They don't do that!'

'Want a bet?' Saul objected fiercely. 'Do a poll amongst all the men you know. Go on. I dare you.'

'Fuck you – don't you dare try to justify or dilute it.' Alice had leapt to her feet. 'It's ridiculous, deplorable, unnecessary behaviour for a man with such a charmed life as you.'

'Alice, I have nothing to say in my defence. But for the record, I never meant to hurt Thea. For the record, there was absolutely no emotional betrayal. My only searing regret is that Thea knows. I don't know how I'll cope with her hurt. And the ramifications. Christ, Alice, I don't know if Thea and I can possibly survive this. I stand to lose the love of my life.'

Alice looked at Saul. There was no solution. There was no point yelling at him. There could be no happy ending. His own acute awareness of Thea's intolerable pain was his own terrible suffering. She could see that, it was written all over his pain-lashed face. No amount of further scolding from Alice could improve a dire situation or make him feel worse. His destiny was that he would lose Thea.

'I have to go,' Saul said, his voice hollow and choked.

'What are you going to do?' Alice asked sadly.

He shrugged. 'I don't know,' he said. 'Allow Thea to call the shots. I have to leave it to her. I don't know – perhaps I should tell her I know that she knows. Do I try to fight for her? Do I try and justify? I don't know. Christ, I don't fucking know.' He stood up and turned to leave.

'Saul, you understand that I can't work with you directly,' Alice said quietly. 'I'm sorry. It's over.'

'I appreciate that,' said Saul as he reached for the door handle. 'I understand. I'll miss *Adam*. I'll miss you, Alice. I can't think about this right now. I'm losing Thea. I have to go. What am I going to do? What can be done? Goodbye, Alice. Goodbye.'

And Saul leaves and Alice feels exhausted. But the underlying emotion worming through her conscience and burdening her soul is Shame. Saul has no shame because he honestly considers he has done no wrong – though he acknowledges it has unwittingly caused his most loved one unfathomable pain. But Alice feels shame like a punch to the stomach. She is winded by it. She can't breathe. She is acutely aware that being so viciously moralistic and heavy-handedly sanctimonious with Saul has an ulterior motive in addition to defending Thea's honour and dignity – it appeases her own guilt. It is as if privately she had placed herself and Saul on a scale of deplorable sins and ensured that, out in the open, Saul lost. His vice is worse. He can go to hell. Alice had accused Saul of 'ridiculous, deplorable, unnecessary behaviour' for someone with such a charmed life. Deep down, she knows she should level the indictment in all its savagery at herself. What was it that he had said? He claimed infidelity was wilful cruelty and devious disloyalty. That it was a crime he was not guilty of. But she was.

Saul had never hurt Thea. If Thea hadn't witnessed him with Black Beauty or Models! top, she'd still be floating in her romantic waft of interior-decorating schemes and dreams of domesticity. Saul's hookers, whoever they were, had never had the wrong idea from him nor wanted anything more than his money. A simple cash transaction. Thanks. Have a nice day. And you. But Paul Brusseque had spent his meagre wages flying himself over to London to be with her. Did Saul send his prostitutes outrageous text messages? Of course he didn't. Did he ever make Thea suffer by cold-shouldering her so he could think of them? Never. Alice feels profoundly ashamed at the hurt and insult she's inflicted on Mark over the months. She goes to the shelf and places the framed first cover of *Adam* face down, and turns her award around.

I have behaved far worse than Saul – my actions have directly caused unhappiness and anxiety. Mark has had to bear the brunt of my impatience, my selfishness and my unrealistic expectations of long-term love. I've used and led on Paul Brusseque and behaved badly to him too.

Alice rests her throbbing head against the window pane. Her office is high up. It's a long way down. There's a long way to go.

Who was it who said something about it's not who you love it's how?

She hums a tune and knows it to be 'Love the One You're With'. Apposite indeed – but she's thinking of another quote, even more pertinent. Slowly, it dawns on her. It is not a lyric or film quotation – it is from an article she'd published. Christ – wasn't it in *Lush* years ago? She vaguely recalls she and Thea perusing the article while eating soup. She'd just split up from Bill, hadn't she? When was that – four years ago? Almost. Alice goes to the *Lush* offices two floors below and rifles through their archives.

From Heartbreak to Happy-Ever-After – 7 Steps to Take You There.

'Number 5: *It's Not* Who *You Love It's* How *You Love*,' she reads under her breath, in no mood to pronounce the excessive exclamation marks. 'Number 6,' she continues, '*Change What's on Your Wish List*.' Genius. Who wrote it? She recognizes the name – a staff writer long since lured away to *Red* magazine. However, Alice has always believed that her magazines' ethics are directly her responsibility. 'As publisher, I should practise what I've preached.'

Peter's 4.26 p.m.

'Souki, can you take my four o'clock, please?'

'Are you OK? You look dreadful, Thea.'

'I have to get some fresh air. I don't feel so good. Can you?'

'Well – OK. It's the ballerina, isn't it? Sure. You go. Oh, by the way, Saul phoned – *again*. You haven't fallen out, have you?'

'I'm just stressed about selling my flat.' Thea bent the truth while wanting to yell why the hell does everyone see us as this golden couple – it's a sham!

Thea walked quickly down Paddington Street, jaywalked over Baker Street and practically jogged along Crawford Street. She knew exactly where she was heading though she'd never been before, had no appointment and would be wholly unexpected. She'd taken the address from the files at work and had double-checked it on her pocket A–Z. Turn left. Straight on. Dog-leg right. It's here somewhere. But there's a few of them along this street and it's difficult to tell the numbers on these buildings. There! That's it. Here.

Thea burst into the offices of Henderson-Goode.

'I need to see Peter Glass!' she declared.

'Do you have an appointment?' said an enormous vase stuffed with overpoweringly scented lilies which Thea presumed was some high-tech gimmick until she spied a tiny woman with too much make-up sitting at the desk behind.

'No,' Thea said, 'just tell him Thea Luckmore is here.'

'What's it in connection with?' the painted pygmy enquired.

'Stuff!' Thea said, levelling what she hoped was a menacing 'I'm bigger than you – do it!' expression.

When Peter appeared Thea was taken aback. He seemed half his usual height and, as he walked towards her, it was without his usual swagger. In fact, amongst the other sharp-suited agents in the hyper-plush office, Peter seemed to lose some of his brash-bold expansiveness he brandished around the Being Well.

'Thea?' he asked, looking rather alarmed.

'I need to talk to you!' Thea tried to whisper though her breathlessness and agitation turned it into a hoarse hiss.

'Come over to my desk,' he said genially, but Thea eyed the open-plan office suspiciously and shook her head decisively. 'Come on, let's go outside for a mo',' said Peter, catching the receptionist's eye and splaying his fingers to signify five minutes. He guided Thea with his hand at her elbow, as if she was a loopy but harmless elderly relative.

'Come on, babes – the Beemer is as good a place as any for a chat.'

With a key that looked nothing like a traditional car key, he bleeped the car into life and opened a door for Thea. By the time he had walked around to the driver's door and slid into his place, Thea was banging her head on the dashboard, sobbing uncontrollably. 'Babes, babes!' Peter tried to comfort. 'Easy, easy. Come on now, babes – you'll set the air bag off in a minute.'

'I'm not a prostitute. I need somewhere to live. I'm single. I'm homeless.'

Peter wasn't sure which of the four revelations he should tackle first, nor really why it was to him that Thea had come. 'Slow down, darling, take a deep breath. Shit, I haven't a tissue. Hold on.' He sprang out of his seat and went round to the boot, returning with a butter-soft, relatively clean chamois leather. 'Here you go, you can use this.'

Thea blew her nose gratefully. He offered her a piece of mentholated chewing gum, popping two tabs into his mouth when she declined. He chewed thoughtfully and tapped her knee while her sobbing subsided into sporadic shudders and erratic gasps.

'Please could you help me,' she asked softly. 'I sell my house in just over a week but I have nowhere to live.'

'What about the ritzy-glitz apartment with your fella?' Peter asked carefully.

Thea looked at him, wide-eyed and fragile. 'I found out something a couple of weeks ago,' she whispered, 'that as well as professing to love me and proclaiming I could trust him, he uses prostitutes too.'

'Christ, babes, that's not good timing, not good timing at all.' Peter assessed how ghastly the situation must be for Thea and in an instant he understood both her recent, bizarre behaviour during his session and also her probing the ramifications of breaking an exchange of contracts. But just then, he had no answers and was for once stunned into silence. It was such an eerie sound for Thea that she felt compelled to continue. 'Look, I'm horrified I gave you the wrong idea the other week at the Being Well,' she confessed. 'I was in such a muddle – I don't know. My mind was wandering and I guess my fingers followed. I wasn't thinking straight.'

Peter tapped her knee soothingly while telling himself not to be such a prat for being momentarily offended that Thea didn't want to have sex with him at all. 'Nothing happened at the Being Well, darling,' he assured her with soothing equanimity. It was true. Nothing had happened. 'What a wanker!' Peter said with derision. 'I mean me – not your bloke. Your bloke is a wanker too. Actually, I'd say he was more of a prat. Poor old babes; there you were, stressed and in shock and therefore coming on to me in your sudden madness – but there was me turning you down! In your hour of need! I'm so sorry, sugar.' Thea wasn't sure what to make of Peter's take on the situation, his confession. It was as if he was apologizing for not having undertaken a charitable act. His expression softened and he squeezed her arm. 'I'm joking. I'm being an arse. I'm not much of a comedian, am I? I was trying to make you laugh. Thea, forget what happened – in the circumstances, I can quite understand you suddenly going full-on doolally.' Thea nodded. 'But you mustn't take it personally that I declined. I mean, look on it this way – I see you as this beautiful, classy bird way out of my league! You're priceless, babes, priceless. Not that I thought you were a real tart anyway. God, no.'

Thea smiled meekly. Peter was trying so hard to be comforting, to say nice things to pep her up, that it was irrelevant his chosen words were in such a sweet muddle. It was comforting to be sitting there, in the neutral but safe territory of his Beemer, all cream leather and overpoweringly air-freshenered; with Peter himself, gold signet ring, slicked hair and wide-boy accent at odds with his decent, endearingly artless character.

'Anyway, down to business,' he said. 'We need to find you a place to unpack, don't we? When do you complete? Next *week*? Well, you've struck gold, babes. I'm the daddy when it comes to short lets and fast service. No shit. I've got contacts all over this city – the best. Name your postcode, say your price and leave the rest to me. You'll have keys before you can say please.'

The fact that her load had been immediately lightened enabled Thea to slow down and walk calmly back to the Being Well. She'd be in good time for her six o'clock, time enough to go to the newsagent's and buy *Heat* and a chocolate bar – neither of which she'd fancied of late. Trying to choose between an Aero and a Biscuit & Raisin Yorkie, she spied a roll of Refreshers. But rather than make her want to cry, the sight of them made her seethe. She felt relieved.

Anger is good. Anger feels empowering. I can act on anger. Sadness and tears are destructive – I can only be shrunk by them.

She left the shop with a triumphant toss to her head. The smile, however, was wiped clean away when she came face to face with Kiki.

'Hullo,' Kiki said shyly, scurrying past, as she had done so many times on this street. Thea was rooted to the spot while Kiki walked onwards to the massage parlour. Despite the sky-blue day, out of nowhere fat raindrops suddenly fell, spreading in globs on the warm pavement like ink on grey blotting paper. From the depths of Thea's subconscious, memories of the Shipping Forecast exhibition sprang to the fore.

Bitch! She was there. That whore said hullo to Saul and then she saw me and scurried off. Fucking cow.

'Oi!' Thea pivoted and yelled after Kiki just as she disappeared into her place of work. 'Oi – come back here!' Thea shouted though her target had gone. Without a second thought, Thea marched her way after her. She didn't look twice at the door, she didn't stop to consider if she had to press a bell, let alone have an appointment. She pushed; it opened; she was in. It was like a takeaway restaurant where you can't see the kitchen but you can sense what's cooking. Only it was very quiet. The subdued lighting, dark-red walls and screened windows contributed to an atmosphere of perpetual twilight. The air was overwhelmingly perfumed by cheaply produced, synthetically scented oil. Behind a bland office desk unconvincingly veneered as mahogany, sat a nondescript middle-aged woman dressed conservatively in a black polo neck. She was obviously startled by the sight of Thea. Not their usual walk-in – but not unheard of, either. All types catered for, and the like. She might even be after a job.

'Where is she?' Thea barked. 'That one?'

'I'm sorry, love?' the receptionist replied.

'The one that just came in!' Thea said, hands on her hips. 'Short one – oriental.'

'Kiki?'

'I don't know – the one who came in two seconds before me!'

'Yeah – that'll be Kiki. But Kiki doesn't do – well, you'd be wanting Miss Lula.'

When Thea grasped the receptionist's allusion, she suddenly felt her stomach twist and her inner voice scream what the hell am I doing in here. 'I need to see Kiki,' Thea said in a calm and measured voice. 'I need to talk to her.'

The receptionist shrugged. 'Who are you?'

Christ. I don't have time for this. I am the girlfriend of a man who may well have paid her for sex.

'Kiki!' Thea hollered in the vague direction of whatever was behind the stud wall demarcating the reception area. 'Kiki!' As footsteps could be heard descending a staircase, Thea and the receptionist stared at each other, mirroring expressions of agitated bewilderment while they anticipated the imminent entrance of a girl, hopefully Kiki.

It was. 'Yes?' she said, looking first to the receptionist and then, visibly confused, to Thea. 'Hullo?'

'Kiki?' Thea asked, her eyes darting with adrenalin and unease.

'Yes, I am Kiki?'

What was Thea meant to say now? She had no idea. She wanted to insult the girl, challenge her, shame her, shove her, make a citizen's arrest. Actually, Thea felt supremely anxious, as though she was being sucked into the vortex of a nightmare. She wanted to run out. But Kiki was standing in the way.

'You need me for something?' Kiki asked in shy, broken English; her face under the make-up legibly sweet and way too young. You dirty old fucker, Saul.

'You!' Thea started, pointing at her and wagging her finger in warning simultaneously. 'You! You!' Kiki didn't understand. Nor did the receptionist. But neither could afford for a punter to enter into this fray. They'd turn and take their money elsewhere.

'Lady,' the receptionist said, 'I think you'd better leave now.'

'But he was *mine* – and I loved him so.' Forsaking the velveteen-covered bench, the pile flat and sheened from where punters sat and waited, Thea crumbled dramatically to the floor, sobbing. The receptionist's priority was to get the girl out of reception, out of the house, preferably. Kiki's instinct was to crouch beside the weeping wreck and place a gentle hand on her shoulder.

'I take her,' Kiki told the receptionist. 'You give work to Lula or Mitzi, yes? I take her for ten minutes, yes? Come, lady, please you come.'

Thea was so tired with it all, she didn't bat an eyelid at being led by the hand deep into the brothel by a young prostitute she presumed her ex-boyfriend to have patronized.

Kiki took Thea right to the top, to a room not dissimilar in size or outlook to the one Thea gave her own massages from. Both had a bed. Both had a sink. But Thea's therapy table wasn't a small double bed laid with a pink sateen coverlet and matching pillows. Thea had a pump bottle of Carex handwash by her sink, not a large tube of lube. This room had a shelf with towels too, but in place of Thea's lotions and potions, was a rather paltry selection of dildos. Curtains, discordantly floral, lined heavily with blackout material, were drawn closed. The room was shadily lit by a single, central light bulb with a cheap lampshade and a fringed gypsy shawl draped over it.

'Please – you sit,' Kiki invited, placing herself demurely on the edge of the bed. Her soft voice, neat petiteness and incongruous politeness reminded Thea of the oriental air hostesses on TV adverts for their airlines. 'You would like water?' Kiki offered. Thea shook her head. 'You feeling better?' Thea shook her head forlornly.

Slowly she raised her eyes to meet Kiki's. 'Have you?' Thea whispered. 'Did he? My? With you?' Kiki's brow furrowed; Thea wondered if she had compromised the girl's integrity; client confidentiality. Actually, Kiki was trying to recall what this lady's man looked like. 'We broke up,' Thea continued. 'I need to put phantoms from my mind – OK? I need to know. Did he? Here?' Kiki didn't appear to recall Saul. 'Do you remember you saw me and him at a photography exhibition?' Thea prompted. 'And perhaps you've seen him along this street?' Still Kiki looked blank. With a sigh, Thea took the photograph of Saul from her wallet and without looking at it, passed it to Kiki.

Kiki concentrated hard and then she nodded and smiled. 'Never with me,' Kiki was pleased to confirm. 'Before here I work somewhere else – I think this man came there. But never with me.' Kiki watched Thea slump. She wondered how to explain in her poor English to this broken, sad lady that she shouldn't doubt the man's love for her. How could she put it to her that men like him were nothing special to any of the girls. And nor would any of the girls be remotely special to him. It was like paying in money at a bank – but he received a flesh receipt, not a paper one. A simple, invariably swift transaction. Kiki knew she'd be hard pressed to explain eloquently and she couldn't expect the lady to understand anyway.

'How many times?' Thea whispered.

Kiki shrugged. She didn't actually know the answer but thought the lady would want to hear 'Once? Twice?' so that's what she told her. 'But you work same street here,' Kiki confirmed, 'that is more why I know him.'

'What did he want?' Thea asked.

Kiki looked embarrassed. 'I don't know,' she answered honestly.

'How much? Don't answer,' Thea said hurriedly, 'I don't want to know. It's enough that I know for a fact that he has.' She put her hands over her ears and rocked as she wept.

Kiki sat herself close next to Thea and gently pulled her hands away, placing them in her lap with hers covering them. Thea considered how pretty Kiki's fingers were. 'I come from the forest,' Kiki began, 'and in the forest we say that true love is one soul in two bodies and that whole love allows the bodies to go this way and that way but the soul always remains. Men they need to—' Kiki stopped. She clenched her fist and then flicked her fingers to signify what she meant. 'They just do.' She shrugged. 'I am sorry for you. It is most hard to understand.'

'Do you like them?' Thea asked her. 'Your clients?'

'They are fine – I am careful. This place is good, the girls are good girls. Clean. I am lucky. Many girls like me not lucky, in danger.'

'Do you hate men?' Thea probed.

Kiki smiled and shook her head. 'No – I don't hate men!'

'Do you pity them?' Kiki didn't seem to understand. 'Do you feel used?' Kiki looked a little taken aback. 'Are you really into sex?'

Kiki laughed and shook her head. 'The feeling of sex is nothing special to me. This job is easy. I never feel it in here,' she says, tapping her heart, 'I never feel it in here,' she continues, tapping at her temples. 'I come from simple family in the forest,' she qualified, 'I can send them much money. They are proud of me.'

'Where is the forest?' Thea asked. 'Do they know what you do?' Kiki's fleetingly downcast look answered her. 'But don't you want a husband? A boyfriend?'

'Oh, I have a boyfriend!' Kiki glowed.

Thea looked horrified. 'But does he know what you *do*?'

'Yes, he knows. He knows this is just my job and all the love I have I give to him.' She regarded Thea. 'We are one soul in two bodies and our love is whole. I go to work and so does he.'

'What does he do?' Thea asked, half expecting Kiki to say 'pimp'.

'He owns two shops for sports shoes,' said Kiki, 'in Ealing.'

'But,' Thea sighed heavily.

'Lady – you are beautiful and clever and with special gifts,' Kiki said softly. 'Maybe my world seems dark to you? It frightens your soul? It is not so. Mostly it is boring! And mostly the men are just bored. Perhaps a little lonely.' Kiki laughed shyly. 'You want to watch? You can watch – I don't mind. You will see it is not – *exotique*! Sex this way is just very boring.'

Thea was bizarrely touched but she shook her head to decline. She'd seen and heard enough. 'You are beautiful too,' she told Kiki, and she meant it. 'And you are very kind. I'm sorry for shouting. I am just hurting so much. My world has imploded. Perhaps the truth is that I am weaker than you because I just can't grant Saul the freedom to be himself. I want him to read a book or something when he's bored.' Thea spoke too fast, too eloquently for Kiki but she could understand her sentiment implicitly.

Thea's gaze fell on an old travel alarm clock placed surreptitiously in the corner on the floor. 'Oh Christ, I'm going to be late for my five o'clock,' she exclaimed. 'And you will be too,' Thea regarded Kiki with a brave smile.

'I take you out private way,' Kiki said. Before they left the room, Kiki turned to Thea. 'Please, you will remember one soul in two bodies? Men are not bad – they are just being men.'

'Thank you,' said Thea, touched, utterly exhausted and still unconvinced.

The rain had stopped. The daylight was dazzling. Thea squinted as if she'd been in the dark for a long time. One more client and then she could go home and resume packing. There were two messages on her phone.

hi hon. shall i swing by 2nite – help u pack? missing u, v v much Sxxx

fancy supper chez me? wine + dvd? Axxxxxxxx-xxxxxx

She phoned Alice to say she'd be round at eight.

She sent a text to Saul as she rushed back to the Being Well. not 2nite – flat chaos Tx

His reply buzzed through just before she entered her room to commence the session.

but me going 2 b'ham & glsgw 2moro x2 nites for FMAP focus groups . . . Sxxx

Thank God for that, thought Thea.

Alice, Thea, Mark and Saul

'Mark, can you set up the DVD for Thea and me?' Alice called from the bathroom. 'She's coming over while you're at that golf thing. I'm having a Jo Malone luxuriate in the bath – the Tube was mobbed today.'

'No problem,' Mark replied from the bedroom, changing

out of his suit into something more appropriate for a golf expo at the Business Design Centre in Islington. Saul had sent him press tickets. 'Is she OK, our Thea?'

'She's bored of packing,' Alice said. 'Mark – we might need to put her up here with us for a while?'

'Is she OK?' Mark asked again, his concern genuine. 'Has something happened with Saul?' Alice said fine, fine hurriedly. Mark was well aware how Thea and Alice had always been thick as thieves together – momentous events befalling one or the other to be dealt with together in exclusion of the world around them. He both admired and gently envied the self-sufficiency the two of them gained from their friendship. When they'd fallen out a couple of months ago, Alice had seemed so displaced, so at a loss, so narky. He still wasn't any clearer on the cause of their impasse nor did he expect Alice even to sketch Thea's current predicament. Mark considered how, on a scale of intimacy, there was a gulf between men and their close mates and women and their best friends. He could acknowledge that Alice possibly needed Thea in her life more than she did him. But it was easy for him to feel gratitude rather than resentment. Thea was Alice's great leveller; Thea was the one person who could chastise his wife; Thea was Alice's enduring ally and, Mark knew, an important fan of his. He knew only Thea could chide Alice for her impatience and calm her hot-headedness, that Thea could scold her when she was being churlish; he'd heard her admonish Alice for sulking with him and he knew that Thea reasoned with Alice on his behalf when it came to the pressures and commitments of his job. Good old Thea – he hoped she was all right.

A buzzing caught his attention; it came from under his discarded work shirt, placed for the moment on the floor until he could transfer it to the laundry basket once Alice vacated the bathroom. Under his shirt he found her phone. He picked it up. `Message,` it flashed. `Paul B`, it said. `Read now?` it asked.

Paul B?

Yes, pressed Mark.

`ur a bitch - but gr8 tits`

It took a while for Mark to actually translate the message, being unaccustomed to the abbreviations of text messaging. He was shocked and indignant. Poor Alice being bombarded by filth – like those obscene pop-ups that occasionally assaulted their home computer screen, worming their way onto some seemingly innocuous website or other. He was sure there must be a way to block them from mobile phones. He was about to call through to Alice about it when he stopped and sat down heavily.

Message Paul B Read now?

It wasn't unsolicited.

It couldn't be.

For the phone to recognize Paul B, Alice needed to have inputted his details. Paul B, whoever he was, was known to her and her tits were known to him. Mark felt less insulted that this Paul B thought his wife was a bitch than he felt mortified that this man was commenting on her breasts. How the hell would he know? Alice was saying something.

'What?' Mark asked, distractedly, his eyes fixed on the screen of Alice's phone.

'I said, don't hang on for me – I'm sloshing on an intensive pro-vitamin hair-restoration mask and it needs to stay on for ten minutes, then have three rinses.'

Ten minutes and three rinses. How long did a rinse take? Multiply by three.

Mark's dilemma lasted seconds. Spy and perhaps suffer? Or ignore and forever wonder? Ten minutes plus triple rinsing was time enough but there wasn't a moment to lose. He scrolled through to the envelope icon. His thumb hovered. Stop singing, Alice. I can't read your text messages with that racket going on.

fancy a fuck?

Another.

u know u want it

Another.

can i c u?

Another.

fuck u! come on! i go 2nite . . .

Gutted, winded and blown apart, Mark was crippled by a searing pain in his stomach. He wanted to ask himself what it all meant but he knew not even he could be naive enough to expect an innocent explanation. No matter how much he loved Alice, no matter how much he'd love to give her the benefit of his confounded doubt, the meaning of it all was clear as muck. He couldn't even read between the lines – the nature of text messaging presenting stark facts in black and white. There wasn't the space for purple prose, just a tiny screen filled with `fancy a fuck?`

My wife.

My wife is having an affair.

My wife has been sleeping with someone else.

Who is Paul B?

How dare he call them 'tits'.

Mark was devastated. Over and above the scorch of pain and the nausea of disbelief was the horror of feeling a total fool – the quintessential cuckold of a piss-taking young wife conducting her affairs via the puerile medium of text messaging.

I could never be a Paul B. I'm too old-fashioned. Too stupidly gallant and respectful. Those are the qualities I thought she loved most about me. It appears they mean the least. What an idiot. And one thing I have to ask myself – which plunges the final twist to the dagger thrust – is why has she kept not one of my messages?

He could hear Alice rinsing out the special hair treatment for the second time.

Foolish girl – does she not realize I'd love her were she to wash her hair with Fairy Liquid? Or is it foolish me for even deigning to think she maintains her beauty and sets her standards for me, rather than Paul B? Standards? What sodding standards?

He could hear Alice releasing the bath water.

And I haven't even read the messages she sends.

Mark knew Alice was seconds from appearing. She was the last person he wanted to see. Quickly, he put the phone back on the floor, under his scrunched shirt.

No doubt it'll stay there. Alice is blind to dirty washing. It's always me tidying away. When has she ever cleared up after the mess she makes?

* * *

'Mark set up the DVD for us,' Alice told Thea who'd arrived just as Alice finished a lengthy, meticulous blow-dry.

'Your hair looks amazing,' Thea remarked, holding up swathes of it as if admiring skeins of silk.

'I used some new product we were sent to trial,' Alice said. 'I pinched one for you too. Hang on. Here you go. Now, white or red wine? Look! Mark's even left out the corkscrew so we don't have to go on our usual hunt.'

'Good old Mark,' Thea said fondly, opting for Sancerre and reaching for glasses while Alice uncorked the bottle. 'How are things? How are things with Mark?'

'It's all going to be fine,' Alice evangelized though she busied herself with opening Kettle Chips to hide the slash of guilt, the scorch of pain traversing her face. 'It's going OK, Thea. Things are better – I feel much more balanced.'

'Good for you,' said Thea, 'good for you, Alice – I'm fucked.'

Alice hugged her sympathetically. 'What are you going to do?' she whispered, holding her tightly. 'Are you any closer knowing?'

'No. I don't know. But I could move into rented accommodation for a while,' Thea said, her flat intonation suggesting she'd learnt the sentence by rote to quote while inwardly she had yet to figure out the manifold ramifications behind it.

'Where? How?' Alice asked, wondering whether Thea would be better off moving in with her for a while.

'One of my clients is an estate agent,' Thea said. 'I asked him earlier today to help. He's found me a place in a mansion block in Highgate already. I'm going to see it tomorrow. It's not available for another couple of weeks though. Can I perhaps stay here in the interim?'

'Of course you can,' Alice said, 'but Saul?' Had Thea come to her ultimate decision? Already? Unaided? 'I mean – have you told him? About rented accommodation at the very least? Have you spoken to him, have you talked at all?'

Thea's gaze dropped, her brow creased and she bit her lip. 'Haven't told him yet,' she mumbled. 'Actually, I haven't seen him for days. I keep fobbing him off. I keep putting it off. I don't know what to do.'

Alice wondered whether now was the time to tell Thea that Saul now knew that she knew. No. It wasn't a good idea. 'But –?'

'What am I going to do?' Thea forces a whisper crackled by the imminence of tears. 'Everything was sorted and now it's all a mess. And now it's gone. All gone. My immediate future, my long-term future. I'm scared.'

Alice racks her brains for something wise to say. Thea beats her to it.

'Even if I manage to forgive, even if I get my head round the theory that men can totally divorce sex and emotion, even if I truly believe that I am absolutely the love of his life – I will never, *never* be rid of this suspicion and hurt,' Thea says, 'and my own principles that hold it's *wrong*. It's not *nice*. Good guys *don't*.' She pauses and she and Alice scour each other's faces, their expressions mirroring turmoil.

Alice watches Thea's face crease with despair. And suddenly she is looking at Thea aged fourteen years old. Almost twenty years later, her eyes are filled with the same dreadful fear, exquisite sorrow and terrible bewilderment as they had been when her father had left home. It makes Alice shudder and be thankful not to be Thea. Just as she had been at the age of fourteen. Just as she had been grateful that her father was nothing like Thea's. At fourteen, she'd rushed home from school and flung herself in his arms, held him tight, felt so lucky that she had him for her father. And now, aged thirty-three, Alice desperately wants Mark to be home soon from the golf show, so she can hold him and rejoice that he is nothing like Saul.

Alice thought it might well be a good idea to inform Thea that Saul knew she knew – it might just facilitate Thea to come to a conclusion. 'Saul was in for a meeting yesterday,' she began.

'I went to a brothel today,' Thea butted in because it was actually far easier to discuss than her relationship.

Alice was suddenly incapable of any sound, let alone speech itself. All she could manage was a silent, gaping jaw-drop of prodigious proportions. Thea couldn't help but giggle at her dumbstruck expression. It was perhaps the first time she'd been the one to shock the other into silence. In fact, it was probably the first time she'd actually done anything categorically shocking. Alice took a gulp of wine. 'Where? Thea!' she managed to gasp. 'What the *fuck* were you doing there? Thea!'

'I went to confront the enemy,' Thea said, 'so I went to that brothel just near the Being Well. I needed to face my fear. *I destroy my enemy when I make him my friend*.'

'Who?'

'Abraham Lincoln.'

'What are you on about, Thea – you're inspired by the founding father of the United States to take yourself into a brothel in Marylebone and befriend the prozzies? Are you *crazy*?' Alice was desperate for details yet wondered what on earth she was about to hear.

Thea looked a little sheepish. 'Not crazy – I just needed proof that this never had anything to do with me.'

'And?'

'It was the best thing to have done,' Thea proclaimed. 'It was horrendous and surreal but in retrospect, I have a sense of peace now.'

'Jesus, Thea!' Alice couldn't disguise the admiration in her voice though she worried it was inappropriate. 'Why didn't you tell me! Why didn't you phone! What was it *like*?'

Suddenly, Thea looked back on her visit as a veritable expedition, an adventure. She'd been in a brothel, for heaven's sake! She'd sat on a bed and held hands with a hooker! Surely she was the only person she knew to have done anything like that. Apart from Saul, of course. And perhaps half the men she knew, if statistics were true. 'I've seen a couple of the girls around,' she told Alice, 'you know, buying chocolate, posting letters – just like me.' She didn't want to tell Alice about the Shipping Forecast, about Kiki greeting Saul. She didn't want to force herself to see how blind love had clouded her view of reality for so long.

'Christ!' Alice marvelled. Sod watching *Ocean's Eleven* on DVD as planned.

'Today, I caught sight of one of them and I don't know, I just went a little mad,' Thea admitted sadly. 'I wanted to insult her. I wanted to hate her, I wanted to blame her, I wanted it all to be her fault. But I couldn't and I didn't – because it isn't. Now I see how she doesn't go out soliciting men. Their predilection is not her fault, not her responsibility, not of her creation.'

'Who *is* she?' Alice gasped, wanting to forsake the academics in favour of specifics. 'What's she like? How old? What's her name? What does she look like? What did you *ask* her? What did she *tell* you? Oh my God, did you see any of the clients?'

'She's young – I didn't ask how young because I didn't expect her to answer truthfully,' Thea said. 'She's called Kiki but I don't expect that's her real name. She says she's from a forest.'

'A *forest*?' Alice exclaimed, imagining Little Red Riding Hood in a crotchless basque under her scarlet cape.

'That's what she told me – that her family still live in the forest and she assists them financially. Her take is that a man's sexual needs are distinct from his emotional allegiance and need never impinge on his commitment as a husband.'

'Right,' Alice said, thinking that's as may be but I couldn't cope with it.

'I asked her if she was a sex maniac,' Thea said.

'You didn't!'

'I asked her if she hated men.'

'You didn't!'

'I asked her if she hated women.'

'You didn't!'

'She held my hand.'

'She didn't!'

'I asked her if she enjoyed her work.'

'Does she? What did she say?'

After a week or so of comforting her friend, sharing her pain, letting her cry but feeling powerless to really help, Alice rejoiced in the apparent return of Thea's initiative and strength. After a fortnight of not really knowing how to advise Thea, of being unable to hearten or soothe her, it transpired that the answer lay in a tour of a brothel.

'The strangest thing is that actually I liked her,' Thea concluded, half an hour later. 'She's sweet and kind. She's nothing like the stereotype.'

'God, you're gracious,' Alice marvelled.

'You know, they used to call prostitutes "erring sisters". And actually, I did feel a sense of kinship – I don't know – collusion? She's *not* my enemy, she's a girl,' Thea shrugged, 'doing a job there's a demand for.'

'God, I think you're brave and amazing,' Alice said with great tenderness and pride. 'I wonder where this forest is?'

'I don't know,' Thea said. 'She's oriental so I suppose it's in Thailand or somewhere.'

Alice nodded. Then she stared at Thea. Though she sucked in her lips, she was helpless to prevent an almighty snort of laughter. She bit her bottom lip hard but she knew she was moments away from an uncontrollable fit of giggles.

'What?' Thea asked, confusion making her eyebrows stutter.

'Thea,' Alice squeaked, 'the *forest*?'

'Yes?'

'Do you think she might have been saying "Far East"?'

Thea frowned. Then she groaned. Then she covered her face with her hands while Alice pronounced 'forest' again and again in a mish-mash Malaysian accent. Soon enough, Thea tried it. Far East. Far East, of course!

'Oh God,' Thea didn't know whether to laugh or cringe, 'oh God. What a day. I'm going mad.'

* * *

'Oh God, what a day,' Mark said to himself as he walked around the golf expo aimlessly and with no interest. It seemed the most sensible place to go, in the circumstances. He didn't want to pace around and around the block. He wasn't in the habit of sitting by himself in bars, let alone drowning his sorrows. So he meandered through the stalls and stands with Paul B's text messages leaping out at him wherever he looked. 'There must be some mistake,' he repeated as a whispered chant, 'there must be an explanation.'

Alice wouldn't do that to me. Alice wouldn't do that to me. Alice wouldn't do that to me.

'Mark! Hullo, mate.'

Mark looked up and saw Saul. 'Saul,' Mark shook his hand, 'I didn't realize you were coming. Were we meant to meet?'

'I only decided at the last minute,' Saul assured him. 'I had nothing else planned. And it's sort of en route to Thea's – I'm going to pop by later and see if I can help with the packing.'

'Oh, sure,' said Mark, 'she's at ours, having a chick-flick comfort-food evening with Alice.'

While Saul was struck by the fact that Thea had lied to him about how she was spending her evening, Mark suddenly wondered if Thea knew Paul B. And if Thea knew, then did Saul too?

'Seen anything you fancy?' Saul asked.

'Fancy?' Mark barked with a deep frown.

Saul regarded him quizzically. 'New balls?'

'New balls?' Mark snorted with derision. He pinched the bridge of his nose and rubbed the corners of his eyes.

'Are you OK, Mark?' Saul asked. 'Are you all right?'

'Fuck knows,' Mark replied hoarsely. Saul reeled from the response. He'd never heard Mark swear, he'd never known him to be anything but composed and always all right. He was thoroughly taken aback.

'Come on, buddy,' Saul said with a hand on Mark's neck, 'let's get a drink.'

Saul didn't think spirits were Mark's thing yet he watched as he downed two neat vodkas in as many gulps. 'I think Alice is having an affair,' Mark announced, his voice rasping from the scorch of alcohol.

Saul was startled. '*Alice*?'

'You see her,' Mark said, 'what do you think?'

'She's never given me any reason to think she's having an affair,' Saul declared. She hadn't. Nor had Thea.

'Look, I don't want you to feel compromised,' Mark said, 'but has Thea mentioned *anything* to you?'

'Not a sausage,' said Saul, attempting to discredit Mark's suspicion by making light of it. 'And she tells me everything.'

Does she, Saul? Are you sure about that?

Mark sunk his head into his hands. 'I don't know,' he said, 'I don't know.'

'What *do* you know, exactly?' Saul probed.

'She can be pretty moody,' Mark said.

'Yes, but all women can be,' Saul pointed out. 'Alice is naturally slightly highly strung,' Saul countered. 'The fact that she's spirited makes her attractive.'

'She can be a flirt,' Mark stated. 'I've known her for years, remember.'

'There's flirting,' Saul reasoned, 'and there's putting your money where your mouth is.'

There speaks an expert. Except you don't flirt, do you, Saul, you don't really have to. Your girls are a sure thing. We know where you put your money and we don't really want to know where you put your mouth.

'I swear to you, Mark,' Saul said, placing both hands flat on the table for emphasis, 'I've never seen even a *hint* of anything untoward – and I've been around her at work *and* play, remember.'

Mark nodded but Saul could see he remained unconvinced. 'I found something,' Mark said darkly. 'Her phone. I found a text message from someone called Paul B.' Saul could only listen – the image of Mark covertly burglarizing his wife's telephone was so atypical as to be frankly disturbing. 'Who's Paul B?'

'Paul B?' Saul thought hard. 'Honestly, Mark, I have no idea. There's no Paul B on the mags that I know. I've never heard Thea mention such a person. Look, can I ask what the message said?'

'Oh, you know,' said Mark with cutting lightness, 'the usual – fancy a fuck, great tits, when can I see you.'

Saul was stunned. And a private part of him wanted to phone Alice immediately and accuse her of hypocrisy of the highest degree, declare her misdemeanour a crime far worse than his.

'What drove you to read them?' Saul asked. 'Have you been going through a bad patch?'

'Not really. I mean, I'm used to her blowing hot and cold – she always has done and I've loved her for years. As you say, she can fly off the handle and she can be moody. It was a bit rocky a few months ago but actually, recently, it's been quite nice and even.'

'I'm sure there's an innocent explanation,' said Saul, though he wasn't so sure and was keen to know more.

'I mean, we've been through much stickier periods – when I've been abroad a lot or working crazy hours,' Mark continued, 'but I've cut down a lot on the travelling – and I'm delegating more now I have a wider team.'

'I'm sure it's not what you think,' Saul said, because though he'd now quite like to doubt Alice, he liked Mark and felt he didn't deserve this angst, however unfounded.

'Do I turn a blind eye?' Mark said, asking himself more than Saul. 'Even if evidence to the contrary is staring me in the face?'

'You know what,' said Saul, 'it's far easier to flirt in emails and texts than face to face. Maybe it's some bloke at the printers or in distribution that Alice keeps sweet. I'm sure it's harmless.'

'How do I find out?'

Saul was stuck. 'I don't think you should go looking for answers unless you can ask the questions directly,' he said after much thought. 'Can you ask her to her face? Will her trust be undermined that you've been searching through her things?'

'I don't know,' Mark shook his head, 'I just don't know what to think or what to do.'

'Listen,' Saul said, 'it's not as if the messages said "great fuck" or "thanks for showing me your boobs". There's no *real* evidence, Mark. You work with numbers, Alice works with words. I assure you our industry is full of boozing, flirting reprobates – and that's the blokes!'

'And my industry is full of strait-laced boring fucks like me,' Mark declared morosely.

If we were girls, Saul thought to himself, *we'd be giving each other a hug at this point. If this was Thea and Alice, they'd be holding hands, their heads together, physically backing up the emotional support.*

Suddenly, Saul thought how much he loved witnessing Thea and Alice's friendship, the intensity of their relationship even when they bickered or, as recently, fell out. Was this Paul B the reason why they fell out? Possibly. Saul thought of Thea's proud-held standards on fidelity and loyalty and what love meant and required. He felt hollow and desolate. He was going to lose her.

'I'd better go,' said Mark. 'Thanks for the drink – and the, you know.'

'Any time, mate, any time,' Saul said earnestly. 'How about one for the road?' He didn't want Mark to go. Mark's quandary was a distraction from his own predicament. Mark, however, declined. 'Listen – don't delve,' Saul advised. 'It won't get you anywhere but the wrong end of the stick.'

Mark nodded and left.

When he returns, Mark finds Alice and Thea snuggled up on the sofa, wineglasses drained and a monster-sized packet of Kettle Chips empty.

'Hullo!' Alice greets him with an expansive smile though Thea seems almost too exhausted to even look up.

'Hiya,' he says.

'Have you had a nice evening?' Alice asks. 'Were there some gloriously naff golfing trousers to buy?'

'Plenty,' Mark says, 'but none in my size.' Alice laughs. Mark analyses it and deduces it to be genuine. It makes him feel confused. 'I'm going to turn in,' he tells them because he wants to see if Alice's phone is still lying under his shirt just up the stairs.

'Thea's going to crash in the spare room tonight,' Alice calls after him.

His shirt is where he left it. Alice's phone is where he'd put it. Keeping an ear on the sounds of life downstairs, Mark takes the phone and scrolls to the envelope icon. He selects her Inbox again and rereads the messages. Perhaps Saul is right – there's nothing that unequivocally confirms anything has actually happened. He scrolls to Sent Items, his heart thudding so loudly it almost drowns out the sound of Alice and Thea chatting. His thumb hovers. This is not right. This is like sneaking a read of a diary. This is not the thing to do. But to Mark it seems like his only option. He has to. And he makes a pact with himself that he must deal with what he might find. He presses the Select button and Alice's sent messages flash up. Thea Thea Mark Thea Mark Thea Paul B Paul B Thea. He can't open them fast enough, his hands are shaking.

no Paul – not poss. pls, pls undstnd

Another.

cant – sorry. Ax ps: no more txts etc PLEASE

He scrolls back to Paul's messages and from the times and dates of these he can equate Alice's answers. He asked to see her. She said she can't. She's asked him not to contact her – even by text. She's adamant – see, PLEASE is in upper case. There are five from him but only two from her. He was the instigator. Both her replies are rejections. There is no reply to his fancy-a-fuck message, no response to his compliments of her breasts.

She hasn't dignified his advances with replies!

Mark is so relieved he could almost cry. And once he's read Paul's messages and Alice's a final time, he feels desperately guilty.

What was I thinking? How could I! I'm married to the most beautiful woman on earth – of course men will be falling in love with her, left, right and centre. Of course they're going to try it on. But see – she's my wife, her home and her heart are with me. I can't believe I pillaged her privacy. I can't believe I doubted her. What was I thinking?

* * *

Saul has sent Thea a text message to say he's been at some golf thing in Islington and he might as well take a bit of a detour and just pop by for five minutes. He is desperate to see her, even if it all comes out. He misses her terribly and is so anguished by the pain she must be feeling that he needs to hold her despite being the unwitting perpetrator. He must be capable of making things better, he must be able to make amends – surely? He wants to hold her even if she hits him. He's willing to proclaim the purity of his love for her even if she hurls hatred back at him and finishes the relationship there and then.

But he's walking down her street, checking his phone and she still hasn't responded. She must be back from Alice's by now. She must have loads to do. He so wants to see her. He rings the bell, knocks and then uses his set of keys to enter. He's always done so. Thea's always been at ease with it. Always welcomed him with a kiss, chatter and the flick of the kettle button. But she's not here. He can't even see the kettle. Just boxes and crates and piles of belongings. It's crowded and messy but it's stark and impersonal. Thea really isn't here. She's packed her life up. She's moving on.

Cold Feet

What do we want most? Alice to be punished though she's already walking with conviction along the road to her marriage's salvation? Shall we have Mark remain content, safely just beyond the reach of hard facts? Do we want Saul to suffer – to atone, to learn, but be damned? Do we think that Thea might be able to put it into some perspective of sorts, better still could she put it into a box labelled The Past and discard it? Is it possible that she could accept, understand, forgive and move forward positively into their long-planned and potentially sparkling joint future? Or are we rooting for Thea to deliver the ultimate scathing soliloquy as she dumps him? Do we want her to destroy him? Do we feel Saul deserves that? Do we want to see Saul foundering in the gutter, weeping and broken, while Thea waltzes away triumphant but with dignity? What is appropriate comeuppance for Saul – and what reward would be appropriate for Thea? Should Saul be allowed to confront Alice and declare a pot-kettle-black situation? Is it deluded to hope for happy-ever-afters all round? Is it right that Alice could get away with it? Are we ready to consider that Saul and Thea might need to have futures without one another?

Thea has already phoned the Being Well to see if her nine- or ten-o'clock slots have been filled since last night. Souki confirms they're still empty.

'I'll be in later, then,' says Thea. 'I have things to finish.'

She's already phoned Saul to say the words he's been dreading but anticipating.

'Saul? It's me. Are you back now? From Glasgow? Good. Are you busy? Oh. But I need to see you. We need to talk.'

She phoned from the bus as it approached Tufnell Park. Saul estimates she'll arrive in twenty minutes. He paces his flat, he's choked. The wait is unbearable though he dreads her arrival. What will you do, Saul?

She's the love of my life.

Will you fight for her?

I wish I could.

Why don't you?

No. I can't. She knows. Don't you see? She knows but she doesn't know that I know that she knows.

Do you not believe you can somehow get round that?

If she ever knows that I know that she knows, her self-respect will be compromised. The subject will be open for discussion and dissection and what good would that do? No amount of debate can repair us or soothe her. So I've decided it would be best if she never knows that I know that she knows.

So that's it? You'll let her end the best two and a half years of your life? Strike out that match made in heaven? Are you sure you're not just being a coward – justifying what can be seen as an avoidance of confrontation?

You don't understand. I know that girl. I know that her trust in me has gone. I don't want to be only half loved. And I know she won't settle for half her dream.

Here she is, Saul. Can you hear her coming up the stairs?

Please use your keys. Please let this still be your home.

The doorbell rings out. Reluctant but resigned, Saul goes to answer it.

'Hiya,' he says, his heart rejoicing at the very sight of her, despite the thud of imminent futility throbbing in his head.

'Hullo,' Thea says. She doesn't want to look at him. It's too painful. He was her dream come true but she was plunged into a nightmare and it's time to make sure she's wide awake. She stands awkwardly, as if she has an infernal itch at the back of her knee, a stiff neck, slight paralysis of the face. It makes Saul feel discomfited but impotent: if he makes it easier for her she'll know he knows she knows and yet he's convinced that ultimately that will be worse for her. Though Saul would be pleased to fall on his sword right now to save her the agony of what she needs to do, he can't help her. The balance of her future, the ease of her upturn, is what matters to him most.

'Babe,' he says quietly, hoping he's managed to etch a look of concern over the expression of dread he's keen to conceal. 'What's up?'

Thea shakes her head and regards her toes. 'I can't,' she croaks, 'I have cold feet.'

Should I ask her why? I would, wouldn't I – if I didn't know that she knows.

'Why?' Saul whispers, taking her hand. 'I can warm them

up – your cold feet.' Thea keeps staring at her toes, peeping prettily through sandals. She's been incapable of planning what to say. 'Thea, please,' Saul pleads, 'don't.'

Fuck it. I don't care now what she finds out. I just need to keep her. I must. She has to keep me.

'Saul,' Thea whispers, 'something's not right.' She glances up at him and looks away. 'It's better this way – before things get messy with mortgages and stuff. It's just not right.' The silence that ensues is so loaded it's deafening and time stands still, choked by the fog of neither person knowing what to do or say next.

'You know, Thea – nothing you can do could make me love you less?' Saul declares, gripping her arms to pull her close. 'Do you want some space? Some time out? Take what you need, sweetie. Anything. And I promise you I'll back off – but I'm telling you, I won't stop loving you.' He steps towards her and gently touches her chin.

Tell me it never happened, Saul. Tell me I'm mistaken. Promise me you've been faithful to me. Promise me you're an ordinary, good boy. Say it out loud and I'll believe you because I believe you'd never lie to me so if I ask you, you'll tell me the truth.

But Thea knows what the truth is so she encircles his wrists to keep him at bay – it would be too easy to melt into his arms and then too difficult to extract herself again. 'I'm not as tolerant as you,' she explains. 'I can't love you unconditionally.'

'Have I ever given you reason to doubt the sanctity and totality of my love for you?' Saul asks her hoarsely. 'Have I ever given you *direct* reason?' Saul emphasizes. He needs to be pedantic and semantic because otherwise he knows she can say to herself yes yes yes you have you whoremonger.

Let her go, Saul.

'Saul, please,' Thea starts to cry.

Please Saul, let her go.

'I don't love you enough,' Thea sobs, 'I don't love you in the way you love me. I don't love you enough to allow you your entire personality.'

Saul, you have to let her go.

'Will you change your mind?' Saul asks. 'Ever?' He pulls Thea towards him and she yields into his embrace. He is not going to let her go. 'Please, Thea. Just take time out – as much as you need. I'll wait. You can't let Us go.' She buries her face in his chest and he kisses the top of her head. He's always loved kissing the top of her head. He's always marvelled at the way they fit. Snug. They're just right. They're just so right. But it's all gone horribly wrong. 'I'll wait,' Saul repeats.

'Don't!' Thea cries.

'You come to love not by finding a perfect person but by seeing an imperfect person perfectly,' Saul proclaims. Thea raises a tear-stained face to him. 'It's a quote,' he admits with a humble grin, 'I found on the Internet.'

How very Saul, Thea thinks.

Once upon a time it would have made me love you even more.

'I can't go through with this,' Thea says, 'I can't.'

'Please, please don't do this, Thea,' Saul begs. 'Whatever has happened, I can fix. Whatever's happened, we can get through.'

Thea shakes her head.

'Talk to me,' Saul implores. He's ready for anything. He's fighting for his life. 'Thea, think about it – your flat sale, all that stress. You sell in three days' time. We're days from exchanging. You can draw a line under whatever it is. Let's just go for it. Start our life.'

'I don't want to live there,' Thea says. Looking alarmed, as if she'd forgotten all about the place of their dreams being at their fingertips.

'OK,' Saul says, 'it doesn't matter. We'll let it go. We'll buy somewhere else. It doesn't matter where. We just have to stay together. Don't let Us go.'

'Let me go,' Thea pleads sorrowfully, imploring him, seeing eye to eye. He looks six years old, with his blotched cheeks, twitching lips and eyes springing with tears. The last time she saw Saul cry was at Juliette Stonehill's baby blessing. He looked so happy then, when he was crying. He looks devastated just now. Really wrecked. Thea shakes her head. And Saul shakes his.

WHAT CAN I DO?

You can let me go.

Saul lets her slip from his hands. He has to. He has no choice. He has no control over this decision.

* * *

Tomorrow, Thea will move in with Alice and Mark for a fortnight or so until the nice rented flat in a mansion block in Highgate Village found by Peter Glass becomes available. Yesterday, she walked away from Saul. Tonight, she is sitting in the middle of her landing, appreciating a final moment or two of Lewis Carroll Living. Actually, there's no room to sit in the living room anyway, it's piled high with packing boxes. Sitting there, on the landing, with the doors closed in a teasing whirl around her, she spies a bent nail lying on the floor. She looks up at the wall and deduces that this nail is the one that held up her framed autographed photograph of David Bowie. She picks up the nail and fiddles with it absent-mindedly, her mind ricocheting from one monumental issue to the next yet unable to alight constructively on any. It's too strange to think philosophically that her flat is sold, it's no longer her home, bye-bye. It's too soon to consider she'll need to tick the 'single' box when filling in forms. It's too raw to realize she has no soulmate called Saul, no soulmate full stop, no more soulmate. It's not possible to think straight at all, really.

Time for bed. It's late and tomorrow will be tiring and trying. But she wants just to sit here a while longer. It's nice and quiet – and anyway, every decision she makes – even to stand from sitting – necessitates untold energy.

The pain weighs heavy. Crying hurts. The pain underscores everything she does. It's the punctuation mark at the end of every thought. It catches in her throat and alters the timbre of her voice. It stumbles her walk and has decimated her posture. It prevents her digesting her food. It inhibits her hearing the loving support of Alice, of Sally, of Souki, though she attempts to listen. It is the bed of nails on which she tries but fails to sleep. It hurts, it hurts. It hurts all the time.

Thea looks at the nail, bent and discarded. With a calm, considered intake of breath, she scores along her roping scar with the nail. She doesn't need to puncture deep enough to draw blood; a simple, long, sharp scratch through the sensitive and fragile keloid surface is sufficient agony. The immediacy and the shock and the uncompromising reality of pure physical pain somehow provides instant respite from the agonizing twist of emotional anguish.

Avon Calling

Thea regarded her two holdalls which contained everything she'd possibly need for the moment. She now thought she probably could have been far more ruthless when packing up her flat. The local charity shops hadn't done very well by her at all yet the storage company was making a fortune out of her. Each bag was heavy, yet when lifted one in each hand, the weight evened out and dispersed a little. There was a sense of symmetry, a feeling of balance. Anyway, she wasn't walking far, just downstairs to the waiting taxi.

Thea had said goodbye to her flat so many times over the last few weeks that when the time came she found it quite easy to simply lock up and leave. There was just time for a backward glance and surreptitious little wave as the cab headed off. Thea had two sets of keys in her hand, one to be relinquished at the local estate agent for the new owner of the Little Bit of Lewis Carroll Living, the other set to let her into her temporary home with the Sinclairs in Hampstead.

'Love, I'm going to have to put the meter back on in a minute,' the taxi driver cautioned as Thea sat still and continued to stare at Alice's house. Suddenly, she was feeling peculiarly light-headed and refreshingly unburdened. Her belongings were in storage, she was rid of her mortgage and had been given time off work on compassionate grounds with the Being Well's blessing. There wasn't much to do at all really. Apart from watch daytime television on Alice's vast plasma until she came home from work. Or, God forbid, mope.

'Actually,' Thea said, as a thought seeded itself, 'drive on, please.'

'You pay for this journey first, young lady,' the cabbie retorted gruffly, 'and then I'll drive you wherever you want.'

'Fine,' said Thea, refusing to round the fare up to the nearest pound, let alone add on a tip.

'You women,' the cabbie muttered with intentional audibility, 'you can never make your bleeding minds up.'

'Oh yes I can,' Thea muttered back, certain that she didn't

want to watch daytime television and definite that she didn't want to mope. 'Drive on.' She texted Alice to tell her of her change of plan and then she switched her phone off before Alice could call her to workshop it.

'Are you going somewhere nice for the weekend, dear? They say the weather is to be very good. I'm going to stay with my son for a week – see my grandchildren.'

Thea turned from gazing out of the train window to regard a neat elderly lady, who must have boarded the train at Reading, sitting opposite her and keen to make conversation. Thea accepted a digestive biscuit and settled herself in for light chat about this and that as Great Western rail continued to carry her away.

'I'm going to see my mum,' she told the lady. 'I haven't seen her since Christmas, it's a surprise visit.'

Gloria Luckmore didn't much like surprises. She liked arrangements and she liked them well in advance. She liked to be able to balance the kitchen calendar with her pocket diary and she did not like having to cross things out. Gloria did not like mess. She would always pencil something in, in the first instance, then carefully rub it out and rewrite it in black ink once it had been confirmed. She considered impromptu to be the bane of modern living. She deemed the concept of popping in or just dropping by to be insulting – something a person decided to do at the last moment because they had nothing better to do. Despite her stringent parameters for socializing, Gloria Luckmore's calendar and pocket diary were actually extensively crocheted in black ink. However, she never organized anything for six p.m. She had a permanent arrangement with herself for that slot – the meticulous ritual of a gin and tonic sipped listening to the Radio 4 news whilst looking out of the sitting-room French doors to the garden. Thus, she felt sheer indignation that her doorbell should compete with the Greenwich Mean Time pips. Defiant, she sipped her drink and listened hard to the headlines, blocking out another round of ringing. What Gloria loved about Radio 4 was the dignified pace of announcement which bestowed equal dramatic impact to each news headline. Nothing could possibly be so important as to interrupt it. Whoever wanted her at her front door would jolly well have to wait. She sipped and listened and ignored the rapping of her letter-box.

'Mum?'

The voice drifted through the hallway and suddenly filled the living room, interrupting the radio voices and rendering Gloria's G & T temporarily undrinkable.

'Thea?'

Gloria went to her front door, slightly alarmed. She didn't need to consult her calendar or her diary. She knew her timetable by heart and a visit by Thea hadn't even been suggested, let alone arranged. Why was her daughter outside at six p.m. without warning, request or invitation?

'Hullo, Mum.'

With two large holdalls.

'I was going to ring but –'

And significant weight loss.

'I need somewhere –'

And a dullness to her eyes, dark shadows surrounding them, alluding to much crying and little sleep.

'I broke up with Saul.'

'Come in.'

'My flat was sold today.'

'Come on in.'

'I've been given time off work.'

'In, darling, in.'

It wasn't as if Thea had nowhere to go – Alice and Mark had been looking forward to laying their home and their friendship at her disposal for the couple of weeks before the rented flat was available. It wasn't as if Thea had bolted back to her childhood home to snuggle down in her old bedroom, to be surrounded by furling posters of David Bowie left in situ over the years, shelves brimming with the friendly familiar faces of dusty soft toys, dressing-table drawers revealing a treasure trove of forgotten trinkets, boxes under the bed containing teenage diaries and years of letters. Thea had never actually lived in this house – her mother had moved here from London once Thea had left home for university. So it wasn't the reassurance of nostalgia that Thea craved. It wasn't even as if Gloria was her enduring confidante – as fond of each other as mother and daughter were, they were actually pretty self-sufficient and private. However, as Thea unpacked in the small spare room, she felt pleased to be there. It was nice to look at the old framed photographs – when she still had a pony-tail, her brother long before he grew his terrible beard. This wasn't running away, this wasn't hiding in the past, this was instigating some space from London, putting necessary distance in time and miles between what was and what soon would be. This was a prudent thing to do. However long she decided to stay, Wiltshire would provide a sensible hiatus. A breather between the chapters of her life.

'Now darling, my day is chock-a-block,' Gloria said apologetically the next morning over a breakfast of triangles of toast queuing politely in a toast-rack and leaf tea brewed correctly in a china teapot. With a twitch of the lip and a light hum, Gloria consulted her pocket diary as if to see whether she could possibly slot her daughter in somewhere between her ladies' guild meeting at quarter to eleven, lunch with Sandra Langley at twelve o'clock and her voluntary work at the Leonard Cheshire home from two till four.

'I'm fine, Mum,' Thea assured her, 'I just need a bit of a rest. I'm fine pottering around by myself.'

'Go for a nice walk,' Gloria suggested. 'I'll be back at four fifteen. I'm playing cards this evening but I don't need to leave until quarter to seven.'

'I'll go for a nice walk,' Thea confirmed, really quite relieved that time would be her own, that she need answer to no one but herself, that it wasn't her mother's style to ask questions in the first place anyway. Gloria's concern was registered as an anxious glance at her daughter. They smiled at each other quickly and then Gloria was on her way.

The village of Wootton Bourne, positioned on the Wiltshire–Avon border, resembled a ribcage: the remaining buildings of the original three-hundred-year-old hamlet forming a spine, the newer buildings branching off in a hug of ribs to either side. The village green, bisected by the main street, was the lungs, the duck pond the heart, the war memorial the sternum, the bourne a small stream like an artery or vein (depending on which direction of approach) running along one side then under the road and out of, or into, the village. The lifeblood flowed from the inhabitants' love of their village and keen sense of duty to its appearance. The communal verges were now, in June, on the cusp of their floral magnificence. There was no village pub, no shop at Wootton Bourne. There was one post-box with a daily collection – a bright red rectangle flush against Mr Kington's wall. Wootton St Mark, the sister village only a stroll away but over the bypass and consequently rarely walked to, had a picturesque church, a pub and a small shop.

Other than residents, no one really needed or much wanted to travel through Wootton Bourne. It had no brown leisure signs heralding it, and maps showed no pub, no shop, no pottery, nothing. Thus, with scant traffic, there was no need for pavement or even footpath. The tarmac simply petered out into the lovingly maintained verges and the villagers were pretty much left alone. The precious pace of life they attained was deeply valued and painstakingly protected and Wootton Bourne had the air of a private manor.

Whatever their age or style, all the buildings were constructed from Bath stone: the detached eighteenth- and nineteenth-century cottages, the one small run of terraced housing sitting impishly like Victorian children on a grassy bank, the Georgian farmhouse, the Edwardian school house, the sixties squat boxes, the modernist barn conversion. Initially, Thea had been disappointed that, in a county of postcard perfect cottages and in a village of classic and varied vernacular architecture, Gloria had bought herself a modern house, set along a lower rib of the village. Actually, though, it suited her needs perfectly and the mellow tones and subtle hues of the masonry gave a tangible softness and pleasing warmth to an otherwise plain design. The rectangular garden was flanked on three sides by easily maintainable borders, on the fourth by a square of patio accessed from the sitting-room French windows. Gloria could tinker with her perennials and evergreens without stressing her back and it didn't take much effort to manage a pleasing display perfect for gazing at while having one's G & T at six each evening.

Everyone knew everyone in Wootton Bourne but no one had the slightest desire to know anyone else's business. There wasn't a village busybody, there was no grapevine, no gossip-mongering, no rival cliques. If there was a local cad or village trollop or resident bankrupt or community bisexual, it was of no interest. This wasn't village life as most city dwellers imagined it according to the standards misleadingly set by *The Archers* or *Heartbeat* or *Balamory* or *Midsomer Murders*, this was village life precisely as the inhabitants of Wootton Bourne wanted it. It was refreshingly, fundamentally, dull. It was the environment Thea needed and, as she meandered around the lanes until peckish for lunch, she congratulated herself on her sensible decision to stay awhile.

After Thea's initial doorstep revelations, nothing more had been said on the subjects and Gloria wasn't quite sure how to go about counselling her daughter who was so guarded. Gloria's schedule, the routes of Thea's daily walk, what to eat morning, noon and evening and the occasional shopping list was ample discussion.

'I've been wondering, darling – where's your car?'

'Back in Crouch End.'

'Is it running all right? Why did you decide not to drive?'

'It's fine. I didn't drive because I didn't know I was going to come here until I was sitting in a cab outside Alice's. And I hadn't taken my car there because it's Residents' Parking or two-hour limits in Pay and Display.'

'Fancy having to pay for the privilege of parking outside your own house.'

'Ridiculous, isn't it, 20p for five minutes.'

'Good God. Well, you can drive my little Micra if you like.'

'Thanks, Mum. Would you like me to pop into Chippenham to pick up a few things for supper?'

'Yes, darling, why don't you do that.'

It was only speaking to Alice a couple of days into her stay that Thea realized just what a tonic a dose of this particular village was just then. Alice of course wanted to know how Thea was, what she'd been thinking about, whether she'd heard from Saul, how long she thought she'd stay, if she was feeling low or feeling any panic or anger or regret.

'We're running an article in *Lush*, you see,' Alice said, 'called "*Five Minutes to the No Entry Sign*". It makes a lot of sense – when you're suffering a trauma, as you are, you should allow yourself five minutes twice a day to thoroughly immerse yourself in all manner of related angst but then you have to envisage a No Entry sign over the subject at all times in between.'

The surprising thing was that during her first few days, Thea had hardly touched upon thoughts of Saul. She'd been too preoccupied walking down this lane and over that field, appreciating that hedgerow or this brook, to navel gaze at her past or flinch from her future. She hadn't tripped at all. But she didn't want to workshop the fact with Alice, who would no doubt worry she was in denial and have another article to quote on the matter. So Thea murmured appreciatively but non-committally and reminded Alice it was her mother's phone and she ought to keep it short.

'But are you OK, Thea?' Alice pressed. 'Because I could always come and see you this weekend.'

'I'm fine, Alice,' Thea said.

'Well, just phone if you stumble, or text if you have a signal,' Alice implored her. 'Say hi to your ma.'

'Will do – she sends her regards. Love to Mark.'

'Bye, sweetie – I'll call again soon.'

'Thanks Alice, thanks.'

It wasn't that the novelty started to wear off, it was that as Wootton Bourne became more and more familiar, there were fewer new details to note and absorb which meant thoughts in abeyance now had the space to resurface. 'Look! Kestrel!' she would hear Saul announce at the split-second she spied the bird. And then she'd go off on a tangent wondering if there were any parakeets in Wiltshire because Saul had told her there were ten thousand in Richmond Park and a fair few on Hampstead Heath. And suddenly she'd profoundly mourn the fact that they'd never seen them on Hampstead Heath and they'd never made a trip to Richmond. And now they never would. And if she positioned her hand in a certain way whilst walking, she could conjure the feel of Saul's hand holding hers. And if she tucked the single duvet against her back, she could convince herself of Saul's presence as she drifted off to sleep. But such imagining had a precise and limited time constraint. The loneliness at admitting that actually you were walking all by yourself, or waking alone in a single bed, was extreme. Thea became frustrated that she should suddenly be craving so intensely the presence of the person she thought she never wanted to see again. It was bizarre to not know where he was or what he was doing at that precise moment but to know for a fact that they were living in tandem. Parallel lives for Saul and Thea? No happy ever after? That can't be right. No entwining? No two equals one? No. Two distinct bodies, two separate souls, two unconnected lives to be getting on with.

I miss you, Saul, Thea could admit out loud in the discreet privacy of a solitary beech clump, weeping into the shoulders of the trees. She knew it wasn't so much cathartic as dangerously isolating to choose to cry where no one could hear. She tried to think of Alice's No Entry signs as she walked vigorously along the Ridgeway by herself. It was comforting to be striding along this ancient right of way, negotiating its chalky furrows kidding herself with excessive interest in the country's ancient history. If she kept walking and watching and observing and humming she couldn't dwell on the fact that she and Saul had never walked the Ridgeway together. Yet she found herself positioning the fingers of her right hand in such a way as to clearly imagine Saul's fingers interwoven with hers. His voice so vivid. His presence so tangible. He's here. Next to me. Look, Saul – kestrel!

I'm alone.
I'm on my own.
I'm in the middle of nowhere.
I don't know where I'm going.
Oh Saul, oh Saul. What happened to us?

Gloria was concerned to see that, despite her daughter's hearty tramping of the surrounding countryside, Thea's complexion was palling visibly. Gloria could tell that it wasn't blisters or aching limbs which caused Thea to walk so slowly towards the house after four hours on the Ridgeway, it was the weight of angst that her daughter was shouldering. It pained her to realize that Thea was trying to conceal her torment; it shamed her to admit that by acting jolly and keeping conversation light herself meant she could veer away from saying but darling tell me what happened with Saul that you should look so fragile and have nowhere to live for a fortnight. The amiable chitter-chatter of fortnightly phone calls and thrice-yearly visits was the blueprint for their relationship and Gloria didn't want to jeopardize that. Even if she did probe, her daughter most probably wouldn't confide anyway.

'Are you all right, Thea? You look a little peaky.'

'It's probably just a cold or something.'

'Sit yourself down and I'll bring you a nice cup of tea. We've been invited to the Craig-Stewarts' tonight. Drinks and nibbles. I've said yes. Won't that be nice?'

'Lovely.' Thea continued to feel it her duty to keep her grief and confusion concealed until she had the house to herself and she could slump to the floor in her mother's spare room, hurl her forehead against her knees and cry her heart out.

The Craig-Stewarts' drinks and nibbles evenings were eagerly attended by their wide social circle. Nibbles was an understatement. Nibbles was a risibly modest term for the lavish finger buffet laid on. Their lovely manor house was on the periphery of the idyllic National Trust village of Lacock. The level of chatter in beautifully rounded vowels complemented perfectly the stately yet comfortable furnishings. The Craig-Stewarts themselves were gracious, effortless hosts bestowing genuine interest and generous cheer on all their guests. It wasn't that they wanted to put on an impressive spread, they simply wanted their house to be populated with their friends, and the sumptuous food and flowing drinks were far more a symbol of their gratitude than a mark of their prosperity.

Thea fixed a smile to her face and tried to make it seem that her non-existent appetite was being sated by a single filo tartlet. Every time Mrs Craig-Stewart wafted past, Thea would busily nibble and sip and grin. She wished she hadn't come. These lovely, kind, happy souls. She was the youngest there by at least twenty years. *When I grow up, I want to be Mrs Craig-Stewart.* To be surrounded by such gaiety, such exemplary domesticity, the furnishings of such a happy and long marriage, were discordant to someone with a heart as lacerated as Thea's. She tried not to be spoken to, taking great interest instead in the affable assembly of benevolent ancestors whose portraits lined the walls, and the framed photos of flatcoat retrievers, springer spaniels and good horses convening on the occasional tables, mantelpieces and window sills.

'She was a poppet, was our Maisie, an absolute poppet,' Mrs Craig-Stewart was saying, suddenly at Thea's side and gazing tearily at a photo of a dog. 'Now Chip here, he was a thug! Huge character but what a yob! Do you like dogs? And horses? Let me show you something, let me show you the photograph of Max and Poppy.' Politely, Thea allowed herself to be led by the elbow to another table of photographs, preparing herself to coo at a photo of two labs or thoroughbreds. Instead, she was shown the wedding photograph of Poppy Craig-Stewart. Last summer. Three years younger than Thea. Gazing adoringly at her brand new dashing husband. What a gorgeous dress. What a beautiful couple. What a wonderful day. What a perfect match. She wished she was Poppy Craig-Stewart. Though Thea genuinely wanted to congratulate Mrs Craig-Stewart and tell her how stunning her daughter looked, how handsome her son-in-law, she found herself gripping hold of her hostess and hollering out uncontrolled sobs.

'What am I going to do what am I going to do what am I going to do?' Thea wept. Momentarily, Mrs Craig-Stewart didn't know what she was going to do either.

'I'm going to find your mother, that's what I'm going to do,' she assured Thea soothingly, relaying the strategy to her husband by a subtly coded raised eyebrow.

'Thea, gracious,' said Gloria, just as alarmed by the spectacle as by her daughter's distress, 'goodness. Thea. Oh, dear me.'

'What am I going to do, Mum?' Thea hyperventilated.

'I'm going to take you home,' Gloria said decisively, glancing apologetically at the kind concern of her social set.

The fifteen-minute car journey allowed Thea's weeping to abate but left her so exhausted that she just about made it upstairs to bed unaided. When Gloria came in with a cup of hot chocolate, she found her daughter fast asleep. She drank the hot chocolate herself, feeling a touch guilty that she should be relieved not to have to counsel her daughter just then.

'Are you OK, darling?' Gloria asked over breakfast the next morning.

'Fine, thanks, Mum,' Thea replied.

'The fish-and-chip van goes to Wootton St Michael this evening,' Gloria announced, 'if you fancy it?'

'Maybe,' said Thea.

'Gosh, I must crack on – another chock-a-block day! See you later, darling. I'll be popping back mid-afternoon, then back for G & T by six.'

'Bye, Mum,' said Thea. When her mother left, Thea wondered if she had the energy to drag herself from kitchen table to sofa for a dose of inane morning television. It appeared she didn't. She'd just have to stay put and concentrate on finding tessellations in the rattan table mats instead.

Gloria tootled along the lanes making a large effort to praise out loud the beauty of the day and the glorious landscape. Off she went to the library, to pick up and then deliver books ordered by the ancient but still formidable Mrs Frederick. That done, she headed to her friend Elizabeth's for morning coffee.

'Is your daughter all right?' Elizabeth asked. 'Poor duck.'

'Oh, she's fine this morning,' Gloria assured her. 'A good night's sleep.'

Next, Gloria headed to Margaret's. They were to have a long-planned meeting about the hanging-basket design for the summer fair at the school where they were governors. She needed to collect Sylvia en route and fill up with petrol. Gloria was motoring along, humming to Classic FM, when she found herself pulling abruptly into a lay-by. It wasn't actually a lay-by at all, it was the pitted sweep before the rutted entrance to a farmer's gate. But it served the purpose for Gloria to swerve and stall her car while her mind racketed and Beethoven's *Pastoral* soared out. She didn't have to think long about what to do. She started her car and hared off the opposite way, without a backward glance in the direction of Sylvia's house, without a second thought for arrangements made and committed in black ink.

'Thea?' Gloria says, shutting the front door quietly. 'Darling?'

Her daughter is still sitting at the kitchen table, pronging a fork into the spaces of the rattan table mat.

'Thea?' Gloria sits down and shuffles her chair close to her daughter. 'Darling?'

She places her hand on her daughter's and just as Thea absent-mindedly wonders how many seconds it now takes for an age-revealing pinch of skin to flatten on the back of her mother's hand, she finds that tears are falling without warning.

'Oh, poor darling,' Gloria whispers, 'you poor old thing.'

'What am I going to do?' Thea croaks.

'I don't know,' Gloria admits because she doesn't know what's been going on anyway.

'Love isn't meant to go wrong,' Thea objects, 'not when it's true love.'

Gloria sighs. 'That's what one would think,' she says, 'but believe me, however good we think we are at being in love, the rules are not of our making and are thus beyond our control.'

'He was unfaithful to me,' Thea whispers. 'Saul.'

Gloria was immediately indignant that history should be repeating itself. 'Oh, Thea, he left you for another woman? When you were on the point of setting up home together? That's beastly. Beastly.'

'No!' Thea objects. 'I've left him. I don't want him now.'

Gloria paused. 'But does he want you?'

Thea hasn't been asked that question before. She nods and shrugs.

'But do you still love him?'

Again, Thea shrugs but finds she can neither shake her head nor nod.

'But darling,' Gloria objects as if this is all a regrettable storm in a teacup, 'forgive him, have him back and forget it. For heaven's sake. Life's too short. Love's too precious. Goodness.'

'No!' Thea protests.

'But he hasn't left you for someone else,' Gloria states, 'and he still loves you and wants to be with you!'

'You don't understand,' Thea counters.

'Oh, yes, I do, my darling,' Gloria says in a hollow voice. 'Your father left me. He no longer loved me. He fell in love with someone else and nothing I could do could win him back. It was irrelevant how much love I still held for him – it was actually worth nothing. He didn't fool around and regret it, he wholeheartedly bestowed his love on another woman.'

'Are you saying that's worse than Saul fucking women behind my back?' Thea bites back from adding 'and he pays for it' because she deems that far more offensive than having uttered 'fucking' out loud in front of her mother. The truth is that Thea feels deep shame at Saul's transgression. Alice can be the only person she'll ever tell – and even then, she's left some details undisclosed. Why couldn't Saul just have had a simple affair? Such a crime was far more normal, far easier to deal with, surely?

Her mother, it appears, vehemently disagrees. 'I am saying precisely that. Men can do that whole physical sex thing – you have to realize that. *You* are still loved,' she declares in an uncompromising tone, warning Thea not to controvert the luck and fortune and love she was denied. 'Goodness, it wasn't so long ago that women knew to allow their menfolk visits to prostitutes!' Thea looks up sharply. Gloria brushes at the air dismissively. 'In France, those French men all have mistresses. And I really needn't comment on our Royal Family. Think about those colourful tribes in Africa – or those Mormen in America – they all have umpteen wives. Under the same roof!'

Suddenly, Thea loves her mother and her logical pluralization of Mormon. And she really doesn't want to tell her all of it. Not just because she's ashamed of the raw truth; she also does not want to distress her mother unduly. If Gloria didn't need to know, then Thea didn't need to say it all out loud again.

'Darling,' Gloria butts in, 'if Saul was a stupid man but begs your forgiveness and lays his love, his apology, his commitment at your feet, please don't stamp on him or, worse, step over him. If what he did has absolutely no bearing on how he feels about you, I implore you to be philosophical about it all. It's such a waste otherwise.'

'But I can't forget,' Thea says.

'You can, with time – it's worth it,' Gloria insists. 'Do you not realize that you can't make someone love you? Do you not appreciate, therefore, how you are truly blessed? I loved your father but he didn't love me. It's far harder for me to cope with the knowledge that his heart, his soul, his intrinsic emotional pull, was to a woman other than me. How I wish he'd just had lots of silly sex elsewhere but come home to me with his emotional loyalty intact. Instead, the man I assumed I'd spend the rest of my life with, the father of my children, left me because he fell out of love with me and in love with someone else.'

'But my trust is gone,' Thea says, 'and so is my dream.'

'Well, if there's one person who can help you find them again,' Gloria says empathically, 'it's the man who loves you. You should not compromise your future happiness because of some sanctimonious adherence to unrealistic expectations of Romantic Love,' Gloria all but chides. 'Crikey, you're so vehemently moralistic you're almost a prude, darling.'

'But you don't understand,' Thea pleads.

'Oh, but I do,' her mother claims impatiently, while taking a Biro and scribbling fractiously through the failed arrangements so clearly written on her calendar. 'It's *you* who doesn't understand. How I wish your father had merely done a Saul. I wouldn't have been on my own for almost twenty bloody years.'

Gloria wasn't sure about going away that weekend but the trip to Bournemouth had been planned for months. It was only for two nights and Thea had mentioned Alice might come to stay. So Gloria left her daughter in charge of the Micra and the hanging baskets and set off with Lorna and Marion.

Though Alice was half expecting Thea to call and cancel the arrangement, she was pleasantly surprised, as she stepped into a cab for Paddington station, that she hadn't heard from her. However, her phone rang as the taxi lurched along the speed bumps in Maida Vale. It was Thea. Christ. Give her the benefit of the doubt.

'Alice?'

'Are you going to blow me out, Miss Luckmore?'

'Yes.'

'Thea, I'm in the bloody cab! I bought first-class tickets.'

'I'll pay you back.'

'It's not the point, silly. Why are you cancelling? It's not good to spend so much time on your own being maudlin. You promised your mum – you promised me.'

'I – it's just. Actually, if you want to know, I've phoned Saul. Alice? Hullo? Why? Because I need to see him. So he's coming.'

'Thea, hang on – excuse me, can you stop the cab please – Thea? Talk to me. What are you going to do? When did this all come about? Are you sure?'

'No, I'm not sure. But I need to see him.'

'Look, you phone me, OK? If it all goes pear-shaped. First-class rail tickets have no restrictions.'

'OK. I'm sorry, Alice, for being so flaky. I'm sorry about the taxi. It just suddenly seemed the right thing to do.'

'Don't worry about it,' Alice said, wondering if she should take the train anyway, hide around the corner in case she was needed.

Saul couldn't focus on anything; not his newspaper, the view from the window, his fellow passengers, his revolting coffee nor the myriad thoughts thundering around his head. It seemed adrenalin had replaced blood in his veins and it surged through his body causing him to feel unnervingly light-headed and hollow. All moisture was being rapidly perspired leaving him dehydrated and nauseous but too agitated to drink. He hadn't known where she was, this last week or so. He'd stopped texting. He'd relinquished hope and taken his flat off the market. When a call came through that morning showing a provincial number, he'd assumed it to be a freelancer.

'Saul Mundy speaking.'

'It's Thea.'

'Thea? Christ!'

'Saul, might we talk? Could you come to Avon?'

'Avon?'

'I've been at my mum's.'

'Your mum's?'

'She's away for the weekend.'

A weekend with Thea?

*

Saul wasn't sure whether he felt optimistic and excited, or apprehensive and pessimistic. He'd already been dumped so she could hardly be summonsing him to dump him again. Though he felt that it had to be positive that she was asking to see him, he didn't dare take it as given. He packed slowly, aiming for an early-evening train, to avoid the aggravation of rushing, the hassles of rush hour, the frustration of a full-price ticket. Perhaps she'd had enough space and thinking time to come to terms with everything. It might not be too late to resuscitate the purchase of the apartment. Justifying it as a purely practical measure, Saul packed the estate agent's particulars just before he left. He was looking forward to seeing Thea, just to look at her, to be with her; whatever the outcome.

When he reached Paddington and found himself a seat on the seven-fifteen train, he couldn't stop his heart from speeding up, though his head warned him to slow down. However, the further the train took him from London, the more apprehensive he became; stabs of caution and surges of pessimism mingling acidly with the adrenalin. Just let her talk. Just don't let her go a second time. Don't tell her you know she knows. Just head for the future and bypass the past. Powers of persuasion, the power of love. What on earth would he feel when he saw her? What would she say? What could he say? What was she expecting him to say?

When it came to it and they met outside Chippenham station, Saul could not take his eyes off Thea and Thea couldn't look at him at all. It was as if he wanted to soak up all the glorious details he'd been denied recently yet she could only flinch away from the personification of heartache that was staring her in the face. On the drive back to her mother's house, Saul didn't know whether to take Thea's lead and speak when spoken to, whether to fill the silences with ingenuous chatter, or try to thaw the situation with a pre-emptive outright declaration of love. However, it appeared not possible to be simply himself in such an unexpected, portentous situation. He found himself wittering at length about minutiae of articles he'd written and articles he'd read. He sounded like a bore and in spite of his jolly countenance, he felt depressed. He didn't know Avon. He'd only visited Thea's mother a couple of times. He could sense Fate lurking just out of view. From Thea's lack of expression, Saul had no idea whether his future was about to be blessed or cursed. It wasn't in his hands, that was for sure. He felt nervous – it was an emotion he was not familiar with.

'I've put you in here,' Thea said politely, showing him the spare room; guest towels folded neatly on the edge of the bed.

'Thanks,' he said. 'I'll just sort my stuff out then.'

'Would you like some supper?'

'It's a bit late,' Saul said. 'I haven't an appetite anyway.'

'A cup of tea?'

'Sure.' What was this? A B&B?

They drank their tea and avoided eye contact. They watched the ten o'clock news and didn't comment. They took undue interest in the weather forecast.

'Thea—'

'Saul, I'm tired. Let's just get some sleep tonight.'

'Sure. I understand.'

'Have you everything you need?'

What a fantastically loaded question but Saul knew Thea was too tired and wary for him to comment. 'I'm fine,' he said, 'see you in the morning. Sweet dreams, hey.' They went to their separate beds and slept fitfully. The tangibility of their physical proximity was exasperating – how easy would it be to creep from one room to the other, from solitariness to togetherness? How tragic that, currently, the chasm between them meant that such a passage was impassable.

'How did you sleep?' Thea asked, feeling a little shy of Saul the next morning.

'Not well,' Saul admitted wearily, half tempted to cut straight to the point and prevent this ambivalence being prolonged. He wasn't good at waiting, at feeling nervous, at not having control.

'Shall we go for a walk, then?' Thea said. 'We can go along the Ridgeway.'

'Sure,' said Saul, 'whatever.'

Thea wanted Saul to take the initiative and hold her hand. But today he seemed more distant, somewhat guarded, so she contrived to bump into him once or twice, to have her arm brush his accidentally-on-purpose, to position her hand enticingly close. Though Saul of course wanted to hold Thea's hand, he'd rather it wasn't snatched away so it seemed safer not to in the first place. It was down to Thea but she couldn't quite do it either.

'Hear that?' Saul asked, suddenly animated.

'What?'

'Listen – there. That *mew! mew!* Plaintive calling. Where is it? There, Thea – look! Buzzard.' With Saul's arm outstretched over her shoulder and alongside her cheek to provide a direct angle of view, Thea saw the buzzard circling, now so close that the calligraphy of dark markings and fawny dapples on the underside of its wings were clearly visible. Are there any buzzards on Hampstead Heath, Saul, any in Richmond Park – is this our only chance to see one? Unable to resist, Thea gently cocked her head so she could rest her cheek against Saul's arm as she observed the bird. She could sense him gazing at her. If she didn't know what she knew, if she hadn't seen what she'd seen, this would all feel so perfect. Just then, she found she could pretend that it was; she found she could forget what had been. Lightly, Saul kissed her temple and she turned towards him, sinking fast into his enveloping embrace. She clung to him, her eyes closed, her face pressed into his chest. If she didn't pull away now, she knew she would never be able to. She needed to try to pull away without actually pushing him away. When she did, she saw the buzzard perched on a fence stake amazingly close. Look, Saul, look.

'*My heart in hiding/ Stirred for a bird*,' he said to her, '*the achieve of, the mastery of the thing!*'

'Don't tell me – you dug it off the Internet?' Thea found she could tease him.

'Gerard Manley Hopkins,' Saul objected. 'Funny what you remember from A-level English.'

They walked on, in awkward silence. Thea quietly engrossed in trying to recall quotes from her English A level. Saul wondering whether he was correctly reading her signals to hold her hand. He tried it. Initially, she didn't resist.

'Let's go to the Polly Tea Rooms in Marlborough,' Thea announced, now finding an itch on her shoulder which required both her hands, 'though it may be full of tourists.'

'We'll put on our best American accents then,' Saul said, taking her hand again as they walked back to the car.

When they arrived in Marlborough, they did just that. They passed the infernal wait for a table by saying things like 'Gee, honey, I sure am hungry' and 'How damn cute is this li'l ol' town?' Thea only just managed to keep giggles at bay. Saul was bolstered. It simultaneously heartened but alarmed Thea how easily, how quickly, she could merge back into the familiar and effortless dynamic with this man.

How Saul wanted to rush back to the house and take Thea to bed. He wasn't particularly horny – the oversized scones and gluts of clotted cream hampered that – rather he was flooded by a desire to display the veracity of his love through quiet intimacy. He just wanted to lie with her, allow his touch and his gaze to say it all. However, Thea's hands were beyond reach, fixed as they were at ten-to-two on her mother's steering wheel. Thea in the driving seat. Thea stalling. Thea putting the brakes on. It was only when they arrived back at Wootton Bourne that Saul realized that actually, he held the key.

'I think I'll just tidy up, do some hoovering.'

'The house is immaculate, Thea.'

'I must water Mum's hanging baskets.'

'Not in direct sunlight – you'll scorch the plants.'

'Well, in that case, I think I'll just have a quiet hour or so with the papers until the sun goes in.'

'No, Thea, talk to me. Talk.'

Thea frowned and flinched and shook her head. She felt trapped. Tidy. Hoover. Water the garden. Read the papers. Quiet hour. Be quiet. She glanced at Saul, who was holding his hand out to her. She spun from him.

'Thea – we can't let this go. It's too good – we must be able to find a way.' Saul was standing close behind her. 'Our lives were sorted – our future was all mapped out. It was brilliant.'

'It was the best thing that ever happened to me,' Thea said hoarsely.

'Well, don't let it go!' Saul exclaimed gently, as if to a simpleton.

'Easy for you to say!' Thea balked, rushing through the French windows into her mother's garden. Saul followed her. 'Fuck off and leave me alone, can't you!' she hissed.

'Excuse me, but it was you who invited me here,' Saul corrected. 'Why was that, Thea? Why summons me?' She couldn't answer and she didn't want to say I don't know. 'We can work through this,' Saul said, 'we must be able to. We were the strongest couple I know – we were the envy of so many. We had everything.'

'I loved you enough to spend the rest of my life with you,'

Thea said sadly, 'and now I face a precarious time on my own. At the age of thirty-bloody-three. When I should be feeling settled and calm.' She took a petulant kick at her mother's Impatiens.

'For Christ's sake, Thea,' Saul said, 'you're answering all your questions and doubts. That's precisely what we are, that's precisely why we should try and sort it – we're now at an age where we don't have the luxury of our twenties, of all that over-wrought drama and game playing and emotional self-indulgence. Perhaps there isn't time to split up. Long, drawn-out conflicts are a waste of time. It's all semantics. Let's get on with life. Let's get through this. Let's sort it out. Let's get on with growing up and growing old.'

'I don't want to get old with you,' Thea stamped.

'Why not?' Saul asked. 'Why not, Thea? What have I done?'

His words hung in the air like laundry on a line. He'd asked her outright, he'd put himself on the line. He was hanging his dirty washing out in the open – possibly for her to tear down and hurl back at him. He was laying himself bare. It's your chance, Thea. Insult him, blame him, shame him, curse him, listen to him, forgive him.

'I never doubted it. I never doubted you,' she said flatly, 'but now I do and that's the end of the story. That's the close of our fairy tale. We didn't live happily ever after. The End. Deal with it.'

'You sound horrible,' Saul frowned.

'*You're* the horrible one,' Thea shouted and she bolted through the house and out.

Traversing the ribs of Wootton Bourne, Thea initially stomped fast, muttering insults under her breath. Soon, her pace slowed and she reflected on what had been said. Saul was completely right. They were a brilliant couple, they were at an age where such a sound union should be valued, snapped up and for ever treasured. But she knew too that she wasn't hastily throwing it out like the tantrum she'd just had. Over the last few weeks, through Kiki, through Richard Stonehill, through Alice, through the rawness of her own desolation, through a naked need to face fact, Thea had gradually accepted that Saul's particular take on what was morally acceptable grossly conflicted with her own deeply revered ethics. She was satisfied that she'd come to terms with her own limitations as well as those she perceived to be Saul's. Ultimately, it was not so much the fact that she knew what Saul was capable of; it was that she finally knew what she was incapable of. Unconditional love.

I can't do it. I'm not that generous, that liberated, that laid back. I used to feel that being in love was enough, but now I know that it isn't. There actually needs to be more to love than love itself.

She knew unequivocally what she believed in and what she needed and she was adamant that, for her, moral compatibility was a fundamental requirement.

She looked behind her. There was no one there. She realized she'd been expecting him to follow. Had he packed up and left? Without them getting to the heart of the matter? She returned at a brisk pace.

'Everything changed,' Thea explains, coming in to find Saul sitting exhausted on the stairs. 'It wasn't right. I couldn't do it.'

'Then why the fuck drag me up from London?' Saul sighs. 'It wasn't to go bird-watching on the Ridgeway.'

Thea fidgets and shrugs and tries to look at him and can't.

'Do you realize this is the first time *ever* that you and I have actually had a full-blown fight?' Saul says. 'That's why all of this is so stupid.'

'I'm sorry, Saul,' Thea whispers, 'it's not you, it's me.'

'I know, Thea,' Saul announces in a hollow voice. He lets it hang. He could be simply acknowledging that yes he knows it's her, not him. But then he turns it into a noose by which he may well hang himself. 'I mean, I *know*, Thea, I know that you know.' He nods to himself. Thea's eyes flick over to his and are caught, like a startled doe in car headlights. 'I know that you know,' Saul says quietly, hating it that Thea looks so appalled, so terrified. 'I know that you saw me. All right?'

It is Saul's final bid. He is standing tall, his honesty a sword which, depending on Thea's reaction, he will either fall upon or brandish like Excalibur. Saul watches as she slowly hauls her gaze away from the middle distance, where it's been fixed for loaded minutes, back to him. He must meet it, he tells himself; he mustn't flinch from it.

When Thea finally looks at him, he is winded by the hurt and trauma which striate her face. When Thea finally looks at him, all she sees is Saul. Good old Saul. The same Saul. Her old Saul. And then she alights on the greatest, most tragic irony – that looking into the heart of undeniable truth really does mean that all hope is lost.

It is simply Saul himself standing before her. The unmistakable reality is out. She'd have to love him for who he is. But the reality is, she knows she can't. It's asking too much. It's demanding too substantial a compromise.

'I'm sorry, babe, I'm sorry. It must have half killed you,' Saul says, visibly racked by his awareness of her pain. 'It meant nothing – please, please believe me. It's just the stupid boy-bit in me.'

'I don't want a stupid boy,' Thea says quietly, 'I want a nice man.'

'I am a nice man,' Saul says with conviction.

'Nice men do not do that.'

Saul sighs. 'Look, we could discuss the psychology behind this – and the facts and statistics that clearly define just what nice men do,' he says evenly, 'but I don't think that's the point. The only point is if you feel there's an inkling of hope we can make our relationship work in the face of this. If I swear it won't happen again – and with or without you, I doubt it will – would you believe me? Can you trust me? Could you remember how you used to love me? Should we try going to Relate or some other counselling?'

'I don't want to *workshop* the fact that you pay for sex!' Thea protests in a whisper. 'I'm not prepared to hear your gory details just so you can assuage your guilt!'

'Thea, I know you're hurting,' Saul tells her, 'I know I caused it but I know I can be the antidote.'

'No, Saul – you can't,' Thea's voice fragments, 'as much as you'd like to be – and I'm sure your self-belief is honest and good in intent – but you can't make me feel better because you made me feel this wretched in the first place.'

'I didn't mean to,' Saul says firmly.

'Well, directly or indirectly you have,' Thea says levelly.

'But I love you, Thea,' Saul says. 'Surely such roots form a basis for survival, for growth?'

'Saul,' Thea says, 'that's what *you* want. You love me. You want us to work through this. You want to make me feel better, feel safe with you. You want us to live happily ever after. But I'm not that strong a person to forgive and forget. And I'm not like you – my morals are different.'

'That's where therapy might come in,' Saul suggests.

'Oh, shut up about sodding therapy,' Thea says. 'You read

too many magazines. My heart is broken, my dreams are smashed, my trust is decimated and my hope is shattered. It's going to take more than an agony aunt or psycho-babble Superglue to fix it.'

'I devote my life to building you up again,' Saul declares.

'But Saul,' says Thea, though she knows it may well be the last word on the matter, the last thing she says to him, 'I don't love you enough to let you.' They stare at each other in horror. 'I'm sorry – the weakness is mine,' Thea admits, 'my love is not unconditional. I don't love you as much as you love me. We are not compatible. I'm a girl who's always believed in knights in shining armour, in fairy tales, in good old-fashioned fidelity, in swans mating for life, in lovey-dovey monogamy. *Amor Vincit Omnia*.' Thea paused. 'But I've come to see that actually love doesn't conquer all,' she says, 'not for me. Not now.'

They slump over each other in the hallway of Gloria Luckmore's pristine house, Saul and Thea. Like two boxers in the fifteenth round, bruised and bloodied, exhausted brains addled with the battering of their first, last, fight. Nobody won, both lost. They look a mess, they really do. You flinch from the sight of them. But given time, the scars will heal and gradually fade. Ask Thea about that.

Friends

'It's weird,' Alice remarked, handing Thea her olive stone because she couldn't see where else to put it, 'I know you don't own this place – but actually, it's much more *you* than your old flat.'

'It's funny,' Thea agreed, delicately spitting an olive stone into her hand, alongside Alice's, 'but I'd have to agree. I thought I'd miss the Gothick quirkiness; I thought I needed my little slice of Lewis Carroll Living; I thought I'd find the ordered layout here boring; but over the last couple of months I've actually grown to love it – it's bright but quiet. I like having the long hallway and the feeling of flow, a sense of space. There might be a flat two floors above coming up for sale – the same size as this but positioned on the other side – with an even better view.'

'Would you buy it?' Alice asked, popping another olive into her mouth and racing ahead with a thought that she and Mark could assist Thea financially.

'Maybe, if I can afford it,' Thea said, knowing she probably could because Mark and Alice would happily help.

'I'd buy you an olive bowl as a house-warming present!' Alice said, tipping another two stones into Thea's hand.

'Hold on, let me grab a saucer from the kitchen,' Thea said.

Alice followed her. 'Come for dinner on Saturday night!'

Thea wiped her herby, oily hands on her jeans and raised an eyebrow. 'Oh God, you're not going to try and set me up, are you?'

'I'm thinking of having all my hair chopped off,' said Alice, making a glaring attempt to change the subject.

'It's too soon, Alice,' Thea said quietly.

'I've been growing it for four years!' Alice objected.

'I'm not talking about your hair,' said Thea.

'I know,' Alice replied with quiet insistence, 'but perhaps I'm allowed to be your judge, Thea. It was ages ago – back in the spring. Now it's practically autumn.'

'It's not even September for another two days!' Thea objected. 'Next you'll be telling me you've been married for five years.'

'Well, I have, in a manner of speaking,' Alice retorted, having a grin at her own expense. 'It'll be three years this year, so I can indeed say the year after next I'll have been married five years.'

'Look, please,' Thea said, opening bread sticks and a tub of houmous, 'I just don't feel ready. And I don't want to analyse it any more. I'm not living in the past. I'm not mourning. I'm fine, now. I just don't fancy having to decide whether I fancy someone or not just yet. I'm not in the mood.'

'It's only Mark's cousin anyway,' Alice said. 'Harmless. Practically family.'

'The American one?' Thea asked.

'Yes,' said Alice, 'one of them.'

'Not the one at your wedding who then emailed me, by

which time I was already with Saul?'

'No, a different cousin. Mark has about sixty-seven of them.' Alice paused. 'Have you heard from him, from Saul?' After weeks when Saul had been Thea's only topic of conversation, there had followed the more recent weeks when his name hadn't been mentioned.

'No,' said Thea evenly, 'no.'

'When did you take off your ring?'

'After the last phone call. Four or five weeks ago.'

'What have you done with it?'

'I've put it in my odds-and-sods drawer.'

'Odd sod indeed.'

They munched on vine leaves thoughtfully. 'You'll be proud of me,' Thea said. 'I even bought the *Observer* today for the first time in ages and found I could skim through Barefaced Bloke's column with no need to read between the lines.'

'He still freelances for *Adam*,' Alice admitted, 'but I don't speak to him directly and I haven't seen him. He sends me his work as simple attachments.'

'A simple attachment was the pinnacle of my hopes and dreams,' Thea said, a sad glaze to her eyes suddenly dulling the ease of their afternoon. 'It's still bloody scary, Alice.'

'I know,' said Alice, giving Thea's leg a comforting squeeze, 'but someone or other said we don't have dreams unless we have the power to fulfil them.'

'Someone else said love is a grave mental illness,' Thea rejoined, 'Plato, I think.'

'Yes, but while you're waiting for the right man to come along, you can have plenty of fun with the wrong ones,' Alice said, 'according to Cher.'

'I'm not entirely sure that Cher and Plato equate on the philosophy stakes,' Thea remarked, 'and I'm not waiting for Mr Anyone, anyway.'

'Well, Woody Allen is arguably the Plato of our age and he says that love may well be the answer but sex raises some good questions while you're waiting for the answer.'

'Alice!' Thea chastised. 'Stop it with the American rent-a-quote, would you? I'm *not* looking for love and I'm *not* in need of sex and I'm not questioning anything – I'm just getting on with things.'

'So just come eat with us Saturday, huh?' said Alice. 'A girl's gotta eat.'

'Why are you talking in an American accent?'

'I don't know.'

'You have to promise me you're not match-making,' Thea warned her.

'Cross my heart, hope to die, bla bla,' said Alice, thinking a little white lie never hurt anyone. 'Come on, I'll help you clear the lunch stuff away. Then I'd better go and help Mark pack. Poor bloke having to fly to Hong Kong on August bank holiday. Oh well, at least he's only going for three nights this time.'

Thea awoke in the small hours with a start. She sat bolt upright in bed with her heart racing at the sense and suddenness of the idea that had woken her. She glanced at the clock. It was just gone four in the morning. She dressed. She rummaged in her odds-and-sods drawer and then she left her flat and drove to Hampstead. She sat outside Alice's house for a while, wondering how best to wake her. She wanted her P.I.C. but she needed her in good humour, not grumpy and shocked. If Thea rang the doorbell, or called her by phone, Alice might panic that something had happened to Mark who was currently en route to Hong Kong. For an hour she sat in her car, fingering the nap of the dark blue velvet box. She sent Alice a text.

r u awake? txxxxxxxx

No reply. She sent another.

r u awake for a chat? Txxxxxxxxx

No response. She sent another.

r u awake? am in my car outside your house . . . txxxxx

Thea saw the curtains at Alice's bedroom window ripple. Then she saw one side flung back as bed-headed Alice peered out. Thea leapt from her car and waved. The curtains closed. Thea made her way to Alice's front door.

'Thea, it's fucking six o'clock!' Alice bleared. 'What's going on?'

'It's my ring,' Thea told her. 'I know what to do with it and I want to do it right now. With you. Get dressed.'

'Don't be stupid – I'm going back to bed. You go and shape your idea in the living room and I'll see you in a couple of hours. It's a bank bloody holiday – I don't have to get up at all.'

'No, Alice – no!' Thea said. '*Now*. Get dressed. It won't take long. You can have a lie-in later.'

'Oh, bloody hell,' Alice said, padding away stroppily to do as she was told.

*

Thea and Alice drive to Primrose Hill. It's deserted apart from a couple of insomniac dog-owners, or perhaps it's the dogs, taking each other for a walk.

'I can't believe you're making me do this,' Alice says though actually, now she's dressed and in the fresh air, she's alert and feeling quite affable.

At the top of Primrose Hill, in the dawn of August bank holiday Monday, Thea and Alice take a seat on one of the benches with a view. Alice gazes at the ghostly panorama of London. The design of the rubbish bins on Primrose Hill echo the shape of Canary Wharf. Everything seems a little unreal, distorted.

Thea opens the small, navy velvet box. She removes the ring and lays it in the palm of her hand, offering it to Alice to inspect. Alice takes it and looks it over thoroughly, reads the Yeats inscription silently. She puts it back in Thea's outstretched hand.

'I didn't want to throw it away,' Thea says quietly, seemingly to the ring itself, 'because I don't want to rubbish what I had with Saul. I didn't want to bury it because that seems negative – vindictive, almost. But I don't want to keep it. I need to do the right thing by it. I just want to let it go – just let it all go.'

Thea stands and then, with a competent throw, launches the ring as high as she can. She turns away. She doesn't need to see where it lands, she's pleased that she's released it to a place, a time, sacred to when she and Saul were very very happy. Now she's spread their dreams under other people's feet. She hopes they'll tread softly. She faces Alice who has tears in her eyes.

'Ready?' Alice asks, linking arms with her.

'Yup,' says Thea, leading the way.

'The thing is, I do really want to love again,' Thea said a little later over a Starbucks latte and supposedly healthy muffin despite its monstrous proportions. 'I'm very good at it. But I don't want to *just yet* – do you see? I have to have faith in my own time frame. I've done the mourning and the grieving and the anger and the desolation. I had that frightening but thankfully brief period of denouncing all men as bastards and condemning love as ridiculous. Now I'm back on an even keel but I don't want to force my passage through.'

'I understand,' Alice assured her, 'I do, truly. I know I tease you for being soppy but actually I've always admired your tenacious pursuit of romance.' She dunked her croissant into her cappuccino. 'Though I have always warned you against setting fairy-tale standards for matters of love and eternity.'

'It's weird – because I've actually taken a leaf out of your book,' Thea confessed. 'I used to think that falling head over heels in love was the benchmark. But it wasn't head over heels, it was heart over head and actually, I like your idea that you should use your head so as not to lose your heart.'

'Love and marriage, or longevity, or whatever you want to call it, do go hand in hand,' Alice assured her, 'but perhaps it takes a certain type of love to succeed.'

'I'm not going out there armed with fixed criteria on what makes a Potentially Good Husband-Type!' Thea objected.

'I'm not saying you should,' Alice stressed, 'but don't hold it against a nice chap if you don't necessarily feel that elusive tingle of yours on day one.'

'I know. I agree. But I still think a shared belief in fidelity, in the value of companionship, the notion of pairing for life, is a good starting point.'

'Yes, but so is acknowledging practical issues,' Alice said, 'careers, money, long- and short-term goals. Respecting each other's lives independent of the union.'

'I do still love the idea of being in love,' Thea said.

'You wouldn't be you if you didn't,' Alice assured her warmly, 'but be prepared now for knights in shining armour to come in many guises,' she added knowingly. 'Some of them aren't conventionally dashing – they don't suddenly sweep you off your feet and whisk you away on a gallant white charger. I should know. Believe me.'

'You mean he might be wearing a suit and driving a nice Lexus,' Thea said, 'like Mark.'

'I do,' Alice agreed wholeheartedly.

'I guess you've always thought that there are rules for love,' Thea mused, 'while I've simply believed that love just rules OK.' The Starbucks in Belsize Park was starting to fill up but such is the quality of that branch's milk froth, Alice and Thea were still lingering over their first cups of coffee and had no intention of relinquishing their seats. 'Oh Alice, bloody hell – of all our years, hasn't this one been the maddest for both of us?' Thea proclaimed wistfully.

Alice cast her gaze out the window and nodded. Mad was

only one word for the year they'd had. She still wasn't sure it was plain madness that drove her to Paul. In retrospect she acknowledged that the affair itself was madness but perhaps what drove her was insecurity. Or her sex drive. Or her own unrealistic expectations of love and marriage due to impracticable emphasis on sex and lust.

'How are *you*?' Thea asked her quietly, having skim-read her thoughts. 'Have you heard from That Paul?'

'No, I haven't,' Alice answered truthfully. 'It's so weird how I went from deifying him like he was Love God Number One to being really quite irritated by him. I was so impressed by his visible masculinity, I was so swept away by the physical roller-coaster thrill, it was bizarre to discover so suddenly that I didn't really like him all that much. In fact, he got on my nerves.' She was just about to denounce his taste in trainers and mock his inability to navigate the London Underground system when she stopped. It shocked her to remember she never told Thea about Paul's impromptu final trip, though she'd spent her lifetime telling Thea everything; the mundane to the outrageous all in the most intimate detail. Yes, Thea was going through the vortex of suffering back then, but also Alice had known all along what she was doing was wrong and she was ashamed. She hadn't wanted to talk about it. She was doomed to have it as her guilty, gut-twist secret.

'You look a bit sad,' Thea said, 'a little distracted.'

'If I had an itch after two and a half years of marriage, what'll I feel like after seven?' Alice admitted sheepishly. 'Say I meet another Paul-type at some point,' she said, 'and I'm lured into another crazy shag fest.'

'But *you* did the luring, Alice, didn't you? If you're honest.'

'I did,' Alice confessed, 'but in a perverse way, that's the point and that's what unnerves me. Though I admit it was crazy and dangerous, it was fun too. Initially. I suppose I'd tucked that side of me – the flirt, the sexy minx – out of sight while I busied myself setting up home being a married woman. It's like the two can't coexist. But actually, it's a side of me that makes me sparkle. And that's what scares me. I must keep a lid on it for the sake of my marriage, but doesn't keeping it in check also sacrifice a little part of me? I don't know if that's a good thing.'

'I think it is a difficult thing – but I don't think it's a bad thing. Look on it as being abstemious and, by definition, as being good for the soul,' Thea said. 'You and Mark are such a *team* – more so now than ever I've known. If you hadn't challenged it when you did – and with thankfully no fallout – perhaps you wouldn't be as content as you are now. I'd hope that Brad Pitt himself could accost you and you'd turn him down without a glance or falter. I suppose you'll have to train yourself not to let the thought cross your mind; train yourself to find the inclination unappetizing.'

'I feel it's really insulting to Mark to say this,' Alice confided, 'but I can admit to you that the thought I'll never again have that rampant, urgent, animal sex makes me feel low. Isn't it wrong to cauterize one's passions? I *love* that sense of being ravished, being someone's fantasy incarnate, being fucked within an inch of my life.' Alice shrugged. 'Pure sex without the encumbrance of love is the most massive turn-on.'

She stopped abruptly. Simultaneously, she and Thea fell on the silent connection with Saul. Was it something to declare out loud? Was it something they could constructively discuss? No. It wasn't the same. Alice acknowledged how Mark didn't know about her fling into adultery whereas Thea knew way too much about Saul. And then Alice thought about how she and Mark had such a charmed life while Thea had been through hell. And the horrible knowledge that, if she'd been caught, Mark would have been as distraught as Thea. She wondered whether Thea ever wished she'd never come across Saul that ghastly day.

I suppose I'm wanting her to say yes, she wishes she hadn't. Ignorance being bliss, and all that. But actually, despite the anguish of it all – the loss, the trauma, the disbelief and the shock – I know Thea is relieved that she did. She's right to expect back the dedication and commitment she bestows. I was going to say 'you get what you pay for' but it seems a bit close to the bone though I suppose in some ways that is precisely what has happened to Saul. I suppose 'what you settle for is what you get' is more appropriate. And Thea shouldn't have settled for it. Nor should Mark have to either.

'I guess I have come to see it's not about getting away with it,' Alice declared, 'it's about not fucking it up in the first place.'

* * *

Saul was looking forward to seeing Ian. It had been quite some time since they'd descended on the Swallow for an evening of pints and sausages. Over recent months, Saul had generally eschewed offers of company and declined invitations to socialize, using deadlines as an accurate though not entire excuse. The only thinking time he wanted was that devoted to articles and columns – life without Thea was so sterile, he needed to fill it with creativity. Since Thea had left him, Saul had immersed himself in his work, diversifying on the way. In addition to his regular columns and freelance features, he took on work for other magazines and also landed himself a weekly slot on Robert Elms's radio show, bantering on London legends, scruffing down his accent to deliver all manner of anecdotes. Most gratifying was the publishing deal he'd landed to collate a charity anthology of men's magazines columnists.

It wasn't that work was fantastically stimulating, Saul just needed as much of it as possible to fill his time. As chuffed as he was about his radio slot, as proud as he was about the book deal, the satisfaction was tempered by having no Thea to share it with. No excited girlfriend jumping up and down, hugging him with congratulatory delight. Ian's interest, Richard's praise and his parents' pride didn't really amount to much in comparison. So Saul took on more commissions and touted for even more work to try and slake the void. If he didn't have time to notice he was on his own, he wouldn't have the time to feel lonely. So, when Ian phoned him on the off chance he was free that night, Saul didn't hesitate to suggest the Swallow.

'How about *Not the Top Shelf*?' Saul tried another possible title for the book.

'It would probably put off half the readers you're trying to attract,' said Ian.

'True,' said Saul, 'perhaps a shout-line like we'd use on a mag – something like *What a Bloke Wants*.'

'That sounds more like an article in *Cosmo*,' Ian said. 'Another pint?'

'Thanks.'

'I ordered food,' Ian announced when returning with two pints. He regarded his increased girth forlornly. 'Not that I need it. Call me Fat Bastard.'

'How about *Five-Bellies Ashford*,' Saul teased.

'It's being married, mate,' Ian rued with a not unhappy sigh. 'My wife is such a good cook it would be rude to refuse and she takes it personally if I leave a scrap.'

Saul laughed. 'How is Karen? When is the baby due? And shouldn't it be Karen eating for two, not you?'

'I'm eating for three, mate,' Ian bemoaned. 'She's either feeling sick or else she has indigestion – she tells everyone "Ian's certainly pulling his overweight in this pregnancy". She's funny, my wife. And God, pregnancy suits her. Her hormones have gone haywire – to my advantage, if you get my meaning!'

'When's the baby due?' Saul repeated. It was strange but since splitting with Thea he'd developed an interest in all topics nuptial or domestic. After squash with Richard, he really liked to hear about Sally, about Juliette, about the trials of sleepless nights, the stress of teething, the nightmare of flying with a baby, the all-consuming exhaustion of it all. It was affirming, not depressing, to hear of such things. For Saul, it was far more constructive than going on the rebound. Case histories of those he knew enabled him to hold on to his faith and believe that love could work.

'Valentine's Day, would you believe it – blimey, four months today exactly,' Ian was saying. 'How are things with you?'

'Busy,' said Saul.

'Seeing anyone?'

'Christ, no,' said Saul.

'What – just lots of no-strings sex, then?'

'Hardly,' said Saul, 'I'm so busy with work.'

'Have you – can I ask about Thea?' Ian asked. He'd be informing Karen that Saul looked wan, thinner, but he didn't think he'd make a point of it to Saul.

'We don't really speak now,' Saul told him, 'at her instigation.'

Ian contemplated his pint. 'It's a shame,' he said, 'I liked her. We all did.'

'You're not the only one,' Saul said glumly, looking at his pint and not fancying another sip. However, as a matter of habit, he raised the glass to his lips to mirror Ian.

'Perhaps if you give her a little space,' Ian suggested, not really knowing what else to say but knowing it was the sort of advice Karen would dispense.

'It's not that simple, believe me. Even now, four months on, my head says let her go but my heart says fight for her,' Saul said. 'How's work?'

'Manic,' Ian said, hardly realizing they'd changed the subject, let alone left the previous one hanging. 'They've made me a partner.'

'Congratulations.' Saul chinked Ian's glass and they drank a toast. The beer tasted fine now. And the sausages looked mouth-watering.

'Look,' said Ian, having wolfed down his portion, 'just tell me to fuck off if I'm speaking out of line, but I don't know if you remember Karen's friend Jo?'

'Jo?' Saul said with no recognition.

'We were trying to set you up with her at much the same time as you and Thea got together. Brunette. Quite busty. Attractive. Bubbly.'

'Vaguely,' Saul said. 'Has Karen got you match-making?'

'Not just Karen,' Ian said cautiously, 'we both reckon the two of you might have a laugh together. Nothing heavy – just some company. Sex, if you're lucky!'

Saul drained his pint. 'Maybe,' he said. 'I'm not in the mood, really, if I'm honest with you. Perhaps in a little while. I don't know. But not just now.'

'My round, mate,' said Ian, rising to go to the bar. 'Same again?'

* * *

It was the first time in a couple of months that Saul thrashed Richard with ease at squash. Richard was pleased to lose in such dramatic style, it could only mean that his friend's spirit was restored.

'Time for a swift half or five?' Saul asked.

'I'll just phone Sal,' said Richard.

'So, how's the family?' Saul asked, thinking there were few things as pleasurable as a long, thirst-quenching drink of lager when one had so earned it. He and Richard drank down half their pints in affable silence.

'Really well,' Richard replied with a friendly burp under his breath. 'Juliette is just adorable – I reckon she'll be walking by her first birthday.'

'How's Sally?' Saul asked.

'She's talking about going back to work part-time,' Richard said. 'She loves teaching – and I love it when she teaches because I don't bear the brunt of her bossiness.'

'I don't think of her as bossy,' Saul mused, 'not on the Alice Sinclair Scale of Bossiness.'

'She comes a close second, does Sal, I assure you,' Richard

said, finishing his drink and heading to the bar to buy the next round. 'How's it going with you?' he asked Saul on his return. 'How's the book coming along?'

'Good, great,' said Saul, 'though I'm struggling for a title.'

'How about *Between the Sheets*?' Richard suggested.

'Bloody hell,' said Saul, 'that's not bad at all. Christ! Cheers! I'd got as far as *Do You Like My Column*?'

'Sounds gay to me,' said Richard.

'You're right,' Saul acquiesced.

'Is it all work and no play?' Richard asked. Saul shrugged. 'Makes for a dull boy,' Richard warned.

'Life *is* dull,' Saul admitted, 'unless I fill it with work. I spend my weekends writing articles on "The Whys and Wherefores of Wi-Fi" – and the like. Mind you, I'd rather do that than mope or get bladdered for the sake of it.'

'Do you hear from Thea?'

'No. Not now.'

'Do you miss her?'

'What do you think?'

'Sorry. I'm sorry. But what the fuck happened, mate?'

'Do you really want to know?' Saul regarded Richard levelly. 'I was seen. With my pants down. Literally.'

Richard was baffled. 'You were playing around?' It seemed inconceivable. 'On Thea?'

'No,' Saul declared, 'I wasn't. But I was paying around.'

Richard only gawped because suddenly he recalled that bizarre drive back to Thea's when she cross-examined him on the theories behind modern man and the oldest trade.

'You seem surprised,' Saul defined.

'I guess I am a little,' Richard admitted. It didn't seem right. It didn't seem right to tell Saul about his conversation with Thea. It didn't seem right at all.

'You don't?' Saul asked. 'Not your thing?'

'Nah,' Richard confirmed. 'Why pay for junk food when I have fillet steak at home?'

'Because sometimes you crave the plastic ease of a Big Mac,' Saul said, 'even if you end up questioning your purchase when it repeats on you, quite unpleasantly, afterwards.'

'I understand,' Richard shrugged, 'it's just never been my scene.'

'Thea would never, ever have understood,' Saul shrugged, 'and I can't blame her – she's a girl, I understand the impossibility of her getting her head around the theory. There was no chance. Her sense of betrayal was complete. She could never trust me again and I'd never be able to override the hurt and horror she feels.'

'And since?' Richard probed. 'Have you been bingeing on junk food?'

Saul laughed bitterly. 'Hardly. You could say I've become something of a health-food freak. I haven't been near a woman since.'

'Are you ready to?'

'I don't know – probably,' Saul theorized, 'but I can't muster much enthusiasm.'

'You should,' Richard encouraged. 'I mean, in between junk food and home-cooked dinner, a nice wholesome snack might do you good.'

Sally was in bed when Richard returned. She was sitting up, engrossed in a book about taming toddlers.

'Hullo!' she said, as if she was pleasantly surprised to see him.

'All quiet?' Richard asked.

Sally nodded. She put down her book and held out her arms. Richard went over to her. 'One day,' Sally said coyly, 'when you've played squash, *don't* have a shower – come home with your sweaty pheromones and ravish me.'

'Strange request,' Richard mused, 'but one which I'll be happy to grant.'

'How was Saul? What is his news? Did he say anything?'

'He's fine. He's cool. He's still working like an obsessive.' Richard paused. 'He didn't really have any news.'

'Did he say *anything*?' Sally pressed. 'You know – about Thea, or something?'

Richard thought for a moment and was careful to make it look as though he was racking his brains. 'No,' he concluded, 'he didn't. You know us blokes, Sal – we don't talk on that heart-baring level you girls do.'

'But he's all right, is he? Is he seeing anyone?' Sally asked.

'No,' said Richard, 'but I did ask.' He kissed her shoulder. He felt uncomfortable about being economical with the whole truth. It felt odd not to tell his wife everything. But changing the subject in his head helped, and the sight of her silken skin, the glimpse of nipple half revealed by the bed linen was irresistible.

'I'd love to have sex,' Sally said apologetically, 'but I'm

absolutely exhausted.' She snuggled close to Richard. 'Us mums seem to expend more energy at Tumble Tots than the tots.'

Richard liked hearing Sally refer to herself as a mum – as their marriage lengthened it had strengthened. He had so much more than he started with. He still had the cute girlfriend but he also had a beautiful wife, a great shag, a best friend and the mother of his child. Amazingly, they were the same woman.

'Night,' said Sally, half asleep already.

'Night, babe,' said Richard. He sat up in bed unable to read the new issue of *Adam* or the last chapter of the John Irving, both of which lay open on his lap. He had lied to Sally and he couldn't really lessen it by philosophizing whether he had truly *lied* or just pertinently withheld elements of the truth. Why exactly had he not revealed his discovery of the true reason for Thea and Saul's split? To protect Sally? Yes, partly. She'd be really quite shocked to learn that Saul did *that* – she'd be distressed on Thea's behalf and she'd take against Saul. Richard was immensely fond of Thea too and, thinking back to that conversation in the car, he shuddered at the level of torment that poor girl must have gone through. It occurred to Richard that Thea had not specifically divulged her discovery for a reason: she was keeping it secret precisely so that she didn't have to discuss it. He had to respect that. Finally, he thought of his mate, Saul. Poor bastard. God, how Richard sympathized. It may not be *his* thing – but he was actually at ease with the notion that for Saul, as for other men he knew, paying for sex was a mindless bit of recreation. For Saul, though, it had now destroyed the dreams he'd so cherished, and Richard felt for him. Maybe the main reason why Richard hadn't told Sally was respect for Saul. After all, Saul had confided in him. And actually, Richard held fidelity to a friend to have equal gravitas, commensurate inviolability, to that with which he honoured his wife. Funny thing, fidelity.

* * *

'Can I do something sneaky?' Alice asked Mark in a beguiling voice, phoning him from her office on a late November afternoon.

'Oh God, what have you done?' Mark said, hoping Alice hadn't done something so sneaky as to take too long to divulge. He had a meeting starting in five minutes and through the clear logo on the frosted-glass door of his office, he could see his secretary to-ing and fro-ing with plates of biscuits and jugs of tea and coffee.

'Nothing yet,' Alice remonstrated, 'but I was thinking about booking a table for six on Saturday night,' she told him.

'Saturday night?' Mark questioned.

'Yes,' said Alice, 'I thought I'd phone Janine and Laurence.'

'*Janine and Laurence*? But I thought you found them dull,' Mark protested, 'after they organized that murder-mystery dinner that went a bit wrong?'

'That's the point!' Alice revealed excitedly. 'I thought I'd invite them *and* Thea! But I've told Thea that *you* organized it and she has to come to give me moral support.'

'Darling, apart from the fact that you've given me the role of Big Bad Wolf, why on earth do you want to spend our third wedding anniversary forcing your best friend to socialize with a couple you don't much care for?' Mark despaired. 'Anyway, I have a reservation at Claridges, you daft girl – you're not going to have me cancel it, are you?'

'Yes, cancel Claridges,' Alice said, 'we can do Claridges next year. Because you see, I was thinking you could invite Joel too! Sneaky old me!'

'Alice Sinclair!' Mark exclaimed. 'Joel is only over for a brief visit – I have a feeling he flies out at the crack of dawn on Sunday.'

'Oh, he travels Business Class,' Alice brushed, 'he can always change his flight. Please phone him, pretty please?'

'But more to the point, darling,' Mark said, 'I thought you'd approached Thea about meeting Joel when he was last over and she'd rejected the idea.'

'That was ages ago,' Alice told him. 'She's my best friend. I know her. And I know this is good timing.'

Mark sighed with happy exasperation at his wife. 'I have to go, Alice – I have a meeting.'

'OK!' Alice chirped. 'I'll see you later. Do you think I'm the sneakiest minx in the world?'

'Yes,' said Mark, 'I bloody do. You're like a maverick Jane Austen busybody.'

'But you love me anyway! See you later, darling.'

Funny thing, friendship, Mark thought as he made his way to the boardroom. In the past he'd felt excluded from Alice and Thea's intimacy. He'd also been privately envious of their bond. He had many friends himself but none with whom the tenets of friendship ran so deep. Over recent months, however, he'd been touched by the unstinting support Alice offered Thea and he'd been moved at Alice's private distress for her friend. He decreed it the mark of a good person when dedication to the deeds of friendship was obviously so paramount. He knew that Alice saw him as her best friend too. She'd told him so one morning over the Sunday papers. He felt greatly honoured by such a role.

However, it transpired that Thea had already organized a weekend in Wootton Bourne with her mother. And Janine and Laurence couldn't make it anyway. And Mark never did phone his cousin Joel. So Mr and Mrs Sinclair celebrated their third wedding anniversary in style at Claridges. Just the two of them.

The simple lack of her is more to me than others' presence

Edward Thomas

I've been thinking about fidelity. I've been thinking about love. I've seen Ian and Karen's friend Jo a few times. We have a laugh, we have good sex, she's interesting and attractive. I have to admit that it's a relief, refreshing even, that she's so different to Thea. However, sometimes I feel like I'm cheating on Jo by missing Thea still. And, conversely, occasionally I feel I'm betraying Thea by enjoying my time with Jo.

I do miss her, my Thea, my ex. I love saying her name. I hate saying 'ex'. When I least expect it, I get winded by a sudden pang. When I heard Lynne's terrier Molly had died, I was grief-stricken because I was transported back to that disastrous second date with Thea. And then on to thoughts of her scar. I felt bereft. I thought, did I kiss that scar enough? And I couldn't quite remember if it snaked this way or that. Ultimately, Lynne ended up comforting me even though her dog had just died. If I'm carrying tension in my shoulders I have to tell Jo: no, left a bit, up a bit, over a bit, deeper if you can while I remember how Thea knew instinctively what to do. I gave my Armani jacket away. I buy *Heat* magazine every week.

But it's not that I harbour even the most silent of secret hopes that Thea and I will be together. I don't because we won't. I'm OK about that. I understand. I've come to terms with it. I now believe that the love of one's life may not necessarily be the person one ends up with. And we have to work bloody hard not to make that fact a tragedy. It's no reason to be maudlin or unprincipled, it's no excuse to reject or downplay the potential of future relationships. I have come to acknowledge that the intensity of the love I had with Thea – that perfect blend of companionship, desire, affection – has become a yardstick. It's something to aspire to because I know it exists – after all, for a blissful two and a half years I was lucky enough to come by it.

I know I won't ever feel for Jo the way I feel for Thea but I suppose that doesn't mean that we can't have an enjoyable relationship. I know intrinsically that the love I felt for Thea can never be equalled. But it's not something I should continue to mourn. It's not something to bury. It's something to revere. It's a legacy. Being in love with Thea Luckmore has made me a better, more complete person. The experience enhanced my life.

And do I still pay for sex? I haven't since I split from Thea. But, if I'm honest, that's not because I'm a reformed character who's learnt his lesson. That would imply conscious misbehaviour. For me, such purchases were a simple and non-invasive way of sating a peculiar yet common hunger. Read my column in last month's *Esquire* – 'Love and Sex – hands up who can do the one without the other?'. I suppose it is one of my life's great ironies – I may be a hard-working bloke but I'm a lazy wanker. Literally. I still don't consider it a crime or a sin or genuine adultery. To me, emotional infidelity is heinous – the ultimate betrayal – and I can never be accused of that. Christ, that one time years ago I came close to feeling it, I felt a moral obligation to finish with Emma immediately. That's why I feel uncomfortable about really liking Jo but still missing Thea. I don't fuck Jo and imagine I'm making love to Thea. I don't compare Jo unfavourably with her. I don't see Jo so that I don't have to think about Thea. It's just I do still miss

Thea, I really do. We were very much in love, we really were. It was beautiful. Perhaps I need to be patient. Perhaps next month I'll find that I think about Thea less than I do now.

Has Thea met someone? I don't know. I don't know how I'd feel about it – whether I'd want to punch the bastard or shake his hand and tell him to look after her. In fact, I can't actually think about her with another man. So I don't. I've decided not to and, being a bloke, I can do that. You should read my column in the *Observer* magazine this Sunday: 'Barefaced Bloke wonders whether his ability to compartmentalize is a skill or a weakness.'

Love is the triumph of imagination over intelligence

H. L. Mencken

I saw Kiki today. I mean, I saw her as a client – my client. Poor girl had ricked her ankle tripping on the kerb. Bloody Westminster council – I told her to write to them, I've told her I'll check the letter for her. Anyway, I didn't charge her for the treatment – I figured I owed her, minute for minute, for the time she gave me. She's a lovely woman. I don't feel sorry for her or sad, I don't feel threatened or repulsed, it's her career and she doesn't regard herself as a victim at all. I see now how my turning on her – and then turning to her – enabled me to let go of Saul. That day, she seemed to represent every prostitute in the world and I felt rage and hatred and fear. I really felt that, as a woman, she was letting us all down. Until I stopped and sat on her bed and let her hold my hand. Don't you see, as in all trade, the control is with the purchaser not the provider? The instinct is within the punter, it's not forced by the prostitute. Demand. Supply. It is absolutely not a case of chicken and egg. Man came first and Woman saw there was – quite literally – a hole in the market and, to put it crudely, a market for that hole.

Saul Mundy was the love of my life. I was deeply in love

with him and it was a glorious state to be in. I was so looking forward to running headlong, hand in hand, into our future. And then I found out. And I cannot begin to describe the untold shock. He wasn't who I thought he was. Worse still, he didn't see love the way I see love. How can you look forward in the same direction if you don't see eye to eye? I know all the theories that it's a bloke thing to be able to keep sex and love apart. I know all the facts about how many men use sex workers. I know that it needn't mean that their wives don't satisfy them, or they have secret perversions, or they're lonely. They do so simply because they can. And they can do so with fundamentally no ramifications on their home life.

But do you know what, there are many men who *don't* pay for sex and, actually, I'd like one of those. The control is with the purchaser, remember, not the provider. I know Saul wanted to provide me with more than all the love I could ever need but actually, I'd rather invest in someone else. Saul was my long-held dream, my fantasy incarnate, who swept me off my feet, who made my spirit soar and my heart fly free. Ultimately, I suppose it was me who didn't love him enough. I couldn't allow him his entire personality. I couldn't love him unconditionally. He was just being himself but I didn't like him enough to let him.

I'm so glad that I experienced the level of love I attained with Saul. It gave me proof it exists. And I'm glad that I mourned Saul so deeply – thoroughly enough to visit a brothel in my quest to confront my fear and understand him. I'm so relieved that my belief in love remains unsullied. Actually, my belief in love has strengthened because it's deepened. It's had to. True love needs to be more than a feeling, more than that rush of phenylsomething. I must have Alice tell me how to pronounce it once and for all. I can see now that the success of love is dependent on the sum of its parts; on the presence of friendship and affection, understanding and tolerance, moral compatibility and practical support. Essential elements in balance.

I wonder whether Mr Mencken meant it derogatorily, that love is the triumph of imagination over intelligence? Wasn't he the man who said marriage is a wonderful institution 'but who would want to live in an institution'? How awful to be so cynical and so decided against love. Did he not read *Sense and Sensibility*? Did he never soar with another person? What is life worth if you don't believe in happy-ever-after? Is that deluded – or is such hope positive and affirming? I have come to see that the course of love might be a tough climb and we have to accept that it might lead us to pastures new rather than the fields carpeting our previous dreams. Life might be easier if we lost our need to find love – but I feel for those who shun the fantasy. The earth can't move for those who don't believe that love makes the world go round.

Love is that condition in which the happiness of another person is essential to your own

Robert Heinlein

I like to believe that if we're good in life, if our thoughts are honourable, our goals worthy, our deeds and dealings principled, then happy-ever-after is our reward.

Would you just look at me and what I have. A beautiful wife, a career which is well paid and stimulating, a large circle of good friends, a stunning home. It is a charmed life I lead. I am the envy of many. I feel truly blessed.

Twenty years ago, we did 'The Miller's Tale' at school for our A-level Chaucer. I vividly remember thinking silly carpenter, let that beautiful spirited Alyson run free. Can't you see she will indeed cuckold you if you repress her spirit and try to cage her like that. Don't deny her that feistiness. If you corral that filly you'll destroy her spirit, and she'll just stand there, beautiful but broken. A façade. She'll hardly love you for it.

Did my wife have an affair? She may have done. If I'm honest with myself, I'd have to admit that I had reason to suspect so. But the point is I don't know for sure. What I do know is we are very happy now. We were going through a bad patch back then – as I expect all marriages do. We were distant – very literally, in my case, with all that travelling for work. She was stroppy and needy. I was too busy, too tired, too stressed to pay attention.

Was I turning a blind eye or was I just choosing wisely not to look? I admit I didn't try too hard to find out. Instead, I found it easier to look for evidence to the contrary. Because I'm an optimist. And what I do not know cannot hurt me. Where is the sense in panic when there is no real proof of transgression? I don't think that to hold on to an element of naivety is foolish; I think it's sometimes wise.

I love my wife and I admire her. Whatever she did or didn't do, she never made a fool out of me. She came through it all with her spirit intact and my love for her not damaged, her love for me rejuvenated. And she does love me. I know she does. She tells me often enough.

Love is often the fruit of marriage

J.-B. Molière

I laughed. I thought it was not just pretentious but also rather incongruous to see my local grocer using a quote by Molière to advertise exotic fruit baskets. But, as I walked back home with my ridiculously expensive Charentais melon and out-of-season cherries, I committed that Molière quote to memory and I refer to it often. It's become the blueprint for my marriage.

When I proposed to Mark, I suppose you could say I was on a reverse-rebound. God – that sounds like a shout line for an article in *Lush* – maybe I'll even suggest it at the meeting on Tuesday. What I mean is, rather than getting over my then-ex Bill by shagging around or serial dating to distraction, I grabbed the antithesis of every man I'd ever had because I realized I'd never found happiness with any of those men I'd fancied rotten. Call me self-centred and manipulative but I calculated that Mark would never leave me, never behave badly, that I'd never have to feel that gut-hurling insecurity again. So I decided that to marry him would be an excellent idea. I knew that he'd always held a torch for me. And it was precisely that. Mark was a beacon of light when I was stuck in a murky place. Deep down I know I was not actually 'in' love with him and for a long while I felt privately ashamed about that. Until I was at the grocer's and saw the Molière quote a couple of weeks ago. I can see now that I proposed to Mark because I knew that he was the one man I sensed I could love deeply.

Perhaps I was naive to think that love would flood me on our wedding night, or on our honeymoon, or on our first anniversary. For something to grow, roots are needed and for roots to establish, time, effort and care are needed. For a long time, I didn't bother to feed or water or protect it from storms and frost. I'm a lazy gardener, as Mark's mum Gail can attest. I now marvel at my fortune to have such a fine man as my husband. Mark Sinclair is kind and sensible and mannered and loving and principled and loyal and steadfast. He's my husband and my best friend and I'm a lucky girl. He is always consistent in his love for me. He allows me to be spirited, he tolerates all my temperamental, attention-seeking nonsense and when I say sorry he accepts without compromising his self-respect.

But I don't find him particularly sexy. For a horrible and dangerous period early in our marriage, I tried to equate not fancying Mark with being his fault. I thought if I didn't fancy Mark, how could I truly love him. And if I didn't fancy Mark, I blamed him for a core part of my personality he was failing to satisfy. So along came Paul in all his brawny glory and I thought that to succumb to pure physical attraction was my *right*. It wasn't. It was my greatest wrong.

Thank God Mark never found out because actually, I was treading a precarious tightrope by which I could so easily have hanged myself and, worse, Mark too. Thank God he never found out because I can't start to imagine his hurt. Thank God I saw that sex for the sake of it wasn't the answer.

I do sometimes miss that energizing sensation of animal magnetism. I do sometimes wonder if I'm OK with Mark not exhibiting wild desire for me. I do sometimes worry that if someone else did, would I be able to resist? Because I love being the centre of attention and I love the physical charge of sexual electricity. Will I crave it again? I don't know. The only thing I crave at the moment is Marmite on chocolate biscuits – but that's because I'm pregnant. Now I know what sex is all about – it's about making babies.

But say some swarthy, well-hung warrior came along, brandishing his lance and thrusting his dagger? Would I want to be swept off my feet? Actually, I feel confident that I'm stronger now and I have the weapons to fight it. I have the fortress that is my marriage. My home – my castle. My impending child – my future. My very perfect gentle knight – my husband. Stay inside, Mark, I'll pull up the drawbridge against intruders.

Christ, I sound like Thea.

Mr Alexander's Three O'Clock

Souki booked Mr Alexander in for a three o'clock with Thea. 'He's over on business,' she told her, 'and slept awkwardly on the plane. Apparently you were recommended by someone he knows.'

'Gabriel Sewell, probably,' Thea said. 'We seem to have a steady stream of clients connected with him.'

'Do you know, I always quite envied you Mr Sewell,' Souki laughed. 'I thought he was scrummy.'

'Well, if his back ever plays up again, I'll book him in with you for acupuncture,' Thea assured her. 'Good Lord! Peter Glass, you're *early*!'

'Hullo, babes,' Peter said, 'my neck is killing me. But I have to leave at two thirty – I'm about to do a major *major* deal on the most fuck-off-gorgeous apartment I've ever handled.'

'Peter,' Thea bemoaned as she climbed the stairs, 'you know I like having you for the full hour – you know you need it.'

'What I need is the commission from this sale, sweetheart,' Peter enthused. 'Then it'll be Maserati time.'

'Oh, right,' said Thea ingenuously, 'is the food good there?'

'It's a *car*, you dumb bird,' Peter said affectionately as he undressed, wincing in pain.

'I'm sorry I'm late,' Mr Alexander said, his American accent reminding Thea of an actor she couldn't quite recall. He was certainly handsome enough for Hollywood though it transpired he was a university lecturer and lived in New York.

'I had the most God-awful sleep,' Mr Alexander explained, while Thea put her notepad on her knee and wrote down *Mr Joel Alexander, 37.*

'That's the horror of long-haul economy seating,' Thea said, 'not that I've ever had the luxury of business class.'

'This *was* business class,' Mr Alexander shrugged, 'but I guess I fell asleep whilst reading and spent the whole flight slumped upright. What kind of dork doesn't take full advantage of fully reclining seat–beds?'

Thea laughed. 'How long are you over for?'

'A week,' he told her. 'I come over every now and then – lecturing.'

'What in?' Thea asked.

'A plane,' Mr Alexander replied, deadpan. Thea looked up from her notes and was greeted by his wry smile. 'Classics,' he told her.

'Oughtn't you to be grey-haired, stooped and wrinkly?' Thea remarked, thinking she might have swapped to Classics herself if the lecturer had looked anything like Mr Alexander.

'Botox, hair dye and marathon running,' Mr Alexander shrugged.

Again, Thea was momentarily taken aback and she found herself glancing suspiciously at his forehead and hairline.

Mr Alexander held up his hands in mock surrender. 'Hair is natural,' he assured her, 'as are any wrinkles, or lack of, that you see or don't.'

'And the marathon running?' Thea asked.

'That's true. I run three a year,' he told her. 'Next up is the London Marathon next spring.'

'Golly,' said Thea, slightly surprised by her choice of word and the sudden plumminess of her accent. Why was she going all English Rose? Was it to counterbalance his All-American Hunk? 'Isn't that a frightfully long way to fly for a jog around the block?'

'A *jog around the block*!' Mr Alexander laughed. 'Actually, I'll be living here by then, I'm taking a visiting post at Oxford.'

'Jolly good for you,' said Thea, hoping she sounded more Jane Austen than St Trinian. 'Righty-ho, let's have a look at you. Face the wall, please.'

Tall, broad-shouldered, athletic build. Very good musculature.

'And turn to the window.'

Good posture – all the way up and all the way down. Nice profile.

'And now turn to look at me.'

He really is handsome.

As Thea massaged Joel Alexander, she tried to temper her smile. She thought it was somewhat unprofessional – though of course he couldn't see her, lying face down as he was. However, she was smiling because when she'd asked him to turn to face her, the masseuse in her had taken a good long considered look at his body but the girl in her had felt a dormant fizz of attraction. And when she had told him she could alleviate the discomfort he felt because actually it was only a tightness in the thoracic, she'd smiled in triumph, he'd smiled in relief and then they'd smiled at each other for a second or two longer than was necessary. In the past, Alice had asked her if she fancied any of her clients. And Thea had primly rejected such an unethical suggestion. But here she was, thinking Christmas had come three weeks early. Santa had brought her a gorgeous surprise. And she hadn't even put him on her list.

'There you go,' Thea said quietly, placing her stilled palms on his back before lifting them away gently and covering him with a towel. 'Dress when you're ready. Take your time.'

'Thanks so much,' Mr Alexander said, sitting comfortably in one of her plastic chairs when she came back in. 'Thanks.'

'Hot and cold, if you can,' Thea advised, 'though I don't know how easy it is to lecture with a pack of cold peas strapped to your shoulder.'

Mr Alexander laughed. 'I don't need to be in Oxford until tomorrow – so I'll have room service bring me up frozen peas and a hot-water bottle. I'm sure they've had stranger requests.'

'Well, have a good trip,' Thea said. They stood and shook hands but loitered. 'And have a great Christmas,' she added.

'Yeah, you too,' he said.

'Oh, and good luck with the Marathon,' Thea added.

'You can always meet me at the finish line and give me a rub down,' Mr Alexander said, 'if you're free next spring.'

Thea blushed. Wasn't this flirting? Was there loaded meaning in the 'if you're free' bit? Was she meant to flirt back outright, or act all demure? What were the rules again? It seemed all she could do was blush like a teenager. And no doubt that was simply down to phenylethylamine.

'Or perhaps you'd just have a quick drink with me sometime later this week?' he said.

Oh stop blushing, you stupid girl! He's only a bloke. It's only a drink. For heaven's sake say yes, thank you, that would be nice.

'Yes, thank you, that would be nice.'

'Good,' said Joel, 'cool.'

'Oh, I forgot to ask,' Thea said, as they headed downstairs to reception, 'which of my clients do you know?'

'I'm sorry?' Joel said.

'Apparently you were referred by a client of mine?'

Joel looked at her. 'No, not a client. A friend of yours. Mark Sinclair. He's my cousin – actually, he's more than that, he's a very good friend of mine too.'

Acknowledgements

Special thanks to Bethia Hope-Rollins, Laura Curry and all at the Pilates Place in Crouch End. Also to Dan Rollins – masseur extraordinaire – and Brent Osborn Smith – genius osteopath – thank you for helping me (and my thoracic . . .). Many thanks to Dawn Gobourne at Haringey Library Services for making me her unofficial Writer in Residence – and providing all those cups of coffee. I'm indebted to my support network: the team at HarperCollins, especially my brilliant editor, Lynne Drew; my wonderful agent, Jonathan Lloyd, and my team at Curtis Brown Ltd; my copy-editor the ever-meticulous Mary Chamberlain, and the tireless and jolly Sophie Ransom at Midas PR. Discreet but sincere thanks to the prostitutes, their maids and their clients in Swindon, Peterborough and London who were willing to talk to me with such honesty, humour and good grace.

Home Truths

For Georgia
my beautiful, beautiful girl

Write your sister's weak points in the sand
and her strong points in stone.

Anon

Prologue

'How do you say goodbye to a mountain?'

From her vantage point, Cat York looked across to the three Flatirons, to Bear Peak and Green Mountain. She gazed down the skirts of Flagstaff, patting the snow around her and settling herself in as though she was sitting on the mountain's lap. 'It's like a giant, frozen wedding dress,' she said. 'It probably sounds daft, but for the last four years, I've privately thought of Flagstaff as *my* mountain.'

'There's a lot of folk round here who think that way,' Stacey said. 'You're allowed to. That's the beauty of living in Boulder.'

The sun shot through, glancing off the crystal-cracked snow on the trees, the sharp, flat slabs of rust-coloured rock of the Flatirons soaring through all the dazzling white at their awkward angle.

'When Ben and I first arrived and I was homesick and insecure, I'd walk to Chautauqua Meadow and just sit on my own. It felt like the mountains were a giant arm around my shoulders.' Cat looked around her with nostalgic gratitude. 'Then soon enough we met you lot, started hiking and biking the trails and suddenly the mountain showed me its other side. You could say it's been my therapist's couch and it's been my playground. It's now my most favourite place in the world.'

Stacey looked at Cat, watched her friend cup her gloved hands over her nose and mouth in a futile bid to make her nose look less red and her lips not so blue. 'This time next week, the only peaks I'll be seeing are Victorian rooftops,' Cat said, 'grimy pigeons will replace bald eagles and there'll just be puddles in place of Wonderland Lake. Next week will be a whole new year.'

'Tell me about Clapham,' Stacey asked, settling into their snow bunker.

'Well,' said Cat, 'it's a silent "h" for a start.'

They laughed.

'God,' Cat groaned, leaning forward and knocking her head against her knees, 'I'm still not sure we're doing the right thing – but don't tell Ben I said so. I can't tell you about Clapham, I don't think I've ever been.' She paused and then continued a little plaintively. 'God, Stacey, I have no job, my two closest friends don't even live in the city any more and I'm moving to an opposite side of London to where I used to live, where my sisters still live.'

'It's exciting,' Stacey said, 'and if you don't like it, you can always come back.' She tore into a pack of Reese's with her teeth, her chilled fingers unfit for the task. 'And there's some stuff that's really to look forward to.'

Placated and sustained by the pack of peanut butter, the comfort of chocolate, Cat agreed. 'I've missed my family – by the sound of it, my middle sister Fen is having a tough time at the moment. And it's going to be a big year for Django – he'll be seventy-five which will no doubt warrant a celebration of prodigious proportions.'

'I'd sure like to have met him,' Stacey said and she laughed a little. 'I remember when I first met you, I thought you were like, so exotic, because you came to Boulder with your English Rose looks and a history that Brontë couldn't have made up. You with the mother who ran off with a cowboy, you who were raised by a crazy uncle called Django, you and your sisters brought up in the wilds of Wherever.'

'Derbyshire's not wild,' Cat protested, 'not our part. Though there are wallabies.'

'What's a wallaby?'

'It's like a mini kangaroo,' said Cat. 'They were kept as pets by the posh folk in eighteenth-century Derbyshire – but some broke free, bred, and now bounce happily across the Dales.'

Stacey took a theatrical intake of breath. 'So we have you and your sisters, living in the countryside with your hippy dude uncle and a herd of mutant, aristocratic kangaroos because your mom eloped with J. R. Ewing?' She whistled. 'You could sell this to Hollywood.'

'Shut up, Stacey,' Cat laughed. 'We're just a normal family. Django is a very regular bloke – albeit with a colourful dress code and an adventurous take on cuisine. I'm starting to freeze. Let's go into town and get a hot chocolate. My bum's numb even in these salopettes.'

'Weird, though,' Stacey said thoughtfully.

'What is? My bottom?'

'Your butt is cute, honey,' Stacey assured her, as they hauled each other to their feet. 'I mean it's a little weird that your mom runs off with a cowboy from Denver when you were small, right?'

'Yup.'

'And you've been living pretty close to the Mile High City these last four years, right?'

'Yup.'

'But you never looked her up?'

'Nope.'

'Never even thought about it? Never went shopping in Denver and thought, Hey, I wonder if that lady over there is my mom?'

Throughout Cat's life, it had always been her friends who'd been far more intrigued by her family circumstances, her absent mother, than she. 'But I never knew her. I was a baby. I have no memories of her,' Cat explained. 'I'm not even curious. We had Django, my sisters and I – we wanted for nothing. Just because we didn't have a "conventional" mother or father didn't mean that we were denied a proper parent.'

Stacey linked arms with Cat. 'Conventional families are dull, honey – stick with your kooky one.'

'Oh I'm sticking with my kooky one all right!' Cat laughed. 'I love them with all my heart. And now that Ben and I want to start our own, it feels natural to want to be within that fold again.'

At the time, Cat and Ben York had argued about putting the set of three matching suitcases on their wedding list. Cat had denounced them as boring and unsexy and why couldn't they peruse the linen department one more time. Ben told her that some things in life were, by virtue, boring and unsexy and he pointed out there were only so many Egyptian cotton towels a couple could physically use in a lifetime. Three years later, Ben and Cat are contemplating the same three suitcases: frequently used, gaping open and empty, waiting to be fed the last remaining clothes and belongings. The process is proving to be far more irksome than the packing of the huge crates a few weeks ago, now currently making their passage by sea back to England.

'Weird to think that this time next week we'll be back in the UK,' Ben says.

'Weird that we both now refer to it as "the UK" rather than "England" or simply "home",' says Cat. 'Stacey and I went for a fantastic walk this morning.' She looks through their picture windows to the mountains, a huge cottonwood tree in its winter wear with stark, thick boughs boasting sprays of fine, finger-like branches, the big sky, the quality of air so clean it is almost visible. 'God, it's stunning here.'

'Hey,' says Ben, 'we'll have Clapham Common on our new doorstep.'

Cat hurls a pillow at him. He ducks.

'We can always come back,' Ben tells her, 'but for now, it is time to go. We have things to do. That was the point, remember. That's why we came here in the first place. It's the things we do now which provide a tangible future for our daydreams. That's why it's timely to return to the UK.'

'Do dreams come true in *Clapham*?'

Ben hurls the pillow back at Cat. She hugs it close and looks momentarily upset. 'I don't even have a job to go back to,' she says, 'and not from want of trying. And I'm not pregnant yet – not from want of trying. I feel like I'm just traipsing behind you.'

'We're a team,' Ben states, 'you and me. I've been given a great job which will be big enough for both of us. I've taken it – for the both of us – so you can take your time and think about you.'

'I know,' Cat smiles sheepishly. 'But what'll I do in Clapham all day? Are we packing the pillows?'

'I don't know – do furnished flats come with pillows?'

'I'm not sleeping on pillows used by God knows who,' Cat protests, though she calculates that three pillows will fill an entire suitcase.

'You do in hotels,' Ben reasons, with a frustrated ruffle through his short, silver-flecked hair. 'It's not as if we're going to some boarding house – I told you, the flat is really quite nice. And when I'm up and running, we'll look for somewhere to buy.'

'In *North* London,' Cat says and Ben decides not to react to the fact that this is emphatically not a question. 'Pip says she's worried about Fen.'

'Your eldest sister worries about everyone,' Ben says, remembering that, actually, these pillows came with this apartment. He doesn't comment.

'But she says that Fen and Matt aren't getting along. Since the baby.'

'You're not your sisters' keeper,' Ben says carefully.

'Oh but I am,' Cat says, as if she's offended, as if Ben's forgotten to understand the closeness between the McCabe girls, 'we all are. It's always been that way, it had to be.'

Ben decides to change the subject. He knows that when his wife is emotional, the legend of her family can be detrimentally overplayed. But he knows, too, that once she returns to their fold again, all the normal niggles and familial irritations will surface and Cat will no doubt be glad of Clapham. He wedges socks into spaces in the cases and then crosses to Cat. 'Your family won't recognize you,' he says. 'They'll be expecting that blonde girl with the pony-tail they saw last summer – not this auburn pixie. Mind you, they won't recognize me – you couldn't call my hair "salt and pepper" any more, it's just plain grey.'

'Makes you look very distinguished,' Cat says, brushing her hand tenderly through Ben's hair. She tufts at her elfin crop with a beguiling wail. 'Do you think mine's too short? I told them to cut it shorter than usual, and colour it stronger than normal because I wouldn't be coming back for a while. It's like I forgot that the UK basically *invented* places like Vidal Sassoon and John Frieda.'

'You look gorgeous,' Ben says, 'really sexy and cute and fuckable.' He's behind her, nuzzling the graceful sweep of her neck that her cropped hair has exposed. He fondles her breasts and then takes his hand down to her crotch and cups at it playfully.

'Dr York!' Cat says. 'I have packing to do.'

'And I want to fuck my wife,' Ben whispers, with a titillating nip at her ear lobe.

Cat resists theatrically but he catches her wrists and suddenly he's tonguing her hungrily. 'Come on, babe. Procreation is top of our list after all, remember.'

'Making babies is a very serious matter, Dr York,' says Cat with mock consternation though she is wriggling out of her clothing.

Ben plugs her mouth with a kiss and takes her hand down to his jeans where his hard-on wells at an awkward angle. 'Well then, we'd better commit ourselves to honing our technique.'

'You're the doctor,' Cat says, dispensing with her knickers. Ben's hands travel her body, he gorges on the sight of her. He loves her naked when he's still fully clothed, the tantalizing interference of fabric between him and his wife's silky skin. She squats down and unbuckles his belt, makes achingly slow progress with the flies of his trousers, easing down his boxer shorts as if it's the first time she's done so. She's on her knees. His cock springs to attention. Her mouth is moist but teasingly just beyond reach.

'Christ, Cat,' Ben says hoarsely, clutching her head and bucking his groin to meet her.

'Blow-jobs don't make babies,' Cat tells him artlessly, but she kisses the tip of his cock and follows this with swift, deep sucks that make him groan. She stands and looks up at him. His height has always turned her on and when he dips his face down to kiss hers it darkens his brown eyes. 'Isn't there some position that's meant to facilitate fertility, doctor?'

'Yes, Mrs York,' Ben confirms, turning her away from

him, running his hand gently up her back, pushing between her shoulder-blades so that she is bent forwards, 'there is. Just. Like. This.'

He takes her from behind. The sensation is so exquisite that, for a while, they are silent, motionless.

'Dr York? Are you sure doggy-style is medically proven to assist conception?'

'No,' Ben pants as he thrusts into her, his hands at her waist to haul himself in, 'but I'm quite certain that the sight of your immaculate peach of an arse improves the quality of my load.'

Django McCabe

Often, making light of the dark makes good sense. When Django McCabe was trekking in Nepal in the early 1960s, en route to some saffron-robed guru or other, he came across a man who had fallen down a screed slope along the mountain pass.

'Need a hand?' Django had offered.

'Actually, wouldn't mind a leg,' the man had responded. It was then that Django saw the man in fact had only the one leg, that his crutch had been flung some distance. Django learnt more from his co-traveller than from the guru: not to let hardship harden a person, to keep humour at the heart of the matter, to make light of the dark. A decade later, when Django found himself guardian to three girls under the age of four, the offspring of his late brother, he thought about his one-legged friend and decided that the circumstances uniting him with his nieces would never be recalled as anything other than rather eccentric, strangely fortunate and not that big a deal anyway. 'I know your mother ran off with a cowboy from Denver, but . . .' has since prefixed all manner of events throughout the McCabe girls' lives.

I know your mother ran off with a cowboy from Denver,

but crying because I accidentally taped over Dallas *is a little melodramatic.*

It was mid-morning and Django McCabe felt entitled to a little sit-down. But there wasn't time for forty winks. It was Monday and if the girls were coming home for the weekend then he needed the week to prepare for their visit; he couldn't be wasting time with a snooze. However, to sit in a chair and not nod off was as difficult, perhaps even as pointless, as going to the Rag and Thistle and not having a pint of bitter.

'I'll multi-task,' Django muttered. 'Apparently it's a very twenty-first-century thing to do.' And so he decided to combine his little sit-down with doing something constructive, in this instance scanning today's runners. After all, studying the form would stop him dozing off.

And there it was. Staring him in the face. 2.20 Pontefract. Cool Cat. Rank outsider – but what did they know.

'It's a sign,' he said, patting himself all over to locate his wallet which, after an extensive grope through the collection of jackets draped over most of the chairs in the kitchen, he finally found. 'I'll put a tenner on the horse. In honour of Cat. I need to pop into town anyway so either way, it won't be a wasted trip.'

Django would never place a bet by phone. He doesn't trust the telephone. He says, darkly, that you never know who may be listening. But his Citroën 2CV he trusts with his life and, along the lanes of Farleymoor and the roads around Chesterfield, the little car filled to bursting with Django is a familiar sight. At seventy-four, Django is physically robust. Tall and sturdy, affably portly around the girth and crowned by a mane of grey hair always pony-tailed. He toots and waves as he drives. He thinks fellow drivers are slowing down to let him pass, to wave back. Actually they're swerving to keep out of his way, holding up their hands in protest.

There are people in every continent who regard Django as their friend, though his travelling days ended with the arrival of his three small nieces some thirty years ago. He has rarely left Derbyshire since and it is the area around Farleymoor, on the Matlock side of Chesterfield, where his warmest clutch of friends are massed.

'Morning, Mary, and don't you look divine for a Monday,' Django says, entering the bookmakers.

'And don't you look colourful for January,' Mary says, wondering if he's warm enough in his paisley shirt and tapestry waistcoat.

'From Peru,' Django tells her, opening his waistcoat wide, like a flasher. 'I had to trade with bandits on a mountain pass.'

'And what did they get of you, duck?'

'My passport,' Django says and he roars with laughter. 'A tenner on Cool Cat, if you please.'

'Rank outsider,' Mary warns him.

'I know,' Django shrugs, 'but the odds were worse for Fenland Star yesterday and truly terrible for Pipistrelle last week and they both won.' He hands over a ten-pound note. 'She's flying home as we speak, you know. Cat. I have all three girls descending on me for the weekend.'

Mary knows Django's girls. They were at school with her daughters. 'No doubt you'll be cooking up a treat for them, then?'

'She's been in America for four years,' he says, leaning on the counter and beckoning Mary closer. 'That's an awful lot of McDonalds. Apparently her hair is now red.'

Mary can't see the connection between McDonalds and hair colour. If she remembers correctly, Cat is the sporty one who married the doctor of a professional cycling team.

'So I am indeed preparing a Spread to welcome her home and put back some nutrients,' Django is saying. 'Oh, and let's have a tenner on Three's Company at Fakenham. Good little horse, that.'

Django McCabe hasn't had a beard for over twenty years, yet still, in moments of contemplation, he strokes his chin with fingertips light and methodical as if his goatee still sits proud on his face. The habit is one that he uses for all manner of pontification, from selecting horses according to their names or the form given them by the *Racing Post*, to his choice of the next domino at the Rag and Thistle. Currently, he is toying with his chin while wondering what to cook. Laid out before him are all the foodstuffs from the fridge, most of those from the larder, and a few from the capacious chest freezer too. He doesn't believe in shopping according to a recipe, he cooks to accommodate available ingredients; he invented food combining in its most oblique sense. He fingers his invisible beard and begins to make his considered selection, as an artist might choose pigment for the day's palette. Indeed, Django feels at his most creative when cooking – he sees blending, mixing, combining, concocting, as art, not science. Thus he never measures or weighs and he believes cookery books are to cooking what painting-by-numbers kits are to painting.

Whenever his nieces visit from London, it warrants a Spread. And as the forthcoming weekend is to be not just an ordinary visit, but a homecoming celebration, it has to be a Monumental Spread. Django hasn't seen Cat since the summer. None of them has. Christmas was peculiar for her absence. She'd turned thirty-two years old in the autumn and he hadn't been able to make her a birthday cake. On top of that, Pip implied recently that Fen has been a little down. He knows of no way better to warm the heart and feed the soul than to fill the stomach with all manner of home cooking first.

Django is at his happiest when cooking for his girls, even though they are all in their thirties, with homes of their own, and their health has never been of concern.

'It's habit,' he'll say when they say he needn't have, when they say a pub lunch or ready-meal supper would be fine by them, when they say they are too full for seconds let alone thirds. 'I'm old and stuck in my ways,' he'll declare. 'Humour me.' He'll say the same thing when presenting them with carrier bags bulging with Tupperware containers when they leave again for London.

Django McCabe is their family tree. The desertion of their mother, the death of their father gave him no choice – but ultimately gave him his greatest blessing. His arms, like great branches, have been the protective clasp, the loving embrace of mother, father, confidant and mentor to Cat, Fen and Pip. He provided the boughs in which their cradles were rocked. His are the roots which have always anchored them and kept them safe.

Tuesday

Fen McCabe used to enjoy looking in the mirror. Far from it being a vanity kick, she'd found it an affirming thing to do. In the scamper of a working day, to grasp a private moment to nod at her reflection was sustaining. Hullo you, she'd sometimes say, what a busy day. And in the heady period when Matt Holden had wined, dined, wooed and pursued her, she'd frequently nip to the loo in some restaurant or bar, for a little time out with herself. He likes me, she'd beam at her reflection, you go girl! She'd wink at herself, give herself the go-ahead to party and flirt and charm the man who, soon enough, wanted to be with her for life.

Since having a baby six months ago, Fen has hated looking in the mirror. Not because she finds the sight depressing but because she finds the sight so strange. She doesn't so much wince away from the sight of a few extra pounds, the limp hair, the sallow skin, the dark and puffy eyes, as glance bewildered and wonder who *is* that? How can this be my reflection when I don't actually recognize the person staring back? And mirror mirror on the wall, wasn't I once a damn sight fairer than *this*? So it's something of a relief not to have the time during the day and to be too tired in the evening to face the facts staring back from the looking glass.

The phone is ringing, the baby is crying. Fen is nearer to the phone and Matt is nearer to the baby. Matt knows that Fen can find little wrong with the way he answers the phone so he's happy to swap places here in the kitchen.

'Hullo?' he answers. 'Well hullo!' He looks over to Fen. She's wearing truly awful pyjamas. Even if they'd been a matching set they'd have little to commend them. The bottoms have polka dots on a sickly lilac background. The top is littered with cutesy cartoon animals, a strange hybrid love child of a dog and a rabbit and even some teddy bear chromosomes somewhere along the line. 'Hold on, I'll just pass you over.' He holds out the receiver.

'Who is it?' Fen mouths but Matt will only cock his eyebrow and grin. As Fen shuffles over to the phone, the placated baby at home on her hip, Matt notes her slippers. The grey, felted monstrosities he once termed 'eastern-bloc lesbian clogs'. He'd had her in stitches at the time, she'd done a bastardized folk dance in them and had him in hysterics, before she'd banished them under the bed. For good, so he'd thought, until just then.

'Hullo?' says Fen.

'Boo!' says the voice.

'Cat?'

'I'm back! We're in a cab, on the M4. Heading for Clapham.'

Matt watches the smile warm her face. He thinks how clichéd it sounds to say that the sun comes out when Fen smiles. But in his eyes, it does. And suddenly he forgives her the pyjamas and the clogs and he feels bad for having felt irritated with her and now he wants to go to her and put his arms around her and kiss the asymmetric dimples on her cheeks, brush her overlong fringe away from her forehead and kiss her there too, scoop her hair into a pony-tail and bury his nose in her neck. She's hanging up the phone and he thinks that, though he's now ready to leave for work perhaps there is time for a little spontaneity, for affection, for physical and emotional contact. The baby can stay on Fen's hip. They're a family after all. Group hug and all that. So he crosses the kitchen and he's about to reach for her when her nose wrinkles.

'Gracious,' she's saying to the baby, 'how can someone so little and cute make such a revolting smell.'

'I'll change her,' Matt offers.

Fen falters. 'It's OK,' she says, 'I'll do it. I want to check that her nappy rash has cleared.'

She may only be six months old but Cosima Holden-McCabe has decided, quite categorically, that she will not be eating anything unless it is orange in colour. Fen is fretting over whether puréed carrot and mashed sweet potato for the fourth day running – and currently for breakfast – might give her baby carotene poisoning. Or have caused the nappy rash. Or created the current extreme pungency of the nappies.

'Wouldn't you rather have a nice squidgy banana? Are you OK, pumpkin?' Keeping her eyes on her baby, waggling a spoon loaded with orange mush, Fen speaks to Matt. 'Does she look orange to you?'

'Pumpkins are orange – you're probably giving her this complex.'

Fen looks at him for a loaded moment.

'Joke?' Matt says with a sorry smile. 'She looks bonny – she has a lovely glow to her fat little cheeks.'

'She's not fat!' Fen protests.

'It was a compliment,' Matt assures her. 'I meant it affectionately.'

'But do you think the glow to her cheeks is a bit orange?'

'No, Fen, I don't.' Matt peers in close to his baby and kisses her cheek. 'She looks fine.' He glances at his girlfriend. 'I think Cosima is happy and healthy and that carrot-and-sweet-potato mush is her favourite food of the moment. I reckon it's because you look peaky in comparison, Fen.'

'If I do look peaky,' Fen says defensively, 'it's because I'm so bloody tired.'

'I know you are,' Matt says and it irritates him that Fen heard an insult instead of the concern intended. He wants to say, I'm tired too, you know; but he hasn't time for a petty dispute over who is the more exhausted. 'Why don't you ask your sister if she's around today? You can have a little time to yourself?'

'She's only just got off the plane!'

'I meant Pip.'

Somewhere, Fen knows Matt's intention is sweet. But lately, unbridled sensitivity has lain far closer to her surface than sense. 'You don't think I'm coping, do you?' she says.

'You're doing brilliantly,' Matt says, because the books and the magazines have instilled the sentence in him and advised him to ignore the ironing mountain, piles of toys and general debris. 'I'm late. What are you doing today? Is it Musical Minis?'

'No, that's Thursday.'

'TinyTumbles?'

'No, that's tomorrow. I may meet up with the baby-mums this afternoon.'

'That'll be nice.'

Fen shrugs. 'I always come away feeling a bit insecure,' she confides. 'Their babies apparently sleep through the night and most have at least one tooth. And I'm not really sure about the women – I can't find a connection apart from the babies being the same age. They're forever trying to out-purée each other with increasingly exotic organic recipes. But all my baby wants is orange stuff.'

'You're being unnecessarily hard on yourself,' Matt says, 'and on Cosima. And possibly on that bunch too. Stop being silly. You're wondermum and we love you.'

Fen can't hear the last sentence. Her ears are ringing with the fact that Matt says she's silly. She wants to say, Well fuck you. But they've made a pact not to swear in front of their child.

'I'm late.' He gulps his coffee. 'Work is mental at the moment – I'll try and leave early, cook us something nice.' He kisses the top of Fen's head and brushes his lips over the peach fuzz adorning Cosima's. 'Bye, girls. Have fun.'

* * *

Tom Holmes likes Tuesdays very much. He doesn't like the fact that at school Tuesdays mean dictation followed by football. Tom finds it difficult to coordinate hearing a word, then assessing its meaning in context and having to write it down, all in the space of about two seconds. It thus seems entirely logical that instructions for rigging a yacht could well be 'Pacific' instead of 'specific'. It frustrates him that he never does well in dictation and that there's no opportunity in dictation to saliently reason that 'Pacific', taken contextually, is just as appropriate as 'specific'. He's slightly taken aback that Miss Balcombe won't at least acknowledge that 'Pacific instructions for rigging' sounds fairly logical. He doesn't like it that there's no room for manoeuvre with meaning where dictation is concerned.

Football makes Tom miserable, more so because he's acutely aware that a nine-year-old should never admit to being miserable in the context of football. He supports Arsenal, which has won him friends at his North London prep school, but he hates playing the game. He hates playing because his limbs are often sore from eczema. Mud can actually sting but tracksuit trousers can catch and snag on chapped skin. Though his teammates are pals enough not to comment, Tom still catches them glancing at his body, unintentionally repelled. However, what makes dictation and football bearable is that, on Tuesdays, he stays with his dad and stepmum at their cool place in Hampstead.

They actually only live a mile or so from his home in Swiss Cottage and, though Tom spends every Tuesday, Wednesday and every other weekend with them, and any time in between that he fancies, the novelty value is still high. His dad's place is closer to school than his other home so instead of his mum slaloming her Renault through the school run (which has its plus points because she appears unaware how much she swears) Tom strolls down Hampstead High Street with his stepmum. And, without actually holding hands (he's nine now, someone might see), Tom can still subliminally tug her into a detour to Starbucks for hot chocolate.

Tom's had Pip for nearly four years. Her presence at the school gates continues to provide much intrigue. Being a clown by trade, Pip is well known to many of Tom's classmates from the birthday-party circuit of their younger years. She's also been to assembly to talk about the other work she does, as a clown at children's hospitals. She did the splits and a flikflak on the stage, bonked the headmaster on the head with a squeaky plastic hammer, made a motorbike from balloons in four seconds flat and Tom was the centre of attention all that day. His friends still make a point of saying hullo to her when she collects him. Invariably, she has rushed to school from the hospital, with her hair still in skew-whiff pigtails and traces of make-up on her face. Far more exotic than the widespread Whistles and ubiquitous Nicole Farhi worn by the other mums.

*

This Tuesday was no different. There was Pip, eye-catching in orange-and-purple stripy tights and clodhopping boots, chatting amiably with the other Hampstead mums.

'Hi, I'm starving. It was shepherd's pie for lunch. *Heinous*,' said Tom, keen to drag her away.

'Dear oh dear,' said Pip, 'heinous shepherd's pie? I'd turn vegetarian, if I were you.'

'No *way*, José,' Tom retched. 'The veggie option is always vomtastic.'

'Vom*tastic*,' Pip marvelled, planning to use the word in her clowning. 'How was football?'

Tom gave a small shrug. 'Cold.'

'Are you angling for a brownie and hot choc?' Pip nudged him.

'If you say so,' Tom said.

'Well, your dad won't be home till sevenish,' Pip reasoned with herself, as much as with Tom.

'It would be very good for my energy,' Tom said not entirely ingenuously. 'Starbucks would *really* help my homework.'

Pip laughed. 'Come on, tinker,' she said. They walked towards the High Street. 'I had a sad day at the hospital. It's lovely to see you.'

Tom slipped his hand into hers. Just for a few strides or so.

Pip looked at the kitchen table laden with the remains of supper later that evening, then she looked at her husband and his son embroiled in PlayStation. She put her hands on her hips and cleared her throat. They didn't look up.

'Hullo?' she called, as if testing whether anyone was there.

Zac glanced up briefly from the console, but not briefly enough to prevent Tom taking advantage.

'Dad!' Tom objected. 'Concentrate!'

And then Pip decided she'd just smile and ask if anyone

wanted a drink. She still found it difficult to gauge her boundaries as a stepmother. Her own standards, based on her childhood and her family's dynamic, said that a nine-year-old should help clear the table, or at least ask to be excused a chore. But she also acknowledged that this father and son hadn't seen each other for a week and Zac had been first down from the table challenging Tom to a PlayStation final-of-finals. So she tidied up and allowed them their quality time.

She glanced at the clock and felt relieved that it really was nearing Tom's bedtime. Zac had worked so late the last couple of nights she felt she hadn't seen him at all. 'I'll run your bath, Tom,' she said.

'One more game,' Zac called to her.

'I'll run it slowly,' Pip said.

Despite actually trying his damndest to win, Zac lost at PlayStation. Far from being wounded, his pride soared at Tom's skill and after a noisy bathtime, he cuddled up with his son for a lengthy dip into *James and the Giant Peach*. Pip could hear the soft timbre of Zac's reading voice. She poured two glasses of wine and organized Tom's school bag for the morning.

Zac appeared and made the fast-asleep gesture with his hands. 'He was tired,' he said.

'Well, it's late for him,' said Pip, offering a glass of wine.

Zac looked at his watch. 'I just have a little work to do,' he told Pip who looked instantly deflated, 'just an hour or so.' He took the wine, kissed Pip on the lips, squeezed her bottom and disappeared with his laptop. He's happy, Pip told herself. She looked on the bright side, which was very much her wont. At least it gave her the opportunity to phone Cat, as long as her youngest sister had been able to resist the jet lag on her first day back in the country.

*

Many would say that being a high-flying accountant would have its ups and downs: financial remuneration in return for long hours and often relatively dull work; a bulging pay packet to compensate for a dry grey image. How else would accountants have become such a clichéd race? But the only things grey about Zac Holmes are his eyes which are dark slate to the point of being navy anyway, and the only dry thing about Zac is his sense of humour. If Zac's looks and his personality had dictated a career, it would have been something on the funky side of creative. But Zac's brain, with its amazing propensity for figures, decreed accountancy from the outset. Anything else just wouldn't be logical. Zac likes logic, he likes straightforward solutions and simple answers to even the most complex of problems. Consequently, he never judges anything to be a dilemma because he knows intrinsically that there is always a way to work it all out. Zac believes that problems are merely perceived as such. If you just sit down and think carefully, there's nothing that can't be solved. Problems don't really exist at all, it comes down to attitude. That goes for his personal life as much as his professional. So, when ten years ago, his on-off girlfriend announced she was pregnant a few weeks after a forgettable drunken friendship fuck, Zac welcomed the news with a shrug and easily devised a formula that would suit them all.

2 firm friends + 0 desire to marry/cohabit
(+ never ÷ by £/♡ issues)
= great + modern parents
= 1 lucky child.

June, the mother of his child, can never be an ex-wife or ex-girlfriend because she was neither when Tom was conceived. She's Zac's friend and Zac is her friend and for Tom to have parents who are friends is a gift. Tom also has two step-parents. Everyone is friends. It might appear unconventional, but it works. A large family of friends.

Django McCabe may have trawled the sixties, trekking from ashram to commune, hiking from yurt to kibbutz, in search of the same. But he was happy to admit that his eldest niece had found its apotheosis in London NW3.

Pip is hovering. Zac's hour at his laptop has turned into two.

'Coffee?' she offers.

'No, ta,' says Zac, 'need to crack on.'

'Tea?' she suggests.

'Nope, I'm fine thanks, Mrs,' says Zac. 'I have to knock this on its head.'

'Whisky?'

'No, nothing – I'm good. Thanks.'

'Rampant sex?'

'Tempting – on any other night. I have to work. Seriously.'

'One of my very special blow-jobs?'

Zac looks at his screen. He has a very good head for figures. But if there's one figure that gives very good head, it's Pip. His eyes don't leave his laptop, his finger hovers above the mouse-pad. 'A special blow-job?' Zac asks, as if it's a deal-breaker. 'Not just a standard one?'

'Trust me,' Pip winks.

'Because,' says Zac, 'if it's just run-of-the-mill sucky-sucky, I'll pass. This audit is crucial.'

'I'm not capable of run-of-the-mill sucky-sucky,' Pip clarifies, hands on her hips, chin up.

'I mean, I'm talking *cosmic*, Pip,' Zac stipulates with a lasciviously raised eyebrow. 'It needs to be mind-blowing.'

'I assure you it's not just your mind I'll be blowing.'

Finally, Zac looks from his laptop to Pip, then back again. Contriving a sigh, as if he was doing her the favour, he logs off. 'I'm sure the powers that be will understand,' he says.

'I'll write your boss a note,' says Pip. 'I'll tell him the dog ate your homework.' She takes Zac by the hand and leads him to the bedroom. They undress silently and have rude sex as quietly as they can.

* * *

Matt had come back from work early, made sausages, mash and onion gravy. Perfect for a cold January night and essential for his girlfriend who'd told him she hadn't had time to eat more than toast and Marmite during the day. He'd bought a DVD too, which Fen managed to stay awake through despite snuggling up against the cosiness of Matt's chest. Now she's reading in bed and Matt is nuzzling the fragrant softness of his girlfriend's neck. His cock is surprisingly responsive. He'd only intended to kiss her goodnight. He didn't know he had the energy to feel horny.

'How did we make Cosima again?' Matt whispers, running his hand the length of Fen's thigh, spooning against her, the sensation of her buttocks against his erection causing his pelvis to rock automatically, his hands to travel up along her torso. He bypasses her breasts. They're Cosima's for the time being. He doesn't really mind, it's lucky he's always been a legs and bum man. And his hands sweep down to Fen's thighs again, and over them, and around. And he walks his fingers up through the fuzz of her sex then attempts to tiptoe them down in between.

Fen's hand joins his. 'I do want to,' she announces, a tinge of apology, a ring of reluctance, which stills Matt's hand immediately. 'I'm just really really tired. Sorry.'

'I bet I can have you in the mood; bet you I can have you hollering for mercy,' he tells her. He always used to be able to. He leans across her and kisses her, pulls her to face him, holds her against him. He rocks his groin gently against her, takes her hand down to his perky cock and works his hands over her body. He is not sure whether he's taken her breath away or whether she's holding it to pull her stomach in. But he feels her stiffen, and a glance at her face, where anxiety is mixed with reluctance, causes him to turn away from her, to stare at the ceiling with a sigh.

'Do I feel different to you?' she asks. 'I'm still so squidgy and unattractive.' And then she mutters that she shouldn't have had all that bangers and mash.

'You look gorgeous,' Matt says, 'I keep telling you. God. Wasn't my raging hard-on proof enough how much I fancy you?'

Fen shrugs and looks downcast. 'I know you do,' she says quietly, 'but I have to fancy myself, too, to feel horny.'

'Will you give yourself a break,' Matt says. He switches off the bedside light and kisses her lightly on the shoulder. 'Stop being silly.'

Fen lies in the dark, wide-eyed and confused and wishing they had a spare room she could withdraw to. She encourages a hot, oily tear to sting its way from the corner of her eye and slick down her cheek and onto the pillow. She knows it's bizarre, but rather than being bolstered by Matt's assurances that he loves and lusts for her however she feels she looks, she's cross that he appears to trivialize her concerns, her loss of confidence, her fragile self-image.

He called me silly. For the second time today. Silly is a stupid, insensitive word to use. He just doesn't understand.

God. It's gone midnight. Cosima will wake in a couple of hours. I have to get some sleep.

Django McCabe and the Nit-Pickin' Chicks

Though only three years separated the oldest and youngest of the McCabe sisters, Cat had always been very much the baby of the family. She was a little shorter than Pip and Fen, her features more petite. She lacked Pip's aptitude for performing, to entertain, which gave her eldest sister her apparent sassy confidence. Nor did she have Fen's self-containment, her ability to seem so quietly self-possessed, so attractively serene. While Pip and Fen had encountered the various dramas in their lives head-on and for the most part single-handedly and discretely, Cat had always simply stood there and cried loudly for help. It wasn't that she was particularly feeble, nor was she excessively attention-seeking or spoilt; Cat was accustomed to being looked after because there was something about her that inspired others to care for her. Ben believed it was to do with the arrangement of her features; her large eyes set winsomely around the childlike upturn to her nose which led down to the natural pout to her lips. It compelled one to offer protection, even if it was not specifically needed or asked for. However, Cat's strength was that she was never too proud to ask. She'd grown up knowing that what made her feel strong and able was the presence of her support network, her sisters in particular.

When Cat had gone to live in America with a relatively new boyfriend (as Ben was then) and brand new job, everyone anticipated floods of tears to wash her soon back again. But the anticipated plea to be rescued never came. Her letters and e-mails and phone calls attested to her happiness, and her occasional visits home confirmed this. Her apparent self-sufficiency was a source of joy and relief for her family and soon enough they were delighted for her that she'd gone. Not half so thrilled as they are now, four years later, that she has come back.

Being swept north by rail for their family reunion, the McCabe sisters were initially preoccupied with three-way inane grinning and quietly assessing physical details and changes.

'So.'

'So?'

'So!'

'You're back.'

'I am.'

'For good?'

'Indeed. For better, for worse.'

'I do love your hair,' Pip told Cat. 'When you e-mailed to say you'd gone short and red, I had visions of a ginger buzz-cut.'

'It's very gamine,' Fen said whilst hastily retying hers into a hopefully smoother pony-tail, 'very Audrey Hepburn. God I feel a dowdy frump.'

'You don't think it's too short?' Cat asked them. 'And you're sure you like the colour? Yours is so much longer,' she said to Fen, 'and darker.'

'That's probably because it's greasy,' Fen said. She took a

twist of her hair and scrutinized the ends. 'I can't remember the last time I went to the hairdresser.'

'Go this weekend,' Pip said. 'Django will know somewhere.'

'When did he last go to a barber?' Cat interrupted. 'You're not telling me he's chopped off his pony-tail? I expected things to change while I've been abroad – but nothing that drastic.'

'It's still his crowning glory,' Pip assured her with a smile.

'How's he been?' Cat asked.

'Fine and dandy,' Pip said. 'Same as ever, really.'

'It's funny, initially I'd curse him for not having e-mail, but actually I loved receiving his letters and writing back,' Cat said. 'I've kept them all. They're hysterical. He'd send me the TV listings page every single week so I could keep up with *Corrie*.'

'Zac and I bought him an answering machine for his last birthday – but he took it back,' Pip said. 'I suggested a mobile phone – but you can imagine what he said.'

'Talking of birthdays, I wonder what we'll do for his,' Cat said brightly. 'Can you believe he'll be seventy-five this spring?'

'He'll either throw a huge party – or go on a retreat,' Pip said. 'In which case we'll make him a surprise party.'

'Yes!' said Cat. She gazed at the sleeping baby nustled up to Fen in a papoose. 'Cosima is so beautiful,' she said dreamily, watching Fen's fingers tap out a mother's instinctive, gentle rhythm against the baby's back. Absent-mindedly, Cat rolled her thumb against her wedding ring. 'Still no plans to wed then, Fen?' She felt Pip glance at her.

Fen balked. 'What an odd thing to say.'

'Sorry – I just mean, you know, since you now have a baby.'

'Shock, horror, an *illegitimate* child? Is that what you're implying?' Fen said.

'Blimey Fen, I was only teasing,' Cat said, because she had been. She glanced back at Pip who, ever the diplomat, decided it was a good idea to change the subject.

'I'm hungry,' said Pip.

'I'm hungry now too,' said Fen. 'Do you think Django's made a late lunch for us?'

'Followed almost immediately by an enormous tea with just time enough to burp before a Spread for supper?' Cat laughed.

'I'll go and buy sandwiches for us,' said Pip.

'And salt-and-vinegar crisps!' Cat called after her. Fen smiled at her. Cat turned her gaze out to the English countryside zipping by outside the train. So different to Colorado, where she had remained in awe of her surroundings. Here, the scale was comfortingly familiar, if a little tame by comparison, the colours darker, damper.

'Sorry about before,' Fen said. 'I've been horribly snappish, lately. I hate it and I can't help it. I'm just so tired. And – well – things at home have been a little strained.'

Cat watched Fen's gaze drop. She'd been shocked by the physical change in Fen, the wan complexion, the dark eyes, puffiness here and a general lankness there. Objectively, Fen had always been the true beauty of the three of them; her features and complexion adding refinement where Pip was just pretty, where Cat was simply cute. Today, though, Cat noticed a certain pallor now veiling this.

'Is it Matt?' Cat broached, though she'd intended to seek details from Pip later.

'I don't know, Cat,' Fen said, a tear clouding one eye, 'but I think it might be me. My love for my baby is so primal and complete that sometimes I feel like running away so it's just the two of us.'

'Don't do that,' Cat said and she reached across the melamine for her sister's wrist, 'please don't do that. I've just come thousands of miles to be back in my family fold. I want Cosima to get to know her Auntie Cat. And when I am pregnant, I'll need you within arm's reach to tell me how to do it all properly.'

Fen smiled. 'I'll need bloody long arms to stretch to Clapham from East Finchley,' she said.

'Clapham is not, I repeat *not*, permanent,' Cat said. 'You know I've always had a thing for Tufnell Park.'

'It's good to have you home,' Fen said, 'but it'll be even better to have you on the doorstep.'

Pip returned. 'Cardboard bread with rubber cheese in between,' she announced. 'Don't anyone tell Django what we're about to eat.'

Peeping through the window, it is a joy for Django to behold his three precious girls spill out of the taxi. Momentarily, he turns away from the sight and offers a prayer of sincere thanks to all the gods and spirits who have ever interested him at any stage during his life. He can hear their laughter and their excited chatter. Will you look at Cosima – how she has grown in the last month. How naturally Fen has the baby against her. See the sun spin gold through Pip's hair. And Cat, that can't be Cat! Cat was the little girl with the jaunty pony-tail. Who is this beautiful woman? And what's with the red hair!

Django had intended to position himself in the hallway, so that when the girls opened the door he'd be there; his arms flung wide, like a celebrity tenor on an album cover. In the event, he is as excited as they are and he strides out to meet them, booming his welcome. The only member of the family who does not cry is Cosima. She regards the grown-ups with her solemn unblinking eyes, absorbing all the facts and details as if logging the information that when you haven't seen your family for a long time, you leap about and sob and touch each other's hair a lot.

'I'm still stuffed from tea-time!' Cat whispered to Pip while Django tinkered in the kitchen. 'Those scones were like cannon balls. Never mind enough to feed an army – enough to sink the navy!'

'Shh,' Pip said.

'Has he been well?' Cat asked quietly. 'Hasn't had flu, or something? It's just that he looks a little tired to me, a bit peaky, since I last saw him.'

'I think he's been fine,' said Pip. 'He certainly hasn't said anything to the contrary. He's probably been slaving over the stove all week, preparing for our arrival.' She spied a copy of the *Racing Post*. 'Or else he's put all his money on some old nag and lost the lot.'

Cat walked around the living-room, fingering objects, lingering over framed photos, feeling the heavy brocade of the curtains, running her hands over the worn warm upholstery, filling her nostrils with the scent of home. It was like remaking her acquaintance with the essential elements of her personal history; reminding herself how everything looked and felt and smelt and should be, while at the same time reasserting her own presence in this sacred family space.

The Spread was simmering and sautéing and roasting and steaming. Elements of it were happily marinating, or being chilled, or else ripening at room temperature. All the pots and pans were in use and every utensil had served many a purpose. The various scents emanating from oven and hob joined forces to create an olfactory explosion that, to Django, was as contradictory yet ultimately pleasing as a jazz chord.

The point of cooking and the point of jazz are essentially one and the same, Django thought to himself as he ran a sink of water and half a jar of Bar Keeper's Friend to soak all the knives. *It's about an element of surprise, of revelation and re-education. Of experimentation. Like when the African pentatonic scale met the European diatonic scale and jazz was born; a sound that was initially bizarre, disconcertingly discordant. It simply required one to open one's ears and one's heart to the flattened third and seventh notes and suddenly the aural pleasure of the blue note coursed through one's veins. Likewise, one's initial concern that Tabasco and tuna may be odd accompaniments to duck with a celery stuffing, dissipates when one shrugs off preconceptions of convention and allows the tastes to speak for themselves.*

'Not too dissimilar to Kandinsky either,' Django mused as he left the kitchen in search of his nieces, 'seemingly an arbitrary cascade of colour and shape yet utterly grounded in structure and purpose. Jazz, Cookery, Abstraction. It's all art.'

He found them in the living-room and observed them unseen for a nostalgic moment. Just then, the girls could have been any age. The scene was immediately familiar and timeless and the continuity was poignant. 'By golly,' Django declared, 'sing hey for the return of the nit-pickin' chicks.'

The nit-pickin' chicks looked up at him. Fen stopped plaiting Pip's hair, Pip stilled her hands from massaging Cat's foot, Cat brought her head up from Fen's lap and ceased tracing patterns on her sister's legs.

'Django, you're not going all sentimental on us are you?' Pip asked, resuming her massage in a businesslike way. The girls laughed. Privately, they each felt suddenly very sentimental, in an affirming way. It had been years since Django had referred to them as the nit-pickin' chicks, because it had been such a long time since they'd sat in their huddle with their hands almost absent-mindedly working on each other.

'Stop fiddling,' Django said. 'Let's eat.'

'I'll just check on Cosima,' Fen said.

'You were only up there half an hour ago,' said Cat, 'and she was quiet then.'

'You'll see,' Fen said, slightly defensively, feeling entitled to her knowing nod, 'you'll see.'

'It transpires that Cat hasn't just come home because she misses your cooking,' Pip told Django, slipping her arm around his waist, 'she's come home to breed.'

Django took a moment. 'Wonderful!' he then said, placing his hand on Cat's head as if blessing her. 'Another reason to celebrate. There's some champagne somewhere. It may well be in the bottom drawer in your room, Pip.'

'I could look in on Cosima for you while I check,' Pip suggested to Fen.

'No,' said Fen decisively, 'I'll go. I'll do both.'

'The meal is organic,' Django told her, 'mostly. Shall I purée a little for Cosima for tomorrow?'

'No, thanks,' Fen said, hoping she hid her alarm.

'The sauce is relatively orange,' Django elaborated.

'That'll be the Tabasco,' Fen said, 'which isn't really appropriate for a six-month-old baby.'

'It's never too early to prepare the palate,' Django said.

Despite the size of the scones, the aromas from the pots and pans were too tantalizing to resist and appetites magically expanded to meet the quality and quantity of food prepared. Though the menu was predictably unorthodox and though they started with dessert because Django didn't want to risk the lemon-and-rum soufflé collapsing, traditional manners had always been proudly upheld in the McCabe household. Don't hold your knife like a pencil, elbows off the table, don't talk with your mouth full. Between courses, after polite dabbing with napkins, news and plans were discussed.

'A toast to absent menfolk,' Django said, charging his glass, 'to the accountant, the publisher, the doctor.' He took a sip. 'There was plenty of food for them, you know, even if you lot want second helpings.'

'But we didn't actually want them here,' Pip said as if revealing a secret. 'We wanted you to ourselves.'

'And Ben's mum wanted him to herself,' Cat reasoned.

'Next time you come, you bring your boys,' Django said. 'This stew will be good for days – you're all to take a tub home.' He topped up his glass again. 'Well, another toast. To the clown.' Everyone chinked Pip's glass. Django cleared his throat: 'To the art historian.' They raised their glasses to Fen. And then they all looked at Cat. 'What shall we toast you as?' Django asked her. 'Sports journalist? Redhead?'

Cat looked concerned. 'I'm not sure.'

'But you so love the cycling world,' Pip said, 'and you had such respect as one of the few female reporters.'

'And you're married to the doctor of one of the world's top cycling teams,' Fen said.

'*Ex*-team doctor,' Cat pointed out.

'No more gallivanting around the globe with that circus of Lycra and bicycles then?' asked Django.

'No,' Cat laughed though she looked a little forlorn. 'I've fallen out of love.' Pip and Fen jerked with concern. 'With the sport,' Cat clarified. 'So has Ben. Too many drugs, too much cheating.'

'So, what'll you do?' Pip asked again.

'I'm not sure – maybe write more widely. Maybe not just yet.'

'And are you back for good?' Django asked. 'Or is this a pit stop?'

'This is home. This is where we want to start a family. Maybe I'll take a leaf out of Fen's book – and yours, Django – and make motherhood my career.'

'No finer, more noble job than that,' Django said, 'mark my words.'

'You forgot to add *knackering*,' Fen laughed. 'Academia was a breeze in comparison. Not that I have any desire to go back to it.'

'But you're so talented,' said Cat, 'you've had stuff published. You've lectured at the Tate. You're the authority on the sculpture of Julius Fetherstone. You have all those hard-earned letters after your name.'

'Art is still my great love – just because I choose not to work in that field doesn't negate that,' Fen shrugged and continued more defensively. 'I've gone for a change of career. Raising my baby is just as challenging, as stimulating – and far more time-consuming.'

'I suppose I'll have to see which comes first – a blue line on the dipstick, or a job offer,' said Cat.

'I'd like to propose a toast,' said Pip, 'to my sisters, to our Django. To family.'

Django makes his announcement over strong Turkish coffee and enormous petits fours. He clears his throat and asks for silence, please, ladies.

'No doubt my impending milestone birthday has been the cause for much speculation – and I hope you haven't already planned a surprise party.'

'You're not going on a retreat are you?' Cat asks.

'On my seventy-fifth birthday?' Django objects. 'Good Lord no. I have no intention of retreating anywhere. Quite the opposite. They'll be coming out of the woodwork, far and wide, because I'm going to throw a party.'

'Here?'

'Of course *here*,' Django says, 'a huge rollicking knees-up that will rewrite the significance of May 16th in history. I'm going to have a party that'll be totally, eye-openingly unsuitable for someone of such an age.'

Cat, Fen and Pip gawp at him.

'You're all invited,' he assures them earnestly, 'along with anyone who thinks they might ever have known me.'

The Rag and Thistle

Early the following evening, Django placed his hands on Fen's shoulders. 'Do it for me,' he said quietly.

'It's only the Rag and Thistle,' said Pip, 'it's only down the road.'

'And it's my welcome-home weekend,' Cat protested.

'I don't *feel* like it,' Fen said.

'Your sisters request your company and I'd like to have my granddaughter all to myself,' Django said but he could see that he hadn't dented her defence. 'You do have faith in my abilities, don't you? Did I not bring up you three single-handedly – and fabulously – when your mother ran off with a cowboy from Denver?' He paused carefully to assess the just perceptible upturn to the corners of Fen's mouth. 'And isn't Cosima already sound asleep and unlikely to waken anyway?'

'It's not that,' Fen said. 'Of course I have faith in you. It's just I don't really feel like going out.' She wanted to sound needy rather than defensive so that they'd sympathize.

'But it's *my* weekend!' Cat reiterated.

Fen looked deeply uncomfortable. 'I don't want to go to the Rag and Thistle because I don't want to leave Cosima,' she explained, looking at the semicircle of her family surrounding her. 'It's not something that I've done. Why can't we just stay here – open some dodgy home-made elderberry wine?'

Her sisters and uncle regarded her while she scrutinized a threadbare patch on the Persian rug. Was that newspaper beneath it? Probably. When from, Fen wondered. She'd known the rug all her life.

'You mean to say you haven't had any time apart from Cosima in six months?' Cat asked.

'No – yes,' Fen elaborated, 'not really. Matt has babysat a couple of times.'

'You mean you and Matt haven't been out *together* since she was born?' Cat asked, thinking it sounded preposterous.

'That's right,' said Fen, with a tightness that told her audience she thought they shouldn't be questioning.

'That's *not* right,' said Cat, 'that's terrible.'

'Fuck off, Cat,' Fen said sharply.

'Don't swear,' Django said.

'I have offered,' Pip said to Cat and Django, 'to babysit.'

'But Cosima was colicky,' Fen said.

'No one's likely to judge your mothering abilities on whether you occasionally have some me-time,' said Django.

'It's not that,' Fen sighed.

'It's good for you,' said Pip, 'it said so in that baby book you keep in the loo.'

'What's all this Fen-bashing?' Fen asked. 'God, you're my bloody family. Cosima is a tiny baby and I'm allowed to indulge my maternal instincts.'

'I simply want the treat, the *honour*, of looking after my first granddaughter, and your sisters just wanted a couple of hours down the local with you to themselves,' Django reasoned. 'As you say – we are a bloody family.'

'It's not a challenge,' Pip said, 'it's just a quick drink down the pub, silly.'

'Christ, why is *everyone* calling me silly these days?' Fen muttered to herself. 'And it *is* a challenge, actually, to me. Do you not think it doesn't disturb me that my self-confidence can leak away like breast milk? That I'd reject my sisters' invitation to go out for a couple of drinks? That a strange and terrible part of me doesn't even trust the man who raised me to look after my baby for two tiny hours?' Her eyes darted around her family from under knotted eyebrows.

'Look – I'm sorry, Fen,' said Cat, who looked it. 'Please come. I'm so excited to be back. I've missed you.'

For a moment, Fen thought she might cry. Then she wanted to stand her ground and refuse. 'I don't know,' she faltered.

'Leave me a long list,' Django said brightly, 'with illustrations.'

So, still a little reluctantly, Fen took him at his word and did just that. When she was quite sure Cosima really was fast asleep, she left with her sisters for the Rag and Thistle.

As pubs go, the Rag and Thistle was both lively yet homey. Having been in the Merifield family for four generations, it retained the charm and authenticity that many brewery-owned pubs never achieve despite trying so obviously to replicate. Thus there were no mass-produced sepia pictures of Street Scene Anywhere but photos instead of Merifields old and young, dead and alive, their various dogs and horses, adorning most of the wall space. The cast of *Peak Practice* had signed beer mats which David Merifield had framed in a jaunty pattern around a cast photo. There was a paper serviette, illegibly autographed by an actress whose name no one could remember and sometimes this was hung upside down in case it was meant to be so. There were no laminated menus with novelty meals and photos of the dishes. Just simple home cooking, available whenever required. The bell for last orders was usually rung when someone remembered to ring it. The Rag and Thistle was a mainstay of the community and its community cherished it. Though the McCabe girls left home over a decade ago, they still think of it as their local and the Merifields welcome them back as if they last served them a drink just the day before.

'G & T,' Pip ordered.

'Glass of house red,' said Cat. 'Fen?'

'Oh go on then,' Fen said guiltily, 'V.a.T. But loads of tonic and easy on the vodka. I'm still breast-feeding, remember.'

'We couldn't possibly forget,' Pip murmured to Cat though it landed her a harsh glance from Fen.

'I'll bring them over,' said the publican Mr Merifield, who always treated the girls like royalty on their visits home. 'You'll be wanting to nab that table that's just come free.'

'So Django's going to throw a birthday party,' Cat marvelled, making a beeline for the table in the corner bedecked with horse brasses. 'Is he serious about having it at home? He could have it here.'

'This place couldn't fit everyone in – they'll be coming from the four corners of the earth,' said Pip.

'Didn't you know the earth was round?' said Mr Merifield, setting down their drinks.

'We're talking about Django's birthday.'

'Ah,' said Mr Merifield, 'and the party. No point us opening the pub that night – everyone will be at yours, if memories of his sixtieth party serve me right.' The girls laughed and everyone buried their heads in their hands.

'Can you believe he's going to be seventy-five?' Fen said, arranging a beer mat in front of each of them and removing the ashtray to the window sill with a look of utter distaste.

'It sounds so old,' said Cat. '*Seventy-five*.'

'He *is* a grandpa,' Fen defined, 'though actually he likes to be called Gramps.'

'Tom calls him that,' Pip explained to Cat. 'Tom calls him Django Gramps which is weird really, because he's even less of a real grandfather, in the literal sense, to Tom than he is to Cosima.'

'I laughed when you told me in that e-mail that Django refers to Tom as his "step-grandsonthing-or-other",' Cat told her.

'I wonder if our children will be confused that they have a grandpa for an uncle, but a non-existent grandmother?' Fen mused.

'They have other grandmas,' Pip said. 'Matt and Zac's mums.'

'It's odd,' said Fen and then she stopped. 'Nothing.'

'What?'

'It's just that, having really thought of her so rarely, just recently I've thought of her more.'

'Who?'

'Our mother,' Fen shrugged. 'Now that I have my baby. I just can't figure out how a mother can leave.'

'That's why we'll all make grade A mummies,' Cat said. 'We'll be automatically compensating for the fact that our mother was sub-Z grade.'

'It struck me recently that the only person I've ever called "Mummy" is myself,' Fen said. It quietly struck her sisters that they hadn't called anyone 'Mummy' at all.

'I can't wait to be called Mummy,' Cat said dreamily. 'Do you realize I was pretty much Cosima's age when our mother left?'

'It's only since having Cosima that maternal instincts, in all their crazy hormonal cladding, have made sense,' Fen continued, 'and to be honest, though previously I never much cared about her, it now makes me shudder. A woman ran off with a cowboy from Denver and left behind three girls under the age of *four*? How could she do it? How can a mother not have maternal instincts? It's *criminal.* They're *chemical.*' Fen looked at her sisters. 'I gaze at my daughter and I think of us three. Three tiny little girls. How could she have walked out?'

'I reckon life would still have been better under Django than under her if she hadn't left,' Pip reasoned. 'His maternal instincts more than made up for her lack of them.'

'It never bothered me before, really, because there were never situations when we wished we had her,' Fen reiterated quietly, 'but now, recently, it's made me utterly bewildered. Indignant too. That's why I don't like to be separated from Cosima. That's why I hold her so tight.' Pip and Cat regarded her and felt bad about before. 'I don't like missing a minute with her – not because I'm a hormonal fruit cake, though you probably think I am. But because, in my book, there cannot be such a thing as an overprotective mother.'

'Do you want another?' Cat asked Fen.

'God no,' said Fen, 'this one's gone to my head already.'

Cat laughed. 'I meant another baby – not vodka.'

'That would necessitate Matt and me having sex,' Fen said glumly.

'Oh God, does all that really go down the nappy-bin?' Cat asked.

'Pretty much,' Fen admitted. 'To be completely honest, we prefer that extra hour's sleep to banging away for an orgasm.'

'The royal "we"?' Pip asked. 'Do you speak for Matt?'

Fen blinked a little. 'You know blokes,' she laughed it off but didn't elaborate. 'The weird thing is, it all seems a bit irrelevant. As if Cosima has shown us what life's all about. It's like, in retrospect, it was all a means to an end. Fancying Matt, falling in love with him, rampant sex, domestic daydreams – it's as if all that was a preamble, all a clever cloak to ensure the continuation of the species. Having

Cosima has shown us that life is about going forwards with her, rather than backwards trying to cling on to pre-baby days.'

'Us?' Pip questioned. 'The royal "us"? Do you speak for Matt too?'

Fen glanced at her with fleeting annoyance. 'Life is more meaningful now that I'm a mummy,' she said to Cat. 'I have a true function, a role. I'm a mummy. I don't feel any need to reclaim my sexuality. This is me now. This is what I was made for. This is the best thing I've ever done.'

Cat thought this sounded extreme, mad even. Pip thought it was sad and she immediately wondered how Matt was. He was going out with Zac for a pint that night. She'd probe. She was fond of Matt and, being the Great Looker-Afterer, she'd see to it that his relationship with her sister did not suffer.

'God,' said Cat with nostalgic admiration, 'and you used to be such a vamp, Fen.'

'What are you talking about?' Fen rubbished. 'Me? A vamp? Hardly.'

'You were a downright slapper,' Pip teased.

'Piss off,' Fen protested, suddenly knowing to what they alluded and not wanting to revisit the past.

'Don't tell me your nappy-addled memory doesn't stretch back four years when you were having to choose between two men?' Pip said.

They looked at Fen who was peering through a cage of her fingers as if shying away from a horror movie that turned out to be her history. 'Stop it you two,' she winced, 'it was ages ago. It was a different me.'

'It was right here in Derbyshire,' Pip said pointedly.

'He moved away,' Fen said, 'a while ago. You know that.'

'Regrets?' Cat asked.

'Don't be daft,' Fen said.

'Does Matt know?' Cat wondered. 'Did you ever tell him?'

'Are you mad?' said Fen. 'It had no bearing on my feelings for Matt. When it ended, it didn't release extra love for me to bestow on Matt. My feelings for Matt never changed – my feelings for the other man did.'

'I love Matt,' Pip said.

'Me too,' said Fen, 'me too. I'm very lucky.' Suddenly she felt overwhelmingly sad. Just then she longed for Matt even more than she longed for Cosima. 'I'm such a crotchety old bag at the moment,' she admitted and her sisters could see fear written across her brow. 'I'm tired and narky the whole time. I can't seem to help it. Who is this Fen who doesn't have the energy to make love to her boyfriend, who has lost the desire to be touched but doesn't really care? I can't remember when I last told Matt that I love him.'

'You should, you know,' Pip said sternly, 'according to that baby book you keep in your loo.'

'Do you and Zac plan to have proper babies?' Cat asked. Fen and Pip stared at their younger sister whose cheeks suddenly turned the colour of her hair and she buried her head in her hands. 'God that sounded awful. Poor Tom – I didn't mean—!'

'It's not in our game plan,' Pip laughed. 'We're a gang of three. I like being a stepmum. It suits me. I'm not really broody, I don't think.'

'You wouldn't have time anyway,' Cat said, 'because you're always so busy looking after everyone else.' Pip looked a little nonplussed. 'It's a compliment,' Cat assured her. 'Even Django calls you the Great Looker-Afterer. You're only three years my senior but you've always mothered me. Capably, too.'

'And me,' said Fen.

'Someone had to,' Pip shrugged.

'To us,' said Fen, now toasting with mineral water, 'to sisterhood and motherhood.'

Pip went to bed hoping everyone was all right. She was worried about Fen. If having a baby had brought such sense and sunshine into her life, as Fen claimed, why did she seem so out of sorts? Alternately under-confident and yet smug, defensive yet somehow needy too. Pip didn't doubt that it was normal and right to be so absorbed in her child, but she was concerned that Fen seemed so defiantly blasé about the other aspects of her life. As if being a mother had given her a superiority complex and inferiority issues in one fell swoop.

And what about Cat and Ben? Pip lay there anxious that her youngest sister had skipped back home hoping to play out a rather unrealistic daydream of easy baby-making and rosy domesticity.

She thought about Zac. And Tom. Just then Pip felt intensely grateful for Tom. Really, what a joy her gorgeous stepson was – what a privilege to have so many rewards without any of the hormonal rumpus apparently affecting her younger sister. She chastised herself sharply for certain occasions when she was irritated by Tom; when he hogged Zac or overran the flat, when Zac all but ignored her, when Tom appeared to think he needn't listen to what she said.

I'd hate anything to disrupt what I have with Zac. There's a safe harmony between us; I know when our tides come in and go out. Tom graces our lives but ultimately, by virtue of the living arrangements, lets them be as well. Zac and I are man and wife in the conventional sense but I still feel we're girlfriend and boyfriend too. Nothing is a chore, nothing is a bore. Everything is a treat. The sexual buzz I feel for him is as charged now as ever it has been. Our domestic set-up is perfect. Nothing can better it. As a couple, we have freedom and privacy and Tom.

As Cat lay in bed, she wondered whether she could still blame jet lag for making her feel suddenly so teary. She considered going downstairs – Django would be up for another hour or so, with his 'medicinal' brandy. Or whisky if he'd used all the brandy in the soup. Or she could knock out the special sequence on the wall dividing her room from Pip's. Pip would remember their childhood code, the tympanic lingo of knuckle against plaster. Long, short, short – Are you awake? Short, long, long – Come in here. Long, long, short, short – Can I come in?

It's just the jet lag. I'll let Pip sleep. I'll let Django relax over the day-before-yesterday's crossword. I won't disturb Fen. Actually, I don't really want to talk to her. I hope having a baby won't make me like her. That sounds awful. Fen's consuming passion for Cosima, her zeal for her role as mother, is beautiful on one level – lucky little Cosima. But where's my sister gone? Where's Matt's girl? Where's Trust Art's brilliant art historian and archivist? I've come home to find that Fen has only half an ear to lend us and half her personality available. That sounds harsh. Perhaps I don't understand. But I don't want it to be like that for me. Cosima has gained a brilliant mother but we've lost Fen. It will be different for Ben and me. A baby is for the two of us. At the end of the day, it will always be Ben and me and when baby makes three, we'll welcome it into our life. I can't wait.

Fen's daughter slept soundly in her pop-up travel cot, making occasional grunts and snuffles. Fen listened carefully, while gazing around her childhood bedroom which Django had lovingly preserved. Above her head, an Athena poster of a semi-nude faceless bloke in peculiar tones of lilac duelled for attention against pouting men with big hair and a penchant for frills who postured down from album covers drawing-pinned to the wall. Teenage angst novels crammed a shelf, flanked by two chunks of Derbyshire stone holding their skinny spines straight. Under the Formica dressing-table, over-sized tiger-feet slippers, padded with scrunches of *Racing Post* from 1989. In her bedside drawer, the jewels of her pocket-money days: a Mexican silver brooch in the shape of a cat, small 9ct gold hoop earrings with a single seed pearl, a silver-plated heart-shaped locket whose hinge broke when she opened it and found it empty, a three-band Russian wedding ring she'd bought for Pip's fifteenth birthday but decided to keep for herself yet never felt comfortable wearing. It was all tarnished, everything was a little bashed.

It felt strange to be in a single bed, strange that only two-thirds of her own little family were together that night, nicely strange to miss Matt. She smiled at the pin-ups of her teenage years and suddenly Matt's face loomed large in her mind's eye. She hoped she loved him as much as she used to. Again, she felt subsumed by a longing tinged with loneliness and she sent him a text message saying night night love your girls xxxx. She looked at it and worried over the lack of punctuation, that he might think she was nagging him to love his girls. Hopefully he'd be distracted by all the x's instead.

Her mind drifted back to a time before Cosima. Not so long ago, really, there was a girl called Fen for whom motherhood had then been such a distant notion as to have had no realism. It was like recalling a best friend she hadn't seen for years, a soulmate who had gone so far away that their paths would never now cross. Just then, it made Fen wistfully sad. She reminisced that there had been fun in all that dangerous gallivanting. It had been liberating and energizing, being responsible for no one but herself.

She thought back to that heady time when she and Matt had just met at work and were embarking on the definitive office fling. She conjured again the feeling of exquisite anticipation, remembered so clearly sitting amongst the papers and pictures and boxes in the archives willing Matt to rudely interrupt her with a furtive snog and a grope. She relived the joy of racing down the corridor to delight Matt with her unbridled enthusiasm about some discovery or other amongst the dust and documents. She felt again the euphoric pride when their romance was exposed amongst their colleagues, when they were the centre of attention, the focus of gossip and approval, soon enough the benchmark for love and romance.

And then she thought back to those short, secret trips to Derbyshire around the same time, to those exhilarating afternoons of sex with another man; the urgency to have her desire sated but to make her home-bound train. It's really only now that she feels horror while she wonders what on earth all that was about, how bizarre it all was. At the time she'd divided her heart meticulously into two and coolly separated her body from her conscience. It had been intoxicatingly exciting for a while. It hadn't felt wrong. But then her sisters found out. And, in retrospect, thank God for Cat and Pip badgering her on the finer points of morality. Thank God she chose Matt and he never found out. And thank God she'd grown out of all of that. And grown up. And most of all, thank God for her beautiful beautiful baby.

As Fen lay thinking, her hands subconsciously assessed the changes in her body. Really, she knew she ought to adore her post-birth figure, her fuller breasts and becoming curves. But lying there, squidging more than an inch to the pinch, she did not. Instead, she tormented herself with clear images of how her body had been when it was the object of all that sexual attention. Pert and lithe and powerful in its energy and desirability. Ultimately, though, it did not come down to aesthetics. Her body was no longer her own now. It was as if, in nurturing a baby, she'd renounced sole ownership. Though she was slowly scaling down breast-feeding she knew she'd never have the same freedom with her body, she wouldn't be reclaiming it as her own.

Does Matt miss it? My body? Does he miss the way we were? I don't like to think that he might. I haven't asked him on purpose. I've just been hoping that his tolerant nature and all those ante-natal classes plus the magazines I leave lying around and the baby book that's in the loo will have filtered through, will have put paid to any resentment or disaffection.

Anyway, what was all that spontaneity actually worth? Was it really such a privilege to be able to do as we pleased whenever we liked? I suppose I'm on a crusade of sorts – that what we have now completely outweighs what we were then. Surely Matt feels the same?

Django pottered around downstairs. He couldn't find the crossword from the day before yesterday. He couldn't even find today's paper. Then he remembered he'd used one to wrap up the giblets. And he'd used another to wrap up the broken wine bottle which had tumbled onto the flagstone floor after he'd sloshed its contents into the stew with excessive flamboyance. Instead, with jazz playing softly, he tidied and swept and took lengthy breaks to sip a little whisky.

He had loved babysitting Cosima. She was an angel who hadn't woken once but still he'd taken his responsibility gravely and hadn't dared tidy or sweep or search for lost crosswords lest she should wake and he not hear her. Sipping whisky any earlier had been quite out of the question. He'd spent most of the evening intermittently creeping up the stairs to the point where he knew the treads would creak. He could sense the baby in the silence and he'd had a lovely evening, halfway up the stairs. He was pleased Cosima hadn't woken because he wanted to be able to reassure Fen on her return. He hoped the fact would bolster her, encourage her to breathe a little more deeply in fresh space of her own, or even breathe a little more lightly in other spaces.

I can reason it out. I can see why. Couldn't anybody? Her mother buggers off with a cowboy so Fen has decided she won't be leaving her baby at all. That's OK. That's OK. It's still relatively early days. But I hope all is well with Matt. I'll invite them for a weekend soon. I'll take him to the Rag. Or perhaps I'll babysit and send the two of them there for a little them-time.

How lovely to have our Cat back in the bag. A relief that her accent is unmodified by her time abroad. She's grown, she's bloomed, she's chopped off her hair and she's home. I must have her and Ben up for a weekend too. He's a good chap. I'll try and find an opportune moment to slip in my little query. I'm sure it's nothing but if he could just pop his doctor's hat on for a minute or two I could ask him a couple of questions and be done with it. I don't want to worry the girls, or waste my own GP's time. It's probably nothing. I'm probably daft for even noticing it. After all, I am growing old – I can hardly expect the rude health I used to enjoy.

Pip looks well. Whoever would have thought that the wilful girl who denounced any merit in love and money, found both in the good form of Zac? And a ready-made son too! Tom may officially be a stepson but that doesn't place him on any lower rung in my affection. He's my grandson-thing-or-other. And I'm most certainly his Gramps. I haven't seen him for far too long, though I wrote him a letter in rhyme last week which I'll try and remember to post when I'm in Bakewell next Tuesday.

Funny thing, blood ties. I don't think of Tom as any less

my grandchild than Cosima. Some pompous old genealogist wouldn't even consider me a grandfather. I'd be stuck out on a limb on a sub-branch of some silly conventional family tree. But the girls do and the children do and that's what counts. My nit-pickin' chicks, back together in the embrace of our funny family.

Penny Ericsson

On the other side of the Atlantic, it is still the day before and Penny Ericsson is wondering how to handle the hollow stretch of another evening alone. This is her twenty-fourth since Bob, her husband of thirty years, died. And though friends have ensured that she does not often spend long tracts of time on her own, Penny has felt utterly alone whether she has company or not.

Her house is immaculate. She is not hungry. She doesn't care for television. There's nothing to do but grieve. In some ways, it makes sense of her life. You love, you lose, you grieve for ever more.

Even the staircase feels longer and steeper now Bob's gone.

'Life's gonna be one long drag,' Penny murmurs as she ventures downstairs because she's been doing nothing upstairs for ages. She rotates all the scatter cushions from resting like squares on the two large sofas to perching like rhombs. She changes the angle of the many framed photographs on the mantelpiece so that they all seem to be standing in line to the right. She chooses two large art books from the shelves to replace the current photography books on the coffee table. She sits beside them and laughs hysterically. So many places to sit, so much time. Too much time. She decides the scatter cushions look ridiculous and they should live up to their name so she chucks them around the sofas until she feels they've found their natural grouping. Still she doesn't fancy sitting there. She gazes at Bob's chair and her laughter is stilled by a sigh that seems to start in the pit of her gut and expels every molecule of breath in her body.

'You know, I always thought you were ugly and nothing but,' she says. 'I mean, my cooker may be ugly but I like it. But you, you I never liked. If I'd had my way I'd've sent you back just as soon as you arrived.' She looks out of the window. More snow. 'Think what I could've had here without you taking up all the space. You're the ugliest chair in the world. With some things, you can appreciate that form simply follows function. My summer sandals for example. If they were pretty I'll bet you they wouldn't be comfortable. But look at you – you're ugly and you don't even look like you'd be comfortable.'

There's someone at the door. A rattle of friendly knocks followed by a ring of the bell.

'Penny? Penny honey – you home?'

It's Marcia and she's gonna let herself in anyway.

'Pen? It's me. I've brought soup. Snow's said to be bad tomorrow. You in here?'

'In *here*,' Penny's voice filters through to the kitchen where Marcia has put the soup on the stove. She goes through to the sitting-room to find Penny.

'Hey you.'

'Hullo, Marcia.'

'You sitting in the dark on the coffee table for a reason? You want me to get some lights on in here?'

'Sure. I didn't see it's gotten dark. I've been sitting here, Lord knows how long, cussing Bob's chair.'

'Cussing Bob's chair,' Marcia says sagely. 'Well, you never did like that thing.'

'If the first sign of madness is talking to oneself, then talking to a chair must make me insane. But hell, it's ugly.'

'Ah – but is it comfortable?'

Suddenly Penny finds she's laughing again. Marcia seems taken aback. 'You know something, I don't know! I never even sat on it! I never tried!'

Marcia's eyebrows, tweezered into supercilious arches, shoot heavenwards. 'In thirty years, you never sat on it *once*?'

'Not once.'

The notion is simultaneously idiotic and rather amazing. 'Was that out of pure stubbornness?'

'A little,' Penny smiles forlornly, 'but then you see, Bob was usually sitting there himself.'

Marcia sits down alongside Penny and places a hand gently on her arm. They gaze over to the chair, both trying to privately conjure Bob – any image of him, at any point over the years – sitting in his chair. Marcia finds she can do so with ease; for Penny it's impossible.

When is his face going to come back to me? Why can't I remember how tall he was? Which way did he position his legs when he sat in that chair?

'Did you ever see Bob sit anyplace other?' Penny remarks wistfully.

'You know what,' Marcia marvels gently, 'no I did not.'

'For thirty years I've been complaining about it – I told Bob over and again that it was a clumpy, ugly thing, out of keeping with all our other furniture. But he wouldn't consider looking at an alternative. He'd sit there, relaxed as you like, while I cussed.' Penny gives just a little laugh. 'I can throw it out now,' she says, with dull triumph, 'I can dump it outside. I can have it chopped up for the fire.'

'Oh don't chop it up, my dear,' Marcia takes Penny at her word. 'Perhaps the refuge – they might find a good home for it?'

'Perhaps,' says Penny. Then she frowns. 'You know something, crazy as it sounds, I couldn't bear to. All these years I've been hating it. But just now, this instant, I love it. It's just where it's always been. And here it shall stay. I'll give it a good home – right here. How insane is that?'

'Honey, are you doing OK?' Marcia asks tenderly, giving Penny's arm a squeeze of wordless sympathy and concern.

'No. I'm not,' Penny states confidently, sucking in her bottom lip so hard her face looks turtle-like and inappropriately comic.

'It's been less than a month,' Marcia almost doesn't want to remind her.

'Twenty-four days,' Penny shrugs.

'Honey,' Marcia tries to soothe though she feels impotent in the presence of such pain.

'What am I going to do without him?' Penny asks. 'What else do I have?'

Suddenly, Marcia is acutely aware of the fact that her own husband is just fine. Just down the street and just fine. It's almost embarrassing. She feels guilty. And she's horribly aware that next week, she'll be swanning off to their winter home in Florida. 'Why don't we all go to Boca for the winter?' she says. 'I mean, Mickey and I are planning to leave next week but there's so much room for you too. Oh say you'll come. Stay as long as you fancy. I'd love it. It would be good, Penny.'

'I'll be fine here,' Penny says, surprising herself at how decisive she sounds. 'This is my home.'

'You know you can just call whenever? Come whenever?' Marcia says. She looks out of the window. 'I'd better go – it's snowing hard now. You eat that soup. I'll call you later. I'll see myself out.'

'Thanks for stopping by,' Penny says and she's ready for Marcia to go. She wants to be on her own, free to grieve, free to drift into a space where just perhaps she might feel Bob still. A semi-dreamland.

She listens to the muffled sound of Marcia's car driving through the fresh snow and away. She turns the lights out in the sitting-room and stands in the darkness quietly. The snow sends silver glances into the room. The moonlight silhouettes the hills as a lumbering but benign presence. Penny wishes she hadn't rubbished clairvoyance and the concept of the Spirit. Because just say it is for real, say it really does exist – has she jinxed herself by being a cynic most of her life? Are you there? Can I sense you? Is that you I can hear? How was your day, honey? Can I fix you a drink? You sit yourself down in your chair. That goddam ugly chair. Let me fetch you a Scotch. Then you can tell me about your day.

'I never even sat in that chair.'

Penny goes to it and sits down. She has no idea whether the chair is comfortable or not. It is as close as she can now get to being with Bob again. She sleeps.

Home from Home

Cat sat at the table, in the furnished flat she and Ben were renting, tracing a pattern someone else had gouged into the wood at some point. Some previous tenant with little respect, she assumed with distaste. As she ran her finger over it, she considered perhaps it wasn't wilful carving, it might even be as old as the table – a slip of the original carpenter's chisel? It was a nice piece of old farmhouse pine. Ben watched Cat work her middle finger along the furrow as if she was gouging it anew.

'Are you OK, babe?' he asked, looking from one tub of fresh pasta sauce to another. He held them to Cat for final selection.

'Arabiata,' she said. 'I'm fine.'

'Liar,' said Ben. 'What's up?' He left the sauce to simmer and sat, cowboy style, astride the chair next to Cat. He brought his face to the level of hers. Cat looked at him, stuck out her bottom lip in an over-exaggerated pout that she knew would invite a kiss, and shrugged.

'How are your sisters?' he asked. 'How's Django? Everything was all right up there, wasn't it?'

'God, fine,' Cat assured him. 'I don't know. It's just that

it's all changed a little since we've been gone. I suppose I was expecting to find my life, my family, just as I left them. As if they'd been happily freeze-framed in anticipation of my return.'

'And?' Ben said.

'Now Django's going to be seventy-five,' Cat said quietly.

'You staying in the UK the last four years couldn't have prevented that,' Ben pointed out.

'And Pip is more sensible than she used to be,' Cat bemoaned. 'By that I mean she's all settled and content with her grown-up role as a school-run stepmum.'

'What's wrong with that?' Ben asked. 'And aren't you settled and content?'

'Of course I am, you know I am,' said Cat. 'But Pip's the one who should be doing cartwheels down the hallway, who makes teaspoons disappear and then reappear from behind my ear. She didn't do one handstand against the wall this weekend.'

'It was the weekend. She was off duty,' Ben pointed out. 'It's normal for people to not want to take their work home with them. Imagine if I came home with my stethoscope, or took the blood pressure of any visitors to our house.'

'But we don't own a house,' Cat mumbled, 'just this horrid rented flat.'

'Cat!' Ben remonstrated. 'We've been back in the UK two bloody minutes.'

Cat ignored him by changing the subject. 'Fen is in the throes of this immense love affair with her baby and she can talk of nothing else.'

'What's wrong with that?' Ben asked. Cat shrugged.

She wasn't prepared to say out loud that though her niece was utterly adorable, she had found Fen uptight, boring even.

'They're not who they were,' Cat said. 'Their identities have changed.' She could hear the plaintive edge to her voice.

'That's par for the course – growing up, growing old,' Ben said, though he saw his wife flinch from his cheeriness. 'Anyway, they probably find you different too. But that's no bad thing.'

'I don't like this place,' Cat said, irritated. 'I don't like other people's furniture. I don't like stupid Clapham. I want to be in our own place, with our stuff. Perhaps we should have rented unfurnished. Perhaps we should have stayed in the US. It's all going to take ages.'

Ben looked at her, suddenly serious. 'Nothing's going to happen overnight,' he said. 'It'll take a while to attain Pip's peace of mind and Fen's healthy baby. Nine months at the very least.'

Cat thought for a moment. Perhaps that was it – perhaps she didn't resent her sisters their changes, perhaps she aspired to what they had. Or there again maybe it was just jet lag.

'I'll tell you what was peculiar,' she said. 'Fen talked about how being a mother had made her really think about our own mother. It had me thinking too.' Her voice dropped to a whisper. 'But say. Just say.' She looked imploringly at Ben, as if he might know what without her having to just say.

'Just say what?' he asked.

Cat paused. 'Just say it's hereditary?'

'But you just said that Fen is a caring mother to the point of being obsessed,' Ben said carefully.

Cat glanced at him shyly. She shook her head. 'I don't mean Fen. Say it runs in the family. Say I'll be a crap mother? Maybe I should concentrate on my career for the time being.'

Ben thought for a moment, scratched his neck. 'Actually, genetics rarely play a part in such extreme behaviour,' he said. 'For all you know, your mother sucks in her bottom lip – like you do – and that's the only family trait you've inherited from her. Think of Fen – mother superior, however much she might irritate you. Think of Pip – her maternal connection with Tom is great and there's no blood there. You McCabe girls are all destined to be extraordinary mothers – by virtue of the fact that your own set such a poor example.'

He watched Cat start to thaw. He ruffled her hair and she ruffled his. Then they put their foreheads together for a moment.

'Being a mother is a state of mind, a condition of the heart, as much as it is biological,' Ben said. 'Christ, look at Django – he's the best mother you girls could have wished for. Stop worrying, Cat. You'll be a star.'

'Do you really think so?' Cat asked, a little bashful but privately delighted.

'I do,' said Ben, 'but we have to get you pregnant first.'

Cat propped her head, chin in her hand, and looked over to Ben. 'It's what I love about you,' she said in an intentionally dreamy tone, 'that you know me inside out but I never feel I'm getting on your nerves. You love me in spite of my foibles. You're so tolerant. That's what I so love about you – that you so love me.'

'Stop it,' Ben joshed, getting up and checking his pager, 'you make me sound a wuss. And anyway, I thought you loved me for my enormous dick.'

* * *

'I cannot believe that I'm going to spend my Saturday traipsing around Alexandra Palace at a convention of model railway nutters and their train sets!' Pip declared, only half joking, surveying the hall and its eccentric population.

Zac raised his eyebrows. 'Firstly, it's the Thames and District Society of Model Engineers. Secondly, if it wasn't for me, you'd have to spend *every* Saturday dressed ridiculously trying to entertain roomloads of sugar-crazed party children.'

Pip fanned out her fingers in front of her sulky expression, then furled them away to reveal a winsome look with much batting of doe eyes. Zac crossed his arms and regarded her sternly. She fanned and then furled her fingers once more, reinstating a natural grin to her face.

'Thirdly,' Zac continued, 'we haven't had Tom for two weekends in a row.'

Pip nodded. 'I know,' she said, 'I'm only joking.'

'Look at him,' Zac said softly, noting that his son had teamed up with a new-found posse of young rail boffins, 'he's in his element.'

Tom was a thoughtful child; not shy, popular at school, but thoughtful. Zac had a theory that boys were divided into two camps: football and fantasy. His nine-year-old son was firmly in the fantasy camp. It wasn't that the restrictions of his eczema ruled out football, it was that Tom's natural interests were dominated by trains and dinosaurs. *My son the trainspotter who knows his connector rods from his couplings*, Zac would say with pride. *My son who could spell pterodactyl before he could spell his own name*, Zac would beam.

Watching an animated Tom admiring the array of essential pieces of kit and name-dropping each model engine from at least fifty paces with his new pals, Pip was consumed by a totally unexpected pang. It was like an electric shock and she jolted physically.

'Are you OK?' Zac asked.

Pip nodded earnestly and went off at a tangent to dislodge the thought. 'Django called us lot the "nit-pickin' chicks" last weekend.'

'That's a fine Djangoism if ever I heard one,' Zac laughed, strolling on to the next stand.

'He hasn't called us that for ages. Mind you, it's been a while since the three of us sat like that,' Pip said wistfully. 'We always used to, when we were little – gravitate into a huddle, play with each other's hair, trace patterns on each other's clothes, tickle each other's forearms. We do it absent-mindedly.'

'Nit-pickin' chicks,' Zac mused. 'I'd've called you a bunch of monkeys, I think. Did you ever actually *have* nits?'

Pip laughed. 'I do remember that we all had them at the same time – some epidemic at school. But of course Django couldn't be doing with those torture combs and vile chemical shampoos so he doused our hair in some bizarre concoction of mustard powder and bicarbonate of soda. Or something. Tabasco. I don't know.'

'Did it work?'

'The daft thing is, I can't remember,' Pip laughed. 'I can only remember feeling slightly miffed that not even a case of head lice was going to make Django conform to conventional methods. I do remember the three of us having pretty short haircuts soon after. Django appeased us by saying our hair was so glorious that he'd been able to sell the offcuts to a master upholsterer in London and we would each be paid £5. We believed him. Even though the salon junior was sweeping it all away.'

'And you were £5 richer?'

'We were,' Pip laughed, 'though of course, Django made a rod for his back because we expected payment for every haircut thereafter.'

'You must have done well, between the master upholsterer and the tooth fairy,' Zac said.

'The tooth fairy never paid cash,' Pip bemoaned.

'Can I have some money?' a flushed and rather breathless Tom jogged over to ask. 'I'd like to buy the guys a juice. They're 50p each. I need about £2.'

Pip looked over to where the other three boys were loitering by a spectacular G Scale display. 'They seem nice,' she said, 'nice guys.'

'They are,' said Tom proudly. 'They're coming again

tomorrow. It's the last day of the show. There's a prize draw. A model of Lampton Tank. Can we come again too?'

'Sure,' Zac told Tom, and Pip took a deep breath. Hadn't they planned to take Tom to Tate Modern and then have lunch with Cat and Ben? Yes, father and son hadn't had a whole weekend together for three weeks but Tom had met Cat only a handful of times over the last four years. However, watching Tom belt off to buy refreshments for his steam gang, Pip let her breath and the objection go. He was a sweet, sweet boy.

Again, the pang confronted Pip and she shuddered. Zac sensed it. 'Pip?'

'Do you think Tom minds?' she asked Zac. 'I mean, do you think he ever minds being an only child?'

Zac looked at Pip and frowned into thought. 'I don't think so,' he said at length, 'I mean, he's never mentioned it. He has plenty of pals and he's thick as thieves with his first cousin.'

'I know,' Pip rushed, 'I just meant. I was just thinking about my sisters. Our closeness. I read a lovely saying the other day – Vietnamese, I think. *Brothers and sisters are as close as hands and feet.*'

Zac kissed Pip. 'Well, worry no more,' he said, 'because Tom isn't to be an only child for much longer. I mean, he may be *our* only child, but he's soon to have a sibling. June is pregnant. She told me this morning when I picked Tom up. He doesn't know yet – June wants to wait till the tests are all-clear. Rob asked me if we'd mind having Tom an extra night now and then while June is feeling ropy.'

Pip was dumbstruck, felt flushed and suddenly light-headed.

'Are you sure you're OK?' Zac pressed. 'You look a little odd, Mrs.'

'I'm fine. Good for June. Great news. I'll call her later.

Odd, though,' Pip said, though she was aware that her thoughts were unreliably half-formed and should stay silent until worked through, 'odd that Tom's being was the result of two friends getting drunk, feeling horny and being careless – yet his half sibling has been meticulously planned. I wonder how he'll feel about that later on.'

Zac stopped. 'What a weird take on it all, Pip,' he murmured.

Pip shrugged. 'I used to wonder if I was planned, you see,' she said. 'I used to presume that I *wasn't* planned – because that meant my mother had some kind of excuse for buggering off.' Pip linked arms with Zac. 'But then I think of Fen and Cat and my theory goes out the window. No one could be that careless.'

Zac slipped his hand into the back pocket of Pip's jeans and gave her buttock a light feel. 'Well, I'm pleased for June and Rob. And I'm made up for Tom.'

'Me too,' Pip said, 'me too.' But she turned away from Zac to conceal the prickle of tears, feigning interest in a Hornby set-up, while trying to figure out the provenance of these tears. And whether they were happy or sad.

Cosima was fed orange food, entertained, fed more orange food, played with, bathed, given some bosom, sung to, cuddled, cuddled some more and placed gently in her cot where she'd promptly fallen into a blissful sleep with the revolving night light and an *Elvis for Babies* CD playing softly.

'Perfect *perfect* baby,' Fen thought to herself as she padded out of the room. 'Bloody awful day.'

She went to the bathroom and tidied up, catching sight of herself in the mirror.

'Yuk. You haggard old bag.'

With a rubber duck in one hand and a Miffy flannel in

the other, she peered closer at her reflection. Sallow and saggy, limp and lacklustre, hollow and haggard, she thought. Then she thought, poor old Matt. Fancy coming home to *this* every evening. Not much to fancy at all. So she rummaged around in her long-forsaken make-up bag and turned to her faithful Clarins mainstays for assistance. Just closing her eyes and slowly, properly, cleansing her face felt as heavenly as a spa facial. Exfoliate. Moisturize. A careful dab of concealer under the eyes, a swipe of mascara, a lick of lippy for the hell of it. Lastly, a few pinches to her cheeks which made her eyes smart a little but gave her cheek-bones a comely emphasis. Matt's key in the door. Hear Matt sigh. A dormant butterfly taking wing in her stomach. Here, Matt, this'll make you feel better.

'Hullo,' Fen said, walking downstairs, carefully tucking her hair behind her ears.

'Hiya,' Matt replied. 'You look – have you got make-up on?'

'Yup.'

'Why?'

Fen frowned and wondered which way to take this. She felt helpless not to opt for the wrong way. 'Because I feel a frump and I feel I look worse than I feel,' she snapped.

'Are you fishing for compliments and craving attention?' Matt teased her. Fen felt embarrassed.

'Well, I think you look very pretty,' said Matt, 'and it's a nice distraction from the baby puke on your top.'

Fen didn't know which to take off first, the make-up or her messy top.

By the end of a rerun episode of *Taggart*, Fen was chanting to herself, *I will instigate sex; I will, I will.* But by the end of *News at Ten* half an hour later, she was willing herself to simply stay awake.

‘Tired?’ Matt asked.

Ruefully, Fen nodded.

‘Go to bed,’ he suggested with a friendly pat to her knee.

And therein lay the calamity. As much as Fen feared the platonic mundanity of Matt’s knee-patting, she loved his suggestion that she go to bed. She still wanted Matt to desire her, she thought she wanted to desire him, but actually her strongest inclination at the moment was to go to sleep. She sat beside him, torn between what her body was shouting at her and what her conscience was whispering and what her partner was sweetly telling her.

‘I was trying to be all vampy for you,’ she confessed, ‘like the girl you fell for. But I’m just a tired old frump.’

‘Fen,’ Matt said, ‘don’t worry about it. Just go to bed.’

Fen had looked nice. Matt thought about it as he zapped TV channels. The messy top didn’t matter. He felt a little badly for her – she’d made an effort but an effort it had obviously been. There was nothing on television. Matt looked around the living-room. A soft towelling rabbit on the armchair, one tiny sock under it. A muslin square, scrunched up, on top of yesterday’s *Evening Standard*. A glob of something orange just above the skirting board. The all-pervasive scent of laundry washed in hypo-allergenic powder. But suddenly, Matt didn’t want to smell drying babygros. He snapped his eyes shut. He didn’t want to see any of these accoutrements of fatherhood. Actually, all he wanted to see was tits and arse. Quietly, he tiptoed up to the bedroom. It was dark, Fen was sleeping. Could he wake her? Would she mind? Dare he risk it? But realistically, was there really much point trying? He went instead to the cupboard, eased open the door, waited a moment to see if she’d woken. She hadn’t. By feel, he differentiated between the suits that were hanging there, found the Paul

Smith one according to its superior cloth. He slipped his hand into the pocket and tiptoed his fingers along the edges of some discs. One would do. It didn't matter which. Though Fen slept on oblivious, Matt still felt obliged to tuck the DVD up his jumper and hurry from the room as noiselessly as he'd entered.

Porn. Odd stuff, really. In reality, pneumatic women had never been Matt's type, let alone the stuff harboured in secret fantasies. He'd never pursued a situation of sharing a girl with another bloke, exotic underwear had never really turned him on and he could take or leave the thought of getting down with a pair of rampant twin sisters. But Matt had always enjoyed porn. He'd been sustained by top-shelf supplies as a teenager, even wondering if sex for real could ever match up to the thunderous wanks he indulged in. And then in his early twenties, purchasing hardcore videos by mail order became a rite of passage. Did he dare? Yes he did. Matt Holden became Mr M. Smith and Mr M. Smith shared his consignments amongst the lads with whom he lived. By his mid-twenties, Matt was a serial monogamist and there were rarely fallow periods long enough between girlfriends to warrant the purchase of new porn. But then his girlfriend had become the mother of his child, their sex life had dwindled and porn had progressed to DVD.

Tiptoeing back downstairs, he didn't check which disc he'd pulled out. He'd never been one for the stories; he never had to start a scene from the beginning. He wanted cunts and cocks to fill his screen just as soon as he pressed play; fast forward any kissing or slinky foreplay, just delve in deep to the fucking and sucking. Matt loaded a disc and, with the sitting-room door ajar and the TV volume low, skipped forward until a mêlée of bodies was having sex in his face. Fantastic, he commented under his breath, as a variously pierced woman with a shorn head and spiked dog-collar was simultaneously being double penetrated, wanked upon, and orally stuffed from an incongruously orderly queue of erections.

Matt masturbated frantically and synchronized his orgasm with a generalized spurting from the remainder of his on-screen cohorts who were not yet spent. Their spunk was gobbled up; Matt had to mop up his from his belly. He didn't realize until he'd done it that he'd used the muslin square his daughter nustled up to, not the sheets of kitchen paper he'd prepared in advance. He was aghast. He put the soiled muslin into a plastic bag, knotted it and then threw it away in the dustbin outside. He wouldn't even want it washed on the hottest cycle. He took his DVD and made his way quietly upstairs, putting it back in the pocket of his Paul Smith suit before going in to check on Cosima. He slipped into bed and lay in the dark, staring at an approximation of the ceiling. He felt utterly empty.

I've always thought a wank to porn is similar to a curry. The sort of thing one craves, one hungers for. You're absolutely in the mood, so looking forward to it, ravenous to the point of visible drool – poppadams or a smooth little blow-job scene to whet the appetite and get you started, then straight for the glut of hot and spicy. Stuff it in. Gorge. But like a curry, once you've had your fill you really don't want to look at what's left on your plate; so it is with hard-core – once you're done you just don't want to see any more.

I feel grubby and not nice. I wanked into my baby's muslin. Fen's asleep upstairs while downstairs I'm shooting my load with a bunch of blokes over some really quite ugly woman. Physically I'm relieved, sated. But I feel a bit, I don't know – sad.

He listened to Fen's breathing, soft and shallow. Turning

towards her he spooned lightly against her. The sleep-scent wafted from her neck. Matt closed his eyes.

My sexy girlfriend who I used to fuck became this amazing vessel who carried and bore my child. But I miss fucking my sexy girlfriend.

Winter Ice

'Perhaps I'll thaw when spring comes,' Penny muttered to herself, a gaze at the wide white world beyond her picture windows informing her that she could thus stay exactly as she was for a good couple of months still. Her solitude and grief felt cathartic, they were becoming a way of life though she quietly wondered if they risked becoming a habit that would soon be hard to break. Penny Ericsson may have lived in the States for most of her adult life and though her accent was commendable and she had not left the country for practically thirty years, she displayed a control when it came to expressing emotions that her friends fondly remarked was transparently English.

'Oh honey,' Marcia once laughed, 'you fool no one with your rhinestones and your blue jeans and your Chevy and all. You're still an English Rose at heart – and that's because you keep your heart all polite and proper.'

'You mean to say that English women are incapable of expressing their emotions?' Penny had retorted.

'Heavens no,' Marcia had said, 'it's just we *guys* gush, while you *chaps* are more, well, *sparing*. It's genetic, is all. Nothing any of us can do about it. We are who we are. Can't deny that.'

And yet just recently, Penny felt her all-American friends, with their gushing and their ability to frequently say *I love you*, now seemed to expect her grief to have lessened. That she ought to feel able to find closure, be ready to move on, and confront a host of other emotional achievements carrying the Oprah Winfrey seal of approval.

Noni had left her a message, inviting her to see a movie at the Mall.

'I'll not go,' Penny told herself and justified that it was because she didn't share Noni's taste in film. Really, she didn't want to have to act upbeat and lie that she was doing just fine. But what else to do? What might pass time, occupy a couple of hours of her day which would be otherwise devoted to the futility of missing Bob? Where could she go in her snowbound county on a bright February afternoon and not bump into a soul?

'I could go for an ice cream,' she said, and she found that the notion was sweet. In fact, she was nearly excited. She'd go in honour of Bob, who had always loved the stuff, and by venturing by herself back to their favourite parlour she'd be simultaneously closer to him while also laying just a little more of him to rest.

There was only the one road into the mountains, with three communities of decreasing scale placed along it. They'd developed organically but a town planner could not have done better. Nothing was duplicated. Everything was shared. Lester Falls, where Penny lived and the largest town, had the Mall and a cinema and a Pack'n'Save on the outskirts. The smaller Hubbardton's Spring, further along and higher up, had a great fish place, a lively pizzeria, a gallery and a hardware store amongst its amenities. The last village, smallest in population but servicing the wider community no less, was Ridge. There, on Main Street, cosy alongside the bookstore, a small theatre, art supplies and a cheese maker, was Bob's favourite ice-cream parlour, Fountains.

Supply and demand. Make superior ice cream from the finest ingredients and people will want it, whatever the weather. The parlour wasn't busy, but it was by no means empty and Penny was relieved to see it wasn't patronized solely by brave widows out for day-trips. Recently, when browsing at the Mall, or strolling the nature trail to the panorama, or visiting the library, Penny had passed other women who'd catch her eye and hold her gaze with a searching nod of recognition. Yes, I lost my husband too, you know, they seemed to say. Join the club.

But I don't want to join your club, Penny would divert her gaze quickly, *I'm not ready to be a widow. It's different for me. You wouldn't understand. I don't want to nod knowingly back at you. I don't want to learn to play bridge. I'm not going to buy a little dog to give me a reason to leave the house every day and join communal walks. I'm perfectly content to pop out for an ice cream. By myself.*

'You want a taste?'

Penny looked up. The waitress behind the counter was offering her a pink plastic spoon on which was a furl of ice cream the colour of butter and the texture of suede.

'It's a new flavour. Banudge-Nudge.'

'Banudge-Nudge,' Penny marvelled at the appetizing name, accepting the sample.

'Banana, double fudge – half fat. Delicious, hey? You want a scoop?'

Penny glanced swiftly along across the colourful tubs like a pianist travelling the length of a keyboard with a single finger. 'You know what,' she said, 'actually I think I'll sit and have a sundae.'

'You take a load off,' the woman encouraged her. 'Menus are on the tables. Juliette'll be right over.'

Aren't the staff great, Penny thought, they give you long enough with the menu so that you're truly salivating and desperate to order. 'I'll have Chippy Chippy Bang Bang, please,' she said, just as soon as she was aware that the waitress hovered, 'with hot chocolate sauce. And nuts. And Lucky Charms. Hell, why not.'

The waitress brought over the sundae, perfectly presented in a pretty frosted dish, oozing with sauce and smothered in extras.

'Enjoy,' she said.

'Oh, I will,' Penny assured her, 'thank you very much.' She sensed the waitress linger, so with the long elegant spoon she dug up a glut of sundae and held it aloft as if to say cheers. Penny experienced a sensory burst that was delicious and exquisitely sweet and intensely painful. She closed her eyes. She closed her eyes to appreciate the taste. She closed her eyes because it hurt, because she suffered from sensitive gums and always seemed to forget the fact where ice cream was concerned. She closed her eyes because she used to bring Bob here when ice cream was the only thing he found digestible and that didn't taste metallic from the chemotherapy. That was the sweetest thought, and that's what hurt the most.

When Penny left, leaving an empty dish and a grateful tip, the waitress Juliette who had served her turned to Gloria behind the counter.

'I recognize her – do you?'

'Not especially,' Gloria said.

'Sure you do – she used to come in, with her husband I guess. You *do* remember him. He was sick. They used to sit right there. Sometimes she'd spoon it for him, feed him. Like a child.'

'Hey, I do remember,' said Gloria, 'but that was a few months back.'

'Yes. But today she comes in on her own,' Juliette said.

'You think he died?'

'I guess,' said Juliette. 'Sad.'

Noni invited Penny to the cinema again the following week but Penny thanked her and declined, citing other plans. She took herself back to the ice-cream parlour, which was no less empty though the day was dull and the weather was now too cold to snow.

'Hi,' said the counter waitress, 'have a taste.' The pink spoon, today laden with an ice cream the colour of coal, was passed to Penny.

'Liquorice,' Penny said, having assessed it with the commitment of a sommelier.

'And?' said the waitress.

Penny tasted it again. 'I'm not sure – there's something. I can't—'

'Raspberry.'

'Raspberry,' Penny marvelled, 'and liquorice. Fancy that.' And she went to the same table she'd sat at the week before. The one in the window, furthest from the table in the corner she used to seat Bob at.

'Hi, I'm Juliette,' the younger waitress came over to take her order. 'How are we today? You set?'

'I'm good,' said Penny, 'and I'd like a scoop of that liquorice one.'

'You should get a sherbet with that – brings out the flavour.' Juliette was quite forthright about that. Penny looked up. The girl looked like a confection herself, in her uniform striped the colours of apricot and strawberry, her hair in a high pony-tail, a jaunty little pink-peaked thing on her head, her name in copperplate across it. 'I'd recommend lychee,' Juliette said and Penny nodded.

When Juliette brought the bowl over, Penny took a small

taste and nodded her approval. Her gums didn't seem so sensitive today. She didn't have to close her eyes so often. But there again, she'd abstained from hot chocolate sauce or candy toppings. And Bob had not liked liquorice at all. She felt relaxed, as though she needn't scurry away just as soon as she finished. So when the waitress suggested a cup of coffee, Penny accepted.

'Excuse me, ma'am,' the waitress said after placing the cup and turning the saucer so that the handle was correctly placed. Penny looked up and read the girl's name again. Juliette. Well, Juliette looked a little concerned. 'I don't mean to – well, Gloria and I, we just. We remember you from the summer, from the fall. You used to come in with the gentleman? He was – he was.'

How old? Penny thought. Early to mid-twenties, she guessed. Nice-looking in a plain way, perhaps nicer-looking on account of her politeness and her slightly shy sweetness.

'Is he?' Juliette was bending down a little, as if in a reverential curtsy. 'Was he?'

'He was my husband,' Penny told her. 'He died. Near enough two months ago.'

'Oh I'm so sorry,' said Juliette, instinctively clutching her heart for emphasis. It touched Penny. It was as if everyone, no matter how little they knew Bob, had been rooting for him to pull through.

'Thank you,' said Penny. 'He sure loved this place.'

Penny returned two days later. Not to avoid any social invitation, nor because she had a craving for ice cream, but because Fountains felt like a nice place and seemed a good space to be. Comfort and warmth. Lovely warm chocolate sauce. Beautiful, pastel-coloured candy. Ice creams whose names brought a smile. Everything sweet. If you licked the blossom-coloured walls or bit the backs of the chairs, you'd probably discover they were made from candy. Everything there was sweet. The staff especially. They were like a personification of some of the ices. Pink Wink. Smile Sweetie.

When Juliette brought over Honey in Heaven, with chocolate sauce and marshmallows, Penny spooned into it but then spoke before tasting. 'We were married thirty years nearly,' she said. She looked up. Juliette didn't seem taken aback by the information, her expression invited Penny to continue. 'He called me dear. Always did, right from the start. Good morning, dear. Well dear, I'll be off to work now. I'm home, dear. What a nice supper, dear, shall I fix the coffee? It may have sounded formal, but I always heard it as charming and old-fashioned.' Penny tasted the ice cream. Heavenly indeed. She had two more spoonfuls but Juliette stood beside her, quietly attentive. 'I guess you wouldn't call us a lovey-dovey couple. But we were a good team.'

Juliette was shaking her head shyly. 'I watched you feed him,' she said very quietly. 'That's far more beautiful than lovey-dovey. It must be so hard – but I guess it's a blessing that his suffering should be over, that he is at peace.'

'I'm not a superstitious type,' Penny said, working her spoon busily against the sundae as she spoke, 'I don't believe in astro-mumbo-jumbo, I pooh-pooh voices from the dead, I don't do karma and yin-yang spirit guides; you know? But when Bob was fading I'd whisper to him, over and over, *Find a way, Bob, find a way to be with me. Stay in touch. Send a message. Show me a sign. Promise me*?'

'I *believe*,' Juliette confided with quiet earnestness, while Penny ate.

'Nothing,' Penny said gruffly as if disappointed by Juliette's response. 'I haven't seen *any* signs, I haven't felt warmth – nothing at all. Just the icy emptiness of being on my own.' Her hand formed a fist around the spoon, the skin so taut across her knuckles they looked like the snow-sharp mountains outside. 'There is no blessing,' she ridiculed. 'He shouldn't have suffered in the first place. Death is not a good thing. It's very cruel and it's a waste.' She didn't finish her ice cream and she didn't leave a tip. And she didn't go again the following week.

But she did return the week after that. And she felt her eyes smart at the bright sweetness of the welcome Juliette gave her. Fountains, she decided, was better than any support group. 'Hey stranger, you missed out on Chuckle Berry last week. Gloria will give you a taste. You sitting?'

Penny sat. She managed to make the sundae last an hour and at any opportunity, she passed the time with the waitresses about the weather, or about ice cream. Then she ordered coffee. And a refill. She was obviously lingering but no one, herself included, was quite sure for what.

'My father passed,' Juliette told her, when she accepted a second refill.

'I'm so sorry,' Penny said, genuinely shocked. She'd practically forgotten that grief could befall other people. 'Can you sit awhile?' Penny asked. Juliette glanced around the parlour, raised her eyebrow at Gloria who gave her a nod. 'When?'

'Coming up to a year and I need to tell you that I think death is a great thing. He was a rotten drunk and he hurt me and my mom. So I guess I envy you a little,' Juliette said with a reluctant smile. 'Not your pain, not the longing that must weave the minutes into the hours and drag your hours into these dark days right now. But I envy you the fact that your loss is so great because your love itself was so great. I never had that.'

Penny didn't know where to put herself. For the first time she experienced the guilt that she assumed her own friends were feeling. The guilt at one's own good fortune. She put her hand over Juliette's wrist because she was lost for words. She didn't know what to say because recently Bob was all she really talked about. Just then, though, she wasn't actually thinking about him at all.

Road Kill

Pip butters toast, Zac is skim-reading the *Financial Times* and the *Today* programme drifts sedately through the kitchen; not loud enough to be an active part of breakfast but audible enough to be an integral component in their morning routine. Pip knows to savour these few minutes before Tom breaches the peace.

And here he is. Hastily dressed for school. His nine-year-old physique spurting in fits and starts; just recently his feet have apparently doubled in length yet the softness of his peachy cheeks remains unchanged from when he was a toddler. His fingernails exhibit the indelible grubbiness commensurate with a boy of his age but the pale pitch of his voice seems so pure and clean. His hair truly has an energy of its own and Tom is not yet of an age to exhibit much interest in styling or even basic control. Consequently, it tufts itself into increasingly haphazard configurations, caused as much by spasmodic keratin production as by the freedom of such deep sleep. Today, it resembles something that the forefathers of punk rock spent hours trying to achieve.

'Happy St David's Day,' Tom announces. 'We're doing it in school today.'

‘Good Lord,’ Pip declares, ‘it’s the mad March hair.’

Zac looks up from his paper. ‘Or the mad March heir,’ he quips though neither Pip nor Tom cotton on to the pun. It’s too early to hear silent ‘h’s. It’s too early to have to explain, thinks Zac, returning to the pink pages.

Pip attempts to smooth down Tom’s hair with her hand. He shirks away and ruffles up Pip’s meddling. ‘Toast?’ she asks.

‘Yep,’ Tom says. Zac glances over his paper. ‘Please,’ Tom adds with a sigh.

‘Do you want to go through your piece?’ Pip asks.

Tom looks alarmed. ‘My piece?’

‘For assembly this morning? On the patron saints of the British Isles. Aren’t you St George?’

‘Oh. That. I thought you meant my piece of toast,’ says Tom. ‘Digby says that the dragon is a metaphor. But he doesn’t even know what a metaphor is.’

‘And do you?’

‘No,’ says Tom, ‘but it sounds boring, like something Miss Balcombe would go on about. And on and on. Yawns-ville.’

‘Well, would you like to go through your piece about St George?’ Pip asks.

‘I know it off by heart,’ Tom says proudly, and launches into a fast, monotone delivery. Pip can see the *Financial Times* quivering. She surreptitiously kicks Zac under the table. Tom finishes his recitation to applause from the table and the 8 a.m. GMT pips from the radio.

‘If babies are such a great thing, if they’re such a miracle and stuff – why do they make their mums so poorly and so mega grumpy?’

Pip wasn’t prepared for this. Usually when she walked Tom to school she was entertained with a diatribe of the personal hygiene habits and physiognomic misfortunes of his teachers, which merely required tuts of her disapproval whilst she bit back laughter.

'Seems a bit stupid to me,' Tom continued darkly. Pip wasn't sure what to say. Was Tom about to probe for the facts of life? She felt uneasy, having not yet discussed with Zac the information and terminology he was prepared to give his son. 'Did I do that to her, to my mum, do you think? When she was having me, did I make her puke like mad and be a grumpy old moo?'

Tom was asking Pip about something on which she had actually no authority to answer. 'Perhaps,' she answered cautiously, having never actually discussed the vagaries of June's first pregnancy, 'but excuse me, young man, your mum is not an old moo.'

'But she *is* grumpy,' Tom muttered. 'I thought she would be chuffed about having a baby but all she does is grumble and puke.' He allowed Pip to take his wrist as they made to cross the road. 'There's going to be buckets of blood too, of course, when the baby comes. And do you think Mum'll scream her head off – like that woman on *Holby City* last week?'

Pip couldn't really answer that one, not knowing June's take on epidurals.

'I can see why *you* don't want all that madness,' Tom said darkly, with much sage nodding.

'Pardon?'

'You and Dad,' Tom shrugged. 'Don't tell my mum I said stuff like that about her and stuff.'

Pip and Tom were about to step off the kerb when they saw the squirrel. Tom was still young enough to point and declare 'Hey! Squirrel!' as it bolted into the road. And then came the car at the same time and they both foresaw the death of the squirrel by a second or so.

'Oh God,' Pip gasped, helpless not to be transfixed by the

spatter of guts, the barb of torn limbs, the stark stare of sudden death.

'Gross!' Tom said, not quite sure if he was thrilled or distraught.

'We'll cross the road further down,' Pip said.

'Do you think it's really dead?' asked Tom.

'Yes,' said Pip, 'I do.'

'Oh.'

'Poor little thing.'

'Poor little thing. Do you think it was a boy or a girl?'

They crossed the road and Pip began to gamely tell Tom that babies didn't cause their mums to feel poorly and be grumpy, all that was down to chemicals causing a lady's body to be able to grow and carry a baby. And anyway, mums and dads so want to have babies that a bit of yukkiness now and then didn't matter at all in the long run.

'Tom?'

Tom was quietly sobbing though the school gates were in sight.

'Your mum is fine – please don't you worry about her. She doesn't mean to be grumpy and she can't help feeling a bit yuk.' Pip gave Tom a hug. 'Do you want your dad to talk to her? I promise you she can't wait to give you a little baby brother or sister.'

'Not the baby,' Tom sniffed, 'the squirrel.'

happy st david's day!!! Pxxx

Fen stared at the text message Pip had sent her and wondered for a moment whether St David's Day was something she'd forgotten that they celebrated despite having no Welsh blood in the family. Funny old Pip, Fen smiled, texting back.

and to you. F + C xx

Fen knew Pip would start to text her at length but soon

tire of the thumb effort and phone her instead. The call came a couple of minutes later.

'Happy St David's Day.'

'Same to you, with bells on.'

'What are you up to today?'

'Oh, the usual – puréeing things, changing nappies, singing daft songs, spending the afternoon with women I have nothing in common with other than postcode and the fact that our babies were born in the same month.'

'Shall we meet up, then? I'm not clowning today – and I'd love to see Cosima. And you.'

Fen looked around her home. It was a tip. She ought to prioritize the chores and say no. 'OK,' she said, 'that'll be lovely.'

'Kenwood?' Pip suggested. 'It's equidistant. Let's have coffee and cake. See you in an hour or so?'

Fen looked at the clock. It was ten o'clock and though Cosima was dressed beautifully in Catimini, Fen was still in her dressing gown. She opened her wardrobe and perused her pre-pregnancy Agnès B skirts and John Smedley cardigans. It was a perverse, masochistic ritual she taunted herself with almost daily. She didn't dare hold them against herself, let alone try them on; scrambling instead into yesterday's cargo pants. Packing Cosima in a snowsuit that made the baby resemble the offspring of the Michelin Man and Laa-Laa the Teletubby, Fen crammed essentials and non-essentials into the changing bag and just about remembered to grab her own jacket before heading out of the house.

Big Red Bus, Cosima!

Look at that little fluffy doggie!

Can you see the blue car, baby girl? Yes, it is a blue car, a nice blue car. Blue, blue, blue car blue.

Walking through East Finchley, Fen and Cosima passed buses and dogs and cars of various descriptions. However, there was little to point out to Cosima about the Bishops Avenue other than Great Big Houses and Great Big Trees and Great Big Cars.

But then Fen saw the young man with the flowers.

She slowed her pace. He was some distance ahead, fixing a bunch of flowers – tulips, they looked like – around the trunk of a tree. Fen was captivated; how often had she passed by a tree, some railings, displaying a bunch of bedraggled flowers as a memorial to a life lost? But such flowers had simply been there and, usually by the look of them, for quite some time. Had she ever actually seen someone placing such flowers? No, she hadn't. Had she ever seen flowers tied to this tree-trunk? She didn't think so. Not until today. She was approaching him, the man now fixing a bunch of daffodils alongside the tulips. Fen was close enough to see that some had orange trumpets, others white; a cut above the bog-standard yellow for sure.

Should I cross the road? Should I treat him as the bereaved – give him space and peace so he can have his ritual as solemn as is fitting? He looks so young. Who did he lose?

And the young man was offering a daffodil with a broken stem to Cosima. 'Happy St David's Day,' he was saying.

'Oh!' Fen chirped. 'A lovely flower! A lovely daffodil. Are you Welsh?'

'No. Will she eat it if I give it to her?' the man asked.

'Probably,' said Fen.

'Here, you have it, then,' he said, worrying his hand through his already tousled jet black hair as if he was genuinely concerned. 'Put it in her room. Or something.'

'Oh. OK. Thank you.'

The man paused. 'My sister would like it.'

Fen looked at him. Christ, how awful. Suddenly she wanted to know details; how awful. She should say something. 'I'm sorry for your loss.'

‘Thank you,’ the man said, and he genuinely seemed touched. ‘She was twenty and was killed three years ago. My mum lives in Manchester and I’ve promised her that I’ll replenish the flowers each anniversary.’

‘Was it a car?’ Fen asked, cringing that this sounded both tactless and interfering.

‘No, a motorbike,’ the man said.

Fen regarded him. He was fresh-faced and slightly gawky, looked as though he should be putting up leaflets about drama soc at Oxford or Cambridge, rather than road-kill flowers in East Finchley. How old was he? Early twenties? Had he been a younger or older brother to his late sister? ‘How long do the flowers last?’

‘Longer than in a vase, bizarrely,’ he replied, ‘but I hate seeing commemorative flowers all withered and limp. I always come back and check. I take them down before they’ve passed their best. You could say my sister was in full bloom when she was cut down. So I don’t think she should be remembered any other way.’

‘What was her name?’

‘Kay. What’s your name?’

‘Fen.’

‘Short for Fenella?’

‘Yes,’ said Fen, charmed. ‘Not many people know that.’

‘I was at college with a Fenella.’

‘What’s yours?’

‘Al.’

‘Short for Alan?’

‘No, Alistair.’

‘Ah.’

‘Know any Alistairs?’

‘Nope, you’re my first.’

‘What’s the baby’s name?’

‘Cosima.’

'That's pretty.'

'I think some people think it's a bit pretentious.'

'Is the mum a bit arty-farty then?'

'The mum?' Fen was simultaneously shocked and charmed again. 'I *am* the mummy.'

'No way! I thought you were the nanny.'

'No. I'm the mother all right.'

'Cool. I see. Wow.'

There followed a pause that was simultaneously awkward yet heightened as they both scrambled around for some other common ground, just something to say, to prolong conversation.

'Anyway, we'd better go – we're meeting my sister at Kenwood,' Fen said, as if she'd been miles away and had suddenly come to. 'It's been nice talking to you. And I'm sorry – about Kay.'

'Thanks. Thanks. Nice to meet you too – and Cosima. How old is she?'

'Eight months old,' said Fen, now really wanting to know how old Al was and whether he was younger or older than his late sister. They'd paused too long for her to ask now. 'Bye, then,' she said, a little reluctantly. And just a little coyly too.

Fen walked on. She stopped and turned. Al was looking after her. She waved and he raised his hand. She strolled onwards to Kenwood House, breaking into a sudden grin every now and then. Flattery. How good it felt. 'I don't know whether to be charmed or insulted,' she said to Cosima as she walked. 'I thought I had "Frumpy mum" written all over me.'

The unusual incident, the unexpected attention of a stranger, the break from the drag of just a normal day, served as a tonic that Fen wanted to keep private for utmost potency. So when Pip said how bright she looked, Fen didn't mention

Al. She didn't say that attraction is a peculiar, sly thing that can work wonders on the complexion. She pointed instead to a good night's sleep at last and that Cosima had gobbled up pear purée that morning that had no orange tinge to it whatsoever.

'It wouldn't be wise to tell Auntie Pip anyway,' Fen chattered at Cosima as they walked back. 'Auntie Pip would only give me her worried look – her "Motherhood has made my sister loopy" look.' Fen stopped at Al's flowers. Cosima was fast asleep. Fen tucked the fleece around the baby and stroked her cheek. 'I feel a bit ambivalent that I should feel just slightly flattered that Al thought I was the nanny, not your mother. He said "Wow" when I corrected him. What did that "Wow" mean exactly? That I look good for my age? That I'm a yummy mummy? That I'm the first person he's met with an eight-month-old baby? I can't remember the last time I wowed someone. Daddy just calls me silly.'

Waterworks

'Mr and Mrs York! Mr and Mrs Holmes and Master Holmes! Mr Holden, Ms McCabe, Miss Holden-McCabe! Welcome one and all.' Django genuflected flamboyantly throughout his roll-call, much to everyone's amusement. He was wearing the jeans he'd worn to Woodstock, tessellations of denim patchworked together, teamed with a shirt swirling brightly with paisley motifs. His belt was all buckle, in the bashed bronze form of a mounted Red Indian, bow and arrow poised. Pip had seen similar go for princely sums on ebay. 'Cuppa tea? Something to dunk?'

'Can I have squash?' Tom asked, but directed the question to his father. 'And something to dunk?' Although Django was certainly the most exotic adult he knew, Tom still passed all requests via his father first.

'You can, my boy, you can,' Django responded to Zac's nod, 'but you'll have to tell me how to squash it – I'm sure to have the ingredients.'

'You just untwist the bottle top, pour in about a centimetre and then top it up with water. Even water from a tap,' Tom explained helpfully despite being somewhat incredulous. It occurred to Django only then that they were talking different types of squash. He realized with some relief that he needn't attempt to juice the pumpkin. And he realized with some disappointment that he did not own the bottled cordial to which his step-grandson-thing-or-other alluded. Good job, really, because he hadn't a clue what a centimetre was anyway. A dash he knew intrinsically, a dollop too; he could do a smidgeon blindfolded and had always denounced the pinch as miserly. Feet and inches he was fine with, metric however was another matter; one he staunchly felt did not matter. 'I have some cherry syrup,' he said quietly to Zac. 'Do you think that might do?'

'I'm sure it will,' Zac said, laying an affectionate hand on Django's shoulder. 'But what on earth do you use cherry syrup for?' he asked as they walked on up the path and into the house.

Django stopped. 'Do you know, I don't think I've used it for anything. I think it's unopened. I've had it ages.'

In the event, Django couldn't find the cherry syrup but he did have cherry brandy and decided that a smidgeon watered down excessively with flat R White's lemonade wouldn't do the boy any harm at all. He was right. Tom acquired a liking for it and asked for more.

'I hope you left the beds for the blokes to do,' Pip said, all stern, 'like I suggested in my letter and on the phone.'

'Yes, I have,' Django sighed, 'but only because you're so bossy I didn't dare do otherwise.' He didn't confess to certain relief at Pip's directive; that he didn't actually feel like shunting and shifting divans about any more, didn't feel he could. 'There's a zed-bed out in the shed,' he added, 'though I've used its mattress to lag the water tank.'

'Can't I sleep in the shed?' Tom sighed, looking imploringly to Zac before winking beguilingly at Django.

'Have you been incorrigible?' Django asked him.

'No, actually, I've been *exemplary*,' Tom said. 'Miss

Balcombe told me that's what I am in some things – like maths. It's just that Pip told me all about the shed.'

Django's contrived haughty expression softened. 'In the summer,' he said, 'if you promise to be as incorrigible as Pip was when she was young, before she was bossy, I promise to banish you to the shed for a night. Now come along, troops, we have a party to plan. There's only two months to go.'

No one would hear of Django sleeping on the sofa; they were reluctant enough to let him give up his bed but the deal was settled on Django sleeping in Fen's bed and Tom sleeping in Fen's room on the zed-bed plumped up with two sun-lounger mattresses, Fen and Matt in Django's bed with Cosima in her pop-up travel cot, Zac and Pip in her old room with Cat's bed dragged through, Cat and Ben on various cushions and beanbags in her room. 'You're the youngsters,' Django had told them, 'you won't have the spinal issues of those over a certain age.'

'Shall I point out that I'm older than Matt?' Ben joshed.

'No, don't do that,' Django replied. 'You know how I enjoy my theories.'

At the crack of dawn, Django came across Fen boiling a kettle in the kitchen.

'Did Cosima wake you?' she asked, alarmed.

'No darling,' Django said, 'just the infernal need to pee. Not that you'd want to know the finer details of my water-works. It's an age thing.'

'And a pregnancy thing – I remember it well,' Fen groaned. She took the kettle from the hob. 'Can we buy you an electric kettle for your birthday?'

'No thank you,' Django said, 'far too dull.'

'I don't suppose you'd like a microwave then?'

'Absolutely not. What would a seventy-five-year-old want with one of those?' Django said.

Fen poured boiling water into a Pyrex jug and immersed a baby bottle to heat through. 'I'm trying to reclaim my boobs,' Fen explained, with a tone of regret and a look of guilt, 'not that you'd want to know the finer details of my lactation.'

'Quite,' said Django. He paused. 'Matt must love it – the bottle feeding – enables him to feel hands-on and useful.'

'Absolutely,' said Fen. 'I like watching him.'

'Watching or checking?' Django posed. 'It's good for him to feel *useful* – because, you see, you are so very *capable*, Fenella.' Fen was taken aback by the use of her name in full and she detected a subtle note of warning from Django. 'It must be easy for Matt to feel left out a little – on account of you being so very capable.'

Fen felt a little defensive but it was too early and she was too tired to express it with much vehemence. 'It's not that Matt does things wrong,' Fen attempted to explain, 'it's that he doesn't do things quite right. It's often easier for me just to do it in the first place. It saves time. And tears.' With that she took the warmed milk upstairs to feed a now grumbling Cosima.

Fen gazed down at her daughter, sucking contentedly on the bottle, locking eyes with her and sharing silent waves of intense love. She looked over to Matt who was sound asleep. How strange to feel simultaneously grateful but also resentful of the fact. Though nothing, not even a much-needed simple lie-in, was worth trading these silent waves of love, yet still Fen felt a little put upon that Matt never woke instinctively in advance of the baby stirring. However, though she knew that he'd be happy for her to boot him out of bed and be on early-morning bottle duty, she also knew she'd only lie there wondering if the bottle had been mixed correctly, whether it was the right temperature. She'd end up double-checking anyway. So what was the point in not doing it herself in the first place? There was no such thing as a lie-in. Did it slightly offend Matt? She rubbished the notion – he understood, didn't he? He understood that it's a mother's prerogative to be finicky. It's out of love for the baby anyway. No bad thing.

An hour later, swathed in his voluminous velvet dressing gown, his hair not yet pony-tailed and so fanning around his shoulders in silver skeins, Django sat in state, in the huge old Windsor chair in the kitchen. He looked like a Norse god, or straight from a William Blake painting, receiving his house guests one by one. First Tom, who scampered down, hair in hysterics, to see where his roommate was. Then Zac, to check his son hadn't actually woken Django. Then Pip, to check Zac and Tom were helping themselves to breakfast though of course she found Django busy rustling up his panffles, because he'd offered to make his highly complicated hybrid of pancake and waffle and Zac and Tom had readily accepted. Cat and Ben appeared because the scent of maple syrup warming over pancakes or waffles or some such, had drifted evocatively into their room and filled them with hungry memories of American breakfasts. Next came Fen and Cosima, the baby dressed immaculately down to the colour-coordinated tiny hair grip gathering together the few strands she had, while her mother wore mismatched socks. Finally, Matt emerged, still sleep-crumpled but characteristically cheerful.

'The morning is for Chatsworth, the afternoon is for lolling and party planning, and the evening is for the Rag and Thistle – for men who are over the limit,' Django announced.

'Over the limit?' Zac and Matt asked.

'Over the *age* limit,' Django said, with an apologetic ruffle to Tom's wayward hair.

'I see,' said Cat, hands on hips with consternation that wasn't wholly mock, 'while we womenfolk keep the home fire burning?'

'And do the washing-up,' Django added calmly. The men cheered. The baby cried. Let the day begin.

* * *

If Django was a perk of being married to, or partnered with, a McCabe girl, it was definitely a high point of a trip to Derbyshire to share an evening at the Rag and Thistle with their eccentric host. While Zac, Matt and Ben donned a change of shirts, Django certainly dressed for his big night out; watched by Tom fascinated with the provenance of each article of clothing. Django gathered this was a delaying tactic but it was his pleasure to spin yarns about his threads. Whether they were fact or fancy was of little relevance to Tom. He'd further embroider it all at school next week anyway. Tales of Django Gramps and his pink shirt with the gold buttons. Real gold. A gift from the King of Kathmandu.

To Matt, Ben and Zac's urbane, understated signatures of Ted Baker, Gap and Paul Smith, Django added a certain flamboyance with his Astrakhan waistcoat, his Pucci neckerchief, his peculiar multi-seamed corduroys and yet another great big fuck-off belt, this one with an amber-encrusted buckle. The only item no one had seen before was the excessively floral shirt.

'I knew a woman who worked at Liberty's,' Django explained nonchalantly. 'Her name was Maureen. The summer of 1970. She was *spectacular*.' And with that, the men left.

While Fen checked on Cosima, who was compliantly sound asleep, Pip served up the casserole Django had left simmering and Cat poured the wine.

'Come on, Fen,' Cat muttered to herself, 'I'm starving.'

'Cravings?' Pip probed.

'Unfortunately not,' Cat said, 'but not for want of trying.'

'Django's recipes would be perfect for pregnant women,' said Fen, who'd appeared and sat herself down in a chair with a great exhausted sigh, 'on account of all his bizarre combinations.'

'I've just found a walnut,' Cat said, chewing thoughtfully. She detested walnuts and was privately slightly irked that Django appeared to have forgotten this. 'God, I've only been away four years.'

'They're very good for you,' said Fen.

'Isn't there stuff one should eat if you want to have a boy, and other stuff if you want to have a girl?' Cat asked her.

'Apparently there is,' said Fen, 'but I couldn't tell you which was which. Would you like one more than the other?'

'No, no,' Cat said, 'but I would like just the one – I don't think I have the space for twins.'

Fen glanced at her sister's slender frame with gentle envy.

'You certainly wouldn't have the space in that Clapham place,' Pip remarked. 'What's happening with all that?'

Cat sighed. 'Apparently, we're under contract until June. I keep telling Ben it's never too early to scout around. There's no harm in planning. It's fun. I've always really loved Tufnell Park,' Cat enthused, 'and Parliament Hill. I know it can be expensive – but what an investment. Then we'd all be within a mile or so of each other. And I'd have Hampstead Heath on which to push my pram and have picnics. It's Nappy Valley, isn't it?'

'You need to conceive first,' Fen said.

Cat giggled. 'Each time we have sex, I hold my legs up for about five minutes. Ben thinks I'm daft.'

'It'll happen when it happens,' Fen tried to reason.

'I hope it happens soon,' Cat said wistfully. 'I'm doing everything right with the folic acid and the yoga and the magazines. Or watching repeats of *Location Location Location*. I've always had a thing for Shaker kitchens and tumbled mosaic tiles in bathrooms.'

'You need to find a job,' Pip interjected. 'You have a little too much time on your hands at the moment, methinks.'

'And expensive taste,' said Fen.

'That's easier said than done,' Cat muttered. 'I have looked. There's nothing. Not even freelance work.'

'Maybe you should think tangentially,' Pip suggested.

'You mean settle for less?' Cat said gloomily.

'No,' Pip said gently, 'but perhaps you have to consider the bigger picture rather than fixate on details.'

'You're so sensible,' Cat muttered with slight irritation.

'What do you expect me to say?' Pip said.

'It was something he said,' Fen interrupted.

'Who?' Cat was confused. Hadn't they been focusing on her?

'Django,' said Fen, 'about that flowery shirt. About a woman called Maureen.'

'Who was *spectacular*!' Pip mimicked.

'I wonder who she was,' Fen said. 'A spectacular woman called Maureen, who defined Django's summer of 1970.'

'We can ask him,' Cat suggested. 'He's bound to be fantastically verbose when he comes rolling home with the boys later.'

'Come to think of it, I do remember him in other floral shirts,' Pip said. 'They were probably all Liberty. Perhaps they were all from this Maureen.'

'When you have children, there's so much you leave by the wayside,' Fen said pensively.

Instinctively, it didn't seem right to Pip or to Cat to tease their sister just then for contradicting her previous conceit.

'Flowers by the wayside,' said Fen, her voice cracking. 'Sorry,' she mumbled, 'sorry.'

'Are you OK?' Pip asked. 'Is everything all right?'

'Are things no better with Matt?' Cat asked.

'I don't know,' said Fen, 'I don't know. I'm just tired, I suppose.'

Django's posse was the centre of attraction at the Rag and Thistle, especially when it became known that the main topic of discussion was the forthcoming infamous seventy-fifth birthday party to which, it seemed, all the clientele and staff of the Rag and Thistle, plus their pets, had already been invited.

'I was thinking of three marquees,' Django proclaimed, accepting a complimentary pint of Guinness with effusive thanks, 'the Good, the Bad and the Ugly.'

'But Django,' Zac pointed out, 'how will you decide which guest goes in which tent?'

'Marquee!' Django objected.

'Marquee,' said Zac. 'It's rather subjective. I mean, take Matt, he's bad *and* ugly.' Matt raised his pint.

'I didn't see it like that,' Django mused, as if he now found Zac's take rather interesting. 'I envisaged a natural progression from tent to tent—'

'Marquee,' chorused Ben, Matt and Zac.

'Mar-bloody-quee,' Django sighed. 'You know: a suitable, conducive environment to assist the three key stages of any good party. Conduct starts off good, behaviour then worsens until hopefully proceedings become downright shameful. Each marquee would have food to facilitate, cocktails to complement and soft furnishings to, well, accommodate.'

'McCabe,' said Mr Merifeld the landlord, with a grave shake of his head, 'sounds right costly to me.'

'Merifield,' said Django, 'what's money? I can't take it with me and I *am* well into my eighth decade.'

'Marquees don't come cheap,' said Mr Merifield.

'Tents it is then!' Django exclaimed, to much raucous approval.

By the time the four men made their somewhat unsteady passage up the garden path after a lock-in at the Rag and Thistle, Django's party had been planned to an imaginative degree; the minutiae mapped out down to the wording of the invites, the order of speeches and cleverly themed play-lists for each hour.

'The devil is in the details,' Matt justified, with drunken solemnity.

'Then the devil can come too!' Django proclaimed. 'Who's for a cup of tea or a nightcap?'

'Nightcap,' said Ben.

'Nightcap,' said Matt.

'Nightcap,' said Zac.

Ben gave Django a hand, while Zac checked on Tom and Matt tiptoed in on Cosima and Fen, who sleepily protested that he reeked of booze.

'Django,' Ben said cautiously, while he searched under the kitchen sink and found a bottle of cognac shoulder to shoulder with Domestos, 'are you happy with your health? Is all well?'

In the context of the lightness of the evening's conversation, Ben's question surprised Django. 'I'm in rude health, doctor,' he declared, placing four enormous brandy balloons on a tray.

'Any concerns?' Ben pressed. 'However minor?'

'I can't shift and shunt the beds about like I used to,' Django joked.

'It's my job to notice that you appear to go to the loo a lot,' said Ben. 'Have you noticed an increase in this? Pain? Discomfort? Any change in the old waterworks?'

'You cheeky whippersnapper,' Django protested, 'don't you go calling my waterworks old.'

'I'm just saying perhaps a check-up might be a good idea,' Ben said evenly.

Django didn't reveal that he'd thought the same himself. He didn't tell Ben he'd gone so far as keeping an appointment with the GP.

But the GP turned out to be a girl who looked no more than twelve. Don't doctors seem younger and younger these days? I'd really rather not discuss my waterworks with a young lady. I had to invent a sore throat as the purpose of my visit. She told me to go easy on the Tabasco. And she recommended Strepsils. Jolly nice they are too.

'Django?' Ben was saying. 'There are basic steps you can take – restrict fluid intake after 6 p.m., cut down alcohol and caffeine. Limit spicy food. Increase fish, carrots, broccoli. And exercise.'

Django nodded thoughtfully. 'Life would be a bit of a bore,' he said.

'Just cut down on some stuff and increase other things. Invent new stews,' Ben suggested.

Django was about to respond but then Matt and Zac were joining them again, switching the conversation back to party planning.

He's Not There

If the devil is in the details, if the pleasure is in the planning, then the fun is in the fantasy. Though Fen knew well enough how reality can let a daydream down, that Monday she made sure she forgot. Though she was aware that the planning might well be pointless, she happily indulged herself. Though she knew that her own guardian devil was guiding her, she turned deaf ears to her conscience. All her conscience wanted to say was *Think about it – what is the point?* But for Fen, just then, the point was that her imagination had been ignited and running with it was fun. And wasn't it refreshing to have the energy and the desire to spend a little time choosing what to wear? And didn't it seem entertainingly decadent to put mascara on in the daytime? And wasn't it fun to think about something other than baby food for a little while? And when it all seemed suddenly fanciful, questionable even, Fen simply justified that Cosima needed some nice fresh air. And wasn't a stroll up Bishops Avenue as good a route as any? And if further corroboration was needed, then a date with Cat at the café in Kenwood House provided it.

*

'He's not there,' Fen said to Cosima as they walked up the Bishops Avenue, 'but there again, why would he be?' She walked on, mulling theories on coincidence, unrealistic expectations and downright improbability. She stopped to pick up Cosima's teething rings. She looked back over her shoulder to the tree and the flowers. 'Shall we leave a little note?' she asked. 'There's no harm in that. It would be friendly, wouldn't it – might make his sad task a little less so.' She turned the buggy and retraced her steps.

Hi Al!

Cosima and I were passing.

I noticed a couple of Kay's daffodils were looking peaky so I've removed them.

Hope that's OK.

Fen.

'Shall we leave Mummy's mobile number too? I mean, it's no big deal, is it, it's just a friendly gesture – communication being a global thing.' Fen added her number after her name.

She set off for Kenwood in earnest and thought to herself how she'd just done the right thing.

It's not like I'm hoping he'll call. It's not like I'm swept up in daft daydreams. She spent the rest of the route distinguishing between the Daydream and the Distraction.

There's a major distinction between the two. A daydream can be pointless, a distraction useful.

It was with a spring in her step that she crunched along the sweep of gravel driveway heralding Kenwood House.

Cat was already there, sitting in the converted coach house, caressing a cup of tea. Fen zoomed the buggy over to her, mimicking a screech of brakes with her voice. An elderly couple looked slightly alarmed, as if that was no way to handle a buggy, as if babies should be in nice coach-built prams, not bizarre three-wheeled monstrosities.

Though they'd spent all weekend together, Fen gave Cat a kiss and a hug. She took Cosima from her buggy.

'Here, you cuddle your Auntie Cat,' she told the baby. 'Mummy's going to get herself an enormous slice of cake.'

'You're chirpy,' Cat told Fen on her return, declining the gateaux that Fen had bought.

'And you look miserable,' Fen commented, giving Cosima an organic sugar-free rusk. 'Everything OK?'

'I feel glum,' Cat admitted, 'and I want to be allowed to feel glum. So thank God you're not Pip.'

'What's up?' Fen asked, spooning butter-cream from the cake's surface directly into her mouth.

'I'm not pregnant. I don't have a job. I don't like Clapham. Ben's never home and I wish I'd stayed in Colorado,' Cat declared.

'Cat,' Fen said, 'you've only been home two minutes.'

'It's been three months,' Cat corrected. 'I've had sex forty-two times and have sent out nineteen pre-emptive letters for jobs. Nothing.'

'Cat, you make the former sound like a chore and you're being unrealistic about the latter,' Fen admonished her lightly.

'And you sound like Pip,' said Cat, 'so stop it because I need you to be the one who there-theres me.'

Fen paused to consider this. It was true. Go to Pip for practical advice and accept her authority. Go to Fen for a hug and be assured of some plain sympathy. 'It takes time,' Fen soothed, 'both take time.'

'You got pregnant overnight!' Cat objected.

'It wasn't planned,' Fen said.

'Then it's not fair,' said Cat.

Fen looked at her younger sister apologetically and put

her hand over Cat's. 'Come back to mine this afternoon,' she said. 'Let's look at my books and magazines. There's sure to be Ten Top Tips For Tip Top Fertility or something.' Though Fen made it sound as though she was doing Cat the favour, privately she liked the idea of a way out of the mums-and-babies group.

'What's wrong with Clapham anyway?' Fen asked. 'I thought it was meant to be quite a happening place?'

'I stick out like a sore thumb,' Cat said. 'All the women bustle about with perfect children, or sit smug behind the wheels of their SUVs.'

'But that's your goal too,' Fen said, 'that's what you're hoping for. And actually, it doesn't sound dissimilar to this part of North London.'

'But while it's not happening for me, it makes me feel so isolated,' said Cat, 'and it's made me realize that I really want to be nearer to you. And Pip. I felt less far away when I was living in Colorado – how mad is that? I feel lonely stuck over the river. Ben's really upbeat about his job but he's working really long hours. I haven't made any friends. I miss Stacey and the gang in Boulder. And I miss my mountain.'

'Your what?' Fen asked.

'Flagstaff. Remember that hike we went on? That's my mountain. You saw where Ben and I lived, Fen. You saw the awesome wilderness right on our doorstep. You filled your lungs with that crystal-pure air. You stayed in our gorgeous apartment. You hung out with our mates. You saw how people drive SUVs out there because of the terrain, not fashion. You had a taste of our quality of life.'

'But you wanted to come back,' Fen pointed out. 'It was part of your game plan and you were adamant.'

'I know,' said Cat, 'it's true. We had a purpose. A goal. Hopes and dreams. Absolutely. But you see, it's March, it's been three long months and none of it has happened. And in that context it's really difficult to like Clapham. And it's bloody easy to wonder whether we've done the right thing. You know me – I love planning in my head but in reality I can't set the pace. I was so eager to return, I suppose I've been a bit deluded too – thinking nothing will have changed, like everything has been on hold for four years, awaiting my return.'

Fen nodded. She rubbed her sister's knee. She wondered what constructive advice she could give. But then she thought, that's Pip's job. What Cat wanted her to be was typical Fen just then. 'I understand,' she said, with a ruffle to Cat's hair. It was still short, but longer than that stunning elfin crop she'd arrived back in the UK with. 'It will happen, Cat. I promise you. Everything will be fine. Don't worry – that's the main thing. You'll make a wonderful mummy. We'll pick up brochures from estate agents on the way back to mine. Make some appointments for next week. There's a new kitchen design shop in Muswell Hill – we could go there after Cosima's nap.'

'Thanks, Fen,' Cat said, squeezing her sister's hand, 'that's just what I needed to hear.'

Walking back down Bishops Avenue, Fen considered crossing the road as they neared Al's flowers. It was as if they suddenly personified Al; that Cat might see something she shouldn't, make something out of nothing. While Fen didn't want Cat even to comment on the flowers, she knew she needed to bite her tongue herself. Must not make a bouquet out of a hasty posy. Must not read into this. Must not say anything out loud.

Her note had gone.

A piece of folded paper was tucked between the stems of a few daffodils and the trunk of the tree. As they passed by, Fen could see her name written on the paper. Neat and bold handwriting. There was no way she could take it just then and though she didn't resent Cat, she reprimanded herself for having invited her forlorn little sister back home with her.

I wonder what it says?

I suppose I'll have to wait until Matt's home before I can retrieve it.

But say that's too late? It's windy. It looks like it might rain.

It's exciting!

Of course Fen couldn't wait for Matt. Could you? She nipped out while Cosima slept, supposedly to the shops, leaving Cat snuggled up on the sofa with back issues of *Prima Baby* and the property section of the *Ham & High*.

The note just said 'Thanks, Fen. Alistair.' There wasn't much to read. Certainly, nothing could be read into it. But she quickly reconfigured a crashing disappointment into no big deal. It was nice, anyway, wasn't it? Nice of him to reply, and nice to have a tiny, harmless secret.

However, it was difficult not to feel a little glum when, a week later, Fen saw that the flowers had been taken down. That there'd been no phone call to her mobile phone. It made it difficult to know what to do with his note. She'd kept it folded and tucked into a book of stamps in her purse. She'd have to throw it away, and her silly fantasy with it. The note was only three words long, after all, and you could hardly read into those. It wasn't as if it was even long enough for there to be any lines to read between.

April Fool

Penny had specified no flowers at Bob's funeral. She didn't much like flowers – not cut ones. You cut flowers and then the natural process decrees that you witness them die. Why be reminded of death by things that are themselves dying? Much better to say '*No flowers. Donations to the Lance Armstrong Cancer Foundation*'. Lucky Lance – cancer hadn't killed him, like it had Bob. Perhaps if other mourners over recent years had boosted the funds of cancer charities, rather than the coffers of the funerary florists, then things might have been different for Bob. Wishful thinking, perhaps – but what else could she think about or wish for?

She didn't feel like going out. But she knew it wasn't sensible to mope around the house. Not at this time of day. It would make the wait until bedtime interminable. Marcia was back from Florida and Penny thought to phone her, but they already had an arrangement for the next day and she didn't want to come across as needy. Marcia would worry. And when Marcia worried, she would fuss. And Penny had never liked being fussed over. So she summoned up some sense and energy and went out for a drive. Just a drive, she told herself, no rush to be anywhere specific. It was a fine day, though there was a chill to the air – the sharp brilliance of April sunshine issued a defiant dismissal of winter. Just beyond Hubbardton's Spring, Penny stepped from the car to admire the herd of unusual red-and-white Holstein cattle peacefully chomping away at the lush spring grass. She gazed at the cows for a while and found she was often gazed back at. 'I'll see you in a moment, ladies,' she said, marvelling how beasts so lumbering and lugubrious could also be unequivocally female. She walked to the famous covered bridge a few yards ahead. She read from the plaque aloud because she didn't want to hear Bob's voice in her head. He'd loved this spot: postcard perfect yet untainted by commercialism. '*1872. Horsemen keep at a walk,*' Penny read. She glanced around her. 'If they went at a trot, the bridge would bounce,' she explained conversationally, though there was no one around. 'It was used as a boxing ring too, you know.' Suddenly, she found the sound of her voice a little embarrassing – talking to no one sounded worse than talking to cattle – so she walked briskly back to the car, nodding quickly to the cows on her way. Making much of the correlation between the rich Holstein milk and the ingredients for Vermont ice cream, Penny headed off for Ridge as if the idea to drive there for an ice cream had only then occurred to her.

'Hi Penny,' Juliette said casually, whilst taking the order of another customer. Penny nodded without checking if Juliette had seen. She didn't go to the counter where Gloria was already preparing her a taster of that week's special flavour but when Penny realized that someone sat at her table – a mother and toddler – she felt so discombobulated as to be tempted to walk straight out of the shop.

'Penny,' said Juliette kindly, guiding her to a table with no fuss. She came back a few minutes later with a pink plastic taster spoon, mounded high. 'It's a new flavour,' she told Penny. 'It's called Sing for Spring. It's pistachio and meringue – boss says it symbolizes the spring pasture peeping through the snow fields.'

Penny sucked the glob off the spoon. 'I'll have a banana split, thanks,' she said flatly.

'Banana split for Penny,' Juliette called and Penny detected excessive jollity and loud kindness in the girl's usually soft voice. Simultaneously, Penny felt her eyes smart and her toes curl.

'It's April Fool's Day,' Penny told her with a shrug. 'In Britain everyone plays pranks – practical or intellectual.'

'I knew it,' said Penny, triumphant. 'I says to Gloria, that Penny's not from around here. You're English? How cool is that?'

'A long time ago,' Penny confirmed.

'I'm sorry – I interrupted. You were saying about playing tricks?'

'I made an April Fool of Bob one year,' Penny shrugged. 'He took it well – but I know he was a little upset. I never said sorry for it.'

Juliette wasn't quite sure what to say. 'Bob won't have taken anything by that,' she mumbled.

'That stupid movie *Love Story* got it wrong,' Penny frowned. 'Love means you *must* say you're sorry. I never said, *Sorry Bob – that wasn't funny and I apologize*. I've been saying it over and over today. But it's too late.'

Juliette hovered. Penny had barely established eye contact with her this visit. Juliette glanced over at Gloria who used her eyebrows and vigorous tilting of her head to signify for her to sit down. She slid into the chair next to Penny. 'My dad used to tell me I was a fool the whole time – he didn't need April 1st,' she told Penny. 'He used to tell my mom she was a fool as well. Actually, he didn't use that word. He called us dumb. Dumb-ass bitches.'

Penny jerked and locked eyes with Juliette.

'When he said sorry, he never meant it so I stopped believing him quick,' Juliette said with a shrug. 'He'd even try tears, get down on his knees and holler that he was sorry. He was a better actor than Ryan O'Neal, I'll say that. It's a crap film anyway.'

'I left my husband on April Fool's Day,' Penny suddenly interrupted in a hoarse whisper. Juliette's eyes darted in confusion. 'Not Bob,' Penny hastened to add. 'I left this other man for Bob. I left this other man for Bob thirty-three years ago today.' She tucked into her banana split that was on the verge of being renamed banana spilt. 'I'm sorry,' she said to Juliette, 'I interrupted you. It's just I never told a soul about this until right now.'

Two weeks later, when Penny caught sight of Juliette at the Pack'n'Save, a world away from Fountains Ices, she wasn't sure what to do but she didn't think she wanted to be recognized. Fountains had become a sacred space for her, her visits there sacrosanct. She liked the anonymity, the sense of sharing but of confidentiality. She'd come to feel that it was as close to a support group as she would ever come by. And it was a comforting thought that wherever she was, whatever the time, the candy-coloured parlour where everything was sweet and pretty, existed. So, it didn't seem right to see Juliette in Pack'n'Save. But Juliette was apparently pleased to see Penny there as she'd made her way over, an older woman with her.

'Hi Penny.'

'Hi Juliette.'

'This is my mom, Cyn.'

'Hi Cyn.'

'Hi Penny.'

'You shopping?'

'I am. You too?'

'We are. My aunt's coming to stay.'

'That's nice.'

'Honey, I'm going to pick up some soda.'

'OK Mom, I'll be right there.'

Penny and Cyn nodded at each other, smiled cordially. Penny thought about the woman's deceased husband calling her a dumb-assed bitch. It chilled her. 'Well, you have a nice weekend,' Penny told Juliette.

'Thank you,' Juliette said, 'and you. You doing something?'

'Not especially,' Penny said.

'Oh. Oh. Well, see you next week, I guess.'

'Yes,' said Penny, 'goodbye.'

But Juliette loitered. 'Bob sure was special,' she said to Penny. 'I mean – for you to up sticks and leave like that. Your home, your country. When you were so young.'

Penny was taken aback. She couldn't possibly comment.

Juliette tipped her head to one side and regarded Penny. 'I know you can come across a little frosty and all,' she said with kindness, 'but I say it's a shame you never had kids of your own. You'd've been a good mom.'

Penny was so stunned she hadn't the self-possession not to let it show, scrambling around for her composure whilst scrabbling for something to say. However, her feelings of disarray obviously didn't offend Juliette who smiled sweetly and made to go.

'Don't you go thinking you and your mom aren't special just because your daddy didn't say so,' Penny suddenly said.

Juliette was visibly touched. 'See you next week, Penny,' she said.

'Actually, I won't be here next week,' Penny heard herself telling Juliette though she knew the thought was unformulated.

'Oh?'

'No. No. I'm going to be in England,' Penny told her, 'I haven't seen my family in many many years.'

Juliette smiled and placed her hand warmly on Penny's arm. 'You do that,' she enthused, 'you do just that.'

My Round

Predictably, it had been Pip's idea to encourage the menfolk to meet.

'You always say what a good bloke you think Ben is,' she said casually to Zac as they dressed for work: Pip braiding her hair tightly into pigtails and securing them both ends with polka-dot ribbons, Zac donning a sober navy blue suit enlivened by a Paul Smith tie emblazoned on the underside with a 1950s pin-up girl. 'You should get together more often with him and Matt. You're brothers-in-law.'

'That's stretching it,' Zac laughed, peering over Pip's head to check his reflection in the mirror.

She twisted around and looked up at him. 'Well, whatever you are officially, you are certainly family,' she said. Zac kissed the bridge of her nose as the tip of it was already painted red. 'Anyway, you three need to meet up to discuss the music for Django's party. It's less than a fortnight away. He'll be digging out the gramophone and all his scratchy old vinyl if you don't.'

'Good thinking, Mrs,' said Zac. 'Remember to pick Tom up later.'

What a stupid thing to say, Pip thought.

*

To meet at the Mariners was Zac's suggestion and it was a good one. Tucked away up a side street off the Embankment, it was a hop across the river from Ben's hospital, a walk through the City for Zac and a quick taxi ride for Matt, better locating him for the journey home anyway. The establishment itself, though categorically a pub, had the feel of a gentleman's club, with walls panelled in oak, tub chairs set around tables placed discreetly apart and booths upholstered in dark green leather along the back wall. There were no fruit machines, no television, no music, no menu. The landlord and bar staff were male and conservative, in their waistcoats and ties and neat moustaches and referring to their clients as Sir. There was no active misogynism in play, indeed the landlord was somewhat mystified that the various girls to whom he'd offered bar work had turned him down. His bar, it seemed, was simply not conducive to a female clientele.

'It's what the young people refer to as the "vibe", dear,' the landlord's wife defined. 'It doesn't have the right *vibe* for the ladies.' Even she preferred to take her occasional gin and tonic at the Kings Head in the parallel street.

'Bitter?' Zac asked.

'And twisted,' Ben quipped. 'Actually, I hate to say it but I'm a bit of a bottled lager man now – those years in the States lured me away from warm beer.'

'You drank pints at the Rag and Thistle when we were there the other week,' Matt commented.

'Country pubs are different,' Ben said, 'and the Rag and Thistle is in a league of its own.'

'Apparently they're providing the beer for Django's party,' Matt said, 'in barrels.'

'We must discuss the music, we only have this weekend to sort it out,' Zac reminded himself out loud of the reason for their meeting.

'I can't do Saturday,' said Ben, 'I have clinics all day.'

'How's work?' Matt asked him.

'Brilliant – but long hours, which pisses Cat off,' said Ben. 'But I'm in my element – I'm pleased we seem to be taking sports medicine seriously in this country at last. It's not so much about treatment – if you get to that stage, you're a little too late. It's about understanding and management – that's why I pressed for the department to be called Sports Medicine, not Sports Injury. If we look after our sportsmen – professional, school, club – we'll see less injury and better results.'

'Interesting,' said Matt. 'God, it's years since I put on a pair of trainers.'

'It's not years,' Zac corrected, 'you and I were playing a bit of tennis last summer – you mean it's since your baby came on the scene.'

'Christ you're right,' Matt chinked glasses with Zac. 'All those things I used to do BC.'

'BC?' said Ben.

'*B C*,' Matt said. 'Before Cosima.' Then he continued, theatrically *sotto voce*, 'Can you slip me a nice little tonic, doctor? Some va-va-voom?'

'Va-Va-Viagra?' Ben asked.

'Sod off,' Matt laughed, 'not for *me*. Something I can slip into Fen's Ovaltine?'

'Oh dear,' said Ben, 'not enough action?'

'None whatsoever,' rued Matt, 'and I'm so bored of furtive wanks in the shower I can't even be bothered to do that any more.'

'Christ,' muttered Ben and Zac sympathetically, grateful it wasn't them.

'Bad patch?' Zac asked, knowing Pip had said so but not wanting to offend Matt by revealing this.

Matt shrugged. 'I don't know,' he faltered. 'It's probably

fine.' He took a sip of his pint. 'Look – it's just I'd rather it didn't get back to Fen,' he said, 'and you know what those sisters are like.'

'Off the record,' Zac assured him while Ben pulled an imaginary zip across his lips.

Matt shrugged. 'To be honest, things aren't as good as they were – dare I say it – BC. I mean, I've read the mags, the books, I went to the ante-natal classes, I cut the cord and I change nappies. I *expect* to be tired beyond belief – I *understand* that tiredness plays havoc with the libido. But actually it's not just about sex. It's more.'

'It's about more sex?' Zac asked and they all laughed before Matt buried his head in his hands in exaggerated woe.

'I love the mother of my child,' Matt said, 'but where the fuck has my girlfriend gone? I feel surplus to requirements, you could say. It isn't in any of the books that when your child has a wonderful mother, you can't have your girlfriend back.'

'She's obsessed with the baby?' Ben said, being careful to turn it into a question though actually he was stating the obvious.

'Yes,' said Matt, 'and nonplussed by me. I must admit, initially I was delighted and relieved by Fen's almost fierce maternal instincts – she's certainly not following in her own mother's footsteps. But now it's frustrating me.'

'It will be temporary,' Ben told him. 'It's hormonal – motherhood is still partly chemical in these months.'

'But we're dangerously close to being in a rut. Don't either of you say "Give her time",' Matt warned them, 'seriously.'

'Have you talked about this?' Ben asked.

Matt looked embarrassed. 'When? How?' he said. 'I arrive home from work and Fen badgers me to have quality time with Cosima. Then we eat in front of the television. She goes to bed early and is out like a light. If I can't use all the tricks of the frigging trade to arouse her for some sleepy shagging, I certainly can't rouse her for a heart-to-heart.'

'You two need time together,' Zac said, 'grown-up time away from home.'

Matt looked deflated. 'I know,' he said, 'but she doesn't trust babysitters.'

'We'll do it,' Zac offered.

'Us too,' said Ben.

'Thanks,' said Matt, 'thanks. The thing is, she doesn't seem interested. She just wants an early night. Every night.'

Ben took a long pull at his bottled beer. He shook his head with a sorry smile. 'I tell you, Matt,' he said, 'it's a cruel irony – but I'm having so much sex I'm rapidly going off it.'

'You total wanker,' Matt laughed, a little bitterly.

'It's no laughing matter,' Ben assured him. 'Cat's constantly analysing calendars and her temperature and demanding sex at scientific moments and weird angles. I'm seriously thinking of providing her with samples and a turkey baster. We've stopped making love, we're "trying for a baby". And I'm the sperm bank.'

Zac laughed. 'Not really Kama Sutra, then, Ben?'

'It's about as far from the Kama bloody Sutra as *A Nun's Story* is from *Debbie Does Dallas*. All this sex – it's not fucking or shagging or making love. It's purely mechanical. But of course she also wants me to gaze at her in a deep and meaningful way because we're baby-making.'

Zac had a contemplative sip of his pint. 'Much as I do love my two sisters-in-law, I thank heavens Pip doesn't want to procreate. I have my son and my wife and life is very very good.'

'You smug git,' Ben laughed.

'Isn't June pregnant?' Matt said with a sly edge to his voice.

'June?' said Ben. 'Remind me?'

'Tom's mother,' Zac said and Ben slapped his forehead and said, Of course. 'Yes,' Zac confirmed, 'she's due this summer.'

Ben and Matt exchanged glances and eyebrow-raises.

'What?' said Zac.

'It won't be long before Pip's going to want to keep up with the June-ses,' Matt said.

'Pip?' Zac was incredulous. 'Pip isn't remotely broody!'

'Have you asked her?'

'We discussed it before we got married,' Zac said.

'Tick-tock tick-tock,' said Ben, with a shrug. 'Biological clock, mate, biological clock.'

'We have Tom,' Zac exclaimed, 'our family is complete.'

'Talking about tick-tock,' said Matt, glancing at the old clock above the bar, 'one for the road? My round. We need to discuss the music for the party.'

'A soundtrack to Django's life?' Ben said.

'It's going to be a memorable night,' Zac said. 'Take tissues. You know how over-emotional the McCabes become en masse.'

'Has Django been all right?' Ben asked. 'His health? The last couple of years?'

'I think so,' said Zac and Matt nodded. 'He always has a comedy moan about gammy hips and old bones and such. Why do you ask?'

'It's probably nothing,' said Ben. 'I'm trained to notice things, I suppose. Age can creep up on a person in quite a sudden way.'

'Pip grills him about how he is on a weekly basis,' Zac said. 'She goes through a checklist which covers everything from the freezer to the hot water to his bones and brain.'

'The trouble is, though Django's such a big character and he appears so robust – he's seventy-five.'

'Or at least he will be next weekend,' said Matt.

'Here's to a great party,' said Zac, 'and to Django McCabe's very good health.'

'Here's to Fen,' Ben said, knocking his beer bottle against Matt's pint glass.

'And to Cat,' said Zac.

'And Pip,' said Matt. They drank.

'Swing Out Sister,' said Ben, 'remember them? Are they in your collection, Zac?'

'Sisters of Mercy,' said Matt.

'Sister Sledge,' said Zac.

'Scissor Sisters,' said Matt.

'As if having two older sisters wasn't enough,' Ben laughed, 'I have two sisters-in-law too.'

Zac thought about what Pip had said that morning and he realized how much he liked Matt and Ben. He chinked his glass against theirs. 'Brothers in Arms,' he said and called it a night.

Freeze a Jolly Good Fellow

The fact that Django McCabe's seventy-fifth birthday party happened at all was a feat of some engineering and community spirit. On the Monday he had to admit that to single-handedly cater for over a hundred people was a tall order for anyone, let alone a man of his advancing years; but to request outside assistance was such an affront to his pride and his culinary standards that temporarily he thought he'd rather cancel than do so. On the Tuesday, the Matlock Marquee Company went out of business and though Django left a message saying he'd buy the bloody tents for cash, no one replied. On the Wednesday, the storms came with such ferocity that only an extreme heatwave could prevent the lawn becoming a quagmire on the night. However, by the Thursday, the sun indeed blazed and by Friday morning, Babs Chorlton had already made the spiced-chicken-and-white-chocolate vol-au-vents to Django's stringent specifications. By lunch-time, Mrs Merifield was baking Bakewell tarts with the quince jam and crystallized ginger that Django provided, and the Blakes car dealership in Chesterfield were installing their marquee on Django's lawn. He didn't mind in the slightest the ubiquitous Vauxhall branding emblazoned all over it – it brought back very colourful memories of playing jazz with Vauxhall Vinnie and the Bebop Boys.

Cat and Ben arrived at tea-time on the Friday; Zac, Pip and Tom were in time for supper – a vast, misshapen pie using all leftover ingredients, from pickles to plums, chillies to cherries. The beds were shifted and shunted, Pip turned her hand to floral arrangements, and Tom painted an old sheet with '!!! go Django !!! go Django!!!'. Cat managed to persuade Django to put the heirloom canteen of cutlery back under his bed and let her buy plastic cutlery, rather than silver polish, at Morrison's tomorrow. Fen, Matt and Cosima arrived in time for the institution of After Eights with *News at Ten*, and the family were sleeping soundly by midnight.

The day of the party dawned fine and the family gathered for a civilized breakfast. 'Speeches,' Django announced as if he was requesting the jam, please.

'Before or after the food?' Zac asked, noticing that the sisters were motionless in shocked silence.

'There will be no *before* or *after*,' Django said, 'the food is to be a constant for the duration of the party.'

'After the savoury and before the sweet, then?' Matt asked.

'I never make such distinctions,' Django said. 'One must respect one's taste buds – if one fancies Bakewell tart *before* Scotch eggs, then there's probably a jolly good reason for it.'

'When would you like the speeches to happen?' Ben asked him.

'Before we're all too blotto,' Django reasoned.

'What time is kick-off?' Tom asked, already anticipating this party to be the highlight of his life so far.

'Seven thirty,' Django told him.

'Cool!' said Tom, looking forward to staying up well past his bedtime.

*

While the menfolk, accompanied by Cosima and a long list of Fen's handwritten notes taped to the buggy, spent the morning chuffing between Matlock and Rowsley on the Peak Rail steam train, the sisters took up position under the apple tree with notebooks and pens and adjectives scattered around them.

'I don't know what to say,' Cat wailed. 'I used to write for a living and I don't know what to say. I feel pretty emotional, I must admit.'

'Me too,' Fen said, 'and I've never written a speech – only dissertations and academic lectures which are easy compared with this.'

'And here's me, able to juggle, do flikflaks and balloon-modelling in front of an audience, but I shudder at the thought of an ode to Django in public,' Pip declared.

'He'd love it in rhyme,' Fen smiled.

'We haven't the time,' rued Cat.

They looked at each other and laughed.

'Barber's shop?'

'A cappella?'

'God, he'd love that!'

'No bloody way.'

When Django and the others arrived back, he requested a run-through of the speeches. 'Just to check your chronology,' he said, 'and to approve the length and breadth of superlatives. You only have a few hours to perfect it, you know.'

'Django,' said Pip, 'if it's a dress rehearsal you're after, you need to follow suit – literally. We'll read our speeches – if you give us a twirl in what you'll be wearing.'

Django looked outraged. 'And spoil the surprise? Philippa!'

Pip gave a triumphant shrug and rolled her piece of paper tightly into a scroll. Cat and Fen copied her.

'I do hope everyone will come,' Django said thoughtfully. 'I'm looking forward to it immensely.'

*

And they came; they came from all over the county, from up and down the country, from further afield too. Jim McKenzie came down from Glasgow in his kilt, and Bibi came from Paris swathed in the shawls and jangling with the bangles the girls remembered so vividly from their childhood. Gregor and Ferdy brought their banjos and strolled amongst the guests like minstrels. Landed gentry rubbed shoulders with rogues; lifelong friends mingled with folk of a more recent acquaintance; musicians and artists vied for eccentricity – it wasn't officially a fancy-dress party but the colourful flamboyance of many guests suggested otherwise. Pip, Fen and Cat were embraced constantly as faces they'd forgotten beamed back into their lives. People ate and ate and their eyes watered; they drank and they drank and their tears rolled, theatricality seamlessly blending with genuine emotion.

Django coasted around; resplendent in voluminous batik trousers from the Caribbean, a floral shirt that was alarmingly diaphanous, a suede waistcoat in colours of fire and a trademark neckerchief in incongruous toile de jouy. He kissed everyone regardless of their sex or age, how well he knew them and whether he'd kissed them already. He sang and he danced, he improvised impressively on Ferdy's banjo and the sound of his laughter became the underlying theme tune to the party. He could not pass Cat, Fen or Pip without hugging them – and if he hadn't seen them for a while, he searched them out.

'Where's your sister?' he asked Pip who was mopping a splodge of mayonnaise from the knee-skimming hem of her black shift dress.

'Which one?'

'The Fenella one,' he said, having already noted Cat jiving with Joe and Jack, still nimble on their feet at seventy-five.

'Checking on Cosima, probably,' said Pip, scanning the

throng and noting Bibi encircling an entranced Tom in one of her shawls like a wizard taking an apprentice.

'Fetch the girl,' Django said. 'I feel a speech coming on.'

Pip made her way through the marquee and over to the house. She called Fen softly from the hallway and made her way upstairs. She trod a careful path along the corridor, knowing which floorboards to avoid. From Django's bedroom, she could hear gentle music. The door was ajar and Pip tapped out a little rhythm on it.

'Shh!' came the response. Pip put her head around the door. 'Oh it's you,' Fen whispered.

'Do you always hiss at Matt?' Pip asked quietly.

Fen put her index finger to her lip. Pip looked over to the travel cot where Cosima was evidently sound asleep. 'Just changing the CD,' Fen whispered. Pip frowned and mimed that the baby was fast asleep. 'In case she wakes up,' Fen mouthed. Pip looked at the CD case of *Elvis for Babies*. To the sound of 'Love Me Tender' being played out on a glockenspiel, Pip raised her eyebrows and made the universal symbol of insanity; corkscrewing her finger against her temple. Fen stuck her tongue out at her, and gazed down at her baby for a long moment before tiptoeing from the room.

'What's wrong with "Baa Baa Black Sheep"?' Pip said as they went downstairs.

'Nothing,' Fen said, 'but a girl is never too young for Elvis. Django will back me on that one.'

'Talking of Django, he sent me to fetch you. It's time for the speeches.'

'God,' Fen groaned. 'Hang on, I'll just double-check the baby monitor. Stay here.' She placed a plastic egg-shaped receiver in Pip's hand. 'I won't be a moment.' She went back upstairs. Pip held the machine to her ear. She could hear heavenly angels la-la-ing to 'Suspicious Minds'. Then she heard Fen's whisper crackle through. 'Pip? Pip? Code word: Tabasco.'

'Tabasco,' Pip declared, as soon as Fen joined her again.

'Good,' said Fen, 'now I can relax.'

'No you can't,' Pip said. 'It's the speeches.'

Django's speech was surprisingly short but effusive with thanks and characteristically emotional. 'But enough from me,' he concluded, 'let's hear all about me instead! I hasten to add I've paid them proudly so I'm confident they'll be extravagant with the compliments. Ladies, gentlemen, troubadours and one important young man of nine years old – I give you my three exquisite girls, Pip, Fen and Cat.'

The sisters weaved their way to the head of the gathering, turned to face the guests and curtsied to much applause.

'As you all know, my sisters and I are famous for having the mother who buggered off with a cowboy from Denver when we were small,' started Pip, clutching her hands in front of her and then behind her and not really knowing what to do with them.

'And a father – Django's brother – who died not long after,' Fen said, nervously tying and retying her pony-tail.

'But far from being poor little orphans, or being remotely rootless or in any way scarred,' said Cat, fiddling furiously with the beads decorating her cardigan, 'our glory is that we had Django.' There followed much applause and whooping from those gathered and the three sisters felt each other relax. The smiles broadened, their confidence and showmanship blossomed and they started to enjoy themselves.

'Most of you know Django as a friend, a musician, an artiste, a culinary superpower,' said Pip. 'For my sisters and me, he's all of these – but he's also our parents. A good father makes you feel safe, he provides for you and protects you.

He teaches you about trust and explains fairness so clearly that you can understand it even if you don't agree. He teaches you to ride your bike without stabilizers, he makes you a sledge by adapting the old garden slide, he takes you out for your first driving lessons and doesn't protest when you crunch his gears or clip his wing-mirror. He gives you pocket money when you're young, bales out your overdraft when you're a student and helps you with your first mortgage when you're trying to afford to be a grown-up. A father instils your sense of right from wrong.' Pip smiled and winked at Cat and Fen. 'You grow up hoping the man you'll spend your life with might possess even half the qualities of your father. We three are true daddy's girls. Thank you, Django, for being Superdad.'

Pip stepped back to whistling and clapping, stamping and banjo-strumming. She saw Zac wink, watched Tom clap his hands high above his head and Django dab tears from his eyes with Ferdy's polka-dot handkerchief.

'Encore!' Django cried. 'Encore!'

'A good mother,' Fen began, 'nourishes you.' She let it hang and raised an eyebrow. Laughter was spontaneous, followed by a tide of applause, just as she'd hoped when she'd practised it silently in the bathroom mirror earlier. 'When it came to love and food, Django ensured we were fed like royalty. A mummy strokes your hair when you've had a nightmare and mops up after you when you're sick. A good mother soothes your heart when some cad or other has broken it. A mother hands down prized recipes – be they for beetroot crumble or fish pie with olivey hollandaise – and has a snack waiting for you when you get home from school. A mother takes in your jeans to drainpipe proportions, lets you borrow Pucci scarves for dressing up, and French-plaits your hair perfectly before you go to school. A mother makes curtains for your Wendy house and clothes for your dolls. A mother brings you hot chocolate when it's that time of the month. You should always feel that a mother loves you more than anything and anyone. A mother must make you believe you are the purpose of their very existence. A mother is a daughter's best friend.' Fen looked at her sisters and giggled involuntarily, shrugging helplessly as tears spiked her eyes and caught in her throat. 'I raise my glass to the best mother in the world.'

Fen grinned at Django who clasped his hands against his heart while coos and ahhs resonated through the marquee.

'Encore!' Django croaked. 'Encore.'

'A friend,' said Cat, as if she was about to recite a poem at school assembly, 'is there whether you need them or not.' She paused and looked imploringly at Fen and Pip, biting her lip. She scanned the crowd for Ben, who gave her an encouraging nod when she found him. She plucked at her cardigan and faltered. 'I can't remember what we wrote.' The crowd laughed soothingly. 'Something about it's our friends who make our world.' She winced. Fen whispered something to her. Cat shook her head adamantly. 'But the thing is, usually you choose your friends – but Django McCabe had no choice when we had no one else. He created our world for us. And what a world. How fucking amazing of him was that!'

'Language, Catriona!' Django called from the throng, cupping his hands over the ears of an obviously delighted Tom.

'Django – you always said we could swear when we really needed to, if a situation truly warranted it. Talking of situations – Christ, you had no choice, Django. You had *no choice*. But look at the life you made for us – our lives are a tribute to your devotion, your friendship, your parenting. And of course your home cooking. You, who are mother, father and friend, to me and my sisters. So you *are* fucking amazing, OK? We couldn't live without you. Does everyone realize that?' Cat looked out amongst the guests. 'Do you? Does everyone realize how great this man is?'

'Never let a McCabe girl near the punch,' Matt whispered to Ben. 'One sip and they're squiffy and hyper-emotional.'

'The sacrifices he made,' Cat continued, 'his generosity, his altruism and selflessness.'

'I've always thought tautology a good thing,' Django nudged Bibi proudly.

'He's always made us feel that we are *his* good fortune,' Cat declared, 'but of course he gave up so much for us.' Thoughts of Maureen and the summer of 1970 sprang to her mind and, momentarily, Cat was unsure whether she'd spoken aloud. 'He's our life-force,' she started to sob.

'Christ,' Ben whispered to Matt, 'never mind journalism, her natural career is Oscar speeches.'

'Django,' Cat declared, 'look around. Look who's here. From far and wide. From over the sea. From over the years. It's because you are so *fucking* amazing.'

Pip patted Cat's shoulder and interrupted. 'Could you all please raise your glasses and toast Django McCabe's seventy-fifth birthday before my sister swears any more and is sent to her bedroom.'

'To Django,' said Fen, tears making a mockery of her mascara. 'Happy, happy birthday.'

The adrenalin from speech-making, combined with the gin, vermouth and some strange green liqueur from Grenada in the punch, had a fast-acting intoxicating effect on the McCabe girls though their reactions differed. Fen became physically demonstrative, offering hugs and hand-holding to whomever was within arm's reach. Pip became affectionately animated. Cat was simply over-emotional.

'I do so love my family,' Cat declared to Pip who was trying to French kiss a bemused Zac much to Tom's jaw-dropped delight. 'Family is everything,' she said, looking desperately fondly at Ben. 'The family you have, the family you create.'

'Family is what matters,' Pip agreed. 'You're so right.'

'Oh God, not the waterworks,' Ben groaned passing Cat a serviette to mop her eyes.

'I can't believe you said "fucking" *three* times in front of *everyone*!' Tom marvelled.

'Fucking fucking fucking fucking,' Cat laughed. 'There, that's another four.'

'Cat!' Zac protested, shooting a glance to Pip for back-up.

'Cool!' Tom laughed, deciding Cat was definitely his favourite step-aunt-or-something.

Cat hugged him. 'I just can't wait to have a little Tom or a little Cosima of my very own,' she told him. 'Family is what matters most in life.'

'I agree,' Tom said earnestly. 'I've got loads.'

'That's what they should teach children in school,' Cat said. 'Are you excited about your new baby?'

'Mega excited,' Tom said. 'I don't even mind if it's a girl.'

Zac laughed. 'That's only because you think your train collection will be safe.'

Tom grinned and shrugged.

Cat and Fen are teaching Tom how to swear in German and French. Matt and Ben have snuck behind the marquee for a secret spliff. Pip's arms are about Zac's neck again. 'Why don't we do it?' she whispers, whilst nuzzling his ear lobe.

Zac regards her with a lascivious grin. 'Sneak away for a quick knee-trembler against the oak tree?'

Pip frowns fleetingly. 'I don't mean that,' she laughs, 'I didn't mean a shag. I meant why don't *we* do it, Zac. You and me. Us. Have a baby?'

What was previously but the hushest of whispers in the furthest recesses of her own mind, is suddenly out in the open. Though she has enunciated the question mark and made it sound like a request, her words are less a suggestion and more a proclamation of intent. And Zac must respond, he must answer, he must acknowledge her invitation. And for Pip, in an instant, it is irrelevant whether Zac's expression is specifically one of shock, one of bemusement, one of aversion or an amalgamation of all three. The significance is the absence of a smile. It's shocking. Zac's smile was what she'd first fallen in love with. It can't have gone.

'You're drunk,' he's saying, 'you're joking.'

'I'm not,' Pip protests. 'Well, maybe I am drunk. But I'm not joking.'

'Don't be daft,' Zac says and he plugs her mouth with an affectionate kiss. 'And stay off the punch, Mrs.' He looks around while Pip stares at his shoes and quashes a sudden desire to scuff their well-tended shine. 'Have you seen Tom?' he asks her. 'There he is. Can you keep an eye on him? I'm going to find Matt and Ben for a crafty puff.'

Pip weaves her way to Tom. She feels winded. She hadn't known she was to make her revelation so of course she couldn't reasonably anticipate his reaction. But the reaction, when it came, flummoxed her more than her revelation itself. She's embarrassed. And a little hurt. It's a sensation she does not like, one that she won't allow to show because she'd hate anyone to pry. She's always been very committed and particular in her role as the eldest; she's taken it to mean that she must appear infallible and in control. How would Cat and Fen cope if she wasn't? They depend on her. It's their family way.

And here they are, her little sisters, their arms around her stepson.

'Where's my dad?' Tom asks.

'I don't know,' Pip says, 'and you should be thinking bedtime.'

'But it's not ten o'clock,' Tom protests.

'It's five to,' says Pip.

'But Dad says I can stay up until ten,' Tom moans.

Pip bites her lip. Fine. Whatever. What does my opinion matter anyway? I'm not your mother. I have no natural authority.

'Pip?' Fen asks. 'Are you OK?'

'What? Fine,' Pip says and she walks away.

'Go after her,' Cat nudges Fen.

'You,' says Fen. 'I need to check on Cosima.'

'Come on, kiddo,' Cat says to Tom whom she's noticed has much the same hairstyle as her – though his here-and-there tufting is beyond his control while hers requires expensive products and much time. 'Let's go and find some crazy chums of Django's to chat to.'

'It's my bedtime,' Tom says gravely.

'Fuck bedtime,' Cat says with a wink and a nudge. 'Let's pretend we can't tell the time.'

'You're wicked,' says Tom, beaming, as Cat puts her hand on his bony little shoulder and guides him into the party.

'Sleeping peacefully?' Matt whispers.

Fen turns from the travel cot and puts her finger to her lips. She nods. Matt comes over. He doesn't glance in the cot. He has eyes only for Fen. She looks so pretty tonight and he's feeling so horny, a bit drunk and stoned too. He comes up to her, tucks a straying lock of hair behind her ears and cups her head in his hands. He winks suggestively. The gesture is partly comic but engaging too. Over her clothes, Matt's hands peruse her breasts while his mouth finds hers. To his surprise and delight, suddenly she's tonguing him greedily, grasping his buttocks and pulling his pelvis against hers. Privately, he salutes the punch and the green stuff from Grenada. He thinks he'll ply Fen with alcohol on a regular basis. She's wearing a soft skirt and all evening he's been noticing how it catches the curves of her bottom, the sides of her thighs. No panty line. No panties? He explores. A thong. God, when was the last time he saw her in a thong? His hands move over her bare buttocks, he slips his fingers under the fabric of the thong and starts tugging it gently, knowing it creates tantalizing friction for her.

Fen's hands are all over him. Sweeping over his torso, grabbing his neck to pull his face even closer to hers, fondling the bulge in his trousers. He fumbles with buttons while Fen drops to her knees and tugs down his boxers. There's no preamble. No inner-thigh massage or ball-licking or shaft-caressing. She takes the entire length of his tumescent cock in her mouth and sucks so ravenously that he has to desperately conjure an image of the mad old woman near work, to stop him coming right then. He pulls Fen up to him, pulls at her top and fiddles with her bra cup to release her breasts. Her nipples are hard between his fingers and his cock is now achingly erect. He'd love to spend time sucking her tits, fingering her sex, maybe go down on her, some reciprocal oral sex, perhaps some mutual masturbation but actually all he wants to do is fuck her, get his cock up inside her in some primal urgency to reclaim her as his own. They fall onto the bed, not bothering about what clothing is on or off, just as long as there's no fabric restricting entry. Fen pulls her G-string to one side, fleetingly Matt brushes through the fuzz of her mound, to confirm the ready ooze from her sex. Her legs are spread, their eyes are locked, their lips are parted and wet. He thrusts into her and they hump vigorously. Usually, Fen likes to go on top. Usually, she wants to go on top, to dictate the pace and the angle to facilitate her orgasm. Usually, she needs penetration interspersed with manual or oral stimulation to climax. Tonight, it is as if she has started to come as soon as Matt is inside her. The longest, most overdue, most body-racking orgasm. She gasps and bucks and scratches and yelps and she's pretty sure she's just come again instantaneously. Yet despite this fantastic vast throbbing wet pleasure zone electrifying her body, her mind tunes into her baby's cry the millisecond before the sound is made.

And then Fen's eyes are wide open and she's shoving and pushing Matt off her. He's a matter of thrusts away from his climax but the strength of a mother is no match for him. She's gone. She's gone away. He lies there, his balls aching with unspent sperm, his cock more flaccid by the second. He thinks it's an amazing but dreadful feat, the way she can flit between sex-greed and maternal obsession. It's really quite some skill. One to revere, but not necessarily like. What he doesn't like at all is a lurking sense that while he was compelled by passion for her just now, she was pursuing only her own physical gratification. I've come – you can go now. Matt feels used, really. As let down and deflated as his ignored, limp cock.

Once Cosima has settled again, Fen offers herself to Matt; caressing his wilted cock, taking it in her mouth. Though she performs a variety of usually fail-safe tricks and techniques, it is not possible to disguise her drive as one of desire rather than duty. She's not even half-hearted; her heart obviously isn't in it.

'Moment has passed,' Matt shrugs, tapping her head.

Fen looks up. His cock snuggles against his pubic hair like a little creature asleep in a nest. He thinks it looks pathetic. He closes his eyes.

'Don't I turn you on any more?' Fen says and he looks down at her pouting up at him.

He knows she's trying to be cute but he wants to tell her,

Actually, sometimes no you don't, especially not when you reject me to faff with the baby. But it's not worth it. It's Django's birthday party. Matt can't possibly instigate a confrontation, or even a heart-to-heart.

'You can owe me one,' he tells her as he rearranges his clothing.

She gives him a quick kiss on the cheek. 'Deal,' she says warmly, led by growing guilt. She's horribly aware that throughout the fuck she was abandoned to the fantasy that Matt was someone else. No one whom she knew. Just someone specifically not Matt. But now is not the time to worry and analyse it. There's a party out in the garden. She double-checks the baby monitor and returns to the mêlée.

Django is telling Tom somewhat fanciful stories about his time with the Beatles. Bibi is nodding earnestly, adding details of her own which she's pretty sure must be true. 'The thing about the sixties,' she confides to Zac, 'is I can't remember a bloody thing about the sixties! I think LSD may well have been a terrific trip – but the downside is I don't honestly know which memories are real and which are purely chemical.'

'Where's Ellisdy, Dad?' Tom asks Zac, wondering if such a trip might be something they could do over the summer holidays. Zac is momentarily thrown. Now does not seem an appropriate time for the 'just say no' lecture.

'Ghastly! Don't go there!' Django rues, which is good enough for Zac and good enough for Tom.

'Gracious me, look at the time – it's nearly midnight and I'll turn into a pumpkin. Or, rather, seventy-five years old officially.'

'I thought it was a birthday party?' Tom says, confused. 'You can only have a *birthday* party if it's on your actual birthday. Otherwise it has to be called a *party*.'

‘My seventy-fifth birthday is actually tomorrow,’ Django says. He looks at his watch and counts down the seconds with theatrical nods of his head. ‘No. I tell a lie. It’s now today. I’m now seventy-five years old.’

‘So it *is* a birthday party,’ says Tom, dreading his father hearing all this talk about what the time is.

‘Whatever you’d like to call it, I had an absolute blast,’ said Django. ‘And now I’m going to bed.’

Derek

Often, a great party is defined less by the event itself, than by the calibre and longevity of subsequent reminiscences. A balmy May Sunday morning in the idyllic setting of the house and grounds at Farleymoor, provided a conducive carte blanche for lounging, lazing and recounting. Of course, this could not be done on an empty stomach, nor with a hangover, so Django had prepared his remedy for both – a vast breakfast of sausages, eggs, bacon, champ and beans, all flooded with Henderson's Relish and roofed over with slabs of toast plastered with marmalade. His family lolled about outside, turning their faces to the sun, chatting. Behind them, the Blakes of Chesterfield marquee seemed to breathe; its sides swelling rhythmically in the gentle breeze, as if still sleeping off the excesses of the night before.

'You said "fucking" *seven* times!' Tom whispered to Cat who winced, covered her eyes and apologized profusely.

'Did anyone video the speeches?' Fen wondered, hovering her hand an inch above Cosima's head so that the baby's downy hair caressed the palm of her hand.

'Video?' Django balked. 'Gracious no, though the Ravellas brought their Super8. Doubt whether it had film in it. They've taken that thing everywhere with them over the years, amassing a footage that runs into – well – *minutes* on account of their forgetfulness.'

'Bibi's dancing deserves to be documented for posterity,' Ben marvelled. 'She's more loose-limbed than Josephine Baker.'

'Actually, she really was a contortionist in her prime. That's how we met. It was some festival or other. She was doing frightfully bendy things whilst saluting the sun, or the moon, or something similarly yogic. However, she ended up making quite a few bob as many people presumed she was busking for tips.'

'What a character,' Pip said warmly. 'I hope she pops in sometime today, to say goodbye again.'

'Look, here are Ferdy and Gregor!' said Cat.

'No banjos,' Tom remarked sadly.

It took some time for the couple to kiss everyone on both cheeks. They then made much of how ghastly their headaches were and that the least Django could do was provide hair-of-the-dog by way of compensation. Zac's constitution was far too delicate just then, to withstand an explanation of the term to Tom, though Matt promised the boy he'd tell him later, when his own headache had subsided.

'Will you be having an eighty-fifth birthday party?' Tom enquired. 'In a decade?'

Django considered the question carefully. 'I can't see why not,' he reasoned, 'as long as I'm still relatively hale and hearty.'

'I'll be nearly *twenty* by then!' Tom said. 'How fucking amazing is that!'

'Tom!' everyone remonstrated, before levelling accusatory glares at Cat.

'Goodness me, I need a cup of tea,' Django declared.

'I'll make it,' offered Pip.

'You stay put, darling,' Django ordered. 'I may be old, but I'm not incapable.'

'Can we just have Darjeeling, please?' Fen requested as diplomatically as she could.

'She means not that weird purpley stuff that smells like stewed grasses,' Cat laughed.

'I didn't bring you up to be dull,' Django protested, though he had to privately agree with the stewed-grass analogy. 'Might you settle for Lapsang?' he asked. They'd have to.

'Do a flikflak, Pip!' Tom implored his stepmother. Pip looked at the lawn: soft, level and inviting. It was where she'd taught herself all manner of tumbling over the years, but she didn't much feel like demonstrations today. She had a hangover and what she wanted was to have a private moment with Zac so she could say *Did you mean what you said last night? Because, actually, I meant what I said*. But Zac had been infuriatingly cheerful all morning, tactile and attentive, thus allowing her no recourse to challenge him.

'Please do a flikflak?' Tom pleaded. 'It makes sense to do flikflaks *before* you have a cup of tea.'

'I wasn't actually considering doing any after,' Pip pointed out. And then she looked at Tom's disappointed little face and flikflaks suddenly seemed a tiny price to pay for his smile. 'I want applause,' Pip stipulated, 'cheering and whistling, if you please.' And off she went, executing a perfect line of four.

'I used to be able to walk on my hands,' said Ben. Rolling his head, giving his wrists and ankles an energetic shake, to gasps of admiration, he found he still could.

'I can cartwheel!' said Cat, scrambling to her feet and doing just that.

And when Penny Ericsson came through the garden gate,

that's the scene that greeted her: a laughing bunch performing amateur acrobatics in the early summer sunshine.

No one knew who she was. Why should they? But the appearance of a stranger didn't surprise them. People had been calling in all morning to thank Django for the party and wish him many happy returns. Some hadn't even been present the night before, but still they came with their birthday greetings. So the group on the lawn didn't bat an eyelid at the woman. She was just another friend of Django's, wasn't she? Someone from his dim and distant past, from some far-flung shore, no doubt. Relatively conservatively dressed for a friend of Django's. Silvering blonde hair cut close. Small tortoiseshell glasses. A tunic top and cropped trousers in the same honey-coloured linen. Sensible sandals. Interesting jewellery. She had stopped some distance away. She raised her hand. Fen raised hers.

'Hi,' the woman called.

'Hullo!' called Cat.

'Hi,' she said, coming nearer, 'hi.'

An American. Django had plenty of friends from the States. Perhaps this was the famous Toni from Squam? Or the infamous Rayner from Sausalito?

'Hi,' she said, once again, slightly breathless, squinting in the sunlight.

'Hullo,' said Fen. And Cat. And Pip. And the men. And Tom.

It is often a peculiar surprise to hear the sound of one's voice on a recording. The sound doesn't make sense. I don't sound anything like that. Sometimes, a mirror presents an image so far from one's perception of oneself that the reflection could well belong to a stranger. But that's not how I feel I look.

However, for Ben, Matt and Zac, a glimpse of the future,

of seeing how their partners might look in twenty-five years' time, was immediate. But that wasn't the shock of it. The fundamental shock was that this woman's resemblance to their girls was so striking that there could be but one explanation. And yet the girls obviously hadn't noticed a thing.

But what when they did?

What then?

The three men could do little more than glance at each other and feel their heart rates thud like the countdown to a detonation.

'So,' the lady said, 'where is the birthday boy?'

'He's making tea,' Cat said. 'He'll be out in a mo'.'

'He always makes plenty,' Fen assured her.

'Sorry – were you at the party last night?' asked Pip.

'No,' she said, 'no.' And she fingered the cord of silver around her neck while being smiled at.

Tom wondered whether this new lady might be interested that Cat had said 'fucking' seven times.

'Here he is,' Fen said, before Tom had a chance to find out.

Django was far too busy balancing the tray with all the cups and saucers and teapot and plates piled high with biscuits to notice his guest at first.

'Hi Derek,' the lady said, 'happy birthday.'

Derek?

Who's Derek?

I don't think we know a Derek.

There's no Derek here.

In severe electric shocks, it is impossible to let go. Such shocks are, literally, riveting; they simultaneously root you to the spot while they decimate you. Django didn't drop the tray, he didn't faint or fall to his knees and he didn't wail or gasp. He couldn't. He couldn't make a sound, let alone say a word. He couldn't drop the tray. He couldn't move. He stood there, momentarily paralysed.

'This is *Django*,' Cat was saying to the lady, 'Django *McCabe*.'

'If you're lost, there are loads of Ordnance Survey maps in the house,' said Fen helpfully.

'I think they're in that trunk in the shed, actually,' added Pip.

'Girls,' said Django, and the pureness of his audible pain was not for himself, but for those he loved most on whom he was about to inflict it. 'Girls.' Carefully he put the tray down. He did not know in whose eyes he should look. So he looked at her. 'Girls. This is your mother.'

* * *

Where were you when Princess Diana died? What were you doing when the planes struck the World Trade Center on 9/11? Were you sitting down to Christmas Day leftovers when you learnt about the Asian Tsunami?

On Django's seventy-fifth birthday, Cat, Pip and Fen wouldn't have had a clue where they'd been on those landmark moments. For them, history ceased to be defined by such events. On Django's seventy-fifth birthday, history was retold.

Our mother ran off with a cowboy from Denver when we were small.

And then she came back.

Then What?

Then what? No one could actually say a thing. Time had stopped, the temperature had dropped and Pip, Cat and Fen were paralysed in a state of frozen panic. If the magnitude of the situation was beyond belief, it was certainly beyond words. They had never imagined this occurrence, never craved it, never dreaded it. Therefore, they had never bothered to prepare fanciful speeches in the event of their mother showing up. They'd never even wondered 'What if?' This sudden reality was so far from their expectation that they were utterly ill-equipped to deal with it. They could only sit and stare, with time suspended while their hearts thumped with disbelief. No one wanted to break it. In the silence, they were still safe. If anyone moved or any sound was made, time would have to resume. Nothing would be the same again. This they knew. And yet Cat, Fen and Pip hadn't ever wanted anything to change in the first place.

Penny stood there and deduced which daughter was Cat, though just then she didn't know Pip from Fen. It also occurred to her, with unexpected pleasure, that she appeared to be a grandmother too. The particulars of her gene-pool were immediately legible; her three daughters had paired up and had two offspring between them. The bare facts were pleasing. The girls appeared in good health. Their men looked nice. Everyone seemed happy. It was a soothing scene to behold but one she suddenly wished she was seeing as a fly on the wall. Home seemed very far away.

'Hi,' she said, focusing on the baby, 'and aren't you a cutey?' She stooped to Cosima who was gurgling and bashing her pudgy legs with her little fists. Penny offered the baby a finger. 'Hi, hi, cutey-pie.'

Fen grabbed her baby away before she could grasp her grandmother's finger. She staggered to her feet, the brittle rubber of one flip-flop ripping away from the sole as she did so. Her face glowering with mistrust and animosity. 'What the fuck?' she managed in a hoarse whisper.

Tom gave a delighted gasp. 'Fen said f—'

'Tom!' Zac hissed, now in no quandary over whom to protect. He took Tom away, to the tyre swing at the outer edge of the garden. He could only touch his wife gently between the shoulder-blades as he went.

'You're Fenella?' Penny deduced. 'And look, you have a daughter!'

Fen couldn't respond, she could only hold Cosima protectively. What did all this mean? What was going on? Matt rose and stood oak-like and silent behind his family.

'You're Philippa?' Penny asked Pip.

Pip was unable to give much more than a childlike shrug. Where was Zac? Where should she be? By her sisters? But they had their partners. No one was looking to her for help. They were each in a constrictive space of their own. Pip felt entirely alone. Zac was in another space, protecting his son. She was surrounded by a family in splinters and for the first time she had no idea how to go about putting it all back together again. She felt very cold.

'And I guessed you were Catriona,' Penny gave a small smile. She turned to Django. 'She has your eyes, hey?'

1960s and All That Jazz

If ignorance had been the background to the bliss in the McCabe sisters' lives until that moment, knowledge was its polar opposite and it suffused them with panic and pain. In desperation, they tried to plead ignorance. If they pretended they didn't know what she meant, everything might be all right.

'What are you doing here?' said Pip.

'Who's Derek?' said Fen.

Say something Cat. Quickly. You need to say something naive and pedestrian. Why not tell that woman she simply has the wrong family. But Cat's voice was horribly noticeable for its silence. Her sisters turned to her. She looked back at them, imploringly. 'What does she mean about me having Django's eyes?' said Cat, capable of little more than a whisper. They turned to Django who was staring at Penny. They turned to Penny who was gazing at the three of them.

'I had to come,' Penny told them. 'I know it must be a shock and all. But could we talk? Might you listen?'

The sisters turned to Django but his head hung low and his eyes were fixed on the ground.

'If you're on some mission to appease your guilt, you've

wasted your journey,' said Pip flatly. 'It has nothing to do with *us*.'

'What are you doing here?' Fen said so icily that Cosima wriggled and began to cry. 'What are you implying about Cat? Why do you call our uncle "Derek"?'

'You did not know?' Penny appeared shocked. 'Did you God-honestly not *know*? Your whole lives – and you did not *know*?'

'Know what?' Cat asked, her voice barely audible.

The faintest of whispers coursed through Fen and Pip, but they blocked it out, not ready to listen.

If we did not know any of this, what else might we not know? The thought was trying to sidle.

Cat now had her hands clamped over her ears, her eyes screwed shut. She did not want to hear them and she did not want anyone looking at her eyes.

'I am *sorry*,' Penny said with a hand at her heart for emphasis, 'this must be a terrible shock. Derek – could you not help me out here?'

All eyes turned to the man in the candy-striped cheesecloth smock, the man with the moccasins on his feet, wearing patched cords with fraying seams and a faded CND patch appliquéd under one knee. Whatever his name was. There had to be an explanation. He was the man who had always made everything all right. Who had made sense of everything. He had always told them, when they were hurt, that he was there to make them better. That it was his job to kiss that bruise. That he was the world expert in cuddling away tears. There there. There there. Django is here. Don't cry. Don't worry. Django's here.

Except he isn't.

Some bloke called Derek is standing in his moccasins.

*

He suddenly looks very old and tired, thought Pip.

He doesn't look well, thought Fen.

I hate him, thought Cat.

Christ, this is one crackpot family, thought Ben.

Bugger, Cosima needs changing, thought Matt.

'I,' Django said. 'She.' He paused. 'You,' he said, though he focused on no one. Silence fell and Django felt powerless to do anything about it.

She took off her glasses. 'My name is Penny Ericsson,' she told them, 'and I am your mother.' Her voice was gentle and clear, tinged with reflection but underscored with relief; a timbre that told everyone that the truth was being told. 'I was married to Nicholas McCabe when I was a very young girl. I was seventeen and pregnant – not with you, Philippa, with another child. I miscarried. I had you. I had Fenella. I had Catriona. And I left.'

The silence, no less heavy, was calmer.

'Why do you say that Cat has Django's eyes?' Pip asked finally, the reluctant spokesman for the sisters.

'You have Nicholas's chin, Philippa,' Penny said levelly, 'Fenella has Nicholas's eyes.' She stopped. 'And Catriona has Derek's eyes.'

'What are you *saying*?' Fen then turned to Django who finally met her gaze. 'What is she saying?'

Django looked around him. His home. His garden. His girls. His grandchildren. All that he loved. He was soaking up the sights, as if within seconds he'd be denied them for ever. All that he held sacred, all he had hoped to keep safe, was teetering on a precipice that was as much of his own making as of Penny Ericsson's. He wasn't sure if he'd be able to step in as protector or if he was about to push what he held most precious straight over the edge. He stumbled, grabbed the cold edge of the curlicue garden chair and sat down heavily. With a hand on each knee, and rocking gently, he spoke with audibly heart-heavy reluctance. 'My name is Derek McCabe – or at least that's what it says on my birth certificate.' Suddenly, it seemed like a good if desperate idea to fixate on the triviality of this particular revelation, to step outside the bigger picture and the graver question. A glance at his girls suggested they were almost glad of the diversion. 'Look at me, I hardly look like a Derek, do I?' he tried a meek smile. 'Derek was my given name – but Django is my true name. Can we settle on that?'

'*Django*?' Pip enunciated the word as if it sat awkward on her tongue, as if it were no longer a name. 'How the hell did you go from Derek to Django?'

Django looked hurt. 'Jazz,' he declared, as if to prompt, '*jazz*.' Fen and Pip nodded as if they thought they understood. 'When I heard the music of Django Reinhardt, the colour and spirit at my core leapt free,' he explained, 'and in the sixties, to be who you felt was the easiest thing in the world. You think Bibi's parents called her Bibi when she was born in 1939? They called her Doris, but what did they know? Can you imagine Bibi being called Doris, for goodness' sake? One day she said, Hey call me Bibi, so we said, Cool. And one day I said, Hey call me Django, and they said, Cool. Feel the vibe. Tune in. Dig it.'

Too many psychedelic drugs, Ben mused in a quick, private glance to Matt.

Good thing his hero was Django Reinhardt and not Bix Beiderbecke or Thelonious Monk, Matt thought as he raised his eyebrow to Ben.

But for the sisters, Django's eccentricity was suddenly baffling and irritating. Throughout their lives, in spite of his quirks, he'd been utterly reliable and had ensured consistency in their lives. Now they felt conned.

'But are you?' Cat's voice suddenly rang out, far stronger than Pip's, much calmer than Fen's. She locked eyes with Penny. 'Is he?'

'I am,' said Django.

'How long have you known?' Cat asked.

'I've always known,' Django said.

With that, there was now nothing else to misconstrue, nothing to cling to in the faint hope of a mistake. And in the here and now, the hear and now became far too onerous for Cat. Burying her head in Ben's chest was her only option because, just then, he was the closest she felt she had to proper, genuine family.

Penny cleared her throat, to invite all eyes back to her. She looked from Fen to Pip, gazed at the back of Cat's head, at Ben's hand holding it protectively against his chest, his wedding ring glinting in the sunshine. Then Penny glanced at Django. 'He's kinda right,' she said. 'I don't know.' She stopped. Attempted to speak again. Stopped. 'Nowadays there's Prozac,' she said, 'and therapy. But back then, there were magic mushrooms and acid and free love. Only it wasn't free. None of it was free or liberating. The cost was high.'

'But why are you here?' Pip asked.

'You're screwing up our lives a second time around,' Fen cried.

Penny looked crestfallen. She hadn't anticipated this and she certainly had not intended this. Privately, she cursed Grief for having centred her world around herself. 'If I could try to explain?' she asked them and continued before they could deny her. 'Despite the fog of my screwed-up 1960s state, I met the love of my life. The love of my life. The light in my life. A beautiful man called Bob Ericsson.' She looked around her. Their faces wouldn't be blank if they'd known him, she thought. 'He died, you see. He died five months ago. The light in my life went out. And I am here because suddenly I don't want to be hated like Juliette hates her father.' Penny faltered. So much to explain. How could she have suddenly arrived at Fountains ice cream when there was over a quarter of a century's details to divulge? 'Juliette is this young woman I've met,' she said, a little meekly. 'She's about your age, Fen, I would imagine. I don't actually know.'

'Don't you even know how old I am?' Fen cried.

'Oh, I know *exactly* how old you are,' Penny said, her voice so hoarse it had no tone, 'to the day. The minute. I just don't know how old Juliette is, precisely.'

For the sisters, details were now irrelevant. Other people's sob stories were irrelevant. The quandary all three shared was who to feel most betrayed by. The mother who had abandoned them when they were small? Or the man who had lied to them, to a greater or lesser degree, throughout their lives? In their past, at tumultuous points in their lives, there had always been that one place to go to – home, Derbyshire, Django. Now it was the one place they wanted to run from. Their hearts were not here so how could it be home? Their hearts had been fractured into splinters and shards by the arrival of this woman saying she was their mother, and this man called Derek admitting he was Cat's father.

'I want to go,' Fen told Matt.

Pip looked over at the tyre swing. 'Zac?' she called. He looked up. *We're going*, she mouthed with an urgent beckon.

She and Fen looked at Cat, at the back of her head, Ben's chest keeping her face from view, her hands still protecting her ears. 'Us too,' Ben nodded, kissing the top of his wife's head again and again.

Where were you when you found out that Pip and Fen were only your half sisters? That your father was a man called Derek McCabe whom you'd known your whole life but was now a complete stranger?

I was listening to Ben's heartbeat, sixty-two beats per minute. Strong and steady. Take me away from here, Ben. Quickly. Back to Clapham – that's fine. Wherever. As long as I'm with you. Home is where my heart is. And it won't ever be here in Derbyshire. Never again.

* * *

From standing stock still with time suspended, suddenly the emphasis was on movement, on going, on getting away and fast. There was no flouncing, no histrionics, just calm and purposeful organizing.

'Have you had a wee?' Pip asked Tom.

'I'll just change Cosima,' said Matt.

'It's OK, I'll do that,' said Fen. 'You pack the car.'

Finally, the sisters hugged each other and pointedly stayed beyond arm's reach and avoided eye contact when muttering goodbye to the approximate location of Django and their mother.

How can something planned to perfection go so horribly wrong? Though the thought had conflicting relevance in terms of timescale, both Django and Penny pondered as they stood in the garden transfixed by the space made by the girls' leaving.

'Oh dear,' Penny said, 'this I did not plan. How dumb am I?'

'Ditto,' said Django, 'still. Still.' He sighed and glanced at her. 'One can't expect to hoick secrets one's whole life. They're far too cumbersome.' He spoke for them both. She nodded and hung her head. 'Though I'd say I'm more deluded than dumb,' Django said. 'I've spent over thirty years keeping them from hurt. How conceited I must be to have assumed I could maintain this.'

He looked at her. Penny at fifty-three. She hadn't really changed. Physically, the years had apparently treated her relatively well but a good complexion could not mask a certain delineating sadness. And it was precisely this that he remembered, from thirty years ago; more than the colour of her eyes, the set of her mouth. Still the same sad, mixed-up girl, currently hiding behind a more weathered façade. 'Why on earth did you come back?'

Penny looked at her sandals, looked at Django's moccasins, made an oddly childish semicircle in the grass with her foot. 'I don't really know right now.'

'Well it can't have been to wish me happy birthday.'

'No,' Penny agreed, 'I'd already booked my flight when I remembered your birthday and realized it was your seventy-fifth.'

'Why come?' Django asked. 'Why now?'

'Because Bob died,' Penny shrugged, hastily blinking away tears and feigning that it was the sunlight bothering her.

'I am sorry for your loss,' Django said, his eyes and his voice softening a little.

'I tend to lose most things, don't I?' Penny remarked. 'But I really did try to take good care of Bob, you know.'

I've just lost the lot, Django thought sadly to himself.

The M1

Junction 27

Guns N' Roses was a very odd choice. Odd, because Ben had no idea that Cat particularly liked their music. Odd because they'd always favoured Moby for motorways. Odd because the thrash and slash of heavy rock should surely be utterly at odds with the fragile, solemn mood. Wouldn't Cat want to listen to something more ambient, something to soothe the scorch on her soul? Obviously not. Sweet child of mine.

At first, Ben thought she was singing silently. From the corner of his eye, he assumed Cat was miming along to Axl, imitating his physiognomic contortions. But a swift glance across at her and he realized she was hyperventilating, tears streaming, her face racked in torment.

'Oh babe,' he said, while thinking to himself that he was driving at eighty miles an hour and wondering if he could pull over to the hard shoulder. He placed his hand on her knee. 'It's OK. It's OK.'

'It's not!' she cried. 'Nothing's OK. And I can't breathe. Help me.'

'In through your nose, out through your mouth, in through

your nose, out through your mouth,' Ben chanted at her, calm but insistent. 'Cat, breathe into that paper bag. Down there – that the bananas came in.'

'It has rubbish in it.'

'Take the banana skin out. Throw it on the floor. Put the bag against your mouth and breathe into it. Come on Cat – in through your nose, out through your mouth, in through your nose, out through your mouth.'

With the music hammering and Cat sucking and blowing into the bag, Ben thought it ludicrously plausible that she should look like some solvent-abusing rock chick.

'I want to stop.'

'Babe, I can't stop on the hard shoulder. There's a services in a couple of miles. In through your nose and out through your mouth.'

'I need to stop,' Cat gasped. 'Stop the car.' Ben swerved the car to the hard shoulder. He flicked on the hazard lights, unclipped his seat-belt and leant across to hold his wife. However awkward and uncomfortable the angle for him, he knew it was nothing compared to the pain she was in. There were hundreds of questions he wanted to ask but of course he refrained. There'd be time for that. Way too much time. Just now, he knew there was not much he could say at all. His job was to hold her and fill her ears with comforting hushing, place the tender kisses on her forehead and keep her freezing cold hands warm within his. He promised her, over and over again, that everything would be all right though he hadn't the faintest idea how to fulfil such a pledge.

'I can't believe it. I don't know what happened. What does it all mean? I don't want anything to change. Life will never be the same again.'

No. Oh fuck no. Not the fucking police. Blue lights flashed up behind Ben's car and an officer walked over. Ben racked his mind for explanations, excuses, lies – anything would do. He wound down his window.

'Everything OK?' the policeman asked, peering in to the interior of the car and politely overlooking the state of Cat's tears-ravaged face for the time being.

'Yes,' said Ben, 'fine.'

'Your car OK, sir?' the officer asked. 'Broken down?'

Ben faltered. It was his wife who had broken down. Wasn't that glaringly obvious?

'Everything all right?' the officer asked again, now looking directly at the sobbing, shivering heap of Cat half in Ben's arms.

Ben didn't know what he ought to say. 'I. It's. She.' He shrugged. 'It's personal.'

Suddenly Cat looked up. 'Someone died,' she told the officer. 'I've only just heard. It's my uncle, who brought me up. He's now dead.'

The officer spoke quietly to Ben. 'You need to move along, sir. It is an offence to stop on the hard shoulder. There's a services a few miles on. Take her there.'

Back on the M1, Cat continued to sob, alternating sucks on the paper bag with great soul-crushed wails while Axl Rose still blared out about bad apples and dead horses.

'It hurts,' she cried. 'Christ the pain, Ben.'

'I know, babe, I know.'

'You don't! You can't possibly! No one does!'

Ben thought about this. It was true. 'I know. You're right. I can only begin to imagine. I'm sorry. But *they* know,' he said, 'your sisters.'

'It's not the same, I'm nothing like them. They're the ones who are sisters. They still have an uncle called Django.'

Ben drove on in contemplative silence, one hand on the wheel, the other on Cat's knee. Perfectly true. The mother's reappearance was to some extent irrelevant. Much more of a shock to discover at the age of thirty-two that your father is in fact alive and that half of each sister didn't actually exist.

'In through your nose, Cat, out through your mouth. Good girl. Good girl.'

'I don't know who I am,' Cat sobbed. 'I'm not who I grew up thinking I was.'

Junction 23a

Matt's eyes scanned a constant triangle: ahead to the motorway, sideways to Fen, to the back to Cosima and then forward to the motorway. The traffic was light and driving conditions were good. The baby was dozing contentedly – her thumb had fallen from her mouth but her sucking reflex continued regardless, her cheeks dimpling and the underside of her chin pulsating rhythmically. Fen's gaze was directed out of the window but it was obvious she wasn't admiring the view. She usually commented on the cooling towers near Nottingham but they'd passed them, solid and peaceful and elephantine, yet she'd said nothing. Nor had she remarked on the radio listening station outside Rugby, as she was wont to do; today the slightly alarming, sci-fi forest of antennae in the lie of the two motorways was spared Fen's customary comparison with a Ridley Scott film set.

Every few miles, Matt had placed his hand on her knee with a supportive stroke or squeeze and asked her if she was OK. Each time, she'd reply that she didn't know. And Matt would ask if she wanted to talk. And she'd shake her head and return her attention to the hard shoulder.

Matt scanned his triangle of interest again. The motorway and Cosima were doing as he wanted, Fen remained beyond reach. He put his hand over hers.

'You OK, Fen? Do you want to talk?'

Don't block it out, Fen. It's not healthy. Don't block me out, Fen. It's not good for us.

'Fen, you OK?'

'Life will never be the same again, Matt.'

That's what worries me, Fen, that's what worries me most.

Junction 16

Aren't grown-ups odd. It's not a question, it's a statement. We'd already been in the car for years and I was trying to ask what name I should call Django Gramps from now on. Dad gave me one of those looks with his eyebrows that told me to zip it. Then Pip suddenly starts talking about dandelions. But the thing is, she finished talking about dandelions ages ago and we are all still sitting in silence. It's boring. Motorways are for singing and 'I-Spy' and playing 'I-love-my-love-with-an-A' all through the alphabet. I'd even secretly practised in case I had 'q' or 'z'. For 'z' I found the name 'Zuleika'. Imagine that! You'd change it wouldn't you, change it to something like Zara or Zoe. Like if you were called Derek it would certainly be a good idea to change it to something like Django.

I couldn't even join in about the dandelion – I was going to ask Pip if it was a metaphor because I thought it probably was because Miss Balcombe was teaching us about metaphors in English last week. But just as I was about to, Dad gave me another 'zip it' look with his eyebrows. I wonder if it is a metaphor or whether it is a simile or something. I'll ask my mum. Anyway, Pip starts going on about how in an instant her family is suddenly scattered and flung far beyond reach. She says she and Fen and Cat were like the seed head of a dandelion, that Django was the stalk around whom they gathered and clung to. And then that woman comes along and blows them away and Pip doesn't know where they'll all fall but that she does know it is now impossible for them to be the same dandelion ever again. Or something like that.

'Dad, I really really need a wee soon.'

'Can you hang on until the next service station – about ten minutes?'

'OK. Dad?'

'Yes?'

'Shall we play I-love-my-love-with-an-A?'

'Er. Not just now.'

'I'm bored.'

'For goodness' sake.'

'It's natural for a kid to be bored in a car – that's why they invented games like I-Spy and I-love-my-love. And now they've invented cars with DVD players in the seats for the kids – so I suggest you get one of those next time.'

'Could you please pipe down, Tom. I'm driving.'

'Tom, I'll play I-love-my-love with you.'

'Well, if you're going to do "u", I'll do "z" – we don't have to do it alphabetically, Pip. We can make it more complex.'

'I meant *you* not "u".'

'Oh. I'll start with "z" anyway. But can I just ask one very quick, small question first?'

'OK.'

'Am I still his grandsonthing-or-other?'

'I'm sure you are.'

'Phew. One other minute question – can I still call him Django Gramps or do I have to change it to Derek? I've been thinking about it and Derek Gramps doesn't sound right – but I was thinking Grandpa Derek sounds all right.'

'Tom, will you please just button it.'

'It's OK, Zac, it's OK. Tom – I don't know. It's very complicated and I can't tell you anything at the moment. I'm sorry.'

'I was just thinking that it would be as strange as having

to call you Philippa all of a sudden. I mean it *is* your name but it's *not* your name. You're Pip. Do you see?'

'Tom – last warning.'

'Zac – it's all right. Tom, listen, I need some grown-up time to come up with some answers for you.'

'Oh. OK. The very very last thing I was just going to ask – is Cat still your sister, though?'

'Tom!'

'It's OK, Zac. Of course she is, Tom. She'll always be my sister.'

London

In previous times of crisis, the siblings had always turned to each other, and of course Django, for support and advice. In the past, there had always been an easily accepted hierarchy of need because crises had never befallen them simultan-eously. They've always had each other to turn to, to consult. They've never had cause to crave attention; they've never had to shout to be heard. Never had to face fears alone or mop tears unaided. Long distance, middle of the night, intrusive, time-consuming, occasionally expensive, sometimes frustrating – but always there, always there. That's what families are for. Families matter. But until now, the McCabes have never confronted family matters. Nor have their crises collided.

They have not been shaken to the core. It's far worse – now their core has gone. Like a split atom: something previously so complete suddenly obliterated; propelling components so far flung that they are surely destined to remain beyond reach. The destruction unfathomable.

No one phones anyone that night. This is not denial but a heart-rending clutch at survival in a world they don't under-stand. The only way to cope with a world you don't understan-d is to do something completely different. Reinvent yourself anew.

Dovidels

There were some crude similarities with a hangover in that, the next morning, Cat awoke feeling wretched, with details of the previous day swarming over her in bilious waves. Like a hangover, the easiest way to react initially was to pull the duvet over her head and beg for a dreamless sleep to numb the pain and drive the memories away. Unlike a hangover, there was nothing that could combat her fuggy head and untold nausea when she finally awoke at noon. No hair-of-the-dog equivalent to settle the soul from the shock of meeting your long-absent mother and being told that your father is not dead but standing right in front of you. A mammoth fry-up might be a miracle cure for a body depleted by alcohol, but it doesn't work when a mind racing with hideous facts ties a stomach in knots. None of the painkillers in Cat's medicine cabinet would have the slightest effect on the anguish choking her.

She deleted the voicemail messages on her mobile phone from her sisters without listening to them and she left the envelope icons of their text messages unopened. She sensed their contact was one of love and support but just then she felt too raw and bewildered to receive it at all. She phoned

Ben though she had nothing to say and clung to the receiver, eyes closed to direct the sound of his voice straight to her heart.

You're all I have, she said to herself when she hung up, *you're all I really have.* When the phone rang again, she didn't answer it. If it was Ben, she'd only break down. If it was anyone else, she didn't want to speak to them anyway.

There was a loaded pause, followed by an uncertain 'Hullo?' It was Django, famously suspicious of answering machines, leaving a message for Cat nonetheless. 'Hullo? Is that Ben? Oh, it's the whatsit. Is there anyone— Hullo? Hullo. This is Django McCabe. I'm leaving a message for Catriona. This is Django. Just leaving a message to say— Blast these blessed machines. I'd like to leave a message to say I hope your journey was OK yesterday. That was Sunday. And I'm. Thinking.' He phoned again almost immediately afterwards just to say, 'Monday. It's now Monday.' For the first time, Django's trademark flummoxed messages brought no smile to Cat. She deleted the messages immediately and switched the answering machine off.

I'm Cat McCabe. I'm thirty-two years old. I never wanted to meet my mother. I thought I was brought up by my uncle. I thought I had two sisters, that I was one amongst equals, in the same boat, cut from the same cloth, sharing the same blood tie. This is the opposite of finding out you're adopted. There's no one out there for me to find and I can't bear the sight of those staring me in the face.

Roof upon roof upon roof. Obnoxious pigeons the colour of concrete. Where was a mountain when a girl needed one most? Flagstaff. The Flatirons. Bear Peak. Where was the exhilaration of feeling so tiny in the great wide open, the comfort of feeling so alive surrounded by vast natural wilderness? It was time zones away. A whole day on a plane away.

In Boulder, there'd still be snow on the peaks but the

pastures would be so lush they'd be positively luminescent. Nowhere had Cat seen colours in nature clash so cacophonously and yet so pleasingly as in Colorado. Nature's daytime fireworks. She looked out of the window. Rust-red roof tiles smudged with lichen here, dull grey mass-produced slate tiles there, ugly dormer windows, redundant chimney-pots, bird shit, the spike and clutter of too many aerials. She looked at her watch. Stacey would be awake. And even if she wasn't, she wouldn't mind Cat phoning her.

'Did I wake you?'

'No – I'm just back in from a run. Seven-miler – the killer loop. I wiped the ass off your best time, lady. How *are* you!'

'Miserable,' Cat said. 'Where are you? In your kitchen? By your fridge? Will you look out of the window and tell me what you see? Tell me everything.'

Stacey's description was soothingly detailed and Cat listened with her eyes fixed on the roof network outside.

'I hate it here, Stacey. I want to come back.'

'You serious?' The surprise in Stacey's voice was edged with excitement and it heartened Cat.

'Yes,' said Cat, 'desperately. For good.'

'You OK, hon? Ben OK?'

'He's fine,' Cat said.

'And you?' Stacey repeated, a soft insistence to her voice, a perceptiveness that Cat was so grateful to hear.

'No,' she said, 'I'm not doing so good. Life's gone pear-shaped. In fact, there's no shape at all. It feels like my world has imploded. Can you talk?'

'Sure,' Stacey said. 'What's happened?'

'I want to run away and start afresh,' said Cat.

'What's happened?' Stacey repeated.

'You'll never believe who I met yesterday,' Cat said and out the story tumbled.

*

Ben came home to find Cat curled up on the sofa in his towelling robe looking as though she had flu. He put his hand against her forehead and then stroked her cheek.

'How are you, babe?' he asked. 'Did you have much of a day?'

'I spoke to Stacey,' Cat told him, 'for over an hour. Sorry – I know it's long-distance.'

'Don't be daft,' said Ben. 'It was probably a good thing to do. Have you – Fen? Pip?'

Cat shook her head and scrunched her eyes. 'Can't do that just yet,' she said.

'Did you tell Stacey everything?'

'Of course,' said Cat, 'and that I wanted to go back to Boulder for ever.'

'Would you like that?' Ben asked thinking the timing was lousy but he loved his wife and would move mountains for her, or move back to the mountains with her.

Cat gave a forlorn smile. 'The thing I love most about Stacey is that she's so good at the caring sympathy but she's also brilliant at common sense. She has Fen's and Pip's qualities perfectly combined.'

'What did she say?'

'She said going back now would be running away. She said if I don't face facts head-on, they'll hunt me down and haunt me.'

'And how do you feel?'

'I don't care if I'd be running away,' Cat said thoughtfully, 'but I trust Stacey and I know what she says makes sense.'

Ben put his arms around her. 'Bloody hell, babe, what a total palaver.' Cat snuggled into the crook of his arm. 'For the first time, I actually give thanks for the dullness of my own family,' he told her.

'For the first time in my life, I wish my family weren't

who they are. For the first time ever, I curse all those eccentricities and unconventional quirkinesses that I used to feel so proud of.'

'You have me,' Ben said, tufting life into the flatness of her hair, 'and for me, you're just what this doctor ordered.'

Ben could not reach Cat on her mobile phone the next day and it unnerved him. He had considered going in late but there was a departmental meeting he could not miss. She'd assured him she felt fine, that she'd slept well, that she felt much better than she had the previous day. He'd studied her face carefully. Pale but not drawn; her eyes dull but not so desperate now; she'd washed her hair and styled it.

'I'll be fine,' she told him. 'I'm going to fanny around the flat for a bit, do some ironing then go through the jobs in yesterday's *Guardian*.'

'I'll phone you later,' he'd told her, with a glance at his watch and a tender kiss.

And he had been trying to. But her phone was off. Now he wasn't sure what to do. Nip home during his lunch-hour? Not practical, as the afternoon surgery was always a busy one. Phone her sisters? He didn't think she'd thank him for that, at the moment, though he felt they would. He tried both phones again and left messages on each. Over lunch by himself in the canteen, he wondered if Cat had found much demand for sports journalists in the job pages of yesterday's *Guardian*.

Ben tried her phone a final time, five minutes before his afternoon appointments were due to commence. She answered. Thank Christ.

'Hi, just me,' he said, feigning a casual tone.

'Oh. Hi.' She sounded odd.

'You OK, babe? I've been trying all morning.'

'I'm fine. I can't really talk right now.'

Was she whispering? Why was she whispering? Ben shook his phone. 'Hullo? Where are you? Are you all right?'

'I'm fine. I'm at work. I don't know their policy on personal calls.'

'At *work*? What work! Cat?'

'I'll tell you when I see you tonight. I finish at 6.30. I'm fine. See you later.'

At *work*? Cat had a *job*? What sort of job? How could she find one and start there and then? What was she doing? This time last week he would have been delighted for her to have been so proactive and successful in finding a job. Instead, he worried that her haste was indicative of some state of denial. It was only forty-eight hours after meeting her mother and father for the first time.

Ben's secretary was buzzing through the first patient. Ben glanced at the notes. Ah yes, the male ballet dancer with the tendonitis. Later, between patients, Ben sent Cat a text message; hopeful that she'd be able to respond, whatever her employers' take on mobile phones.

job wot job? DrB x

The answer came an hour later.

Dovidels!

There are eighteen branches of Dovidels, up and down the country, comfortingly uniform in their classic bookshop interiors, a brave and stubborn reaction to the cavernous bookstores found in city centres and commercial parks. In design, Dovidels shops are bright and stylish; burgundy-coloured shelves edged in maple, limestone floors, leather armchairs and sofas. For Cat that day, it was the lure of such a chair and the opportunity to flick through a new Lance Armstrong biography in an amenable environment. Over an hour later, she was still there and the friendly manager who'd said hullo to her earlier now remarked in passing that there was a job going.

'You look part of the furniture already,' he added.

'Have I outstayed my welcome?' Cat worried.

'Not at all,' he said.

'Are you serious about a job?' she asked.

'Yes. Do you love books?'

'God yes,' said Cat, 'but I don't have any experience – I was a journalist. A sports journalist.'

'Hey – you wrote words, now sell them. Are you interested?'

'I think I am. Yes. Yes I am.'

'When can you start?'

'Now?'

'There speaks a Dovidels girl. Welcome.'

Kate and Max and Merry Martha

Over the time that Cat had spent analysing the roofscapes, making long-distance phone calls and finding herself a job, Fen and Pip had been trying to find their feet too, seeking a balance of their own amongst the debris of their family trauma. They've left messages for Cat by phone and text and they've been in touch with each other to say, Hullo, how are you feeling, what should we do. But the truth is, they don't know how they're feeling or what they should or can do.

Like Cat, their initial and instinctive priority is to establish firm footing in their individual lives before they can tackle their wider roles as sisters, half sisters, nieces, daughters.

'Fen, well *hullo*! We haven't seen you in ages! Come on in, come on in. Just wait until you see Max – he has four teeth and another two breaking!'

Previously, Fen had found Kate somewhat overpowering, her house a little intimidating and little Max rather annoying. Kate's life was all so fastidious, so impeccably ordered, so terribly grown-up. Kate's life, it seemed, barred tiredness, fretting and mess. The walls and floors, an elegant chorus of ochre and taupe, were miraculously unscuffed and gunk-free. There must be rusks and rice cakes in places other than labelled Tupperware in the meticulously organized cupboards. Mashed into the rug, perhaps? Down the sides of the sofas, surely? Apparently not. Max's hand-crafted wooden toys were so tasteful and so amazingly unchewed. How could Kate's baby never be sticky? How had he managed to sleep through the night since ten weeks old? And have four teeth and another two breaking? How did Kate have a wardrobe free from stains and why did her hair always look so good? How on earth could a baby co-exist so happily with decorative pebbles placed on the side of the modernist fireplace?

Fen had been avoiding these mums-and-tots gatherings at Kate's because invariably she left feeling personally unkempt, grubby even, self-conscious about her surfeit of stained clothing and split ends. She also felt petulantly discomfited with her own home: shelves yet to be painted, cushion covers in need of a clean, gaudy plastic toys with tinny electronic jingles and indeterminate stickiness, beakers with mismatched lids, no ensuite utility room, an ooze of Johnson's baby shampoo treacherous on the bathroom floor. She tried to rationalize how, if Cosima was partial to the woodchips in the playground, what a meal she'd make of decorative pebbles at home. After gatherings at Kate's, Fen would return home convinced her organic food wasn't organic enough, her baby wasn't teething quickly enough and that somehow she as a mother wasn't doing anything quite well enough at all.

Fen didn't much connect with Kate, didn't care for her plasma TV, shared nothing in common with her birth story, was irritated by her success with broccoli and her smugness with Max's centile chart. But more than her hair, Fen envied Kate her composure; her ability to achieve so much with so little visible expenditure. How could Max have four teeth and two breaking yet his mother have no dark circles around her eyes? How was it possible for Kate to prepare such successful dishes utilizing organic vegetables of every colour when there was no evidence of it daubed on her kitchen walls? How did Kate get so much enjoyment out of these banal gatherings when Fen left them feeling inadequate and insecure yet bizarrely envious? How was Kate able to be constantly so gracious? It made Fen feel all the more frazzled and fractious.

However, the day after Fen discovered Derek and met her mother, she made a beeline for Kate's and was the last to leave. Suddenly she found all the tasteful, neutral loveliness utterly soothing. She coveted Kate's walls and rugs and home cinema system, the shiny Lexus jeepy vehicle parked outside. Fen now felt slightly in awe of it all, as if here was a proper and conventional grown-up environment to which to aspire. She found herself far more conversant with the group than she'd ever been, happily imparting her recipe for carrot-and-sweet-potato fritters to a cheerily receptive audience. She made plans with Beth to take their babies to SplashyKins at the local swimming pool the next day and even suggested to the group at large that they all meet at the café in Highgate Woods the day after that. She asked Joanne for her hairdresser's salon, she wrote out Susie's salmon pie recipe, she took down the number of Kate's decorators and made a note to phone Lexus for her nearest dealership.

Fen suddenly didn't mind that Cosima had fewer teeth than her contemporaries, nor was she remotely worried that her baby was happy to sit Buddha-like whilst the others were keenly attempting to crawl. Fen's overwhelming ambition, just then, was not to compete but to blend in, to fit the scene as evenly as Kate's walls ran from soft ochre to antique buff. To dull down elements of her sense of self in return for an environment of safety and belonging seemed no compromise to Fen. It wasn't too dissimilar to her first days at university, when she chattered to anyone even if she sensed little in common, let alone any potential for lasting friendship. Just having company was the key. Thus she joined practically every university club, from Cycling to Cluedo, Wine Soc. to Winnie-the-Pooh Soc. – £1 for a sense of belonging was a small price to pay. It all helped to pass the time in a new world and made it seem not such a hostile place. Over a decade later, Fen found herself a new club out of necessity; Yummy-Mummy Soc. (London North branch), with daily activities to tag along to. Blend, blend until all is refreshingly bland.

Pip McCabe's career was an odd one. There is little true structure to being a clown. Children have birthdays but once a year and being married to a well-off accountant had enabled Pip to cut right back on her weekend work. Tuesdays and Thursdays she worked as Dr Pippity, her clown-doctor alter ego, a vastly different form of clowning for which she was rigorously trained to bring an alternative form of therapy to the children's wards at St Bea's hospital. During school holidays, Pip was rushed off her stripy, clodhopping feet, performing as Merry Martha in Golders Hill Park, on Parliament Hill, at Brent Cross shopping centre and the KidsKorners in theme-pub gardens.

Often on a Monday, she'd visit Fen, or spend hours on the phone nattering with Cat, since her return. However, the day after Pip met her mother, lost half a sister and discovered Django was called Derek, her appointments diary was frustratingly bare. It wasn't as though she had an agent she could phone to ask, 'Any jobs going for today?' But Pip had to get out of the house because thoughts were starting to lurk around her soul, badgering her mind and hurting her heart, and once they took hold, she feared they'd never let go of her. Where better to hide than behind a slather of slap and motley.

So Pip undressed. She pinned back her hair with kirby-grips, laid out pots and palettes, sponges and brushes and slowly masked Pip McCabe from view. She pulled on a pair of lurid tights that she'd customized from two pairs – one leg green and sparkly, the other red and stripy. She put on a polka-dot ra-ra skirt and a lemon-yellow top bedecked with patches of orange material. She rejected the multi-coloured waistcoat because it was an old one of Django's and she did not feel like having him around her today. Finally she plaited her hair into pigtails so tight they stood out at right angles to her head as if she'd suffered a comedy electric shock or was the head of the Pippi Longstocking Appreciation Society. Before she left the house, she took the bucket from under the sink. She drove to Brent Cross shopping centre and spoke to management about loitering with intent to raise money for charity. They gave her the go-ahead, knowing her well.

Four hours later, Barnardo's was £193 richer. She took the loose change to the bank and sent the charity a cheque immediately. The next day she dressed as Dr Pippity and immersed herself into her ward rounds at St Bea's. The following day, Wednesday, she was back at Brent Cross as Merry Martha but raised a disappointing £109.56 for Barnardo's. She drove back to Hampstead, parked the car outside the flat and, still in full clown guise, walked up the High Street with her bucket of change. She queued at the bank before brandishing the bucket at the teller and being invited to take a seat whilst the money was counted.

It was a beautiful afternoon. Tom would be finishing school, just up the road, in an hour or so. But today was not a Dad and Pip day, it was a Mum and Rob day. So Merry Martha swung her bucket and headed off for a stroll on the Heath. She decided to walk to Kite Hill, overlooking Parliament Hill fields, because the Kenwood side was out of bounds on account of it being the space she traditionally shared with her sisters.

Preschool children pointed at her, delighted, and she happily performed impromptu tricks and mimes much to their delight. Finding a bench, Pip sat. She turned her face to the sun and attempted to smile at its warmth, despite the risk of make-up meltdown. A cloud came and her face chilled. She opened her eyes and tried to see. She couldn't see the view. She could stare right into the mess of it all but was unable to deflect her gaze. Tears started to well caustically in her throat, impervious to any attempt to swallow them down. They squeezed themselves out of her eyes, resistant to frantic blinking and the digging of nails into the palms of the hand. Attempting to stem the impending flow only provoked her nose to clog with snot that impaired breathing and crackled audibly. Pip realized she could no longer break it all down into objective physiology. She'd just have to break down. Her throat was aching and her nose was running and her eyes were streaming because she was crying. She swiped at her wet cheeks and itched her nose vigorously against her arm. Then she buried her head in her hands before rubbing and rubbing her tired, hot eyes.

'The clown is crying!' Pip heard a child's delighted whisper.

'It's all part of an act,' Pip heard a parent explain. 'It's called *miming*, darling.'

'Does she have a red nose?' the child continued. 'I can't see – her hand is in the way.'

'We'll have to wait and see,' the parent enthused.

Oh shit, thought Pip, *can't a clown sit in a public space and cry in private?*

Of course not.

And then Pip thought, *Oh shit, when I look up, my slap*

will be smudged to gruesome effect and will surely frighten the child.

Well, you'd better make sure that isn't the case.

Slowly, Pip unfurled her crumpled form and lifted her head. Her histrionic sigh, her expression of highly theatrical grief, were so fabulously comic that parent and child were delighted and the blurred make-up was an irrelevance. Pip stood and clutched at her heart while contorting her face in the universal mime language of 'Woe is me'. Then she stooped to the child and pulled her most beseeching face. She pointed to her nose and pressed it lightly. The child looked to his parent for guidance.

'I think the clown wants you to press her nose,' the parent whispered.

Gingerly at first, the child eventually did so. Suddenly, there was a chorus of great honking from a small horn hidden in Pip's pocket. Her face broadened into a smile of prodigious proportions and she outstretched her arms in triumph, performing a jig of merriment on the spot.

'I did it! I did it – I did a happy spell on her nose!' the child shrieked with delight, clapping and jumping. The parent put £1.70 into the empty bucket, nodded gratefully at the clown and led the child away in the direction of the ice-cream van.

Pip walks home and finds Zac already there. He looks at her askance.

'Merry Martha again?' he asks, privately thinking she looks more like Miserable Molly.

'Yup,' says Pip.

'Blimey, £1.70,' Zac says.

'Plus £109.56,' Pip protests.

'Are you OK?' Zac asks her. She looks a fright.

'Fine,' says Pip.

'You look as if you've been – well – crying,' Zac pauses. 'Your slap is all over the place.'

'Oh,' says Pip, thankful she has her mask still on, however blotched and smeared it may be, 'it's all part of today's act.'

'Oh,' says Zac, unconvinced, 'do you want to talk? I want to give Tom a call and I have a little work to do – but I could crack on with it while you're in the shower.'

'I wasn't thinking of having a shower,' Pip mutters and she leaves the flat, silently cursing Zac for making her feel so low down his list.

Zac takes a beer out onto the balcony and dials Matt's mobile.

'Hiya mate,' he says, 'it's Zac.'

'How are you doing?' Matt greets the call.

'Fine, fine. Listen – I don't want to speak out of turn or anything, but I'm wondering how Fen is? You know, since all the drama.'

There's a long, loaded pause. Matt clears his throat. 'She's gone absolutely barking bloody mad, if you ask me. Not that she'll talk to me.'

'Thank God for that,' Zac says. 'What I mean is, Pip too. Bonkers. The only time she's not being a clown is when she's asleep. And I can't get anything out of her.'

'Fen keeps putting rocks and pebbles everywhere,' Matt says.

'Why?'

'I don't know why – but they're everywhere. On the side of the bath. By the fireplace. On the mantelpiece. That's not all – suddenly I'm being asked to pay a fortune for some interior designer to go all Laurence Llewelyn-Bowen on the flat. 'And she keeps baking all this – stuff. I think she's joined the Women's Institute or the Stepford Wives or something.

Have you spoken to Ben at all? Because if our two are like this, can you imagine how it is for Cat?'

'No, I haven't,' says Zac.

'I'll give him a call tomorrow,' says Matt.

'I'll give him a call now,' says Zac. 'Pip's stormed off somewhere. Looking like Smarty Arty on acid.'

Sweet is the Voice of a Sister in the Season of Sorrow

Fen overheard Matt's conversation with Zac and she was pissed off. It wasn't because Matt thought she'd gone mad which annoyed her, just then she was far more riled that he didn't like her pebble motifs. And couldn't he see that her grand designs for their house were much more Kevin McCloud than Laurence Llewelyn-Bowen? What did he know anyway? Pebbles weren't indicative of insanity and nor was Pip choosing to dress as her clown character. It occurred to Fen that no matter how deeply they were loved by their menfolk, she and her sisters were fundamentally misunderstood. She realized then that the only people who could possibly appreciate how she was feeling were those feeling just like her. Suddenly she longed for Pip and Cat and realized the last few days had been all the more lonely for lack of them.

Traditionally, Pip had always been the one to take the mature option and decide what to do, taking all matters onto her own shoulders and then dispensing constructive and logical advice. Cat had always simply cried out loud for assistance, inciting the others to rally round. But Fen had customarily kept herself to herself, until her sisters instinctively came looking and coaxed her out into the open.

Well, hadn't so much changed. She dialled Pip. Zac answered.

'Is Pip there?'

'Fen?'

'Yes?'

'Hi – how are you?'

'Very well, thanks Zac. Is Pip there?'

'She's in the shower.'

'Please could she call me once she's dry.'

She dialled Cat. Ben answered.

'Is Cat there?'

'Fen?'

'Yes?'

'How are you?'

'Well, you know. Anyway, is Cat around?'

'She's not back from work yet.'

'Work? She has a job?'

'Yes. In a bookshop.'

'Oh. Good for her. Will you ask her to call me when she's back?'

'No problem – good to hear you, Fen.'

While Fen waited for either sister to call, she played with the configuration of various pebbles and analysed the Farrow & Ball colour chart through slanted eyes. What gorgeous names: Clunch, Mouse's Back, Dimity, Cornforth White, Porphyry Pink, Sutcliffe Green, Cook's Blue. Names are everything. If Dulux or Crown also did these particular colours, Fen reckoned she'd still buy the Farrow & Ball version, even if they were more expensive, on account of them being so inspiringly named.

'Do you like the sound of Ringwold Ground?' she asked Matt.

'Shouldn't the question be do I like the look of it?' Matt said. Fen thrust the colour card at him. The shade looked like unpainted plaster to him, though he realized that was probably the point and chose therefore to nod and not comment.

'For our bedroom?' Fen furthered. Matt considered this. The bedroom looked fine to him. Though of course he wanted to make her happy, to see her smiling, this was becoming costly in a single-salary household. He was about to allude to this but wisely bit it back. After all, hadn't he actively encouraged her change of career, from art historian to mother? Realistically, her freelance wage would mostly cover just childcare; the amount she'd bring home would be paltry enough not to be worth the separation anxiety. He thought about asking if B & Q did their own version of Sugar Bag Light but was saved by the bell. Pip was returning Fen's phone call.

'Hullo. It's me.'

'Hullo, you,' said Fen. 'I think it's time – don't you?'

'Yes,' said Pip, 'we'll go in our car. I'll pick you up.'

'Thanks.'

From the first-floor window of the flat, Ben watched in disbelief but with great relief Pip and Fen walking up the street. He glanced across to Cat, engrossed in a copy of the *Bookseller*, and could not anticipate how she might react. Did he have a duty to tell her they approached? Or did he owe it to all of them not to interfere? His wife would be better off for the company of her sisters, of that he was sure, no matter how over-emotional the proceedings might be. It had been difficult enough to gauge her reaction when told that Fen had called. And now the doorbell was sounding. He looked over to Cat and she looked up.

'Shall I get it?' he asked and she looked at him with a

slow nod as if it was a pretty daft question as he was nearest and it was gone nine o'clock and who could it be.

Fen and Pip filled the room. Cat's heart heaved with relief. Here was Fen, and Pip too, the promise of their familiar smiles, side by side. And Cat hadn't even needed to cry out loud, she hadn't asked for help, she hadn't said a word. Still they'd come. How lovely to feel so second-guessed, to be known so well, to be loved so fully.

'We thought you probably wouldn't return Fen's call,' Pip explained, walking straight over to her little sister and kissing both cheeks.

'So we came to you,' said Fen, glancing around the flat and thinking it would be really quite nice if it was given a lick of Joa's White. She went to Cat and hugged her close. 'I hear you have a job,' Fen said, 'in a bookshop?' Cat gave a nod. 'Do you get a discount?' Fen asked slyly.

'Signed copies?' asked Pip.

'I think I'll just pop out. To Waitrose,' said Ben, but the girls hardly heard him. Fen was fussing at Cat's tears with a tissue and Pip was fiddling with mugs and the kettle.

'Our blokes think we've gone nuts,' Fen said indignantly once Ben had gone. 'I heard Matt and Zac discussing it.'

Cat still hadn't said a word but it didn't bother her sisters. Her tears, and the way she clung to them, told them enough.

'I mean, Fen and I are entitled to have flipped out,' Pip reasoned, 'but you're allowed to go loop-the-frigging-loop, my dear.'

'I think we'd be far madder if we were untouched by this,' Fen said.

'Anyway, we're not mad, we're not insane, and we're certainly not over-reacting,' Pip decreed. 'It was a huge shock. When you're a child, normal is whatever you know. We've suddenly had everything we've ever known stripped away from us.'

Cat regarded her. While she felt the official age gap between her and Fen had lessened as they'd become older, she still revered Pip as very much the eldest and wisest – her keeper, her protector. How she loved her. How safe she made her feel, safe enough to finally find her voice. 'Do you love me less?'

Pip and Fen could clearly hear the quiet fear beneath the plaintive timbre of Cat's voice and they could see right through her beguilingly mournful expression to the presence of panic. Cat might be dressing her question with a certain theatricality, but the question was no joke. Her sisters let her ask it because they knew she had to. They were well aware that she'd probably tortured herself with the possibility of the notion, since the revelation. Pip folded her arms and raised her eyebrow. Fen put her hands on her hips and looked at Cat. 'Stupid question,' Cat answered shyly, on their behalf.

'Do you need us to answer?' Fen said softly.

'Would you like us to answer?' Pip asked.

Cat shrugged. 'Yes, please. I think I would.'

'You're our baby sister,' Fen said, nudging her gently.

'Nothing can ever change that,' said Pip.

'I've been wanting to be a grown-up so desperately,' Cat croaked. 'All these thoughts of baby-making and house-hunting. But now I feel like a crazy mixed-up kid.' She stopped. The faces of her sisters were close to hers, their eyes large with love and concern. 'I feel I've lost what I had – and what I had I loved.' Cat continued. 'Django is a liar. I've been lied to my whole life.'

'This will not come between us,' Pip said sagely, unfurling her sister's clenched fists, 'between us three. It wouldn't matter to me if I shared no scrap of DNA with you.'

'But suddenly our stupid little family seems so dysfunctional,'

Cat said quietly, 'whereas before, I was proud – I felt it was joyously eccentric.'

'Wonderfully unconventional,' Fen mused sadly.

'I agree,' said Pip. 'It now seems messed up to the extreme. Remember how we'd vilify those prim mothers of some of our schoolmates for assuming that our family was somehow substandard, not real because of it being not proper? Well, now it's hard not to think that they were right. I can't help but feel it's all been a bit of a farce.'

'But what can Django have been thinking?' Fen asked, sitting heavily on a kitchen chair. 'Did he really believe we'd never find out? Part of me would hope that it was irrelevant to him that one of us was biologically his child. I certainly never felt his love for us wasn't utterly equal and unconditional. But actually, it appals me that fatherhood didn't make a difference to him. Sorry Pip – but don't you feel he should've loved Cat more? Or differently? Or something? Sorry Cat – but you're his *daughter*. A parent's love for their offspring should be omnipotent, it should be chemically impossible for it not to be. So is he an amazing man for loving us the same, or is he downright neglectful for that very reason? I can't work it out. I can't.' She laid her head on her folded arms and focused on the grain of the kitchen table.

Pip wanted to argue that a stepmother's love for her stepchild could be just as true. But she was aware that this was not the forum for hypothetical discussion.

'I don't know how to handle any of it,' Cat said with a frantic shake of her head, 'and we haven't even spoken about *her*.' She began to pace the room.

'The odd thing is, I'm not so curious as to why *she's* returned, why *she* showed up on his birthday,' Pip said. 'Perhaps I would be, had the Django stuff not transpired. I just don't know what to do about him.'

Cat looked taken aback – how could Pip not know what

to do? She always knew what to do. Cat stomped around the room again.

'He's called *Derek*,' said Fen, lifting her head from her arms only temporarily. 'It's so *weird*.'

'Why didn't we ever wonder why he has an Italian gypsy name,' Pip said, 'when his family were from Sutton Coldfield?'

Cat stopped pacing and burst into tears. 'All these years I've wept for the father I never knew, now I'm presented with one I'd rather not have.'

'Don't cry,' Pip tried to soothe her.

'We're here,' said Fen, feeling desperately in need of being soothed herself.

'I never want to see my father again,' said Cat. 'I want Django back. I don't know. I really don't. It's what Ben would call a complete and utter headfuck.'

'How very medical that sounds,' Fen remarked.

'The thing is,' said Pip to Cat, with a glance at Fen, 'it's your call, Cat, in the first instance. We can cease all communication, if that makes life easier for you. Or we can roll up our sleeves and dig around the mystery.'

'But I can't make the call,' Cat said slowly. 'I can't. I can't.' She fingered Pip's wedding ring. 'But you can.'

Their gaze alighted on the telephone and Pip sensed her sisters look imploringly at her, of course.

Pip wants to duck out. She wants to protest, 'But what will I say?' but she can't. That wouldn't do at all. Pip has always had the answers for Cat and Fen. She's grown up knowing that even if she doesn't have the answers immediately, she has to find them for the sake of her sisters. But today she doesn't know what to say – and what she'd like to say is that she doesn't know what to do. There's been little opportunity for vulnerability in Pip McCabe's life; the occasions when she's felt fragile have been kept carefully out of sight and out of earshot. She's always liked being the Big Sister, she's found it preferable to be the solver of other people's problems, she's been flattered to be hailed as the Great Looker-Afterer. But just now she curses these roles. Actually, she wants someone's lap for herself to curl up into, to assure her that it'll be OK.

Zac?

But she's been distant with Zac since he rubbished her revelation at the party that she just might like to make a baby. She's hidden behind her slap and motley and let him have Merry Martha or Dr Pippity for company since then. The sad irony is that, traditionally, when issues have been just too heavy for her to shoulder herself, it has been Django to whom she has turned.

'Ah, my precious caryatid,' he would soothe, 'whose burden is too much to bear. Let me help. Offload, pet, offload.'

I can't, Django. You're the burden.

You have to, Pip. See how Fen and Cat are depending on you?

So Pip dials. She'll know what to say, she tells herself, when he answers. Please let him be out. Be out be out be out. Dominoes. Something. Fen and Cat crowd around the receiver. They hear the click as the phone is answered in Farleymoor.

'Hullo?'

But it isn't Django. It isn't Django. The voice is female and American.

Pip hangs up in a fluster. 'She's still there,' she tells them, incredulous. Now she's bemused, very bemused. 'I have to phone again,' she says already dialling though she has no idea what she'll say when the American woman claiming to be their mother answers Django's phone. But the phone is ringing. And now it is being answered.

'Hullo?'

It's Django.

'Hullo?'

Pip glances at Cat and Fen but their wide-eyed gazes seem to mirror back her own question. *What do I say next? What was I going to say in the first place?*

'Is this a trickster?' Django is asking. 'Hullo? This is Farleymoor 64920. If you are going to sell me something, you can bog off.' He hangs up.

'He's hung up on us,' Pip tells Cat and Fen who've heard every word anyway.

'Phone again,' they urge.

Pip dials. No one answers. She dials again.

'Great Gods!' Django barks. 'Who *is* this? I'll have the police track you! This is *trespass*. Now bloody bog right off.'

'It's us. It's me. It's Pip.'

Now no one knows what to say.

'Hullo?'

'Hullo?'

Pip is clutching the receiver tightly, Fen has grabbed her wrist and Cat's face is so close Pip can tell she's had milky coffee before they arrived.

'Pip?'

'Yes. We're all here.'

'I see.'

'What's *she* doing there?'

'She? Oh. Packing. She flies home tomorrow.'

The girls send each other thank-God-for-that but what-the-fuck-is-going-on glances. 'What's she doing there anyway?' hisses Fen. Pip repeats the question down the receiver.

'She needed a holiday,' Django says.

For Christ's bloody sake. 'There are too many secrets,' Pip says, the words oozing acidly from between clenched teeth, 'and true families don't have so many secrets.'

'Nothing is secret,' Django replies steadily. 'You have only to ask.'

'Maybe we shouldn't have to ask,' Pip says, while Fen and Cat nod earnestly.

'That's because you're not sure you want to hear,' Django says.

Pip shrugs. Fen and Cat shrug back. Django can sense them, in a huddle in a muddle, clutching at each other.

'When you're ready,' Django says, 'I am here. You can ask all you like. And I will tell.'

Coupling

Bizarrely, in times of extremis, there is always sex. Actually, it's not all that bizarre at all. It floods the body with feel-good endorphins and releases reassuring opiates in the brain. It feeds the soul and occupies the mind. It infuses the spirit with a sense of well-being, it enhances communication, it builds an appetite, it facilitates sleep. Not tonight, dear, I have a headache, is one of the greatest misnomers. An orgasm can alleviate a headache far more efficiently than paracetamol. Sex is good for mind, body and soul. Sex is both a leveller and a lift; it soothes as it soars. Sex is necessary. It's natural and base and when the fundamentals of life have been challenged, sex takes an instinctive, primal function. If life is under threat, then make more life. Regenerate. That was the point of sex in the first place: the survival of the species. The fact that it also felt so good was life's great added bonus. The fact that it felt so good inspired people to connect on a spiritual dimension in addition to the primary physical level. Sex ceased to have the sole role of procreation. Sex, it transpired, was extremely good for the heart. And so sex evolved into making love, the most sublime form of communication. Words can be so clumsy. Action can be far more productive.

'Are you OK?'

Hold me, Ben, hold me. My head is killing me. Envelop me and keep me safe. Now I am OK. Yes, kiss and kiss and kiss the top of my head. Oh, the smell of you. Heaven scent. I can close my eyes and melt into you. If I raise my face I find your mouth, your lips meet mine with so much more than a kiss: a whisper of tenderness, the taste of love. I hear all that you say, you needn't utter a word. The touch of your tongue causes my hands to move, to search and feel and squeeze and stroke. Now your hands too. Traverse my torso in a caress so fluent, the flow of your touch, the walk of your fingers, the feel of your skin – the softest, warmest substance I know. The smell of you. The taste of you. The strength of your limbs, your manliness alongside my femininity. My breasts the most perfect shape for the precise cup of your hands, my sex soft so that yours can be hard. The yin and the yang. The ebb and the flow. The up and the down. The ins and the outs. The peaks and the troughs. The thrill of the thrust. We fit and flow, we fit and flow. You and me into you into me.

I'm going to come. Oh God I'm going to come. And as I come I go, my soul floats into yours. The synergy of it all, the rhythm of Us.

'How did it go?'

Oh Zac – you waited up, you noodle. You needn't have. You have that conference call first thing. But thank you. It's so good to see you, to be home. I don't really want to talk about it. You talk to me. I'm happy to just listen to the mundanities of your day. Just keep talking facts and figures while I listen to the timbre of your voice. I don't know why

I'm shivering slightly. It's May. But I sense your warmth and you sense my chill and you are doing something about it – now I'm not cold at all.

I love it when you tiptoe your fingers along my arms. I love it when you absent-mindedly finger my nipple. So instinctive for you, so exciting for me. This is a position I like so much – you on your back, me on my side, the lolling of limbs. I rest my outer leg on top of you, I stretch my arm along your torso, have my hand cup your neck, my fingers playing with your ear lobe. And when you talk I touch your lips and I know that before long you'll be unable to resist kissing my fingertips. Then you'll flick your tongue tip over them and then my face will look up and your face will look down and our mouths will be magnetized. Your hands will search out the parts of me that excite you and thrill me. Secret pathways to electrifying pleasure. You found them – I never knew they were there. I find myself rubbing against you. And my hands will seek your beautiful hard cock. Pull me on top of you, then you can sweep your hands up and over my buttocks. You love them, don't you. Makes me love them too, makes me believe they're the most shapely pair on the planet.

I like being on top. There's no psychology to it, it's not a control thing or a domination thing, it doesn't make me feel empowered or emancipated. I just like the angle of you inside me. Instinctively I move, I undulate and rock against you. I hold myself up on my arms because it increases the intensity and it enables you to fondle my breasts, to reach for them with your mouth by raising your head – which serves to increase the intensity of the angle even more. Christ I could come right now. Or I can push you down and still my body so I can build for a more exquisitely potent orgasm alongside yours in a while. Let's do that.

Let's do doggy.

God, you're close. I can sense it in the fluidity of your thrusting, I can hear it in the rasp of your breathing. Wait. Missionary – and quickly! I love it that you sense I'm on the verge of orgasm. I love it that you know my body inside out, that you know to push in and up, your balls nustling against my buttocks, your cock suctioned into perfect position. And your gaze penetrates me one way as your cock penetrates me another and you stare and it's so intense and you let me rock and writhe as you see deep into my soul while I come.

And then you trace a tenderness of kisses all over my face as the throbs of my body subside. And I love you and I fold my arms around your back and I move against you, letting you pick your rhythm. I love feeling you come. I love hearing the abandon and the desire. Come on, Mr.

Oh. You're spurting on my stomach.

God, are you that risk averse, Zac?

I'm stuck for words and I feel like crying.

'Do you want to talk?'

I thought you were asleep, Matt. Did I wake you? I tried to be quiet. I tiptoed in to see Cosima and tripped over her plastic turtle but she didn't stir. I'm exhausted. I have a headache. But I can't possibly sleep. There's so much in my mind, running rings around me, too much to fathom. From the dishwasher to Django, from Cat to Cosima; from stupid meanderings to portentous thoughts. If I bury my face in your chest, can I pretend that everything is OK? Because the sound of your heartbeat can block out all the other stuff. I think sometimes – recently – I don't listen carefully enough to your heart. Are you tired, Matt? Because quite to my surprise, I feel rampant and horny. So actually, Matt, no I don't want to talk, I just want to fuck. If I imagine myself a porn star, can I forget that Fen is just a frazzled mum with a pile of washing she's forgotten to hang out and a heap of shit on her shoulders?

On the Phone

Fen was standing in the middle of her sitting-room, looking from a pile of laundry yet to be ironed, to a heap of toys, to a mound of papers and magazines that she'd half sorted into recycling or keeping sub-piles the day before yesterday. She looked at her watch. 10.30 a.m. Was it really worth tidying the toys at this end of the day? No. Was there any real chance she'd do any ironing during daylight hours? No. Was there any point saving papers to be recycled when the bin-men were due to come tomorrow and she'd already missed the recycling service for this week? No.

'Don't eat the pebble, Cosima – Mummy give you a rice cake instead.'

Fen looked from rice cake to pebble and thought there probably wasn't much in it, taste-wise. The phone was ringing.

'Hi Fen. It's me – Kate. How are things? How's little Cosima?'

Fen imagined Kate in her tidy house, her perfect shades of unstained neutral, her toothsome ten-month-old baby happily doing algebra. 'Oh, great,' Fen breezed, 'and you? And Max?'

'We're wonderful. Listen, I was wondering – do you fancy coming to the Chelsea Flower Show tomorrow?'

She may as well have said Australia. Or the moon. A lovely idea but somewhat implausible. 'I'd love to,' said Fen, 'but how baby-friendly is it?'

Kate laughed. 'It isn't. That's the point. Can you get babysitting? We can make a girls' afternoon of it.'

Fen thought for a moment. She and Matt didn't have much of a garden, let alone the time or inclination to work the little they did have. But there again, she didn't have much of a social life either so, though her interest in horticulture and her friendship with Kate were both limited, the notion of an away-day from toys, recycling issues and laundry taunts was certainly attractive. Fen was surprised to find that the thought of being apart from Cosima for more than an hour didn't seem so unthinkable. She'd phone Pip; wasn't her sister always offering to babysit after all?

'Fen?' Kate prompted.

'I'd love to,' Fen said. 'I'll phone my sister and let you know this afternoon. We're meeting at Anna's at three, aren't we?'

'Yes. But actually, can you text me as soon as you know? Because if you can't make it, I'd like to offer the ticket to Ruth.'

'Oh. OK. Of course.' It did then occur to Fen that she herself may not have been Kate's first choice. But she didn't dwell on it. She fancied the invitation at any cost, even if she'd been Kate's last resort. Anyway, she couldn't be – because apparently Ruth was lower down the rungs than she. It made Fen feel rather smug.

'Hullo Pip?'

'Hullo Fen. How's you? I spoke to Cat on her way to work. She sounded a little brighter.'

'Good, that's good.' Fen paused. 'Pip – any chance you could have Cosima tomorrow afternoon? It's just that one of the mums in my group has tickets for the Chelsea Flower Show. And she's invited *me*.'

'Chelsea? Are you now doing a Charlie Dimmock outside, in addition to Sarah Beeny-fying inside?'

Fen laughed. 'It just sounded different and fun. And aren't you always telling me I don't get out much?'

Pip looked at her Filofax. 'No problem,' she told Fen. 'We have Tom tomorrow but Cosi can do the school run with me. Can you drop her off?'

'Of course,' said Fen, loving Pip's intimacy with her niece but hating the way she abridged her daughter's name. 'Thanks, Pip. There's a bunch of daffs in it for you.'

'Daffs,' Pip said, 'are out of season. You'd better gen up before you go or they'll make compost out of you.'

'Dovidels, can I help you!'

Cat had been manning the phone all morning. It was her shift on the information desk at the back of the shop. She was loving her job: the books, the customers, her colleagues. It was more than a distraction, it was a revelation. And she found that to immerse herself in this new world, this lovely space, afforded her hours and hours where she didn't have the time to think about anything else. No one asked her about herself, they just asked her about books. The information desk put her in good view of the entrance and each time a customer came in she'd fling over a smile, hoping to lure them over, promoting herself as a preferable alternative to shelf-browsing. She unpacked the special orders with enthusiasm, lovingly handling the books and taking much pleasure in announcing their arrival to the customers, as if the books were one-offs, written to order. *Mrs Cohen, I'm pleased to tell you that your Laurie Graham is here. Mr O'Connor, good news – your Tom Holt has arrived.* And when they came in to collect their copies, she'd hand them over in a most midwifely way. Enjoy, she'd tell them, as she embraced the cover, enjoy.

Jeremy, the manager, was charmed by Cat. He'd never had a writer who wanted to be a bookseller; it was far more usual to be the other way around. He loitered as the phone rang again.

'Dovidels! Can I help you!' Cat answered.

The great thing about Cat, thought Jeremy, was that there was never any question mark. Just enthusiasm and energy. She might as well be saying *Dovidels! I* can *help you!* and he was in no doubt that, subliminally, this was the way most of their customers heard it. He'd never caught her picking her nails or gazing into the middle distance or clock-watching. During quiet periods, she busied about tidying shelves, checking orders and asking him the secrets of successful bookselling. She was in early, back promptly from her breaks and often stayed late.

'One moment please,' she was saying to a caller, 'the computer says we have two copies – but let me do a shelf check.' She scurried away, soon racing back, triumphant. 'Sorry to keep you on hold but yes! We do! I have a copy right here. I'll put it on one side for you. Pardon? It's my pleasure! No, thank *you*.'

'Cat,' Jeremy said, 'head office are coming in this afternoon – I'm going to recommend you for assistant manager.'

Cat blushed and gawped but the phone was ringing and it was her duty to answer it.

'Dovidels! Can I help you!'

'You might as well be trilling *hi-de-hi*,' Ben's voice told her. 'I'm just between patients – thought I'd give you a bell. Your mobile is off, as per usual.'

'I can't talk now, Ben,' Cat scolded him. 'We're very busy. The phone hasn't stopped ringing and head office are coming in this afternoon.'

'I just wanted to ask—'

'I'll call you later, Ben,' Cat said sternly, hanging up with an irritated sigh she ensured Jeremy could hear, lest he felt she condoned or, worse, encouraged personal calls.

'Dovidels! Can I help you!'

When Ben's mobile phone rang a minute or two later, he assumed it was Cat returning his call from the sanctuary of a storeroom or somewhere.

'Babe, I'm just about to see a patient,' he said. 'I'll call you at lunch-time.'

'Actually it's not Babe,' said the voice, 'it's Django. McCabe.'

For a suspended moment, Ben found himself wondering why Django had emphasized 'McCabe'. He really did know just the one Django. And it would only make sense to stress McCabe if the man was now going to refer to himself as Derek. Which, obviously, he wasn't. Ben's receptionist was buzzing through the arrival of a patient.

'Django – good to hear from you,' Ben said, 'but I'm just about to see a patient – can I call you afterwards?'

When it came to returning the call, Ben wondered whether to phone Cat first. But no doubt she'd give him short shrift for not being a bona fide Dovidels caller. He dialled Derbyshire. The phone rang unanswered. Ben dialled again, intrigued but slightly uncomfortable. Regardless of his affection for the old man, his allegiance was to Cat and she might well disapprove of this exchange. He'd just see what Django wanted. No harm in that. Keep the call short. He could always press the buzzer himself and invent a patient if the call was lengthy or the subject contentious.

'Django? Hullo – it's Ben. Sorry about before.'

'Hullo Ben, thank you for calling back. I'm no good with these telephone things. I always seem to use them at an inconvenient time. That's why I don't trust the blighters.'

Ben smiled at Django's characteristically convoluted theory. 'Don't worry. It was just a slightly neurotic dancer anyway. Now, what's up?'

'I,' the line went very quiet. 'Well.' Django cleared his throat. 'Are you still there?'

'I'm still here,' said Ben continuing to hope that whatever it was that irked Django wasn't going to take too long to reveal, and would not compromise his loyalty to his wife.

'Well, I'm telephoning you at work because I appreciate it isn't appropriate to telephone you at your home,' Django said, 'on account of Cat's needs. I fear my tones would not be dulcet but despicable to her ears – you needn't comment. But actually, the main reason I'm telephoning you at work, is because this call is in fact a work call.'

'I see,' said Ben, who didn't, and whose stomach was telling him it was past lunch-time. 'Django?'

'Yes?'

'A work call, you say? Hullo?'

'It's my waterworks,' Django said, his anxiety transmitting straight through the receiver. 'And. Well. It's just.'

'Django,' Ben said, with bedside manner expertly employed in an instant, 'has there been a change in the situation?'

'Oh, just a very minor one,' said Django.

'And that would be?'

'Well, just a little bit of, you know, something a little like blood.'

'There is blood in your urine?'

'Possibly.'

'Discomfort?'

'No. Not really. Though I'm rather irked by having to spend so many bloody pennies. Especially at night.'

'When did you first see the blood?'

'A couple of visits ago.'

'And since? Is it still present?'

‘A little. I suppose. But you know I am partial to beetroot – and that certainly discolours one’s water. Almost gave me a heart attack, when *that* first happened. Far more alarming than the effect of asparagus.’

‘Have you eaten beetroot, Django? In the last thirty-six hours?’ Ben asked.

‘No. No. But I am fond of it and have eaten a lot of it in my time.’

‘Django, did you see your GP about your waterworks? After we had our chat?’

‘Well. I did go to my GP. But it’s all changed. Dr Sutton isn’t there any more. In his place, just some lovely young doctor but she really is too young to be dealing with me, you know.’

‘Django, I really do want you to go and see a doctor. It’s probably nothing. But at your age, we need to check your prostate. It’s very easy to do.’

‘Is it? I see. But I don’t think this very young lady doctor should be bothered by me because as you say it’s probably nothing.’

‘Is there another doctor at the practice you might prefer to see?’

‘I don’t know. It’s all changed so much. In Dr Sutton’s day, you knew them and they knew you. Now they don’t even tick you off – you have to tap in your name on a computer screen yourself. You know how I hate newfangled technology.’

‘Will you phone them?’ Ben pressed. ‘Request a male doctor, if you prefer?’

‘I could do that, I suppose.’

‘You do that, Django, you do that. It’s a very simple thing to test PSA. It’s just a quick blood test to measure levels of a particular antigen associated with prostate conditions. Plus, an examination.’

'An examination?' Django said vaguely. 'I don't know very much about my prostate, I'm afraid. Or prostates in general.'

'No, Django,' said Ben, 'not that sort of exam.'

'No. I didn't think so.'

'It's just a very quick digital exam.'

'Oh a *digital* exam. Well. Isn't that marvellous. All this technology. Computers to sign you in and computers to diagnose your prostate. Marvellous. They say we're living in the digital age, don't they!'

'Django, I'm sorry – I've misled you. Digital – as in finger.' Ben closed his eyes and pinched the bridge of his nose. 'It's the best way to check your prostate gland.'

'Oh. Oh dear. A *finger*.' There was a horrified pause. 'The doctor's?'

'The doctor's,' Ben confirmed. 'The doctor will need to insert a finger into your back passage to assess your prostate gland.'

'Oh.'

'Django, I know it sounds ghastly but it's fast, gentle and diagnostically efficient alongside the blood test. I really do want you to see a GP. Prostate conditions are common but some can be quite nasty if they're left too long. I think we'd like to rule out anything more untoward.'

'You know, I'm just thinking here – but actually, I *may* have had beetroot.'

'Django – would you like me to phone your practice? Make you an appointment?'

'No thank you.'

'But you will phone them directly?'

'Well, yes I will. If that's what you say, doctor.'

'It is. I'm sure it's probably nothing – it might just be a minor kidney infection. But combined with your increased bladder activity, I would really like you to have a prostate check-up.'

'Yes, I see.'

'So will you phone me when you have an appointment?'

'Well, OK then.'

'OK then. Good. And if there's anything that worries you or you don't understand in the consultation, will you please call me? Take notes – doctors don't mind.'

'Righty-ho.'

'OK. OK. Good. I'm glad we're agreed. But don't you worry – as I say, it's easy to diagnose and sort out.'

'OK, Dr York. Thank you.'

'I'm glad you phoned me, Django.'

'Yes.' There was a pause. 'Ben?'

'Yes?'

'And how is Cat?'

'How is Cat,' Ben had to think fast how to answer. 'She's up and down, Django. But she's working at a bookshop and she's enjoying that.'

'A bookshop you say?'

'Yes, she's really taken to it. Very busy and enthusiastic.'

'Good for her. Good for her. Is she also – well – OK?'

'She'll be OK, Django,' Ben said carefully. 'She's still very confused. We'll just bide with her, I think. You know how emotional she can be.'

'Yes. Yes I do. And the others? Might you know?'

'They're OK too, as far as I'm aware.'

'Good. Good.'

'It's all been a little – odd.'

'More than a little odd, dear Ben. On paper, it's downright preposterous.'

'Well, you know those McCabe girls – they need to vent their emotions before they can settle down and consider hard facts.'

'Yes. But the facts are very hard, Ben, for them. Very hard.'

'I know. But rest assured we're looking after them. Zac and Matt and me.'

'Bless you all,' said Django, 'bless you all.'

'Django – will you call your surgery now?'

'I will.'

'And we'll speak later today?'

'We shall. Goodbye.'

Ben sat and stared at his mobile phone. Ought he to phone Cat? But would it alarm her? Perhaps he should phone Pip and ask her the best tack to take. But Pip would no doubt be struggling with her own reactions. He wondered what would alarm Cat most – that he was phoning her, again, at work? That he'd had the call from Django? Or that there was some concern for the man's health? Ben decided it might be prudent to wait until Cat had left work and he'd next spoken to Django.

Cosima and her pals were alternately gnawing on wooden spoons and bashing them, or their fat little hands, against a variety of Tupperware containers provided by Anna.

'We could call them the Rhythm Method,' Fen remarked, clicking her fingers as if the babies were jamming a catchy beat.

'Hardly,' Kate commented. 'It's a contradiction in terms. If us lot had kept up the tempo of our Rhythm Method, this little lot wouldn't be sucking our kitchen utensils.'

Momentarily, Fen thought this was slightly harsh. But then she told herself it was just Kate's manner. She was to let nothing detract from her excitement for tomorrow afternoon's excursion.

'We heard from Highgate School,' Ruth was saying. 'Josh is in in in!'

'Good for Josh, it'll suit him. We turned down Highgate, because Jacob's more of a UCS boy, we feel,' said Anna.

'Fen, have you put Cosima down for Channing?'

'Um. No. No,' Fen said.

'God – you must.'

'Oh?' Fen felt all the other women nodding at her.

'Where *have* you put her name down?'

'Well. Nowhere, actually. As yet.'

'You are *joking*! You must have her down for nursery places, surely. The Avenue? Rosemount?'

'I haven't – as yet. I might not send her to a nursery,' Fen said quietly.

They stared at her.

'You're mad!'

'Or a liberal. Don't tell us you're a home-education type?'

'Fen – *honestly*, you must start calling around. You owe it to Cosima!'

Fen looked down at her spoon-sucking daughter. 'I suppose – but she's only—'

'No she's not – she's *old*! Believe me! I was phoning schools as soon as the pregnancy-test dipstick went blue.'

'I've spent over two grand on deposits at various schools – but it's money well spent, I reckon.'

'Fen you really should – whose phone is that? Mobile alert! *Mission Impossible* ring tone!'

'It's mine,' said Fen, wondering if 'saved by the bell' had ever rung truer, 'it's mine.' It was a mobile number she didn't recognize. 'Hullo?' she answered.

'Hi,' it was a man's voice, 'is that Fen?'

'Yes?'

'Hi – it's Al.'

Who is Al? I don't know an Al.

Yes you do.

'Al – with the flowers. On Bishops Avenue.'

'Hi! Hi! Of course! Sorry – it's a bit noisy. Hold on.' Fen moved out of Anna's sitting-room and into the hallway, turning her back on a particularly vile arrangement of orange amaryllis, red gladioli and yellow something-or-others. 'Hullo? Al? Are you still there?'

'I am. How are you?'

Oh you know, my mother popped in to see me after thirty years, I found out my uncle fathered my sister, I've been told my daughter stands to be denied a decent education and my partner and I live parallel lives under the same roof which I'm madly redecorating in my misplaced desire to fit in with a group of people I have little in common with.

'I'm fine,' said Fen. 'How are you?'

'Cool. I'm cool. I've been meaning to call,' he said, 'say hi.'

'Hi.'

'Hi.'

Fen could see Cosima. She loved watching her baby, unseen. Who cared about waiting lists and sodding private schools.

'I was just wondering if you fancied a quick drink. Sometime,' Al said.

'A quick drink?' Fen was about to add 'What for?' but she stopped herself.

'Yeah – you know. If you were free.'

Free? Free from whom? Free for what? If there's no such thing as a free lunch, does the same apply to a quick drink? 'Oh,' Fen said, delighted, flustered, 'well – I think so.'

'Babysitting permitting, I guess.'

Now that's good. His invitation is above board. He's just being friendly, isn't he. And I'll accept because there's no harm in a quick drink. It'll be nice. I'd like to go out for a quick drink. I don't get out much – as I like to say.

'OK – thanks Al. That sounds great.'

'Cool! When are you free?'

'Actually,' said Fen, glancing through the glass door at Kate, in all her sumptuous beige and stain-free white, preening her lustrous hair, 'I'm free tomorrow, Al. I have babysitting – I'm going to the Chelsea Flower Show. We could meet afterwards, for a quick drink.'

'OK, you have my mobile number now. Let's touch base sometime tomorrow and take it from there. Hook up when you're done with the flowers.'

Fen was helpless not to giggle a little. The last time anyone had spoken to her about touching bases was her second boyfriend who sent her a postcard of the Venus de Milo and a stick of Bazooka bubble gum with the priceless message: 'Show us your bazookas! Second base? How about it!'

But it's not what Al meant of course. Gracious no. Just touching base to hook up for a quick drink with a sweet boy I met laying flowers for his late sister.

'OK,' said Fen, 'I'll call you tomorrow.'

She felt flushed. It was suddenly all rather thrilling to have a proper little secret. A tiny harmless one, but fun all the same.

'Everything OK?' Kate asked her.

'Fine!' Fen exclaimed. 'Just an old pal. Might meet up for a quick drink after the flower show tomorrow.' Kate glowered at her and in an instant Fen sensed the other mums look up, offended, but swiftly pretending not to have heard. Fen scooped up her baby and cuddled her whilst babbling sweet nothings.

'Come on, gorgeous girl,' she whispered, 'let's head home.'

Ben hadn't heard back from Django and he was about to leave work. Cat was working late as the honchos from head office were in the shop and there was an after-hours team-bonding or book-binding or something. Ben felt irritated. With all aspects of the situation. He loved the responsibilities of his job, but not when they compromised his family life. Had Django even made the call to his GPs? Ben doubted it. This irritated him. And at what point would he be telling Cat of the call? This irked him. And the cause? This worried him. And how could the cause be any clearer if the old man won't visit his GP? But what could Ben do about any of it at this precise moment? If he called Derbyshire, would Django even answer? Six o'clock. He'd probably be cooking. Ben didn't want to make the call from home. Or from his mobile. It felt slightly disloyal to Cat to do so. But he wanted to go home; it had been a long day. It was that time of day when he sensed the smell of the hospital seep through to the fibres of his clothes.

Cat's phone was switched off. Dovidels' phone rang through to a chirpy message with opening times and website details. The phone at Farelymoor rang and rang. Ben persevered.

'Hullo – this is Farleymoor 64920.'

'Hullo Django, it's Ben.'

'Ben! And how are you?'

'I'm fine. And how are you?'

'I feel much much better, thank you.'

'Did you phone your surgery? Django?'

'I said – I feel much much better.'

'Right,' said Ben, rubbing his temples, pinching the bridge of his nose. You daft old man. 'Right. Oh, Django – can I call you back in two minutes? There's someone to see me.' There wasn't. But there was someone Ben wanted to see.

A few minutes later, the phone rang again at Farleymoor. That will be young Ben, thought Django. And though he really would rather not answer it, it was impossible not to. Ben knew he was there. And Django knew the wretched phone would just ring and ring until he picked up.

'Farleymoor 64920?'

'Hullo Django – sorry about that. It's Ben.'

'Hullo Ben. I'm cooking a stew. Pots of it. *Sans* beetroot.'

'Good, good. That's very good. Look, Django – I know how awkward all of this is for you. And I don't know your GP but I respect that you do. But I do know an excellent chappy down here. And he was just passing by my rooms while we were on the phone before. And I nabbed him and he'd be delighted to see you. He's a *he*,' said Ben. 'He's in his late fifties, I'd say. And he sees chaps like you all the time. He's a dab hand, a first-class doctor.'

'I see.'

'He really is,' said Ben, 'he's a specialist. A very nice man. I like him. You would, too.'

'I would?'

'Yes,' Ben said, 'you would. He's what you'd class a "proper" doctor. You'd feel comfortable with him. Confident too.'

'I would?'

'Will you come, Django?' Ben asked very gently, the tone of his voice full of the same soothing care and concern he'd invested the carefully chosen word 'chappy' with.

'To London?'

'To see my Mr Pisani,' said Ben. 'A quick consultation.'

'Is he foreign?'

'He's Scottish,' said Ben, 'he's excellent.'

'I see. But he's only a "Mr" not a "Dr"?'

'He's a consultant. Mr is far superior to Dr.'

'I see.'

'A day-trip,' Ben said, 'that's all. The trains are marvellous. Frequent and fast.'

'I haven't been to London in years,' Django said. 'The girls have always come to me.'

'I think you should come. I'm happy to accompany you to the consultation,' said Ben, 'or not. As you wish.'

'You won't tell anyone, will you?' said Django after a while.

'You have come to me in my capacity as a doctor,' Ben said evenly. 'I am bound by the Hippocratic oath.'

'Perhaps I will come,' said Django.

'I think so,' said Ben.

'All right,' said Django.

'I will make an appointment and telephone you tomorrow. I'll telephone you at this time. Then you'll know it's me.'

'Yes. OK, Ben.'

'Good. That's settled.'

'And Ben?'

'Yes?'

'Well – thank you.'

'Don't mention it, Django,' he said, 'it's nothing.' And Ben sincerely hoped that it was.

Seeds Sown

It wasn't so much a case of Fen not being able to see the wood for the trees, more that she couldn't see the flowers for the florid meanderings of her overactive imagination. It was a waste of a ticket, really. From the moment she arrived, Fen was planning her escape. She walked around the Chelsea Flower Show, her head nodding like a fritillary, while she pretended to listen to Kate's ostentatious commentary. Scandalously, Fen barely noticed the displays. She was aware of the scale of it all, of a certain cacophony of colour and fragrance, but ultimately her senses were set aside, held in abeyance, until later. She didn't actually have time to marvel at all this horticulture haute couture; she was too busy preparing for her next appointment. She'd been musing scenarios in her mind's eye of the various ways to sashay into a bar, finally favouring her version of a classic Western – stranger enters the saloon and all fall silent. It was compulsive to envisage being the centre of attention, to imagine Al give a double take, bowled over, greeting her with an appreciative 'Wow! I didn't realize it was you!' Fen couldn't actually remember what Al looked like and she was rather hoping he couldn't remember what she looked like either. After all, when they'd first met she'd been head to toe in frumpy mummy guise. Today, hopefully, she'd appear a vision in floaty bias-cut and dainty kitten heels.

God – hi, Fen. You look great. Let me buy you a drink.

She'd carefully blow-dried her hair and had spent as much time as Cosima had allowed her, to blend and blend the Mac and Bobbie Brown mainstays of her neglected make-up bag.

Fen? Blimey! I didn't recognize you. What are you drinking?

While Kate went into paroxysms of wonderment for the Great Pavilion, Fen convinced herself that Al would be currently awaiting her call. She was to let him know when she was free, and he was to tell her where they were to meet; that was the plan. As she was pushed along by the throng, Fen was too busy musing over the best way to touch base with Al to notice the gardens, or that she was being vigorously poked and shoved by all those green fingers. Fen suspected Kate was well able to appreciate the displays *and* eagerly eavesdrop her call, but Fen thought she'd be far more conspicuous standing stock still frantically texting in the midst of all this magnificent flora. A man next to her sneezed. And sneezed again. And suddenly Fen had her motive. She began to rub her nose, to feign a look of discomfort entailing much blinking and nose-twitching.

'Isn't it stunning? Who'd've thought to bind akebia quinata through actinidia? Inspired!' Kate gushed.

Fen realized she couldn't even pronounce let alone identify the majority of the exhibits. 'Kate,' she sighed, 'I hate to say this – but I think my hay fever is about to take hold with a vengeance.'

'At Chelsea Flower Show?' Kate looked at her, horrified, as if the salubriousness of the event surely counteracted such a vulgar affliction.

'I can't bloody believe it,' Fen bemoaned after an impressive chain of sneezes. She blinked and rubbed her nose. 'I'm going to have to go,' she apologized, with a woeful expression.

'OK,' said Kate glumly, 'OK. Come on then, let's go.'

'Kate – you needn't!' Fen rushed. 'Please stay – I'll be fine. My bloody hay fever shouldn't spoil the day for you too.'

'Are you sure?'

'Very.'

Both women quietly considered just then how Ruth would have been a far more worthy recipient of this spare, precious ticket.

As Fen fought her way out, she thought about flowers and gardening and pomp.

Give me a wild-flower meadow over formal planting any day; give me a thatch of heather on a moorside over topiary and edging. I've never been one for bouquets. I'm more of a daisy-chain girl. Pip and I once made one with daisies and buttercups that was almost two yards long. Django pressed the entire thing, between volumes of Encyclopaedia Britannica *set out for weeks in a long line down the hallway. He even contacted the* Guinness Book of Records *about it. I bet he has it still.*

For a while, Matt and I couldn't decide between Cosima and Daisy as names.

I do not want to think of family today.

Fen aimed to come across as imperturbably casual to the point of downright cool when she phoned Al from a side street and said yeah, wine bar coffee shop whatever. However, her stomach was flipping, her conscience was goading and her handwriting was scrawled with adrenalin as she attempted to jot down the location of the bar Al suggested. And then she stood there, palms clammy, heart pounding, wondering how to kill time for the next hour.

You are on the King's Road, Fen. Window-shop? Impulse buy? Full-on Retail Therapy?

Look, Daisy & Tom – their kids' stuff is adorable.

But today isn't about babies.

At first, she was tentative; nipping in and out of L.K. Bennett as if she was being monitored on CCTV beamed straight to all who knew her. She settled into browse mode after circumnavigating the collection at Jigsaw, and in Karen Millen she relaxed a little more, gently running her fingertips along the racks of garments like a pianist from one end of the keyboard to another. Though nearly everything struck a chord with her, still she didn't try anything on. It wasn't the price tags, or the fact that all the pieces she fancied were in implausible shades of white, it was her perceived decadence of the situation that prevented it.

I shouldn't be trying on organza cream shift dresses with bugle beads under the bust; I should be hurrying home to mash sweet potato with organic crème fraîche.

However, Whistles seduced her away from all thoughts of domesticity, luring her into a luxurious world lined with wafts of chiffon and silk, floating with sequinned butterflies and populated by retro imagery woven with humour and imagination into lovely skirts, groovy tops, heavenly knitwear and divine undies. So absorbed was she in the gorgeousness of it all, it was with some consternation that she noticed time had flown and she had five minutes to find the bar and no time to try anything on.

It felt as though a stampede of butterflies, sequinned or otherwise, had suddenly taken flight in her stomach, causing havoc with her ability to walk without tripping and interfering with the demure smile she'd planned. And so, with a slightly twitching physiognomy, she hurried into the bar. The first thing she noticed was the smell. It was overpowering; at once nostalgic and now faintly intimidating. When on earth had she last smelt that wine-bar smell: alcohol, cigarettes, olives in garlicky marinade, leather slouchy sofas? When? *When?* It was evocative – but unnerving – to realize it was not since her pre-pregnancy days. The Rag and Thistle, with its aroma of stale beer and fags partly soaked up by carpet and beer mats, was somehow a warmer, more welcoming smell. Similarly, the sounds at the Rag and Thistle were more affable, as if the carpet and the beer mats absorbed some of the volume and infused the interior with a convivial resonance, a hubbub of cheer. In this bar, however, with the obligatory stripped floorboards, the volume was unmoderated and the clatter and chatter of the clientele were staccato, loud and slightly inhibiting.

Fen was desperate to come across Al without having to search him out; she didn't want to have to stand there, staring from clique to clique, strangers glancing back disinterested. She'd envisaged simply waltzing in, calm, confident and eye-catching, for Al's eyes to alight in delight before she saw him. It appeared, however, that he had yet to arrive. Fen scanned the crowd again. No. No Al. She might not be able to remember precisely how he looked but she was quite sure that no one here just now was him.

'Fen? Hi!'

Oh here he is. Of course. I remember now.

'Sorry I'm late. Drink?'

He hasn't said 'Wow' or anything. What shall I have? What's the time?

'Just a glass of white for me,' said Fen.

'Do you want to grab that table over there – with the two leather cubes?' Al said.

Fen sat a little gingerly on a leather cube, which looked more stable than it felt, but was probably more stable than she thought. She wondered how many people toppled off them on a nightly basis, once balance was compromised by a couple of drinks. She'd be having just the one glass, she wouldn't be wobbling anywhere. She wouldn't even teeter. She had an image to maintain. And a baby to get home to.

She looked over to the bar. She'd define Al as 'cute' – a term men detested but women understood. She hadn't remembered just how lanky, how boyish, he was. His jeans hung a little baggy, his hair was becomingly unkempt, his skin soft and young. Fresh-faced and cute. He was an attractive package and she really *really* mustn't assess him as such.

'Sauvignon, madam,' he announced, beer slicking over his fingers from his glass as he sat down. Fen saw that he wore chunky Mexican silver rings on two of his fingers and one of his thumbs. She didn't like jewellery on men; she didn't like thumb rings at all.

'Cheers,' said Fen, diverting her gaze as she sipped. Revolting wine. Not cold enough. Never mind. Maintain eye contact, slide him a coy smile and ask what he's been up to.

'Oh, this and that,' he replied. 'Busy at work. Moving house.'

'Where do you live?'

'Now? In Camden. We've just taken on a house, five of us plus the occasional surplus body kipping on the sofa. It's good – it's a laugh.'

It sounded slightly unsavoury to Fen and she conjured an image of batik wall hangings, dog-eared posters of Jim Morrison, a chaotic fridge, forgotten washing-up and contrasting music reverberating from each room. She shuddered at her thought of what the bathroom might be like.

'It's not studenty,' Al was saying, as if sensing Fen's reservations. 'We're all a bit obsessed with cleaning, actually. It's a gorgeous house – all polished floors and high ceilings. It belongs to Jed's parents. They're collectors. Anyway, what have you been up to? How's your kid?'

Fen detested children being referred to as kids. 'She's wonderful,' she smiled suddenly missing Cosima terribly. What was she meant to say now? What had she been up to? Was Al really remotely interested in her daily grind of cleaning and tidying, of wiping bottoms and shovelling organic mush into a little mouth, of stocking the fridge and socializing with people to keep herself from going mad? She doubted it. And she was hardly likely to tell him all about the Mother, the Uncle, their Affair and her Half Sister. In an instant Fen assessed that for this afternoon to work, for it to have the function she hoped for, truth and veracity were not essential. 'I've been bloody busy,' she heard herself saying. 'I'm planning to go back to work.'

You are?

No.

'Work?' asked Al. 'What do you do?'

Fen reckoned 'archivist' sounded dull but 'art historian' sounded pompous. 'I lecture,' she embellished, 'in art.'

'Wow! Where?'

'Oh, the Tate usually,' she said with nonchalance, 'the Courtauld.' Partly true. She'd studied at the Courtauld and had frequently given talks as a student to people visiting the Institute's collection.

'What do you lecture about?' Al seemed impressed and genuinely interested.

'The European *Rappel à l'Ordre* of the post-war years,' Fen announced elaborately, simply repeating the title of one of her undergraduate courses, 'and Fetherstone too.'

'Who's Fetherstone?' Al asked, endearingly sheepish.

'A student of Rodin. Late nineteenth, early twentieth

century,' Fen discoursed. 'Famous – or notorious – for his exquisite feel for form, his intensely erotic subject matter.'

'Cool!' Al marvelled, his pupils dilating as he hung on Fen's words and gazed at her lips. 'I'll have to come along to a lecture, then.' Fen tossed her head and laughed and told herself to go easy with the exaggeration and embellishment. Instead, she turned to questioning him, flattering him, expressing great interest in all he said. And she took to touching his arm at times when he made her laugh. And laughed in excess of the cause. And licked her lips becomingly every time she sipped her wine. And lowered her eyes at opportune moments. And pouted now and then.

'Do you have to get back?' Al asked her eventually. 'To your kid?'

'Yes,' said Fen, with a shrug.

'Who's looking after her? Do you have a nanny?'

'No,' said Fen, 'my sister is.'

Al drained his beer glass. 'Is it tough? Being a single parent?'

Something Fen couldn't pinpoint, and hadn't the time to analyse, made her not jump to Matt's defence. It occurred to her only then that Al had never asked about the father of her child. But there again, she didn't wear a wedding ring and she'd never mentioned Cosima's father. Why wouldn't he suppose she was a single mother? Fundamentally, why would a mother in a relationship take up an invitation for afternoon wine, flirting and flattery in a bar? She wondered what to do. To whom did she have the greater duty to set the record straight – Al? Matt? Herself? Cosima?

But can't I just play a while longer? I'm not ready to go home. It's fun, liberating. It's just harmless acting. It's not like I'm telling lies. Or doing anything wrong.

'No, it's not tough,' Fen finally answered Al. 'I'm very close with my sisters. I have two.'

Al nodded. 'Shall we meet again?' he said.

Fen looked at him. It was all appealing and a little dangerous and all the more tempting for it. 'But I'm a frumpy old mum!' she protested with a winsome pout and a flutter of her eyelashes. 'I'm almost thirty-four!'

Al shrugged. His eyes sparkled. 'I think you're cool,' he said. 'I think it's sexy that you're a mum.'

'I'll call you – when I'm not so madly busy,' Fen all but purred, standing, leaning to kiss him on the cheek and making sure her lips just caught the side of his mouth in the process.

Al didn't say anything in response. But his eyes followed her as she left the bar.

He's looking at my bottom, she thought, unsure whether to enhance her wiggle or screen it with her handbag. He gave her a wry, desirous smile when she turned to wave before she sashayed away.

No one has called me sexy for ages. I can't even tell if I actually fancy Al – but I am turned on by the fact that he fancies me.

With a spring to her step, a sexy sway to her stride, she grinned her way along the King's Road, tossing her head and tempering her smile into a pout every now and then. She felt like pouting, she felt coquettish. Someone found her sexy. How thrilling! She enjoyed catching sight of herself in the shop windows. Oh look, here's Whistles. And look at that divine dress.

Did she dare?

Yes she did.

She didn't have to spend money to waste time, or spend time to waste money. She could just try something on, take window-shopping one logical stage further. Flushed with anticipation, Fen headed to the changing cubicles.

She was crestfallen. How stupid had she been? It was as if her trip away from home to an area far from her stamping ground, her shrug from responsibilities, had falsely invested her self-image with extra inches in height and fewer pounds in weight.

Nothing bloody fitted.

She denounced herself for being too round of figure and too square of image. She felt she looked ridiculous. The confines of the clothing made her feel saggy and squidgy and unrefined. And so she stood; horror-stuck in the cubicle, clammy and depressed, confronting all the bumps she could see and a fair few she imagined.

'I'm fine!' she all but yelled to the sales assistant hovering.

What Fen couldn't see was that if she tried a larger size, just one size up, she'd look wonderful. She couldn't see that the dress suited a fuller figure anyway. Designers don't want bagginess in a forties-style tea dress; the cut craves curves and the material needs undulations to flow to its best advantage. But Fen was defiant that once a size 10, always a size 10. And if she didn't fit a size 10, she simply wouldn't be able to have the bloody dress.

If nurturing a foetus required padding to the hips, surely running around after a baby should take it off again? If hormones had encouraged her ribcage to expand during pregnancy, then why hadn't hormones shrunk it back to normal after the birth? Ten and a half sodding months after the birth. Standing there, she scowled at her reflection, rounding her shoulders and relaxing her belly to compound her fears and loathe herself more. She felt resentful and out of sorts and dreaded leaving the changing room, the sparkle of the shop, the clear light of day.

I'm not sure it should be the fit of frock that makes you loathe yourself, Fen.

Seeds Not Sown

'Give us a hug,' Pip cooed and clucked. She scooped up her niece and pretended to gobble her cheeks. The baby giggled. Pip gobbled some more. 'You are scrumptious,' she said, 'but we'd better think of something to do before I eat you up.' Pip and the baby regarded one another, as if considering various options. 'I know,' said Pip, 'how about we pop over to Auntie June and save her the journey here?' Cosima didn't appear to object. 'She left a message to say Tom had left his cricket stuff there, which he'll need for tomorrow.'

For June and Pip, Zac had swiftly ceased to become part of their equation. June didn't think of Pip as the wife of her ex who was the father of her child; Pip had no issue with June being the woman with whom Zac had a baby. Not for June or Pip the dropping-off of Tom with cordiality. Sharing Tom was easy because the women liked each other; to some extent, Tom was both central and yet oddly irrelevant to their friendship.

June cooed over Cosima, marvelled at how much the baby had grown, in much the same way as Pip fussed over June's bump. 'It's not so much a bump,' Pip said, 'it's a perfect medicine ball. So neat!'

'I'm enormous,' June remonstrated, 'and I still have eight weeks to go.'

'You're gorgeous,' said Pip wistfully.

'I think I'm practically due on Cosima's first birthday,' June said.

'Well, we'll cancel the clown if needs be,' Pip said, 'and relocate the party to the labour ward.'

'Or I could just set up my birthing pool in Fen's back bedroom,' June said.

'Are you going for a water birth?' Pip asked.

'You must be joking,' June said. 'I'm going private this time so I can have all the fancy drugs available. I don't do pain.'

'Listen to you,' Pip chided in jest.

'Believe me,' June said, 'Tom's birth was a nightmare. This time, I don't want plinky plinky music, whale song and yoga – I just want drugs.'

Pip glanced from June's bulge to Cosima and back again. *I wonder what sort of birth I'd go for?*

'Do you ever think about it?' June asked.

'About?' Pip busied herself fussing over Cosima.

'About having a baby,' June said.

'Zac loves having just Tom,' Pip said.

'But that's not what I meant,' June persisted.

Pip wasn't sure if she wanted to answer fully or not. 'Sometimes,' she said. June said nothing. 'Recently?'

June clapped her hands and grinned. 'And?'

'Zac loves having just Tom,' Pip reiterated.

'Have you asked Zac?' June asked.

Pip shrugged. 'Sort of,' she said. June looked confused. 'I think he thought I was joking. And then I think he thought I was drunk. And ultimately I think he thinks I'm barking.'

'Well, he sounds complacent,' said June. 'You should keep the pressure on – you'll make a great mum.'

'I hate confrontation,' Pip said, 'and anyway, it's probably just a hormonal thing.'

'You know what,' said June, 'you're right it's probably hormonal but I for one think it'll be a shame if you let it pass.'

Pip wanted to cry. This was the first she'd said out in the open and it was being met with such tender but unswerving support it was rather overwhelming. 'The thing is,' she said tentatively, 'since the woman who is my mother barged back in, I've had something of a confidence crisis. Am I fit to be a mother? Say there's some rogue part of our DNA that dictates otherwise.'

'Rubbish, Pip,' June said, not intending to sound so sharp but she was beginning to feel a little tired. 'Look at Fen – she's a fabulous mum. Your mother – literally – has nothing to do with you. I think you should go for it. And I think when that stuffy old accountant comes home all hassled from work tonight, you meet him in an outrageous negligee and you demand that he impregnate you with his finest.'

Pip looked utterly disconcerted.

'Believe me,' June continued, 'and it's not because I'm an over-heating, hyper-hormoned pregnant woman. Well, perhaps it is – but that's no bad thing. But what I want to say is this – that urge to breed is one you *must* heed. Breeding is your *raison d'être,* Pip, it's your right.'

Pip pushed Cosima's buggy along Hampstead High Street. It was a glorious day and she'd toyed with the notion of taking the picnic blanket and lolling about on the Heath. But what swung it for the High Street were the shops. The shops provided one thing that the Heath didn't. Windows. And reflections. And every shop she passed boasted back an image of Pip pushing a buggy. It was visible proof, as if it was needed, that it suited her. She proudly told the first admirer that Cosima was her niece. But when the sales assistant in BabyGap cooed over Cosima and asked Pip how old her daughter was, Pip told her ten months and agreed with the assistant that she was quite the most beautiful baby girl in the world.

And Cosima ate everything Pip offered her, even if it wasn't orange.

And Pip could soothe the baby's tears quickly.

And Cosima needed minimal lulling to drift off to a lovely afternoon nap. She didn't need her *Elvis for Babies* CD which Fen had packed, nor flopsy bunny. A personalized rendition of 'I Had a Little Nut Tree' from Pip was all it took.

Pip let the answering machine take the call because she and Cosima were engrossed in *Teletubbies* and something extraordinary with the Tubby Custard machine was about to befall Po.

'Shall I pick it up?' Tom asked, looking up from his maths homework.

'That's OK,' said Pip. 'You crack on with your work, young man.'

It was Fen leaving a message to say she was running late and how sorry she was but she'd had a lovely day and would be there soon.

'Never mind,' said Pip to Cosima, 'you can have tea with Tom.'

'Am I her big cousin?' Tom asked because he was stuck with his maths but knew that Pip was no use to him whatsoever. 'Am I her big cousin officially? Or am I a step-cousin twice removed or something?'

Pip paused. 'Well, let's work this out. I think you're her step first cousin.'

'Will my new brother or sister be her step second cousin, then?' Tom asked.

'No, I don't think they'll be cousins at all.'

Tom looked perplexed. This was becoming more complicated than the maths homework. 'Of course they will!' he declared. 'It's all about family.'

'If I had a baby, then the baby and Cosima would be full cousins. I have you which makes you half a full first cousin. Step.' Pip and Tom looked at each other, brows furrowed. 'Or something!' Pip said and they laughed.

'Why do babies like eating such weird things?' Tom asked.

Pip looked over to Cosima who was sucking the remote control. 'Shit – that's Bang & Olufsen.'

'You said "Shit"!' Tom whispered, impressed.

'Don't tell your father,' Pip warned him.

'If you had a baby, I'd have two half brothers or sisters, wouldn't I?' Tom mused. 'I'd have brothers and sisters from all directions. That would be funny.'

Pip couldn't think how to respond.

'Why don't you have one, then? With my dad,' asked Tom.

Pip couldn't think how to respond, but Tom seemed happy to wait. 'Well,' she said, 'because he hasn't asked me.'

'Why don't you ask him?' asked Tom.

'I half have,' Pip admitted and wondered if she should now backtrack.

'I'm getting confused with all these halfs,' Tom laughed.

'Me too,' agreed Pip.

Fen appeared slightly flustered when she arrived to collect Cosima, mumbling something about wanting to die in Whistles.

'But how were the flowers?' Pip asked. 'Can you now tell your larkspur from your delphinium?'

'What? Oh. The show. Was – great,' said Fen, 'huge. Amazing.'

'Are you OK?' Pip asked. 'Want a cuppa?'

'I'm just a bit – stressed,' said Fen, looking very discomfited. 'You know – Tubes and rush hour and escalators that aren't working.'

'Welcome back to the real world,' Pip laughed.

'To think I did the rush-hour thing every day,' Fen remembered. 'Madness.'

'Would you like that cuppa?'

'We'd better go – Cosima needs her supper.'

'We fed her!' Tom announced, triumphant. 'She had scrambled eggs just like me!'

'Scrambled eggs?' Fen looked at Pip.

'Was that OK? The eggs are free range.'

'Well – yes. But did she eat?'

'The lot!' Pip said.

Momentarily, Fen felt put out, having had limited success with scrambled eggs. 'Organic milk?' she asked shyly.

'Of course,' said Pip.

'You're a star,' said Fen looking at her sister with affection and at her baby with pride.

'Any time,' said Pip.

'You're a super star,' Fen said, wondering if Pip really meant it when she'd said, 'Any time.'

Zac returned to find his wife and son embroiled in a backgammon tournament; a pile of pennies at Tom's side and a fraught expression etched on Pip's face.

'Hullo,' he said, scanning his son's impressive defence and two of Pip's counters desperate for access.

'Six, two,' Pip muttered at the roll of the dice. 'Blast and double blast, I can't bloody move!'

'That's her fourth "bloody", Dad!' Tom informed Zac, Pip's language obviously giving him far more pleasure than his victories or winnings.

'I'd say a "bloody" is worth 10p, Tom,' Zac said, taking

off his jacket, loosening his tie, opening his post. 'How's your mum?'

'She's like a great big beached whale,' said Tom, rather proudly.

'Tom!' Pip and Zac remonstrated.

'But she says so,' Tom protested, as if it were a standard description of her particular stage of gestation.

'June looks wonderful,' Pip told Zac. 'I babysat Cosima today and we met up. She's absolutely blooming.'

Zac regarded Pip. 'Oh Christ,' he said, with mock consternation, 'you're not going to go all broody on me, are you?' He winked at Tom, planted an affectionate kiss on Pip's forehead, bypassing her mortified expression, before heading to the kitchen to make coffee.

'What does "broody" mean, exactly?' Tom asked and Pip wished he hadn't because she didn't want to hear Zac's reply.

'Broody?' mused Zac. 'Broody is when hormones and BabyGap turn women into mad things.'

'What exactly are hormones?' Tom asked, knowing precisely where BabyGap was but not hormones.

'You'll learn about them in science, soon enough,' Zac assured him.

'Have you gone broody on my dad, then?' Tom asked Pip though he was still unsure to what it precisely alluded.

Pip wanted to cry out, Yes! yes I have – I am seriously broody. But she did not. She assessed that the circumstances were inappropriate. And though part of her resented Tom's presence, felt that it prevented her confronting Zac, she put the child's best interests first.

What I want to say is, For fuck's sake, Zac. I'm thirty-five years old and maybe my sodding hormones are *hounding me. Most of the people I know have children. I would like to increase our family – a brother or sister for Tom, a baby for us. What the fuck is wrong with that? Why won't you take me seriously? All you say is 'Oh Christ you're not going all broody on me?'*

So why don't you talk to him, Pip? You who are so adept at being a shoulder, an ear, an embrace for the needs of others; you who can listen so well, mediate so constructively when it comes to the strife in other people's lives. You've spent your life arbitrating other people's discord, sorting out the ways forward from their crises, dispensing wisdom, advice, support and affection. You can gently coax others down off their high horse, you can enable them to see clearly without their rose-tinted glasses. But you have no faith in your ability to stand your own corner and proclaim what you feel. You have self-awareness in that you know what you want; but you lack the self-confidence to express it.

She can't concentrate on her game. She thinks the right thing to do is to hide her hurt from Tom. It's much easier to put Tom at the centre of her equation than herself.

'I won!' Tom proclaims. 'Pip is such a complete walkover,' he says to his dad and the two of them disappear to play PlayStation, leaving Pip on her own.

Seeds in a Packet

'You're hot and you smell of – toast?' Ben remarked with pleasure, in bed, spooning up against Cat, nuzzling her neck.

'But I haven't eaten toast,' she said.

Ben took her hand to his nose. 'Toast,' he declared. He kissed the palm of her hand and flicked his tongue tip at the centre. Then he kissed her fingertips and sucked softly on her middle finger.

'I've got a sackful of seed,' he murmured, pressing up against her. 'I've been saving it up for the last – Christ – *week*.' Cat giggled. She travelled her hand down to Ben's hard cock, experiencing a buzz of excitement between her legs which caused her to turn towards him and find his mouth immediately. His hands caressed her breasts and she began to moan softly as his finger nudged at her clitoris, dabbing her with her own expectant moistness.

'What do you say, babe,' he whispered, 'want to mate?' He grazed at the side of her neck, dipped his head down to tease her nipple with his tongue tip. 'Want to mate?'

But Cat didn't writhe in reply. She didn't gasp the affirmative. His words had stilled her and his actions ceased to elicit a response.

And then she sighed. 'I do feel horny,' she whispered back, 'but I don't want to *mate*. I'd rather fornicate.'

'What you're saying is that you want me to give you a good seeing to? You don't want to make love – you want me to shag you senseless?' Ben gave a dirty laugh, his hands resuming a dexterous exploration of her erogenous zones. He rolled on top of her, his pelvis rocking as his cock probed its way between the lips of her sex. 'You want me to fuck you, then?'

Yes, that was precisely what Cat wanted and when Ben talked crudely to her, she wanted it all the more. And harder.

'Shall I fuck you?' Ben asked, desirous and gruff, doing precisely that with eager, ravenous thrusts.

'With strings attached,' she whispered, gasping as he powered into her. She bucked against him instinctively.

'Strings, hey?' Ben said. 'Tie you up? A little light S & M on a warm June evening?'

That's not what she meant at all.

I meant, yes fuck me – but with conditions. But I'm so close. I'm so fucking close and my body is tingling with the anticipation of orgasm. It's welling. Fuck. God. Ben. Oh Christ.

Ben felt Cat's sex close around his cock, every pulsation pulling him deeper inside her, luring his sperm, starting to suck it from his balls up his shaft; nearing the point of no return.

'Christ Cat,' he panted as his thrusts automatically increased in pace, 'Christ.'

But then Cat did something with her hips. And her knees. She'd never done it before and it took Ben by surprise, weakened as he was by being in thrall to his imminent orgasm. She levered him away and all of a sudden he was coming in the open, nowhere near her dark, damp gorgeous pussy. Instead he was spurting his load God knows where. In between her and him. Instantly, the orgasm became purely perfunctory. Not even as good as a wank. Simply as physical as a wet dream. A waste. He switched the light on, blinking, pissed off. He pulled the duvet off and regarded the sticky mess in Cat's pubic hair, caught too in the fuzz of his stomach.

'What was that all about?' he asked, flushed and frustrated.

'It's not safe to come inside me,' Cat said, disconcerted that Ben looked so displeased. She felt a nag of guilt over the greed for the quality of her own orgasm at the expense of his and it was spoiling the post-coital moment.

'What the fuck do you mean, Cat?' Ben objected. 'What are you on about? Our sex life has been ruled by your charts and temperature.'

'I'm not ready,' Cat said gruffly, 'not any more. Not without a condom.'

'Cat,' said Ben, sitting up, reaching for tissues, mopping at his belly, 'I thought *we* wanted to start a family. *Our* game plan. We make decisions *together*.'

'Bloody hell, Ben,' she protested, 'are you thick? In the light of recent events, why would I want to be pregnant?' He stared at her, shocked by her aggression. 'Parenting is a dangerous thing. Can't you see that?' she shouted. 'Believe me. It's not worth it. I should know.'

Ben waited a moment and spoke calmly. 'Cat, that's not an informed view – you're very tired and too emotional.'

'You cold bastard!' Cat hissed. 'Can't you see what I'm going through?'

'Of course I bloody can,' Ben said calmly, 'but now you're being a drama queen. Christ if ever there was a time to take the "sins of the fathers" and make something good from them, then this is it.'

'Fuck off.' She turned away from him abruptly. 'You don't understand.'

That last comment hurt Ben the most. He had no desire to spoon against her or nuzzle up to see if she still smelt of toast. If only this sodding rented flat had a spare room. He switched off the light, plumped his pillow and made an irritated grab at the duvet. And when all was still, he sighed emphatically.

'For fuck's sake,' he said, as if to himself, but loudly enough for Cat to hear. He sensed she was only pretending to be asleep.

They didn't speak when they woke up. Ben didn't wake Cat with his customary 'Rise and shine, sleepy head'. He went to have a shower and didn't pour her a cup of coffee, leaving the cafetière and its tepid contents on the table instead. Get your own mug.

'See you,' he said, already on his way out. Cat didn't look up from the newspaper. She continued to read, continued to sip her lukewarm coffee long after Ben had gone. The newsprint was illegible because the bruise of tears impeded her sight and the coffee caught harshly on the lump in her throat. She struggled with her tears as she walked to work, biting hard on the inside of her lip during the managers' meeting. She didn't want to be on the information desk. Couldn't she unpack deliveries instead? It wasn't beneath an assistant manageress to unpack deliveries in the back, you know. But Jeremy wanted her up front and the customers did too. Cat muddled through the morning, hauling a weak smile to her face and disappearing to the toilet on her break for a private cry.

Pip would know what to do. She'd know what I should say. She'll be able to tell me if I'm in the wrong, or a little right. She's my big sister. I'll listen to her. She's the wisest person I know. She can tell me what to do.

*

In her lunch break, Cat phoned Pip. Privately, it rankled Pip to hear about loving husbands actively wanting to make babies. But she had to listen because it was her job and her youngest sister was sobbing at the end of the phone, pleading with her to tell her what to do. Over the years, she'd conditioned herself to stop what she was doing, put thoughts of herself to one side, whenever she received those calls from her sisters that said, Pip? Pip? I need you. Can you help?

'I thought I was ready,' Cat cried, 'but I'm not. I don't even feel broody any more. I can't figure out this whole mother–father business. I'm scared, Pip, and confused.'

Quietly, Pip considered her sister's predicament. 'I understand, I do,' she soothed, because on an academic level, she did, 'but how I see it is that you've been gravely let down by a total lack of communication within our family – and the only history about to repeat itself is precisely this.' She paused. Why couldn't she herself boldly practise what she so gamely preached?

This isn't about me. It's about Cat.

'Don't let that happen, Cat. No secrets. We were kept in the dark – we weren't even lied to. We were ill-informed and misled. But Cat, don't take that with you into your life. Don't let that same lack of communication decimate what you have with Ben. It sounds clichéd, but *talk* to him.' She paused again.

That's what June told me.

'Tell him how you feel. He's your man, Cat. He's your future. You can turn to him. You must.'

'But he's not speaking to me,' said Cat, now smarting about the lack of coffee that morning. 'He's mad at me. We never row. It was horrible. I feel sick. Suddenly Ben and I want different things, Pip. We're totally incompatible.'

'It's not about how compatible you are, Cat – it's about

how you deal with incompatibility,' said Pip. 'When did you last tell him you loved him?'

When did Zac last tell me?

'I don't honestly know,' Cat was saying, 'but how do I start talking? And what do you think I should say?'

On the other end of the phone, Pip was pinching the bridge of her nose and trying to strip her mind of Zac so she could concentrate on Cat.

'You have to do the right thing,' she heard herself say. 'You have to open up and lay yourself bare – if you can't do this in front of your husband, then you are in serious breach of the trust and honesty you promised him when you married him.'

Which makes me a fucking hypocrite.

'Shall I phone him at work?' Cat pressed. 'Shall I ask my manager for a break?'

'Yes,' said Pip, 'do.'

'And tell Ben how I feel – even though some of it sounds daft?'

'Yes,' said Pip, 'you must.'

'Say he disagrees? Say he objects?'

'Say he doesn't?'

'Say he's cross?' said Cat.

'Say he isn't?'

Cat paused. The notion of Ben's love being just at the end of the phone, of his support and understanding being just a phone call away, of her being just moments from the comfort of his companionship, was thrilling. Suddenly, she wanted Pip off the phone.

'Thanks,' Cat said cheerfully. 'I'll phone him right now. Can I phone you again, though?'

'You know you can,' said Pip.

Pip hated herself for hoping that Cat wouldn't phone her again. She didn't want to listen to how the heart-to-heart had gone and she didn't have the energy for further counselling. But Pip hated herself more for her intrinsic inability to take her own sound advice. How easy it was to see the right thing to do. Crystal bloody clear. Talk it through. Lay yourself bare. Show your soul and open your heart to the person closest to you, the person who transcends a need for blood ties to create a bond. How pathetic, she felt, to be fundamentally incapable of doing this herself.

Behind the information desk, Cat contrived to look important and busy. She wasn't. She was utterly absorbed in the pleasure of planning the reconciliation. She hadn't asked for a break because it was premature. She had to know exactly what she'd be saying before she phoned Ben. She had to be word perfect and her words needed to be honed for ultimate poetic and meaningful impact. He'd be in afternoon surgery. She couldn't phone now, she needed the best forum and no time restraints for her soliloquy to resound. But say he was still pissed off and went to the pub instead of coming home? And say he was pissed when he then came home? She couldn't endure another cold-shouldered night. She had to let him know that she was sorry, and soon. That there was an explanation. A text message could work – something sweet and slushy. But texts were somehow too easy to send. Who hasn't used a text message to avoid having to talk to someone?

As she hung up from telling a customer's answering machine that their books were awaiting collection, Cat thought about message services. About telegrams and messengers and couriers. She phoned Ben's hospital and asked for the Sports Medicine department and when a female voice answered, Cat put on her most friendly, conniving voice.

'Hullo? Is that Marjorie?'

'Yes? Sports Medicine clinic – how can I help?'

'This is Cat – Ben's wife. We haven't met but he speaks highly of you.'

'Oh!'

'Can you help me, Marjorie? I did one of those silly things – those over-emotional daft-cow things.'

'Ah,' said Marjorie, who had been no stranger to the syndrome in her younger days.

'Ben has speaker phone, doesn't he – is that how you announce his patients?'

'Yes, that's right, dear.'

'Before the next patient can you tell him that his wife loves him and she's sorry for being a madwoman and that she can't wait to see him later?'

'I can,' Marjorie said with slight reluctance.

'Oh,' said Cat, forlorn, 'is it something to do with hospital policy?'

'No, dear,' said Marjorie, 'but can I reword it? I think I should say— In fact, he's ready to see his next patient. You can listen in.'

Cat pressed the receiver hard against her ear, giving Jeremy who was loitering an irritated 'Shh!' before turning her back on him.

'Dr York,' Marjorie could be heard to say, 'before I send in Miss Drew, I have been entrusted with the following announcement.'

Cat's heart raced. Marjorie's pitch changed, as if she was having to be heard across a football pitch. 'Your wife wishes you to know that she loves you truly, and that she is extremely sorry for her behaviour. She would like you to know that she looks forward to your homecoming tonight – and that she would be pleased to talk through the circumstances.'

Cat couldn't hear Ben's response, but she fully approved Marjorie's handling of the situation. 'You're a genius,

Marjorie,' she said, and she planned to send her some books in gratitude.

'Cat!'

Cat turned to see Jeremy looking put out.

'We do not, as a rule, take personal calls – let alone make them.'

'I know,' Cat beamed, 'I'm sorry – there was a family crisis. It's all sorted now. It won't happen again.'

The manager thought she spoke of the personal calls.

Cat stopped beaming on her journey home. It struck her that nothing was actually solved. All she'd done, hopefully, was give Ben an inducement to come home, pacify his anger and open a door to communication. They still had to talk. And reach an understanding, an agreement.

But he wasn't home and her confidence was instantly sapped. She started to allow herself to feel the wounded party. Why hadn't he figured out why she might now be reluctant to start a family? Why hadn't he been instinctively more supportive? Her mobile phone buzzed through a message.

U ok? Here 4 u. P xx.

Good old Pip, coming to the rescue. At least someone knows me inside out and understands.

'He's not home yet,' Cat phoned Pip in a whisper, in case Ben should be just about to come in. She told Pip of Marjorie. She could sense her sister's smile, her approval. 'But suddenly I don't know what to say when he does come home. Say he's still cross. Say he didn't like my message? Say we can't sort this out?'

'If you look out your window, will you see him walk up the street?'

'Yes,' said Cat.

'So, the sight of him will incite an emotional reaction in you. Act on it.'

I speak from experience. I could hardly bear to look at

Zac when he came home half an hour ago. So I invented some urgent shopping. And I'm now advising my sister from the canned-goods aisle in Sainsbury's.

'You're a genius,' Cat told her. 'Thank you. God, thank you, Pip.'

'Call if you need me,' Pip said, by rote. But Cat had already hung up.

Cat has been gazing out of the first-floor window for almost half an hour. She's elaborately decided that if three red cars pass in succession, Ben will be the next pedestrian to walk down the street. But blue cars and white vans and the occasional candy-coloured scooter keep interrupting and there's no sign of Ben. What a gorgeous evening. How lovely to see a couple of children playing hopscotch on the pavement. Clapham doesn't seem so unattractive today and Boulder doesn't seem so far away. The world seems smaller, more friendly, more manageable. Listen! That evocative jingle – an ice-cream van! When had she last had a gloriously synthetic whippy with a Flake? She can't remember. But she heads out of the flat and down to the street. She's second in the queue. She's first. She's being served.

'A medium 99, please,' she says.

And Cat sees Ben.

He's turned the corner.

He's only a hundred yards away.

'Two!' Cat says. 'Make that two!'

Can Ben see me? Has he seen me yet?

He has.

But is he smiling?

He is.

Cat walks fast towards Ben who is strolling along the street with his shirtsleeves rolled up, his jacket slung over his shoulder. All her words have gone, her memory stripped of the soliloquies she's spent the day perfecting. All she can do, within yards of Ben, is brandish the ice cream she's bought for him.

'Look!' she declares holding out the ice cream. Ben thinks she looks like the Statue of Liberty in jeans and a T-shirt. 'I didn't even take a bite of your Flake.'

'Well,' says Ben, 'if that's not a sign of your true love, then what is?'

Cat blushes and doesn't know what to say and Ben thinks it's funny so he dabs the tip of his ice cream against her nose. Then he kisses it off. 'Thanks for your message,' he says. 'You're a madwoman. But I've given Marjorie a promotion.'

They sit, busy licking, on the low wall outside their flat. Cat bites the bottom of her cornet, looks at Ben and then sucks until her cheeks pucker and the ice cream scoots down the cone. Her daft face makes Ben laugh.

'I can't believe you save your Flake until last,' Cat says, knowing she'd never have the self-restraint to push the chocolate down the centre of the cornet and studiously eat around it.

'I don't think I have a system,' Ben says, 'but I'm doing it because I know it'll wind you up.'

'Bastard!' Cat says softly. She's finished her ice cream now and she lays her head against Ben's shoulder. 'I'm sorry,' she says.

'Me too,' says Ben. 'I hate falling out with you.'

'Me too,' says Cat.

'It's not what we're about,' says Ben. He offers his cornet to her, he's nibbled down so the Flake, somewhat phallic, stands proud. Cat takes a bite. It's a beautiful evening. If they go inside, there'll be the television to flick on, supper to discuss, post to open. If they walk on, they'll hit that long patch of shade as the street bends right. So they decide to stay put, to sit on the wall and wonder what to say and who will speak first.

'Do you not want to have a baby?' Ben asks outright, because actually that's the basic question he needs answered.

Cat looks uneasy. 'No,' she admits quietly, 'I don't. Not now.'

'Not now, not *never*?' Ben probes gently.

It strikes Cat she hasn't actually thought about it to this extent. 'I'm so caught up in the mess of the moment,' she admits, 'I can't see beyond the immediate future.'

Ben nods. 'I know how awful all these revelations have been for you,' he says. 'Actually, I don't – I can only begin to imagine.'

'It's thrown into turmoil all my plans, all my previous beliefs,' Cat explains.

Ben nods.

'I'm not ready to be a mummy,' Cat says sadly.

'Because you're not ready to accept your own parents?' Ben suggests. 'In retrospect, your childhood may not have been perfect, but it is over.'

Cat shrugs. 'It's all been so – shocking.'

'I know. But you need to confront it all,' Ben advises, 'somehow. Stacey said the same, didn't she? I don't know if that's by soul-searching or full-on confrontation. You need to decide. But being in this vortex of bewilderment isn't good, Cat. If you're stuck in a downward spiral, it figures you can't move forward.'

Cat nods. Ben wonders whether to tell her about Django's call. But he can't really, the call was in confidence.

'You have all these strands of your life, flailing around,' he says. 'You need to either tie them up, or cut them off.'

'I know,' says Cat, 'but that's terrifying.'

'You need to face facts – quite literally,' Ben says. 'You should go and see Django – just you. Without me. No sisters to hide behind. Talk. Shout. Cry. I don't know. But you must have a million things to ask and he probably has a million things to tell.'

'I can't believe my father is alive,' Cat tells him. 'I can't believe I am Django's daughter. I don't want to see him, Ben. Should I have known? Shouldn't I have wondered at least?' Ben shrugs and places his hand over hers. 'Now that I know where I come from, I don't quite know where I'm going.' She pauses and rests her head on his shoulder. 'That's why I feel ambivalent about starting a family.'

'I understand you may feel this is not the right time to have a baby just now,' Ben sighs, because actually he'd truly love to have his family under way soon. He's thirty-four years old, he feels it's right, logical, that he should feel broody himself. 'But I also need to know that you are open to change. And most of all, I need to know that, theoretically, I'm still the bloke you'd want to have a baby with.'

Cat jerks her head up from his shoulder and looks at him, shocked. How could big strong Ben doubt this?

Ben shrugs. 'You have to hug me back, sometimes, you know,' he explains.

She looks at him again and despite his strong physique, his handsome face, his silvering hair, just now he looks like a little boy. Cat stares at her knees, ashamed. Regards a smudge of ice cream on her jeans. 'Of course there's only you,' she whispers. 'My family begins with you.'

They sit on the wall and like the words.

'But listen,' says Ben, 'I hate condoms. And pulling out is grim – and not sodding fair. Messy too.'

'Blow-job?' Cat says with meek coyness.

'Swallow?'

She giggles.

'The pill?' Ben asks.

'But I put on weight and got spotty last time,' Cat says.

'I still fancied you,' says Ben.

And Cat knows that he did.

'Perhaps,' she says.

'For the time being, hey?' says Ben.

Cat gives a small nod and slips her hand into his. It's a good enough answer for Ben.

Bad Seed

And where is *she*? The mother who ran off with the cowboy from Denver when her daughters were small, who reappeared with bombshells to drop thirty years later, has since returned to the United States. It's now June and Penny has been home for a couple of weeks and though the weather is glorious, Penny hasn't once been for ice cream. Not even a pink taster spoon. Though she'd love a sundae, nowhere but Fountains will do. Once tasted, never forsaken. However, she hasn't felt like going there but she'd rather go without ice cream than compromise with a tub from her local store. And she'd rather go without than confront sweet Juliette and her hopes of hearing that closure was a magical thing.

The house was sparkling, the fridge was full, the washing was done and the garden was so tidy that short of untangling blades of grass with a toothcomb, there was nothing more for Penny to do. The silence in the house was deafening but a coffee morning with Marcia and Noni would be more so. So she drove. All the way to the state line. Then she drove back and sat in the drive and berated the lawn for still looking so manicured and thus unmowable. She sat in the car with the engine running calculating the hours and hours until bedtime. A beautiful home, spick and span, empty and soulless. She phoned her home number from her cell phone and listened to Bob's voice on the answering machine. She phoned her home number again and cursed technology, denounced it as trickery that she could hear Bob's voice so clearly when the man no longer existed. She knew she ought to re-record the message. Some might think it macabre to hear a dead man's voice on it. And there was new information to record. She'd have to reword the message in the first person. No more 'we'. But how could she wipe Bob's voice away?

Penny started the car and headed out of town. She arrived at the intersection and turned right with a bit of a sigh and soon enough turned onto the mountain road. She wasn't heading for ice cream, or Ridge, she'd just stop at the first village, Hubbardton's Spring. There was an easy trail there that would take her to one of the most gorgeous panoramas in the vicinity. She drove through the village and along a no-through-route, parking up soon after the road petered out into an unsurfaced one. Her eyes were filled with the lushness of early summer; sumac trees and maples cloaked in such verdant hues it was difficult to imagine them ablaze in gold and scarlet and amber in a few months' time. Her sensible summer sandals were soon filled with powdery earth and the occasional small stone, viciously sharp despite its size. She headed for the vantage point high over the river, the land then surging and swooping to the mountains. It was one of Bob's favourite paths. Maybe he'd meet her there. She walked with hope though she chided herself an idiot for doing so. Wasn't she done with retracing old footsteps? After all, wherever she went now, she could look behind and see the unmistakable truth: there would only ever be one set of footprints.

There was nobody there. Of course there was nobody there.

Penny scrambled down to the cluster of flat rocks and took a seat. The purity of the air, the vividness of the view, the reality of the chill and scuff of the rock on which she sat, infused her with the clarity she needed.

I guess there's no point in mourning him any longer, because he's not coming back. There's only photographs and memories. I can close my eyes and try to recall the sight and sound and smell of him but I can't hope to conjure him.

I need to draw the proverbial line under it all. Re-record the answering machine. Find different trails to walk. I need to keep on going. Move on. I guess that's a positive thing to do – even if at the moment there seems to be a futility and finality to it which seems negative. If I can't hope for Bob – if I admit he's dead – will it somehow kill him off entirely? Death might be ultimately the simplest, truest thing we'll ever know – but it's way too complicated for the living.

People are coming. I can hear them. I want to curse them for stealing my moment. I want to tell them they're trespassing. This is mine – take your picnic and your laughter some place else! But Bob and I often shared this hike with other people – friends and strangers – so I can't expect Bob's death to bequest it sacred, private land. I'll go. I'll nod at these people. Maybe I'll even say, Hi, enjoy the view, it sure is pretty today. Perhaps I can smile at them too.

Penny could have gone home. Hubbardton's Spring was pretty much equidistant from Ridge where Fountains was, and Lester Falls where she lived. But it was a fine afternoon. And there was nothing to do at home. And still there were hours until bedtime. Anyway, perhaps Juliette didn't work Sundays. And with the trails now fully open, the parlour would be fuller anyway. Though there were more cars parked along the way, people were obviously out and about on the trails because Fountains was no busier than when Penny had last been in.

'Well look who it is,' said Juliette, rushing to the counter to have Gloria load a taster spoon with Coffeebanoffee. 'So good to see you!' she told Penny. 'Sit! How was your trip?' Juliette's mousy little face, with her generous smile and button-black eyes, was alert with anticipation and affection. Penny fixed a beatific smile to her face which she hoped would tell the girl all she could possibly want to know. And shut her up. She sat at the table and chided herself for not ordering her ice cream to go; for coming here in the first place.

Juliette returned with the sundae and loitered, waiting for Penny to engage her in conversation or even invite her to sit. But Penny appeared not to notice her, so engrossed was she in a leaflet she'd picked up outside the gallery in Hubbardton's Spring. When Penny noticed that Gloria was busy serving at the counter and Juliette had gone through to collect orders, she left the parlour and her uneaten sundae.

'Hey – Penny? Wait up.'

Penny turns to see Juliette hurrying down the street, with her sweet smile and a warm wave and something held aloft in her other hand.

'Hey Penny,' says Juliette, a little breathless, 'here. You hardly ate a bite.' She hands Penny a polystyrene block encasing the tubbed-up leftovers of her sundae. Juliette regards her, tilts her head, frowns a little whilst smiling. A contradiction in terms, Penny thinks to herself, like so much of life.

Love blossoming from a bad seed.

'You crying?' Juliette seems perturbed.

Penny touches her cheeks and swipes away the tears.

'I don't know whether our relationship was blessed or doomed,' Penny announces and is helpless to stem the flow of words streaming out. 'I try and defend my actions, I try to justify that I was young, that it was the 1960s, that I was a crazy mixed-up kid, that I wasn't in love with Nicholas anyway. But actually, what Bob and I did was *wrong*. Love blossomed from a bad seed – it screwed with the lives of others.' She stops abruptly, gasping a little.

'I think you have it wrong, Penny,' Juliette says with a caring tilt to her head. 'It's not your fault Bob died – and it's not your fault that you guys fell in love,' and she touches Penny's arm tenderly.

Penny feels surprisingly irritated. How bizarre to feel the need to defend the bad in herself. 'But my dear, you really don't know me,' she protests in an accent more English than at any time over the last three decades.

'Sure I don't know the ins and outs – who does? But I'm a good judge of character,' Juliette says, a little defensively, 'and I sense you and Bob shared something beautiful.'

'We did,' Penny says flatly, 'but at a high price. And I'm sorry, Juliette, but you are *not* a particularly good judge of character – you have me all wrong.'

'Great love isn't given to those not worthy of it,' Juliette says. Then she quickly regards her feet and looks a little bashful. 'That's a song lyric by my favourite band, actually. But it says what I believe. You *were* lucky, you and Bob. You were blessed.' She looks up and gives Penny, who is glowering, a little grin.

'But those around us weren't,' Penny says stonily. 'Juliette honey, I'm tired and I just want to drive home.'

'Sure, sure,' says Juliette, but still she loiters. 'It's just I didn't like to hear you say you were a bad seed – you're not, you're what me and my mom call a *good egg*.'

Suddenly, Penny is disconcerted that her words have been listened to so earnestly but that the impression they've given is erroneous. And that this sweet young girl, troubled by the death of a useless alcoholic father, should have Penny so wrong too. Penny might once have been wryly amused at being glorified, but just now it seems immoral.

'You draw a picture only from what you've heard,' Penny tells Juliette. 'Believe me there's a whole bunch of stuff you wouldn't want to know.'

Juliette looks a little taken aback. 'But I like you.'

'Juliette,' Penny says, scrunching her eyes shut against the headache of it all, 'if I told you I had three daughters – whom I *abandoned* when the youngest was just a baby, would you believe me? Would you like me then?'

Juliette balks. What a weird question. 'Of course I wouldn't believe you,' she says.

'Well, I did,' Penny declares hoarsely. 'I did the unbelievable, OK? I walked out on three little girls. And you know something, I actually never regretted it. Now you stand there and tell me that the love I had with Bob was a good thing. You stand there and tell me I'm not a bad seed. You tell me you like me now.'

'But—'

'I'm no better than your father – in fact I'm worse. He treated you bad when he was drunk and in some ways not accountable for his behaviour. I walked out on my children when I was stone cold sober.'

Juliette stares; disbelief and hurt and horror striating her face. Penny perversely welcomes the scorch of shame which cuts through her. 'You know what,' Penny mutters, 'I have to go.' And though Juliette stands there motionless, dumbstruck and bereft, Penny walks the short distance to her car, dumps the polystyrene container in a trash-can on the way and drives off without a backward glance.

What is one more person hating her? What is one more person to have let down? Join the queue, Juliette, join the queue.

*

Penny is still awake in the early hours of the next morning. She's sitting in the dark, in Bob's chair, wondering why. In the last twelve hours, she's said goodbye to Bob at the vantage point near Hubbardton's, she's revealed the ugly truth of her life to Juliette and she's re-recorded the answering-machine message. So why does she feel so anxious and fretful? Why is there no sense of peace, of relief, of lightness, of that oft-bandied term *closure*?

Penny knows why. She can't achieve closure because the door cannot yet be shut. It is jammed with issues she must confront and own, see in black-and-white in the clear light of day, acknowledge out loud. Where she'd gone that previous afternoon, what she'd spoken of to Juliette, what she'd recorded into the answering machine, were single strands in a knot of loose ends which need to be untied.

Stray Cat Blue

Ben hadn't asked Cat what she was going to do on her day off which, this week, fell on a Wednesday. He hadn't asked and she hadn't mentioned it because he seemed a little distracted anyway, somewhat stressed. He was sitting at the kitchen table, flicking through the newspaper as if every item of news irked him.

'Everything OK, doctor?' she asked, handing him a mug of coffee and then giving his neck a quick rub.

'What? Oh, fine,' said Ben. 'It's probably going to be a bit of a full-on day, babe. I may be home late.'

'I'll have your pipe and slippers waiting,' she laughed, stroking his closely cropped hair; the flecks of grey catching glints of silver as she did so.

'That's my girl,' he said.

'Although you may have to fetch your slippers yourself – I might be late home too,' Cat said.

'Oh? Staff meeting or something?' said Ben.

Cat shook her head. 'It's my day off,' she said. She took a seat beside him, pulled the chair close so their knees touched. He looked at her: her cheeks were a little flushed, her eyes flitted with whatever she was on the verge of saying. She gave a quick shrug. 'I'm going to go to Derbyshire. Just a day-trip.'

Ben stared at her, fighting hard to keep horror from his face. He must not let his dismay show. He must say nothing. He must smile and nod and instead say, Wow, babe, wow. He must fight the urge to say, Don't! You can't! Not today, Cat! He can't warn her that today's not a good day for a round trip to Derbyshire. Because then she'd ask why. And he couldn't say, Because Django's coming to see me. Because, as a doctor, he was bound by the Hippocratic oath. And anyway, just look at her, all flushed with the supreme effort of arriving at such a proactive and possibly tough course of action. How much late-night thinking had she done to come to this decision? How much soul-searching had she accomplished to be ready to go home and face her father? Ben loved her so much for her courage and her reckoning, but as full as his heart was for her, it bled for her too. Ben had been so anxious that Django might not make this trip – but suddenly he was hoping this would be the case precisely. Ben felt torn and compromised. He'd made the appointment on Django's behalf and without Cat's knowledge because he was worried about Django. Because he had thought it was the right thing to do. Just now, though, he wondered what right he had at all. He felt quite sick.

'What?' Cat said, her eyes darkening to khaki as her brow furrowed and she regarded Ben anxiously. 'Don't you think it's a good idea?' She looked crestfallen, her lips pouting inadvertently.

'It's an amazing idea,' Ben assured her, though his instincts goaded him otherwise. 'I'm so proud of you. Sorry – I've just got stuff on my mind. Sodding politics with the Trust and the NHS. Budgets. Funding. Targets. Sorry.'

'That's OK,' said Cat, 'but you do think I should go, don't you? It's not so much a gut instinct I'm acting on – my gut is in a knot right now – it's a carefully considered decision. The timing seems good to me. It feels like it's the right thing to do.'

'Have you told your sisters?' Ben asked. 'Are you going alone?'

'I am going alone,' Cat said, with slow, awkward nods. 'I haven't asked them along. I haven't actually told them I'm going.' She looked a little unnerved, trying to find twists of hair to bind around her finger though mostly it was too short and quickly sprung free. 'Do you think I should have told them? Or asked them along?'

'Not if you don't want to,' Ben told her while his mind sped through a variety of plausible suggestions to dissuade her from going. But it was too complicated. He needed more time to figure it all out. But Cat needed his advice. Now. 'This particular side of the story is yours,' he told her. 'You need to act on what feels right.'

'It's a rare old thing for me not to feel I have to analyse such a momentous decision with Pip and Fen first,' Cat said. 'I was proud of myself for having arrived at it on my own.'

'I'm proud of you, too,' Ben repeated. 'You'll be even more proud of yourself when you step down from the train at Chesterfield station.' And he wondered whether he should be phoning Django and alerting him. Ben's sense of duty, always hailed as one of his key qualities, was today giving him a headache. He rubbed his eyes. Not a good sign to feel this knackered at only breakfast-time. He suddenly loved his own family for being so conventional and dull. He must phone his mother, it was a good couple of weeks since he'd done so. He wouldn't phone Django. He couldn't. Ultimately, it wouldn't be fair on Cat. He rapidly justified that his duty to Cat was partly to ensure that Django kept the appointment he'd made for him.

'I don't know what I'm going to say,' Cat was saying, 'but

I feel ready to talk. To listen. I just need to make sense of my past, Ben. I feel in limbo until I do.'

Ben put his hand around the back of her neck and pulled her face close for a kiss. 'I hope you have a good day, babe,' he said. 'I hope it feels good to go back there, whatever you hear or don't.'

'Thanks,' said Cat. 'If you wait, I'll walk to the Tube with you.'

We know Django won't be there. But Cat spent the train journey alternately smiling and frowning as various scenarios came into her mind's eye. She even laughed out loud at a fanciful scene in slo-mo, she and Django running down the platform into each other's arms. Daft. She hadn't even tried the Farleymoor number from her mobile phone, let alone announced her visit to him in advance. She didn't want to give him a shock though she knew he'd be taken off guard. She anticipated his initial concern would be that he hadn't prepared anything special for lunch. What was she going to ask him? What did she hope to learn? She gazed out of the window and watched the landscape rush past, slip seamlessly from one landscape into another. The flatness of the South-East, the uniformity of the Midlands, soon enough the rolling promise of the Derbyshire Dales.

She thought about phoning from the station. Then she thought about phoning from the cab. But soon enough she was within ten minutes of the house and if she phoned now, the adrenalin coursing through her would surely give her voice little more than a whisper. The house came into view, sitting solid and squat in the grounds, as indigenous to the locality and as comfortable in the landscape as the moorland ponies or hardy little sheep.

'Just here is fine,' she told the cab-driver. She needed the walk up the drive to take deep breaths, plucking at the ivy which clustered along the drystone wall. If Django wasn't looking out of the window, she'd have the chance to stand awhile on the doorstep and collect her thoughts. As she walked up the path to the front door, she could only fix her sight on her feet. Her teeth chattered. *It's June!* she told herself, *and it's only Django*.

No Django.

No one at home.

She's been sitting on the great grey flagstone doorstep for some time, hugging her arms around herself. She'd envisaged a bear-hug from Django. It had been one of the driving thoughts that had got her here. She'd thought that no matter what she might say, or hear, that hug was a given. Only it wasn't. Because Django is not here.

The courage Cat had summoned to make this journey, the pride and excitement she'd felt in a huge affirmative surge when she'd stepped from the train at Chesterfield station, have now dwindled into disbelief and deep loneliness and despondency. Where could he be? Cat circumnavigates the house, peering into all the downstairs windows. Were there no clues? A pot of jam is on top of the *Racing Post* on the kitchen table. Not much to read into that. The living-room is extremely tidy. The flip-flops that Fen was wearing on Django's birthday, one broken, are on the bench in the utility room with other variously sized footwear neatly laid out to either side. The opaque window to the downstairs toilet is fixed ajar but though Cat squints inside, she can't really see anything, certainly no pointers to the whereabouts of the master of the house.

I don't believe this. Where can he be? Where does he go on a Wednesday? Dominoes is Thursday afternoon and he usually shops on a Tuesday and a Friday.

She taps on all the windows as she makes her way back

round to the front door. She raps on that and calls through the letter-box. She has a long look through, but the hallway is empty of details.

'Django!' she calls. 'Django!' She waits and listens. 'Where the fuck are you?' she mutters under her breath because she knows Django is not here to admonish her language. 'What am I going to do?' she sobs, sitting heavily on the doorstep.

You could go to the Rag and Thistle?

But I wanted Django to myself. And if he's not there, word will soon be out that I came looking. But that I didn't stay. Stupid man for not having a mobile phone!

Are you not going to wait awhile? Write a note?

And say what? 'Hi, Dad, I summoned every ounce of courage to come and see you. Oh well, never mind, I'll try again tomorrow?' No. *I may as well just call a cab to take me back to the station. My gesture was meant to be momentous. But all that's happened is that the moment has passed. It's all been spoilt. It's no good. I just want to go home to Ben.*

If only Django had said yes to the answering machine Pip wanted to buy him, hey?

Whatever. It was probably a stupid idea of mine anyway. Perhaps I should've run it by Pip first.

A Fish Out of Water

Django had always liked trains, but recently he liked them more so on account of Tom's fervent and endearing obsession with them. As he boarded at Chesterfield station early that morning, Django thought of Tom, thought how much he'd like to see him that day, to tell him about the Virgin train ferrying him to London and back. Wouldn't it be nice if Pip brought Tom to meet him at St Pancras? She might well have done so, had he not been Derek, the father of her youngest sister. Half sister. Anyway, they didn't know he was coming to town. Only Ben knew. He'd sent Django the ticket. Django felt uncomfortable about this. He would reimburse Ben the price of the ticket. He had the cash on him. Most, though, he felt uncomfortable about the trip itself; he didn't like London, he didn't like hospitals and he didn't like it that Ben felt it necessary to send him a ticket to ensure he'd keep the appointment.

As he settled into the seat, arranged the *Telegraph* and his Thermos flask in front of him, he tried to think of trains and tracks and north and south and not that he hadn't spoken to his girls since Pip's call to him over a fortnight ago. He curtailed the thought that told him he hadn't seen them for a month. Customarily, their visits home were every two months or so. But, devoid of all contact, this one month seemed the longest separation yet. Django thought about Cosima, wondered if she was crawling by now, imagined Fen dressing her in sweet, pink cotton creations. Did Cosima have more teeth? Did they make her grin look different? He smiled sadly but gazed out of the window as if he was particularly interested in the passengers alighting at Derby station. And was Cat perhaps pregnant, Django wondered, taking a long time to pour a cup of tea from his flask, trying to counteract the careen of the train. How wonderful that would be – although no more wonderful than Fen having Cosima or Pip having Tom of course – just a blessed situation for all three girls.

'The continuation of family,' Django said quietly, 'that's what it's all about.' And he felt appalled that his family were continuing without him. And he felt appalled that the purpose of this trip was not to visit family but to see Dr Mr Pisani. And he felt extremely disconcerted that the emotion this raised was fear.

I am seventy-five years old. I am frightened.

At Leicester, a young girl came and sat opposite Django, smiling politely before burying her nose in a novel with a candy-coloured cover festooned with illustrations of handbags, high heels and squiggly writing. So squiggly that Django had to squint hard to read the words, wondering which was the author, which was the title.

'Sandwiches, snacks, cold drinks, tea and coffee.'

The refreshments trolley was announced in robotic monotone by the stewardess, who was less trolley-dolly, more sturdy dinner-lady. Django had a good look at what was on offer because he could not believe that food could appear so unappetizing. The girl sitting opposite bought a can of fizzy something, tapping the ring-pull sharply before opening it.

'So it doesn't go insane,' she announced and Django realized he must have been staring. He felt a little awkward. Does aluminium have sanity to lose? Is this a technique that everyone knows about, instilled in all teenagers along with the importance of condoms and just-say-no when it comes to drugs? Why don't the manufacturers do something about the design, if drinks go mad unless tapped sharply? Django knew his thoughts were meandering excessively so that his mind could be diverted from Dr Mr Pisani. He rummaged around in his old canvas knapsack, the one that Pip, Fen and Cat had each clamoured to use at some point or other during burgeoning teenage trendiness. He took out a Tupperware container and regarded the selection of sandwiches he had packed. The fizzy girl was looking too.

'Carrot, cheese and Marmite,' he told her, 'or tuna, piccalilli and tomato.'

She looked at him as if he might be one of those dreaded loonies that seem to inhabit every carriage of every train journey one ever takes. Django showed her the sandwiches. 'Would you like one?' he offered. 'They're mostly organic.' She shook her head though her gaze remained fixed on the sandwiches, intrigued. 'Go on,' said Django, 'they're easy on the calories and whatnots.' She smiled meekly and shrugged, peering into the container and asking which were the carrot and cheese. Django felt a sense of triumph that she took one and, though she nibbled gingerly at first, finished the whole thing, inch-thick crusts and all. She offered Django a Malteser but he declined, saying forlornly he was watching his weight, which made her giggle.

'I'm going to see my nan,' she told him, unprompted. 'She lives near Luton.'

'I'm going to see my girls,' said Django, 'and their offspring.'

'Are you a granddad then?' asked the girl.

Django nodded proudly.

'My granddad died when I was small and I don't remember him,' the girl said with regret, 'though I tell my nan that I do, of course.' Django didn't want to talk further on this. He was now worried he'd tempted Fate and tampered with Fortune with his white lies to the girl. But what was he meant to say – that he was going by himself to St John's Hospital so that Dr Mr Pisani could put a finger up his bottom?

'Your beads are cool,' the girl was saying.

Django touched the nibs of tiger's eye and turquoise, strung on leather around his neck. 'There's a story behind them,' he said. 'It starts in New Mexico.' And he set off on an extravagant elaboration of the truth which saved him from ruminating on whether or not he'd see his girls and their offspring ever again.

'Ta for the sarnie,' said the girl, as she disembarked at Luton, 'and have fun with your family.'

'Thank you,' said Django, 'you too.'

The train shuffled into St Pancras a quarter of an hour late. Django felt agitated; which was itself exacerbated by the unfamiliarity of the emotion. He observed people in his carriage, making calls on their mobile phones to alert whomever to the train's delay. Django would have liked to have warned Ben, but he didn't have a mobile phone. He thought of Pip offering him one as a birthday present and remembered denouncing them as preposterous, invasive and unnecessary. How his girls had laughed at him. Cat had said, Nonsense Django, you won't have one because you know you won't know how to make it work. And Fen had said, Yes yes, the apotheosis of mobile communication was via smoke signals at the reservation in North Dakota so do tell us the story featuring you and Chief Lone Hawk for the umpteenth time. And Pip had said, But Django, why don't you have one just for emergencies. And he'd been comically huffy while they teased him relentlessly and laughed. They all laughed. How they laughed. Always laughter when his girls were around.

Now he felt anxious. Leaving the train, stressed passengers bustled and shoved. Django did not like London, the pace of it all intimidated him. He felt apprehensive about taking the Tube to the hospital, with two changes of lines and escalators and people rushing and being underground. And he was already fifteen minutes late, at least, though Ben's ticket had afforded him plenty of time. He kept to his regular walking pace and attempted to wear an expression that said I know where I'm going, I'm savvy, don't shove me – and there's no need to stare.

When did buskers become beggars? I busked with Flint Maystone in Paris and we had a following. We made music. We were respected. I would go so far as to say we were the precursors of skiffle. But this isn't busking, it's begging and it's threatening and how can someone so unkempt and unsightly dare to stare at me?

But the chanting, ranting beggar wasn't the only person to stare at Django. Everyone who passed him gave him more than a passing, smileless glance. You'd've thought Django would have been more of a talking point, an eyesore even, in the calm backwaters of Derbyshire, than in the swirl of London where his physical eccentricities shouldn't raise an eyebrow or bat an eyelid. However, right from the start, when he moved to Derbyshire in 1969, hirsute and kaftan-clad, with beads clanking and pony-tail flowing, they welcomed him for bringing moccasins and Pucci neckerchiefs, Astrakhan waistcoats and voluminous, embroidered flared denims to their dale.

However, on the Victoria line decades later, people steered clear of Django, as if he might bark, in case he smelt. To his consternation, he realized they held him in the same regard as they held the ranting stinking beggar on the platform. He hardly felt that a Liberty shirt, suede waistcoat and green linen drawstring trousers warranted such suspicion. Yet it made him suddenly fret that perhaps protocol dictated the wearing of a suit to see a consultant. Soon enough he was embarrassed, ashamed even, of his apparel, denouncing himself a stupid bugger and feeling miserable. Would Ben be disappointed? Would Ben have to apologize on his behalf? If he had a mobile phone, Django supposed he could have forewarned Ben of his sartorial gaffe. Perhaps Dr Mr Pisani would decline to see him. And then he could go straight back home again.

But Ben is delighted to see Django, mainly because he'd been quite convinced that he would not appear. He's been loitering around the hospital's main entrance and silently praises Django's dress sense for holding him aloft from the crowd; a beacon of colour walking awkwardly amongst the drab bustle of everyone else.

'How was your journey?' Ben asks, guiding Django through hallways and corridors to his own office. 'Would you like a drink?'

'Scotch?' Django asks hopefully. Ben laughs. 'Is the tea plastic?' Django asks. 'Do you press a button for it?'

'No,' Ben assures him, 'Marjorie makes it in a teapot. She insists. It's why I gave her the job – that perfectionism.'

'I should like a cup of tea,' Django says and Ben calls through to Marjorie.

'How are you feeling?' Ben asks.

'Oh, you know – a little like a fish out of water,' Django confides. 'I don't like this town at all.'

'And how are you feeling otherwise,' Ben asks, 'in yourself?'

'Oh, you know,' Django dismisses any gravity, 'rather good for a gent of seventy-five. Can't complain about a rickety hip, gammy knee and mischievous waterworks.'

Ben nods and smiles. 'I didn't know you have a gammy

knee and rickety hip,' he says conversationally, though privately this concerns him.

'All that thigh-slapping to Lonnie Donegan,' Django says, 'all that toe-tapping to Namesake Reinhardt.'

'Ah,' says Ben. 'I made the appointment under *Django McCabe*.'

'Bless you,' Django says quietly.

'But do you know under what name your GP has you listed?' Ben asks.

'Well, Dr Sutton always called me *Mr* McCabe in the surgery and Django at the Rag and Thistle,' Django tells him, 'but that new young girl called me *D*. McCabe. So it could be the one, or the other.'

'OK,' says Ben, 'don't you worry. I'll handle it.' Ben looks at his watch. 'Do you have any questions? About the appointment? I'll come with you – all the way, if you like.'

'Yes, thank you, Ben,' Django says with a light laugh that belies the slight tremor of his hand when he raises the tea cup to take a sip. 'Will you tell Dr Mr Pisani that you are my personal physician and anything he says to me he can say to you too? I'm no good with medical jargon.'

Ben nods.

'Thank you,' Django nods back.

'Cat is well,' Ben tells him, 'but she doesn't know you are here.'

'Thank you,' says Django.

'And Fen and Pip are well too,' says Ben.

'Thank you,' says Django.

Ben glances at his watch. 'Well, I think we'll mosey on over now,' he says and Django is so thankful that he has Ben with him today.

Mr Pisani's appearance surprises Django who had envisaged an elongated Frankie Dettori. The consultant is in his late fifties, short and round with a very shiny pate ringed by a smile of neatly slicked grey curls. He's wearing a suit with an orange tie, has a wedding ring on his plump finger and looks like a bank manager. His accent is Scottish and his voice is quiet. Django likes him immediately though the imminence of the examination dampens much banter on his part.

Notes are taken. Information is given. Django tells Mr Pisani that Ben is his personal physician. Ben nods but also offers to leave the room, anticipating that Django might play down his symptoms if he is there. But Django says, Please stay, and he furnishes Mr Pisani with a host of details – apologizing intermittently about whether they are relevant or not. He admits that perhaps his hips and knees aren't so much rickety or gammy as really fairly painful. His lower back too. And he adds that he has steered clear of beetroot so yes, he's fairly sure it's blood in his urine.

'Prostate problems are common,' Mr Pisani smiles as if Django has something akin to a simple cold of the gland. 'Today, I'll be determining if your prostate is enlarged. And if it is – which I expect it is – what the reason may be. Most chaps over the age of fifty have an enlargement, you know, and mostly it's simply a benign condition. I'm going to take blood too. With those results – and the findings of the examination – we'll be able to see what's what and what to do.'

'Righty-ho,' says Django, looking to Ben for the nod and smile which he gives.

'I think Ben has alerted you to the procedure?' Mr Pisani asks with a sympathetic raise of his eyebrows. Suddenly, Django is concerned about the plumpness of Mr Pisani's fingers, and wishes for a tall thin Frankie Dettori. 'It may be uncomfortable – but it shouldn't be painful.'

'Django?' Ben asks, noting the colour has drained from his face.

'You will stay, won't you?' says Django.

Ben tells Django fascinating anecdotes about his time with the professional racing cyclists; he speaks quickly, jauntily and in great detail, maintaining eye contact with Django who is lying on his side. And, without asking, Ben takes his hand at the opportune moment, holding it firmly yet tenderly, talking at Django the whole time.

'Thank you, Mr McCabe,' Mr Pisani says eventually. 'I'm done. Do dress. There are tissues there. Take your time.'

'Can I help?' Ben asks Django.

'No, that's OK,' says Django. Ben sees he has a tear coursing its way down his nose.

'You did brilliantly,' Ben tells him as he pulls the curtain around to afford Django his privacy. 'Take your time.' Ben takes a seat and glances at Mr Pisani who raises his eyebrow and busies himself with his notes.

Oh Christ, thinks Ben.

'Now,' Mr Pisani says chattily when Django reappears and takes his seat, 'generally speaking – *generally* speaking – an enlarged prostate ought to feel firm and smooth. Yours feels rather hard and knobbly.'

'I see,' says Django, though he doesn't know quite what he's meant to be seeing, or what Mr Pisani was meant to be looking for.

'This may suggest something a little more serious than prostate problems,' Mr Pisani continues, 'which is why the blood test is important.'

'OK,' says Django. 'You can take an armful, if you like.'

Mr Pisani smiles and nods and says a test tube will be plenty. 'Now, you see the *symptoms* of both a benign enlargement and a malignant tumour are similar. And you have presented those symptoms. But a malignant tumour *feels* rather different to a benign enlargement.'

'A malignant tumour?'

'Most prostate cancers grow very slowly indeed, Mr McCabe.'

'*Cancer?*' Django stands up and looks at Ben in bewilderment. 'Who said anything about cancer? It's my waterworks. I'm just old.'

Al and the Girl from Purley

Despite all manner of skewed rationalization, Fen felt uncomfortable and at a loss. In the past, at such times, there was always Derbyshire to escape to – even if only in the realms of her imagination – but now not even that seemed an option. She was hardly likely to phone Django, nor did she consider the cause of her discomfort an appropriate topic of discussion between sisters. What was she meant to say? She told herself her sisters wouldn't understand – they'd go on about rocky patches and she didn't want to be judged or lectured.

Fen had long had an idiosyncrasy of looking from one hand to the other when weighing issues which irked her, to assist her in making a choice. Some saw it as an affectation, but it had proved a fail-safe method for her. For the second time in his life, Matt unknowingly was being held in Fen's left palm. Four years ago, a man called James Caulfield had been in her right palm. For a while she fought against having to choose, railed against her sisters' accusation of immorality, disputed their allegation of duplicity. She'd made her choice only when she realized the love she felt for Matt was more ordinary, thus somehow deeper and more true. And she has never looked back, never wondered *What if*, never doubted her decision. But now Matt is unwittingly back in one hand, and this time Al – whose surname she doesn't even know – is in the other; yet this time they weren't unsuspecting pawns competing for Fen's love. Love wasn't coming into it at all. On the one hand, Fen feared love was lost from her relationship. On the other hand, she feared the lure of lust. Left, right. Love, lust. Right, wrong. Her scale of values was unbalanced and tipping dangerously in favour of Al.

The easiest way to keep guilt at bay and to give her feelings for Al credibility, was to blame Matt for the irritation she felt increasingly towards him. She begrudged his freedom to go to work but also resented him for not being around more, for not helping enough, for not spending quality time with Cosima. Yet when he did, his ways got on her nerves, he got in her way and ultimately, she didn't trust him to be doing things quite right so she brushed him away, did whatever it was herself, felt put upon, then resented him. In Fen's eyes, Matt couldn't win, and she felt that this was his fault. She didn't like the sound of him eating and yet she'd never noticed it before. At night, she slept with a pillow half over her head because the incessant sound of Matt sleeping kept her awake. She didn't like the monotony of their communication; his daily question of 'And how are my girls?' set her teeth on edge – Fen didn't like it that he lumped her and Cosima together, that he only half listened to her answer anyway while he opened post or checked the television listings in the newspaper. He didn't seem to notice if Fen's hair needed a wash and she was wearing stained clothing, or there again if she'd made an effort with mascara and had changed before he arrived home. She was aware that her friends and sisters would proclaim her lucky indeed to have a man who never judged her on her looks but Fen interpreted it as Matt not really noticing her at all.

Left hand, right hand. Good, bad. Right, wrong. Harmless,

dangerous. Fen's scales appeared to be peculiarly calibrated at best; at worst downright faulty. On the one hand, the marks Fen placed against Matt became blacker, on the other hand the warning signs she'd seen in Al became fainter. Taken together, their collusion was dangerous and deluded, exacerbated by the fact that it had been almost a week since she'd seen Al and she'd heard nothing. Al's desirability increased the longer the message box on her mobile phone remained empty. The less he appeared to want her, the more she wanted to pursue him. These last few days, during which she'd consulted her phone with frustration and growing insecurity, and analysed the palms of her hands with increasing regularity, Fen had reinvented Al and invested him with much more bearing than his actual gaucherie. She reassessed his shared living arrangements in deepest darkest Camden as funky and intriguing, and in her mind's eye he'd become far more buff and beautiful. She had transposed her previous image of him as a fairly nondescript young bloke, into a vision of an arresting enigma. When Matt attempted to travel his hands over her body last night, she'd initially flinched but then an image of Al's hands came into view and even all the silver rings suddenly seemed achingly sexy. So she fucked Al while Matt made love to her. She squirmed away from Matt's post-coital cuddle and then she'd put the pillow over her head to block out the warning bells as much as Matt's breathing pattern.

Fen convinced herself that her self-esteem depended entirely on Al desiring her, that if she could just seduce him, her sense of her own femininity and self-worth would be restored. And, with her head under the pillow muffling any sound of chastisement or ridicule, she gamely justified that it would do her disintegrating relationship with Matt the power of good. She'd often read about stale relationships being rejuvenated by one or other partner having no-strings secret flings; heartening accounts of how people fell in love with their partners all over again in the aftermath of affairs. If she had a fling with Al, she'd see sense, wouldn't she? A fling with Al would prove what Matt truly meant to her, wouldn't it? A fling with Al would have a positive impact on her libido and this in turn would have a positive effect for Matt. Fen was convinced that if she had a fling with Al, she'd be doing everyone a favour.

But it had been three days since she'd seen him. And because it had been three whole days and because she'd heard nothing, Fen found it easy to transform Al from a bad idea best forgotten into an exciting challenge. She convinced herself that actually, hadn't *she* told *him* that she'd be in touch?

1.12 p.m.

hey Al, ta 4 drinx. See u soon?

7.56 p.m.

If Matt had at least forewarned me that he was going to be home late, I wouldn't be sitting here, feeling neglected.

8.00 p.m.

'Oh, hi – is that Al?'

'Yes?'

'It's Fen.'

'Oh – hi Fen.'

'I just thought I'd give you a quick call – I sent you a text earlier but I think I forgot to put my name to it.'

'Ah.'

'Anyway, just thought I'd give you a quick call. How are you doing?'

'Yes – good. And you?'

'Oh, you know, busy.'

'Cool. Cool.'

'Anyway – I'd better go, I suppose. I just thought – maybe meet up for a quick drink or something?'

'Cool – I'll give you a call.'

'Great.'

'OK, Fen – bye then.'

'Bye. Oh. When? Ish?'

'Sorry?'

'Us fusty old mums need time to organize babysitters – so I was just wondering if you had an idea of when? You know – when you'd be calling and when we'd meet up?'

'Oh. Soon. Next couple of days?'

'Great. Bye Al.'

'See you, Fen.'

That call was crap. Ought I to text him to rectify? Should I just compose one and see how it looks on the screen? Or should I sit on my hands and watch Grand Designs *and keep shtum?*

Who are you asking, Fen?

And by the way, where is Matt?

Matt is having an impromptu drink after work with an old mate, Jake, with whom he shared a flat and a certain level of rakishness in their twenties. Though their thirties have led them onto divergent paths, their friendship continues and they like to meet up every now and then and live vicariously through one another, just for the duration of an entertaining evening. Jake has taken to calling Matt 'Daddy', and Matt calls Jake 'Twat'. They are in Soho and the area is buzzing. Matt hates to admit even to himself how long it has been since he last had a night out in town; he hadn't thought he'd missed it, he wasn't aware of having craved it but it's reviving to be back here, heading through the colourful milling crowd to a bar, past shops specializing in everything from whisky to ship's chandlery, gay paraphernalia to hip and costly trainers, from sushi to sex. The bar is new to Matt though Jake informs him it's been open awhile, and is *the* place to drink and Where the fuck have you been, Daddy – it's where all manner of media scandal and celebrity debauchery are often chronicled. Shut up, Twat, and buy me a beer.

While Jake orders, Matt quietly wonders if he looks out of place, whether it's obvious that he's more accustomed to slouching in front of the television with a ready meal and being in bed by midnight. He scouts other people's clothing and footwear, feeling slightly faded and last-season in comparison; resolves to spend a lunch-time and a wage packet in Paul Smith the next day. Does he feel out of place? A little, just a little at the moment. But beer will help and make all equal.

'They only do bizarre beer in piss-pale shades from places like Latvia,' Jake apologizes, setting down two over-designed bottles in front of them. 'Cheers anyway.'

'Cheers mate,' says Matt. 'How's it going?'

'Madly busy at work,' Jake rues, 'and complicated as ever at play.'

Matt laughs. Jake lights a cigarette and offers one to Matt who falters for a moment and then takes one. He was only ever a social smoker but the arrival of Cosima stipulated a nicotine-free zone and now, the head rush he experiences after the first few drags is slightly disconcerting yet nostalgic and oddly liberating.

'There's this girl,' Jake is saying, clasping the cigarette between his lips as he describes her assets crudely with his hands. 'She's a total babe – Suze – pretty young but bloody bright. Anyway, I thought she was just after a good time, you know?'

Matt nods sagely as if he does.

'Suited me fine – absolutely. You know, finally a woman after my own heart – or rather, not after my heart but only my body. No-strings sex and the like. But the weird thing is,' Jake continues, *sotto voce*, 'increasingly I find myself wanting a bit more.' Jake slaps the table and roars with laughter. 'What the fuck is all that about then? Usually they harp on at *me* about mini-breaks and meeting my parents and bollocks, and here I am, toying with the idea of asking her to move in. Here's *me*, pissed off if *she* hasn't phoned all day!'

'Bloody hell!' Matt marvels, with a glug and a drag.

'Bloody hell is right,' Jake says darkly. 'Wedding bells and babies.'

'Have you talked to her?' Matt asks. Jake answers him with a look of ridicule.

'As I say, she hasn't phoned all day,' says Jake morosely, 'but I'm damned if I'm going to call her.'

'I meant,' says Matt, 'have you talked to her about – you know – how you feel? Longevity? The C word.'

'Cunt?' says Jake.

'*Commitment*,' says Matt. 'Twat.'

'Well. Almost. You see, what complicates it,' Jake says, 'is that Ellie is still on the scene – casually.' Matt covers his eyes in mock distaste. 'I mean, I never ring her, really. Well, not really,' says Jake. 'Sometimes I do – if I'm bored or drunk or both. And when she rings me – well, it's a bit mad to turn it down, isn't it?'

To Matt, Jake's life sounds dictionary-definition mad. Momentarily, it all seems a little unsavoury too, unnecessarily complicated and way too tiring. It's not a been-there, done-that derision Matt feels as he never quite subscribed to Jake's low-level ethics, more it's an uncomfortable feeling of what the allure can still be for Jake. Isn't he bored after well over a decade of bawdiness? Oughtn't he to have outgrown such philandering? Doesn't he aspire to a more grown-up way of life? A quiet side of Matt is slightly insulted that his own lifestyle, the developments and changes, the achievements and differences, appear to hold little attraction for Jake. Though Jake usually asks after Fen, after the baby, after the mortgage and the mundanity, Matt detects a perfunctory edge before Jake deviates to humorous accounts of his own ongoing hedonism. Jake is a great raconteur – and that's the point of such evenings. But Matt has to admit that the fact that their lives are now so disparate is also the reason that they now meet so infrequently.

However, alcohol is a great leveller. Once a certain level of inebriation has been reached, Matt finds he and Jake are blokes with equal charisma, wit and highly entertaining neuroses. So they drink and they smoke and they banter. They put the world to rights, they re-train the England soccer squad and they recite lengthy tracts from *The Office*. Jake confides that he had to be treated for chlamydia after a mad week in Aya Napa and Matt reveals that a baby and a sex life is a contradiction in terms.

'Do you not fancy Fen like you used to?' Jake asks, with slurred concern. 'I've heard about this – it's a syndrome, mate. Once you've seen what her vagina is really for, you can never see it as your playpen again.'

But Matt shakes his head.

'Oh!' Jake whispers. 'Oh.' He nods his head earnestly. 'I've heard about that too,' he says. 'It's another syndrome – that childbirth alters, well, the feel of the fuck. Like a familiar room with all the furniture moved around. Or, worse, *gone*.'

Matt laughs but shakes his head. Jake looks a little surprised that he's wrong again.

'Too tired?' he tries.

'Partly,' says Matt.

'Oh God – she's not up the duff again is she?'

'Hardly!' Matt snorts. He contemplates the cocoon of ash lying pristine on his knee. He flicks it away. 'I'm not getting it because Fen seems to have gone off me.'

'Maybe she's still – you know – *sore*?'

'What, ten months on?' Matt argues. 'Mate – it's like her opinion of herself has altered. She has this whole new identity. She loves being a mummy but she's not that into being my girlfriend.'

'She turns you down?' Jake is appalled.

'I guess,' says Matt, 'yes. And when we do have sex – I sense it's more like she just wants a simple shag. An orgasm – and quick.'

'Man,' sighs Jake, 'I've been searching my whole life for a simple shag.'

Matt shrugs. 'You know what I mean.'

Jake doesn't, but he nods anyway as he's not particularly interested in developing this strand of the conversation.

'You know something,' says Matt, 'I wonder if we hadn't had Cosima whether we'd have split up by now.' He picks at the label on the beer bottle. 'But I also wonder if our relationship would have been better without having a baby. Terrible thing to think, really.'

'Like you can't have the one without the other – or you can't have both? Or something?' Jake asks, his eyes drawn to three girls ordering at the bar.

'Something like that,' says Matt.

'Fantastic,' says Jake. Matt frowns until he realizes he's referring to the girls who are sending lascivious glances in their direction.

Usually, the point at which Jake starts to prowl is when Matt decides to bale out and go home. He tends to glance at his watch and calculate the maximum sleep he needs against the hours of sleep he's actually going to have. This is when Matt usually slaps Jake on the shoulder and tells the girl, or girls, to look after his mate. And this is the point when Jake says 'Goodnight, Daddy' and feels a slight sense of relief that he's free to continue the evening in his own inimitable way. This is when Matt goes home. As you'd expect. He's a father after all. It's not seemly to drink into the small hours; it's irresponsible. So go home, Matt.

But Matt sees little point in going home. Fen will just say he stinks of booze and fags and forbid him from going anywhere near the baby and then reproach him for the fact that it all amounts to her being the one who's always up at the crack of dawn despite her matchless tiredness. So Matt doesn't go home because just now he doesn't like who's at home; what he likes more is the upbeat revelry of his immediate milieu. And he likes the girls who have come, pouting and posturing over to him and Jake. He likes the way one of them licks her lips while he's speaking. She's hanging on his words and his arm because she's a little unsteady on her feet; not surprising, considering the combination of cocktail and the precarious height of her fuck-me shoes. Matt doesn't quite know what he's talking about but she seems to find him scintillating and hysterically funny. When she throws her head back like that, her throat looks so lickable. He likes her pierced navel, there's a sparkly dangly thing hanging from it. And look at the tantalizing wobble of her high, nubile – oh Christ – braless breasts.

What did you say her name was, Matt?

'Are you married?' she's asking him.

'Nope,' Matt says.

'Is your mate?' she asks, trying to focus on Jake who has an arm around each of her friends.

'God no,' Matt laughs.

'I'm so pissed,' she complains, lolling into Matt's chest.

'Me too,' Matt agrees, using it as an excuse to drape his

arm around her and flop his hand down to the small of her back. If she brings her face up, he knows they'll snog. In fact, he wants her to, so he strokes the small of her back and extends his fingertips beyond the unmistakable boundary to her buttocks. Up comes her face and in slips Matt's tongue. He can taste Bailey's and Marlboro Lights. For the first time in five years, he is sharing his mouth with a woman other than Fen.

'Hey! Daddy!' says Jake. 'Let's go to Eddie's.'

Matt takes his mouth away from the girl's though his hand keeps her clasped against him. 'Who's Eddie?' he asks, wondering why Jake isn't raising eyebrows at him, or looking remotely shocked, or even amused.

'It's this late-night drinking den in Dean Street,' Jake says with a glance around, as if embarrassed to be in the company of someone who's never heard of Eddie's.

'Why did he call you Daddy?' the girl is asking Matt, who ignores her.

'Nah!' Matt says to Jake. 'I'm going to head home.'

The girls with Jake look at their friend. 'You coming to Eddie's?' they ask her.

'Nah,' she says, just like Matt.

Jake and the girls shrug, say a brief goodbye and head off.

So, Matt, are you going to head home then?

Yeah, I'll just have one for the road first.

One what?

When it's very late and you're drunk and horny in a bar in Soho, where do you go? As Matt snogs the girl, he asks himself this question. They're still in the bar, but they've found an enclave with a curved leather banquette. He's bought them a drink which they haven't yet touched. They've been groping at each other while sucking face; there's a teenage randiness to it all which Matt is, literally, lapping up. He is sitting, legs spread, with a hard-on bulging shamelessly through his trousers. Every now and then, the girl sweeps her hand over it in a kind of maintenance check. Matt's been feeling her breasts through her top and because it's so skimpy and because she's not wearing anything underneath, she's as good as naked to his touch.

'Let's go back to yours,' she suggests.

Matt looks at her as if she's mad. But how's she to know his child and the mother of his child are there? He's told her Jake calls him Daddy because he's the eldest. He's told her he calls Jake Twat because he is one.

'Can't,' he replies to her, 'there are people there.'

She shrugs this off.

'Where do you live then?' he asks.

'Purley,' she says.

Even in his drunken state and despite his aching balls, Matt assesses that Purley is pointless. The taxis would cost a fortune. 'Purley,' he says. 'Oh.'

'There's the loos here,' she says. 'They're big and posh and this place turns a blind eye to people going in pairs.' She taps the side of her nose as if she knows a secret and it takes a while for Matt to realize she's alluding to cocaine.

'Have you got any?' he asks, actually feeling his desire for drugs is more iniquitous than the adulterous lust bulging in his trousers.

'Ruby's got the wrap,' she says forlornly, 'but I reckon your mate had most of it anyway.'

Matt thinks he's probably relieved. At the same time, he's slightly disconcerted that he didn't realize Jake had been doing drugs that evening. That Jake hadn't offered any to him. Though, in all probability, Matt would have refused. If this girl had in fact had some, would he? He's too drunk to debate it. She's winking at him, nodding her head in the direction of the toilets.

And off they go, hand in hand, no one is in the lead.

The cubicle is spacious; faux panelled with strangely subdued lighting. There's loo paper on the floor and a Vent-Axia whirring away, affording a contradictory soundproofing of sorts. As soon as they're in, with a giggle and a fast lock of the door, they're snogging and fumbling and grappling and groping again. Matt has pulled her top to one side so he can see her tits in the flesh. They're fabulous: sizeable but pert with keen dark nipples craving his attention. While he sucks, she ruffles his hair through her fingers, backs up against the wall and spreads her legs, guiding his hand up in between. He rubs his fingers ravenously against the gusset of her thong. She gyrates against him and his thumb probes under the material to the lips of her sex. She's shaven. He's aching, there's a sackload of spunk which has been cramped in the holding bay of his balls for what seems like hours.

'Have you got a condom, then?' she asks. Matt frowns. 'You've got to pull out then, all right?'

In spite of the alcohol, Matt's inner voice is suddenly sharply lucid. The harder the facts of the imminence of infidelity, the softer his cock becomes. Man's best friend. Warning balls. He's far more grateful for his flaccidness than he is embarrassed by it.

'Don't worry,' she says sweetly, glancing at Matt's limp penis and she sits on the toilet and takes a pee. 'Another time, maybe? Shall we go to Eddie's?' she says conversationally, while wiping herself with loo paper and righting her thong. 'See if Twat and the girls are there?'

'I'm going to head home,' Matt says.

'Will you see me into a cab, then?' she asks.

And he does. And he says that of course he'll call her though he's aware that she's not aware that she hasn't given him her number nor asked for his. He flags down a taxi for her and watches it go. He finds that he's now utterly sober. So sober that his mind is reeling with frantic theories on what constitutes infidelity. He doesn't want a cab, he wants to walk and think and fast. As he marches up Wardour Street, weaving his way through all the people, he wonders if he just cheated on Fen. He justifies that he was drunk. He reasons that it wasn't sex anyway, in the penetrative sense. When push was about to come to shove, he had not wanted it, regardless of the state of his cock. But had what he had done amounted to being unfaithful? Was it possible to rank degrees of infidelity and if so, how far down the scale had he just stooped? He'd snogged another woman, had a grope and a feel. So his heart hadn't been in it, his mind hadn't been on it, his dick hadn't been sucked and his conscience had remained firmly trothed to Fen. But the urge had been there and whose fault was that? Could he blame Fen? Or had he only himself to blame? Or should he marvel that his love for her had caused his inner voice to yell out, Stop? He crossed over Oxford Street and walked briskly along Tottenham Court Road, feeling slightly hostile towards the pockets of pissed-up people for whom a night out in town was still young and promising. Despite the crowds of people, no one but him had any thoughts of home so he flagged a taxi with ease.

'Good night out?' the cabbie asks him chirpily, having passed comment on the weather, the traffic conditions and Ken Livingstone.

'Crap,' Matt says, glowering at his reflection in the window.

'Coming home empty-handed are we?' the cabbie chuckles. 'Your powers of persuasion let you down tonight?'

Matt looks up, straight into the eyes of the cabbie staring back at him from the rear-view mirror. 'Quite the opposite,' Matt says. 'She was up for it. I wasn't.'

'Heart strings not plucked, then?'

Christ will he not just shut up!

'My heart's at home,' Matt says while wondering why he hadn't shut up, himself.

'Ah,' the cabbie sighs, 'so you knocked temptation back to touch. Good for you, mate.'

'I had a touch,' Matt mumbles, 'it didn't feel good at all.'

'Precisely,' says the cabbie, 'so it *was* good for you.'

Cat Out of the Bag

The last thing Matt felt like doing, two days later, was to go out again. However, the choke of guilt, the nauseated regret, became more severe in Fen's presence. When he was at work, he longed to be at home, as if he imagined Fen and, to a lesser extent Cosima, suddenly unprotected without him there. When he was apart from her, he desperately needed her in sight – even if this meant apologizing to her photograph which he carried in his wallet. He stroked the image with the tip of his little finger, proclaiming to her that he'd never drink again, that he'd see no more of Jake, that he'd re-focus his eyes for Fen alone. What had happened was nothing, just stupidity; it had felt vile, a lesson had been learnt. Or so he kept telling himself. Yet in Fen's company, he couldn't even meet her eye, so convinced was he that he wore his sin as a sandwich board, guilt writ large all over his face. All he could do was feign tiredness as the cause for his uncommunicativeness, close himself off by watching *The West Wing* on DVD, while Fen made much of doing all the tidying up, all the cooking and all the laundry. When Matt did glance at her, hoping to bestow a loving, affirming smile, he found himself flinching away, as if her top was emblazoned with You fucking bastard how could you. So, though a part of Matt felt he should go home directly, to silently beg her forgiveness and declare his utter steadfastness and enduring loyalty, when Ben phoned and suggested they meet at the Mariners, Matt embraced the opportunity to be distracted from both his atonement and culpability.

Ben had beers waiting for them.

'How's life?' Zac asked. 'Pip told me about Cat's non-trip up North. Is she OK?'

Ben took a visibly deep breath. 'She'll be fine,' he said, 'but I have to tell you both something and it's about Django.' Ben looked from Matt to Zac and saw the same look of surprise and enquiry. 'He's told me to tell you. It's not nice. The long and short of it is he came to the hospital for some tests and he has prostate cancer.'

'For fuck's sake,' said Matt, closing his hand over his eyes.

'Cancer?' said Zac. 'Jesus.' Ben let the news sit with them a moment. 'Hang on,' said Zac, 'he was down *here*? In London? When?'

'The day that Cat went up to Derbyshire,' Ben said, shaking his head. 'Last Wednesday. I made an appointment and sent him a train ticket. It was the only way I could be sure he'd have it looked into – he wouldn't go to his GP. And I'd noticed some signs a while ago – before all the Derek–Mother shit.'

'Does Cat know now?'

'No. He didn't want anyone to know. And now he wants me to tell you. And us to tell them.'

'Christ,' Zac and Matt said in unison.

'Poor sod,' Matt said sadly. 'What's the prognosis?'

'It's difficult to say at this stage,' said Ben. 'It's not uncommon and it's usually very slow growing – sometimes the effect of the treatment is much worse than the symptoms of the cancer itself. Often sufferers can live out a normal lifespan. However, he has pain in his hip, leg and back which suggests it may have spread to the bone. He's only had a physical exam and blood tests. Now he needs an ultrasound, then we're into the territory of biopsies and scans. The results will take a while but they'll show the grade and stage of the cancer.'

Matt and Zac sat silent and shocked. 'I can't believe this,' Matt said with audible alarm.

'What treatment will he have?' Zac said.

'It depends on what the tests reveal,' Ben said. 'It's not my area. But I know around one in twelve men are diagnosed with this illness. He may have had it for years – it tends to be without symptoms in the early stages.'

'I can't believe it,' Matt rued again. 'What are we going to do about the girls?'

'I have no sodding idea,' Ben sighed, 'which is why I thought we should meet. Cat is up and down at the moment.'

'Fen too,' said Matt.

'And Pip,' said Zac.

'Is he OK?' Zac asked. 'You know, psychologically?'

Ben smiled sadly. 'Beneath the neckerchief and dodgy trousers, there's an ill man of seventy-five. And unfortunately, the tests are pretty unpleasant.'

'Is he coming back down for the tests?' Zac asked. 'Perhaps we could arrange for him to see the girls then?'

'He's been referred to his local oncology department,' Ben said.

'He needs support,' Matt said, 'he needs his girls.'

'So what are we going to do about them?' Zac asked. 'I could tell Pip,' he offered, 'then she could tell the others? She's suggested to them that the three of them should go up to Derbyshire soon, anyway.'

Matt nodded but Ben shook his head. 'I don't know. I

know their traditional dynamic is to look to Pip for advice – but that dynamic was turned on its head by the mother showing up and the Derek business and the whole parentage thing. I speak for Cat, of course,' said Ben, 'because I think somewhere, deep down, she just can't help fearing that she's slightly less of a sister to your two than they are to each other.'

'Which is horse shit,' Matt assured him, backed up by Zac raising his glass.

'I know that,' said Ben. 'It's stupid, I know, but it's where her mind is at just now.'

'They should know at the same time,' Zac said. 'I could do a dinner gathering and we could tell them all together.'

'I don't know,' Matt said. 'It's going to be such a massive thing – we don't know how they'll react individually. And then there's Cosima – if we're round at yours, Fen will have half her mind on how the baby is.'

'Good point,' said Ben, 'and I think Cat might feel a bit compromised – like we've engineered a situation. She's very particular about her comfort zone at the moment – even if it is behind the closed doors of our rental place in Clapham.'

'The thing is, we *are* going to need to engineer it,' said Zac.

'Meticulously,' Matt agreed.

The three men sipped their beer contemplatively, half their thoughts directed to Django, half to their girls. 'I reckon we tell them separately but at the same time,' said Ben. 'We agree on a time, and specific information – perhaps down to the very wording.'

Matt and Zac nodded in agreement. 'I think we also let them know that we met to discuss this,' said Matt, 'that it's what Django wants. And that they're each hearing the news at the same time in the same way.'

'OK,' said Zac, 'this is good. We also need to decide which

order they'll phone each other. I know it sounds contrived but our McCabe girls have a tendency to leap on their emotional high horses and bolt. We can't have them all in a scatter – they're going to need each other.'

'Agreed,' said Matt and Ben.

'You find in traumatic situations, those involved need assistance in deciding what to do and how to do it,' said Ben. 'Cat is still insecure, somewhere, about the dynamic between her and her sisters. Perhaps she should make the first call. I'll have her phone Pip – and then Pip can phone Fen?'

Matt and Zac nod. They've gone off their beer.

'This is crap news,' Matt said forlornly. 'Really horrible.'

'It'll be the making or the breaking of them,' Zac agreed.

'As a family,' defined Ben, 'as well as individually.'

They dreaded being grilled by the girls when they arrived home because it had been settled that nothing would be said until 9 p.m. the following evening when the situation would be revealed according to the information advised by Ben, the precise wording honed by the three of them.

When Zac arrived home, Pip was watching a cable health channel about having babies, but she zapped over to E4 hurriedly.

'How was your evening?' she asked casually, reducing the volume.

'Fine,' Zac said, 'but you carry on. I have a little work to do.' And he disappeared with his laptop to sit on the edge of the bed, feeling winded and sad.

Matt came home to find Fen already asleep. He spooned up gently against her and mouthed 'Sorry' over and over again into her hair.

'You reek of booze,' she muttered sleepily, hitching her shoulder up a little to block him out.

Cat was full of beans when Ben returned because Jeremy was leaving to run the Basingstoke branch of Dovidels and had intimated to Cat that she should apply for his post.

'Everything's looking up,' Cat exclaimed, giving him a hug.

The Ten o'Clock News

Fen's morning started very well indeed. It was warm enough to dress Cosima in a broderie anglaise sundress with matching puffy knickers and frilled cloche hat which Matt's mother had bought her. The baby looked adorable and her matchless beauty in her mother's eyes made the day seem even more balmy. There were new gurgles, from which Fen could deduce a private language of sorts and she conversed with her daughter enthusiastically, not caring how daft she might sound. Cosima was also trying out a commando slither pre-crawl and Fen could not be more proud had her baby stood up and danced a jig. Strolling along to Musical Minis, chortling to Cosima in gobbledygook, pointing out the red letter-box, the nice mister postman and the big yellow truck, Fen felt her mobile phone vibrate through a message. She retrieved it from the back pocket of her jeans, the pair she'd been able finally to fit back into today, oh joyous day, for the first time, not minding that they felt comfortably snug.

Hi f - drinx 2nite? Al

Feeling comfortingly smug, Fen spent the next half-hour composing various answers whilst singing the tunes at Musical Minis by rote. Her walk home had her weigh up which order was best – phone Pip to check babysitting was possible, or text Al first to accept and then work through babysitting options later. Her sense of maternal duty was far stronger than her sense of adventure so she called Pip first.

'Shouldn't be a problem at all,' said Pip.

'Are you sure you don't mind coming to mine, though?' Fen double-checked. 'I'll be able to give Cosima her supper but then you'll be in charge of bath, bottle, bed.'

'No probs,' said Pip, 'we'll flood the house, drink the fridge dry and have a pillow fight. Who's this friend?'

'Oh, just Al – we meet up every now and then.'

'Have I met her?' Pip asked.

Fen realized that if she denied Al a gender, she could further avoid revealing her agenda to Pip. 'Probably,' she said casually. 'Thanks – you're the best auntie in the world.'

'You mean the best auntie north of the river,' Pip laughed. 'Have you spoken to Auntie Cat?'

'Yes, we had a chat yesterday when the boys were out,' said Fen.

'I think she sounds a bit brighter,' said Pip.

'I agree,' Fen agreed.

'We really should think about making a trip home,' said Pip, 'the three of us together.'

'You're right,' said Fen. 'Tell us when.'

The morning had not been going well for Matt and just before lunch-time, it became worse. The network at the office was still down, the art editor had thrown up in the corridor, the printers were breathing down Matt's neck and the news about Django was playing on his mind. So when he saw it was Fen bleeping through a text message, what he really hoped for was the tonic of sweet nothings. After all, it had been her speciality in their courtship days – daft e-mails and cute texts and the occasional soppy card sent by snail-mail to work. Old-fashioned and romantic was the girl he'd fallen for. He had to admit, sadly, that since having Cosima, if texts came from Fen at all, they were usually asking what time he'd be back and could he detour via Marx+Sparx. What Matt needed just then was a thnkng of u F xxx. What he read was something else.

havng drinx w/ old pal Al this pm – wont b late. Pip bb-sittng – don't rush! F x

Matt swivelled in his chair and racked his memory for an old pal called Al. Then he re-read the message and wondered why just the one kiss. Then he thought, Shit! she can't – not tonight, sorry Al – and he phoned Zac directly.

'Slight problem,' he said to Zac. 'Fen's organized a drink with some old friend and has roped Pip in to babysit until I'm back.'

'Damn,' pondered Zac. 'How can we prevent this without suspicions being raised?'

'I don't know,' said Matt. 'It's so rare for Fen to go out anyway. Any ideas?'

'I could call Pip,' Zac said, 'think of something that makes babysitting not possible – make her let Fen down?'

'Great,' said Matt. Then he paused. 'No it's not. We can't have anything come between the sisters today – and you know their potential to strop and sulk with each other.'

'God, you're right,' said Zac, who privately didn't want anything to come between him and his wife at the moment either. Recently she'd been not so much distracted as frosty.

'I'll phone Ben,' said Matt, 'and get back to you.'

'I was just about to call you,' Ben responded calmly to Matt's concern. 'Panic not – Cat called to say she's working a late shift to impress some honcho or other from head office – so let's just change mission time to 10 o'clock?'

'Twenty-two hundred hours,' Matt said through his fist to sound like a war film fighter-pilot, 'roger that.'

'Will Fen be back by then?' Ben asked. 'And sober?'

'Nowadays she is practically asleep by 9.30 and decrees more than two glasses of spritzer to be anathema to motherhood,' Matt said. 'You wait and see – Cat'll be the same.'

Privately, Ben hoped Cat wouldn't keep him waiting too long on that front. 'Listen,' he said to Matt, 'hope it goes well.'

'Yes,' said Matt, 'for you, too.'

'We'll touch base later,' Ben said.

'We will,' said Matt. He phoned Zac. 'Sorted. We have a later kick-off set for 10 o'clock.'

'Good,' said Zac, 'thanks for that.'

'Bizarre, isn't it,' Matt said darkly, 'to make light of it is the only way I can deal with it at the moment. Because actually, I'm fucking dreading it.'

'Me too,' Zac agreed. 'God – me too.'

'Speak later,' said Matt. 'Good luck.'

Matt and Zac and Ben sat there, in their offices, their working day stretching ahead replete with other people's problems. Ben had a wincing queue of twisted ankles and torn ligaments clamouring for his attention; Zac had corporate clients shirking millions of taxable pounds onto his shoulders; Matt had the irate printers and the hacking wafts of his art editor's vomit to deal with. But it all seemed like child's play in relation to the task and trauma of the evening to come.

'She's eaten loads,' Fen said proudly, delighting in her sister's obvious adoration of her daughter. Pip took Cosima from Fen and pulled what her family call her Guppy Face. Cosima glanced at her mother, as if to double-check this gurning lady was indeed funny, as if to seek parental go-ahead to chortle at this fish-faced auntie. Everything was making Fen laugh today and she and her baby squeaked with delight as Pip ran through her entire repertoire of animal impersonations, from chameleon to tortoise to two-toed sloth.

'She's so gorgeous,' Pip declared mistily, stroking Cosima's silk-fine hair.

'I know,' Fen cooed, 'she's the best little girl in the world.'

'You are *so* lucky,' Pip said while giving Cosima an affectionate squeeze.

'I made a list,' Fen said, with apologetic guilt, glancing towards the sheet of paper on the kitchen table. Pip raised her eyebrow. She could see it was densely written and awash with asterisks. 'Humour me?' Fen implored.

'If it says, Check milk temperature – I'll be offended,' Pip said.

'Of course it says, Check milk temperature,' Fen said, 'and the bath temperature too—'

'Use the inside of my wrist for the former, the outside of my elbow for the latter,' Pip mocked before Fen could say just that. 'Go and get yourself ready,' Pip chided, 'or you'll be late. I think I have met Al.'

'Yes?' Fen said vaguely. 'We're not that close – just fun to meet for a quick drink every now and then. We're hardly bosom buddies.' And suddenly an image of Al getting to know her bosoms simultaneously horrified yet thrilled her and she hurried away to change.

Pip couldn't decide whether to continue cuddling Cosima or to flop to the carpet and play with her. It was 5.30, just a precious hour and a half to fit in games, baths, bottles and bedtime cuddles. Fen was certainly indulging in a long shower. 'Hope she doesn't take all the hot water,' Pip said to Cosima, 'because I'm going to make you a great big bubbly bath.' She had to admit Cosima didn't seem remotely bothered and smelt good enough to eat anyway.

When Fen reappeared, Pip was quite taken aback. She hadn't seen her sister look like this for a long time. And she looked great. Her hair was glossy, having been blow-dried to perfection, and she'd eschewed her customary pony-tail to wear her hair loose and lovely. Her make-up was subtle but meticulous. She was in a dress Pip was sure she hadn't seen before though quite when Fen had taken herself shopping she didn't know. And wasn't it just a week or so ago that she'd endured that unsuccessful trip to Whistles?

'You look amazing,' Pip said. She frowned. Odd to make so much effort for someone who was hardly a bosom buddy. 'Is that dress new?'

Fen nodded guiltily. 'You can borrow it if you like.'

'Well, you look particularly gorgeous –' Pip said and though she'd intended to finish the sentence there, the niggle at the back of her mind made itself heard, '– for a quick drink with someone you only see once in a while.' Just then, Pip couldn't work out if her sister feigned not to hear or did not deign to comment but she did note that Fen did not want Cosima's dribbly kisses or sticky fingers anywhere near her frock. 'Doesn't your mummy look pretty!' Pip cooed to Cosima, trying to hand the baby over, but Fen busied herself with a glass of water. 'Where are you meeting?' Pip asked, because it was a reasonable question. She set Cosima down at Fen's feet.

'Some bar in Camden,' Fen replied, stooping awkwardly to stroke her baby's head whilst tucking the fabric beyond her touch.

'Why Camden?'

'Oh, Al suggested it,' said Fen casually, 'it's his stamping ground.'

'Well, that sounds like your cab,' Pip said airily though she was awash with the information confirming Al as male. 'Have a great time – and don't worry about Cosima.'

'Thanks,' said Fen, gazing reflectively, momentarily guiltily, at the baby in her sister's arms. 'Thanks. Nighty-night gorgeous girl.'

Pip marvelled that Cosima waved to her mummy all by herself. It seemed just the other day that her chubby little arm had to be held aloft on her behalf. It felt so nice to have the weight of the baby hitched on her hip. Once she closed the door, she went to the mirror, delighted that the sight looked as natural as it felt.

'So,' said Pip, taking the baby upstairs, 'so Al's a "he". If your mummy tried to hide the fact from me, what can she have told your daddy?'

Pip trusted the veracity of her vibes in the same way that Fen trusted the palms of her hands, and just then Pip's vibe was one of warning. Her instinct to protect kicked in, but she wasn't sure who warranted it first or the most. Cosima? Matt? Or in fact Fen? If she was to protect Cosima from a misbehaving mother, if she were to protect Matt from abandonment, and both Cosima and Matt from potential heartache, she should reach out to Fen first. But Fen was being evasive, Fen was being deceitful, Fen wouldn't look her in the eye and give her a straight answer. Fen had everything to hide and thus nothing to confide. Though Pip felt very angry with her sister she felt impotent too; if her sister felt beyond reproach it was because she'd carefully taken herself out of sight and far from earshot, down to Camden for a secret rendezvous with some bloke called Al.

'She's made me an accessory to her crime – roping me in to babysit,' Pip said in a sing-song voice. She mounded bubbles on Cosima's head. 'Poor Cosi. Am I facilitating this – unwittingly or not – whatever it may be?' She sponged the baby gently. 'It's bad enough your mummy is using me – it's worse that she's consciously deceiving me too. But would I feel differently if she had asked outright, if she'd said, Cover for me, Pip? Would I have covered for her then?'

Pip smiled at the baby. One of a clown's skills is to multi-task, to juggle whilst singing, to converse solemnly whilst limbs veer off on an energetic mime of their own, to talk to the audience earnestly whilst concentrating on sleight of hand, to tell jokes with a straight face, to appear to be doing one thing yet enabling something else to be happening. So while Pip bathed the baby and sang about the AllyAllyOh, she thought about Fen. And Al. As much as she wanted to denounce her, she had to consider how lovely Fen had looked. It was so much more than the sum of a gorgeous frock, clean hair and careful make-up. She glowed on account of her demeanour. Pip had to concede that Fen appeared hearteningly, refreshingly ebullient.

'I remember that Fen,' Pip said nostalgically, 'but I'm worried about this one.'

Fen was right on time and momentarily she wondered whether to tell the cab-driver to go on a little, so she could walk back and not risk arriving before Al for a second time. But then she reasoned that if Al was there already she'd be denying herself his company. So she went in. And of course Al wasn't there yet.

She bought herself a tonic water because she wanted to pace herself and anyway, she could always say it was vodka and tonic. The bar was painted purple and, with the dark red plush booths and tea lights everywhere, the interior seemed far more convivial to a winter setting than the gorgeous June evening. Fen told herself that perhaps she'd simply brazenly suggest they have a quick one here and go on somewhere else.

I only want a little bit of fun; I hope to take home something I can call upon and remember when I'm feeling frumpy or weighed down by the drudge of the day – something to raise a private smile when it's most needed. Isn't everyone entitled to a small, risk-free escapade? Don't little secrets go a long way? I can feed my soul without hurting a soul.

She checked her phone. No messages. Al was now ten minutes late. And her tonic water was nearly finished.

Here he is.

'Shit – Fen, I'm so sorry,' Al flustered. 'I just completely – well, anyway, I'm sorry. How are you? Can I get you a drink? What's that?'

'Don't worry!' Fen implored him, dismissing his apologies as unnecessary. 'No problem! I was late myself! I'd love a drink – vodka and tonic, please.'

She snuck a glance at him while he ordered. He looked different to last week. Shorter, younger, plainer. That ghastly, cheap, tinny jewellery. Momentarily, Fen felt disappointed, as if all her efforts were somewhat unwarranted. But when he brought her drink over, set it down, kissed her cheek as he sat and commented on how nice she smelt, she called herself a daft cow and told herself to have fun because she was in control.

And she did have fun. She had fun because she could not afford for the evening to be anything but. She contrived to come across as lively and feisty and before long, she believed that she was. She ignored it when Al said things that were slightly puerile or rather dull and she tried not to waste time feeling irritated by him drumming along to music she didn't know, his index fingers chopping the table edge, his top teeth biting down on his bottom lip as if he were in torment. Her job was not to judge Al, but to present herself. So she tossed her hair and dipped her head coyly and licked her lips lasciviously and fluttered her eyelashes becomingly. It didn't really matter what she thought of him, just as long as she could weave some kind of spell that had him craving her. She knew to flatter him, to pout a little while he spoke, to laugh in excess. And to touch him. Every now and then she laid her hand on his arm, his wrist, nudged his knee. When he teased her about her not knowing some new band or other, she flicked his chin with her finger. And he caught her hand and while he held it for a suspended moment, she had the presence of mind to raise her eyebrow cockily and belie the welling adrenalin causing her stomach to flip.

'Shall we go on somewhere?' Fen asked because a football match was now being shown on the plasma screen and Al's eyes were drawn to it. He looked at her. 'Silly game,' she said.

'Go back to mine?' Al suggested, a little drunk by now. 'My place is just around the corner.' Fen stood up as her answer, smoothed her dress and jutted her bust just within the ambivalent side of perceptibly.

After the gloom of the purple interior, the bright evening was dazzling. A small voice told her to suggest a walk along the canal, a snack at an outside table, an ice cream from Marine Ices, but Al's hand around her waist led her away from such thoughts.

I won't stay if there are batik bedspreads as wall hangings.

There aren't.

I won't stay if there are lads lolling about.

There are lads lolling about, watching the football, but they appear not to notice Al come in. Or you.

I'll go if the kitchen is grimy.

It is surprisingly spruce.

I'll say I'm fine if he offers me a drink.

He's handing you a glass of wine whether you've asked for it or not.

Well, I won't drink it.

Al is rolling a joint.

And I won't be smoking that.

'Come on, let's go upstairs.'

Not if it's to your bedroom.

Well, you never know, Fen, perhaps the house has a delightful roof garden and that's where he's taking you.

But he isn't because it hasn't.

And remember, no batik bedspreads – I'll leave directly if he has one on his bed, let alone on the wall. Same goes for joss sticks. And Jim Morrison posters. Or Che Guevara. Or that Andy Warhol banana.

Where do you stand on mattresses-on-the-floor?

I hate those.

Al has one. But it is covered with a Conran bedspread.

That's different, then.

Be careful Fen.

She tinkers with his things, peers at photos of strangers she'll never meet but who grin alongside this man in whose bedroom she's mooching. Al is sitting on a pine trunk, having problems lighting the joint. She's planning to take a drag without inhaling. She never liked weed, it always made her feel discombobulated and queasy. She's intending to say something funny, like, I only do Class A drugs. But then she worries this might run the risk of him or his friends brandishing wraps of cocaine or handfuls of E.

'Fen?'

Al was looking at her in a dopey haze, offering the spliff. She saunters over but soon realizes that to puff without inhaling is harder than it seems. Oh well, one drag won't hurt. One drag and that's it. God it is strong.

She smiles and goes away to look at an abstract print. This is the wrong thing to do as the trompe l'oeil of prismatic colour exacerbates her headrush. She's pretending to look at old concert tickets, Blu-tacked to the wall, but actually she's staring at the white paint in between. She feels a little nauseous. Silently, she vows not to touch spliff from this day on if only the nausea would please just abate.

Al is behind her. He has slipped his hands either side of her waist. The surprise of him there, his lips at the back of her neck, have straightened her head and she finds she can close her eyes and concentrate on his touch without feeling dizzy. He's travelling his hands, down her hips, around the front of her thighs, inner thighs, oh God even inner more. He's missed out her stomach and gone straight for her breasts. He's now sucking and kissing at her neck and he's turning her to face him. Fen is suddenly terrified. Does she really want to kiss him? She hasn't time to figure it out because his tongue is in her mouth and she keeps her eyes closed and momentarily envisages Brad Pitt because she's not sure she wants the reality of kissing a bloke called Al whom she hardly knows. Luckily, the weed has fired Fen's naturally vivid imagination and she finds Brad is an excellent kisser. It's thrilling to feel his hands caressing, groping, being led by his excitement for her. With her eyes closed, she sucks Brad's ear lobe and grazes his neck with her mouth while he undoes the zip of her dress. The dress falls away and Fen keeps her eyes shut because she's conjured an airbrushed and idealized image of her figure in her mind's eye and she daren't open her eyes and find her physique causing anything other than awe and delight. But Brad is gorging on her breasts and searching for a way underneath her panties, so she needn't worry. Fen is wet and suddenly she wants to be fingered and sucked and fucked and she's so hot and turned on and slightly woozy that she no longer cares if it's Brad Pitt or Al.

And then a mobile phone rings and she knows that it's hers. She'll let it ring out. It does. They'll leave a message. No, they won't – they're ringing again. Sod off. They ring again.

'Shit, sorry, I'd better just see,' says Fen, opening her eyes, locating her bag, catching sight of Al's reflection in the mirror and feeling immediately shy. She goes over to retrieve her phone, holding her crumpled dress against her body.

'Hullo?'

'Fen – hi sorry, it's me.'

It's Pip.

And here's Al, slipping his hand down the front of her knickers and tugging cheekily at her pubic hair. Fen glowers at him in the mirror but he closes his eyes, bites her shoulder and works a finger through the lips of her sex.

'Can you hear me OK, Fen?'

'Yes.'

Fen is turned on by the sight of her body being ravished by this person. It doesn't matter that he's not Brad Pitt any more. What matters is that he's not Matt. He's secret. She spreads her legs, permits him easier access.

'Is everything OK, Pip?'

'Well,' Pip says, 'I wouldn't have phoned – but I can't seem to settle Cosima.'

Fen tries to still Al's hand, grabs at his wrist. She's doesn't want to be fingered in the same breath as talking about her daughter. She steps aside and is vaguely aware that he's now unbuttoning his trousers.

'What do you mean?' she asks Pip.

'Well she just seems restless, a little fretful.'

'Is she hot?'

'A little.'

'Shit. OK. I'm on my way.'

Fen shrugs apologetically to Al who is standing there with an impressive hard-on which she considers probably looks bigger because his body is so thin and hairless. Nothing like Brad Pitt. Or Matt Holden.

'My kid,' Fen shrugs and instantly detests herself for referring to Cosima as such, for all but blaming her baby for coital interruption. Al is absent-mindedly caressing his cock and Fen wonders, a little pathetically, whether he'll wank in her honour once she's left. 'I'm sorry,' she says, 'I'm really going to have to go.'

She dresses and as she does, she looks at a framed photo of a young woman.

'That's Kay,' he tells her. Al is still naked, his cock now at half mast. It seems disrespectful, really.

Fen looks at the photo. She was pretty, his sister. And as she sees herself out, she thinks how death distorts. She knows she was enamoured with the idea of Al because he was this brave boy who'd faced tragedy head-on. She loved the sight of him placing his flowers around the tree-trunk; his story. But she knows now he is rather immature, a bit boring actually, and a little too puny for her taste.

She heads out into the street, flags down a cab mercifully easily and phones Pip to tell her fifteen minutes. Fen gazes out, her head rests lightly against the window, being juddered; as if she needed physical discomfort to bring her to her senses. Yes, she feels guilty for the pleasure she's just had, the illicitness of it, the excitement and attention. She feels badly for Matt and she fears Cosima's unsettled state is directly attributable to her bad behaviour. But Fen's anxiety runs deeper too and it occurs to her that it is rooted in something far more ominous.

Is history repeating itself? Is this what my mother went through? Did her cowboy come riding by just when she was becoming stifled by the drudge of it all?

But did he lure her away or did she seek him out?

Pip tapped the phone against her lip. It was difficult to know what to do.

Should I wake Cosima in ten minutes or so? Or is that too cruel?

Because, in reality, Cosima had actually been sound

asleep since Pip laid her in her cot after her bottle two hours ago.

Matt came in half an hour after Fen. He'd left the bus early and taken a long walk to settle his nerves and ensure he was word perfect. He was dreading being the harbinger and he was dreading seeing Fen distressed, yet he hoped it might engender an opportunity to put his arms around her and hold her close. That she might feel safe. Protected. If she'd let him.

'You're back early,' he said.

Fen nodded. 'Pip couldn't settle Cosima.'

'Is she OK?'

'She's fine – she was fine by the time I arrived back. Probably tummy troubles or something.'

'Did you have fun with your friend?'

Fen looked at Matt and wondered if fun can only be fun if it's still fun in retrospect, in the aftermath. She nodded because she didn't want to say yes out loud. Because if she did she'd be saying to her partner's face, Yes it was fun to have some bloke I've met three times finger my vagina and fondle my boobs.

Matt looked at his watch, as if Fen's answer was a long time coming. 'Ten to ten,' he said. 'Do you want a cup of tea?'

'Please,' said Fen, 'thank you. I'll just pop upstairs and take off all this stupid make-up.'

'You look nice,' said Matt. 'I like your dress.' Shit – how long does make-up take to remove? More than ten minutes? Matt had no idea. 'Leave it on!' he exclaimed. 'You look nice.'

Fen found this touching. But she was desperate to remove the knickers tacky with the juice of infidelity. 'I'm just going to the loo,' she told him.

'You feeling OK?' Matt asked. Timing was everything but he really didn't want to ask her outright, Number One or Number Two.

'Just a bit tired,' said Fen.

When she came back downstairs, a cup of tea and a biscuit were waiting. And so was Matt.

When Pip arrived home from Fen's, Zac was already there, engrossed in some scintillating spreadsheet or other on his laptop.

'You're back early,' he commented, glancing up.

'Fen came back early,' Pip said tonelessly.

'How was Cosima?' Zac asked, squinting as he pulled the cursor around the screen.

'Cute as a button,' said Pip.

'Did it all go smoothly?' said Zac.

'Of course,' Pip said defensively.

'She is a poppet,' said Zac, 'a real little munchkin.'

Pip looked at her feet. 'I want one,' she said quietly.

Zac laughed a little. 'Oh God, one night's babysitting and you're all broody on me again!' he declared, returning his attention to his work.

'Oh will you just fuck off,' Pip stormed.

Zac looked up, startled. He'd been joking – hadn't that been obvious? Because hadn't she been joking too? It was some sort of shared joke, wasn't it? 'Pip!' he began to remonstrate.

'I'm sick of you not taking me seriously! I'm fed up of you demeaning how I *feel*,' Pip said and she flounced off to the bedroom with a slam to the door.

Zac was dumbstruck. He was amazed. He was worried – hadn't he discussed with Ben and Matt to keep the girls calm and enveloped with love and support? Most of all he was bewildered; Pip's words were in some ways irrelevant to the violence with which she'd expressed them. Pip rarely raised her voice. She loathed arguing; even mundane bickering upset her. She avoided confrontation and was the person to whom others turned for assistance in deflecting situations. Pip was the least argumentative, least aggressive, most easygoing person he'd ever met. That's why he'd married her. She was also, in his eyes, so beautifully readable. That's why he loved her. But this he hadn't seen coming. And try as he might, it seemed illegible to him. But it was ten to ten and Django mattered most. Further discussion or shouting or whatever would just have to wait.

Cat floated in at quarter to ten. 'I've had the most brilliant day,' she beamed.

'Are you hungry?' Ben asked her.

'Nope.'

'Have you eaten?'

'Nope – I'm too excited to eat.'

'You ought to eat, babe.'

'Oh be quiet, you fussy old doctor.'

'Cup of tea, then?'

'That would be nice.'

'And then you can tell me all about it,' said Ben, glancing at the clock and hoping Cat could do so within ten minutes.

At 10 p.m. on 15 June, Ben put his finger over Cat's lip and said, 'That's wonderful news but you need to sit down. Babe, I need to tell you something.'

At 10 p.m. on 15 June, Matt switched off the TV and turned to Fen and said, 'Fen, I need to tell you something.'

At 10 p.m. on 15 June, Zac had to deny Pip her post-argument privacy. He went into the bedroom and sat alongside her. With tenderness and scorching regret, he put his arm gently around her. 'I need to tell you something, Mrs,' he said.

Where Were You When You Heard that Django McCabe Had Cancer?

In all his purple splendour, with his eternally optimistic smile fixed across his plastic face, Tinky Winky gazed kindly up at Fen. He was lying at her feet, she was sitting on the sofa, her hands clasped together tightly in automatic supplication. Matt was at her side, stroking her arm, her leg. It was ten past ten. Fen bent and picked up Tinky Winky, Cosima's favourite Teletubby, and hugged him tight. She pressed her nose to his head. He smelt of her baby. Just then, she gained more comfort from him than from Matt.

Is this my fault? In some horrible skewed scheme of things, I think it probably is. I feel sick. I shouldn't think of Django and Al in the same context but it all makes horrible sense if I do. Isn't this what they call karma? Or else, divine retribution? Of course I must have my comeuppance for all that stupid, stupid stuff with Al – but why does it have to be via Django?

'Is prostate cancer terminal? Where is the prostate exactly?' Fen turned to Matt, her eyes fixed warily at his groin. 'What does it do – can you live without one? Like an appendix or gall bladder? Is that what they'll do – chop it out? But they will be able to fix him, won't they?'

If I feel I am being punished, how must Django be feeling?

'He's on his own,' Fen continued, her voice cracking with emotion. 'He hates doctors and hospitals.' She looked at Matt, seeing worry and tenderness written all over his face. 'He'll be redefining cancer "a spot of the lurgy",' she said with a sad laugh. 'He'll tell us not to worry. What has he ever done to deserve this?' She stood and paced the room, clutching Tinky Winky to her breast like a prayer book. 'I think I know that he never meant to hurt anyone,' she said, 'so he changed his name from Derek and had a fling with his brother's wife. But he is a brilliant parent – he couldn't have been a better father to us, to Cat. His love was perfectly equal.'

'I know,' said Matt, 'I know. It seems so unjust, Fen. He's always looked after himself, what with his cooking and his love of Derbyshire air. He's one of the good guys.'

'Please don't let him die,' Fen pleaded, bursting into tears. 'I don't want this to be happening. I want Cosima to grow up knowing her Django Gramps. I can't believe we've been so horrible to him. We have to go up there, immediately. It's our turn to care for him.'

Matt went to her and pulled her into his embrace. She sobbed, knocking her forehead against his chest again and again. Snotty and tear-stained, she took deep breaths. 'If he could see me now he'd be saying, "Stop it with the sobbing, you'll ruin the carpets." Fuck, Matt, I'm terrified.'

Matt offered his arms to her but this time Fen stepped back and turned away, burying her face in Tinky Winky's tummy and sobbing anew.

I feel as if I don't deserve the comfort of Matt's arms, as if I've forfeited my place within his embrace because I've abused his trust and sullied our love for a pathetic fumble with that stupid Al. What sort of mother was I to Cosima earlier this evening? I have to change, for her sake. But actually, this isn't about me at all. It's about Django. And Django has to make it through, for her sake too.

'Pip's going to phone you,' Matt was saying, 'in a little while – once Cat has phoned her. We had to contrive it this way – it's why I met up with Ben and Zac yesterday.' And he told her about Django coming to London which made her cry; of Ben arranging for the consultation, that Django wanted the boys to tell his girls.

'He hates the city,' she cried. 'He must have been so anxious. He must be feeling so alone.'

I can't believe this is happening. And I can't believe it's still the same evening that I faffed around with Al. All that seems unreal, now; distant and past. Totally over and done with. Thank God Pip phoned me when she did. In some ways, she's always been there to pull me or Cat out of harm's way, to steer us clear of trouble.

'Pip will be phoning soon,' Matt said, and Fen shuddered at how close Matt seemed to her thoughts. 'Then you'll be able to decide what to do.'

'But even if we band together, can we help Django? Are we a match for cancer?' Fen whispered. 'Cancer happens to other families, Matt. Not ours.'

* * *

Pip was frowning so hard her head ached and the corner of her eyelids twitched.

Zac just said something like Django has cancer. I think I heard him right. But Django can't have cancer because I saw him a month ago and he looked as fine then as he has looked for the past however many years. And Django can't have cancer because he isn't the type. He's fantastically robust. You wouldn't believe he's seventy-five.

'But the most ill he's ever been is a head cold, which he cured overnight with his concoction of Caribbean Hot Sauce, brandy and an egg yolk whisked together and served in a

Babycham glass,' she said, a tone of protest to her voice. 'He made the concoction for me once – just before my A-levels. I swear my cold went before the glass even touched my lips. For Christ's sake, Zac – Django McCabe found the cure for the common cold. He can't have cancer.'

She looked at her husband, sitting beside her on their bed, and all the wariness and annoyance she'd harboured for him over the last month evaporated. Suddenly, she doubted she had the strength or the nous to fulfil her role as Great Looker-Afterer and she knew that, without having to be asked, her husband would take on that role. She knew that as soon as her tears came, Zac would be there, solid and close. She began to cry, lowered her head and crumpled into Zac who was there for her at once. She sobbed for a couple of minutes before physically pulling herself together.

'It's fine. It's fine,' she said loudly, sniffing away her fragility. 'If Django does have cancer or something, then he'll sail through it and no doubt discover some history-making, Nobel-prize-winning potion in the process. It'll be the new penicillin. It's all going to be OK.'

'Ben says that prostate cancer is not uncommon,' Zac said.

'Then it won't stand a chance in someone as rare as Django,' Pip said.

'Ben said often it is slow growing and the man can live out his normal lifespan in spite of it.' Zac matched her optimism because he sensed it was what she needed.

'And he certainly won't tolerate the ignominy of losing his trademark pony-tail during treatment,' Pip continued, almost brightly. 'I can just see him in a hospital gown, brandishing a Thermos of home-made soup, saying to the doctor, "Blast me with whatever but don't touch the hair, son." Can't you?'

Zac said yes he could, and he chuckled because he knew the sound of it would be a relief to Pip.

'He'll be fine,' Pip declared. 'Everything will be OK. It's a nasty, nasty shock. It's a terrible way to reunite us all, but reunite us it will.'

'Cat's going to give you a call, then you're to call Fen,' Zac explained because he deduced that facts and the opportunity to be proactive was what Pip wanted. 'We discussed it last night, Ben, Matt and I.'

They've thought it all through, the boys, bless them.

'Django McCabe will give cancer an unceremonious boot,' Pip said. 'Come on, Cat, ring me won't you? I think I'll make a cup of tea. Want one?'

'I'll make it, Mrs,' said Zac, kissing his wife's shoulder.

'We'll go up to Farleymoor at the weekend,' Pip said, 'and sort everything out.'

* * *

'Babe?' Ben looked at Cat who was standing as motionless and emotionless as a wax statue. She could hear him, but it sounded as though he was in a different room. She couldn't locate his voice or his presence and it felt safest to just keep standing still and staring straight ahead.

I'm sort of speechless and thoughtless. I can only compute facts at the moment.

I have been made manager at work.

Django has cancer.

'Babe – prostate cancer is not uncommon. It may have no great effect on Django's lifestyle or lifespan.'

Ben says prostate cancer is common.

'And I'm sorry, Cat, that I just couldn't tell you of his phone calls to me, of his trip down to St John's.'

Django came down to London on a train and went back home again.

My father is Derek McCabe.

The man who is my father has cancer.

I haven't seen Django for a month.

I thought I never wanted to see him again but just over a week ago I yearned to see him. Only he wasn't there because he was down here, with my husband, who helped him learn he has cancer.

'It broke my heart to know that you were going to Derbyshire, that he wouldn't be there. That there was nothing I could do about it.' Ben put his hands on Cat's shoulders and kissed the top of her head. She was stiff to his touch. 'Babe?'

'I have to be at work an hour early tomorrow,' Cat said.

'You need to phone Pip, when you're ready. Then she's going to phone Fen. We arranged it that way, the guys and I. With Django's approval.'

'OK,' she said, picking up her mobile phone and pressing the speed dial for Pip, whose number Cat currently had no chance of recalling otherwise.

Testing Time

The McCabe girls usually let BBC Radio Four pass the time when they made the journey to Derbyshire by car. That Saturday morning, though the radio was on and Ben was doing the driving, it was no more than a background sound to the lengthy loaded silences. What they wanted to tune into most were Ben's pragmatic facts about what Django was facing.

'So he may have had it for a long time?' Pip asked from the back of the car.

'Yes. Quite possibly,' said Ben, nodding at her from the rear-view mirror. 'Actually, a large percentage of men over eighty have a small area of prostate cancer.' She nodded back at him.

'But Django is only seventy-five,' Fen said. Ben looked at her too, but unlike Pip by whom she sat, Fen didn't meet his eyes. She was frowning intently at her hands.

'Many men can live out their normal lifespan without it causing any problems,' Ben said though he immediately regretted the joint sigh of relief from Pip and Fen. False hope could be a cruel thing. Also, despite being a level-headed scientist, Ben had always feared that Hope without Fact tempted Fate. 'But we are still unsure of what's what with Django,' he continued. 'He needs more tests. The results can take a couple of weeks to compute. There are all sorts of treatment possibilities, sometimes they even opt *not* to treat – and nothing drastic happens.' Ben had repeated the facts so often over the last few days he hoped his voice still sounded convincing.

'That's good, that's positive,' said Pip, leaning forward and nodding at him assertively. 'When can he have these tests? Can we bring him to your hospital? I suppose I'm asking if you can organize special privileges?'

'There are excellent urology and oncology departments local to Chesterfield,' he said. 'He's already been referred and tests have been set up. It's better for the patient to be closer to home.'

'Has he had them? These tests?' Fen asked quietly, disturbed by the thought of Django, on his own, being probed and scanned.

'I don't know – he was due to have some yesterday,' Ben said, trying again to encourage her with eye contact but she continued to look down, her hands now tight fists in her lap. 'I tried to phone a couple of times but he didn't answer.'

'Maybe now he'll buy a mobile phone,' Pip said, with a woeful laugh.

Ben was acutely aware that Cat had not reacted, let alone spoken and they were now just north of Junction 24, the eight mammoth cooling stations sighing out steam in slow motion. He glanced at his wife sitting beside him and wondered how much of the conversation she'd listened to. Though she appeared to be gazing out of the window, obviously it was not at the view. Much as Ben was fond of her sisters, and hoped they found comfort in his honest answers, so he also wished he had Cat to himself that journey. Over all others, his duty was to her. This he did not feel was an obligation of marriage, but a reason for it. In Cat he'd found a person other than himself, or anyone he had ever known, whom he wished always to put first. For Fen and Pip, cancer might well cure the situation between them and Django, and Ben understood that by genning up on details and prognosis, they might feel better equipped to make their reacquaintance. What could be more shocking than cancer of a loved one? In the scheme of things, didn't cancer cancel out all other ills?

For Cat, though, cancer had been thrown into a mix already clouded by complex fears, mistrust, hurt, shock and disbelief. Ben wondered whether, for Fen and Pip, Django's cancer in some way provided an easy way out, an excuse to move away from the disruptive revelations of the previous month; that cancer rewrote all scales of gravity. Django's cancer could also redefine their roles as nurses, and not accusers. In a bizarre twist, cancer might just make everything better. Ben felt that for Cat, however, cancer was confusing the ambivalence she was entitled to feel. If she wasn't yet ready to accept the shock of her parentage, the untruths she'd grown up believing, the hurt and the deception – then she certainly wasn't going to be prepared for the hard facts of cancer.

Suddenly, Ben resented her sisters for not being aware of this. Then he asked himself if he would still feel it was worse for Cat than for her sisters, was Cat not his wife? The truth was, he didn't want to talk about cancer any more because privately his concerns for Django were more grave than he was prepared to reveal before the tests were done. He was beginning to feel tired and irritated by the drive. Why couldn't Cat take the wheel?

Because she never did.

When the two of them were in the car, it was always

Ben who drove. A silly little quirk of marriage, of their dynamic, he'd never really thought about until just now. He didn't really mind. He was glad to be able to do something.

'He's going to die, isn't he?' suddenly Fen sobbed. 'Oh God, he's going to die.'

'Fen shut up and stop that,' Ben snapped. 'You're being hysterical and that kind of thinking is no good to anyone.'

'I'm sorry. I'm sorry,' Fen gasped, and she turned to Pip. 'Do you think everything will be OK? Pip?'

Pip had to gather her thoughts. It struck her that Fen was reacting in much the way she would have expected Cat to. Yet Cat, sitting in the front passenger seat, was currently doing the deeply thoughtful gazing out of the window more usual for Fen. It was as if the events of the past month had transposed her younger sisters' traits. It was Cat guarding her emotions now, and Fen spewing out hers. 'It'll be fine,' Pip told Fen in the tone of voice she'd often employed for her youngest sister. 'It's a nasty shock. Can you imagine Django as a cancer patient?' She waited for Fen to shake her head. 'Nor can I. It doesn't happen to people like him.'

'We were just this ordinary bunch, this normal family,' Fen said croakily, 'and in a matter of weeks, it's all fallen apart.' She thought of Matt and Cosima at home, suddenly praying hard that her other little family would never fall apart, shuddering violently at how close she'd come to ripping them asunder herself.

'We have to hold it together,' Pip said, misreading Fen's shaking. 'That's the point of family – one is duty-bound to hold it together to prevent it falling apart.'

I am duty-bound to hold it together to prevent it falling apart, Fen said to herself.

She gazed at the back of Cat's head, the soft auburn

spikes of her hair, the gold butterflies at the back of her ear lobes fixing her earrings. 'Is it harder for you, Cat?' Fen asked her gently, leaning forward between the front seats. 'You know – because of—' She paused. 'What we found out.'

'He's just my biological father,' Cat said quietly, her voice sounding new and emphatic after two hours of silence, 'and that can't mean much because Christ, we didn't even suspect, let alone know, until a few weeks ago.'

'Pit stop,' Ben announced, deciding to pull in to the services at the last minute. There was so much stress and emotion and anticipation in the car it was now making driving difficult. Part of him was dreading the weekend, part of him wanted to take Cat back to Boulder for good, far away from her first family so that he and she could settle down and make a new one of their own. He felt slightly burdened though it had been his decision to accompany the sisters, his advice to Zac and Matt that they stay at home with their children, his offer to be the chaperon, the doctor-on-call. He loitered behind the sisters as they made their way in to the services. He observed how Pip had put her arm around Cat's shoulder, that Fen's arm was around his wife's waist. And the sight released a surge of relief.

She'll be OK. They'll all be OK. Whatever happens, they have each other. They always will.

'Stop!' Cat suddenly said, anxiety riding high in her voice, as the car pulled along the one-in-ten drag to Farleymoor. Ben pulled over to the verge. The girls staggered from the car, allowing the sight of the dip and roll of the ancient and familiar dales to calm their nerves, the sweet soft air to fill their lungs and steady their minds; while goose grass, licked with flashes of silver as the sun and the wind played on it, whispered comfortingly against their legs.

'Why don't you three walk the last mile,' Ben suggested. 'I'll drive on. And pave the way.'

Django peered at length and with theatrical curiosity into Ben's car. He stroked at his non-existent goatee and frowned. 'Are they dieting?'

Ben laughed. 'They wanted to walk the last bit.'

'Dragging their heels?' Django asked.

'Steadying their nerves,' Ben said diplomatically.

'It's nice to see you,' Django told him, 'but I'm wondering whether you are here as intermediary or physician?'

'I have many caps to wear this weekend, Django,' Ben said. 'Chauffeur – currently.'

'You're very skilled,' Django told him, 'and you are of course most welcome, bless you. But your services as intermediary and physician won't be called upon. You see, I'm feeling dandy. Furthermore, I've made curried trout for supper. And Eton Mess. It's their favourite. Guaranteed to break the ice and melt hardened hearts.'

From the garden, they could see the curve in the road as it started its long, meandering descent to Two Dales. And just then the sisters came into view as they mooched their way closer.

'It's funny how it never changes,' Django said. 'Whatever their age, wherever they've been, it's always Pip leading the way, Fen bringing up the rear and Cat, protected, between them.'

'Cat's extremely nervous,' Ben told Django, his wife's welfare his main consideration.

'I'm sure she is,' said Django, 'but there's so much ground to cover and most of it is a wasteland there seems little point in revisiting.'

'But they need to know,' Ben told him, a little irritated by Django's whimsy.

'If they ask,' Django said.

'They might not,' Ben said, polite but firm, 'but still they need to know. It's part of the point of this weekend – you must realize that.' He paused. 'How were the tests?'

'Tests?' said Django. 'I'm feeling dandy, my boy – and look, here come the girls.'

The girls were now walking up the drive. Pip. Fen. Cat lagging behind. The disruption to the familiar order perturbed Django. The pace was less their usual brisk walk, more a reluctant amble, and that vexed him too. And as he watched the girls approach in this awkward, unnatural arrangement and faltering gait, he sensed it was mostly down to him to realign it all. If only life could be like jazz. If only he could gather together these disparate components. If only he could make a sweet chord from discordance, a new melody from dissonance. Perhaps he could.

The girls stood before him.

'Hullo, chaps,' Django smiled. 'Cup of tea?'

It was incongruous; to drink tea so politely, in such silence, when the tea was so uncouthly strong and served in the great clunking stoneware mugs Django had made during his mercifully brief foray into pottery in the late seventies. But they sipped away and smiled awkward half smiles while waiting for the scald on their tongues to subside.

'Well, I think I'll unpack,' said Ben but immediately the girls left the table too, which had not been his intention at all. He'd assumed he'd simply be on-call, in any capacity, but he had hoped this meant waiting in the wings, a step removed, while the action played out elsewhere. Django took the teapot and poured out the amber-coloured dregs into the curry sauce, desperately annoyed at the nag of his bladder. He dropped a mug on the floor, yet not even the flagstones could break it. Django wondered if he was allowed to read into this – that something rather old and odd-looking should be so strong and resilient. He'd made the mug himself. He looked at his hands, glanced around the kitchen to check he had no audience, and then he pressed his hands hard against his heart, his brow, his groin.

Cat watched Ben unpack. 'I wish I'd never come,' she whispered.

Ben nodded, shook the creases from a shirt and hung it on the back of the door. 'I'm sure, babe,' he said, 'but you need to stay open. Don't close yourself off, OK?'

'His birthday and all that – it seems a lifetime ago,' Cat said.

There was a gentle knock on the door and then Fen came in. 'You OK?' she asked Cat.

Cat shrugged. 'You?'

Fen shrugged back. 'I thought it would be easier, I thought there'd be tears and hugs and we'd all know what to say. It's all so formal. And awkward.'

'I wish I hadn't come,' Cat confessed. 'I thought everything would seem magically clearer, everything would be fine. But it's not.'

'We have to be here,' Pip, suddenly in the doorway, spoke strongly and a little irritated. 'Of course it's awkward. Come on. We need to go downstairs and help.'

'In a sec,' said Fen and she turned to Ben. 'Does your mobile have a signal? I want to phone home.' Ben handed his phone to Fen. There was no signal and she looked crestfallen.

'Come on,' Pip said to Fen, 'let's go downstairs. You can use the normal phone. But we'll lay the table first.'

'Isn't all of this freaking you out?' Cat asked her.

'Of course it is,' said Pip, 'but we have to do something about that. That's why we're here, remember.'

When Pip and Fen had left the room, Cat went over to Ben, laying her head against his chest. 'I don't even know where to look, let alone what to say,' she muttered. 'I can't seem to look him in the eye. It might make me cry and I don't want to. And I might see that I have his eyes and I don't think I want to see that either.'

'Yet,' Ben qualified gently.

Matching cutlery had never really been a priority in the McCabe household, nor had the resultant assortment ever been particularly noticeable. Food was the all-important element of mealtimes at Farleymoor, and though the laying of the table held some ritual, the lively clatter of crockery and cutlery was in anticipation of the repast itself. Cutlery was a means to an end, a way to expedite the passage of food from plate to palate. It was mostly irrelevant whether it was steel from Sheffield or silver from Harrods, ivory stems or antler handles; as long as the pieces could prong, scoop or cut.

That Saturday night, between silences as thick as Django's Christmas gravy, the cutlery provided a cacophonous and alien soundtrack. On account of each piece being unique, no two clinks or clatters were the same. No one had noticed this before, but they all tuned in to it now. The racket was irritating, so annoying that everyone tried to scrape and clang their cutlery the loudest to obscure the sound of the others and perhaps signify their own unrest as well.

'And how is little Cosima?' Django asked Fen who nodded her answer while making much of chewing concertedly. 'Good! Splendid. And how is young Tom?' Django asked Pip who, for some reason, smiled her answer to Ben. 'Super!' said Django, turning his attention to Cat. 'And I hear congratulations are in order, Cat.'

'I'm not bloody pregnant,' Cat retorted with her mouth

full, which in the first instance irked Django far more than the facts of her answer or the sentiment by which she expressed it. 'I meant your promotion,' he said. She shrugged, as if it were no big deal, as if he should expect her to be capable of such accolades.

The grating scrape of cutlery; the grate of non-communication anathema to this kitchen, this family. Ben asked for another helping, not because he was still hungry but just to break the awkward silence. In the most stinging indictment Django had yet been savaged by, each girl left part of her meal on her plate.

Django fetched the Eton Mess and placed it with justified pride in the centre of the table. Pip patted her stomach as if she were full, Fen burped politely into her napkin as if she didn't fancy it anyway and Cat wouldn't even bring her eyes to glance at Django's trademark triumph of a dessert. He sat down heavily and, with a great sigh, placed his head in his hands. And there they all sat, in a suspended moment of extreme unease. The silence was choking but with a cough, Django cleared his throat and let rip a roar the likes of which the girls had never heard and could never have imagined.

'Enough!' Django slammed his hand against the worn wood of the table. 'Enough. My name is Derek McCabe – it's a ghastly name and there should be a law against it. I have three daughters one of whom is biologically mine. I have cancer.' He rose. 'With regard to your blood lines, on my gravestone I want it said that I was a good father to my three girls,' he almost bellowed. 'You can punish me and condemn me for the details I withheld; put me in the proverbial stocks and pelt me with how rotten you think me. It was naive of me to believe I could protect you – but then all parents wish to protect their offspring so the whole bloody lot of us must be fools.' He shoved his chair back. 'You tell me – any of you – that our life thus far was not better for turning a blind eye to the finer facts of biology and forenames.' He smote the table. 'Pip – you dish up, I need the lavatory. Bugger the Eton Mess and bugger my blasted bladder.'

When Django came back after an infuriating and unsuccessful trip to the toilet, the Eton Mess was still intact, or as intact as a smash of meringue, gluts of fruit and great clods of cream defining this dessert can be. He looked around the table. Poor Ben, mortified, at the periphery of his comfort zone. The girls, looking glum, staring at their laps. Slowly, Pip stood up and Fen lifted her eyes and Cat raised her head a little. 'It's your job,' Pip said to Django with humility, 'you're head of our family.' And she held out the serving spoon. Before Django took it, he turned his attention to Fen, who could only mouth 'Sorry' on account of the choke of emotion tightening her throat. Then he looked to Cat, whose tears bounced on her plate like hailstones.

'Don't do that, dear,' Django chided her softly, 'it's the best china. And the recipe does not call for salt. Just sweet things.' A glance back at Fen and Pip showed their tears had started to fall too.

'Dear God,' Django exclaimed softly, 'I'm about to do that ghastly Hollywood thing and tell you all how much I love you, how I never meant to hurt you.'

Oh Christ – mass hysterics, thought Ben, *we so don't do this in my family*.

Django went to Pip, took the serving spoon from her hand and embraced her tenderly; then went and stood behind Fen's chair and bent down to kiss her forehead over and again before pulling Cat to her feet and straight into the warmth of his bear-hug.

But nor do we do this, Ben thought enviously and he

moved quietly from the kitchen, taking his dessert into the garden, leaving the McCabes to their ways.

Bolstered by brandy and heartened by After Eights, the girls shyly gathered around Django's armchair in the drawing-room, as if he was about to read a story though it was the truth only that they craved and that finally he was prepared to give. With the apologies and declarations of love now fulfilled, a spew of questions surfaced, though it was only Fen and Pip who could voice them.

'Was it a shock, that *she* came back?' asked Pip.

'Yes and no,' Django told them. 'We've had no contact and yet I must admit to an inkling that at some point, she'd show up.'

'Did he know?' Pip pressed. 'Our father?' She glanced at Fen and then, apologetically, at Cat.

'No,' Django said emphatically, 'he did not.'

'So how can you be sure?' Fen asked abruptly, having slipped her hand into Cat's.

'Unlike me, my brother wasn't very good at maths,' Django said nostalgically. 'Perhaps I would have told him – when the dust had settled. When a little more time had passed. But life was back on an even keel – Battersea had been left, we were all happy here together. And within two years, he was gone.'

'Is it really *really* as you've always told it?' Fen asked, a little accusatorily.

'It really *really* is,' Django said.

'About everything?' Fen pressed. 'About all of you?'

Django nodded. 'Though with hindsight, I suppose one can see that she was on this mission to find herself and all that transcendental nonsense which, in the 1960s, we simply accepted as right-on and far-out. Nowadays I reckon one would call her a crazy mixed-up kid.' There was a pause as the girls tried to tag this description to the woman in her early fifties they'd met for the first time just over a month before.

'Did you actually have an affair with her?' Pip asked. 'A love affair?'

'No,' Django admitted, 'not technically.'

'Just a fling,' Cat commented sadly.

'But did you *love* her?' Fen asked, unnerved by the thought of a reckless one-night stand. She glanced at Cat but could not decipher the emotion that dulled her eyes.

'In a make-love-not-war zeitgeisty kind of way – yes, I suppose I did,' Django said and he could feel Cat's eyes burning into him. He looked at her and nodded again. 'There was a lot of love around,' he continued, 'between everyone in those days.'

'Did you think she'd come back?' Pip asked. 'At the time?'

Django looked upset. 'Of course I did!' he declared. 'Gracious, she had three beautiful *beautiful* babies.'

'Did you think she'd come back for *all* of us?' Fen pressed, squeezing Cat's hand and half hoping her sister would hear that she'd asked the question as much on her behalf as for herself.

'Of course I did!' Django said, a little impatiently. He paused and continued in a softer tone. 'I was mortified that she'd left – but soon enough I dreaded her returning. I didn't want to lose you three. Especially not after my brother passed away.'

'Was it a shock? When you realized about me?' Cat asked. They were her first questions and her voice rang out. Django, Fen and Pip looked at her, though just then she remained unable to establish eye contact with any of them.

'Well, yes it was. Goodness me, yes,' Django told them all. 'Although I didn't know until after she'd left. She told me in a letter. A letter that was unopened for days on end because I was so busy running around after you all.'

'But *why* did she leave?' Cat asked urgently. 'Why did she leave us? Did she say? Do you still have the letter? Why *didn't* she come back for us? All of us?'

What could Django do but shrug? What could he say but, 'I don't know, girls. I don't have that answer. You'd really have to ask her that.'

Time for Tests

After an exhausted sleep in which thoughts of their mother and thoughts of cancer were banished, the family reconvened at the breakfast table where the cutlery could no longer be heard, but could be seen making swift work of the stack of panffles and maple syrup. The C word was now horribly anticipated, but none of the girls could bring themselves to articulate it. Yet it was the news of Django's cancer that had facilitated this return home and they were leaving later that day.

Ben was acutely aware of this fact. And he was eager that the issue be broached with sufficient time to do it justice.

'How are you feeling, Django?' he asked, as conversationally as such a loaded question could possibly sound.

'I had the most dreadful procedure on Friday, truly ghastly,' Django replied in a similar tone, and he pointed his steak knife at Ben. 'You medical men are an imaginative and sadistic lot. Pass the syrup. Thank you, Fen. They trussed me up, Ben, they trussed me up.'

'A TRUSS?' Ben asked.

'Yes,' Django regarded the girls. They'd stopped eating. They looked terrified. 'As you know, I don't trust technology and I'm not one for all these new-fangled gizmos. It was a *camera*,' he muttered, shaking his head, 'at the end of a medical hosepipe.' Fen laid her hand over his wrist. He gave a little shrug. 'Not one for the family photo album,' he said robustly.

'You'll be fine,' Pip said.

'What's next?' Ben asked.

'Toast?' Django offered. 'Fresh tea?'

'I meant for you, at the hospital, test-wise,' Ben clarified.

'Let's see – tomorrow, it's something about "ice",' Django said.

'Isotope bone scan?' Ben asked.

'That's the one,' said Django benevolently, as if he'd been quizzing Ben on his med school revision. 'It all sounds increasingly Ridley Scott to me.'

The sisters stared at Ben intently.

'OK,' said Ben, 'OK. I'm the doctor so you can all listen to me. The bone is perhaps the most common place for prostate cancer to spread to. This scan can detect abnormal areas of bone. A mild radioactive liquid is injected into a vein in the arm and because abnormal bone absorbs more than normal bone, the radioactive stuff shows up as highlighted hot spots.'

'I could bag myself a role on *Doctor Who*,' Django said brightly, 'or audition as the new ReadyBrek boy.' But Fen had now begun to cry. The sudden sound of her distress rang out the truth about Django's alarming situation. 'Poppet,' he tried to protest but when he looked over to Pip for assistance, he saw that she hid her face behind her hands and a glance at Cat showed her tears falling steadily if silently.

'The scan is just diagnostic,' Ben told them, his arm around Cat.

'But what if it diagnoses horrible things?' Fen sobbed. 'We've only just got each other back. We want to rebuild our family, not have it taken away from us.'

'I've always worried that the more they look for the more they find,' Pip said, working hard not to let her voice crack.

'Girls,' said Django, 'it's probably just a spot of the lurgy. I have all my faculties. I just cannot take a pissing leak.' No one laughed. No one said, Language, Django.

'Did they warn you that after the injection you have to wait a good two or three hours before the scan can be taken?' Ben asked Django.

'No,' said Django, a little unnerved. 'I can't remember. Perhaps they did.'

'Nothing sinister,' Ben assured him, 'just a lengthy process – so take a book.'

'I'll stay,' Cat announced suddenly, decisively. 'I have a day off tomorrow. I'll come with you, Django.'

With the car packed and ready to leave later that day, Fen and Pip shuffled around and loitered, having final drinks of water and double-checking the rooms upstairs.

'I could stay too,' Pip offered.

'And me,' Fen added quietly though she was now desperate to see her baby.

'Thank you,' Django said, his hand at his heart, 'but much as I love the image of arriving at the hospital with my entourage, my bevy of beauties, I think you two should be back with your families tonight.' Pip asked him over and again if he was sure, and then she asked the same of Cat. Fen didn't want to ask if Cat and Django were sure because actually she was missing Cosima so much she felt sick.

'I'll call, as soon as there's anything to call about,' Cat told them, transformed into a capable nurse, currently in the arms of her doctor. 'I'll call you anyway.' While she hugged her husband, Fen and Pip said goodbye to Django.

'Oh Django,' Fen whispered, letting him make her feel better in his arms.

'Behave,' Pip told him, giving him the tight hug and brisk kiss to each cheek she gave to Tom when she took him to school. 'Do what the doctors say.'

'She's so bloody bossy,' Django said to Fen.

Fen suddenly felt great affection for her sister. 'And we love her for it,' she said. Pip looked a little embarrassed. Fen linked arms with her. 'Sit in the back with me?' she asked. 'Even though Cat won't be in the front.'

'I have dominoes tonight,' Django tells Cat as they wave the others off.

'*Big Brother* is on anyway,' she tells him, 'and you don't have a video recorder. Anyway, I'm all talked out for today.'

'Me too,' says Django, 'me too.'

They feel awkward but strangely excited to be in such close proximity, to have the opportunity to spend quality time, alone together. It is almost easy to forget the reason why Cat is staying on in Derbyshire.

When she first saw the hospital the next morning, Cat was pleased that Django was having the tests done there and not in London. In contrast to the vertical sprawl of the London hospitals, and the unfriendly busyness of Ben's in particular, this place was welcoming. Set amidst dunes of neatly tended lawns, a series of low buildings constructed in the buff coloured local stone sat peacefully and spaciously, a little like the sheep that grazed the hills just beyond the perimeter fence. Cat wanted to say how she hated hospitals, hated the smell, that they made her feel nervous, but wisely she changed her perspective and wittered on about the landscaping and the architecture instead.

'Prince Charles opened it,' she marvelled, reading from a brass plaque.

'Well then!' Django declared, implying the Royal Family

wouldn't waste their time opening hospitals not at the cutting edge of medical excellence.

It still smelt like a hospital, though. And the sights and sounds were indisputable too. The rubbery squelch of the staff's sensible shoes against highly sheened linoleum; the rumble of trolleys and the clatter of wheelchairs; the whistle and cheeriness of the porters ferrying patients. The universally familiar typeface pointing out departments. Cat wondered whether an element of acting was an integral part of a nurse's training. Like barristers. As if facts and procedures could be dressed up or played down through their performance. But the kindness of the matronly nurse who led Django through, delivered in broad Derbyshire vernacular replete with affectionate monikers, was genuine in its down-to-earthiness. She might as well have been serving him chips in a café in Matlock as preparing his arm for radioactive fluid. And whether Django had been seventy-five, seventeen or seven, she'd still have addressed him as 'ducky'.

And Django was injected. And the wait began. Initially, Cat eyed him vigilantly, as if she'd be able to detect when the liquid came across something sinister, but soon enough the tedium kicked in and disparate topics of conversation were mused over in varying degrees of detail. After they had spent ages trying to remember the various teachers at the girls' school, there was a lengthy and loaded silence.

'Do you – did you ever – oh never mind,' Cat mumbled but she dragged her eyes to Django.

'Did I what?' he asked her gently.

'Doesn't matter. Nothing. Feel differently towards me than Fen and Pip?' Cat whispered. Django took a sharp intake of breath.

'It's just Fen says a parent's love for their child should, by definition, be supreme,' Cat explained in a small, guarded voice.

Django took time to answer. 'Well, I must be an exception to the rule because I have never distinguished between the three of you.' He paused. 'Would you say that makes me a bad parent?'

Cat twisted her fingers and wished she'd not veered from their mild and mundane nattering.

'Did I distinguish between you?' Django rephrased it. 'Do you think I should have?'

'I've always felt an equal,' Cat qualified, 'but it's difficult – it's difficult to wonder whether I shouldn't have. Whether I should have at least wondered.'

Django turned in his chair to face her head-on, wincing as he moved. 'Blasted ancient bones. Sometimes I've wondered, if your mother hadn't left, whether you'd have been told earlier.'

Cat thought about this. 'Would you have told me later, then – would you have told me *ever*, if she hadn't come back last month?' Then she gestured around her. 'With all of *this* now on the agenda?'

'I,' Django paused, 'actually, no – I don't suppose I would. I don't know, Cat. With this cancer business, might I have told you?' Django shook his head. 'I don't know. What's important in all of this? I don't know. I sway from thinking it matters not one jot, to it mattering a lot.'

Cat nodded but she didn't understand.

'I would hate Fen or Pip to think I ever loved them less,' Django said, sounding weighed down and tired, 'because the truth is, I simply couldn't have loved any of you more.'

Cat waited for the information to reach her brain, though she knew it might take a while longer, weeks, months even, for it to settle comfortably in her soul.

'I suppose you girls ought to think of it as you are my daughter and they are my adopted daughters.' Django paused. 'Take Tom – he's about to have a baby brother or sister made by his mother and her new husband but I don't think he'll ever doubt that he's loved equally. And if Zac and Pip ever have a child, I can't imagine that Tom would feel they had more love for their offspring.'

'I hear what you're saying,' said Cat, rubbing her forehead. Over the last month she found she could only spend limited time on the subject before a headache encroached. She felt like a soaked sponge; she'd absorbed so much that she was clogged; if she wasn't careful much of the cherished information would start to leak because she did not have the capacity to hold so much, as yet. 'So who was this Django Reinhardt?' she asked, needing to veer off at a tangent.

Django sighed, partly with relief, partly with pleasure, partly with comfort that this topic was one he could happily and knowledgeably discourse on for the duration of this radioactive trip.

'Django Reinhardt was the stuff of legend,' he began as if starting a biopic, his voice animated in contrast to the hush with which he'd previously spoken.

'When are we talking?' Cat asked.

'Well, he was born in 1910,' said Django, 'to a gypsy family. He was a banjo prodigy by the age of nine, horribly burnt and partially paralysed by a fire in his caravan when he was eighteen.' He checked to see that Cat looked suitably alarmed. 'Because of his handicap, he had to invent a technique to play at all – he'd use a whalebone collar-stiffener as a plectrum and a two-fingered method with sudden explosions of strumming.' Django gave a brief air-guitar demonstration, which made Cat laugh. 'His discovery of jazz – and his friendship with Stephane Grappelli, the great violinist, resulted in a musical marriage which gave birth to a new sound. He wouldn't play tunes *straight*. Gypsy music delights in improvisation and embellishment so Django and Stephane would take the melody of a dance or song as a starting point – "Sweet Georgia Brown", or "Jeepers Creepers", or "Ain't Misbehavin"—'

'I know those!' Cat interrupted, feeling proud rather than embarrassed that other waiting patients appeared to be listening in now. 'The house used to ring out with them.'

'His guitar had a voice that was near-human,' Django said dreamily. 'Everyone wanted to play with him. From trumpeter Bill Coleman, to trombonist Dicky Wells, to harmonica player Larry Adler and, just before the war, the mighty Duke Ellington.'

'I've heard of him!' Cat said proudly, aware that an elderly man sitting opposite was nodding to himself.

'Of course you have,' said Django as if it was the most basic part of anyone's education. 'After the war, Dizzy Gillespie.'

'I've heard of him too!' Cat exclaimed.

'I would jolly well hope so,' said Django, sharing a raised eyebrow with the pensioner opposite. 'During the war, in occupied France, American jazz records were banned but the musicians set up a Resistance of their own – putting out hundreds of jazz records but with camouflaged titles. Silly Huns never cottoned on. After the war, Django and Stephane reunited in London and reformed their old quintet – at the BBC's request. Their apotheosis was to famously rerecord the *Marseillaise* – which had been banned from the airwaves for many years. Django Reinhardt's ultimate triumph, in his final recording, was to reconcile jazz with the electric guitar. And then he died.'

'When?' Cat asked, shocked at the bluntness of the end of the story, horribly aware that they were sitting in a hospital, desperate to be distracted away again.

'In 1953,' Django told her, 'on May 16th.'

'That's your birthday,' Cat noted sadly.

'He was only forty-three years old,' said Django McCabe even more sadly.

'Poor Django,' said Cat. Quietly, she sat and thought to herself that if her Django hadn't had his career cut short by the demands of three small girls, he'd probably still be living in Paris, a life as colourful and creative as his namesake. She glanced at him. She knew every whisker on his extravagant sideburns, every furl and kink of his pony-tail, every dint on his forehead. And she knew that Fen knew them too. As did Pip.

He gave himself to us, he did. Entirely. I don't know anyone as well as I know him. Not even Ben, I suppose. I've had a lifetime of knowing Django.

She linked her arm through his. 'Hum me your favourite Django Reinhardt tune,' she asked him, laying her head against his arm; closing her eyes as the vibration of his humming 'Georgia On My Mind' travelled through to her heart.

I can't believe you're my father. My real father. My own dad. My very own daddy. The thing is, you're so nice to share. Pip and Fen might never be able to say 'my real father' in connection with you – but they'll always be able to say 'our very own father'.

Say it out loud, Cat.

I can't seem to.

'All right petal, time for your photo shoot.' The nurse had appeared, accompanied by a porter with an empty wheelchair. Momentarily, Cat thought she spoke to her. It seemed very odd to refer to Django as 'petal'.

'Your limo awaits,' said the porter, giving the wheelchair a twirl.

'I can walk,' Django objected.

'We'd rather you didn't, duck,' the nurse chided amicably.

'I pride myself on a smooth ride,' the porter protested, with a wink to Cat. 'You'll not find finer in the whole of Derbyshire.'

'Can I come?' Cat asked urgently, not wanting to leave him, or be without him.

'Only room for one,' the porter said, 'and I don't do pillion.'

'I meant—'

'I know,' the nurse said.

'Can she come?' Django asked.

'Of course she can,' said the nurse, 'as far as any of us can go. Come along ducky. How are you feeling, Mr McCabe?'

'Please,' he said, easing himself down into the wheelchair, 'call me Django.'

Cat insisted that she drove the 2CV back to Farleymoor though Django was a notoriously annoying passenger, stamping on imaginary brake pedals and gasping when corners were not taken at the angle he would have chosen.

'Mirror, signal, manoeuvre,' he muttered under his breath at regular intervals.

'It's a beautiful afternoon,' Cat said, when they arrived back in Farleymoor, 'shall we go for a walk?'

'I'm a little tired,' Django said.

'Are you feeling all right?' Cat asked. 'You look a little pale – not the Chernobyl glow we were expecting.'

'Just a little tired.'

'Sit in the garden,' Cat told him, repositioning the ancient Lloyd Loom chair. 'I'll make a pot of tea.'

By the time she came out, Django was fast asleep. She sat on the grass, listening to him breathing, the occasional extravagant, gruffled snore that always made the sisters laugh. Pip tape-recorded him once.

Cat looked at him. His mouth was slightly open, the deep laughter lines around his eyes a map of his life. 'Dad,' she said quietly.

'Daddy.
Dadda.
Pops.
Da.
Papa.
Pa.'

None of them actually suited him. Tellingly, nor did he awaken.

'Derek,' she said softly. Certainly not. On he slept.

'Django,' she all but whispered.

'Yes?'

He could only ever be Django, really.

'Sorry – did I wake you?'

'Heavens, what's the time? How long have I been asleep?'

'About an hour,' Cat told him. 'I can make this into iced tea,' she said, tapping the teapot. 'My train leaves in a couple of hours.'

So iced tea it was.

'I've ordered a cab – I don't want you driving,' she said, 'but I can stay, Django, if you like. I'm sure work will give me dispensation.'

'I'll be fine,' Django said. 'What's a bit of radioactivity? I can drive you.'

'No,' Cat insisted. 'You can – but you won't.'

He shrugged.

'Can I ask you something?' she said, shyly.

'Of course,' Django said, clenching his jaw on a yawn.

'Maybe when you're not tired,' Cat wavered, thinking better of it.

'Ask now,' he told her.

'Do you think it's a bit ominous,' she asked, 'that I wasn't really born of Love? That actually, I was the result of Adultery? A brief fling?'

Django sipped his tea silently. 'Don't be overly biblical and sanctimonious, Catriona,' he said crossly.

She plucked at the grass and thought about it. 'Sorry,' she said after a while.

'Let me ask *you* something,' Django said. He was feeling supremely tired now, a little nauseous too. 'Should I not expect *you* to love me *more* than Fen or Pip love me?' He let the concept hang. 'You're my daughter after all, aren't you? You're my *real* daughter, my *proper* daughter,' he tapped her quite briskly on the shoulder. 'Don't you think *you* ought to love me the most?'

Cat was simultaneously taken aback by his challenge and humbled by the astuteness of the remark. She felt immediate remorse. She'd so rarely been chastised by Django and neither had Pip or Fen. Their family dynamic had hardly ever necessitated it.

'None of us could love you more,' she proclaimed, relishing the new sense of clarity. Her smile grew from her soul and she could see the positive effect it had on Django. 'I'm ashamed to admit that we tried to love you less – last month,' she revealed, 'but we couldn't do that either.'

VT 05154

An early symptom of Django's cancer was to effectively kill off the anger and hurt that Fen and Pip had each experienced towards him since his birthday. It was as if the diagnosis packed up the past and placed life gently on new ground with a firmer footing. Cancer would define them, all of them. They would become nicer people for it. In the meantime Fen and Pip decreed that whatever had happened BC – before cancer – was largely irrelevant. They would pull together; life was too short, family was everything. Cat did so want to flow with their energy but unconditional love and trust were still in a holding bay, guarded by a self-protective wariness. She found herself both chipping away at it but building it back up too.

For Ben and Matt and Zac it was quite simple, really. Men for the most part are blessed with the ultimate take on the situation. Say less. It's not Neanderthal, it's genius. A variant on the theory that it takes a multitude of muscles to frown, but only three to smile. It was far easier to be nice than to be at loggerheads, it was far nicer to just feel love than argue about the vagaries of it. Love wasn't a matter of equality after all, but of equilibrium.

*

However, though Fen and Pip felt a welcome sense of relief at the warm waves of harmony and support, Cat's feelings of unease and dissatisfaction were contagious and before long a gnawing realization crept in that fundamentals remained untreated, unfixed.

So, though Fen acknowledged her present disinclination to even think about Al or anyone like him was due to her overriding concern for Django, the fact that she *had* been indisputably courting infidelity, could not be explained by Django's cancer. Similarly, though Pip now welcomed Zac's embrace and found great comfort in his calm and level-headed assessment of her uncle's illness, she knew too that joining forces on Django's behalf cleverly waylaid them from tackling the impasse existing in their marriage. As for Cat, if she split her time on a purely practical level between being a nurse and a bookshop manager, if she focused on jazz with Django and cancer with Ben and ISBNs with head office, then she reasoned she would have no time for the needling concerns about her own sense of self.

Mothers, daughters, lovers, liars – who were they? And how might Django's illness shape who they could become? In the clear light of each new day, questions yet to be answered came more and more to the fore. Questions to face head-on and answers not to be flinched from. They were prepared, at last, to question themselves. And at last they felt prepared to seek answers from somebody else too.

'What will Denver be like at this time of year?' Pip asks Cat.

'Hot,' Cat says and she doesn't need to say *Why?* It's of sudden comfort to her that the telepathy gifted amongst sisters obviously extends to half sisters too. She's always had it with Fen and Pip. The more recent discovery of specific DNA wasn't going to alter it. 'Lovely,' she says, 'but hot.'

Fen looks from left hand to right, from Cat to Pip, and lets her gaze rest on her daughter who is grabbing at Pip's rug in a bid to get onto her knees. 'I've never left my baby for more than a few hours,' Fen says quietly, attuned to their thinking.

'Could you leave her for a few days?' Pip asks tentatively, burning a knowing look at her sister.

Fen locks eyes with her. She shrugs. She nods. She shrugs again.

Pip turns to Cat. 'Could the shop spare you for a few days? Do you have any holiday entitlement?'

Cat shrugs and then she nods.

'Django will have an address,' says Pip. 'Who's going to call him?'

'You are,' say Fen and Cat together.

Django isn't surprised by the request. But he won't tell them he is relieved until they're back home again. 'OK. Hold on. It's in my address book. Where's my address book?' The telephone receiver is clattered down as he rummages around for some time. Pip raises her eyebrows to her sisters who listen in and smile. 'Here's my address book,' they can hear him say in the background because he's momentarily forgotten to retrieve his receiver. He picks it up. 'Hullo? Hullo? Are you still there? Ericsson. Here we are. Mrs P. Ericsson. 84 Emerson Street. Lester Falls.'

'Thanks,' says Pip, about to change the subject, as if the intended trip is no big deal.

'Vermont,' Django adds, 'VT 05154.'

Pip's pen hovers, frozen. Fen mouths, *What? What!* 'Pardon?' Pip says.

'It's a zip code. VT 05154.'

'I know it's a zip code,' says Pip, 'but what's it doing in *Vermont*?' Cat and Fen now crowd around the telephone, which irritates her. She's trying to concentrate and figure it out. She brushes them away as if they're children.

'Because your mother lives in Vermont,' they all hear Django clearly say, however, 'she never moved.'

'You said Denver,' Pip objects and Cat backs away now, feeling deflated at possibly more twists to the tale.

'I did not,' Django is saying carefully. 'Your mother ran off with a cowboy from Denver when you were small. But you've never asked where they lived. And they lived in Vermont. Never moved.'

Lester Falls

They didn't expect rain. Nor did they anticipate Lester Falls to be so plain. Pip knew better than to expect the maple trees to be ablaze with fiery foliage in June, but she had hoped for pretty weather-boarded houses, Adirondack chairs on porches, the odd covered bridge or white wooden church; it was thus difficult not to feel hard done by with this incessant drizzle in a rather nondescript town. Especially after an arduous three-hour drive from Boston. For Fen, picture-postcard perfect scenery had been an imperative notion when it had come to packing her suitcase and leaving her eleven-month-old baby; her ache for Cosima was now manifest in the gut-hollow, throat-ripped perpetual threat of tears. Cat found herself resenting her sisters for organizing the trip in the first place and she lagged behind, sulking to herself darkly that it must be easier for them than for her. With Fen close to tears and Cat glowering to herself, it was down to Pip to jostle maps and leaflets and figure out what they should do and where they might stay. Privately, she cursed her mother for not living somewhere more picturesque and she cursed her sisters for standing around gormlessly leaving everything to her. She remembered the quote on the mug Fen had bought her last Christmas which said that an older sister helps one remain half child, half woman; just then, Pip wished her younger sisters would opt for the grown-up identity.

'We should have stayed in Boston,' Cat said sulkily. 'A little retail therapy would probably be far more curative than some misguided fact-finding mission with some woman we don't even know.'

'We shouldn't have come in the first place,' Fen muttered, staring at outdated fashions fastidiously displayed in a shop window. 'What do we hope to achieve anyway? We don't even know what we want to say. We'd have been better off spending time in Derbyshire with Django.'

'For God's sake you two!' Pip snapped. 'We're jet lagged and we're nervous. But we're here. So let's find somewhere to stay – and something to eat. It's lunch-time.' She stomped off with Cat and Fen mooching behind her.

There's little a great cup of coffee can't soothe. Especially when served by a friendly soul in the comfortable surroundings of a genuine diner. Combined with a sturdy plateful of eggs and grits to raise blood sugar levels and stave off tiredness, Cat and Fen felt revived and able to assess their surroundings and consider their options with Pip.

'We don't know where exactly she lives,' Cat said, squinting at the map.

'Or if she's even here,' said Fen.

'Please God let her be out of town,' Cat said. 'Then we can justify a weekend's shopping in Boston.'

'If she isn't here, I might just fly back home, actually,' said Fen, brightening at the possibility.

'I'll ask the waitress if she knows where Emerson Street is,' Pip said.

'Don't mention her name!' Cat rushed.

The waitress, who had 'Betty' embroidered on a pristine pale blue gingham uniform, was sorry to be unable to help, but she asked the short-order chef who scribbled down directions on a paper napkin.

'Is it walkable?' Pip asked.

'Joe – lady here wants to know if it's walkable?'

Joe came right out of the kitchen, appeared to evaluate the age and fitness of the girls and nodded. 'I reckon. About a half-hour. Who you looking for?'

The girls paused.

'Oh, no one, really,' Cat said.

'You guys on vacation?' Joe asked. 'In *Lester*?'

'Just passing through,' Pip said lightly. 'A friend of a friend of a friend lives on Emerson Street – we thought we'd look her up.'

'Who's that?' Joe asked.

'Um. A Mrs Ericsson?'

Joe thought hard. 'Nope. Can't say I know her. You know her, Betty?'

'I'm thinking, I'm thinking – but no, don't think I do. Say, are you from England?' the waitress asked with breathless awe.

'Yes,' the girls told her.

'That is just so nice,' Betty enthused. 'I could listen to you speak all day long.'

Automatically, the girls found they rounded their vowels and used choice adjectives, much to her delight. After more coffee and flattery, Lester Falls seemed less dull and their hostility lessened too.

'Well, thank you so much,' said Pip, 'that was simply super.'

'Indeed!' said Cat. 'Splendid coffee.'

'Have a nice day!' Betty said.

'Cheerio,' said Cat.

They strolled along Main Street. The rain had stopped, revealing the town to be less dreary than first impressions suggested. The shops were old-fashioned but quirky, the façades comfortingly indicative of small-town America, as portrayed in so many of the films the sisters had seen. A promising landscape was now impressively visible beyond the town. The mountains so thickly forested that they appeared to be clothed in thick green bouclé sweaters.

'We're in the lie of the Green Mountains here,' Pip looked up from the guidebook. '*Vert Mont* – Vermont! Do you see?'

'Shall we walk then?' Fen asked tentatively. 'Joe said it would take half an hour.'

'But say she *is* in,' Cat said. 'We don't even know what we're going to say.'

'Let's find somewhere to stay first,' Pip said.

Sitting tightly together on one of the beds in the family room they'd found in a decent guest house on a pretty street a short walk from the centre of town, the McCabe sisters pored over the local phone directory. They'd missed the entry initially, forgetting that Bob was most likely a diminutive of Robert, but had then found the entry for R. Ericsson. The address was the same as that which Django had provided and gave the girls a bizarre sense of triumph, as if they were veritable sleuth-hounds. Pip jotted down the telephone number. Then they stared hard at the entry again, as if utter concentration might suddenly provide fly-on-the-wall privilege, some sort of telepathy or more clues.

Pip looked at her watch. 'Shall we mosey on up there now,' she suggested lightly, 'you know – just in time for tea?'

'We have another three days, remember,' said Cat and Fen felt herself lurching to the verge of tears at the thought of four more days until she'd actually be home. 'We could look around the town and get our bearings.'

'Find somewhere for supper later,' Fen agreed.

'This is not a holiday,' Pip said impatiently. 'We're here

on family business. Now come on.' She picked up the car keys and led the way.

Pip crept the car along Emerson Street. The houses, modern but unexceptional, were set spaciously along it, fronted by steeply pitched gardens making the buildings appear more squat than they actually were. Under their breath, the sisters spoke out the house numbers, falling silent when they came upon their mother's home. Though it fitted well with the style and scale of all the other houses they had passed, its blandness took them aback. Fen felt embarrassed that she'd actually thought along the lines of Bates Motel. She realized how, deludedly, she had been expecting something else; presumed that somehow she'd instantly recognize the house where their mother lived. Something more sinister. Something a lot less ordinary. Pip stopped the car at the bottom of the drive and they looked up.

'Doesn't look like there's anyone at home,' said Fen though she could not base this theory on fact.

'Might as well come back later,' Cat said, 'or tomorrow.'

'God almighty, you two,' Pip sighed, 'come *on*.'

They walk up the drive.

They loiter by the front door.

Then they turn on their heels and walk briskly back to the car.

Unseen from an upstairs window, Penny had watched them arrive and now she's watching them leave. And they've gone. She goes downstairs and sits heavily in Bob's chair. What could it possibly mean? It was a sight she has never envisaged, never even thought about, never hoped for, never dreaded. What on earth should she make of this? What on earth is she meant to do? What on earth do they want? Why didn't they ring the bell? Why didn't she open the door anyway? she asks out loud, again and again. But no one answers.

'We could head off to Boston,' Cat suggested, once they were back in the guest house.

'Or we could just go home,' Fen said. 'Do you mind if I do that? You two hit Boston, by all means.'

'We'll call her,' Pip said and Fen glanced with resentment at the phone book still lying in the centre of Pip's bed. 'We can't go without trying a bit harder,' she told her gently. 'We've come this far. And spent a fortune.'

'How about we phone the number at 9 p.m. tonight, and if there's no answer, we pop up there again at 9 a.m. tomorrow and if she still isn't there, we head back to Boston and Fen can make the 9 p.m. flight?' Cat said.

'Cat o' nine tales,' Pip laughed.

'We can send her a postcard, or something,' Fen said quietly, looking from one palm to the other.

'Are you missing Cosima dreadfully?' Cat asked.

Fen nodded. 'You have no idea how much.'

'But Matt's mum said everything was fine when you last phoned home?' Pip said.

Fen nodded and shrugged.

'Weird to think that Cosima's other grandma is just a couple of miles away,' Cat remarked.

'Weirder to think it's our *mother* just a couple of miles away,' said Pip and they stared at the phone book. 'Right, I'm calling her now.'

'What if she answers?' Cat gasped as Pip lifted the receiver. 'What will you say?'

'What if it's an answerphone?' Fen asked. 'Will you leave a message?'

Pip was already dialling. 'Answering machine,' she said, hanging up.

They stared at the phone.

'What did it say?' Fen asked.

'I don't know,' Pip said, 'I hung up on "Hi".'

'Can I listen?' Fen asked. Pip shrugged, phoned the number and passed the receiver over to Fen who glued it against her ear and tried to detect clues from the wording of the message, the timbre of her mother's voice. She hung up in a hurry before the beep.

'I suppose I ought to as well,' said Cat and Pip dialled the number again. Cat listened hard; though she'd heard the voice only once before, it sounded strangely familiar.

Hi. You've reached Penny Ericsson. Can't take your call right now. Leave your message after the tone and I'll call you as soon as I can.

'Hullo – who is this?'

The voice rang through before the anticipated beep. Cat was so taken aback that one hand was paralysed to the receiver, the other frozen in mid-air where it had been hovering over the phone's cradle. The voice filtered out of the receiver, tinny and faint yet filling the room.

'Hullo?'

Fen stared at Cat wide-eyed while Pip mouthed, *Say something Say something* whilst holding out her hand for the receiver.

'Hullo? Who is this?'

Cat cancelled the call.

They sat in silence, staring at the phone with trepidation, as if their mother might suddenly materialize from it, like some wicked genie.

'She was *there*,' Cat whispered, 'she's there right *now*.' She looked at Pip. 'Please don't make us go back up there tonight.' She held her hand out for her sisters to observe how it trembled. Fen took it and held it between hers. Pip sat and wondered what they should do next.

*

It was like a skewed take on Postman's Knock – the resultant addled adrenalin rush caused by the near miss. Derring-do mixed with jet lag and crisp cold beer in a local bar, combined to ensure a lively evening for the McCabe sisters. They picked at peanuts and at the labels on the beer bottles and giggled at the details of the day.

'It's all very Enid Blyton,' Fen said, chinking her beer bottle against her sisters'.

'Woody Allen, more like,' said Cat, with a long drink.

'Let's just hope it doesn't turn Stephen King,' Pip laughed and she put down her bottle and laid her hands on the table as if they symbolized facts. 'Right. We know that she's here but she doesn't know that *we're* here. Do we phone first or just front up?'

'I wonder if she was in all along, this afternoon,' mused Fen, 'spying on *us* stalking *her*.'

'We didn't ring the bell,' Cat said, 'but perhaps she traced our calls. Do they have 1471 in America?' she wondered, hiccing softly.

'The thing is,' said Pip, 'what do we want to say? What is it that we want to hear?'

Tracing the paths of the condensation on their beer bottles, tracing the pattern of the wood grain on the table, making patterns out of peanuts, they could draw no conclusion.

If Pip had been subconsciously looking for any excuse to confront her middle sister, that night it was presented to her on a plate, or rather in a beer bottle, in the guise of four studenty local boys offering to buy them a drink. It wasn't as if the boys loitered with intent. Or made a pass. Or even flirted harmlessly. They didn't ply them with alcohol, just the one friendly round of beers. They weren't suggestive in their conversation; if anything they were refreshingly artless in their questions. After all, three English girls were something of a novelty and buying them a drink bought an evening's entertainment. They asked about the Queen. They asked the girls to say 'squirrel' and 'bath' and 'pasta'. They asked how old were the houses in which they lived. Though Fen's smile and easy chatter was harmless enough, to Pip it seemed otherwise. With her beer goggles on, she computed simple facts into complex danger signs. She fused the tone of Fen's laughter, the slant of her smile and the glint of her eyes, into the image of a trollop warranting chastisement.

'Nice guys,' Fen commented as the boys left the bar.

'You can tell whose daughter you are,' growled Pip.

If this was a saloon in a Spaghetti Western, loaded silence would have met Pip's verbal gauntlet. But in this bar in Lester Falls, time didn't stand still and the din did not abate and Pip's haughty expression was somewhat diffused by the dim lighting. Both Cat and Fen had to squint at her and say, What? because the beer and the bar and the bizarreness of what they thought they'd heard were so distorted.

Pip looked at Cat. 'Why not ask her what babysitters are for?'

Cat looked at Pip, confused. 'What *babysitters* are for?' she asked and Pip nodded gravely. Cat turned to Fen. 'What are babysitters for?' she asked ingenuously, with a conspiring twitch of her face to signify she thought Pip odd.

Fen took a long moment to answer, in which time Pip's point struck her sharply. 'Tell her they're to alleviate the oppressive humdrum a frumpy mum can just occasionally be choked by,' Fen told Cat whilst glaring at Pip.

Cat looked at Pip. 'She says they're to – oh fuck it, did you hear all that? They choke humdrum frumps and stuff.'

Pip folded her arms and levelled a stare at Fen, whilst speaking to Cat. 'Tell her, Oh! Really! I thought that was the function of someone called Al!'

It was well below the belt but it winded Fen all the same, a single spasm deep in her diaphragm forcing her breath into her constricted throat. 'Fuck you,' Fen whispered which was easy enough for everyone to lipread.

'What's going on here?' Cat asked, her gaze leaping from one sister to other. 'Have you fallen out? Have I missed something? Who's Al?'

'Al's your sister's bit-on-the-side,' Pip announced.

'That's not true!' Fen protested.

'*Who is Al*?' Cat repeated. 'What's happened?'

With her hands in her lap, Fen looked deeply into her beer bottle as if hoping for a magical kaleidoscope to transport her away, willing the neck of the bottle to widen and reveal Narnia, Wonderland, anywhere. But it didn't. It didn't even say Drink Me any more. Fen pushed the bottle away and slowly she looked up at her sisters with a smile soft and beatific which she hoped might miraculously solve the issue and change the subject. But it didn't.

'Fen!' Cat implored. 'What's going *on*?'

'Leave me alone,' Fen said feebly as she stood heavily from her stool and made to leave the bar. Almost at the door she stopped. What was the point of this? Storming out would only make her look worse. These were her sisters. Really, she needed their support, not animosity. After all, as the only feeling she harboured for Al was regret, there could be no harm in divulging that at all. Her sisters' friendship was imperative; she hadn't been through life without it and just then she could not contemplate going forward without it. As she made it to the door, she was accosted by the memory of a quote on a tea towel Pip had once bought her, which decreed that anyone who didn't know how a woman could both love her sister and also want to strangle her was probably an only child.

'Sorry,' Fen said, with searching eye contact, as she returned to the table and sat back down for her comeuppance.

'What's happened?' Cat pleaded. 'What did you *do*?'

Fen glanced from one hand to the other and then she looked up. 'There is this bloke called Al,' Fen told Cat apologetically and with a clear shrug of confession to Pip, 'but nothing happened really.' She stopped at her words; glancing back over her memory of the time in Al's room and wondering just what defined something or nothing; what precisely was infidelity. Penetration or intent? Wandering hands or simply straying thoughts? She remembered how she'd deludedly hoped a quick dalliance with Al would provide positive memories that would titillate. But there, in the bar in a one-eyed town in Vermont, the thought of what she'd done, what she'd been on the verge of doing had Pip not phoned her that fateful night, sank a leaden spear of shame right to her core. She dragged her gaze to meet her sisters'.

'I almost cheated on Matt,' she confided with a meek nod and a sad shrug.

'What's "almost"?' Cat asked aghast.

'I met some bloke,' Fen admitted, 'a bloke called Al and he was flirty and young and the opposite of Matt. And I was flattered and tempted. More than tempted. And thank God Pip phoned when she did because if she hadn't I probably would have.'

'Would have what?' Cat asked. 'Phoned Pip?'

'Had sex with Al,' Fen admitted. Suddenly, she realized that she could fob off her sisters with this limited version of events, but not herself. It was time, at last, to change tack and face facts. 'I have to admit, I practically did,' she revealed forlornly. 'If we're talking all the other bases, I'd passed Base 3. We were on the home straight when Pip called.'

'You're joking!' Cat laughed, because Fen's terminology seemed so adolescent and the notion seemed so preposterous. *Fen*? Fen being fingered and having her tits groped while she fiddled with the cock of a bloke called Al? Fen who had embraced to the hilt the all-consuming responsibilities of being a mother at the expense of even a night out at the Rag and Thistle? Fen, the conventional, stay-at-home mummy with lovely Matt providing for her and her perfect daughter?

'I'm not,' Fen said, her eyes downcast as she hid behind her fringe.

'Not what?' said Cat.

'Not joking,' Fen declared.

'But you're not allowed to do that!' Cat protested.

'I lost sight of that fact,' Fen admitted, 'but I swear to you, it stares me in the face every time I look in the mirror.'

'Do you no longer love Matt?' Pip asked carefully, her tone more level, her look softer.

'Of course I do,' Fen said, suddenly realizing she couldn't even consider answering the question any other way.

'But who is this Al?' Cat pressed.

'I don't really know,' Fen admitted, 'just someone who wasn't Matt. Someone with whom I could be more than just me.'

As they walked back to the guest house, Cat and Pip wondered why their sister should think there was anything wrong with just being herself. While Fen just thought there must be something wrong with her. None of the other new mums she had met had gadded off with flower-laying toyboys. The only new mum of whom she knew who had behaved in a similar fashion was her own mother. And Fen and her sisters were in agreement that there must have been something very wrong with her. Fen's last thought on the matter, before she was distracted by the flashing red button on the phone in the room, was to pray that her wayward detour had been temporary and to thank God that it hadn't taken her away from her baby.

But had the woman who had taken herself away from her three babies decades ago, now tracked them down?

Cat, Fen and Pip stared at the flashing red light.

'Could be Ben,' said Cat.

'Or Matt,' said Fen.

'Or Zac,' said Pip.

But there was no message. Just a long recorded silence.

Probably one of the boys.

Playing silly buggers.

Cat looked at her watch. 'If it's 10 o'clock here, it must be three tomorrow morning in proper time.'

'Proper time?' laughed Pip, putting an affectionate arm around Cat.

'Check your mobile for messages,' Fen told Pip, who had the only tri-band phone between them. 'Just in case it's for me.'

Pip took her phone from the bedside drawer where she'd placed it on top of their passports and next to the complimentary copy of the bible which was alarmingly covered in lilac suedette.

The envelope icon signified a message.

'It's just a text from Zac,' Pip told them, opening the message.

Hope all ok. Just 2 say Tom has baby bro!!! Nathan Oliver, 7lbs 13oz. Evryone doing just fine!!! Z xx

'What does he say?' Cat asked.

'Pip?' said Fen, because her sister's face had dropped.

'What? Oh,' said Pip, 'nothing really.'

'Sweet nothings?' Cat smiled.

'Something like that,' Pip said, switching off the mobile and putting it back by the purple bible.

The girls were exhausted. It had gone three in the morning proper time, and they'd had a day beset by travel, jet lag, strange towns, their mother's front door and their mother's voice. Cat and Fen shared the kingsized bed, falling asleep within seconds of each other, within minutes of clambering in. Pip turned away from them in her queen bed. Hot tears seeped silently from tired sore eyes.

Evryone doing just fine. Evryone doing just fine. Welcome little Nathan. But I'm not fine. I'm not doing just fine at all.

* * *

Those three silent calls. Penny guessed it was them, her daughters. Her three girls, silent for almost three decades. She surprised herself by hoping that it was. They just wanted to listen, didn't they? Who dialled last? Who was it who hung up on 'Hi'? She had traced the call, to put a place to the number. Brook Barn Inn. She knew exactly where that was. It was a decent enough place. She had spent the remainder of the afternoon and all evening meandering around the house, walking in and out of rooms that had seen no person other than her for seven months. She went to bed early but couldn't sleep. Nearing midnight, she dressed and drove into town. Parked her car, switched off the engine and just gazed and gazed at the Old Lester Inn; wondering what she should do.

Plastic Tubing

'Are you awake?'

'Yes.'

'Is Cat awake?'

'Yes I'm awake too.'

'Sodding jet lag. It's not even seven o'clock.'

'I bet that diner will be open by now.'

'What day is it – is it Saturday?'

'Yes. I think so.'

'It *is* Saturday. We arrived in Boston Thursday night – then came up here yesterday morning. So yes, today must be Saturday.'

'Perhaps the diner won't open so early on a Saturday.'

'Only one way to find out.'

The diner was open and Cat, Fen and Pip were greeted by Betty the waitress who, bizarrely, had 'DeeDee' embroidered on her uniform today.

'The English Roses return, Joe!' she called through to the back before fussing around them, wiping an already gleaming table and straightening the napkin dispenser and cruets. 'You take a load off, girls,' she said. 'What'll you have? Did you meet with your friend?'

The sisters exchanged glances; if they couldn't refer to her as their 'mother' they certainly couldn't refer to her as their 'friend'.

'She wasn't in,' said Pip, deciding to gloss over the ambiguity by polishing her vowels. 'Frightful shame.'

'Frightful shame!' the waitress repeated, marvelling at the words, not the matter. 'Well, if you're kicking around today, there's a lot of fun to be had round here. There's the Falls for a start – if you guys like hiking that sure is one pretty place. There's also some quaint villages near by – Hubbardton's Spring and Ridge – just like you see on the postcards, though most of the postcards are taken in the fall so don't go expecting those colours. And if you like to shop, you head over to Manchester – the finest outlet village. Puts New York in the shade, I'll say.'

Cat's glance to her sisters was sufficient to say that she for one rather hoped the house on Emerson would be empty again today. She found herself looking at the waitress's left breast as coffee was replenished. 'I say,' she said plummily, 'I hope you don't think me rude – but yesterday you were Betty, today you're DeeDee.'

The waitress looked at her bosom, as if to check herself who she was. 'You're right!' she said cheerily, and busied away to collect the girls' breakfasts from the grill, piping hot and delicious.

After a leisurely breakfast, though coffee was topped up and more pleasantries were exchanged with the waitress, they were no nearer finding if she was DeeDee or Betty. Fen and Cat called goodbye to Betty, Pip called goodbye to DeeDee, all three said see you tomorrow.

'Bugger Boston,' Cat remarked as they walked up Main Street, 'let's just do a day-trip to Manchester. When Betty said "dickny" do you think she meant "DKNY"?'

'Or do you think *we've* been mispronouncing the brand?' Fen challenged and she and Cat laughed in mortification.

'Ralph Law-rn,' said Cat.

'Ralph L'Ren,' Fen said.

'Sad thing is, I don't possess a single item from Ralph or Donna,' said Pip. 'I'm not what one would call a designer clown.'

'So let's go to Manchester!' Cat said.

'Or we could just catch an earlier—'

'Hi.'

It was Penny.

Right in front of them.

Sunlight bouncing off her glasses and flashing platinum through her short, silvering hair; her slim, wiry frame appearing to fill the sidewalk. Fen glancing sharply behind herself, as if looking for an escape route; Cat staring at her mother's feet, ten toes with neat nails; Pip stepping forward just slightly but able to raise her eyes only as far as her mother's tiger's-eye pendant.

'Hi,' she says again, this time with an awkward shrug. Pip can feel Cat and Fen looking beseechingly at her.

'Hullo,' says Pip.

'Fancy seeing you here,' Penny says with what would have been a wry smile though her nervousness and the intense sunlight make it appear more of a grimace and a squint.

'We've just had breakfast,' Pip says, cringing inwardly. Since planning the trip, she's prepared many a soliloquy and rehearsed varying degrees of acerbic wit and biting truths. Not once has she practised the line 'We've just had breakfast'.

'You have plans for today?' Penny asks, steering clear of the undisputable fact that the girls can only be in Lester Falls on her account.

'We were going to go to Manchester,' Cat says shyly, addressing her mother's feet. 'Shopping.'

'Nice,' said Penny, as if this was reason enough to have Lester Falls as their base.

'Perhaps a walk to the Falls,' Fen says, glancing over her shoulder again though that's the opposite direction to the Falls.

'Real pretty,' Penny says, as if a hike to the Falls could indeed be the sole purpose for crossing the Atlantic to this little town. 'You could come for lunch,' she says, 'if it fits your day?'

The sisters regard each other in silent consultation.

'Could do,' says Pip, noting half a nod from Fen and a small shrug from Cat.

'Good,' says Penny, wondering what they like to eat. She's never been much of a cook. Never attempted the eccentric fusion cuisine of Django McCabe. 'You vegetarian or anything?'

'What – having been brought up by Django?' Fen says to Penny's sandals – she remembers distinctly they are the same she wore that morning in Derbyshire.

Penny surprises herself by smiling easily. 'So, shall we say noon? I live on Emerson Street.' She pauses. 'But you know that.'

The sisters consider their mother's slightly cryptic allusion.

'Hey, Penny!'

A young woman, much their own age, has approached and she's smiling at their mother, regarding them quizzically.

'Oh,' Penny flusters, and Cat can see that her toes curl slightly, 'Juliette. Hi.'

'Haven't seen you for a while,' Juliette says warmly. 'How you doing?'

'Fine,' says Penny, acutely aware that the last time she saw Juliette was when she stormed away from her, 'just fine. Real busy.'

'Oh,' says Juliette, 'cool.'

There follows a pause so pregnant Penny fears she is on the verge of bellowing in discomfort. Juliette is looking from the girls to Penny, and back again. Smiling sweetly, genuinely friendly.

'I'm Juliette,' she says to the sisters, with a childish little wave. 'Hi.'

The sisters respond with awkward hand-raising of their own.

'Pip.'

'Fen.'

'Cat.'

'Well, I gotta go,' Juliette says, with polite reluctance. 'Sure was nice to meet you all,' she smiles at the girls. 'Don't be a stranger,' she says to Penny, touching her hand. 'We miss you.'

And there they stand for a mammoth moment or two longer.

Penny, a woman who feels she has no right to introduce herself as 'mother'.

And the three sisters who can't yet bring themselves to be known as her daughters.

Pip walked a large, aimless loop. Fen and Cat followed.

'Christ, are we sure about all of this?' Fen asked, standing stock still. 'Isn't it just too bizarre to be having lunch with her? Too quick? Too – I don't know – normal? Too friendly, too accepting?' Pip sighed as she thought although Fen didn't wait for an answer. 'I don't know about you two but I don't feel prepared. I've run through so many scenarios in my head these last few days and in all of them, I'm this empowered woman brimming with erudite proclamations and condemnation. But now I feel very, very small.'

Pip looked ahead. 'Look, we all feel weird – her too, no

doubt – but we're here and this is an opportunity and we have to take it, whatever the outcome.' She paused, tying and retying her pony-tail while she thought. 'If we don't – if we blow her out – imagine how you'll feel once you've returned home. Jesus – I've said it before, it's not a holiday. It's not a social engagement. It's necessary. It's a summit.'

'What do we do about Django? Say she asks?' Fen asked. 'Are we going to tell her?' She looked at Cat who appeared lost in thought.

'I think we avoid lies,' Pip said, reflecting on it. 'After so much dishonesty, the plain truth will do. But let's not volunteer information. If she asks directly how he is, then we'll answer directly. Agreed?'

Fen nodded. Pip looked to Cat who was still avoiding eye contact or comment. 'Cat?'

'Whatever,' Cat muttered. 'I'm not hungry,' she said, thinking fast that she could find if there was a flight from somewhere to take her to Boulder.

'That's totally irrelevant and you know it,' Pip snapped.

'But we don't know her at all,' Cat said, cross with Pip for her reaction.

'What we do know is that she ran away with a cowboy from Denver when we were small,' said Pip. 'Here's our chance to find out why.'

In their fantasies, over the years, they'd created an image of their mother that was far from flattering. They'd never quite given her form – a stereotypical warted wicked witch seemed too contrived – but they'd created the world in which she lived. Most damning of all, they'd given her a world with no style. With the cowboy-from-Denver situation always to the fore, they'd positioned their mother in a poor and tacky version of *Dynasty*. An ostentatious driveway in a boring flat land. A preposterous fountain flanked by disparate figures from antiquity, poorly copied and made from resin. Fake Corinthian columns and disproportionate pediments. White leather sofas. Reproduction furniture with ubiquitous claw-and-ball feet. Lots of gilt. Lots of guilt. Uniformed staff, who all secretly hated her, addressing her as 'ma'am'. The cowboy himself, laughably repulsive in a rhinestone-encrusted ten-gallon hat; corpulent, porcine and with a gait dictated by gout.

But how reality can let a daydream down. For a start, they had to relocate their fantasy from a dull and nondescript landscape to America's lush and hilly smallest state. Then, on entering Penny's house, the girls were immediately shocked and humbled by the utter contrast to their fantasy. Their sense of control of the situation was compromised. Reality was staring them in the face and they had to swallow hard and meet it eye to eye. No stuffed bison heads. No rifles, criss-crossed, above vulgar stone-clad fireplaces. No white leather anywhere. No staff. Most poignantly: no cowboy. But how they could feel his presence, how noticeable this man was by his absence. The house was tidy and clean, the furniture simple with a slightly dated Scandinavian feel; but no amount of messiness or belongings could change the haunting feeling that this was a lonely house; a place, a space, essentially designed and designated for two.

'Shall I show you around?' Penny offered. The four of them had been gathered in the hallway for some time, taking silent interest in each other's footwear whilst practising what to say. 'We built this house in '74.'

It was the same in every room; the house and its contents seemed to be putting on a brave smile, a bit of a show. Crisp linen, pretty curtains, handmade cushion covers and warmly worn rugs were easy on the eye in a futile bid to keep the solitary sadness from view. Everywhere appeared airy and light but a pervasive sense of melancholy cast metaphorical shadows which were long. Following behind Penny, Pip wondered whether this was their mother's home or her purgatory. Fen thought of their childhood house at Farleymoor; the scamper and warmth there, the welcoming dishevelment, the flow of company; the ring of home. The last room Penny took them to was the sitting-room, with its picture windows presenting a painterly and flawless view to a nicely tended garden rolling gently down to a thatch of trees that swathed its way up to the skirts of the hills beyond.

'Take a seat,' Penny said. 'Can I fix you a coffee? Something soft?' and she hurried off to the kitchen to compose herself and gaze quietly out of the window at the hire car of her daughters who were currently making themselves comfortable just across the hallway.

Cat stared at the chair. It was truly monstrous, the clumpy wood lacquered until it looked plasticized, embalmed even. She couldn't help but admit to herself that it was the sort of piece that Django would declare marvellous. She turned her attention to other features: the low table in burr oak laden with three neat piles of large-format coffee-table books; framed photographs on the mantel that would need to be seen up close; a large selection of board games piled on the lowest shelves either side of the fireplace; a chess set on an occasional table, its players standing to attention as if a game was imminent. Cat would have liked to peruse the photographs but a perverse desire to appear in Penny's eyes not remotely interested in her life kept her sitting on the sofa, looking at the chair.

'So,' said Penny breezily as she came into the room with a tray, 'here's your juice. I mixed cranberry and apple. And some cookies.'

Everyone sipped awkwardly and nibbled self-consciously.

'We were looking at the chair,' Fen said at length. 'It's – unusual.'

Penny regarded it for a moment. 'It's revolting,' she colluded, 'but it was Bob's most favourite possession. And though I found it easy enough to give all his clothes to the mission without so much as a sentimental sniff to his shirt collars – the chair, well, I just couldn't do it. I had to keep it.' They all looked at the chair, as if willing it to talk. 'Try it,' Penny said to Fen, 'go ahead.' Fen glanced at her sisters, then balanced her cookies on the rim of her glass and went over to sit down. 'Well?' Penny enquired.

'It's not designed for my shape,' Fen said diplomatically.

'I'm more of an Eames lounger girl,' said Pip, when Penny gestured for her to try. Cat avoided eye contact.

'My mother used to say every pot has its lid,' Penny said, 'so, perhaps every backside has its chair.'

Pip considered this. Then she thought about their maternal grandmother. 'When did she die? Your mother?' she asked.

'When I was fourteen.'

'Your father?' Pip asked.

'When I was very young.'

'Do you have any siblings?' Pip continued to probe.

'No, I have not.'

'Any other children?' Fen asked.

'No,' said Penny, 'I have not.'

'Stepchildren?' Pip asked.

'Nope,' Penny said, seemingly engrossed in massaging her cuticles, 'none. That's it. No family left.'

Pip thought to herself that if this was Hollywood, there'd be soaring violins and group hugs to accompany them proclaiming *Hey! We're your family! We never stopped loving you! Love means never having to say you're sorry! Oh Mom, it feels like we're home!* But the thought held no attraction and she reminded herself that this was not a journey to reconciliation, it was a fact-finding mission.

'I don't know if I was the lid or the pot,' Penny was saying, her thumb playing anxiously over her fingertips, 'but whichever I was, Bob was certainly the other.'

'We thought you lived in Denver,' Cat said, speaking for the first time. 'I lived in Denver for three years. We thought you lived with a cowboy.'

'Bob?' Penny looked incredulous. 'A *cowboy*?' She mused this over. 'I mean, he looked the part, when I first met him, in his blue jeans and his boots and his buckle belts and bootlace ties. And he *was* from Denver. But he wouldn't know one end of a horse from the other. He never got close enough anyway, on account of his asthma.'

'Oh,' said Cat.

'All these years you've been thinking I've been living with John Wayne on a ranch out west?' Penny started to giggle. It was Fen's giggle – Cat and Pip could detect it in an instant and they both glanced automatically from their mother to their sister; intrigued, disturbed. 'Oh my!' Penny continued. 'Would he have loved that.'

'Was it something to do with asthma?' Pip asked. 'How he died?'

'No my dear, he had cancer,' said Penny. The sisters looked at their laps and said sorry. And then they privately hoped that Penny wouldn't ask after Django because they didn't want to say the cancer word out loud. They hated saying the word. It was impossible to say it without a hush. And that seemed to dignify the dreadful disease. And anyway, his results weren't in. They didn't want to jinx Django.

Penny had crossed to the mantelpiece and selected a clutch of photographs. She passed them around. They studied the pictures, looked hard at Bob. He did not look anything like they'd imagined. The photos showed a tall, slim man in sensible V-necked sweaters, with a tidy slate-grey beard, round spectacles, silver glinting hair neatly clipped short beneath a smooth, tanned pate. Smiling. Easy, open, attractive smile. In most pictures, his arm was warmly around Penny. He looked normal and nice and Pip was surprised by how easy it was to tell Penny so. Cat wanted to say that he looked nothing like Django but she didn't. She felt slightly offended that there was no physical similarity at all. Instead, she focused on an old photo, from the seventies perhaps, in which Penny could well have been Pip, the same tilt of the head, the identical sparky smile.

'If he wasn't a cowboy,' Fen said, 'what did he do?'

'We had a business,' Penny said. 'We were very good at it. Tubing.'

'Tubing?' Fen looked disappointed.

'Yes,' Penny confirmed, 'plastic tubing. Bob Ericsson sure was the king of plastic tubes and components! Now would you look at the time – I'm going to fix our lunch.'

For the first time in their lives, Pip, Fen and Cat did not act like sisters; they did not huddle together to confab and support. They didn't even look at each other. They sat in their own heavy spheres, with thoughts spiralling nearly out of control. It was like having nothing to cling on to after a lifetime of clutching at straws which, when looked down, had opened onto a fantasy world of imaginative exaggeration and convoluted details. All of which had been comforting in their negativity. Yet in the space of an hour, the McCabe sisters had had to let the vulgar cowboy go, and the revolting ranch and the obsequious staff and all the rhinestones with him. Plastic tubes now replaced their hollow straws. They had a face to put to a name and the face was friendly. And though they'd been staring at their mother, noting all the details of her face, computing all her mannerisms, what they could see most vividly was her sadness and loneliness. It was all a bit disconcerting. A great love had been lost, and it was this love which defined this woman – not them. It was clear they never had done. The bluntness of this hurt. But the fact that a great love had existed also gave the protagonists qualities that Pip, Fen, Cat and even Django had spent their lives denying them.

Penny had started to sing. They could hear her. They didn't know the tune. But the sound broke their hermetic isolation from one another.

'I've just realized – we've probably never asked Django much about her or her cowboy because our family folklore of "Your mother ran off with a cowboy from Denver when you were small" had served as an answer in its own right,' Pip said. 'And I suppose we've always held her and the evil cowboy as somehow responsible for our father's death – like they caused the heart failure.'

'But there was never a cowboy,' Fen said flatly, 'there was just plastic tubing and now there's just a lonely widow. Who's currently cooking us lunch.'

'I'm not hungry,' said Cat and her voice was hoarse, 'and I no longer want to be here.'

'We'll go after lunch,' Pip said.

'Yeah right,' Cat muttered. 'I want to go now. Not after lunch.'

'Well we can't,' Pip whispered in a hiss.

'Why the fuck not?' Cat whispered back.

'We can't,' Pip said.

'Don't tell me what I can and can't do!' Cat objected. 'You two bloody stay then – I'm not.'

'Cat!' Pip said.

'Fucking hell, Pip,' Cat said, 'just because I can't be as *big* as you or react in your controlled way.'

'Calm down, for goodness' sake,' Fen said.

'It's hard enough dealing with what I do know,' Cat said. 'It's like with Django – you two want to know all about the tests and the treatment and the prognosis. I don't. OK?'

'I know it's difficult,' Pip started.

'Don't patronize me,' Cat said, pointing her finger. 'I'm going for a walk. I'll wait by the car. Or I'll go back to the hotel. I don't know. But I'm not staying *here*.'

And she left.

And when Penny heard the front door shut, she wondered if they'd all gone. She felt almost jubilant to find that two of her three wanted to sit at her table and eat lunch with her.

'Cat's just—' Pip paused.

'It's OK, honey,' Penny said, 'you don't have to explain for her.'

But Pip felt duty-bound to. 'It's sort of hit her the hardest, perhaps,' Pip said, 'on account of her not knowing about – well, her father.'

Fen was suddenly terrified Penny would say, Ah and how is Django? and she didn't want her to so she changed the subject urgently. 'Gorgeous bread!' she exclaimed.

'Bob's favourite,' Penny revealed and from then on she talked only about Bob. She said she'd map out Bob's route to the Falls for them. She asked how the guest house was – because Bob had always said that the town lacked a really good hotel.

'He'd say, "If you build it, they will come",' she reminisced.

It was more exhausting than tedious – Pip felt obliged to nod sympathetically at every mention of this woman's late husband. They'd long finished eating but they remained at the table, which Bob had shipped over from Denmark where he used to do a lot of business, so Penny said.

'Well, we ought to make tracks,' Fen said after a coded glance to Pip.

'Perhaps we'll take Bob's route to the Falls tomorrow,' Pip said, standing, 'if we decide not to take an earlier flight home.' She gave Fen a little smile.

'When you due to fly?' Penny asked.

'Monday evening at the moment,' Fen sighed.

'The red-eye? You know, Bob swore by Melatonin to combat jet lag. Wait – I'm sure I still have some.' Penny disappeared upstairs, leaving Pip and Fen to stare at each other and shrug.

'Thank you for coming,' Penny said, giving Pip a pot of pills. 'It's nice for me to talk about Bob. Feels like I can honour his memory by recalling the minutiae – like I'm bringing him back to life by describing him to folk who never met him.' She paused, consumed by some deeply private thought. 'Too bad you never met him.'

'I'm sorry for your loss,' Pip heard herself say, edging across the hallway towards the door.

'Thank you,' Penny said, opening the door and shivering a little though it was a warm soft breeze which trickled in.

Fen stopped at the threshold. 'How old was he?' she asked. 'And had he been ill for very long?'

'He was seventy,' Penny said, 'and he'd been ill five months.'

'Five *months*!' Fen exclaimed. 'That's *terrible*.' She thought of Django and felt panic.

Love at Long Distance

'Marjorie? It's Dr York's wife – it's Cat. I'm sorry for phoning reverse-charges. I'm in a phone box and I want to speak to my husband.' She began to cry. 'I want to speak to Ben.'

'My dear, he's consulting at the moment. The Saturday evening clinic is very hectic.'

'But I'm phoning long-distance.'

'Are you all right? Is everything OK? Is this an emergency?'

Cat cried silently while Marjorie said Hullo? Hullo? down the phone.

'How long will Ben be? How long will Dr York be – do you think?'

'Is it an emergency, dear? I can call through if it's an emergency.'

Cat thought about this. And she thought about her husband, with some rugby player's prize tendon in his hands. 'It's not an emergency,' she had to sadly admit, 'I'm just lonely. I miss him.'

'Can I take a number for you?'

'This is a pay phone,' Cat said, 'in Vermont. I can't remember the stupid place I'm staying.'

'And when are you coming back?' Marjorie asked in her best soothing voice.

'We fly Monday night.'

'That's lovely and soon,' Marjorie enthused.

'But I miss him now,' Cat stammered, crying again. 'Is he almost finished? Do you think?'

'I'm afraid not,' said Marjorie. 'All these sportsmen with their strains and pains from today's games. Why don't I send him a nice message for you – like that other time.'

Cat brightened a little.

'I could say, "Dr York, your wife says absence is making her heart grow fonder," or something along those lines.'

Cat thought about it. 'Will you tell him I called, Marjorie? Tell him I miss him. Tell him I love him. Tell him it's rubbish here. But tell him I'm fine. Tell him I can't wait to see him.'

'I've written it down,' said Marjorie, 'word for word.'

'And tell him that for me, family means him,' Cat said. 'Tell him I love him.'

When she stepped away from the hood of the pay phone and turned to consult her whereabouts on the edge of town, Cat saw that the hire car with her sisters in the front seats had pulled up and was waiting. As she regarded them, tears still wet on her face, Pip wound down the driver's window.

'Hullo my pretty girl,' she said in a commendable Bill Sykes voice. 'Want to come and see my kittens and puppies?'

Cat was at once helpless not to giggle.

'Get in the car goddammit!' Fen leant across Pip, drawling in a deep American accent, as if they were about to start a cops-and-robbers chase. 'Get in the goddam car goddammit.'

So Cat got in the car, drying her eyes on the way.

For there is no friend like a sister,
in calm or stormy weather,
to cheer one on the tedious way,
to fetch one if one goes astray,
to lift one if one totters down,
to strengthen whilst one stands.

No-Brainer

Bob's route was certainly scenic and the view from the Falls was postcard wonderful the next morning. Fen stood with her eyes closed, her hands clasped behind her head, breathing deeply, the air feeling thinner, finer, than down in town. Cat murmured that Ben would love it.

Pip thought to herself how Tom would too. 'They look like Hornby model railway hills,' she said, gazing at the spread of tree-clotted hills, 'like great big sponges dipped in green poster paint.' Her voice faltered.

'Are you all right?' Fen asked her, eyes still closed.

'Yes,' Pip said, with some busy blinking, 'I'm just tired. Yesterday is seeming more and more bizarre. I'm fine. Fuck it.' But then she squatted down and took her hands to her face, her shoulders heaving with her tears long before she made a sound.

'Pip!' Fen dropped down beside her and put an arm around her back.

'Pip don't *cry*,' Cat implored, crouching to the other side of Pip.

It was horrible to see Pip cry because she so seldom did. She was, after all, the great Mopper of Tears; a role neither of her sisters felt they could fulfil anywhere near as well. Pip had goose bumps on her forearms. It had been T-shirt weather on the lower part of the hike but the breeze at the top was insistent in its chill. Fen rubbed her sister's arms.

'Don't cry,' Cat continued to plead, as much for her sake as for her sister's. 'What's wrong?'

Pip gave one vigorous sniff, then took the sensible deep breaths she always advocated to others. In through the nose, out through the mouth, in through the nose, out through the mouth. She cleared her throat, stood up with her hands in the small of her back and had a good stretch. 'Fuck it,' she said, her voice now strong and surprisingly indignant, 'fucking *hell*.'

Cat and Fen looked at each other, a little bewildered. Something was coming and they couldn't anticipate what.

'I think she truly believes we've come all this way to offer our condolences on the death of her husband,' Pip laughed caustically. 'Don't you remember, Fen? When she thanked us for coming and said how nice it was for her to talk all about Bob to folk who'd never met him? Do you realize, she never once asked us a single thing about ourselves?' She put her hands on her hips and glared at her sisters. 'She's a self-centred old bag!' Pip rarely spoke ill of anyone, let alone with such a crude insult, and the sound of it was so out of character that Fen burst out laughing. 'It's not fucking funny,' Pip seethed, 'it's fucking sad. The whole thing. Our whole history. The fact that we've spent a small fortune coming out here. What's the prize?' She looked from Cat to Fen. 'Do you feel better? Either of you? Do you think it was a good idea? You were right yesterday, Cat. I should have followed you out instead of sitting politely and being Miss Maturity, Mrs Stupid Fucking Level Head, Mrs Pathetic Giver of the Benefit of the Doubt.' And with that she marched off.

'For fuck's sake, Fen,' Cat said under her breath, 'what are we going to do?'

'Come on,' murmured Fen, automatically stepping into the role as next-eldest and leading the way after Pip.

Pip stomped down from the Falls. 'I'm starving,' her only comment, called over her shoulder. Fen and Cat shot each other worried glances as they tried to keep up. She headed directly for the diner, which had provided their hearty breakfast for hiking a few hours earlier, and slumped down at the table they'd appropriated as their own these past three days. DeeDee, embroidered as Betty again, was delighted to see them so soon, charmed by the flush of their reddened faces.

'Joe – the hikers are back!' she called through. 'My, you girls must have made quick work of our Falls,' she marvelled while cleaning their table unnecessarily, straightening cutlery and presenting the menu though it already stood to attention before them, laminated and clasped between two steel blocks. 'No specials today, on account of it being Sunday, but if you need refuelling, you'll be wanting the burgers. We make them ourselves and the beef is from the Holstein herd just up at Brook Farm.'

'Sounds super,' said Fen, with an anxious look at Pip.

'Super duper,' Cat added, for Betty's pleasure.

'We'll have three, then,' said Fen, 'and a pot of strong tea too, please.'

Cat and Fen sat next to each other. Then leant across the table and took Pip's hands in theirs.

'It's OK,' Fen said to her.

'Pip,' Cat all but pleaded again.

'Fucking *hell*,' Pip growled under her breath. 'The point is – I didn't cross the frigging Atlantic in search of an apology and it may have been a bit hopeful to even expect an explanation. But Christ, to be asked *nothing*?'

Fen wondered what to say. Should she try and calm Pip or bolster her? 'I know,' she said, 'I know. I can see exactly what you mean. I now know all about tubing – but *she* hasn't a clue I have a sodding MA from the Courtauld Institute.'

'I told her I lived in Denver for three years,' Cat said, 'but she didn't ask me a thing about that.'

Pip buried her head in her hands and tugged hard at her hair. 'It's amazing we're as normal as we are,' she said hoarsely, with a burst of hollow laughter. The burgers arrived and she took great snatching bites. 'Christ, this is fucking delicious,' she said. 'Sorry about my language.'

'You swear as much as you fucking like,' Fen encouraged her, anything to restore her sister.

With blood sugar levels raised, stomachs full and nerves settled, they took stock of the situation once more.

'You say we didn't come here for an apology,' Fen said to Pip, 'but you know what, I think we *are* entitled to an explanation.'

'I sort of wish we'd never come,' Cat said quietly, 'but I suppose I'm pleased we are actually here. Thing is, I don't know what I came for – and I'm not really sure what it is I'll be taking home with me.'

She looked at Pip intently, willing her to respond. 'I mean, I'm sorry for her loss,' Pip said in her more usual voice, 'it must be ghastly – but for God's sake I don't even know if she was interested in telling us apart. I tell you something – we're not going home until we've had our say.'

'Are we going back?' Cat whispered. 'To the house on Emerson?'

'Yes,' Pip declared. 'God, don't look so scared, Cat – you're coming too this time, all the way. She's only human. We should use this trip to bury the mystique of her, once and for all.'

From the outside, the house on Emerson Street looked as empty as it had on their first visit. But to the sisters, they sensed it was brimming with information. They rang and they knocked and Penny seemed quite pleased to see them on her doorstep.

'Hi! How were the Falls?' she greeted them. 'Did you take Bob's route?'

All the confrontational power, the burning right to feel cross and cheated which Pip had amassed, simpered away in an instant in the presence of this woman. For the first time in her life she stood on a precarious threshold, wishing her younger sisters were in front of her, and not behind.

'Won't you come in,' Penny asked.

But Pip eyed the open door with suspicion. Bob was in there. This amazing man who looked so nice and who had loved their mother with all of his great big heart. Instinctively, she knew if they went in and sat in the kitchen and said yes to tea or coffee or cranberry and apple, they'd be back in Bob's space where the hurt and the anger that were justifiably theirs would be banned from the home of this widow. Pip reminded herself of her manners, her sense of decorum; both fastidiously instilled by Django.

'Are you OK?' Penny asked her, looking to Fen and Cat who both avoided her gaze. 'Are you OK, all of you?'

Pip was distraught at her emptied mind, her stupid silence. But suddenly Fen was alongside her. 'I have a daughter,' Fen proclaimed with slicing calm. 'Cosima is eleven months old.' Fen locked eyes with Penny. 'I have chosen to leave her for four days and five nights. You chose to leave us full stop.'

Fen observed Penny bristle and though she remained motionless, Fen could detect her pull back. 'It must seem that way,' Penny said, a guarded hostility edging into her voice.

'How did you do it?' Fen asked, genuinely flummoxed, slightly incredulous. 'I just don't know how it is possible, what with all the hormones and the *love*. Christ – the love!

I've never known such love! It's so exquisite it's almost painful. The emotion I feel for my partner is strong and stuff, but the emotion I feel for my child is. Is. God. It's *primal*.'

'You must be a very good mother,' said Penny, an unidentifiable tone to her voice.

'She is,' Cat parried in her sister's defence, 'she's amazing.'

Fen shrugged. 'I'm all right,' she reasoned, 'but I'm nothing special and that's the point. I'm just a normal mum – slightly neurotic, a bit dippy, mostly tired. But you see, I actually don't really care about why you left – it's irrelevant. You ran off with some cowboy from Denver, or the tube man from Vermont – the rest is history. But I've come here – I've left my baby thousands of miles away – because I would like to know *how*. How did you do it?'

Penny did not look discomfited and it irked Fen. In fact, it seemed her mother was thinking about these questions for the first time herself.

'How did I do it? I guess I felt I had no option,' Penny said at length. 'This man was my destiny. Being a mother – glaringly – was not. A man in my situation might have doubted himself to be the real father, on account of not feeling paternal. A man in my situation might have questioned DNA, might have said Are you sure I'm the father. But I couldn't exactly say, Are you sure I'm the mother – though actually, that's how I felt. My body conspired against me. Babies born to the wrong person.'

The sisters were too hurt to respond.

'Did you *ever* think of us?' Pip finally spoke. 'Did you *never* miss us? Did you never waiver? Or wonder?'

'No one ever challenged me,' Penny told them. 'You three were never a challenge – you were, all of you, good as gold. You ate, you slept, you were never ill or fretful. You weren't demanding, you didn't need me. It was easy. Nicholas never tried to stop me. Derek never tried to stop me. No one begged me to stay. It didn't seem to matter to any of you if I stayed or if I went; I wasn't needed. I never felt I made much impact on your lives. But I changed Bob's from the moment he set eyes on me. And that changed me. I found my calling. Does that make sense?'

'So if we'd been colicky nocturnal babies who didn't eat, things might have been different?' Fen posed, thinking of her little daughter's peculiar appetite for all things orange. She remembered how Cosima loved to lie, stomach down, over the boughs made by her mother's arms, like a little leopard in a tree. She recalled her own pure panic when Cosima's temperature rocketed to 104. She thought how, right at this very minute, on the other side of the ocean and the other side of the day, Cosima would be fluffy and fragrant and snuggly in her babygro, ready for bed. 'I don't need to feel needed,' Fen qualified. 'I'm a mother and by definition, that's a sometimes thankless task.' She paused. 'But I don't need to think about the level of love I have for my child. It overrides all else.'

'The primal love you speak of – I felt too,' Penny continued, gently insistent, 'but I felt it for Bob. That was birth in its truest sense for me – I was born anew when he touched my soul.'

'Oh shut up with all the Hollywood bullshit waffle,' Pip snapped. 'Can't you see we haven't come all this way to hear about Bob. We've come for plain, honest answers.'

Penny, visibly affronted by Pip's vitriol, motioned to the house. 'Won't you come inside? Please?'

'No!' Pip said.

Penny sighed. It appeared her daughters had not liked her initial and most honest explanation. In fact, they hadn't believed her. 'It was the sixties,' she tried. 'I was eighteen and I popped you out, 1, 2, 3. It happened so fast, so easily. I don't know. I don't know. Would they call it post-natal depression these days? I don't know.'

'Were any of us conceived out of love?' Cat asked. 'Did you create any of us intentionally – or were we just the inconvenient consequences of some 1960s recklessness?'

'Well—'

But Cat needed to continue. 'Jesus,' she said, 'most of my friends' parents got through the 1960s just fine, with little more than photographic evidence of a dodgy dress sense for proof.'

'I hadn't time,' Penny said slowly, 'or maybe I blocked it out. Who knows. It was such a long time ago. I was so young. So caught up in the shock of the new. I'd never been out of England, let alone on an aeroplane. I filled my every waking hour with Bob.'

'Did you not miss us? Did you *ever* miss us?' Fen challenged her but Penny's face wore no emotion. 'Christ – did you even *think* about us?' she pressed.

Penny thought about it. 'Occasionally,' she said quietly, nodding.

'And?'

'I just occasionally thought about you.' Her voice was quiet.

'You do know our father died of a heart attack quite soon after you left?' Pip declared.

'A *heart attack*?' Penny looked confused.

'Did you ever regret it?' Cat asked. 'Do you have any regrets?' She wanted to ask her if she regretted her fling with Django. But what if she quickly nodded to that too? It would be such a searing indictment of Django. And wouldn't it mean she regretted Cat's birth too? And wouldn't Cat then have to live with the notion that she was never meant to be? So she said nothing. She stared at her mother, hoping to compel the woman to look straight into eyes that were just like Django's.

Penny looked from Cat to Fen to Pip. She looked to the

middle distance and her face crumpled a little as she shook her head apologetically. 'No regrets – not as such. Though I am sorry – but I guess that doesn't help.' The sisters stood, staunchly unmoved. 'How can I explain it?' Penny flailed. 'I don't see it as a sacrifice because it never felt like I had a choice to make. The kids round here have an expression they use when something is glaringly obvious. And for me, back then, it was a *no-brainer*. Bob came along and everything made sense. Sure, on paper, my actions appear inexcusably wicked but, I don't know, it made perfect sense to me back then. Even now. I can't explain. I don't expect you to understand.'

Penny took a step back. 'If I was evil,' she said hoarsely, 'if I'd done wrong then surely the natural balance of the world would ensure I wasn't entitled to a smudge of the bliss I was blessed with?' She felt so tired. She wanted to shut the door and sit down and be on her own. 'Perhaps not all women are cut out to be mothers. Maybe I'm just not maternal,' Penny said, starting to close the door. 'Perhaps there's a flaw in my genes; something missing. But anyway, it appears you three have not inherited it. So there you go. You're the lucky ones. Go ahead and hate me if it helps you bury your past and reclaim your lives. I guess we're strangers, you and me. We always were.'

The three sisters stand side by side. Their mother's door has been shut in their faces. Though their limbs are touching, they stand distinct and alone; each constricted by hermetic self-sorrow.

My mummy never loved me.
My mummy never loved me.
My mummy never loved me.

Freedom Trail

To be homeward bound the next morning seemed all that mattered. It mattered more than delaying their departure from Vermont with a last breakfast at their little diner. Instead they boarded the first bus to Boston hungry but desperate to be on their way, to turn their backs on Lester Falls and Emerson Street. To head home. But they arrived in Boston with a day to get through and even for Cat, shopping held no allure. In the end, Pip suggested they walk the Freedom Trail, not because she was particularly interested in Paul Revere and John Hancock, but because it gave them a red line to follow and she didn't have to think. They meandered and mooched and didn't really take in the culture or the sights. They were wasting a day but they felt there was little else they could do with it. They idled at Rowes Wharf before taking the water shuttle across to Logan airport, still managing to arrive at the airport with three hours to spare.

Penny, however, had arrived a whole two hours before that. The girls didn't see her but she watched them, waiting until they turned away from the check-in desk, before she approached. She could hear Pip suggesting to the other two that they might as well go through passport control immediately. Penny thought to herself how easy it would be to turn away; they'd be none the wiser. Perhaps it would be for the best to go now because all of a sudden she wasn't entirely sure what had possessed her to make the trip anyway. It wasn't as if she had anything new to say. If she went now, she could catch the bus that would go to Lester direct. And she'd be home at just past her usual supper-time. It made sense. She didn't like cities and she disliked airports more. She'd come on a whim anyway, and perhaps it was common sense to turn on her heels and just go. She observed Cat, Fen and Pip from behind, thought how nicely cut their hairstyles were. Pip's neatly French-braided, Fen's light and loose, Cat's softly cropped. And then it struck her that, regardless of their colour being natural or not, she actually couldn't recall the hues of their childhood locks. Cat had been practically bald when she left anyway. But had Pip always had such beautiful glints of caramel? Had Fen's hair been spun with threads of gold from the start?

Something is catching in Penny's throat. And whatever it is has now transferred to her eyes and charged her tear ducts. Passport control is just yards away. And if she doesn't go now she'll have to say something. But if she goes now, she'll never see them again. Maybe that is for the best. They're fumbling with their tickets and passports. If they drop something, they'll see her. If they don't, they'll be gone from view in the next moment or two.

Pip is moving.

'Wait!' Penny cries.

The sisters turn. They turn and they stare. They weren't expecting to see Penny Ericsson again. Not at the airport. Certainly not with tears running down her face.

'Hi,' she offers them, 'hi.' She dips her head and sobs,

buries her face in her hands and half hopes that when she next looks up, these three girls will have gone.

But they're standing here still.

'I,' Penny falters, 'I took the bus.' It doesn't really mean much at all, but it is a short enough sentence for everyone to cope with. 'I didn't know which flight you were on.' This was true. 'British Airways!' she marvels, as if the airline is indicative of the girls' affluence. 'Very nice.'

'We're early,' Cat says but though she's glanced at Pip, it seems her eldest sister has yet to find her voice.

'Oh,' Penny enthuses, 'it's so good to be early. It's a great idea. You get the good seats, with the leg room. You get to shop and relax. Good for you. Good for you.'

'Actually,' Pip says, 'we just want to be on our way. We just want to go home.'

Penny stops, a little startled. 'I'm sure,' she says, 'I'm sure you do. To your families and your children.'

'I don't have children,' says Cat.

'I have a stepchild,' says Pip, 'he's called Tom. He's nearly ten years old.'

'He's a lucky, lucky boy,' says Penny, with such feeling that some of it seeps over to Pip.

'Thank you,' Pip mumbles. 'I feel I'm the lucky one, though.'

Penny is trembling visibly. 'Anyway, I guess I'd better go,' she says. 'Just wanted to wish you a safe journey, and all.' And she turns and starts to walk away.

'Wait!' Fen calls when Penny is precariously close to being beyond earshot. Penny stops and faces them again; this time they move towards her. Fen's hand baggage feels heavy, cumbersome; reason enough to walk slowly, with stilted gait. 'Why did you come today?' Fen asks, busy with the straps of her bag.

Penny is swiping away tears as if they're as irritating as

midges, she's rubbing at her nose as if something has gotten right up it. 'Oh,' she waves the air dismissively, 'you know.' But the look on Fen's face tells her that no, she doesn't know. Penny considers inventing a pal who works at the airport – but what a lame and crazy thing that would be to say. She falters, then she broadens her shoulders and nods emphatically. 'I guess I just wanted to say I'm glad that you girls have had a good life.'

'All things considered,' Pip says bluntly, 'yes, we have.'

'You've been so well brought up,' Penny compliments them.

'That'll be Django,' Fen says pointedly, 'on account of our father's heart giving out not long after you'd gone.'

Penny frowns. She takes a moment, then she nods. 'Yes, sure,' she says, 'his heart.' She rocks gently on her heels, begins to talk with her hands in lieu of words. 'I came here to find you,' she says, her voice breaking, 'to tell you I lied. I *lied*. I wanted you to know that, actually, I *have* thought about you. I have thought about you over the years, but in deep, dark privacy.'

Her daughters glance at each other and then regard her non-committally.

'I was never made to be a mother and I never told Bob I was one,' she confesses and she lets the huge fact hang, lets it resound in the departures hall; declared out loud and never to be denied. 'I never told Bob,' and she shook her head sadly at herself. 'He never knew I had three daughters.' She can see these three daughters of hers balk at this. 'I met him when we were still living in Battersea – I'll bet you don't remember that house? The wallpaper on the ceiling in your room? Floral – yellowy beige? I hardly ever went beyond Battersea but I had to go to Victoria – there was a clinic there that I'd heard of, I guess now they call such places Well Woman or Family Planning. I wanted the pill. But when I got there I just couldn't face going in. And I walked around and I was hot and upset and I went into a hotel and ordered Earl Grey tea. And Bob was there.' She shrugs, as if it had been the simplest turn of events, as if he'd been waiting there for her all along. 'There was Bob. That was it.'

Pip, Fen and Cat regard her. They don't have words just now.

Penny sighs. 'Your life is the richer for having not had me – I assure you,' she tells them, sounding quietly defiant. 'But my life – my life has been the poorer.' Her voice is now hoarse, as if the honesty has taken all her energy. She takes a moment and continues brightly, bravely. 'Look at you!' she marvels in a whisper that is sandpaper yet silk. 'Look at you! Such very fine women. You beautiful beautiful girls.'

I'm so proud of you. She mouths the words. *So proud of you.*

Again, the sisters stand side by side but in their own closed-off spaces. Penny has no voice now. She presses her fists against her heart. She opens her mouth but no sound comes out. Her lips move and her daughters can read what she says.

My beautiful, beautiful girls.

Then she shrugs and begins to back away. She raises her hand in a small, motionless wave and forces her quivering lips into a semblance of a smile while she watches as Cat cautiously raises her hand too. Fen is gazing at her, tears slicking down her cheeks. Pip's head is downcast but she flickers her eyes up to meet her mother's and though there's wariness, there's no hostility now.

Finally, Penny has to turn. She has to go. The scamper and whirl of an international airport takes her away. She goes without telling them that actually their father died of liver failure because he was a drunk – and not heart failure as they thought. It was her gift to them; to Django too. And it could also be part of her penance. She goes without telling them that she loves them, because she doesn't think they'd believe her and she didn't know herself until that morning when she rushed for the bus to Boston.

Red-Eye

The red-eye flights which leave the east coast of the US in the evening to arrive at the crack of UK dawn, offer a peculiar phenomenon of time travel. The flight isn't a long one but each hour it gains, as it races to catch up with GMT, is an hour lost in the lives of those on board. All around Fen, Cat and Pip, fellow travellers were desperate to sleep, eschewing the in-flight entertainment, the meals, to busy themselves with towelling socks and eye masks and fluorescent plugs of foam which, despite moulding and compacting, soon appeared to ooze uselessly out of their ears. Seats were cranked back to the maximum but still allowed only a paltry degree of recline, and small excuses for pillows were wedged around already cricked necks. With thin, static-creating blankets offering a little privacy, but not much in the way of warmth, passengers prayed for sleep and tried not to think that beyond those curtains boastfully closed at the front of the cabin those who never flew cattle class were prostrate under cotton-covered quilts and already fast asleep.

Though there had been an exasperating two-hour delay, and though it was now midnight in Vermont, or 5 a.m. GMT, the McCabe sisters couldn't sleep. Just then, time wasn't one coast or the other, time wasn't passing in minutes or hours, nor was it night or day, not even yesterday or tomorrow, in this hinterland up in the sky. In a twilight zone of sorts, life seemed suspended at 40,000 feet above the Atlantic Ocean. A little like the sensation of jet travel itself. Allegedly, the plane's ground speed is over 600 miles an hour, yet everything feels quite still. It's the same with the sound of flying; it's a little like a dog whistle, neither noisy nor soundless but there, unmistakably, all the while.

In a dimmed cabin, illuminated sharply here and there with the overhead reading lights, the McCabe sisters sat. After thrashing around with the blanket and the pillow and the freebies that were meant to assist her flight experience, Cat now read Fen's magazine; the eye mask propped atop her head making chaos of her hair. Pip and Fen were doing the *Times* quick crossword, having shared the paper and pored over every page as though it was a link with a country they'd been far from for years.

'*Makes world go round*,' Fen mulled, 'four letters.'

'Axis?' Pip suggested.

'A X I S,' Fen spelt, somewhat unnecessarily, out loud. 'It fits.'

But it didn't. Because 4 down had to be 'pompous' on account of 13 across being 'Israel'.

'Shit,' said Fen, 'something O something something. *Makes world go round*.'

'Pole?' Pip said, her mouth busy with a Murray Mint which, along with the round tin of boiled square sweets dusty with sugary powder, was confectionery she'd never normally choose yet always bought for travel.

'Pole,' Fen mused, 'yes, I see. Like North and South. Well, it fits. I'll put it in lightly.' Her biro scribbled out A I X and she wrote P L E in small, light, neat letters.

'Poles don't make the world go round,' Cat piped up. 'It's

gravity, isn't it? What's a four-letter word for gravity?' They thought hard but had no answer.

'Doesn't the earth rotating have something to do with the *moon*?' asked Fen ingenuously, never much of a scientist or astronomer. 'That's four letters, second letter O.'

'Hang on,' Pip challenged, 'is there a question mark after the clue?' Fen confirmed that there was. 'Ah,' said Pip, 'then it'll be a Funny. You know – not a straight answer.'

They pondered what could make the world go round in only four letters, second letter O, that was amusing.

'Got it!' said Cat. 'Money makes the world go round! D O S H.'

'Don't be stupid,' Pip laughed, while Fen's biro was poised, ready to scribble out and reinsert.

'Let's do 17 down instead,' said Fen, 'and come back to it.'

A few clues later, they were still none the wiser. Something O something something. They gave up, and did a quiz in *Cosmo* instead: 'Apron Strings or Fur-Lined Hand Cuffs – domestic dominatrix, or just dull?' Maybe it was a quirk of altitude to reveal more at 40,000 feet than at ground level, but much to everyone's surprise, it transpired Cat was the most adventurous of the lot, even by *Cosmo* standards.

Pip shared out her powdered sweets. 'Love!' she suddenly proclaimed. 'L O V E. *LOVE* makes the world go round. Second letter O.'

'Genius,' Cat declared, 'love makes the world go round.'

'Love makes the world go round,' Fen nodded, writing in the letters to complete the puzzle. 'It would be nice if it did,' she said thoughtfully. She looked from sister to sister and shrugged sadly.

It was probably that quirk of altitude again, of being neither here nor there in time or space; the opportunity of this strange non-Newtonian moment. 'Do you know what I think?' Cat said, leaning in from her window seat to regard Fen. 'I think that you're a bit too in love with the fantasy of being in love.' Fen looked taken aback. 'Remember that Shakespeare sonnet you read at my wedding? About love not changing?'

'*Let me not to the marriage of true minds admit impediments*,' Fen quoted softly.

'Well, you see old Will may be a genius in some respects – all that iambic pentameter and a zillion plays – but actually, I think he was wrong with the *Love is not love which alters when it alteration finds* bit.' Cat paused as if she was guilty of the most appalling blasphemy. 'People *do* change and love has to change with them; it's logical that the process of love goes through changes too, and we have to adapt.' She stopped to give a little shrug. 'I think you're probably frustrated that you don't feel that heady rush for Matt any more, that the butterflies don't rampage around your stomach every time you look at him or he touches you. That instead of floating around the still point of the turning world you now trip over toys strewn over the floor and argue at midnight over whose turn it is to stack the dishwasher.'

Fen's downcast eyes revealed this was obviously the case.

'But I think you've misread the situation as having fallen out of love with Matt,' Cat defined. 'You just need to put on your glasses and read it a little more carefully. I read somewhere that being in love is just a cocktail of chemicals which course through the body for the first twelve months – natural amphetamines. Which is why the sensation is so addictive.'

Quietly, Pip wondered when her little sister had become so wise, but then she had to consider that Cat was thirty-two years old and married to Ben. And she'd lived abroad, not knowing a soul, for four years, striding out in an alien territory, finding friends and making a happy life for herself. She smiled at her fondly.

'Matt gets on my nerves,' Fen was admitting sadly, drawing Pip's attention back. 'He irritates me. In that stupid, clichéd, lid-off-the-toothpaste kind of way. I think I've always known that Matt is the one, but for a while, one wasn't enough.'

'You're bored,' Pip defined.

'Our life is boring,' Fen agreed. 'I think I'm boring. I'm a woman of no substance. And you're right about the dishwasher, Cat.' It felt safe to talk, as if what was to be said would stay there, in no man's land, in no time, sealed in a bubble of altitude. Fen looked from one palm to the other. Talking out loud verified the situation; but it made her feel both a little disloyal to Matt, yet greedy for support. 'I've gone off sex with him,' she admitted, 'it's so predictable. I have to shut my eyes and fantasize. But that stupid thing with Al – it wasn't about sex, it was about me being bored and feeling hard done by because of it.'

'I think we have too high expectations of sex,' Pip suggested. 'Our society is over-sexualized. Something essentially private has become so public – all those sex scandals to read about, from politicians to pop stars, emblazoned everywhere, from the red-tops to the broadsheets, from *Heat* magazine to *Marie-Claire*. What was seedy and underworld has become everyday. Sex shops on the high street. Pole dancing and Pilates sharing gym space. Porn now a middle-class pastime. *Desperate Housewives. Footballers' Wives.*' She gave a shrug. 'It's easy to think everyone's having more sex, better sex, than you.'

'Well I still fancy Ben,' Cat confided, making it personal, 'but I constantly fantasize. God, if I open my eyes when we're having sex, I'm quite surprised to see *him*, my *husband*, not Johnny Depp. Or a Viking. Quite disappointed, actually.'

'A *Viking*?' Fen shrieked.

'Sometimes I leap forward a few centuries and allow Henry the Eighth to overpower me in the maze at Hampton Court,'

Cat admitted and she was absolutely serious, 'codpieces, serving wenches – the lot.'

'Bloody hell, Cat!' Pip marvelled.

'Don't tell Ben.'

'So you're advising me not to close my eyes and think of England,' Fen mused, 'but of Nordic pillagers and fat dead monarchs?'

'Whatever takes your fancy,' Cat nodded with a wink. 'Actually, what I'm saying is you have the power to improve your sex life.'

'Is that a quote from *Cosmo*?' Pip asked. Cat stuck out her tongue. Pip raised her eyebrows and turned again to Fen. 'And on a purely practical level, your life simply *can't* be the same as it once was, not now there's a baby added to the equation.' Fen looked at her sharply. 'Because you're a perfectionist, Fen, it follows that you're not very tolerant,' Pip defined diplomatically. 'I mean, in some respects it's great to have such high standards, but in others it's your biggest hindrance.'

Cat nodded. 'You're a brilliant mother and Cosima is a credit to you, but if Pip, or I, or Matt don't dress her or feed her or play with her or put her down quite like you do, it doesn't mean we're doing it *wrong* – just differently. And your way probably is better – but that doesn't mean we're doing it *badly*—'

'And Cosima doesn't seem to mind,' Pip added, 'as long as she's dry, fed and cuddled.'

Fen, sitting between them, momentarily felt persecuted. But she couldn't flounce off because there wasn't the leg room. And she couldn't block her ears with the foamy plugs because she'd already dropped them on the floor. She'd just have to sit still and work out how to lessen her discomfort. A little shift, here and there. 'Deep down, I know,' she said at length. 'Deep down I think it's a matter of identity and how mine has changed – beyond my belief and beyond my control. An identity crisis, if you like. Suddenly, I'm a stay-at-home mum.' She stopped abruptly and stared at the clasp on the drop-down tray. 'I don't think it suits me,' she said quietly. Her sudden honesty, her clarity of her situation, surprised Cat and Pip. 'I was never a thrustingly ambitious career woman,' Fen said, a little wistfully, 'but I did love work, and my role, and my world in which I excelled. God, I used to be asked to lecture at the Tate Frigging Gallery! I've had papers published! I have a double distinction at Masters level from the Courtauld Institute!' She stopped abruptly. 'How can I say all this – with such longing?' she whispered aghast. 'It's a terrible insult to my little baby.'

'No it *isn't*,' Pip said cautiously, 'it's about *you* – not Cosima. Not Matt. You only think Matt is boring because actually you find your life now a little dull in comparison to how it was. And because you perceive that to be a loaded thing to admit, so you pass the buck and shift the blame.' Pip could see from the wince on Fen's face that the nail had been hit square on the head. 'But a fling is not the answer,' she continued sternly. 'It'll only make you feel worse. You need a deeper embrace – and to feel it, you need to embrace what you do have.'

'I know, I know. God, I can't believe I tried to liven it up by fooling around with that idiot, Al,' Fen said darkly.

'Don't call Al an idiot,' Cat now joined in, 'it's not his fault. He didn't know. It was about *you*. He was just the antithesis of Matt. That was the initial attraction for you – and ultimately, his downfall too. Thank God.'

Fen dropped her head at the weight of the truth. She nodded sadly. 'It wasn't so much that I felt bad about myself, more that I've lost sight of who I am. I wanted to feel more than just Cosima's mother. No one looks at me any more – when I open the door to you, or Matt – whoever – you don't even look at me; attention is focused downwards, to where Cosima is. I don't want attention taken from her, my God she's so amazing she's worthy of day-long marvelling – but I feel I've ceased to exist beyond being her mummy. And after that, I'm Matt's long-term partner. So where's Fen gone?' She stopped, as if about to physically search. 'Can she still hold her own? I suppose that's what I went looking for with Al. A little excitement that came not from Matt, not from Cosima. Something naughty but essentially harmless that would make me feel good.'

'Chocolate makes you feel good,' Pip mused, 'but that doesn't necessarily mean it's good for you.'

'Did you know that those loved-up hormones I was talking about are the same as those released during high-risk sports and eating chocolate?' Cat revealed. 'That's why it's all so addictive.'

'Cat,' Pip digressed, 'how do you *know* all this stuff?'

'My husband is a doctor,' Cat said. She grinned. 'And I have subscriptions to *Marie-Claire* and *Cosmo*!'

'You know how you can feel like a fat lump after a chocolate binge?' Fen said. 'Well, after Al, I felt like a stupid old slag.' She looked miserable. 'You could say I've totally gone off chocolate.' She still looked miserable. 'You could say, I've learnt my lesson. I've had my fill.' She glanced at her sisters for approval. 'I *have* learnt my lesson, you know.'

'Why don't you go back to work?' Cat suggested brightly. 'It gives you a buzz and you love it. It's your world and you're brilliant at it.'

'But what sort of mother will that make me?' Fen protested, defensive and distressed.

'A working mum?' Pip said. Fen shook her head vehemently. 'Cosima is a credit to you,' Pip said kindly. 'That baby is a sweet, easygoing, gorgeous and secure little person. She's not going to feel abandoned.'

'In fact, she'll probably love being socialized,' Cat said. 'She won't notice that you've gone.' But Fen's glare said that, at 40,000 feet, this was the wrong thing to say to a woman who hadn't seen her child for four days and five nights.

'Maybe I just need to learn to fall in love with Matt again,' Fen said sadly, 'but it seems very contrived. And I'm not sure how to go about it.'

'He's just a little older, a little more squidgy than when you first met,' said Cat, 'but that's all. It's not just Shakespeare who got it wrong, Ali McGraw was full of crap too – all that *love means never having to say you're sorry* bullshit,' Cat said, echoing her mother's sentiments about that film, not that she was remotely aware of this fact. 'It's a prerequisite of love that we do humble ourselves when we're wrong, when we've been mean; that we say sorry to those we love – because often it's those we love most who are the easiest for us to hurt. Bizarrely.'

The sisters sat and thought. 'I tell you something,' Fen said, 'and I can't believe I feel this – but I actually envy our mother a little.' Cat and Pip looked unsettled. 'No! Not that she buggered off and abandoned her children,' Fen hastened. 'I envy her the scale of the love she had. It was omnipotent. Call me a daft romantic or a deluded fantasist or whatever, but I wish I could have that.'

'I know what you mean,' Cat said quietly. 'I want to detest her but I have to admit, hers is an awesome and tragic love story. And I can't believe I can say I feel for her – but I do.'

'She has no happy ever after,' Pip said pensively. 'Love is nothing without honesty,' she continued, 'and she never told Bob about us. Fucking hell – can you believe that? I'm still reeling from that one. She was hardly who even *he* thought she was. God, we all have little secrets from our partners, elements of our privacy we don't want to reveal. But not telling him about three daughters is slightly more shameful, more loathsome, than going to base three with some studenty type.'

Fen looked at Pip with gratitude for making light of her transgression, for placing it far down the scale of iniquity in comparison to their mother. 'You didn't buy anything for Tom, did you?' she changed the subject.

'I don't know what to do,' said Pip.

'Buy something from the airline mag,' said Cat, leafing through it.

'No,' said Pip, 'no – I mean I don't know what to do. With Zac.'

Cat looked horrified and Fen looked dumbstruck. Their sister looked distraught.

'We're at the most almighty impasse,' she told them, 'and to be honest I'm starting to worry that we won't get through it.'

'What's happened?' Cat gasped.

'What's happened?' Fen asked Pip tenderly, her hand on her sister's arm.

'He doesn't want children – and I do,' Pip shrugged.

'You want children? Since when?' Fen asked, stunned.

'A few months,' Pip said. 'It surprised me too. I don't know if it's the tock of my biological clock, or a surge of hormones, but yes, absolutely, I want a child.' She paused. 'But Zac just laughs at me and says, No you don't.'

Fen was astonished. 'Zac?'

'Oh, and I found out, on Friday, that June has had the baby.'

'While we were here – there?' Cat asked. 'Why didn't you say? Wow that's wonderful!'

'In theory, yes,' said Pip, 'but it's killing me.'

'What did she have?' asked Fen.

'A boy,' Pip said, 'seven pounds something. Nathan. A baby brother for lucky, lucky Tom. And yet I feel hollow –

hungry – all I can think is it should have been me.' She stopped. 'I want a family. I'm in my mid-thirties. I have to ask myself, why does Zac not want one with me?'

'Why doesn't he?' Cat asked. 'What does he say?'

'Say?' said Pip.

'About not wanting to have a family with you?' Fen asked.

'When I say I want a baby he just laughs and says no I don't,' Pip said.

'But when you've asked him, specifically, why he doesn't want a family with you,' Cat paraphrased, 'what on earth are his reasons?'

Pip stopped. 'I haven't exactly asked him that – in so many words, precisely.'

Fen and Cat looked at each other. 'Why *not*?'

Pip thought about it. 'He'll just laugh it off.'

'That's what you think,' Cat said, glancing from one sister to the other. 'Bloody hell you two, after a lifetime of taking your advice and respecting your pretty astute theories, can I now just tell you both to practise what you bloody preach? You have an aversion to confrontation, Pip – that's why you always immerse yourself in being the Great Looker-Afterer – because if you busy yourself helping others with their problems, you needn't consider your own. But you have to confront Zac – he's your husband after all. It's your *duty*.'

It felt odd yet strangely comforting to Pip to be told what to do, especially by her little sister. 'I'm worried he'll say no,' Pip admitted, 'and then I'll be stuck, with no options. Because I *do* want children.'

'With Zac?' Fen asked.

'Ideally,' said Pip.

'Breakfast!' the air hostess announced.

'Breakfast?' the girls were disorientated.

'We'll be landing in an hour and a half,' the hostess said helpfully. 'Lovely tail wind.'

‘I can’t believe we’ve talked this entire flight,’ Fen bemoaned, wondering how a bread roll could be so cold without actually being frozen. ‘I ought to have slept. I’ll be useless in a few hours.’

‘Well, we have Bob Ericsson’s Melatonin, remember,’ Pip said, unable to spread the pebble-hard pat of butter. ‘It’s in my hand luggage.’

‘What did you get from the USA?’ Cat jested, putting on an accent. ‘Oh just some jet-lag pills from my absentee mother’s late husband.’

‘She doesn’t have a happy-ever-after,’ Fen said. ‘Amor did not vincit omnia for Penny.’

‘So let’s make sure it does for us,’ said Cat, with a nudge.

The reality was that the sisters didn’t actually know or remember the grown-ups as they were thirty years ago. The muddle was of their making and ultimately one of them had run away, two had died and one had kept huge secrets because he thought it was the right thing to do for the girls themselves.

The cabin lights are on, the window blinds are up, the day blazes outside the jet windows. It is morning, unmistakably. Britain will be off to work. Their mother will be sound asleep. Django will be making porridge. Matt will be kissing Cosima and rushing out the door. Zac will be telling Tom to get a move on. Ben will be oversleeping because there is no alarm clock as good as Cat.

They are back on terra firma, on home ground, in the here and now, and they must go their separate ways.

‘Everyone will want to know everything,’ Cat rues, ‘but I don’t really feel like revealing much. It feels private.’ She turns to Pip. ‘But what if Django asks?’

‘Direct question, direct answer,’ Pip shrugs, ‘but it may be prudent to be economical with details.’

'I wonder if his results are through,' Fen says. 'No one's said anything to us on the phone.'

'It's been a mad, extraordinary time, of late,' says Cat.

'It's been life-changing,' Fen qualifies.

'Everything will be fine,' Pip tells them.

And they believe her.

'Everything will be fine,' Pip says again.

'Will it?' Fen asks her. 'Will I?'

'Django too?' asked Cat. 'And you?'

The McCabe line-up is back on its more usual footing.

'Everything,' said Pip. 'We'll all be fine.'

Return of the Natives

Fen adored Matt's mother, Susan Holden; a sparky yet maternal woman, energetic and independent but also warm and calm, who had been widowed before Fen met her. She was perhaps the only person from whom Fen was happy to take advice on child-rearing; but Susan also seemed only ever charmed by Fen's zealous love of Cosima. Fen never had any criticism of Susan's techniques – they were as good as her own. Almost. Susan instinctively unfurled the frill from the elasticated legs of the disposable nappies and Fen felt no need to double-check this, as she still did when anyone else changed her baby. Susan knew exactly how long to immerse a bottle in a Pyrex jug of boiling water and though the temperature of the milk was always spot on, still she verified it with a dab to her wrist. She wouldn't dream of saying, Why don't you get a microwave, it takes six seconds to warm a bottle. Susan never said 'Shh!' to the baby – a sound Fen herself could not abide – but used the more soothing hush and coo to far greater and more expedient effect. And if she watched her son, sweetly cack-handed, feed the baby yoghurt with the wrong kind of spoon and no wipes to hand, she'd throw Fen a conniving look which said *Men! Aren't they useless, the silly sods!* She was unstinting in her praise for Fen. But there again, Susan had always longed for a daughter. Now she had a granddaughter too. She felt that, between her and Django, Cosima would have a colourful yet balanced experience of grandparenting. And she liked the way that Fen ensured every weekend in Derbyshire was balanced with a weekend in Gloucestershire with her. Susan thus appreciated how important it was that Fen's homecoming was just right. The house was spotless and so was Cosima and when Fen came in, Susan diplomatically disappeared to boil the kettle, allowing Fen and Cosima to reunite in utter privacy.

'She missed you,' Susan stressed to Fen, who had eventually appeared in the kitchen clinging to her baby almost as much as the infant snuggled against her. 'She missed you very much. You could tell. She didn't pine – she was happy enough – but look how happy she is to have you home.'

Fen's eyes were wet and her heart swelled. 'Has everything been OK? Did she eat OK? Sleep through? Nappies nice and regular? Afternoon naps?'

'Everything like clockwork,' Susan assured her. 'Look, I jotted down a little résumé of each day so you can catch up on all the intricacies.'

'You are a brick, Susan,' Fen said sincerely.

'Now there's a term I haven't heard for a while,' Susan laughed.

'It's a Django-ism,' Fen said. 'Is there any news, do you know? Results?'

'Not as far as I'm aware,' said Susan.

'Any day now,' said Fen solemnly.

'Well, you're all going to Derbyshire this weekend, aren't you?' said Susan.

'Cosima's first birthday,' Fen smiled. 'Are you sure you can't change your Ladies' Guild thing and be with us?'

'I can't, my dear,' Susan apologized. 'Normally I wouldn't

think twice – only it's our annual dinner and it is for charity. And I can't be doing with being the butt of consternation or gossip – not at my age, and not in a village as small as mine.'

'OK,' said Fen. 'Perhaps we'll come to you the following weekend, then?'

'Lovely. I think all women should be entitled to prolong their birthday celebrations – I'm glad to see you're priming Cosima already,' Susan said.

Suddenly Fen realized she had no idea when her mother's birthday was. Nor was she sure of her precise age. And she felt she'd really quite like to know the day, that she ought to know the day – not to send cards, but just so that she could acknowledge, at some point, *Today is my mother's birthday*. Just so she'd be able to say with authority, *My mother is fifty-something*.

'And how was Cosima's other grandmother?' Susan was asking, astutely casual.

Momentarily, Fen was confused. But Susan was quite right; on paper Cosima had two grandmothers, on paper Penny was a mother and a grandmother. 'She was –' Fen paused. What was she exactly, this Penny Ericsson? 'She was – *there*,' Fen said thoughtfully and Susan sensed this was information enough at this juncture.

'Matt missed you,' Susan told her.

Fen felt her face being scanned for a response. 'He probably didn't notice me gone,' she said and she was surprised to hear by her tone that she alluded more to her own inconsequence, than any derogation towards Matt.

'Oh, he did,' Susan assured her. 'I think it did him good.'

Fen pressed her lips against Cosima's fat cheeks. 'I missed him,' she said quietly. 'It did me good too. I can't wait to see him.'

'If you can stay awake,' Susan remarked. 'Go and have a

power nap – just an hour or two of restorative oblivion. Cosima can take me to feed the ducks.'

'Are you sure?' Fen asked.

'Of course I'm sure,' Susan said. 'She's no trouble at all. She's an absolute pleasure to look after.'

'Thank you,' said Fen.

'Say, *See you later, Mummy*. Say, *Sweet dreams*,' Susan cooed on Cosima's behalf.

'See you later, little baby,' Fen said, with a little wave. Then she turned and went upstairs to bed with her share of the Melatonin.

Pip felt slightly insulted by Tom's clothes, strewn around her home in the most unlikely of places. She wondered if she'd been deluded or just unreasonable to hope that her husband and her stepson might at least have tidied the place for her return, even if a bunch of flowers or just a welcome-home note were beyond their imagination. She loaded the washing machine, checked the fridge and wrote a shopping list, made the bed and tidied wet towels from the bathroom floor. If she went to Sainsbury's now, the washing would be ready to hang out by the time she was home. She could then put another load in and take a quick nap before collecting Tom from school. Was Tom staying over that night too? Was June back home now? She could phone Zac and enquire. There again, she could phone June. Or she could just ask Tom when she saw him. But Pip's mind was too befuddled by travel and tiredness to make a decision. And anyway, she didn't need to know just yet.

In the supermarket, perusing the aisles a little absent-mindedly, a peculiar selection of items in her trolley, Pip stopped and stared. It struck her that there was an almost charming paradox about condoms being placed next to home ovulation kits, pregnancy tests sharing shelf space with tampons, KY jelly and cracked-nipple balm tube by tube. It brought to Pip's mind those adverts for pregnancy tests – they never showed the result on the dipstick that was causing the beautiful couple to hug each other in such joy. Were they pleased it was a false alarm after an unprotected shag? Or were they celebrating the outcome of careful planning for a family? She picked up the ovulation kit and wondered, very privately, about buying it, about getting to know her biorhythms and her hormonal peaks and troughs. But she put the pack back hurriedly and rushed away from the section, as if her not lingering a moment longer could somehow banish the thought of tricking Zac and absolve her of momentary, improper intent.

As June lived in Swiss Cottage, just a stone's throw from Sainsbury's at the 0_2 Centre, and as Pip didn't feel quite so tired any more, she decided that she might as well take a circuitous route home.

June's mother answered the door. 'Pip – how lovely. Is Tom with you?'

'No – he's still at school,' Pip told her, suddenly wondering if her timing was off kilter. She checked her watch. Almost 2 o'clock *proper time*, as Cat would say. 'I've just been to Sainsbury's. Just thought I'd pop by. Just got off the plane, actually.'

June's mother smiled benevolently. 'They're sleeping,' she apologized. 'I don't want to wake them – but June will be so sorry to have missed you. You will come in later, won't you, when you bring Tom back?'

'Of course,' Pip said, not quite knowing if she was disappointed not to be having Tom at her place that night, or whether she was apprehensive about having Zac to herself. 'Can't wait.'

'He's absolutely gorgeous, the little mite,' June's mother said proudly.

Pip drove back with tears streaming down her face. 'It's just jet lag,' she berated herself.

She hadn't seen the note but once she sat down with a cup of tea having put away the shopping, hung out the washing and put the next load in, she found it pride of place on the coffee table.

Welcome home, Mrs.

Would you mind doing the school run – and taking Tom back to June & Rob's?

See you later. Sainsbury's delivering 5–7pm.

I'll cook.

Missed you.

Z xx

Pip sipped her tea and traced the marks of Zac's kisses. And then suddenly she was waking with a start and thinking Christ almighty, I zonked out for two hours and I'm going to be late for Tom.

'He blows bubbles, my baby brother,' Tom tells her.

'Is he gorgeous?'

'He has yellow runny poo,' Tom marvels.

'How's your mum?'

'She says she has udders,' Tom reveals, 'and there's a milking machine she's borrowed from the hospital. No one is allowed in the room when it's on.'

'It's so exciting for you all,' Pip says, glancing in the rear-view mirror at Tom who is gazing proudly out of the window with a great big grin on his face.

'My baby doesn't half burp,' Tom says.

The first thing Pip thought was that June looked as tired, as disoriented, as she felt. The second thing Pip thought was that baby Nathan Oliver was more tiny, more perfect than she could possibly have imagined. Just then he appeared to be the most beautiful newborn baby in the world.

'Do you want a cuddle?' June asked her.

Pip smiled and put her arms around her.

'Not with me, you daft cow, with the baby!' June laughed.

Pip cradled Nathan. She remembered this feel from Cosima – that the bundle could be so tiny and yet feel so heavy, so full of life, so enormously and wondrously and terrifyingly precious. She brushed her lips along the crown of the baby's head, the feel of peach fuzz hair mingling with the incomparable fragrance of a newborn accosting all five of her senses at once. She looked at June, her smile spreading. 'He's absolutely gorgeous,' she said.

'Hug him some more,' June said. 'I'm sure I told you there's some tribe somewhere that hug each other's babies the whole time – apparently it increases fertility like you wouldn't believe.'

Pip thought about ovulation kits; about surreptitious enhancement of fertility. But this wasn't the same. Zac would expect her to be cuddling the baby. After all, he'd probably already cuddled Nathan too.

June nudged her. 'Seen Zac yet?'

Pip shook her head.

'Here,' said June, 'have another cuddle with Nathan before you go.'

There were two messages on the home phone when Cat arrived back. One was from Ben, saying he'd left a message on her mobile too, to say he'd forgotten about a talk he was to give to a local hockey team and he'd be back late. The other was from her assistant manager at Dovidels, apologizing profusely, knowing she'd be jet lagged, but they were short staffed and Lorna Craven was visiting the store and was there any chance Cat could come in. She phoned both back and told them not to worry, she'd see them later.

Lorna Craven was high up in head office but subscribed to a hands-on approach across all the stores and was popular with the staff because of it.

'They tell me you're just back from the US?' she said to Cat, having praised her for the commendable figures last month.

'That's right,' Cat said, 'family business. I took it as holiday, though. And I don't have any other plans for time off for the foreseeable future.'

'Everyone needs a break,' Lorna reassured her, 'though family business can seldom be classified as a holiday.'

Cat raised her eyebrow in agreement.

'I thought your family were in the North somewhere?' Lorna commented.

'They are,' Cat said. She paused. 'They are.' It was on the tip of her tongue. She could bite it back, or she could let it tumble. 'My mother lives in Vermont now,' she said, surprising herself how easy that had been.

'I see,' said Lorna. She tipped her head and regarded Cat. 'You're doing a great job here, well done.'

'Thanks!' beamed Cat.

'We're opening a store in Sheffield – at Meadowhall – do you know it?'

'Of course I know Meadowhall,' Cat laughed. 'I grew up in Chesterfield – Meadowhall was the closest thing to paradise and teenage bankruptcy for me and my sisters.'

Lorna laughed. 'Do you still have family in Chesterfield?'

'Yes,' Cat said, 'I do.' And for the first time she wondered how to refer to Django. Everyone who'd ever known her knew him simply as Django; he'd needed no further clarification.

But Lorna didn't know anything about Cat, really. 'Our father lives there,' Cat told her because it felt right and sounded good and, in essence if not on paper, Django would always be as much Fen and Pip's father as her own.

'You wouldn't have plans to move back to the area, would you?' Lorna asked and before Cat could say, God no, my sights are set on Tufnell Park, Lorna added, 'Because I would give serious consideration to you running the Meadowhall store. It's going to be our flagship. Coffee shop, events hot spot – the lot.'

Cat stood and stared. She wondered if she'd heard right or whether jet lag was now playing tricks on her. She wondered, for one ghastly moment, whether the foam ear plugs were still protruding like fluorescent slugs, from her ears.

'Think about it!' Lorna said cheerily. 'Now let's go through the next month's forecast. Then you ought to go home – you must be exhausted.'

'My mother gave us some Melatonin,' Cat said, clicking the computer into action.

Fen McCabe and Matt Holden

If only Matt and Fen could have known each was as apprehensive about their reunion as the other. If only they could have been privy to the information that they both had tampered with the parameters of fidelity but regretted it deeply. And then have such information magically erased from their memories. It is easy to forgive, not so easy to forget. But in some ways, to live with the guilt, to stomach it and suffer it, to learn from it, guards against further transgression. They'd had five days and five nights apart, they'd been separated by a seven-hour flight and several time zones, but in their souls it now felt that they'd made it across a sea far darker and more inclement to be back home together again.

'Welcome back, cowgirl.'

'Howdy, partner.'

What on earth possessed me? each thought as they kissed hullo and hugged that it was good to see you. *What on earth possessed me to turn away from the love of my life?*

In their eyes, each other was staggeringly incomparable to the dalliances of their momentarily misplaced desire. *What on earth possessed me? I won't be doing that again. Christ, I almost lost my mate.*

'You need to keep her awake,' Susan said. 'She needs to stay up until her proper bedtime or her sleep pattern will be disrupted for days.'

'It is her proper bedtime,' Fen said. 'I was just boiling the kettle to warm her bottle.'

'I wasn't talking about Cosima,' Susan said, 'I was talking about you. And I was talking, actually, to Matt.' She turned to her son. 'Take Fen out for a nice spicy curry. I'll babysit.' Both Fen and Matt sensed that his mother was choreographing the situation, that she had some innate sense that they needed a little time and space to slot back in together, that she sensed their separation had lasted longer than five days and five nights. To be a mother is to be granted a sixth sense. To be a good mother is to use that gift wisely. To use that gift wisely is to have the child's best interests at heart, however old the child. As Fen gave Cosima her bedtime bottle, she thought that perhaps her mother hadn't been granted that sixth sense. As she said goodnight to her dozy baby, she wondered whether her own mother had simply been not a very good one. As she put on a little make-up to mask the jet lag, she wondered if, in fact, her own mother did have a sixth sense and had somehow known intuitively that her daughters' best interests did not feature her. Maybe she had been a good mother in that respect. But spiralling theories could not produce definitive answers and, actually, it didn't really matter. It didn't matter at all, really, any more. Because Fen knew that her own little family was in the safest of hands.

Fen slips her hand into Matt's as they meander back home. Usually, a curry means heads down and eat. Tonight, though, they ate only at opportune pauses in the conversation.

'Can you believe our little girl is going to be one year old?' Matt marvels.

'I hope we have Django's results by then,' Fen says. 'Then it can be a double celebration.'

'Hear, hear,' Matt says. 'I wonder if he'll want to know all about your trip. All in all, was it a good trip, Fen?'

'It was,' she says. 'I feel I have answers now, whether or not they were given directly.'

'Do you think you'll see her again?' he asks. 'Keep in touch even?'

'I don't know,' Fen thinks about it, 'I don't know. At the moment, I can't answer that. I'm still not quite sure what I feel or what I want. We all reacted so differently. I think Cat, ultimately, probably accepted her more. Pip, though, still feels pretty raw. And me? I don't know, Matt. I feel a bit indifferent.'

Matt nods thoughtfully.

She takes her hand from his and puts it around his waist, slowing her pace. 'I think what the trip did for me was finely tune my desire to provide the best for my own little family. For Cosima,' she stops. 'For you, Matt.'

He kisses her forehead. 'That's nice to hear,' he said.

She hangs her head. 'I haven't been very nice, have I? For a while.' Her voice quiet but audible.

Matt is about to protest, but he decides not to. 'I don't think I have either,' he says instead. 'I didn't know it was going to be so tough – so baffling.'

'And I didn't know it was going to be so all-consuming, so exhausting,' Fen says.

Matt gives her pony-tail a gentle tug. 'We'd be pretty daft if we were to let the best thing that's happened to us – as individuals – cause discord for us as a couple. It's not about choosing the one we love, it's about then loving the one we've chosen.'

Fen nods. 'You're so right.'

'We're publishing an article to tie in with the Picasso/ Braque exhibition,' Matt says. 'It's a good piece. One thing struck me so deeply – Braque said it about Picasso.'

'He said, "We were like two mountaineers, roped together" – that's what you're going to say!' Fen interrupts.

Matt looks at her, impressed. Then his expression softens and he regards her more quizzically. 'That's us, Fen,' he says, 'you and me. We're in this together. There's nothing we can't surmount. As for the view from the top – I only ever want to share it with you.'

'I was starting to fall,' Fen's voice wavers, 'I was dragging you down with me.' She turns to Matt and folds her arms around him. 'I'm so sorry. But it was never my heart that grew cold – just my feet. For an unfathomable moment.'

'Me too,' he says to the top of her head, 'me too.'

There they stand, locked in an embrace in the middle of the pavement blocking the way like a couple of teenagers. Passers-by must drop down from the kerb to pass them, but they can't help but smile as they do so. Fen and Matt make a lovely sight.

They walk on, holding hands and swinging their arms, feeling so much lighter for love flowing between them. Fen stops. Matt turns to face her. She looks upset. 'How do you feel about me perhaps going back to work?' she asks.

Matt regards the lines and the squares of the pavement and the furrows of Fen's brow. 'I think it might be a really good idea,' he says measuredly. 'Not because of the money,' he hastens, 'but for you. Cosima will be fine, you know.'

'I know that now,' Fen tells him, 'but more importantly, I now know I'll be fine too.'

'Course you will,' Matt encourages her. 'You'll be more than fine.'

'I suppose until quite recently – well, until right now – I still felt that we're umbilically attached. My little girl and I. You could say it's actually been *me* with the separation anxieties, not the baby.'

'Yes, that's a very valid point,' says Matt sweetly, 'but don't misinterpret your maternal qualities, Fen. Don't do yourself a disservice.'

'I would like to go back to work,' Fen says, 'for *me*. I suppose I romanticized the image of me as a full-time mum. But actually, I think I *need* to work.'

'I think you'd be a happier bunny for it,' says Matt, 'and anyway, you couldn't be a better mummy. Do it for you.'

Fen's eyes are downcast. 'Have I been awful?' she asks him.

'Not awful,' he says, 'not really.'

'Not really?' Fen pursues. 'Or not really awful?'

Matt laughs and pokes her. 'Not really awful,' he clarifies and kisses her on the forehead.

'Becoming a mother has been so monumental. I'm different now from the woman who didn't have a child.' She pauses. She looks at Matt intently. The father of her child – beautiful man. 'I'm worried. Am I as nice as that carefree girl you fell in love with?'

He tips his head and regards her quizzically. 'I see only the girl I am in love with,' he says. 'I have eyes only for you.' He kisses her tenderly and Fen's eyes close in gratitude and relief and happiness. 'Come on,' he says, slipping his hand into the back pocket of her jeans, giving her bottom a friendly and affectionate squeeze, 'let's go home.'

'I was thinking of asking Pip if she'd look after Cosima on the days I go to work,' Fen says.

Matt thinks about it. 'I don't know,' he says. 'The occasional day now and then is one thing – but she has her life too.'

'But she loves babies.'

'So she might then have her own, soon enough.'

Fen glances at him, wonders whether to confide but decides she should honour her sister and moves away from the topic.

'Perhaps you could ask around the other mums,' Matt says, 'nanny-shares and the like?'

Fen considers this. 'I will,' she says. 'Good idea.'

Fen is wide awake at three in the morning. She lies in bed, aware of Matt sleeping peacefully beside her. She spoons up against him. The smell of him, the feel of him, so familiar.

I suppose, for a while, stupidly, I saw monogamy – and domesticity – as suffocating my ability to fly and be colourful and carefree. I feared it would sap me of my individuality. But the truth is I'm not carefree, I have huge responsibilities and commitments and whereas momentarily I wanted to shirk them, actually I want to embrace them, venerate them – and never abuse them again. Life is too short, families are too fragile. You are my One. Crappy pop songs and bad poetry hail love to mean two become one. But look at what you and I did, look what our love did – we two became three.

'Matt?' He doesn't wake. He smells so nice. He feels so good. Fen's arm is around him, it's as if he's sitting on her lap and it's nice to have him there. 'I'm sorry.' She thinks about why she is so sorry. 'I probably gave you leave to doubt my love for you,' she says. She nustles against his hair. She kisses the back of his neck. 'Madness,' she says. 'I love you.'

Matt continues to pretend to be asleep.

Pip and Zac Holmes

Pip was apprehensive about seeing Zac. It had taken her sisters to make her see that she'd need to broach the subject because her husband didn't realize the enormity of it for her. However, he was running late and she was starting to feel very tired and rather emotional. She had been taken aback by how hard she found it to take her leave of Tom at his mother's house. It had been a lonely drive back up Fitzjohn's Avenue and once she was home how she craved the happy distraction of Tom rambling on about the personal hygiene of his teachers, the vomtasticness of school dinners and the outrage of so much homework. There was nothing to do. No one to talk to. Just an awful lot to think about. Pip was immensely fond of June and she'd loved cradling baby Nathan but just now she deeply resented June the apparently effortless perfection of her family and she loathed herself for feeling this. She was appalled that she should think June had more than her fair share.

Zac's dilemma was whether to wake his wife or let her sleep. He stood and looked at her, curled up on the sofa, the remote control tucked under her chin, her lips parted and slightly squashed by the conked-out angle in which she'd fallen asleep. She looked young, childlike almost; peaceful. Perhaps he should leave her be. But he knew her theory on jet-lag management and, though she might be temporarily grumpy with him in her grogginess, he reckoned she'd ultimately thank him for waking her. He tried as gently as he could, by tucking her hair behind her ear, by laying his hand on her shoulder and giving it a little shake. Then he whispered her name and gave her buttock a friendly tap. But still she slept. He decided to start cooking but not even wafts of garlic or the clatter of pans roused her. He watched a little television, laying her bare feet in his lap and lightly fiddling with her toes, but she didn't stir. So, with the supper simmering and the wife slumbering, he cranked up his laptop and did a little work.

'Something's burning!' are Pip's first words to him.

'Fuck!' is his back to her.

The pan is such a mess and Zac looks such a hungry, sorry sight, that Pip can't help but laugh a little.

'I'm starving!' he protests. 'I can't believe I find spreadsheets so fascinating to the exclusion of everything else including my house burning down. I'm a sad fuck,' he rues. He peers in the pan. 'A hungry sad fuck.'

'No, you're not,' says Pip, about to surprise herself, 'you're lovely.'

Zac is quite startled by this; he's become quite used to Pip guarding the affectionate, demonstrative side of her nature. 'Thank you,' he says, coming back through to the sitting area. 'You're not too bad yourself.'

They look at each other, waiting to see who will smile first, who will talk next.

Pip does both. 'We had a mad trip,' she says, 'but it was a good thing to do – though it didn't feel as such when we were in the thick of it.'

'What's she like?' Zac asks. 'And would you like me to refer to her as your mother or by her name?'

'Let's call her Penny,' Pip says.

'What's Penny like?' Zac asks.

'She's all right,' Pip says. 'I sort of wanted her to be evil incarnate, but she's not. She's not actually a *bad* person. I can now allow her that fact.'

'That's good,' Zac says, 'that's closure, I suppose.'

'Actually, it feels like the opposite,' Pip says, 'which is why I still feel so unnerved, I suppose. There's an opening now. I don't know how much contact we'll have. But she really is at the end of the phone or just a plane journey away. I can put a face to her. I will see her again – I don't know when. But there will be a time. And I don't think I mind.'

'That's very noble,' Zac says, with genuine admiration that flatters Pip.

'More importantly, is there any news of Django?' Pip asks.

'Not as far as I'm aware,' Zac says, 'but we're up there this weekend, aren't we – for Cosima's birthday? Talking of news and birthdays – did you get my text, about the baby?'

'I did,' Pip says, 'thanks.'

'He's adorable,' Zac says.

'I know,' says Pip, 'I saw him this afternoon – when I took Tom back.'

'Oh,' says Zac, following it with a little awkward nodding.

'Yes,' says Pip, busy with her lips, glancing all around her.

'He's adorable,' Zac repeats, 'isn't he?'

'Absolutely adorable,' Pip says, 'and Tom is made up.'

'Isn't he just,' says Zac.

Go on, Pip! Go on! The scene is primed for a heart-to-heart. You're calm and Zac seems amenable. Say something!

But Pip is now flipping through the *Evening Standard* and she can't see that Zac is staring at her, hoping to catch her eye. 'Nothing on the box,' she says, having spent an inordinate amount of time scouring the TV listings.

'And nothing to eat,' says Zac.

'What shall we do?' Pip asks, happy for Zac to suggest a takeaway and a DVD.

'We could get a takeaway, watch a DVD,' he says.

'OK,' Pip responds.

'Or,' Zac says, sitting on the edge of the coffee table and cupping her face in his hands, 'or we could just go to bed and make a baby.'

Pip's immediate reaction is that it can't possibly be as easy as this. Surely the wrought confrontation she's been planning, dreading, needs to be played-out. There needs to be some level of workshopping, surely, at the very least. Angst. Tears. Proclamations. Soul-baring. Heart-beating. A fight. Should she say, Are you sure? Should she say, You don't really mean it, what's changed your mind? I thought you thought I was joking? But you said your family is complete with Tom? You're just saying this to keep me happy/ keep me quiet?

But luckily for Zac, and ultimately for Pip too, she's a bit too zonked by all the travel and the enormity of the last few days to decide which sentence to deliver. So, she just sits and gawps and Zac swells more at this sight than when she sat and gawped at the Tiffany box with the platinum-set princess-cut engagement ring four years ago.

'Have you gone all broody on me?' she asks wryly.

'Yes, I suppose I have,' Zac nods. 'I want a baby with you.'

'No you don't,' Pip says, trying not to grin, but Zac knows she's teasing him.

'Yes I bloody do,' he tells her.

'Was it hugging little Nathan?' Pip asks.

'Oh God, June's been on at you with her tribal fertility theories,' Zac laughs. 'To be honest, while you've been away, I just had a long think about it all.'

'Zac,' Pip whispers, her hand on his cheek, loving him so much.

'I wish I'd realized you were serious earlier,' Zac says. 'We've missed out on a lot of mating opportunity.'

Cat and Ben York

Cat was watching *ER* when Ben arrived home. She wasn't so much watching it, as staring at the television with a slightly glazed expression.

'You're still up,' he remarked. 'Aren't you knackered?'

'Is Melatonin safe?' Cat asked him.

'Yes – it's just not licensed here,' Ben told her, 'though I'd argue it's better for you than Temazapan or Valium. Did you buy some in the States?'

'Penny gave us Bob's,' Cat told him.

'Penny gave you Bob's?' Ben repeats, raising an eyebrow. 'Did she give you anything else? Say – an explanation for why she buggered off with the cowboy in the first place?'

'He wasn't a cowboy,' Cat said, 'he was the king of plastic tubing. And she did, actually – she did give an explanation of sorts. She wasn't nearly as scary as I expected. Just sad, really.'

'Do you mind if we switch this off?' Ben said, glancing at the television. 'It's too much like work – but my hospital is not nearly as exciting and my staff are nowhere near as good-looking. I find it a bit depressing.'

Cat laughed. And then bit her lip and tipped her head to

her shoulder which Ben knew to herald a request of some sort.

'What is it?' he teased. 'What do you want? Oh Christ – how much did you put on the credit card?'

'Nothing,' Cat protested, 'it doesn't matter. *Nothing*.'

'Nothing on the credit card?' Ben was aghast. '*You?*'

Cat nodded. 'Honestly,' she told him earnestly, 'we didn't shop, we didn't have time.'

'So what were you going to say?' Ben probed.

Cat thought about it. And then she reckoned that it was such an unexpected and probably daft, impractical and altogether bizarre thought, that she'd be wise to say no more. It was probably just the jet lag speaking anyway. Or Lorna Craven.

'How are you, babe?' he asked her. 'So it was a good trip to make?'

'Yes, it was,' she said. 'I feel a lot more settled. The trip quashed the drama, the mystique. I used to think it was something to fear, to be ashamed of, to run from and yet, I suppose, to be slave to as well. But actually, I had nothing to do with anything. It's just a bit of a sad story, really, but it's a story in which I now realize I actually played no part.'

'I'm so pleased for you,' Ben said tenderly.

'Pip seemed to have the hardest time, but there again, she's always taken on the role as mother so I suppose meeting the real one was a little like coming face to face with her nemesis,' Cat said thoughtfully. 'I had a bit of a hissy fit on one day but after that passed I felt a lot more rational. Fen came out with some cracking one-liners – becoming a mother has made her so much more powerful than she gives herself credit for.'

'Do you think she looks like you?' Ben asked.

'I can see Pip in her,' said Cat, 'or her in Pip.' She paused. 'Anyway, I have Django's eyes, remember. Is there any news, Ben, with his tests?'

Ben shook his head. 'I'm sure there will be by the weekend, though. We'll all be there together.'

Cat was pensive. 'Ben. It's just.' She floundered for words. 'I don't want to know – if it's bad, the news. I've thought about it. My feelings for Django are so fragile, so new, so promising. I don't want that to be taken away. I've only recently found him. I can't cope with even the thought that I won't have him for ever. It sounds pompous but this trip to the States, it was about my identity. Not just mine – my sisters' too. But I see myself for who I am – a young woman with my life ahead of me. I want to live it to the full. I want happy times to outweigh sad times. Those around me – my mother, my father – there's been such sadness and weird stuff. I sort of feel sorry for Penny, for my mother. The time I spend with Django I want to be happy, quality time. Does that sound naive? Does that sound deluded? I don't want dark clouds looming when I'm with him, I want only sunshine.'

Ben took a moment and then nodded. 'I understand,' he said, 'but you know he wants me to know all the details, the facts and the figures?' Cat nodded and shrugged. 'I respect your wishes. And I respect his.'

'Thank you, Ben,' she said. 'It's funny – my family is certainly unconventional. But it's such a relief to finally feel that I don't come from bad stock or from damaged genes.'

'So if there are no hereditary implications,' Ben said, 'are you ready to make babies?'

Cat laughed. 'Dr York, is that as good as your bedside manner gets?'

'OK,' Ben said, 'OK. But I'm actually serious here. You can't deny male broodiness. It exists. It's medically proven. I should know. I'm the frigging doctor – and a broody one. Would you like to have a baby? With me?'

Cat didn't laugh, but she did smile at her husband. 'A

family is a very nice idea,' she announced, which was good news to her as well as to Ben, 'but can we wait a year or two? I only want to have a family with you – but I'd like a year or two to get my career under way first.'

Ben considered this quietly. 'I won't tamper with your pill, then, not for the next year or so,' he said, with a theatrical sigh. She kissed his chin, his lips. 'Now go to bed,' he told her. 'You look absolutely washed out.'

At 3.15 the following morning, the three McCabe sisters are wide awake. When Matt perceives Fen to have finished her declarations, he pretends to wake from a deep sleep and finds her very keen to seal her words with slow and exquisite lovemaking. Zac and Pip substitute the familiarity of rampant sex for the fascinating business of procreation and fall asleep in each other's arms, sticky but hopeful.

In Clapham, Cat lies in bed, awake, and thinks about sex. Sex, she thinks, is about more than just making babies. It's about happiness. About communication on a higher level than language. It's about love.

It's about lust!

She turns on her side and gazes at her husband sleeping. She feels horny. She touches his lip lightly with her fingertip and he gruffles and turns away from her. The sweep of his beautiful back. Slowly she takes her lips to the gentle slope of his shoulder-blade and presses against it. Then she licks her lips and takes her mouth to his skin again. She runs her hand along his arm, his muscles, his strength. She finds his hand, his fingers are sleep soft but she feels along the length of each one. She takes her hand back up to his chest, strokes him and hovers her hand lightly over the little smattering of hair he has there. Carefully, she feels down his stomach. Then along his thigh, as low as she can reach. Does she want him to wake? She's not sure. She's enjoying having him all to herself. She kisses his neck and flicks her tongue over the soft bud of his ear lobe. She feels his arm again, his chest. Down to his stomach. His fingers – still limp. And she takes her hand down lower. And finds his cock straining and erect. *Fascinating*, she thinks to herself, *it has a life of its own. Women often chide a man for thinking with his cock – but I rather think a man's cock thinks for him.*

She encircles his penis and tugs it gently. Still Ben sleeps soundly. She goes beneath the covers and very carefully takes the entire length of him in her mouth. She doesn't know whether to feel a little insulted that not even a surprise blow-job can rouse him. Though he is certainly aroused. She comes back up and spoons against him, her hand loosely around his erection. She lies there, in the stillness and the silence, loving him.

'Is that it?' Ben suddenly says.

And now he's turning onto his back and plugging her mouth with his tongue before she can say, You sod, you were awake the whole time. His hands are everywhere. He pinches her nipple lustily and she gasps. He burrows between the lips of her sex to find her oozing with expectation and desire for him. He fingers her, nudges at her hardening clitoris and she moans and she could come there and then but suddenly his hand is away and he's brought it up to her mouth where her tongue and his lick her juice from his fingers.

'I am going to fuck your brains out now,' Ben murmurs and Cat is too turned on to answer him back, to use her voice for anything other than panting. Hot and sweaty, they giggle and grunt their way through a rude shag.

To the Bone

After Ben's phone call at lunch-time, Matt and Zac spent the rest of the day saying 'Shit' and 'Fuck' at regular intervals until it was time to meet at the Mariners.

'Glorious day,' the landlord enthused.

'Was it?' Matt remarked, realizing he'd taken no notice of the weather, no notice of much else at all.

'It's a shit day,' Zac sighed as they took their pints and awaited Ben, 'just awful.'

Ben arrived soon after, draining his pint to quench his thirst and prepare his voice.

'As you know, Django has requested that I am fully briefed by his doctors,' he started, 'and today we have been told that the grade of cancer in Django's prostate is high: 8–10 and the stage of the cancer is T4. It's not good. There's secondary cancer in the bone – as was feared. It is anticipated that it will spread to the lymph nodes too.' He rubbed the bridge of his nose and winced audibly. 'It's not good. Not good at all. We have nothing we hoped for – nothing that we told him, or the girls, to stay positive for.'

'No treatment?' Zac asked.

'There is treatment,' Ben said, 'but no cure. He'll be offered radiotherapy – as a palliative treatment. It's very effective at alleviating symptoms like pain, especially in the bone. There's some discussion of hormone therapy – reducing his testosterone levels can slow down the growth of cancer cells and can even shrink the tumour and minimize the spread but they need to know more about the spread of the cancer to decide whether treatment is viable.'

'More tests?' Zac said.

'Scans, mainly,' Ben explained. 'They could operate and remove all or part of the testicles – but I doubt they'd do that for Django considering his age and the stage and grade. Then there are drugs given as injections or pellets under the skin of the abdomen, or as liquid injected into the muscle every month or so. Or there are hormone therapy drugs in tablet form.'

'Those sound better,' Matt said. 'He'll find a way to integrate them into some recipe or other.'

Ben smiled only briefly. 'There are awful side effects,' he said. 'Sexual impotence, loss of desire, hot flushes, weight gain, tiredness. Even breast swelling and tenderness.'

'Christ almighty,' Zac said angrily, 'if the poor bugger hasn't suffered enough indignity, enough worry and enough discomfort already.'

Matt spread his hands on the table. 'Look, whatever treatment he goes for, this thing is going to kill him – is that what you're saying?'

'In a hard, hard nutshell, yes,' Ben sighed.

'Django McCabe has terminal cancer,' Matt said, to make quite sure he had the facts. 'And there's nothing that can be done apart from alleviate the symptoms? How the hell am I going to tell Fen?'

'It's for Django to,' Ben said, 'though I know for a fact that Cat won't want to know specifics. Will Fen? Will Pip?'

'You know Pip,' Zac said softly.

'Look,' Ben said, 'when we go up tomorrow, we'll see how he's taking it and perhaps we, as a family, can gauge how to proceed.'

Hard Facts and White Lies

Fen had bought a book for Cosima's first birthday. She'd bought her many other gifts too, predictably, but she felt the book was the central present. She bought it because she liked it though it was arguably beyond the intellect of a one-year-old. Even for a bona fide art historian with a double distinction from the Courtauld Institute, the illustrations were beautiful and accomplished: exquisitely gentle, unwhimsical and somewhat melancholy. Coupled with this, Fen found the tale simultaneously heart-rending yet uplifting – the lonely little beaver who thinks the echo of his own crying is the sorrow of another and sets off across the great lake to see, befriending a clutch of other lonely souls en route. Something about the book struck a chord with Fen and she made Matt read it, cover to cover, who said, Very nice, dear, and returned to his issue of *GQ*.

There was something of the little beaver in each of the McCabe sisters; something of the echo in those who loved them.

When you are sad, the Echo is sad . . . When you are happy the Echo is happy too.

Thus, when they tumbled out of their convoy on a clammy Saturday morning in July, and bounded over to Django like excitable puppies, what could the man do but allow his depleted cells to become bolstered by their happiness.

'Do they know?' Django asked Ben, out of earshot of the others.

'We haven't told them yet,' Ben said.

'But you have told the menfolk, like I asked?'

'Yes,' said Ben, 'I did. Everything is your call, Django. We're here for you. Here to help.'

Django thought about it. 'Let's see how things progress. There's a birthday to celebrate. And tales from their trip to be heard. And why would I want to risk losing their laughter, those expansive smiles, all this happy love by imparting gory details and gloom?'

'How are you feeling?' Ben asked.

'No worse. No better. A little tired, perhaps – but I do find this heat rather enervating. I ache and I creak and I wake up on the dot of 5.15 each morning.' Django paused, then he slapped Ben on the shoulder. 'But other than that, not too bad for a cancerous old septuagenarian. Now come along. I've made Pimm's. I had no mint but there was parsley in the garden so I've used that instead. Let's gather the troops.'

Quite conversationally, after the hors d'oeuvres and whilst serving the main course, Django dished out details of his illness whilst spooning out the fisherman's pie which also had kidney beans added for their gorgeous colour, plus a little chicken for extra protein. 'Good news, the radiotherapy will put paid to the aches and pains. Potatoes, Cat? It's just a bit of a bugger about the other bit – but as Ben said, it's quite possible to live a normal life, to enjoy just as long an innings, in spite of it.'

The McCabe sisters looked from Django to Ben. Ben read

the situation in an instant: he knew that Django was tinkering with the truth just as he tinkered with recipes – all the essential items were used, but in quantities Django had decided were best, with one or two added ingredients to make the flavour uniquely his own. Django's way with cancer was going to be like his way with food. Django would justify to himself that it was a little like jazz, a collection of notes to make into a scale for which he had the freedom, the right, to tinker with the emphasis and the order.

But though the girls had an ear for jazz, medical information was clangorous to their ears. They didn't quite understand what they were hearing, nor whether they should turn to Ben or Django for further information.

'Do you have the results?' Pip asked.

'When did they come?' asked Fen.

Cat said nothing. She couldn't. Her heart pounded in her throat. *Don't let him have results yet. I don't want facts. I just want to have hope.*

Django peered at the potatoes, as if making his selection required utter concentration. He spooned them onto his plate, added a dollop of HP Sauce, motioned to Matt to replenish his glass with Pimm's and then he turned to the girls as if he'd forgotten what they'd asked. 'Oh,' he said vaguely, 'that they can treat my old bones with radiotherapy which will very much help with the discomfort I sometimes experience.'

'Has it spread?' Pip asked. 'Is it not just prostate cancer – is it in your bones too?'

'It's spread a little,' Django said.

'What's the buggery bit – about the prostate?' Pip persisted.

'The buggery bit about the prostate?' Django said, as if trying to recall. 'Oh – that. Yes, my prostate's in a sorry state. But it's a bit like your appendix. Or the Monarchy. Not really needed.'

'Can they treat it?' Pip urged.

'As Ben said,' Django said diplomatically, with the swiftest of conniving glances to the doctor, 'sometimes it's not worth it – the treatments and the side effects are worse than the symptoms of the cancer. And the cancer mightn't impinge on my lifespan anyway. Now come on, Fen, Cat – you haven't touched your celeriac. I mashed it with cottage cheese, the pineapple-y variety – is it not nice?'

Ben follows Django through to the kitchen, under the pretext of carrying the pile of plates and empty bowls, all of which have been scraped pleasingly clean. Django is rummaging in cupboards and drawers, muttering. Ben puts his hand on the man's shoulder. 'Are you all right?' he asks.

'Yes, yes,' Django says, a little irritated. 'Ah, here are the little sods.' He brandishes the jar of morello cherries.

'OK,' says Ben. But his hand is staying put. 'You sure?'

Django thinks about this. 'I'm choosing not to use the word *terminal*. When the girls are sad, I am sad. When they worry, I worry. More importantly, when they are happy, I am happy. And however long I *do* have, I may as well have a gay old time of it.' He pauses, tips his head and regards Ben. Echoing the affection of his son-in-law, Django places his hand on Ben's shoulder. 'But thank you, Ben,' he says. 'The girls – they all seem different. Not just happy and effervescent and back to their old selves – but as if they are proud to be in *new* selves too. It must have been a good trip to the States. It must have been a good thing to do. It would be most fitting if good is what ultimately comes out of it all. My lot screwed it up – but Cat, Fen and Pip are ironing out the creases very nicely. Could you fetch the ice cream from the freezer?'

But before Ben can do this, Django puts his hand on his shoulder again. 'Ben – have I in some way contributed to my condition? I don't mean to sound bonkers or melodramatic but if health is not just about what we put into our bodies but what we do with them, if health is a state of mind—' He trails off to clatter around the cutlery drawer. 'Just deserts,' he murmurs.

'Teaspoons will do fine,' Ben says helpfully.

'No – not *desserts,*' Django smiles. 'I'm wondering whether my deeds and my actions have somehow contributed to my downfall.'

Ben puts the ice cream down on the counter firmly. 'Django,' he says, 'cancer is cancer. It's an insidious, revolting affliction. It's rogue cells. Bastard things. They have no conscience. They certainly don't differentiate between victims. There's no proof that reprobates are struck down more than the virtuous. And my God you have far more bloody virtues than you have sodding faults. There's nothing you could or could not have done. It's not your fault. It's just fucking bad luck, Django.'

Django's eyes are tear stung. 'You do swear a lot,' he tells Ben with a fond cuff to his ear.

* * *

Cosima spent her first birthday picnicking in the grounds of Chatsworth House. Her father and her Uncle Zac spent her first birthday urging her to walk.

'Her knees are too fat,' Ben laughed warmly. 'Look at them – they look like scones. And look at those rolls of flesh around her thighs. A mini sumo wrestler!'

'Fuck off, Ben!' Fen protested, firing cornichons at him.

'Language, Fenella,' said Django.

'I'm teasing,' Ben said. 'She's glorious. Absolutely glorious. She's a credit to you. Skinny babies don't bear thinking about.'

'Talking of babies,' Django said, 'how is Tom – what news of his little brother?'

'He's so gorgeous!' Pip drooled, her accent becoming

alarmingly like Tweetie Pie. 'His weeny teeny toes!'

Django flung Zac a very obvious look of sympathy.

'Pip is currently stuffing herself with alkaline foods and God knows what because she's decided she wants a girl.' Zac paused. 'I'd quite like a girl too,' he said wryly. 'I wonder if cousins warrant a discount from South Hampstead High School for Girls.'

'But we haven't put Cosima's name down!' said Fen, after a pregnant pause and a jubilant wink to Pip.

'Are you trying for a family?' Django's eyes danced from Pip to Zac.

'Absolutely,' Zac told him and the pleasure which criss-crossed Django's face was priceless.

All eyes, with eyebrows raised, were suddenly volleying between Cat and Ben. Ben just grinned but Cat lobbed asunder whatever foodstuffs were still on her plate.

'Leave me alone!' she protested, sticking out her tongue. 'I'm younger than you lot! I assure you Ben and I will pop them out – when we're ready. But I want to give my career a chance, I really do.'

'I'm hoping to go back to work,' Fen announced casually, plucking at grass while a flickering across her face belied an immediate need for approval, 'in the autumn, perhaps.'

'That's wonderful!' Pip said.

'Good for you,' said Cat.

'Part-time,' Fen quantified.

'Well done darling,' Django said, 'it'll suit you.'

'I know,' Fen said, 'I see that. So keep your ears open for a good nanny, everyone.'

'I'll ask June,' said Zac.

'Someone at work is bound to know,' Cat told her.

'I could always help out in the interim,' Pip offered.

'Thanks,' said Fen, having a surreptitious glance from palm to palm, 'thanks, you lot.'

'Hey – did you know they're opening the flagship branch of Dovidels at Meadowhall?' Cat said to no one in particular. 'Lorna Craven from head office told me.'

'Meadowhall, hey,' Django said. 'I remember when Meadowhall was just that – all fields.'

'Django!' Pip and Fen groaned.

Ben observed his wife looking pensive and with an awkward blush.

'Excellent hospitals in and around Sheffield. And the outlying area,' Ben said casually, to no one in particular.

* * *

'It's weird, isn't it,' Zac says to Ben and Matt, sharing more Pimm's, this time with courgette in lieu of cucumber, 'it's a fucking awful time, really, shit news, horrible things to come – but it's been a blazing weekend. Really happy. All of us.'

'I know exactly what you mean,' Matt concurs. 'This will probably sound trite but I just want to say, Aren't families *great*.'

Ben chinks glasses with them. 'It's been a good weekend,' he agrees, 'but more than a weekend. I don't know – it feels like we're approaching this truly privileged time. Many families aren't granted this – loved ones are taken suddenly, violently, by cars or heart failure. Or worse. But we have hindsight before the event has happened – we know from the tragedy of others not to let this man go before we say goodbye. That he'll never wonder how much he was loved. That we – the girls – his friends – will never rue not saying all there was to be said. Managed well – and advances in medicine mean it can be managed well – Django can have a good death. When that time comes.'

'When will it come, Ben?' Zac asks.

'Level with us,' says Matt.

'I don't know,' Ben says. 'I'm not just saying this – truly, I don't know. I don't think it will be a sudden, steep deterioration. But the process has started. We'll have to see. He'll make this Christmas,' he pauses sadly, 'but perhaps not the following one. There's a general reluctance to specify possible time remaining, because it can only sound like a death sentence – *when* you'll die, instead of how much life you can still live.' Ben pauses. 'I think Django's take on it is robust – and I think he's kept our girls firmly in his heart by plying them with ambiguity.'

'You don't feel we're pulling the wool over their eyes?' Matt wonders.

Ben shakes his head. 'No, I think we follow Django's lead.'

'Pip will read up on it,' Zac says. 'If she wants to – can she speak to you?'

Ben nods. 'It seems what Django wants them to know is that though there's no cure, it's quite possible to live a normal lifespan in spite of it.'

'I tell you,' says Zac, 'if ever a man will truly live until he dies, it'll be Django McCabe.'

'Hear, hear,' says Ben.

'To Django McCabe,' Matt toasts. 'Long may he live.' And they chink their mugs of Pimm's together.

Sundae

'Maybe I'll just sell the house and move to a nice condo in Florida. Somewhere near Marcia's place. Buy new things. Have a yard sale before I go. Give *you* away for free,' Penny Ericsson says to her late husband's chair. She crosses to the mantelpiece, but instead of looking at the photos, she raises her eyebrow at her reflection in the mirror.

'Or maybe I'll just stop talking to myself, stop it with the pie-in-the-sky planning and just go into town and do my grocery shopping.'

It was the hottest July on record. It was a day for ice cream. It was the day that Penny felt able to return to Fountains ice-cream parlour. Juliette welcomed her as if she'd only been in the day before.

'Hey Penny,' she said, 'take a seat. I'll be right there.'

Penny perused the menu. There were new additions but she fancied old favourites. 'I'll have a scoop of Banudge-nudge, a scoop of Chippy Chippy Bang Bang and a scoop of Fudge Fantasia.' She stopped, not because she was deliberating over toppings, but because she was suddenly thinking of Derek McCabe and his imaginative take on food.

'Excellent choice,' Juliette said. 'Toppings?'

'Hot chocolate,' said Penny, 'and Lucky Charms.'

'Coming right up.'

Penny sat and gazed down the street, the heat haze wavering the vista.

Juliette returned soon, presenting the sundae with a triumphant smile. 'Enjoy!'

'Thank you, my dear,' Penny said. She paused. 'It's nice to see you again, you look very well.' She unfurled the long-handled spoon from the paper napkin and toyed with the ooze of toppings.

She was aware that Juliette was about to speak. 'I'm getting married!' Juliette announced.

Penny looked up. 'That is just so nice,' she said with genuine warmth. 'Congratulations, my dear.'

Juliette took this as an invitation to sit down and tell Penny all about the proposal and to sketch out her ideas for frocks on the paper napkin. Meanwhile, Penny made headway into her ice cream, feeling obliged to take small, polite mouthfuls though it was so delicious she wanted to wolf it down. She'd started doing that at home, on her own. Sometimes, when she was very hungry, she'd scoff directly from the tub or container or foil tray. Sometimes, her supper was so hot, she'd have to stand there with her mouth agape, fanning her hand at the food scalding her tongue. Occasionally she'd even given out a great appreciative burp. She had no audience, after all. Now that her appetite had returned, she realized how hungry she had been feeling.

'Last time I saw you,' Juliette said, 'I wasn't engaged.'

'That's lovely,' said Penny, thinking that Chippy Chippy Bang Bang was possibly the closest thing to ambrosia she'd ever tasted.

'You were with the three girls,' Juliette continued.

Penny stopped mid-mouthful, a glob of ice cream electrifying her sensitive gums.

'Were they your daughters?' Juliette asked shyly.

Penny waited, using her tongue energetically to calm the flare from her teeth. She nodded. 'Yes, they were my girls.'

Juliette beamed. 'How neat that they came over.' She touched Penny's forearm. 'Did you talk it all through? Did you make amends? All that crap about you being a bad mother,' Juliette chided gently. 'I knew you were nice. I told you so.'

'You're very sweet,' Penny said, feeling very uncomfortable.

'Bet your phone bill is mighty big, what with all those long-distance calls,' Juliette laughed.

It occurred to Penny that she didn't have any contact numbers for her daughters. She did have Django's number. But actually, was there any point in phoning him? And if she did find out her daughters' numbers, whom would she phone first? More to the point, what would she say? What would they say? Reluctantly, she had to admit to herself that she'd already said everything, really, that day at Logan airport. And she knew that she'd relinquished any right to contact when she'd left them all those years ago. It was quite possible that she would never see them again.

Moving On

Ben glanced at Cat who was spooning through her cornflakes as if searching for a more tasty one elsewhere in the bowl.

'Are you OK?' he asked.

'Hmm?' She looked up. 'Pardon?'

'Are you OK?' Ben repeated. 'You seem miles away.'

'Oh, I'm fine,' said Cat, 'just thinking about work and Django and Django and work.'

Ben gave Cat a kiss and headed for the door. He paused and returned to her.

'Pinch, punch,' he said, doing precisely that. 'August 1st?'

'Oh,' said Cat, rubbing her arm. 'Ouch.'

'You're meant to give me a slap and a kick for being so quick,' Ben told her, 'or at the very least, a poke in the eye for being so sly.'

'Ben,' said Cat, who did usually biff and bash him on the first of each month, 'do you think someone ought to be with Django when he has his first radiotherapy next week?'

'Well, what does he say?' Ben asked though he knew what Django had said, having spoken to him about precisely that the day before.

'He says no,' said Cat.

'Let's go up a couple of days after that, at the weekend,' Ben said. 'We'll probably be of more practical use to him then.'

Cat brightened.

'The sales will be on at Meadowhall,' Ben told her, with a wink.

Ben thought about it again all that day. And the next. And he thought about it intermittently throughout the following week, even talked to colleagues and superiors, all of whom listened intently. He thought about it as he drove up to Derbyshire, two days after Django's first session of palliative radiotherapy. But it was only when Cat dragged him around Meadowhall that he knew he had thought about it thoroughly and enough.

All angles. Pros and cons. For and against. On the one hand, and on the other. He'd considered everything to arrive at an informed decision about which he was more than content, he was actually fairly excited.

He'd choose his moment.

'This is where Dovidels' flagship store is going to be,' Cat told him as she tried to peer through some unremarkable boarding.

This was his moment.

'I've been thinking,' said Ben, peering through the gap as well, 'about leaving St John's.'

Cat looked at him, alarmed. 'Why?'

'Because I fancy a change—' Ben started.

'A change? But what would you do? You're a doctor – you're a specialist!' Cat exclaimed, aghast.

'A change of scene,' Ben said. 'Same job – well almost – different hospital.'

'But why?' she pressed. 'You like St John's, don't you? The department? The staff? Your colleagues?'

'I do,' Ben said, 'but an interesting opportunity has been put my way to do something similar elsewhere.'

'Where?'

'Sheffield.'

'*Sheffield?*'

Ben shrugged. 'Makes sense,' he said, 'in terms of *my* career. But of course, you have to feel happy with it.'

'It makes perfect sense in *my* career too!' Cat enthused artlessly. 'Lorna Craven from head office as good as offered me this very store as my own.' And she began to pat the boarding affectionately. 'Best of all, we could be nearer to Django,' she declared, 'nearer home.'

'You won't hanker after Tufnell Park, then?' Ben teased her.

'I tell you something, Dr York, we can multiply our Tufnell Park pounds by three round these parts.' Cat took a step back, crossed her arms and narrowed her eyes, as if envisaging what the Dovidels shop front could look like. 'What a coincidence,' she marvelled guilelessly, 'how very serendipitous.'

Not really, thought Ben, for whom Cat had long been an open book. And his best ever, all-time favourite read at that.

Christmas

'Bugger the brandy butter,' Django said as his family gathered around on Christmas Eve. 'This year we're having good old tomato ketchup with *everything*.'

Tom wrinkled his nose in delight at the deliciously revolting thought of ketchup and Christmas pud or, better still, ice cream and ketchup.

'Did you forget the Bisto?' Pip asked.

'Bugger the Bisto!' Django declared. 'When did you ever, *ever*, know me not to make my gravy from scratch. Bisto, she says, *Bisto*!'

'She has a thing about Bisto,' Tom said darkly. 'It's a mad pregnant-woman thing.'

'She makes it up in a mug and drinks it like tea,' Zac colluded with his son, 'by the gallon.'

'It's just a craving,' Pip shrugged, 'it's only natural.'

'She even drinks it at *breakfast*,' Tom said, with a lively repertoire of throwing-up faces for emphasis. 'That's *so* not natural.'

'Anyway, I've brought my own Bisto,' Pip told them, 'so what's with the ketchup, Django?'

'Lycopene!' Django announced. 'A wonderful antioxidant

to be found in the humble tomato but the potency, the *bioavailability* increases when cooked. So, it's out with the HP and in with the ketchup – I have it with everything now. Ben, I read that Lycopene is twice as potent as the better-known anti-cancer betacarotenes, and one hundred per cent more bioavailable.'

'It sounds about right,' Ben confirmed.

'Ketchup it is then,' Django declared.

'Will ketchup make you better then, Django Gramps?' asked Tom.

Django gave the boy a smile and ruffled his hair. 'It makes me *feel* better,' he told him, employing the gentle ambiguity which his friends and his family had come to respect as his right over the last few months.

'Can I help?' Cat asked. 'Anything I can do? Squirt the ketchup, or something?'

'Everything bubbles and simmers,' Django told her. 'Everyone relax and enjoy. Christmas is coming and the family is here. Supper will be in an hour or so. Don't chew that, Cosima – it's very old. Django Gramps found it in Alaska. In 1965.'

'I'm lucky, aren't I?' Tom announces to Pip who has brought him up a glass of water and a torch, at bedtime.

'Are you? In what way?'

'Some people – actually, what I mean is some *children* – have rubbish families. Like Tom B in my class – he's having a divorce. And Alex doesn't see his dad at all, hardly, now he lives not in London with a new baby.'

Pip tips her head to one side. 'We are lucky, aren't we?' she says warmly.

'But isn't it strange, then, that here's you and your sisters with that mum who ran away with the cowboy, and here's me with two lots of dads and mums – but we're all the happiest bunch I've ever known in my whole life.' Pip smiles and Tom welcomes her ruffling of his hair. 'Because did you know something? Ed's parents have done a divorce too and Ed told me that they try and out-present each other. At first I thought, Wow cool. But then he was really upset and actually told me he *hates* it. He even hates the stuff they buy him, he says. Can you believe that? Even hates his *bike*.' Pip makes sure she looks suitably stunned. 'Ed says all those gifts are like *bribes*. He said they're called guilt-trips. He says "Can't buy me love".'

'That's a song,' Pip tells him, 'do you know it? It's by the Beatles.'

'The Beatles are cool,' Tom tells her, 'everyone knows that.'

'Did you know Django actually worked with them for a short while?'

'No way!' Tom exclaims.

'Yes way,' Pip laughs, 'you can ask him all about it tomorrow.' She kisses him. 'Night night, Tomtom.'

'Night, Pippity.'

Pip hovers in the doorway. 'If I said "I love you" would you squirm and puke?'

Tom takes a moment. 'Nah. You can say it, if you like.'

'I *love* you,' says Pip.

'And I "*el*" you,' says Tom.

Fen snuggled up to Matt later that night. She knew if he kissed her forehead and then kissed the bridge of her nose immediately after, he was feeling horny. If he kissed her forehead twice in succession, he was tired. If he kissed it once, and kissed nowhere else, there was something on his mind. Two kisses it was: one to her forehead and one to the bridge of her nose.

'Wait!' she giggled a whisper and slipped out of bed, tiptoeing from the room which, in an old creaky house like that on Farleymoor, was a pointless exercise really, laughably futile actually. Matt grinned in the dark. What on earth was she up to? He was full – dear God don't let her be raiding the fridge for whipping cream. Or ketchup. Fen returned and padded back to the bed. She ripped back the quilt and straddled Matt, his hands on her hips as he attempted to lever her into position.

'Oh no you don't!' she chided, twisting her body away from him. The room was extremely dark, there was no moon, no street lamps, no night lights. 'Merry Christmas, big boy,' Fen whispered coyly and Matt could feel something caressing his balls, tickling up and down the shaft of his cock. His pelvis rocked in response to his desire. What was it? A feather? Some as yet unidentifiable foodstuff? Something from under the Christmas tree?

'Ouch!' That didn't feel so nice, it felt as though his prick had been pronged, something scratching his balls. 'What the fuck *is* that?' he asked.

'Mistletoe, silly,' Fen giggled, 'it's Christmas.'

'How do you feel?' Zac asked Pip, who was sitting bolt upright in bed, staring straight ahead, while he wrapped Tom's presents on the end of the bed.

'A bit indigestiony,' Pip admitted.

'Nothing that a nice mug of Bisto couldn't cure?' Zac asked. 'Would you like me to make you a mug? I have to go downstairs to nibble the biscuits Tom left for Father Christmas.'

'Oh Zac, would you?' Pip said gratefully. 'You won't mind it stinking the room out?'

'How can I mind,' Zac said, 'when Santa's bought me a Rolex Oyster?'

'But Santa hasn't bought you a Rolex Oyster,' Pip told him sadly.

'I'm teasing,' Zac said. 'I don't believe in Santa. But do you think you could make your next craving camomile tea or something?'

Pip sipped her gravy and Zac wrapped presents. Pip marvelled how someone so precise with figures and percentages could make such a hash of papering a parcel. 'Zac,' she said, 'fold in, fold in, turn up. Here, hold my gravy, I'll do it.'

'Can you believe this time next year a little person will be celebrating Christmas with us?' Zac mused.

Pip smiled. And then she felt very sad. 'I pray that we'll *all* be here, *all* of us.'

Zac took her hand. 'He looks well, I thought. No different to when we were here a month ago.'

'He seems tired, though, don't you think?'

'Christmas is a tiring business,' Zac levelled, 'when you're making it for a big family. He seems very happy, to me.'

Tom and Cosima were sharing Cat's old bedroom. Cat and Ben weren't staying at the house at Farleymoor. They now had their own little house in Darley Dale, just twenty minutes away. But they would be back in time for breakfast with the family the next morning.

'Funny isn't it?' Cat says, jolting Ben from the verge of slumber.

'Hysterical,' he murmurs sleepily, hoping if he agrees she'll say no more and let him drift off to sleep.

'What's hysterical?' Cat asks and with all the movement on the mattress and rearrangement of the duvet, Ben can sense she's propped herself up and is staring hard at the back of his head.

He rolls onto his back with a sigh. Then he turns towards her. 'Are you about to put the light on?'

'Yes,' says Cat, doing just that. 'What's hysterical?'

'What's funny?' Ben counters.

Cat is diverted. 'Oh. I just meant it's funny how everyone is up at the house, and you and I are snuggled up here. Yet this – more than any place I've ever known – this is home. This is my home.'

Ben wonders why this is funny. But he swiftly decides not to ask.

'It's also funny how I thought I had everything meticulously planned – and this time last year Darley Dale was way off my map,' Cat says, beguilingly incredulous. 'Isn't it funny how a year of chaos can actually organize itself into the life that's right? Totally be beyond one's control.' She pauses and then smiles, her eyes closing with the surge of emotion. 'I love this place,' Cat enthuses. 'I *love* this place, Ben. I know it's higgledy-piggledy and the water is sometimes brown and there's that damp problem in the sitting-room and you clonk your head on the beam in the hallway and this bedroom is barely big enough to take our bed – but I love this place passionately. I can't believe anyone other than us has ever lived here. It's our *home*.'

'I don't mind that beam,' Ben says, 'and we do have a preposterously large bed.'

'It's about full circles, I suppose,' Cat muses, hovering the palm of her hand lightly over the surface of his cropped, silver-flecked hair to get that velvety feel. 'Because you see it's only now that I know I could never have settled here – less than five miles from my childhood home – unless I'd done the London thing as a single girl and then had a stint out in Colorado as a newly-wed and then returned to the UK all blasé about what was best for us. And the whole time I was destined to be here. It's *here* that I feel my most centred.'

Ben smiles at her. 'Welcome home,' he says lovingly.

'I suppose it's a similar thing with Django,' Cat muses, to herself as much as to her husband. 'I couldn't love him as unconditionally as I do now – had I not had that dreadful period of absolutely loathing him.'

Ben is pleased finally to have the opportunity to elaborate. He's waited for this opening since the day after Django's party. 'And perhaps you couldn't have come this far in accepting the woman on your birth certificate had you not gone out to find her, stood right there in her territory and felt OK about her and, most importantly, felt good about yourself,' Ben says. 'Our parents do define us. And if we like ourselves, then it means that they're not so bad after all.'

Cat is thoughtful. 'You're so wise,' she says and she gazes at him with dreamy affection.

'And hunky,' Ben adds with a frown.

Cat biffs him with a pillow. She wriggles back down and settles her head into her pillow with a tired, happy sigh. 'Merry Christmas, Dr York,' she says and she touches his cheek.

'Merry Christmas, babe,' he says.

* * *

'Boys,' Django said late morning after the mountain of ripped wrapping paper and redundant packaging had been cleared away, the presents stacked into individual piles at well-spaced positions around the room, 'why don't you go for a blow-through. The girls are going to help me with the lunch. Cosima, you can be an honorary boy.'

'Turtle,' Cosima cooed, which had been her first word and remained her favourite.

'You can be an honorary turtle then, poppet,' Django said. 'Tom, you can lead the expedition. You can take my gnarled old cane – no, not that one. That one is from Selfridges. The other one – it was given to me when I was trekking in Tibet. If anyone can unearth its mystical powers, it's you.'

They stood on the flagstone doorstep, Django and his girls, and waved the party on their way; Tom stomping off at a good pace, the men following behind, Cosima sitting proud on her Uncle Zac's shoulders while Ben picked up one pink welly and Matt the other.

'Shall I lay the table?' Pip said.

'I usually do that,' said Fen.

'We'll do the table later, I need you three in the kitchen with me.'

They are in the kitchen, humming to a CD of Christmas carols that Fen bought from the motorway services. There is food on every available surface, including the window sill and the top of the fridge, and the *Times Atlas of the World* is lain across an opened drawer to provide another surface still.

'Now I want you to know, that the thing to remember about parsnips is they're plain. They even look plain. If you enliven something plain, you forget it was plain in the first place. Like Plain Jane at school – pop a lovely hair band on her *et voilà*.' The girls give each other their secret *he's-nuts* look that they've honed over the years to being all but imperceptible to anyone else. 'And so it is with parsnips,' Django continues. 'Ginger is the key. I always add a little ginger to parsnips. Ginger root, mind you, not that powdered excuse.'

'God, I quite feel like chewing ginger root,' Pip murmurs.

'Well, if there's any left, you can,' says Django. 'And I always like to use this knife for the parsnips. And I find this angle works best. You try, Cat. Now you, Fen. Pip – your turn. Good stuff.'

The girls break into a pseudo-operatic chorus of fa-la-las for 'Ding Dong Merrily on High' and Django conducts them momentarily with the soup ladle before noticing the time. 'Carrots and broccoli,' he says. 'There's a secret here and it's to do with texture. Broccoli can be alarmingly woolly – but I find if you add a little lemon juice to the water in which you steam it, *pas de problemo*!'

The girls nod earnestly and then sing along with 'Good King Wenceslas'.

'Carrots!' Django declares above their din. 'Brown sugar elevates this humble but highly hued vegetable above its common status as horse fodder.' The girls keep singing but they give him the thumbs up.

'Have you a secret for sprouts that stops them smelling like farts?' Cat giggles.

'Catriona!' Django objects. 'We don't do sprouts in this family.' The girls consider this. It was true. 'I think I'll sit down for a moment,' Django says and makes his way, a little falteringly, to the chair.

The girls hurry round.

'Are you OK?'

'What's the matter?'

'What can we do?'

'I'm fine,' says Django, 'it's just the excitement.'

'But you look in pain,' Pip says.

'Just a few aches and gripes,' Django says. 'Don't read into it – I *am* seventy-five. What did I want to say? Ah yes, roast potatoes. Roast potatoes.'

And it suddenly strikes the girls hard in their hearts that, actually, they're not helping Django prepare Christmas dinner. This isn't a cookery lesson. This is not about this Christmas or past Christmases, this is about Christmases yet to come. This is the passing down of family recipes, the imparting of knowledge, the handing over of experience and quirks, the conveying of preference and methods in the sincerest hope that family traditions will continue. The room rings far louder with the resonance of this, the solemnity of such responsibility, than it does with 'Silent Night'.

'Don't cry,' Pip whispers to Django who is dabbing his eyes furiously.

'I'm not crying, darling,' he says, 'it's just the onions. It's just the onions. The buggers. When it comes to onions, my advice is to suck a spoon and chop them in water.'

With the children sound asleep upstairs, their new favourite toys propped up on the bedside tables so that they can be viewed and adored on waking, downstairs it is time for the McCabe yuletide tradition of The Great Ring Round. This is the one occasion in the calendar when Django McCabe cannot be prised off the telephone and it is the one day when the telephone company realizes he is a viable customer after all. Bibi is phoned in Paris, Toni is phoned on the shores of Squam Lake, Rayner is rung in Sausalito. They call Babs Chorlton down the road and then Jim McKenzie up in Glasgow. Django bestows Christmas cheer and chatter before passing the caller to Pip, Fen and Cat; going through the ages, over the years. Gregor and Ferdy stay on the phone for over half an hour. The Merifields laugh and say, Why are you phoning us, McCabe, we'll see you tomorrow for Boxing Day drinks. Django shouts down the phone to make himself heard to Vauxhall Vinnie who is now rather deaf. This year, sadly, there are no Bebop Boys left to phone. Joe and Jack go through their own tradition of asking the McCabe girls to tell them about each and every present and what exactly it does. Everyone adds the word 'healthy' in wishing Django a happy new year.

'I'm all talked out,' says Cat, popping an After Eight into her mouth.

'I don't think Joe and Jack quite got what an iPod is all about,' says Pip, 'though personally, I thought I explained it pretty well.'

‘It was so nice to speak to Bibi,’ says Fen. ‘I don’t think I’ve spoken to her since your birthday.’

‘Just one more phone call,’ Django declares, to groans all round, ‘then I promise you, I’ll put the thing in the broom cupboard.’

‘But we’ve done everyone,’ Pip declares.

‘I thought we might phone your mother, actually,’ says Django. The girls fall silent. It’s one thing to honour the requests of a dying man, to learn his way with roasting potatoes, it’s another to agree to a potentially bad idea. But Django reads their minds. ‘It’s not a bad idea,’ he says quite firmly, ‘it’s the right thing to do.’

Penny had refused Marcia’s invitation to Christmas lunch; it was her first on her own and she wanted to spend it at home, not for any maudlin self-indulgence, but because she and Bob had never made a big fuss about Christmas anyway.

She is eating her lunch, direct from the foil container, when the phone rings.

‘That’ll be Marcia,’ Penny murmurs, ‘hoping to change my mind. Well I’ve eaten now – but perhaps I will join them for cards this evening.’ She walks over to the phone.

‘Hullo?’

‘Penny? It’s Django.’

‘Django?’

‘In England. United Kingdom. Derek McCabe.’

‘No – no, Django is fine. Django is good. My *goodness*.’

‘I’m phoning long-distance – can you hear me?’

‘Yes, I can hear you. I can hear you just fine.’

‘We’re all here, all of us, in Derbyshire, as per usual. We thought we’d give you a tinkle. To wish you a merry Christmas and a happy new year.’

Penny is speechless. But being speechless scares her because she knows Django hates telephones and he might misconstrue it as a fault on the transatlantic line. She must speak. She must. 'My,' she says, 'my. That's very nice of you. I wish you a merry Christmas too. You – plural.'

'This line is very clear, isn't it?' Django marvels.

'Yes it is,' Penny agrees.

'And how are you?' Django asks. 'This time of year – I imagine it can't be easy.'

'Thank you,' Penny says, 'but you know it's OK – it's better than I thought. I've just had my lunch. It was tasty. And I'm going to play cards with friends tonight.'

'You are on your own?' Django queries.

'Yes,' Penny says, 'I am.'

'That's not right, not on Christmas,' Django says. 'Well I'm jolly glad we phoned now, I most certainly am.'

'I'm OK, Dango,' Penny says and she cringes because although she wanted to say Django she started saying Derek instead. 'And how are you?' There's a pause. 'Hullo?'

'Still here,' says Django, 'I'm still here. I've had a spot of bother, but I'm still here.'

'Are you OK?' Penny asks.

'I feel fine,' Django assures her. 'I've had a very happy day. I'm passing you over – we have a tradition on the McCabe Great Ring Round, we go through the ages – so you'll have Pip, followed by Fen, followed by Cat.'

'Hullo?' says Pip.

'Hullo Philippa.'

'Merry Christmas.'

'And to you. How are you?'

'I'm pregnant!'

'Oh! Oh! That's just wonderful news. When are you due?'

'Late June – a week before Fen's daughter turns two.' A pause. 'How are you?'

'I'm great, thank you.'

'Would you like to speak to Fen?'

'I'd like to speak to you a little longer,' Penny says, 'if I may.'

'Oh, OK.' A pause. 'How are you, then?'

'I'm great. I'm great. How nice to hear from you.'

'Yes. And you too. Merry Christmas – I hope you have a happier year ahead.'

'That's kind. Will you – well, will you let me know about the baby?'

'Yes,' says Pip, 'of course I will. I'm passing you on to Fen now. Bye bye.'

'Goodbye, Pip.'

'Hullo,' says Fen.

'Merry Christmas, Fenella.'

'And to you – and a happy new year. I hope it's a good one.'

'Thank you. And how are you?'

'I'm fine. Cosima is eighteen months old. She speaks a little. She says "turtle" quite a lot, actually.'

'How extraordinary! How endearing. Your first word was "apple". Pip's was "goody" and I'm afraid I don't know what Catriona's was.'

'Oh. Quite.' A pause. 'How is the weather?'

'We have snow, we have a white Christmas. It's picture perfect. And how is it with you?'

'It's a little overcast. But quite mild, actually.' A pause. 'Would you like me to pass you on to Cat, now?'

'I'd like to speak to you a little longer,' Penny says, 'if I may.'

'Oh yes. Of course.'

'What have you been up to?'

'I've gone back to work, part-time, I'm enjoying it immensely.'

'Good for you. That's great.'

'Thanks. And you?'

'Oh, I've been painting the house. And hiking. And I went to Florida with my friend Marcia – she has a condo there. Boy was it hot.'

'That sounds good,' says Fen. 'I'm going to pass you on to Cat now. Have a very merry Christmas – and a lovely year to come.'

'Thank you, Fen, thank you,' says Penny.

'Hullo,' says Cat, 'Merry Christmas and a happy new year.'

'Well thank you, Catriona – and I wish you the same. How are you?'

'Great – busy. Ben and I moved to Darley Dale. I'm heading up a new flagship bookshop near Sheffield and Ben is Dr Big in sports medicine at the local hospital.'

'My, you girls – you have so much to be proud of. What achievements. It's wonderful.'

'Thank you.' A pause. 'It's nice to be nearer to Django.'

'Is he unwell? I get the feeling he is.'

'He is.'

'I'm so sorry,' Penny trails off. She doesn't want to hear that it's cancer. But she suspects it is. She feels her instincts are heightened, having lived through Bob's cancer. 'What have you done today – what is Christmas Day like for you?'

'Oh, we've cooked and eaten and unwrapped an obscene amount of presents.'

'Good for you!'

'And phoned all our friends,' Cat thinks for a moment, 'and family.'

'Is Django still there?' Penny asks.

'Yes – do you want a word?'

'A word is exactly what I want,' Penny tells her. 'Goodbye, Cat. And merry Christmas. To you all.'

‘Hullo?’ says Django.

‘Hullo Django,’ says Penny. ‘I just wondered – I don’t know why I just wondered.’ She pauses. She laughs a little. ‘But I just wondered if perhaps you remembered what Cat’s first word was?’

Django pauses. ‘Garden.’

‘Garden,’ Penny marvels, ‘that’s lovely. Well I guess I ought to let you go.’

‘OK.’

‘Thank you so much for calling me. I’m quite – I’m quite. I’m overwhelmed.’

Django looks around the room. All eyes are on him. ‘Maybe next year we can entice you over,’ he says.

Penny is speechless but again she fears Django might presume the line to be dead.

‘Oh my,’ she says quietly, ‘well. That is some invitation.’

‘Good!’ Django declares as he smiles at his girls. ‘That’s settled then.’

In loving memory
Liz Berney
12.2.1968–24.12.2005

Acknowledgements

No matter how deeply I love my characters and believe in them, I must reluctantly admit to spending most of my working life with people who don't actually exist. However, behind the scenes, I am blessed with a dynamic and crucial support network helping to bring my books to life. Sincerest thanks go to my team at HarperCollins – especially my esteemed editor Lynne Drew. My agent, the inimitable Jonathan Lloyd, thank you – your percentage is my pleasure. Dawn Gobourne (and Hilary, Germaine and Ana) at Haringey Library Services – thanks for making my working days so happy and cosy. Mary Chamberlain, my eagle-eyed copy-editor, and Sophie Ransom, my tireless publicist – thank you both for your patience and your attention to detail. I'd also like to extend my gratitude to Bex Lane, Jerney de Vries, Naina Patel, Sue McMillan, Souki Hartigan, Sue McCormack and Sarah Henderson for enabling me, in so many ways, to write this book.

The Holistic Cancer Care Centre, James Cook University Hospital, Middlesbrough (*in memory of David Sutcliffe 1937–2005*).